THE WINGED MAN

OR, 'TWIX MIDNIGHT AND DAWN (1913)

E. DUDLEY. TEMPEST

AUTHOR OF "CAPTAIN PAULINE," IN THE RANKS," ETC

The Spring-Heeled Jack Library: Volume 7

EDITED WITH A NEW INTRODUCTION BY

J.S. Mackley

The Spring-Heeled Jack Library

Spring Heel'd Jack: The Terror of London (1863)*

Spring Heeled Jack: The Terror of London (2 vols.) (1886)

Spring-Heeled Jack: Articles and Short fiction (1838–1897)
The Resident of Peckham letter (1838)
The Spring Jack (1838)
Springheel Jack: The Terror of London (The Origin Story) (1878)
From *Chums* by Harleigh Severne (1878)
Spring-Heeled Jack, from *All the Year Round* (9 August 1884)
Spring Heel Jack, *or* the Masked Mystery of the Tower (1885)
Spring-Heeled Jack (The Dialect Story) (1888)
The Mystery of Spring Heel Jack, *or* The Haunted Grange (1897)

Spring-Heeled Jack: The Human Bat
The Human Bat (1899–1901)
The Black Phantom (1901)

Dandy Dick, *or* The King's Highway**
Dandy Dick (1900)
Dandy Dick's Double (1900-1901)

Spring-Heeled Jack: Man or Fiend (1904)*

The Winged Man; *or* 'Twixt Midnight and Dawn (1913)***

* Complete for the first time
** A story featuring Spring-Heeled Jack as an ancillary character
*** A story influenced by The Human Bat series

First published in Great Britain in 2021

New Edition 2025 Published by Isengrin Publishing
ISBN: 978-1-917130-07-3

www.jonmackley.com

For Nik and Sue

Starts next week in THE WONDER!
The WINGED MAN
The Most Astounding Mystery Story ever written.

INTRODUCTION

The Winged Man or *'Twixt Midnight and Dawn* is the final volume in the Spring-Heeled Jack Library, the aim of which has been to make accessible the major works of fiction featuring Jack in his many guises, from urban ghost and aristocratic prankster, to shadowy avenger, to pursued victim of injustice. The introductions to the previous six volumes have covered the historical sightings of Spring-Heeled Jack, beginning with the first investigations in January 1838, as well as each of the major serials and many shorter articles and stories that feature or are connected with Jack from 1863 to 1904.

In many sightings and investigations in 1837 and 1838, witnesses described a "ghost" and were reported as exaggerated descriptions of terror with no reliable witness to be found: "Not one of the injured people had been known to tell the story. Perhaps they did not live to tell it" (*London Evening Standard*, 9 January 1838). However, in February 1838 the violent assaults on Jane Alsop at her home near Bow, and, a week later, on Lucy Scales walking home in Limehouse, just two miles away, were reported to and investigated by the police, although no one was prosecuted for the offences. After April 1838, the newspapers' interest in Spring-Heeled Jack waned although his notoriety was still circulated through hurriedly produced stage plays. Sadly, the content of these no longer exists.

In 1863, however, the first of the serial stories was published, and it linked back to the original assaults and the suggestion Jack was the *alter ego* of the Marquis of Waterford which had been a frequent and popular, but erroneous idea. This sensational serial fiction appealed to consumers of the "Penny Dreadful" market, although the story content was condemned for its lack of morality by the intellectual elite (*Quarterly Review*, July 1890). Later serials featuring Spring-Heeled Jack were situated earlier chronologically, for example during the early eighteenth century (*Dandy Dick*, 1900–1901); the mid-eighteenth century (*Spring-Heeled Jack: The Terror of London*, 1886) or during the Napoleonic Wars (*Spring-Heeled Jack*, 1904). These stories hark back to a romanticised or less cultured era than the time of writing placing a distance between the reader and the events.

A story where the events are contemporary with the publication is *The Human Bat* (1899–1901). Here the protagonists are plucky and honest characters who represent the British Empire, while "Spring-Heeled Jack" is one of the names of the adversary who stands against order, authority and "Englishness".

The Winged Man was written by E. Dudley Tempest and was first published over 28 issues in the storypaper *The Wonder* between 11 January and 21 July 1913. It is presented here as a continuous narrative for the first time. It is, admittedly, something of a leap to include this story as part of the Spring-Heeled Jack Library, since the name of Spring-Heeled Jack is only invoked on a handful of occasions. However, the narrative is arguably a continuation of the earlier serial, *The Human Bat*, and this serves to demonstrate how the character evolves from the earliest narratives and brings to a conclusion the progression of Spring-Heeled Jack's character which spans nearly eight decades.

Early Twentieth Century 'Sightings' of Spring-Heeled Jack

By the turn of the twentieth century, newspaper stories featuring Spring-Heeled Jack or his imitators were considerably less frequent simply because his name had lost its impact. There were occasional references to *a* Spring-Heeled Jack "type" appearing before magistrates, but the name was simply attached to someone who could run very fast or who was engaged in daring escapades. These types of appearances and false attributions are mentioned in *The Winged Man*:

> Again and again their deliberations were interrupted by white-faced men arriving with the information that the Winged Man had been seen in various parts of the town. Now he was reported swinging on the cowl of the malt-house at the end of Southgate Street; again, clinging to a spire, and yet again in the hospital gardens.
>
> The majority of these reports was simply groundless scares. the Winged Man had got on the nerves of the public. Every blackbird, every crow that flew over the old town was magnified by fear into the fearful, supernatural being. (81)

The principal news story featuring Spring-Heeled Jack was concerning the Leaping Man at Liverpool in 1904. This event, considered the last "canonical" appearance of Spring-Heeled Jack, was almost concurrent with the publication of the 12 issues of the Spring-Heeled Jack serial (volume 6 of this series: and this event is discussed in detail there). There are, however, a handful of newspaper stories from the beginning of the twentieth century which are worth mentioning:

A curious report was circulated in a handful of newspapers in April 1902. Residents of Baker Street of Gorleston near Yarmouth complained an individual would leap out after dark and scare passers-by. This Spring-Heeled Jack imitator was discovered to be a young woman wearing her brother's clothes who was "desirous of indulging a practical joke on behalf of her neighbours". The article ends with the stern assertion that "the 'joke' has now been discontinued" (*Worcestershire Chronicle*, 26 April 1902). Unfortunately, this story is repeated verbatim across several newspapers, and it raises many more questions than it answers: the newspapers at the time simply reported incidents, rather than investigating them.

However, this incident echoes another sighting, this time in Dover back in November 1839 where Jack had appeared to several women in town, conducting himself "in a way that does not admit of specific details". A policeman named Cole apprehended an individual on the pier "dressed in a most grotesque Bavarian costume." (In some reports "he" is referred to as "a demon" and "a monster" when "he" is incarcerated overnight). It was later reported Spring-Heeled Jack had been caught wearing a short red jacket and a light blue frock coat with a head decorated by a woman's nightcap and an old piece of black crepe for a veil and numerous visitors came to the police station to see the sources of their anxieties. The "unveiling" of the "monster" revealed a young woman called Kate (or Kitty) Adams. She was well known in the "classic regions of the pier", although she claimed she was not the "genuine monster", and she was on a visit to her brother and was thus dressed "for a lark". Suitably penitent and severely reprimanded, she was discharged of any wrongdoing as there was "no proof advanced that she was the person who had appeared on former nights to the inhabitants, though her dress corresponded with reports in circulation" (*Dover Telegraph and Cinque Ports General Advertiser*, 23 November 1839; *Kentish Mercury*, 23 November 1839). In the previous month, Edward Adams was discharged from an assault on his sister, Kate, on a payment of costs and a promise not to further "annoy" his sister (*Dover Telegraph and Cinque Ports General Advertiser*, 19 October 1839), and five years later, Kate was imprisoned for fourteen days for stealing a wine glass (*Dover Telegraph and Cinque Ports General Advertiser*, 28 September 1844).

A disturbing story appeared in the *Midland Counties Tribune* in December 1903 which caused an alarm in Loughborough, Leicestershire. A 14-year-old factory worked named Miss Beadman, claimed she was approached by a man on her way home from work, who handed her a note which read "You will only be alive two or three more days". It was later claimed the police received a letter from "Spring-heel Jack" threatening he would murder sixteen women factory-workers before Christmas Eve—just a few days away—which necessitated the terrified women being escorted to and from work. The police denied such a letter existed and, upon investigation, discovered Miss Beadman had fabricated the letter and the rumours after "suddenly taking a dislike to work" (*London Evening News*, 21 December 1903; *Midland Counties Tribune*, 22 December 1903).

The Stockport dog poisoner, September and October 1929

One final example of the name of Spring-Heeled Jack being employed was in October 1929 when a number of dogs were poisoned in the Stockport district. First reported in the *Liverpool Echo*, it claimed forty dogs had died in the Heaton Moor area. Two girls witnessed a man on a bike, who they described as clean-shaven, aged between thirty and forty, and wearing a navy-blue suit and a bowler hat, giving "a white solid substance" to a dog on a Saturday morning and the dog died within a few minutes. The witnesses' own dog had died a few days before. A veterinary surgeon confirmed the dogs had died from strychnine poisoning. A man calling himself "Springheel Jack" telephoned a Manchester newspaper office claiming "There will be no dogs poisoned for four weeks. I have only one more left to do". It was claimed the poisoner also contacted the dogs' owners before his actions (9 September). The following day the *Daily Mirror*'s report including an image:

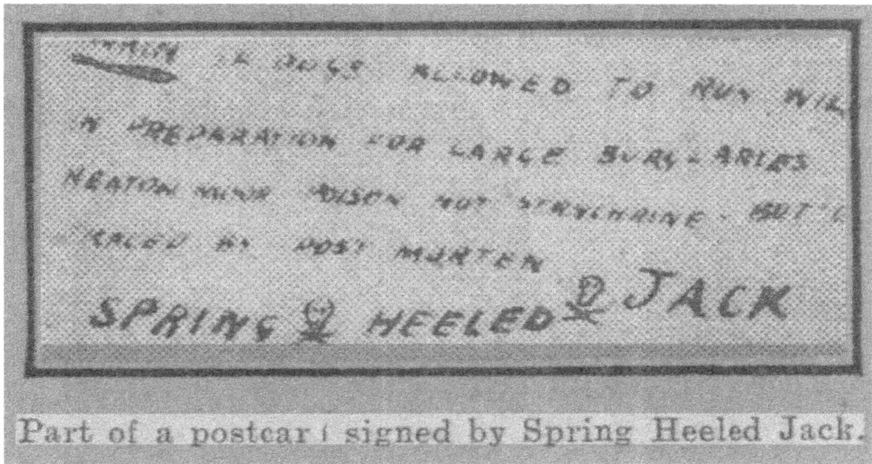

Part of a postcard signed by Spring Heeled Jack.

By the start of October, a £100 reward was offered for information leading to the conviction of "Spring Heeled Jack" noting over thirty dogs had gone missing over the previous weeks, although it could only be proved twelve had been poisoned (*Lancashire Evening Post*, 1 October). At the investigation continued, the description was circulated of an "elderly" man with a "dark mackintosh and a bowler hat" who had "considerable knowledge of the district" but who now operated at night, sometimes dropping meat poisoned with strychnine for the dogs. Some shops which displayed the reward notices had their windows "slashed" with the letter J etched into the glass, prompting other shopkeepers to remove their notices (*Hartlepool Northern Daily Mail,* 8 October). It was claimed the perpetrator was "slighted" the reward was only £100, but he might consider claiming it himself if it were increased to £1000 (*Dundee Evening Telegraph,* 9 October). At the time, £100 reward was also offered for the capture of a murderer from Ilkley, but the reward was offered by a dogs' newspaper, a dogs' food manufacturer, a subscribing dog-owners' society and a group of local dog lovers, "which is why [Spring-Heeled Jack] finds a murderer's price on his head" (*The Guardian,* 9 October)

Some newspapers reported the "ceaseless efforts" of the police in investigating the case, but a Stockport police official admitted "We are only making the usual inquiries … We have so far only two reports of windows being slashed. We do not attach more importance on the whole thing. Someone is out for an advertisement" (*Lancashire Evening Post,* 9 October).

Certainly, the police realised the more publicity the individual was given, the more likely he was to continue with his exploits: "Therefore they depreciate such reports as credit them with having sent flying squads on the track of the delinquent (*The Guardian*, 9 October).

The poisoning incidents continued, however, and it was thought a child had been taken ill when an object containing carbolic acid was posted through his letterbox, although it transpired the child's illness was unrelated (*Daily Mirror*, 11 October). On the following day, two boys were taken to the chief constable for carving the initials SHJ in a shop doorway. The boys claimed they were copying the incidents they had read about, and despite the anxiety and grief of the previous month, the report concludes "the police authorities are inclined to believe that there is no such person as 'Spring Heeled Jack' and that the various acts which have been attributed to him are the work of mischievous boys" (*Hartlepool Northern Daily Mail*, 12 October).

Later that week an RSPCA official from Northenden, a few miles away from Heaton Moor, confirmed ten dogs had been poisoned (*Belfast Telegraph*, 18 October), and more warnings purporting to be from Spring-Heeled Jack had been posted to a number of people including a butcher named Peter Moore who owned a number of greyhounds who found a chilling message attached to his door with a drawing pin: "Your turn next — Spring Heel Jack". Moore promptly engaged a night watchman to guard his dogs (*Leeds Mercury*, 17 October). A "dog fancier" in Blackpool named Holt received the threat "I might see you off yet or your dog. Beware of Spring-heeled Jack" (*Western Daily Press*, 18 October). Curiously, Mr. Holt noted the envelope, which bore a Stockport postmark and was headed "Urgent and Important" had at one time belonged to him as his name and address were printed on one half of the front. Holt suggested the envelope may have been sent to prospective dog-exhibitors from when he was secretary of the Blackpool and District Canine Society some years before. Even at this stage, the police thought the threat "a bit of a bluff" (*Lancashire Evening Post*, 18 October). It was suspected nine other dogs were poisoned in Warrington (*Daily Herald*, 18 October) and residents considered forming a night patrol to protect their pets (*Hartlepool Northern Daily Mail*, 18 October).

As with the original sightings of Spring-Heeled Jack nearly a century before, the dog-poisoner vanished without his identity being discovered, but a series of copycat incidents followed: three boys appeared at the Juvenile Court in Lymm in Cheshire charged with leaving message for a dog owner warning "Your turn next, for Vic will die" (Vic being the name of the dog). It was signed by Springheel Jack and ended with a drawing of a spring, the heel of a shoe and a car-jack. The boys claimed they had read the reports about Spring-Heeled Jack and sent the message as a "trick". The eldest boy, aged 19, was fined 10s and the two younger boys, aged 15 and 12, were ordered to pay 4s costs each and both "undertook to join the Boy Scouts" (*Liverpool Echo*, 20 November). The newspaper reminded readers of the "bogy" from decades before who terrified women by jumping out on them at night and by the time of these incidents, the name has been forgotten "save for the occasional use of his name by evil-doers" (*Hartlepool Northern Daily Mail*, 19 October). There is clearly no logical reason for such distressing actions, but the perpetrator clearly used the name because he felt there was a veil of fear associated with it.

Spring-Heeled Jack's legacy

Often newspapers mentioned events that had happened on that day some years or decades ago. *Pearson's Weekly* (2 March 1901) notes on 26 February 1838 the Metropolitan courts received complaints of outrages committed by Spring-Heeled Jack: "Only a short time before, he had robbed a banker of £700 in Tottenham Court Road" and the article continues with the hyperbolic description of Jack's "marvellous leaps and bounds" and he jumped "clean over a mail coach in the Highgate Road". As noted above, Spring-Heeled Jack's two most notorious assaults took place in February 1838, the first on 20 February, was an assault on Jane Alsop, the daughter of a banker, although this too places the Banker's house between Old Ford and Bow, some considerable distance from Tottenham Court Road.[1] Many of the facts in the *Pearson's Weekly* article are correct; however, the article claims Jack's attack on Jane Alsop was

---

[1] It is noteworthy that the date in the newspaper is obscured. The entries for the week are presented in date order. However, it looks like the date 26 February has been overwritten by 20 February, which would be historically accurate.

repeated from local folklore, rather than historical documents and concludes Jack "robbed only rich people, and many acts of kindness to poorer classes were placed to his credit, although this contradicts the general belief that, while Jack might assault women and even frighten them to death, "he never assaulted anybody for the purpose of stealing" (*All the Year Round* 1884, 346). This shows, by the turn of the twentieth century, historical facts were being dismissed and Jack had taken on the status of the mysterious folk hero, aligned with Robin Hood, even though he had the uncanny ability to "suddenly appear in front of his victims, and make off again by a series of marvellous leaps and bounds" (*Pearson's Weekly*, 2 March 1901). As the authors of the articles remind their readers of stories which happened many decades before, it appears Jack's original appearances and assaults on Jane Slater and Lucy Scales have all-but been forgotten. He was no longer a contemporary figure of fear. As Karl Bell notes, the figure of Spring-Heeled Jack had become "increasingly marginalised as a popular myth that no longer worked" (201) and the "terror of London" was replaced with a new, contemporary and genuinely frightening figure stalking the London streets. One of the letters allegedly sent by "Jack" to the Metropolitan Police (dated 4 October 1888) is headed "Spring Heel Jack: The Whitechapel Murderer" and is signed "Jack the Ripper". In the letter, Spring-Heeled Jack claims to be an American living in London who aims to murder a dozen women, and promising "I will rip a few more so help my God I Will" (MEPO 3/142, 195; Evan and Skinner, 84).

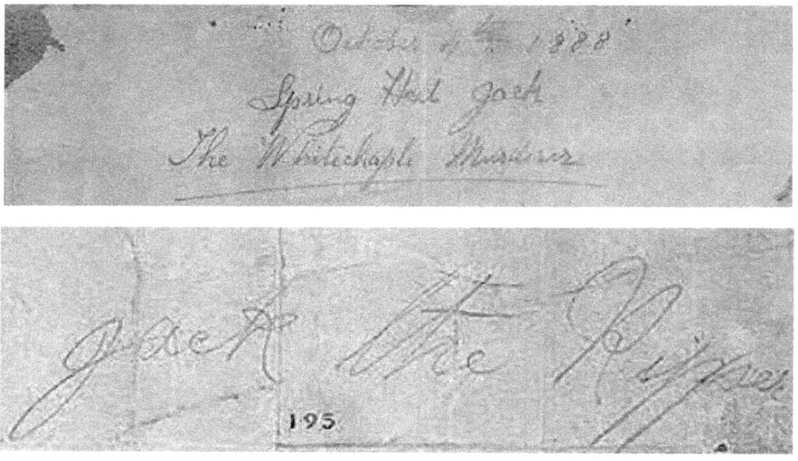

This is arguably the moment Spring-Heeled Jack passed his baton of dread to the new and more terrifying Jack the Ripper. Spring-Heeled Jack belonged to the past and to folklore. And, as noted above, Spring-Heeled Jack's assaults had been largely forgotten and any tales of his jumping out and frightening people were downplayed. On the other hand, reports of Jack the Ripper's victims were circulated with descriptions and illustrations of graphic violence.

Deceptions: Peter Haining and Elizabeth Villiers

Almost all recently published scholarship on Spring-Heeled Jack will often stop and explore details in Peter Haining's 1977 publication *The Legend and Bizarre Crimes of Spring Heeled Jack* which was the first substantial study of Spring-Heeled Jack. Much of Haining's other work focuses on ghosts, monsters, black magic and Sherlock Holmes, and his publications are books he edited while he was Editorial Director at the New English Library. However, his discussion of Spring-Heeled Jack represents his own argument and many of his much the details have been fabricated to substantiate his ideas. Unfortunately, much of the material about Spring-Heeled Jack on the Internet all repeats the same information, and the source for this is often found to be insubstantial.

At the start of his publication, Haining describes an assault on a barmaid named Polly Adams on 11 October 1837. Adams was at a local fair in Blackheath when she was violently attacked in a manner similar to the assault on Jane Alsop – her blouse was torn off and her stomach scratched with claws before her assailant escaped "with huge, bounding steps into the night" (9). According to Mike Dash, there is apparently no evidence for this assault in the newspaper archives (26). This event, if it happened, occurred some months before the investigation into the assaults began and well before the name "Spring-Jack" had been adopted to describe the terror of London: this was first used in the *Woolwich and Deptford Gazette* on 13 January 1838. In addition, the descriptions of Jack's early antics as presented in the Resident of Peckham letter are very different to the assaults on Jane Alsop and Lucy Scales. Furthermore, in Haining's fictionalised description, Polly Adams is able to recognise her assailant as a "pop-eyed, laughing nobleman" which only serves to bolster Haining's assertion that Jack was the *alter ego* of the "mad" Marquis of Waterford, Henry de la Poer Beresford (1811–59). He was known for his pranks and antisocial behaviour, including, quite literally, painting red the town of Melton Mowbray. It is for this reason Haining stresses Jack's appearance on Turner Street in 1838, and includes the (fabricated) detail of the ancestral crest and the embroidered "W" on the perpetrator's coat. Although frequently mentioned in relation to Spring-Heeled Jack's "pranks", there is no evidence to link the Marquis of Waterford to any of the assaults.

Haining, in addition to Polly Adams, Haining cites other assaults, including three unnamed young women who were attacked on Barnes Common. Without naming his own source, Haining acknowledges "these attacks were not reported in a single newspaper" (37) He also describes an attack on Mary Stevens on Clapham Common as well as Jack wrecking a carriage on Streatham High Road, which he derives from a book by Elizabeth Villiers called *Stand & Deliver*. Villiers may have had some access to material that has since been lost, but no contemporary records survive concerning this incident, and, notably, in a short chapter discussing Spring-Heeled Jack, Villiers does not mention any of the *documented* sightings of Spring-Heeled Jack.

However, Haining *does* provide pictorial evidence for the *murder* of a prostitute named Maria Davis in February in November 1845. He claims the woodcut shows of the body of a woman being dragged from an open sewer called Folly Ditch near Jacob's Island in Bermondsey. Consequently, despite numerous reports claiming Jack had scared people to death, Adams was the only *named* victim he allegedly killed. However, Mike Dash's extensive research and analysis shows this woodcut, part of the Hulton Getty Picture Collection, actually shows a boatman collecting water (Dash 26–28). Despite Haining's assertion, there is no evidence Jack murdered anyone, or indeed that any of these assaults actually occurred.

Over the course of researching for this series, it is evident anything in Haining's publication needs to be closely interrogated. For example, as seen in the *Articles and Short Fiction* (volume 3), Haining points to the mention of Spring-Heeled Jack in the novel *Chums* by Harleigh Severne, which was helpful, but Haining then fabricates details of Severne's life to suggest the author was writing about a personal experience. Consequently, when Haining's assertions are investigated the details have the flimsiest of details, if any at all, supported by spurious or contrived evidence and his discussions collapse when his "evidence" is challenged.

Towards the end of Haining's volume, he notes other publications which have featured stories about Spring-Heeled Jack. These include *The Human Bat*. He reveals the Bat's identity as, arguably, his readers would be unlikely to have access to the British Library, or the opportunity to read the series *in situ*. Haining also cites an article promoting the idea that Jack is a visitor from space also gains traction with an article written by J. Vyner entitled "The Mystery of Springheel Jack" which appeared in *Flying Saucer Review* (May–June issue of 1961) which generated interest in Spring-Heeled Jack for a new audience.

However, Haining also lists other stories and features in which Spring-Heeled Jack "appears". His first suggestion is a regular comic feature in *Sparks* entitled "Larkheeled Jack". Sadly, the weak play on words and the pranks Jack performs like a mischievous schoolboy, is where the similarities end. Haining also names two stories published in *Union Jack* and *Detective Weekly* (the same publication, but with a new title). These stories featured Sexton Blake as the detective with thinly veiled parallels to the Sherlock Holmes stories. Haining identifies two stories, "Terror by Night", which appeared in *Union Jack* in October 1929 and "The Seven Matches Mystery" from *Detective Weekly* (27 May 1933).

Haining claims "the agile terror was … pitted against Sexton Blake (129). He even provides the illustrations. Having been through these publications, it transpires this link to Spring-Heeled Jack is another of Haining's fabrications. In "Terror by Night" Blake's quarry is called a "man-bat", but is a circus performer holding a grudge, and in "The Seven Matches" he is identified as a vampire, although he is actually trying to kill members of a corrupt organisation. Haining also identifies another series entitled "The Grey Bat" which was written by Sidney and Francis Warwick and was published in *The Champion* (22 December 1923–23 February 1924). Haining says the Grey Bat was "another mystery crook whose origins could be traced to Spring-Heeled Jack, although the word "could" here is interchangeable as meaning "can" or "might" (one being definite and the other speculative). To my reading, there is little to suggest any influence from any of the historical, fictional or folklore sources in which Spring-Heeled Jack appears, although modern readers may notice a similarity between the Grey Bat's outfit and that of a well-known DC comic superhero.

Illustrations from "The Seven Matches Mystery" and "Terror By Night"

The banner from "The Grey Bat" series

While working on the Spring-Heeled Jack study published in *Fortean Studies*, Mike Dash wrote to Peter Haining asking him to identify his sources. Haining replied he had "ill-advisedly" given the material to a scriptwriter which was never returned. Unfortunately, this "evidence" is often the first information many curious minds might discover about Spring-Heeled, and sadly, it is without foundation.

Another author whose works have found their way into Spring-Heeled Jack mythology is Elizabeth Villiers. Her volume, *Stand & Deliver* is a discussion of highwaymen, which she describes as "Gentlemen of the High Toby" and their adventures which depict them as romantic outlaws in the manner popularised by William Harrison Ainsworth in stories such as *Rookwood* and *Jack Sheppard*. By her own admission, Villiers concedes Jack "should not be included a list of criminal adventurers since, except by very vague rumour, an actual crime was laid at his door" (238). Villiers's survey correctly dates Jack's first appearances as 1838, but nowhere does she mention any of the "canonical sightings" such as Jane Alsop and Lucy Scales or the Aldershot and Colchester "ghosts". Instead, Villiers claims he made his first appearance in Cut-throat Lane near Clapham Common in South London, appearing to Mary Stevens, a young woman in domestic service to whom Spring-Heeled Jack appeared, who caught her by the arms (before she swooned) kissed her "deliberately" on the lips and then "with a loud laugh let her go, and leaping extraordinarily high, vanished into the night as mysteriously as he had come" (242). Mary Stevens was described as a "perfectly sensible, highly respectable girl, not likely to suffer from delusions", but she was the sole witness to this incident. Her testimony is corroborated the following night when a coach was damaged when "some huge creature" leapt in front of the carriage and then vanished over a high wall (243).

A further example of Jack's antics was to leap into a graveyard in Clapham village where an old woman was waiting for her sons' return and where she saw "a black object" leap past her, causing her to scream for an alarm. What is notable about this incident is that when it was investigated, "two deep footprints as those of a man who had alighted heavily from a height" were discovered. Furthermore, their "strange shape" and it this was believed to be evidence of "'machines' or springs attached to his shoes" (245). The inclusion of these imprints may well be a reason for some authors to link Jack with the 'Devil's Hoofprints' which reportedly appeared in South Devon in February 1855, and which have also been extensively researched by Mike Dash.

Villiers's accounts of the reports of Jack's antics become more violent, from an old woman found strangled in a locked room to a young woman found dead on a footpath. Villiers acknowledges these were the "imitators" of Jack's antics which had become women into the mythology of his deeds, and he was only guilty of common assault "since the murder story may be dismissed" (251). However, she concludes with an incident an eye-witness—a "clear-headed, intellectual woman"—recounted to her when she had visited a "gipsy encampment" on Tooting Common with food and medicine. When she wished to return home on a misty evening, she was accompanied by an escort of gipsies, who drove off Spring-Heeled Jack when he came leaping out of the mist. Jack continued his antics for "six weeks only" and then his "hauntings ended as mysteriously as they had begun, and from that time to this the mystery has remained unsolved" (249–50). Villiers offers conjectures about Spring-Heeled Jack's identity, including a suggestion he was a kangaroo which had escaped from captivity (251). Villiers's eye-witness describes Jack as "less tall" than herself (although she was "exceptionally tall for a woman"), bare-headed, wearing dark clothes and having a cloak "swathed around him". A suitably vague description. Significantly, Villiers emphasises Jack's "extraordinarily high" leaps; and yet, in the unembellished first-hand reports, Spring-Heeled Jack rarely *springs*.

As noted above, Villiers does not include any of the reported sightings from 1838 or later. Nor do her accounts appear in any reports prior to the publication of her book in 1928. Peter Haining, however, takes Villiers accounts and weaves them into his own version of the chronology of Spring-Heeled Jack sightings (37–40).

The Winged Man, *The Human Bat* and Spring-Heeled Jack

This current serial story, *The Winged Man,* or *'Twixt Midnight and Dawn,* was written by E. Dudley Tempest about whom almost nothing is known, save he was named as the author of other serial stories including "Captain Pauline" and "In the Ranks." The *Winged Man* serial was first published over 28 issues in the storypaper *The Wonder* between 11 January and 21 July 1913, and is presented here as a continuous narrative for the first time. *The Wonder* was published weekly and priced at 1d. Previously, the storypaper had been called as *The Funny Wonder* and included a story entitled *The Human Bat* between 1899 and 1901 (volume 4 of this series).

At first glance, *The Winged Man* appears to be a continuation of this first story. For the first two issues the antagonist is referred to as "the Human Bat". In addition, throughout *The Human Bat*, the antagonist has many additional epithets: one is "the vampire", and the Winged Man is often described in terms often associated with the undead, such as his white face and his skeleton-like hands. And, of course, another name used is "Spring-Heeled Jack". The Winged Man is only referred to as Spring-Heeled Jack on a handful of occasions, and these are all used pejoratively: he is "but a Spring-heeled Jack from some travelling show!" (48)[2] and "an improved edition of the Spring-heeled Jack of forty years ago" (361), comments that often incur the Winged Man's wrath. Towards the end of the serial, one of the characters refers to the Winged Man as Spring-heeled Jack an insult which dooms the speaker "to the worst the Winged Man could inflict upon him" (582).

Beginning in the third issue, nearly 10% through the overall narrative, the character's name changes to "the Winged Man, otherwise known as the Human Bat" (59), after this there are only three occasions when the title "the Human Bat" is used. The third instalment is the first issue where an illustration featuring the Winged Man appears on the front cover of the storypaper, stressing the importance of the Winged Man's individuality as a principal character in his own right, rather than as a subsidiary to the Human Bat. However, whatever name is used, the characters generate a wave of fear when they are seen.

There are other similarities between the two stories, some more prominent than others: both the Human Bat and the Winged Man have strongholds in Yorkshire, and both series have a character called Nina, and both antagonists use gorillas as prison warders. The detective Danby Druce in *The Winged Man* is the embodiment of Jack Heywood from *The Human Bat* and Heywood's more central role in *The Black Phantom* although, by the end of the serial, he carries a lot of emotional baggage after he has suffered at the Black Phantom's hands. Danby Druce begins his pursuit of the Winged Man without any emotional encumbrance. At one point the protagonist in *The Human Bat* wears identical the apparatus to the Bat which enables them to fly and to face him in the skies as well as on land; Danby

---

2 Notably, on this occasion, the narrator refers to the character as "The Human Bat".

Druce also has access to such a costume so he can face the Winged Man on his "own ground". Both characters attempt to derail a train and to destroy a dam to destroy the lives of the villagers living beneath.

On the other hand, despite the use of the name, the Human Bat, at the outset, and the similarities between plot devices and tropes in the text, we must remember the antagonist of *The Human Bat* had a name and an occupation before embarking on the life of chaos. Some aspects of the Winged Man's past are revealed as the story progresses, but the two characters are very different. The Human Bat's position in the community is well-established, which makes his betrayal of his position and his actions against his community more specifically, and against England more generally, more severe. The Winged Man is very much an outsider, and characters respond judiciously when he threatens "Englishness". We shall return to a discussion of the Winged Man's identity later.

It is impossible to know whether it was the author's intention to continue the story and then changed his mind, or whether *The Winged Man* was always conceived to feature original characters and situations and the opening chapters were written to give the readers a sense of familiarity with the previous serial to draw them in.

The Winged Man

It is difficult to provide a summary of *The Winged Man* as the story is constructed of numerous connected incidents which are sometimes played out over two or three issues and sometimes are dismissed considerably swifter. The story is told through a third person narrative, which mostly stays with the Winged Man. On other occasions, it focuses on Danby Druce and sometimes follows minor characters who frame the narrative until the Winged Man arrives. This said, the narrator is often distanced from the Winged Man, and we never really get close to his internal thoughts, instead, his motivations are often explained through rhetorical questions from the narrator.

There is no logic to the Winged Man's actions. Sometimes his motive is the acquisition of wealth, and sometimes it is about meting his concept of justice. The narrative describes how "wild adventure, hairbreadth escapes were to the Winged Man as the very breath of life. To snatch a victim from the authorities, to beat, baffled, and to defy them, was the greatest joy this strange, weird, unearthly being could enjoy" (184). Consequently, the readers are told the kinds of thrilling adventures they can expect from the story, and, arguably, there is a wide variety of scenes, encounters and challenges the Winged Man faces. These include daring thefts of gold, jewellery and priceless works of art, he undertakes missions of vengeance as part of his heritage is revealed.

The Winged Man also faces personal challenges and initially respects Danby Druce for trying to do his duty as a detective, seeing him as an enemy and an equal and "the only man in the world holds whose brain is worthy to contend with mine". Likewise, after one encounter, Danby Druce reflects: "There was no anger in his heart, no feeling of hatred against the Winged Man. On the contrary, the respect with which he had ever regarded him was increased tenfold. Here was a foeman worthy indeed of his steel. Inch by inch, step-by-step, he would fight him with his own weapon" (268). The two foes, realising they each have a role to play, respect each other for their diligence in fulfilling that role. They are even capable of managing a short treaty between themselves, enjoying an evening in each other's company, which makes the animosity between them more severe and poignant. The Winged Man is unwilling to settle for Danby Druce's defeat or even death. Instead, it is "the humiliation, and not the destruction of the detective the Winged Man craved" (98) Druce frequently falls into the Winged Man's power, but maintains the discipline of the Empire by refuse to plead for clemency, asserting "I will not owe my life to you" (99). As the narrative progresses, the conflict between them becomes personal, and the battles between them take place over land and in the air, at a time aerial flight was still very much in its infancy and the concept of man achieving personal flight was still on the cusp of fantasy.

Published in 1913, there is an undercurrent of paranoia throughout *The Winged Man*, seen particularly in *The Winged Man* when parliament decides to take action against him as a declaration of war (156), tapping into the zeitgeist at the time, while still praising the British Military and their courageous nature. Despite the English King, George V, the Russian Tsar

Nicholas II and Kaiser Wilheim II all being first cousins, there was a sense of xenophobia to the foreign dignities, despite their close familial connection. Rudyard Kipling had warned about the German threat for a decade, including his descriptions of "the shameless hun" in his poem, "The Rowers" (1902), and by the end of 1913, newspapers such as the *Daily Graphic* conmented "wherever we look we see the grim apparatus of war, ever growing, ever more and more viciously on the alert, clogging the wheels of industry and squandering the fruits of peace" (31 December 1913).

As with *The Human Bat*, (1899–1901) *The Winged Man* is a product of its time and there is a strong emphasis on *Britishness* (rather than *Englishness* as depicted in the *Human Bat*). Throughout, there are references to "native courage", "the greatest Empire the world has ever seen" and much praising of the British military and their courageous spirit. There are also, sadly, some shocking comments referring to the "alien scum whom England shelters" (430) half a century before Enoch Powell's divisive Rivers of Blood speech! On the other hand, the details of the Winged Man's past suggest he may have been a king in his own right, which justifies his theft of the Crown Jewels: "And what else is he who rules over the destinies of Britain but the arbiter of the whole world?" Taken together, these elements show the Winged Man as an exile, still believing in his role as ruler. If he cannot be ruler of his own land, he will be ruler of the skies, the land and the seas, He literally wishes to be the ruler over the principal elements.

Of course, stealing the Crown Jewels (just like the character of Colonel Blood who appears in the *Dandy Dick* series) is a symbolic attack on England itself, and while there might be mutual respect between the Winged Man and Danby Druce for the most part of their relationship, when the Winged Man attacks England, the retaliation is merciless. The author employs a useful device in relation to the locations and landmarks around the British Isles. He visits many places in the British Isles where the proper name is used, such as York or Nelson's Column in Trafalgar Square in London are left undamaged. Conversely, locations with fictional names, such as the Cwamba Valley in Wales or Puck's Hill may well suffer from some devastation at the Winged Man's hands.

Who is The Winged Man?

In many, but not all, of the other stories in the Spring-Heeled Jack library, the identity of Jack's *alter ego* is revealed at some point in the narrative, normally at the end. This is not the case in *The Winged Man*. We are told from the outset the Winged Man is "a Strange Genius who, Possessed of Wonderful Powers of Invention," and who "sets forth to deal out Justice to the Evildoers of the Modern World."

The Winged Man often makes no delineation between his enemies and innocent victims: they may simply be people in the wrong place at the wrong time. He is capricious, sometimes downright sadistic and subject to extreme emotions reactions. This is partially explained by his nature of taking "fiendish delight in playing with the hopes and fears of those in his power as a cat plays with the mouse" (573). At the start of the narrative he prevents two burglars from completing a robbery, only to steal the plunder itself. And yet, he not only returns the most valuable of the jewels to the daughter of the house, but also prevents her from having to go through with a marriage against her wishes, and enables her to marry the man of her choosing. Shortly afterwards, his costume is soaked when he dives into a canal to escape Detective Danby Druce. "Without a second thought," he burns down a cottage to dry his clothes, but threatens to throw a villager into the flames for laughing when a cat is discovered trapped by the fire. (59–60). He rescues a criminal from the gallows, but only to extort money from him. He chooses to "avenge a slight" (the nature of which is unknown) by destroying the vats in a brewery, and yet inflicts a terrible punishment on the mill owner who places explosives in his rival's mill. He will chase (or drop) someone to fall from a great height, but will snatch them up, seconds away from death. He will engage in life-threatening activities, simply to feel the adrenalin.

However, through the story, the reader is offered brief glimpses into his identity. He is recognised by Colonel Richbrooke, and the two men pass an evening like gentlemen, although the Winged Man forbids the colonel from repeating his name "on the peril of my displeasure". Here the Winged Man asks the Colonel to tell him of their comrades "we knew in the old days before I died" and reminiscing on events from twenty years beforehand. When the Colonel delivers a message to Count Ixier from the Winged Man, he refers to an event in "a continental town" of twenty years before. "A brother who had sought to seize a brother's throne was preparing to leave his native land, glad to escape with the life he owed to his brother's clemency" (135), and after he left his native land the people suffered "under unjust taxation … prisons [were] filled with innocent men" and graves filled with "countless innocent victims". (139) Count's Ixier, it seems, was part of a plot to usurp the Winged Man, an incident conveyed by music composed by the Winged Man which is filled with contrasts of "an underlying current of deepening sorrow" and "a crash of majestic, triumphant harmony". It inspires the audience to imagine "a king mounting his throne, surrounded by the pomp and majesty of a mighty nation … of a man roused to fight cunning, unseen, unscrupulous foes" (148).

Ultimately, the Winged Man remains an enigma. Perhaps some of the readers would have been disappointed and required a definitive explanation. However, by leaving the Winged Man as a mystery, he is remains something inhuman, something *other*. It is true most of the characters he encounters witness only his vicious and sadistic nature, but he also engages in (sometimes absurd) competitions: if his challengers lose, they stake their lives to servitude to the Winged Man, but if the Winged Man loses, his adversaries receive extremely generous rewards. At one point, the Winged Man declares "Fear nothing. I am a terror only to evil-doers" whereas to others he is "the bearer of freedom" (244). Not everyone whose path he crosses curses his name. A train driver who trusts his instincts that the Winged Man can complete a task for him declares "They speak of you as one without heart, without mercy, incapable of kindly thought towards us human beings! … But your eyes are true, your face bears the mark of great sorrows long endured" (202). Ultimately, the characters who encounter the Winged Man are reduced to their base natures, whether that is courage or the desire to see justice, or loyalty, trust and self-sacrifice, or avarice and murderous deceit.

The Winged Man is a serial made up of a number of connected incidents and encounters which often play out over several episodes; there are very few narrative threads that run through the whole story. The Winged Man's personality changes between scenes and his only sustained relationships are with Danby Druce, Mary Evanson and with his servant, Ghat. In most other cases, the story is also divided into smaller episodes, such as the inventions of Professor Hexmider, the relationship with Annette Royle, the plot to destroy the mill, the exploration of the underground kingdoms, and the Winged Man's vengeance against the American detectives. From a reader's perspective, this type of writing allowed new readers to join the narrative at any stage, without feeling they had not missed too much of the story. From an editorial point of view, it meant the story could be wrapped up quickly after an editorial decision had been taken to finish the story. Consequently, the last two chapters in the final issue (2000 words) complete the story once the last plot strands from a particular episode have been addressed.

The Winged Man is very different to the other Spring-Heeled Jack serial stories of the very end of the nineteenth century and the beginning of the twentieth century. The precursor to *The Winged Man*, *The Human Bat* (1899–1901) demonstrates even though it was published as a serial, the readers it targeted were reading it on a week-by-week basis and were thrilled by the cliff-hanger at the end of each issue, although a mystery at the end of one episode may be completely dismissed in the next. There is little continuity in the story, and characters leave or arrive without explanation. It had all the hallmarks of being written by a pool of authors who were unfamiliar with what had happened before. *The Winged Man* was clearly written by a single author, and the overarching plot—the rivalry between the Winged Man and Danby Druce—is woven through the story. From the outset, it appeared the narrative would gradually reveal more details about the Winged Man's origins, as suggested by the episode involving Colonel Richbrooke and Count Ixier, but the details are instead a lot more subtle. The point of the story is not about revelation and redemption, but instead it is about being forced (and self-enforced) to live on the margins of society, and what happens when such an individual comes out of the shadows and into the light. No matter what their intentions, they are feared and shunned, and therefore their retaliation is unsurprising, and, in their mind, it is totally justified.

Conclusion: The Real Spring-Heeled Jack

Over this series of introductions and stories of the Spring-Heeled Jack library, we have seen a variety of historical representations about Spring-Heeled Jack and his imitators, principally reported in various newspapers, as well as extremely different depictions of the characters in the serial and standalone novels and in the short fiction. The legend of Spring-Heeled Jack most likely started as an urban ghost story such as those circulating around Hammersmith in 1804 and 1824 and developed into a wager between youthful aristocrats to "prank" the residents of the villages around London. There were some notably chilling incidents—violent attacks on young women in February 1838—but afterwards the legend took on a life of its own. The newspapers reported imitators and compared criminal activities with the stories that were starting to build up around Jack. In addition, serial novels and stage plays caught the public's imagination. This meant, nearly a century after the first reports were published, Jack had become a figure of folklore even though there were considerably fewer newspaper reports after April 1838.

Writing half a century after the first investigation into the alleged sightings, a contributor to *All the Year Round* noted "so numerous were the tales told of Spring-heeled Jack that a good many must be supposed to be true; whist on the other hand, great allowance must be made for credulity, some people not being content with the marvellous as they find it, but being only too happy to add thereto" (*All the Year Round*, 9th August 1884, 349).

As for Spring-Heeled Jack, we can reasonably surmise a handful of details from the historical accounts:

- It is unlikely the assaults on Polly Adams, Mary Stevens and the murder of Maria Davis took place. These are most likely fabrications by Peter Haining.
- A series of disturbances *did* take place around London and the surrounding villages in late 1837. These, as noted in the Resident of Peckham's letter, were likely to have been perpetrated by a group from "the higher ranks of life", members of the aristocracy copying the actions of the mohawks.
- The assaults on Jane Alsop and Lucy Scales in February were

genuine and investigated by the police. They were likely to have been committed by the same person or persons. Both Jane and Lucy knew the stories of Spring-Heeled Jack.

- It is likely Payne and Millbank, the two men who were questioned in court, had some involvement in Jane Alsop's assault even though they were released without charge. Thomas Millbank, in particular, is identified as being seen at the Alsop's house at the time of the assault and "the person who had so frightened the Misses Alsop"; furthermore, two witnesses testified he had called himself "Spring-Heeled Jack" (*The Times*, 2 March 1838).

- One of the "Spring-Heeled Jack gang" appeared at the house of Thomas Ashworth on Turner Street on 25 February. Although the property is around two miles from where Jane Alsop lived, and just over a mile from the location of Lucy Scales's attack, the details are different, for example, taking place in a comparatively public location (the corner of Turner Road and Commercial Street), and there not being a young woman involved. However, as the appearance at Turner Street occurred midway between the assaults on Alsop and Scales, the proximity to their location, and the fact all three attacks took place within days of each other between 8pm and 9pm at night, have too many similarities with the other assaults to be coincidental.

- Assaults on women such as Jane Alsop and Lucy Scales ended after Payne and Millbank were questioned. Media interest in Spring-Heeled Jack waned after April 1838, possibly because the days were getting longer. In the stories reported in the newspapers, most were either copycat "larks" or the perpetrators' actions were *likened* to those of Spring-Heeled Jack.

- Despite being named as a plausible suspect, there is no evidence linking the Marquis of Waterford to any Spring-Heeled Jack activity.

- The appearances of the "ghost" at Aldershot and Colchester Barracks in 1877–78 were perpetrated by a subaltern officer. The matter was dealt with "in house".

- The incident of the leaping man at Newport Arch in Lincoln in 1877 was only reported by the sensationalist publication the *Illustrated Police News* and not in any newspaper. Aside from the description of a man jumping to a height of "15 to 20 feet" there is nothing in the article to tie this incident with Spring-Heeled Jack, except the caption on the illustration "Spring-Heeled Jack jumping on Newport Arch" which was added by later editors and not the original correspondent.

- The Leaping man at Everton in 1904 was linked to an appearance of Jack in the park near Shaw Street in Everton. in 1887. The later individual was identified as a man who suffered from religious mania, and his story was woven into the mythology surrounding Spring-Heeled Jack.

Arguably, the folklore of Spring-Heeled Jack derives from many historical reports which have had new elements included and have been woven together to form a loosely connected "canon" list of incidents. Suburban ghost stories from the turn of the nineteenth century were applied to the frightening antics of an individual or group. These "pranks" were investigated, but no reliable witnesses were found. In the meantime, the public found a name for their fears and called him "Spring-Heeled Jack". Over the decades the stories became exaggerated and woven into the tapestry of folklore. Jack became a figure who could "scare naughty children into being good" (*Lancashire Evening Post*, 2 October 1929).

While the intention of the original perpetrators of events described in the "Resident of Peckham" letter was simply to scare the residents of the London villages (apparently scaring them to death), Descriptions of a man tearing women's clothes with claws were likely an exaggeration as no one came forward to the police. These details were picked up by the perpetrators of the attack on Jane Alsop and Lucy Scales.

It is likely Thomas Millbank physically assaulted Jane Alsop on 20 February 1838. It is notable Jack's two other appearances that month—at both Thomas Ashworth's house on Turner Street and in Green Dragon Alley, where Lucy Scales was assaulted—are both around two miles from Bearbinder Lane. Indeed, the report from the court proceedings notes "There was another female"—presumably Lucy Scales—"who had witnessed something similar … close to the residence of Mr. Alsop, so that the case of the Misses Alsop was not a solitary instance" (*London Evening Standard*, 3 March 1838). If there was indeed a Spring-Heeled Jack "gang" as the newspaper suggests, this appearance could have been someone else.

In addition, the Turner Street appearance was on 25 February and the assault on Lucy Scales on 28 February, and all three assaults are reported to have occurred between 8pm and 9pm. If Millbank was responsible for both, he may have been daring the authorities to link him with Jane Alsop's assault, or, if there was a "gang" the other members could have worked on Millbank's behalf to provide an alibi. Millbank's testimony does not hold up under analysis. When answering questions concerning the assault on Jane Alsop in court, Millbank claimed he had been "so drunk, he had not the least idea of any thing that happened", although Jane Alsop and her sister insisted this was not the case (*London Evening Standard*, 1 March 1838).

Furthermore. a witness to the Alsop assault testifies Millbank was present at the time of the assault and he challenged the witness saying "What have you to say to Spring-heeled Jack?" and later challenging the same witness demanding "What do you think of Spring-heeled Jack now?" (*The Times*, 2 March) The "outrage" was described in terms of a "suburban ghost", although Payne and Millbank were told if it were simply a "drunken frolic … it might be looked over by a severe remark of reprobation only" (*Morning Advertiser*, 1 March 1838), Nevertheless, when the court heard a renewed investigation on 2 March, the contradictions in the testimonies and a lack of evidence allowed Payne and Millbank to go free. And the original Spring-Heeled Jack faded out of the public eye to be replaced by imitators. However, because these imitators were caught and questioned, and it became clear Jack was a human agency and not a supernatural figure.

Despite the decline of reported sightings, Jack remained in the public interest through the performance of stage plays and then, a quarter of a century after the original reports, Spring-Heel'd Jack was the focus of a serial story. Here, Jack is a trickster, performing pranks according to his whims, but largely his role is to punish the bullies, the boastful and the malicious characters and to protect the vulnerable. In this story it is strongly inferred Jack is the *alter ego* of the Marquis of Waterford, even though Beresford had died some years before the story was published.

It became easy to connect Spring-Heeled Jack's reputation and antics to an unusual situation. An example is found in *All the Year Round* where a correspondent writes:

A wonderful sight, it was said, was witnessed on Primrose Hill one evening. On the summit appeared a huge figure of a man, in a flame of pale blue; it then assumed the bulk of a massive elephant, then of a windmill in full operation, and lastly, in lessening its dimensions, it became a large ball of snow, which rolled down the hill, and escapes further notice. What Spring-heeled Jack had to do with this dreadful appearance is not at all clear, but it was attributed to him, nevertheless, such was the hold that he had obtained over the public mind. (*All the Year Round*, 9 August 1884, 349)

Newspapers and commentators were willing to attach Spring-Heeled Jack's reputation to any incident. What should have been a ghost story for Christmas was taken too seriously by individuals and it was reported that men, women and children were terrified of leaving their homes for fear of encountering Jack.

Nearly two centuries after the original investigations, we can only suggest the role of Spring-Heeled Jack was played by many people across the so-called "canonical" appearances. Thomas Millbank remains the prime suspect for the Alsop and Scales assaults, and he clearly knew more than he revealed in court. Realistically, however, despite Jane Alsop's middle-class background, these attacks were never seen as more than drunken frolics or "pranks". However, Spring-Heeled Jack's character changed over the decades, according to what the public needed him to be: a wager between aristocratic youths, a menace stalking London and the villagers and frightening women, a ghost frightening the sentries at Aldershot Barracks, a man leaping Newport Arch at Lincoln or a man leaping from the rooftops. The eccentric and illusive nature of these events beguiled the public, and again, Jack's character adapted to what the audience wanted him to be: a masked aristocrat defending the vulnerable and the oppressed, a shadowy figure defending or undermining the rights of an unjustly treated noble, an embittered member of the community who turns against English society, or an ambivalent figure who oppresses or rewards according to his personal (and frequently changing) whims. Karl Bell notes there is no singular explanation for who or what Spring-Heeled Jack was; there are multiple facets to Jack's identity which meant he was 'bigger than any singular interpretation one may care to cage him in" (225–26). Quite simply, Spring-Heeled Jack developed according to the needs of the story. His name once invoked fear, and was used as a means of frightening naughty children into better behaviour. As we have seen, Jack now belongs in the past and his name is more associated with folklore than history. However, he may, one day, come back into the public eye to resume his position as

The *Terror* of London

J.S. Mackley
September 2021

Bibliography

"Penny Fiction" in *The Quarterly Review, July-October 1890.* (London: John Murray, 1890): 150–171.

"Terror by Night" in *Union Jack.*, No. 1357 (19 October): 1–24.

Skene, Anthony, "The Seven Matches Mystery", *Detective Weekly*, No. 14 (27 May 1933): 3–20, 24.

Bell, Karl. *The Legend of Spring-Heeled Jack: Victorian Urban Folklore and Popular Cultures.* Woodbridge: The Boydell Press, 2012.

Dash, Mike. 'The Devil's Hoofmarks: Investigating the Great Devon Mystery of 1855'. Steve Moore (ed.). *Fortean Studies.* Vol. 1. London: John Brown Publishing, 1994. 71–150.

Dash, Mike. 'Spring-Heeled Jack: To Victorian Bugaboo from Suburban Ghost'. Steve Moore (ed.). *Fortean Studies.* Vol. 3. London: John Brown Publishing, 1996. 7–125.

Dickens, Charles. *All the Year Round,* A weekly journal conducted by Charles Dickens. New Series, Volume XXXIV: 9th August 1884. 346.

Dyall, Valentine "Have you a Theory?" *Everybody's* Magazine. 20 February 1954: 12–13, 38–39.

Evan, Start and Skinner, Keith. *Jack the Ripper: Letters from Hell.* Stroud: Sutton Publishing, 2001.

Golicz, Roman. Spring-heeled Jack: A Victorian Visitation at Aldershot. 2nd Ed. Farnham: Don Namor Press, 2006.

Haining, Peter. *The Legend and Bizarre Crimes of Spring-Heeled Jack.* London: Frederick Muller Ltd, 1977.

Matthews, John. *The Legend of Spring-Heeled Jack: From Victorian Legend to Steampunk Hero.* Rochester, Vermont: Destiny Books, 2016.

Villiers, Elizabeth. 'Spring-Heeled Jack: The Unsolved Mystery' in *Stand & Deliver.* London Stanley Paul & Co, 1928, 238–252.

Vyner, J. "The Mystery of Springheel Jack". *Flying Saucer Review* 7, no. 3, May–Jun 1961: 3–6.

THE WINGED MAN
A MASTERPIECE OF MYSTERY
THE STORY OF A STRANGE GENIUS WHO, POSSESSED OF WONDERFUL
POWERS BY INVENTION, SETS OUT TO DEAL JUSTICE TO THE EVILDOERS
OF THE MODERN WORLD

°THE ESCAPED CONVICTS.

Crash!

With a roar louder than the heaviest ordnance, thunder awoke the echoes of night. The trembling trees groaned like souls in torment as they bent before the terrific storm, the terrors of which were quadrupled by thickly-falling snow, that gave the lightning-illuminated field, fell and forest that lay between the ruins of Fermoy's ancient stronghold and the mighty mass of Fermoy Towers the appearance of the dead world wrapped in a ghastly white winding sheet.

An hour before, a belated shepherd, fighting his way against the storm, had seen a bright light shining from a narrow slit in the castle wall, and, terror-stricken, hastened on, for fearful tales were whispered around the cottage fires at night of fearful deeds committed in Fermoy Castle in the old days, and how the old barons' uneasy spirits returned to re-enact on earth the nameless sins that had made men shudder when they walked the earth in mail-clad might.

But, wicked though the dead and gone masters who, in laced doublet and silken hose, had rendered the nights hideous, they were no worse than the five men who, having chosen the base of the ruined donjon keep as a temporary shelter from the storm, were clustered round a fire of logs that sent lurid tongues of flame mounting to the broken roof overhead.

Low-browed, sunken-eyed, big-jawed, the veriest child would have shrunk instinctively from the mildest-looking scoundrel there.

Beneath the well-cut garments, rough overcoats, and ragged cloaks—stolen from hovel, mansion, or cottage—they had donned could be detected the hideous grey cloak marked by the broad-arrow of his Majesty's penal establishments.

Fifty miles from Fermoy lay the great prison from which they had escaped the previous day. A thick fog, a pre-arranged signal, and seven stalwart convicts, wielding spades and pickaxes, had dashed through the encircling line of warders.

Of the seven who had made this bold dash for liberty, one crawled back to the prison, his legs riddled with buckshot; another, stricken by a warder's bullet, would never answer to his number again; but five grey fleeing forms had disappeared in the fog, and, avoiding all public roads and footpaths, had made their way across country to Fermoy Castle.

° 11 JANUARY 1913.

It was Black Jake, the man with the scar, who had led the way.

"Ugh! It is cold—cold as the grave!" shivered a pale-faced convict, as he rubbed his hands over the flames. "What an awful night for anyone in human shape to be out!"

Black Jake laughed.

"Just the night for our job, mates," he began. But ere he could complete the sentence he was interrupted by Big Mike, a burly convict, with a reckless, daring face, springing to his feet and pointing to where an ancient window overlooked the ruined castle's ancient courtyard.

"See—a spy! We are discovered!" he cried, as, snatching up a short, jagged iron bar stolen from a heap of scrap-iron outside a blacksmith's shop, he disappeared into the night, whilst his alarmed comrades, springing to their feet, prepared to follow him.

But ere they could gain the doorway an appalling, terror-laden shriek rose high above the tumult of the storm.

The next moment Big Mike, whining with terror, dashed past them, and clasping his hands at the back of his head, dropped face downwards to the floor.

In panic-stricken silence the convicts looked into the other's pallid faces.

"Cops?" demanded Black Jake at last, shaking the prostrate man roughly by the shoulder.

Struggling to his knees, Big Mike turned a face so full of haunting terror upon his chief that the latter stepped back and cast and in voluntary glance over his shoulder.

"No, no! I cannot describe it! If I think of it, if I speak of it, it will drive me mad!" whined the huge ruffian, who was reduced to a pitiable state of abject fright.

The convicts crowded together—as men will when threatened by some mysterious, some unknown danger.

"Speak up, man! What, Big Mike a coward? What have you seen? If it is anything earthly, I fear it not; if from another world, then it can't hurt us," declared their leader half faithfully, half defiantly.

The other seemed about to reply, but ere he could open his lips, a weird, horrible moan, plaintive as a lost child's despairing cry, shrill yet deep, long-drawn and reverberating, seemed to fill earth and heaven alike, and a shuddering sigh arose from each convict's lips when he saw, enframed in the jagged entrance to the tower, a dark, shapeless form with a ghastly, bloodless, white face, from which a pair of black, piercing eyes shone with a dull, indescribably horrible glare.

Shaking off the paralysis of fear that was robbing him of strength, the leader snatched a knife from his belt, and turned to attack the mysterious figure; but almost ere his advancing foot touched the ground the weird apparition vanished.

Terror and rage fighting for the upper hand in his heart, Jack paused on the threshold and looked around him in speechless amazement. The inner yard was a waste of recently-fallen snow, and the thickly-falling flakes the only moving objects in sight.

"Come, you curs, be men! Whoever it is, he must not leave these walls alive!" he thundered furiously. And his companions, stirred to action by their chief's example, poured through the doorway.

The knife dropped from his nerveless grasp, his whole frame grew rigid, and his blood seemed to turn to ice, as the challenge was answered by a fearful, bloodcurdling laugh, and, looking up, he saw a dark form clambering up the precipitous layers of flint to which none of mortal birth could cling.

Like men in the grasp of some fearful nightmare, the convicts watched the mounting figure until at length it stood, motionless as a statue, on the battlement summit of the tower.

Even as they gaped upwards it stretched out its long arms, batlike wings filled the space between its wrists and ankles, and as, moaning with terror, the convicts retreated in panic-stricken flight into the tower, the mysterious apparition dived from the battlement, glided swiftly across the inner yard, then disappeared over the opposite wall.

THE GATHERER OF THE SPOIL.

A deathlike silence obtained in Fermoy Towers. It was a night those who slept within its walls will long remember. To two people, at least, the past twelve hours had been a nightmare of suffering—a long farewell that shattered a man and a maid's dream of love.

All had retired to rest at a comparatively early hour, for on the morrow Lord Fermoy's daughter, the beautiful Lady Isabel, was to wed Sir Antony Coyle, an old, pleasure-loving libertine, whose evil life was hidden beneath the glitter of enormous wealth.

As the hour of one boomed forth, its echoing notes were taken up by an enormous mastiff chained in the courtyard at the rear of the house. The half-sleeping servants trembled in their beds as its deep-chested bay changed to a prolonged moan, then died away in a whimper of absolute terror, for it had seen a fearful, shapeless form glided towards a long-disused and ivy-hidden portal at the foot of the northern turret.

Two o'clock struck, and, gaining admittance from a door that had been left unlocked by an accomplice, Black Jake and Big Mike—the latter now entirely recovered from his fright—stole with stockinged feet along a dark landing, then up a back staircase, until they stood in a fine old gallery filled with portraits of dead and gone Earls of Fermoy, into which the principal bed-rooms opened.

Evidently Black Jake had the geography of the place by heart, for without a moment's hesitation he made his way to the chamber occupied by Lord Fermoy.

A moment's halt, to assure himself that all was still, and he pushed open the unfastened door. A flickering light from the well-piled hearth showed a room filled with priceless old furniture, such as money could not buy nowadays, the greater part of which had come from the old castle.

In one corner, looking out of place among the age-stained tables and chairs, was a big green safe, and sleeping on a silk-hanged, four-post bed opposite lay an old man, looking stern, grim, and relentless even in his sleep.

Without a word, Black Jake slipped his knife into Big Mike's hand, who, moving with noiseless strides, took his station at the head of the bed, where he stood motionless as a statue, hidden from the view by the silk curtains.

Sleep on, Earl of Fermoy, if you would live to see another sunrise. To awaken means certain death!

Confident that even if the sleeper awakened no sound would be allowed to pass his living lips. Black Jake knelt before the safe, and with workmanlike deliberation spread out a leather case, divided into a score of different compartments, each one containing an instrument of his nefarious art, on the carpet beside him. They were as bright and in as good order as when they had left the maker's hands, though for the last three months they had lain hidden in the outer walls of Fermoy Castle, whither an accomplice had deposited them ready for their master, if fortune favoured him and he made good his escape.

A well-satisfied smile upon his thick, ill-shaped lips—for a glance had shown him that the safe was of an obsolete pattern—the burglar commenced operations upon the lock.

So noiselessly did he work that a mouse nibbling at the wainscoting close at hand was not disturbed. Yet twenty minutes elapsed ere the safe was open, and its precious contents lay at the spoiler's mercy.

Immediately before him was a bag of gold, and this, with a surreptitious glance at his accomplice, the craftsman slipped into his pocket for his own special use and benefit.

Then he pulled out drawer after drawer emptying the contents—tiaras of diamonds, necklaces of pearls, bracelets, charms, snuff boxes encrusted with diamonds—into a stout canvas bag laying, mouth open, at his knees.

From the last drawer he drew a big morocco case, shaped like a large red heart, and grasping it in his knobbly, dirty hands, touched a spring that released the lid.

A low grunt of admiration caused his companion to turn, half wonderingly, half angrily, towards him.

"Jake's luck—Jake's good old luck!" muttered the burglar, in a voice that trembled with delight.

"The Fermoy collar! The Shah's Blood, by all that's ripping! I thought it would have been at the Bank, but I suppose it has been brought down for to-morrow's wedding," he added feasting his eyes upon a magnificent diamond collar four inches in depth, to which was attached as a pendant a magnificent blood-red ruby, worth a king's ransom.

His great prize under his arm, the bag clutched tightly in his left hand, Black Jake noiselessly closed the safe, and, beckoning his comrade to follow, glided from the room, drawing the door to after them.

Rapidly retracing their steps, they reached a diamond-framed window, filtered through which the beams of a newly-risen moon formed a checkered pattern upon the floor.

Unable to keep his good fortune longer to himself, he beckoned his companion to his side, and a volley of whispered oaths attested to Mike's admiration of the gems.

As, their heads together, the two scoundrels gloated over the diamond collar, the canvas of which was painted the portrait of John the Cruel, the seventh Baron of Fermoy, rose like a blind, and the Human Bat, slipping noiselessly through the frame, approached the unconscious burglars.

Then a hand snatched the collar from Black Jake's hand, and a low, mocking voice hissed in his ear:

"Ho, ho Black Jake! You do the work; I, the Human Bat, gather the spoil!"

The Winged Man robbed the thief of his spoils.

With the snarl of a tiger robbed of its prey, the burglar turned upon the new-comer; but only to have the bag of plunder snatched from his grasp.

"The Bat—the Human Bat!" arose from Big Mike's lips; and, turning on his heels, he rushed headlong down the servants' stairs, up which they had crept so cautiously half an hour before.

But Black Jake was made of sterner stuff, so, darting forward, he tried to seize his assailant by the throat.

Elusive as a shadow, the Human Bat soared to the lofty ceiling, and, hanging like a fly from its carved surface, rattled the bag of diamonds mockingly in his face; whilst Black Jake, gnashing his teeth with baffled rage, strove in vain to seize him, until the sudden opening of a door at the farther end of the gallery caused him to turn on his heels and follow his terrified accomplice.

IN THE PICTURE-GALLERY.

Detaching his legs from the ceiling, the Human Bat hung for a moment by his hands; then, ejecting the air from an apparatus which allowed him to cling to the smoothest surface, he dropped lightly at the feet of a beautiful girl, who, clad in a padded-silk, richly-laced dressing-gown, her long hair falling in a golden cascade over her shoulders, stood motionless, her deep blue eyes round and staring with unspeakable terror.

For some moments the lovely girl and the weird, unearthly midnight prowler confronted each other; then, his hand to his heart, the Human Bat bowed low.

"Lady Isabel Fermoy, I presume?" he said.

The most blood-curdling shriek, the most terrible threats, could not have astonished the girl more than this commonplace question, asked in the quiet, refined tones of a well-bred aristocrat.

Instinctively she retreated, but came to a halt as the Human Bat, this weird king of mystery, continued, speaking in the same low, well-modulated tones as before:

"I cannot express my regret that you should have been robbed of your beauty-sleep, Lady Isabel. Believe me, it was not my wish that the slightest disturbance should have broken your slumbers."

The girl looked at the bag and jewel-case hanging to an ingeniously-constructed belt round the other's waist, and despite her terror, braced herself up to speak.

"I can very well understand that," she replied, with a scornful toss of her head. "Thieves do not generally invite detection."

The Human Bat looked admiringly at the speaker. She was pale as death, but the only sign of fear she showed was the terror that lurked in her eyes, and a slight quivering of her upper lip.

"I presume that bag contains the Fermoy jewels. Keep them, but for the sake of an already stricken house, give me back the Shah's Blood. It is the 'Luck of Fermoy,' and terrible misfortune will follow its loss," she continued, looking in eager appeal at the mysterious man.

Without a word the Human Bat released the case from his belt.

"It is yours!" he said, handing it to her.

With a grateful bow the high-spirited girl thrust the case into the bosom of her dressing-gown.

"And now about yourself," continued the Human Bat, in quick but respectful tones. "I hear of a certain fair lady who must wed one I know to be a scoundrel and a callous-hearted villain. Does she do so of her own free will, or is she forced into a hateful union?"

The girl started as though the speaker had lashed her with a whip.

"I know not who you are—I know not whence you come, yet your strange appearance, your ready restoration of the Shah's Blood, proves you to be no common thief, perhaps no common being," she said, in low, excited tones; then stopped for her companion to reply; but the Human Bat stood with folded arms, his coal-black eyes fixed searchingly upon her; and, after a moment's hesitation, she continued:

"Yes, I will trust you. Sir Antony Coyle is repulsive to me. I loathe and hate him, but he holds a terrible power over my father. What it is I know not. It must be something greater even than the power of gold; more black, more terrible than I dare think of."

"And yet you love another?" asked the Human Bat.

A delicate rosy tint overspread the girl's clear forehead and swanlike neck; and then she raised her eyes, and looked unflinchingly into the face of her interrogator.

"Yes, I love Claude Doone, my father's secretary," she replied simply; then started back with a stifling cry of horrified amazement, for, with a warning gesture, the Human Bat wheeled swiftly round, and, springing almost to the ceiling, glided on outstretched wings to the portrait of John the Cruel, through which he disappeared.

As the canvas door closed behind him, the Human Bat drew a small glass stiletto from his belt, and made a tiny peephole, to which he applied his eye for a few moments, then continued his way with a low well-satisfied chuckle, for his spyhole had shown him that the footsteps which had caused his sudden flight were those of Claude Doone, and the lovers were looking into each other's eyes, the flight of time and the girl's late strange adventure alike forgotten in the delight of an interview that might be their last.

In the meantime, lighted by a small but exceedingly powerful electric lamp, that glowed like an enormous single eye from the centre of his close-fitting cap, the Human Bat traversed the narrow, dusty, long-since-forgotten secret passages by which Fermoy Towers was honeycombed, until the ivy-cupboard door by which he had entered was reached.

SIR ANTONY'S VISITOR.

Expelled from school, sent down from Oxford, cashiered[1] from the Army for actions unworthy of an officer and a gentleman, dipped in dissipation to the very lips, steeped in crime, a scoundrel without a heart, Sir Antony Coyle found himself at a comparatively early age a prematurely aged man.

---

[1] Dismissed in disgrace.

His riches had bought him every evil gratification; now they were to purchase a young and beautiful bride. On the morrow he would lead Isabel Fermoy to the altar, and those who knew Sir Antony best shuddered at the fate in store for the young girl.

Stretched on a huge, elaborate the-carved four-post bedstead in his bed-room in Coyle Priory, some ten miles across country as the crow flies from Fermoy Towers, Sir Antony Coyle lay in slumber, rendered restless by an evil conscience.

Presently he awoke with a start, and sat up; then—why or wherefore he could never tell—his eyes wandered to an old oaken press standing against the wall at the foot of his bed.

Even as he gazed the double doors of the press flew open, and a cry of horror, frozen ere it could find utterance, arose to his lips, as a strange, unearthly figure, in shape like an enormous bat, flew out, and perched on the wooden panel at his feet.

Then its outstretched wings changed into legs and arms, and a lithe, active form, clad in black garments which clung loosely about his body, stood revealed.

"Who are you? Whence come you? What do you want with me!" demanded the affrighted baronet.

A loud, unearthly laugh struck like a death-knell upon his ears.

"Who should I be but a self-invited wedding-guest!" demanded the strange visitor. "If you can shake me off between now and the hour fixed for your wedding all may be well. If not—well, the worse for you, the better for Lady Isabel."

"What are you—man or spirit?" demanded the trembling baronet.

For reply, the Human Bat sprang from the footboard, raised Sir Antony in his arms, and threw him as easily as though he had been a child into the middle of the room.

"Could a spirit do that?" he laughed.

But, although Sir Antony had had such striking proof of his weird visitor's earthly origin, the terror of the supernatural was on him, and, whimpering like a stricken child, he proceeded, in obedience to an imperative gesture from his visitor, to don his clothes.

Then, with a wild yell of terror, the baronet dashed headlong from the room.

As he sped down a wide corridor, a number of guests, invited to the Priory for the wedding, rushed from their rooms and stood aghast, as they saw their host fleeing down the corridor before a strange, weird, fearful-looking being that covered the ground in long, loping strides.

Casting a terrified glance over his shoulder, Sir Antony reached the stairhead; then rushed, three steps at a time, down the oaken stairs to the hall door.

Throwing aside the fastening with trembling fingers, he dashed into the night, closely followed by the flying man; whilst the astounded spectators, whose ranks had been strengthened by the arrival of indoors servants, grooms, and gamekeepers, brought up the rear.

Almost mad with fright, Sir Antony made straight for a large sheet of ornamental water, intent upon seeking refuge from the terror that pursued him in death.

With a loud, despairing cry, he was about to fling himself into the lake, when the Human Bat, springing over his head, alighted on the brink of the lake and thrust him back.

Close at hand, hidden from view by a fine belt of trees, was a disused quarry, and thither the tortured man turned his frenzied steps; but the relentless form followed with long, easy strides that cleared a dozen feet at each step, and was before him once more.

Panting and well-nigh spent, huge drops of cold perspiration chasing each other down his pallid face, Sir Antony wheeled round and dashed back to the Priory, which he gained just in time to slam the door in his pursuer's face.

Baffled for a moment, the Human Bat stood gazing with flashing eyes upon the crowd of servants and visitors, who shrunk in terror from him.

Suddenly a huge, bronze-faced man—a world-famed big-game hunter, who feared neither man nor fiend—stepped to the front, and fired a '45 Colt revolver point-blank into the Human Bat's breast.

The spear of flame from the pistol's muzzle seemed to pierce the apparition's very heart; but, with a loud, mocking laugh, he sprang from the ground, and cries of amazement arose from every lip as the spectators watched him climb up the side of the ivy-clad wall as easily as though it was level ground.

"Quick—a light!" shouted the explorer; and a groom, his teeth chattering with terror, thrust a stable-lantern into his hand.

Raising it high above his head, the explorer examined the strange visitant's track, to find that wherever his hands or feet had alighted the ivy was torn away in patches.

"Man or demon, he shall not escape me! Fifty pounds to the man who brings him down!" cried the explorer.

Then, directing half a dozen grooms and gardeners to remain below, ready to seize the flying man if he ventured to descend, he led a dozen men, armed with cudgels, knives, rifles, and shot-guns—in fact, any weapon they could snatch up on the spur of the moment—to the roofs of the big, straggling building.

A WILD RIDE.

Then commenced to chase such as those who took part in it will never forget. The Human Bat seemed in every part of the Tower at once. Now the sullen roar of a gamekeeper's gun would proclaim that he had been sighted on the southern extremity; the next second a white-faced footman would drop his hastily-assumed weapon, trembling, to find that the white-masked face was leering at him from behind some grotesquely-contorted chimney.

Now floating in visible in the darkness above his pursuer's head, now clearing an intervening courtyard at a bound, the Human Bat easily evaded pursuit.

Soon an expected sound fell upon his ears, and a strange, unfathomable smile divided his white, almost bloodless lips.

It was the low "teuf-teuf" of a recently started motor-car. Gliding unseen a few feet above the explorer's head, he took his stand on the pinnacle of the tower immediately over the stables just as, bending low over the steering-wheel, Sir Antony Coyle drove his new forty-horse power Panhard from its garage.

Waiting until the car had got a hundred yards' start down the winding carriage-drive, the Human Bat opened his black pinions and took up the chase.

The trees prevented his sweeping down upon the car at once, but at the park gates he alighted on the back of the vehicle, then thrusting his hand into his chest, his fingers encountered some rough substance, which he drew forth with a smile.

It was the flattened bullet of the explorer's revolver, which had been stopped by a thin but impenetrable steel plate he wore over his chest.

Then, as the fleeing baronet advanced the spark, and the magnificent car tore over the ground at a tremendous rate, he attached one end of a thin wire cable to the woodwork of the vehicle, and, passing the other end through a loop in a belt he wore round his chest, stood for a moment on the back of the car, spread out his wings, and hovered half a dozen feet above the unconscious driver's head.

For some minutes he remained thus; then, descending, reached forth one long, white finger, and touched the driver on the shoulder. With a loud, piercing shriek the baronet released his hold of the steering-wheel. In a moment the car swerved, but ere it could plunge into the ditch the Human Bat's firm grasp had brought it back on to the road once more.

Almost instinctively the baronet resumed control of the wheel, and, his awful companion floating like some fearful bird of prey over his head, the car resumed its fearful journey.

On they flew, on and on. Trees, houses, hedges flew past in quick succession; whilst the car's terror-maddened driver now and again looked fearfully over his shoulder at the relentless pursuer he was trying so vainly to shake off.

Topping the brow of a steep hill, the car flashed like lightning down the opposite side. There was a momentary glimpse of red light, a shock, a crash, followed by the sound of rending wood, and the air was filled with splinters; then, the mud-guards on one side completely tore off, her bonnet bruised and battered, yet with her engines uninjured, the car, having smashed through the stout gates of a level crossing, continued with her mad career.

Another long, stiff climb, and the Human Bat drew closer to the frenzied face of the driver.

"Slacken down, Sir Antony, or you will be over the cliff!" he ordered.

"Ay, ay, I know the road well! A sharp bend, a low wall, a gentle slope of fifty yards, then a fall of two hundred feet over a cliff into the merry, dancing sea. Ha, ha! A grand ride—the ride of a lifetime!" almost shrieked Sir Antony Coyle, who, for the time being, was mad and hysterical through terror of the fearful foe who was dogging him to his death.

Almost ere the words left his lips the front wheel of the car struck the wall of which he had spoken. Fortunately, the terrific speed at which she was travelling saved her.

She rose like a hunter to its fence, struck the ground with a force that almost hurled Sir Antony from his seat, then dashed straightforward over an uneven pasture, beyond which could be heard the never-ceasing roar of billows breaking upon ironbound rocks.

A dozen turns of the wheel, and the car, with that fearful, outstretched form hovering like some awful, shapeless cloud over it, shot over the edge of the cliff, tilted forward, then dashed head-foremost towards the restless, hungry sea below.

The car, with that menacing form hovering above it, shot over the edge of the cliff.

DOOMED.

With starting eyeballs, hair on end, his heart beating like the piston of an engine, Sir Antony Coyle uttered a loud shriek of terror as the car shot over the edge of the cliff, her racing engines causing her wheels to revolve at a fearful pace.

Wildly he glanced around. Above shone the clear, pitiless sky; beneath tossed the restless sea. No hope, no chance of life above or below. He was doomed. A sickening drop through space, a plunge beneath the waves, then—

No, he; he dare not—he would not die! It was his wedding morn. His death would set Lady Isabel firmly free to marry the man he hated, the man she loved.

Suddenly the half-formed curse with which he was about to meet his death died away in a shuddering moan. There was a rustle of wings above his head, the sweeping dive of an enormous black form, and, clasped tightly in the arms of the Human Bat, the baronet was snatched from out the falling car, which, turning twice in its descent, struck the waves with a report like that of a cannon.

A sheep at bay will fight for its life. Like a hard-pressed tiger Sir Antony turned upon his capture, and strove to drag him down to the fearful depths beneath.

Apparently, his vengeful scheme was successful, for the Human Bat ceased to struggle, and the two, turning over and over in the air hurtled headlong towards the sea.

Down they went, down, and down, until, when but a dozen feet separated them from the hungry waves, the Human Bat rolled over on to his back, and his wings shooting out, they alighted on the water as gently as a feather from a wild gull's wing.

All the fight frightened out of the baronet by the fall, Sir Antony clung tightly to the Human Bat, expecting every moment to feel the waves closing over his head. But the watertight wings kept them both afloat, and Sir Antony gazed, wonder-struck into the white, mocking face of the being to whom earth, air, and water seemed alike.

"It is a dream—a fearful dream," the baronet muttered, through his chattering teeth.

"A dream? Ay, a dream that will haunt you until death gives release from my power, unless you swear to give up all claim to Lady Isabel Fermoy!" came in stern tones from the Human Bat.

"I cannot! I am pledged—" began Sir Antony, when, to his horror, the Human Bat sunk like a stone beneath the surface, leave him struggling in the sea.

"Help—help! I am drowning! Help!" shrieked Sir Antony, beating the water, too horrified to even attempt to swim.

"Swear!" cried a solemn voice immediately overhead.

He turned and gasped with horror. The Human Bat, who a minute before had disappeared beneath the surface of the icy-cold, foam-flecked sea, was flying, with slow, regular beats of his enormous wings, just above his head.

"Yes, I will swear anything, only save me!" he yelled.

Even as the last frenzied appeal left his lips he turned a white, pallid face to the Human Bat. Then the water closed over his head, and he would have disappeared from the sight of man for ever had not a long-jointed steel arm, terminating in five iron, finger-like grapples, shot from the Human Bat's side, and, seizing him by the collar of his coat, carried him towards where a mighty rock reared its granite head above the waves, some forty yards from the shore.

Upon this rock the Human Bat deposited his burden.

Barely had his iron arm released its hold ere Sir Antony Coyle sank, a shivering heap of humanity, on to the rock.

Clinging with frenzied strength to a projecting pinnacle, he turned his fear-contorted face towards his terrible foe.

"Don't leave me! I shall be drowned or starved to death! You would not murder me?" he whimpered.

Without deigning to answer the terrified man's appeal, the Human Bat pointed to where a fisherman's boat approached on a course that would bring her past the rock; then, with a warning, "Beware! Prove false to your oath, and it were better you had never seen the light of day!" glided swiftly to the foot of the cliff, up which the astounded baronet saw him clamber, until, the summit reached, he waved his hand—it might have been in menace, it might have been in farewell—ere he disappeared from view.

RECEIVER OF STOLEN GOODS.

Night had fallen over the wealth and poverty, the misery and happiness, the luxury and destitution of Leeds. Already the more fashionable streets of the great Midland town were emptying.

Within, probably, the worst court, abutting on High Street, is a large, ramshackle, old house.

In the basement is a kitchen, where thieves resort, to poison themselves with vile liquor, to lay their plans for future robberies, or to divide recently-gained "swag."

The next two floors are let out to half a dozen families, nursed and brought up in crime and vice.

Above all is a garret, lighted in daytime by a gable window, fifty feet from the ground. To-night a sputtering candle in a black bottle, placed at one end of a rickety deal table,[2] which, save for a broken chair and an old egg-box, was the only furniture the miserable place contains, shed its beams over the scene.

Seated on either side of the table are two men, one with the strong-marked features, hook nose, and long, straggling locks of a Russian Jew.

It is Simon Leichkoff, factory owner and sweater during the day; "fence," or receiver of stolen goods, at night.

His companion is a decrepit old man, with long, white hair. He is clad in a strangely-shaped, cape-like cloak, and ragged slouched hat. A grey beard hides

---

[2] A table made of deal, a type of wood.

from view a face as white as that of a corpse.

The Jew's eyes are bright with greed, his talent-like fingers opening and shutting convulsively, whilst his whole frame trembles with excitement.

Seldom has Simon Leichkoff beheld so valuable a booty, for, looking strangely out of place in that miserable garret, the Fermoy family diamonds are reflecting back the yellow rays of the guttering candle.

"As you have not the money it is useless wasting more time," said the old man, making as though he would sweep the jewels into his pocket.

"Ach, I said not so! Be not in a hurry! I am poor—very poor, and to buy these diamonds will take of my money the whole. But it is here—here in my pocket, all but fifty pounds," he added, after a moment's hesitation.

The old man rose, and swept the diamonds into a heap.

"No, no; go not! Ah, I remember, there is one leetle fifty-pound note I have saved for the day when it rains! You will not take an old man's all?" pleaded the Jew. He knew the deal would bring him a good fifty per cent profit, but yet he was not satisfied.

"Then produced it—quickly, too. I never haggle!" ordered the old man.

Sighing and groaning, Leichkoff drew a dirty pocket-book from an inside pocket, and carefully counted out the desired amount.

His companion watched his slow actions with evident impatience.

Neither man noticed that a square trapdoor immediately above their heads was open, a hand, grasping a shining revolver, thrust through, and beyond it the round, good-humoured face of Sergeant Bride, the smartest detective the Midlands has ever produced.

Patiently Bride waited until the notes had been handed over to the elder man, then uttered aloud "Ahem!"

With a cry of alarm, the Jew clutched at the diamonds as a drowning man would a straw. His companion did not move a muscle, but looked calmly into the threatening muzzle of the revolver.

"Thought you might want a witness to your little deal, gentlemen!" said Sergeant Bride good-humouredly. "Keep your hands from your pockets, and you won't get hurt. Don't try any tricks. The house is surrounded, and—Ah, would you?"

A bullet from his revolver ploughed its way into the floor alongside the Human Bat, as, his hat, false beard, and wig thrown aside, shielding his face with his arm, he charged at the window.

A second shot, a crash of broken glass, and, plunging through the dirty panes the Human Bat disappeared into the black void beyond.

"Heavens, the fool is mad! He will be dashed to pieces!" ejaculated the astonished detective. "Leave those diamonds alone, Leichkoff!" he added sharply, as, taking advantage of the confusion consequent upon his companion's strange and apparently suicidal flight, the Jew tried to thrust a few of the bigger stones into a secret recess beneath the table.

With a groan of despair the Jew obeyed, for the order was enforced by a significant wave of the still-smoking revolver, whilst its wielder, putting a police-whistle to his lips, blew a loud shrill blast.

Then came the sound of many men running up the uncarpeted stairs, and Leichkoff new that it was all up with him. He had been caught red-handed, and must pay the penalty of his many crimes.

"Who was with you? You might as well tell; it won't do him any good to keep silent, poor chap?" asked the detective, keeping his man covered until his assistants arrived.

"By my beard, I don't know! He—" began Leichkoff. He ceased speaking, and gazed in open-mouthed amazement and terror at a white face, lighted up by the powerful white beams of an electric light that blazed from the centre of his forehead, which, despite the absence of the false beard, he recognised as that of the man he believed to be lying a mutilated corpse on the pavement below, that was peering mockingly at him from over the detective's shoulder.

Following the direction of the Jew's bulging eyes, Bride turned to look over his shoulder. Even as he did so the back of his neck was seized in an iron grasp, a strong hand was slid down his arm, and ere he realised what was about to happen the revolver had been snatched from his grasp and hurled into the room beneath.

Sergeant Bride was a heavy man, yet almost without an effort the strange being, who in some mysterious way had entered the skylight by which he himself had gained admittance to the roof, rolled him over on to his back.

"I congratulate you, Sergeant Bride. You have come nearer arresting me than any man I have ever encountered," said the Human Bat tauntingly.

"I'll have you yet!" retorted the plucky detective.

"Never! The man has yet to be born who can capture the Human Bat!" was the defiant reply. "Farewell! We will meet again!"

Suddenly releasing his hold of his prisoner, the Human Bat disappeared through the skylight.

Scrambling to his feet, Sergeant Bride followed.

Half in, half out of the skylight, he paused, a thrill of superstitious terror tingling through his veins.

Standing upright on a stack of chimneys on the opposite side of the street, whither no mortal man could have fled in the time, was the Human Bat.

Even as he gazed a tremulous, mournful cry filled the air, and, spreading his wings to the breeze, the Human Bat flew out of sight into the dark, snow-laden air.

BENEATH THE LEEDS ARCHES.

Alighting in Park Square, the Human Bat walked slowly in the direction of Park Lane. Presently he came to an abrupt halt, then stole noiselessly into a neighbouring doorway.

A few seconds later Sir Antony Coyle walked by his place of concealment with the quick, stealthy steps of one engaged upon a secret errand.

Noiselessly the Human Bat stepped from the sheltering doorway and hastened after the unsuspecting baronet, who, having crossed West Street, and traversed the whole length of Queen's Street, turned to the left, and made his way towards Wellington Station.

Here he left the main thoroughfare, and the Human Bat quickened his steps as his quarry turned down a by-lane that would take him to Leeds' famed arches, gloomy tunnels, through which the River Aire flows beneath the Midland, North-Eastern, and London and North-Western railway-stations.

Ahead loomed a gloomy, circular opening, but ere he ventured on to the wooden platform, or bridge, which has been erected for foot passengers beneath the arches, Sir Antony came to a halt beneath a lamp-post, and carefully examined a small revolver he had drawn from his pocket.

Slipping the weapon up his sleeve, the baronet hesitated, then plunged boldly into the dark, little-trodden path.

The arches of Leeds is a forbidding place even in bright daylight. At night no spot seems a better fitted for the committal of dark deeds.[3]

Unhappy, indeed, the lot of the wayfarer, attacked by robbers on the narrow bridge over those dark, subterranean waters.

No ear can hear his despairing cry for help, no hand will be stretched forth to save him, for the arches are shunned, as though accursed by all who know their evil reputation.

As Sir Antony disappeared in the darkness, the Human Bat sprang to the top of the nearest arch, and, suspended by hands and feet from its slime-covered bricks, scrambled on all fours along it.

Presently the tread of the baronet's footsteps on the echoing bridge ceased. Peering through the darkness, the Human Bat, whose keen eyes could pierce the darkness at night, saw him place his back against the brick wall of the arch, for, echoing beneath the hollow brickwork, came the sound of slouching footsteps.

The Human Bat's instinct had not deceived him. An assignation had drawn the baronet from his hotel.

A meeting at such a time, and in such a place, could but be for some evil end.

Stealthily creeping along the top of the arch until abreast of Sir Antony Coyle, the Human Bat pressed his body close to the dark, time-stained bricks.

---

[3] The "Dark Arches" were constructed in 1869 to support a new railway station, spanning the River Aire, Neville Street and Swinegate.

Nearer and nearer came the footsteps, and soon the Human Bat's keen eyes detected a man clad in rough home spun, with a cloth cap drawn over his eyes, whose face was disfigured by a livid scar that ran from the corner of his left eye to his mouth, approaching.

A tremulous "Hallo!" brought the newcomer to a halt within a few feet of the baronet.

"Hallo yourself! Turned up, eh, Sir Antony Coyle, Bart.?" sneered the Man With the Scar.

"Hush! Not so loud! There's no need to mention names. You can never tell who's about," interposed Sir Antony hastily.

"Why, bless your frightened heart, there's nobody here this time of night! If I wanted to 'out' you, you might scream your gizzard out, and no one would hear you!" was the reassuring reply.

Sir Antony drew back in alarm.

"You needn't be scared!" chuckled the Man With the Scar, evidently enjoying the other's terror. "I ain't a-going to prison for the likes of you, I can promise you brought the notes?"

Sir Antony hesitated, and the Human Bat saw large drops of cold perspiration standing on his face.

"Yes. Have you the—er—letters?" he asked.

"Rather! And the other thing, too! Come, hand over the rhino![4] Here's your lot. I want to be off. I'm a bit particular as to the company I keep, and it wouldn't do my character any good to be seen with the likes of you!" said the Man With the Scar insolently.

Sir Antony thrust his hand into his breast pocket, but withdrew it again.

"How do I know the real letters are there?" he demanded.

"You've got to trust your luck," retorted the villain, "as I do. Mrs. Rupert, of Tinder Street, York, wouldn't ask so many questions, nor would Lady Isabel. There wouldn't be much of a wedding to-morrow if the truth was known."

The Human Bat started, and glared angrily at the baronet, who he now knew had broken his oath.

"No, no; anything that that!" Almost shrieked the baronet. "The wedding must come off, if only to spite the Human Bat. Once Lady Isabel is mine, once I have broken her proud spirit, and brought her grovelling to my feet, you can produce that Mrs. Rupert, and rid me of her."

"Who's this Human Bat you talk so glibly about?" asked the Man With the Scar curiously.

Sir Antony looked fearfully around.

"Hush! Don't speak so loud! He may be listening to us this very minute. He's a thing, a fiend if you like, with the power to fly like a bird, jump like a grasshopper, or swim like a fish."

---

[4] Cash.

"And with a face as makes you shudder to look at?" demanded the Man With the Scar, in a low voice.

"Yes, that's him—" began the baronet, when he was interrupted by a volley of low but fierce oaths from the Man With the Scar.

"Then it's this flying, Spring-heeled demon as robbed me of the Fermoy diamonds!" cried the Man With the Scar viciously. "If ever I come across him again, I will—"

The rest of the sentence was drowned in a shriek of terror, as, with starting eyeballs and pallid cheeks, he pressed against the rail of the bridge.

There was a dead pause, and in the silence from out the darkness somewhere overhead came an ominous flapping, like that of some huge night-bird testing its pinions ere taking flight.

The sound and the darkness was terrible, and full of ominous menace. It was, indeed, a sound to conjure up terrible visions to such an evil conscience as the baronet possessed.

Sir Antony quailed, and his frame quivered as if with ague, as he watched the terror in the eyes of his companion.

"What is it? What do you see?" he hissed between his chattering teeth.

The Man With the Scar made no reply. Only hoarse, gurgling moans were issuing from his foam-flecked lips.

"What is it? Speak, you fool!" hissed Sir Antony again, for the silence had become intolerable. He felt he would go mad.

But it did not require the Man With the Scar to tell him what it was. He knew.

"It's—it's up there—against the roof—somewhere!" groaned the Man With the Scar hoarsely.

And he crouched down lower, his eyes glaring round, endeavouring to pierce the gloom and to locate the ominous foe whom he knew lurked somewhere in the shadows overhead. Sir Antony pulled himself together. He was armed; he had a revolver. True, he had meant it, perhaps, for another use. But there was six barrels to it. He let it slide down his sleeve into his hand. He, too, crouched down.

"That's it," muttered the Man With the Scar—"that's it! You've got a shooter! Good! Give him a taste of it! See once for all whether he's human or the fiend himself!"

There came in answer a weird, mocking laugh, sardonic, and with no ring of humanity at all in it.

The Man With the Scar gave a hoarse howl.

"Fire!" he gurgled. "Fire! It's our lives or his!"

Again, in answer, came only that terrible, uncanny peal of mirth.

Both men came upright to their feet. Their one desire now was to flee the scene.

But they had not the power to move an inch. They stood rooted to the ground, paralysed with horror. For between them both had alighted, silently as ever, a dread, grim, black form—the form of the King of mystery himself—the Human Bat.

WHAT THE BUNDLE OF LETTERS CONTAINED.

Very terrible to the conscience-stricken scoundrels appeared the Human Bat, as he alighted between them, his white face contorted with rage, and the brilliant glare of his electric torch shining like a single baneful eye from the centre of his forehead.

For nearly a minute no sound was heard but the laboured breathing of the two men.

Then the Human Bat spoke.

"I am here, Black Jake; what do you want with me?" he said, in deep, awful tones.

"I—I—nothing. I only—" stammered the dumbfounded man through chattering teeth.

"Pshaw, coward! You are beneath my vengeance," interrupted the Human Bat. "Quick, those letters!"

Cowed and trembling, the Man With the Scar surrendered the tell-tale papers he had taken from Sir Antony Coyle's safe the night following his interview with the Human Bat.

"The notes!" thundered the Human Bat.

"Take them—and this!" shrieked Sir Antony.

As the Human Bat's fingers closed over the rustling banknotes, a spear of lurid flame shot from the baronet's concealed revolver, and a dull, leaden report echoed a thousand times through the domes of the arches.

But ere the thunderous report died away, a loud, shrill cry of pain arose from behind the Human Bat, and the Man With the Scar, stricken in the thick of his arm by Sir Antony's bullet, crashed through the rotten rail into the dark-flowing waters.

Then a loud, mocking laugh turned Sir Antony's blood to ice, as, rising on extended wings, the Human Bat flew unscathed towards the arches.

Cries for help from the river roused Sir Antony Coyle from the stupor of horror into which he had fallen.

It was not humanity that impelled the baronet to hasten to his accomplice's assistance. The loss of the papers must be made good in some way, and the only course now open to him was to employ Black Jake to get Mrs. Rupert into his power without delay.

"Where are you?" he cried, running in the direction from whence the cry had come.

"Here, clinging to one of the supports! Quick! Your bullet has shattered my arm! I cannot hold on a minute longer," came with oaths from out of the darkness. And, groping over the rotten planks, Sir Antony had soon drawn the wounded man from his previous position.

In the meantime the Human Bat alighted on the roof of the biggest hotel in Leeds.

He was far from his usual haunts, and tired with an exciting night's work.

Crawling, flylike, down the wall, he at length reached a window. This he opened by slipping back the hasp with the blade of his knife; then, entering the room, closed the window behind him. The room was empty.

Having locked the door, he turned on the electric light, took out the bundle of letters he had obtained from Black Jake, and went swiftly through them.

As he read, an angry frown darkened the Human Bat's brow.

The letters were from a woman to her husband, begging him, for the sake of the love he once bore her, to return to her child and herself.

There was also an oblong slip of paper—a certificate of marriage, which showed that that husband was none other than Sir Antony.

Thrusting the letters into his pocket, the Human Bat turned a regretful glance upon the luxurious couch he had hoped to occupy till morning, when, as was his custom, he would go by the way he had come, leaving a handsome tip where the chambermaid would see it on entering the room the next morning to pull up the blinds.

There must be no sleep for him that night.

Well he knew that the unscrupulous baronet would not hesitate to murder the unfortunate woman rather than she should come between himself and his marriage with the rich and high-born Lady Isabel.

Cautiously raising the window, the Human Bat stood for a moment balanced on the sill, then spread his wings in flight.

As he soared over the roofs of the town the loud, shrill whistle of a locomotive rent the air.

He turned in the direction from whence the sound came, and saw the Eastern night mail thundering through Leeds on its way to York.

Turning in the direction of the railway, the Human Bat beat the air with his wide wings in frenzied haste. His eyes were fixed upon the sparks from the funnel of the express, like fire from the mouth of some mighty, old-time dragon.

It was later than he had thought. He had hoped to have been outside Leeds ere the express overtook him.

A woman's happiness, perhaps a woman's life, depended upon his getting to York before Sir Antony Coyle's creatures could reach that city.

A WILD RACE.

Straining every nerve, the Human Bat flew as he had never flown before, his mark the border-land between Leeds and her most eastern suburb, where a stretch of comparatively open ground gave room for his contemplated swoop.

As with laboured breath he toiled towards his goal, the rising wind seemed to hold him back. But he persevered, and reached the railway just as, groaning and grunting like some living being, the engine passed beneath him.

Folding his wings, the Human Bat dropped like a stone. As he did so a more fierce gust of wind than any that had preceded it sent him slanting towards the end of the long string of carriages.

An ejaculation of despair burst from his lips.

He had missed!

No!

Even as the last spark of hope died within his bosom, his outstretched hand caught the rail at the rear of the guard's van, and, holding on like grim death, he felt his body swaying like a wet flag behind the train.

The strain was fearful, but only for a moment. The next the Human Bat bent his body downward, his sucker-armed feet fastened on the back of the van, and as he pressed his body against the woodwork his wings draped themselves snugly round his body.

He was safe until the train reached its destination.

It was bitterly cold. The air was laden with frozen sleet, that forced its way into every crevice of his strange garb.

But cold or heat were alike to the Human Bat when he had work on hand, and he held on with all his strength whilst the train rattled and roared through deep cuttings, over bridges, through tunnels, until at last it began to slow down; then, releasing his hold of the van, the Human Bat sailed slowly away in the direction of York's ancient walls.

There was not a city in the British Isles, and few in Europe, unknown to the Human Bat.

Over the city walls he flew, across the Ouse; then, halting for a moment on the highest tower of the old castle, glided swiftly to one of the narrow streets of old-time houses for which York is famed.

It was Tinder Street.

Alighting in the yard at the back of one of the houses, he climbed slowly up its walls, stopping to peer into every window, and flashing a momentary blaze of light from the lantern in the centre of his cap upon the occupants.

Presently he crouched on the sloping sill of a window through which he had seen what he sought—a man sleeping alone.

Noiselessly he forced back the old-fashioned hasp, and, swinging the window open, entered.

With the stealthy tread of a tiger stalking its prey, he neared the wretched bed upon which the unconscious sleeper lay.

Bending over his victim, the Human Bat seized him by the throat, and at the same time flashing his headlights into his eyes, and saying, in low but fearfully distinct tones:

"Remain silent, and fear no harm! A word, even a whisper, and the worst your mind can conceive shall befall you!"

The man gazed at the fearful, white face, tongue-tied with terror.

"There is a Mrs. Rupert in this house," continued the Human Bat, adding, as the terror-stricken wretch looked at him as though he had not heard: "Speak! I can reward as well as punish!

"Yes; top attic," stammered the man.

"Arise, go to her room; say that a messenger from her husband awaits leave to visit her, then return. Beware how you attempt to play me false. The deepest mine, the highest mountain, shall not hide you from my vengeance if you prove false. Go!"

As he felt those iron fingers withdrawn from his throat, the man rose, and, hastily dressing, crept swiftly from the room.

The Human Bat stood with every muscle drawn tight, ready to spring after his messenger if he attempted flight.

But the scared man was duly impressed by the warning he had received, and the Human Bat heard his footsteps sending the stairs.

Three minutes later he returned.

"Well?" demanded the Human Bat.

"She will be ready to receive you in five minutes," replied the man.

"Good! You will remain in this room during the night, and will never tell a soul of my visit, or dread my wrath. Here is payment for your work."

And from the Human Bat two five-pound notes fluttered down upon the floor.

AN INTERRUPTED WEDDING.

Five minutes later the Human Bat entered Mrs. Rupert's wretched attic, and gazed with interest upon a faded, poverty-stricken woman of about thirty, who still bore traces of great beauty.

"You are from my husband?" asked Mrs. Rupert. Then she stopped, terrified by the white, death-like face and the fierce, penetrating eyes that confronted her. Was this a man, or some dread being—a creature of her imagination? She brushed her hand across her eyes.

The next moment the Human Bat's face seemed transformed.

"Yes, Lady Coyle, I have come to escort you to him," replied the King of Mystery, in his deep, sepulchral but organ-like tones.

The woman started, and the pallor on her face deepened.

"You are mistaken. My name is Rupert," she said, one hand on her heart, the other resting on a rickety table in the centre of the room.

"Ralph Rupert and Sir Antony Coyle are one and the same!" exclaimed the Human Bat. "But we have no time to spare. You shall know all later. Entrust yourself to me, and I will take you to your husband."

"But my child?" objected the mother, pointing to a wealth of golden curls peeping from beneath the bedclothes.

"He must accompany us. See, here is the certificate of your marriage. Should we be separated, it will aid you to regain your rights," said the Human Bat, handing a piece of paper to the astounded woman.

"My marriage lines!" gasped Mrs. Rupert. Then, as though the sight of the certificate had opened some old wound, she dropped into a chair and sobbed bitterly. "No, no; I can never return to him. The last time we met he tore this paper from my hand. See, I still carry the mark of the blow he gave me as I clung to him, and begged him not to leave me," she added, pointing to a slight scar half hidden by her right eyebrow.

"Woman, for that boy's sake, as well as your own, you must take your proper station in the world," declared the Human Bat. "Besides, there is yet another reason why you must accompany me to-night. To-morrow at twelve o'clock, Sir Antony will lead to the altar a girl whose father is forcing her to marry a man she hates and despises."

With a low, moaning cry, Mrs. Rupert swayed, and would have fallen, had not the Human Bat caught her in his arms.

Laying her gently down, he held a queerly-shaped glass vial to her nose. A few minutes later her breathing grew deep and regular, and he knew she had fallen into a sleep, from which she would not awaken until he chose.

Leaning gently over the sleeping child, he administered the sleeping-gas to him also, then, having secured him to his mother's breast with strips torn from the bedclothing, he carried the two up a rough ladder which led through a skylight to the roof.

Mother and child clasped tightly in the grip of his steel arms, the Human Bat spread his wings and leapt into the air.

But the wind was now blowing a gale from the east, with the result that it was only by superhuman efforts that he saved himself from being dashed against the roofs and chimney-pots over which he was flying.

Unencumbered, the Human Bat could have laughed at the gale, and, opening wide his powerful wings, have been blown swiftly back to Leeds.

But the deadweight of the mother and child bore him down, and it was with difficulty he kept abreast the gale.

At last, worn out with his fearful fight against the wind, he alighted on the railway a mile beyond the village of Holgate.

Baffled but not beaten, the Human Bat looked about him for shelter, and saw, close at hand, a platelayer's hut. But he did not enter. Lying by the side of the hut was a trolley.

This is the Human Bat lifted on to the rails, then, breaking into the platelayer's hut, he secured a coil of rope, with which he bound his charges to the rough wooden platform, ere, springing on to the trolley, he stood with his feet glued firmly by their suckers to the boards, and slowly opened his wings.

Soon the trolley began to move, and as the strong sombre folds of the Human Bat's wings were opened wider, she dashed over the rails with constantly increasing speed, until at last she rivalled the speed of an express train.

The strain was fearful.

The gale tore at his wings, as though it would tear his arms from their sockets. But the Human Bat stood as firm as an iron mast, his wondrous electric eye casting a shining bar of light over the glistening rails before him.

An hour past; then, with a sigh of relief, the Human Bat drew in his wings, and the pace slackened until at last they came to a halt just outside Leeds.

Turning the trolley which had stood him in such good stead off the line, the Human Bat took Mrs. Rupert and her boy in his arms, clambered to the top of a high building, then launched himself into the air.

A strong wind was still blowing, but it was not so fierce as at York, and ere many minutes had passed, the Human Bat sank, with a sigh of relief, amongst the thirteen bells in St. Peter's Tower.

At noon the following day a large and fashionable gathering was assembled in St. Peter's Church to witness the nuptials of Sir Antony Coyle and Lady Isabel Fermoy.

The bridegroom was flushed and ill at ease; Lady Isabel, white as a ghost, a look of heart-broken despair on her beautiful face.

The eyes of all were fixed upon the bride and bridegroom. None saw, or if they saw, took any notice of what looked like a tarpaulin thrown in a heap on some scaffolding immediately above the chancel.

As, to the strains of the magnificent organ, the couple neared the altar rails, Lady Isabel cast a swift glance round the church.

For a moment her despairing gaze rested upon Claude Doone's pale, miserable face.

She drew back, but her father, his stern face black with anger, ordered her forward, and with drooping head she obeyed.

From the steps of the altar a bishop read the exhortation, finishing with the well-known words:

"Therefore, if any man can show any just cause why they may not lawfully be joined together, let him now speak, or else hereafter for ever hold his peace."

Even as the last words left the prelate's lips, the Human Bat sprang from off the scaffolding, and alighted immediately in front of Sir Antony Coyle.

"Here is just cause and impediment!" he declared, opening his folded wings, and displaying to the astonished eyes of the guests, Mrs. Rupert and her child.

Sir Antony turned deathly white.

"Good heavens, Emily!" came in a hoarse whisper from his lips.

Then he started back. His whole face convulsed with baffled rage.

His involuntary ejaculation had betrayed knowledge of the woman and her child.

Lord Fermoy strode to his would-be son-in-law's side.

"What is the meaning of this? Who is the woman?" he demanded.

Sir Antony pulled himself together.

"An old servant I was obliged to discharge for incompetence and ill-behaviour!" he lied glibly.

"Liar!" thundered the Human Bat, stretching out his long, thin, white hand, as though he would tear the baronet to pieces where he stood. "Lady Coyle, produce your evidence," he added, turning to the white-faced woman, who, with her golden-haired boy clinging to her skirts, boldly faced her recreant husband.

Without a word she drew the precious document from the bosom of her dress.

A shriek that was scarcely human in its intense fury burst from Sir Antony's lips as he recognised the documents. He sprang forward, crying:

"Give them to me; they are my property!"

The woman drew back, and the Human Bat laid his hand on the furious baronet's breast.

Sir Antony staggered back, his eyes fixed in horror on the Human Bat.

"Give me those papers; they will be safer in my charge!" said the Bishop, taking the letters from Lady Coyle's hand turning to old Lord Fermoy, he continued: "Under these circumstances, my Lord, it is impossible for the ceremony to proceed. Will you lead your daughter to her carriage?"

"Stay!" came in loud, commanding tones from the Human Bat. A shuddering cry of horror echoed through the church as, with outstretched wings, he flew to where Claude Doone was peering eagerly through the crowd to catch a glimpse of the woman he loved. "Come, act the part of a man, and the girl is yours!" whispered the Human Bat, alighting by Doone's side.

"Who are you? What wondrous power has brought you here?" demanded Doone eagerly.

"Trouble me not with useless questions," growled the Human Bat beneath his breath. "Come, and happiness awaits you! Stay, and Lady Isabel is lost for ever!"

Then, without awaiting reply, he turned on his heel, and, with folded arms, upright carriage, and a sardonic smile upon his ghastly white face, the Human Bat led the way down the aisle.

Guests and officials alike shrank back from him as from a thing accursed, for they nor none others knew whether he were human or a demon of darkness.

As one in a dream, Claude Doone followed his strange guide. At the steps of the altar they halted.

"Go; and cross my path again on your peril!" ordered the Human Bat, laying his hand on the speechless baronet's shoulder, and whirling him round.

Sir Antony Coyle bared his teeth in an angry, dog-like snarl, but no words escaped his pallid lips, and with a strange expression upon his face he strode towards the door.

Not a word was spoken until Sir Antony reached the church porch. Then the Bishop spoke:

"Why have you brought this man here?" he demanded of the Human Bat, eyeing him with dignity, but, nevertheless, with an inward feeling of trepidation.

For answer, the Human Bat drew a folded document from his pocket, and, opening it, held it before the prelate's eyes.

It was a special licence, filled in with the names of Claude Doone and Lady Isabel Fermoy, and only awaiting the Bishop's signature to make it legal.

For a moment his Lordship hesitated, then a whispered consultation took place between the Bishop and the Earl.

"As you wish, my lord Bishop. The guests are assembled. It would be a pity to send them away empty," growled the angry earl.

Laying the licence upon a reading-desk, the Bishop signed it; then, with a congratulatory smile, handed it to Claude Doone, who turned to Lady Isabel and folded her in his arms.

Suddenly she broke from him, and, dropping on her knees by the Human Bat's side, raised his hand to her lips.

A strange expression flitted over the Human Bat's face.

A momentary gratification flashed from his eyes, then his face became contorted with a look of mental agony terrible to witness.

"No, no!" he cried. "I am a thing apart from men! An Ishmael,[5] an outcast!"

Almost roughly he snatched his hand away.

A few seconds he remained poised above the young couple's heads with outstretched hands; then, with a half-human, melancholy, wailing, eerie cry, vanished through an open window.

---

[5] An outcast, in the Bible Ishmael was disinherited and banished to the wilderness (Genesis 16:1-16; 21:10 ff.).

THE STOLEN MASTERPIECE.

The scene is changed.

A winter's day of fog and sleet is passing into a night of rain and storm.

In Trafalgar Square, the hub of the universe, the centre of the civilised world, the Human Bat peers down upon the busy throng from the top of the Nelson Monument.

Seated on the coil of rope by Nelson's side, his hands clasped round his knees, the Human Bat laughed aloud in fearful glee as a fiercer blast than usual striking the solid column, made it tremble again.

Presently he rose, and, expanding his enormous wings, flew across the square to the steps of the National Gallery.

A woman before whom he dropped shrieked with terror, and seized a policeman by the arm.

"Steady, lady! What's wrong?" asked the policeman, with a good-natured laugh.

"That—that! That thing just walking up the steps! It dropped from the clouds!" panted the alarmed woman.

The policeman glanced carelessly at the tall figure, apparently clad in the wide Inverness cape affected by artists, entering the door.

"Now, look here, lady, there's nothing wrong with that man so far as I can see. The best thing you can do is to let me put you into a cab and go straight home," advised the constable, winking at an old newspaper-seller close at hand, who was evidently of the same opinion; for he raised his hands to his lips with the motion for one draining a glass.

In the meantime, the Human Bat entered the building just as they were about to close for the night.

"Hi! Come back! You are too late!" cried an official. Then he rubbed his eyes, for, springing from the ground, the Human Bat had reached the ceiling, to which he clung, seeming to disappear in the shadows above.

For some moments the man remained gazing around him, rooted to the ground with astonishment; then he walked to the door of the gallery and asked a comrade if he had seen a tall man wearing an Inverness cape pass that way.

An answer in the negative convinced him that he had been mistaken, and he returned to his task of making all secure for the night.

One by one the custodians of Britain's great art gallery took their departure.

Releasing his hold of the ceiling, the Human Bat glided to the floor, and moved cautiously towards a magnificent masterpiece by Titian, which he desired to add to his collection.

Suddenly he sprang upwards and fastened himself to the ceiling as one of the night custodians passed through the dimly-lighted gallery.

As the man's echoing footsteps grew fainter in the distance, the Human Bat dropped to the floor once more.

His single eye blazing brilliantly from the centre of his forehead, he passed from picture to picture until he reached the canvas he sought.

Drawing a sharp knife from his belt, he cut the canvas from its frame, rolled it neatly up, and fastened it inside his tight-fitting coat.

Suddenly he started, his frame became tense and rigid.

A loud, shrill whistle rang out behind him, and a heavy hand was laid upon his shoulder.

Turning, he found himself in the grasp of a burly constable, who nearly released his hold when the Human Bat's ghastly face, fierce, glittering eyes, and weird, bright headlight was turned upon him.

But the British policeman does his duty, even though the powers of darkness be arrayed against him.

With a loud cry for help, he grappled with the mysterious being.

Not a word escaped the Human Bat's lips.

For once he had been taken unawares; for once danger had found him unprepared for flight.

Yet, without a moment's hesitation, the Human Bat flung his arms round the policeman, and strained him to his breast with a force that caused the other, big, strong man though he was, to gasp for breath; then he felt himself being lifted off his feet, and the next moment the two were struggling on the floor.

As they fell the Human Bat's knife clattered on the stone floor.

The constable made a quick dart for it.

The policeman secured the weapon, but the Human Bat was on the top of him, his knees planted on his labouring chest, his fingers clasped relentless round his throat.

Tighter and tighter grew that deadly grip, until, realising that his life hung in the balance, the policeman struck again and again at the Human Bat's shoulder—twice it pierced the folded wings.

But the Human Bat tightened his grip upon his victim's throat as he beat his head on the floor with the force that soon rendered him incapable of further mischief.

The Human Bat had conquered, but only just in time.

Officials and police were advancing upon him from right and left.

A huge doorkeeper, seven medals decorating his breast, rushed at the Human Bat, then came to an abrupt halt, a cry of amazement and horror on his lips as the Human Bat clambered up the picture-laden wall to the ceiling.

"It is no man, it is a fiend!" gasped the medal-bedizened doorkeeper.[6]

"Fiend or not, he has got the Titians!" cried another, pointing to the empty frame.

And six of the seven men dashed in pursuit, leaving one of their number to tend their unconscious comrade.

Filling the air with mocking laughter, the Human Bat led the way to the Octagonal Hall, where, after hanging for some moments from a cornice, he

[6] Decorated.

opened his wings and sprang into space.

It was then that the first spasm of terror the Human Bat had ever experienced chilled his heart.

Slashed by the knife in the policeman's frenzied grasp, his right wing had been so torn and mutilated that it refused to support him.

To right and left he struggled, then rolled over on one side, and fell heavily to the floor thirty feet beneath.

Then might the Human Bat have been captured.

But his weird appearance, his flashing eyes, his grating teeth, struck terror into his would-be captors' hearts, and, panic-stricken, they had turned to fly.

Bruised and shaken, the wounds in his shoulder causing him excruciating agony, the Human Bat sprang to his feet, and, clearing a dozen feet at a bound, made his way to the North Vestibule.

At the head of the stairs a top-hatted, gold-laced official barred his path.

Uttering that loud, piercing, mournful cry which had struck terror into the hearts of so many thousands, the Human Bat clutched the terrified man in his arms, and carried him from the top of the stairs to the bottom.

Dropping his victim, the Human Bat crashed through the glass doors, and reached the entrance just as the doors were thrown open to admit an inspector and a squad of police.

THE DEMON-DRIVEN HANSOM.

Striking sledge-hammer blows to right and left, the Human Bat burst through his foes, and, springing over a parapet between two enormous pillars, alighted alongside an empty cab.

"The Embankment—quick!" he ordered, springing into the vehicle.

The astonished cabman gathered up the reins.

"Stop! In the King's name, stop!" thundered the inspector, rushing down the steps.

"On, on! Ten pounds if I reached the Thames Embankment in safety!" shouted the Human Bat through the trap.

"More than my place is worth, governor. Out you get!" replied the cabman.

The Human Bat glanced through the nearest window.

An inspector, a sergeant, and a couple of policemen were nearly upon him.

Raising his head above the top of the cab the Human Bat glared at the driver.

"Drive on, dog!" he snarled.

"Dog yourself, you walking funeral," retorted the man, aiming a vicious blow at his fare with his whip.

As the blow fell the Human Bat snatched the whip from the cabman's hands, sent him reeling from the dicky[7] by a blow from its butt- end, then sprang on

---

[7] A folding outside seat at the back of a vehicle.

to the horse's back.

With a shrill neigh of terror the horse sprang forward.

Pressing his sucker-armed feet into its flank, he drove in the direction of St Martin's Church.

The road to the Strand and the Square were blocked with traffic.

Narrowly escaping the refuge in the middle of the street, the Human Bat turned up Chairing Cross Road.

A glance over his shoulder showed the Human Bat that the police had commandeered a motor-car, and were following in swift pursuit.

Urging the maddened horse on with cries and blows, the Human Bat whirled through Leicester Square, down a by-street, into the Haymarket.

On they dashed, leaving a trail of shrieking women and white-faced men behind them.

Down the Haymarket they sped, 'bus-drivers and cab-drivers making way for the madly rushing horse and its fearful driver, until Trafalgar Square was reached once more.

Abreast the Nelson Column a gallant constable sprang into the road and snatched at the dangling reins.

Throwing his body to one side, the Human Bat caught the policeman by the throat, dragged him along the ground a dozen yards, then hurled him senseless to the road.

His blood coursing like fire through his veins, his whole body being thrilled with excitement, the Human Bat stood upright on the horse's back, and the blazing light on his forehead sending a spectral glare along his path, guided the maddened beast down Northumberland Avenue.

On he went, and those following in his wake knew not what they were pursuing, whether it was man or demon.

Behind him thundered the motor-car, before him lay the Embankment and Hungerford railway bridge, from whence he intended to board a train that would carry him beyond pursuit.

But as the bridge loomed large before him, the police car flashed ahead. Its occupants alighting, formed a line, across the road immediately beneath the bridge.

It seemed as though escape was impossible.

To the left the police; to the right two huge drays[8] had, in obedience to the inspector's orders been drawn across the road. Loud laughed the Human Bat— a mirthless, fearful laugh. It chilled the hearts of all who heard it.

Swerving neither to right nor left, he turned the horse's head straight to the river. Over the pavement rushed that awe-inspiring apparition.

Then the horse and cab, carried forward by the fearful pace at which they were

---

[8] A truck or cart without sides.

going, crashed into the parapet, went half through, half over, and turned a complete somersault into the river. A cry of horror arose from a hundred lips.

The maniac, as all who had witnessed his wild ride deemed, had paid the penalty of his mad freak with his life.

But no!

In peril the Human Bat was ever certain to find safety. As the horse struck the stonework he sprang from its back and, gliding over the black, swiftly-flowing waters, alighted on the deck of a passing Thames tug.

An alarmed oath burst from the tug-master's lips as the dark, mysterious form alighted on his vessel.

Closing with him, the Human Bat dragged him off the little bridge, and seizing the wheel, turned the vessel's bows athwart the stream.

"I don't care what you are. Ghost or no ghost, here's at you!" howled the tug's skipper, as, seizing a heavy monkey-wrench from the engine-room skylight, he rushed at his uninvited passenger.

But ere his upraised arm could fall the Human Bat, covering twenty feet at a jump, alighted on a moored barge.

A police galley swept forward to intercept him, but the Human Bat sprang over it on to the deck of an anchored wherry,[9] and a few minutes later was clinging, breathless and well-nigh spent, to the wall of a riverside warehouse.

He had triumphed, but at a fearful cost. His wings were slashed and torn, his body bruised and aching, his wounded shoulder stiff and sore, yet he dare not linger there.

Wounded and disabled, he must reach his secret home, his hidden lair.

Yet the place which the Human Bat called "home" was more than two hundred and fifty miles away, on the rugged Yorkshire coast.

°ACROSS THE MOOR.

A dull winter morning was breaking as the Northern Express corridor train neared York.

In one corner of a first-class compartment of a corridor carriage sat the Human Bat.

A felt hat was drawn over his eyes, his cape-like wings were draped round his body, giving him the appearance of a man wrapped in an ulster.[10]

The only other occupant of the compartment was a stout, preposterous-looking man of about fifty, whose massive sleeve-links had long since caught the Human Bat's eyes.

Shortly after they had left London the passenger had tried to enter into

---

9 A light rowing boat or large barge.

° 18 JANUARY 1913.

10 A long, loose overcoat.

conversation with the Human Bat, but his advances had been met with so chilling a silence that he returned to the perusal of his papers in anger.

Now, the Human Bat himself open to the conversation in a way that made his companion wish he had maintained his previous silence.

Rising to his feet, the Human Bat seized him by the throat with one hand, whilst with the other he held a sharp-pointed stiletto to his heart.

"Your purse; your jewellery! Quick!" hissed the Human Bat, in a low, blood-curdling whisper.

"What! You scoundrel, you would—" began the traveller. The sharp point of the Human Bat's weapon, pricking his flesh, warned him that the robber was not to be trifled with.

"Obey, or die! I never speak twice!" ordered the Human Bat. With trembling hands the traveller laid his watch, scarf-pin, sleeve-links, a well-filled purse, and a bundle of notes on the seat by his side.

"Go!" thundered the Bat, releasing his hold, and pointing to the door.

The traveller awaited no second invitation, and quicker, probably, than he had moved for years hastened into the corridor, shouting at the top of his voice:

"Help! Thieves! Murder!"

Calmly the Human Bat swept the booty into a large pouch inside his coat, then turned leisurely towards the door as a guard and half a dozen male passengers burst into the compartment from the corridor.

Turning, the Bat flashed his mysterious headlight into their faces. They drew back in alarm.

"Don't let him escape! He's got my watch and all my money!" implored the robbed man.

Thus abjured, the men advanced, but the door was wide open, and the robber gone.

Once more the injury done to his wing was likely to cost the Human Bat dear.

With only one pinion to steady him, he whirled round and round as he sprang from the flying express, and was only saved from further injury by being hurled head-foremost into a deep snowdrift.

Pain roused the Human Bat to fury. Stamping and raving like a madman he tore a furze-bush to pieces with his naked hands.

As suddenly as it had come, the fit of wild, unreasoning rage left him.

A minute later he was his cold, passionless self once more.

Rising, he covered the snow-laden fields in enormous jumps, each twenty feet in length.

Yet his progress was all too slow. He cursed the hand that had slit his wings, the storm that had swept over the frost-bound countryside, until at last the York and Whitby line was reached, and he crept into a tarpaulin-covered truck attached to a train proceeding northward.

An hour that seemed an eternity to the Human Bat, he lay on the floor of the jolting car. His rapidly-stiffening wounds caused him intense agony.

THE GHOST ON THE FOOTPLATE.

Presently he raised the cover of the tarpaulin. Pain drew an angry cry from his lips, for the covering was heavy with recently fallen snow. A minute later he crept from out of his place of concealment. A biting north wind swept him off his feet.

For a moment the Human Bat hovered helplessly between two trucks. He only saved himself from immediate death by clinging to the end of the foremost truck with his steel grappling irons. As, panting and breathless, he drew himself over the end of the next, he gazed longingly over the snow-covered landscape.

Oft had the Human Bat sprang from a swiftly rushing express at this point, but now he dared not attempt the feat, even from the slow-moving goods train.

It was not fear which deterred him. The Human Bat knew not the meaning of the word.

The rough treatment he had received at the hands of the London policeman, his undressed wounds and want of sleep, had robbed him of strength to perform what he would have looked upon in the ordinary course of events as a mere detail.

The Human Bat ground his teeth in baffled rage. Every revolution of the wheel was carrying him to rougher and more uneven ground.

Had his wings been uninjured this would not have mattered. But he could not fly, and walking caused him intense pain.

However, the Human Bat had no intention of being carried further. As he could not alight from the moving train it must be stopped.

His wings draped closely to his side, the Human Bat sprang from truck to van, from van to truck, until his rapid movements, warming his half-frozen blood, instilled fresh courage into his heart. Ten minutes later he was clinging to the side of the tender.

Cautiously he worked his way forward, until, reaching the engine, he raised his head above the steel guard-rail and looked into the van. His hand on the throttle-valve, his face glued to the look-out, stood the engine-driver.

Beside him the fireman was throwing coal on to the furnace. Suddenly a loud shriek of terror burst from the engine-driver's lips. Icy cold fingers, closing over his head, had drawn the lever back.

Turning, he found himself confronted by a terrible black form with a face as white and drawn as that of a corpse.

Alarmed by his comrade's cry, the fireman turned, then, as the Human Bat advanced towards him, he muttered a loud, piercing shriek of heart-stricken terror. Clasping his hands over his eyes, he staggered back, and would have fallen from the footplate had not the Human Bat dragged him back to safety and flung him on the coal.

"Lie there! Move at your peril!" cried the Human Bat, in a voice that rose high above the roar of the wheels and the shriek of the slow goods train.

Turning to the engine-driver, he commanded:

"On with the brake! Ahead lies disaster and death!"

Scarcely knowing what he did, the engine-driver obeyed.

The train, groaning, creaking, and clanking, came to a halt.

He turned to where he had last seen his weird passenger.

He was gone!

Barely had the engine wheels ceased to revolve ere the Human Bat had cleared the boundary fence at a bound, and was already speeding swiftly over the rugged moor land.

Strange enough, as in awestricken silence, the engineer alighted and searched the rails for the unknown danger against which he had been so wondrously warned, he found a huge tree into which he must have inevitably dashed blown across the rails.

Two days later paragraph headed "A Ghost on the Footplate" went the round of the papers, in which the Human Bat was described by both engine-driver and fireman as a terrible being with fleshless skull, eyes that blazed with living fire, and withered bones in lieu of hands.

ALONE ON THE SNOW-BOUND WASTE.

With long, looping strides, in the face of a roaring blast, the Human Bat forced his way over the moor, now taking a valley in his stride, now scarce able to force one foot before the other as he topped some bleak, storm-swept hill.

There was a strange singing in his ears, a strange mist before his eyes.

Never had he felt so weak and helpless as now.

Loss of blood, loss of sleep, loss of rest were telling upon even the Human Bat's iron frame.

Never before had he stood in such need of his faithful wings.

To rise in the air and be carried on the blast for a few minutes would have been a priceless boon to the worn-out being.

Tired almost unto death, the Human Bat did not stop to rest his weary limbs.

A moment's respite, and he would sink into the sleep from which there is no waking.

With clenched teeth and hard set face the Human Bat pressed on.

Now and again he would stop and shake his fist at the star-bespangled sky, and curse earth and air alike.

It was these paroxysms of rage that saved the Human Bat's life.

They shook off the stupor that was creeping over him, and gave him fresh strength to battle against the storm.

On he pressed, his springs from earth growing more feeble, his alighting less sure with each stride.

Hour succeeded hour. Still the pitiless gale gave him no respite.

At last, on the summit of a rugged hill, he paused and sniffed the air.

His heavy eyelids opened, his face glowed with renewed hope. A tinge of salt on the breeze told him that he was near the sea, home, and safety.

Passing his hand across his brow to clear his eyebrows of the half-frozen snow, the Human Bat sprang forward with a mighty bound.

Some unseen hand seemed to hold his foot in a vice-like grip, and, turning a complete somersault, he rolled helplessly down the steep hillside.

A snowdrift closed over the Human Bat's head; but, fighting for his life, he regained firmer ground; then staggering to a huge stone, seated himself upon it, and raised his right foot on his knee.

Then he knew the worst.

One of the powerful springs in his heel, clogged with frozen snow, had been completely torn off, and with it the sucker-like apparatus attached to his feet.

A mile away lay his goal, but between it and him was a stretch of uneven ground, across which, even in fine weather, he would have been obliged to proceed with caution. Now, with only one set of springs in working order, the task seemed hopeless.

But he dare not stop where he was, so, holding up his useless foot, he sprang forward once more.

The wind caught him in mid-air, and dashed him heavily to the ground.

Twice the Human Bat essayed the task. Twice he fell.

Dropping upon hands and knees, he crawled slowly and painfully towards where a decayed pine marked the vicinity of his lair.

Ninety-nine men out of the hundred would have given up then and there. But was the Human Bat human, after all?

Man or super-man, he possessed an indomitable will.

His hands were protected by the suckers, but his knees were soon torn and bleeding from the rough rocks that protruded from the snow.

Before him lay a large cliff, beneath which thundered and crashed the black waters of the North Sea.

The Human Bat saw it not.

His head bowed to save his face from the stinging spray, he moved as one in a dream.

Suddenly his hands beat the empty air.

He tried to draw back.

Too late!

Turning over and over as he fell, he plunged headlong through the black void into the raging sea.

The shock of contact with the icy water recalled the Human Bat back to life, and to the peril of his position.

Instinctively he draped his wings, as he was wont to do when necessity or inclination caused him to float upon the surface of some sea or river.

Water poured through the cuts in the stout wings, but they did not forsake the Human Bat in his hour of need, and, raising his head, he looked around, to find that he had fallen clear of the rocks that studded, like giant's teeth, the base of the cliff.

Half-way up its white face, and looking like nothing so much as a big ink-stain on a crumpled sheet of white paper, a black spot marked the entrance to the Human Bat's lair.

Striking out with his feet, the Human Bat swam shorewards, then was carried on the crest of a mighty wave to the face of the cliffs.

Forcing his three remaining suckers against the cliff, he clung for very life to the uneven surface. Like some living thing the undertow tugged mercilessly to draw him back.

But the suckers held, and a minute later the Human Bat crawled beyond the reach of the tide.

A triumphant cry burst from his lips.

He was safe now.

In a moment he would have found shelter from the stinging blast in the luxurious haven now almost within touch of his hand.

Crash!

The Human Bat fell heavily against the side of the cliff.

The sucker on his foot had given way.

He had now but his hands to depend upon.

What of that?

It would take a little longer to reach the entrance to the cave, that was all.

Drawing his body up on bent elbows, the Human Bat detached his right hand from the cliff, shot it quickly above his head, glued it to the white surface, then rested a moment ere he repeated the movement.

Foot by foot the Human Bat neared his goal. Another struggle, and he would be in safety.

Swinging his right hand over his head, he sought to grasp the edge of a whole, but in vain.

No matter. The next upward movement would carry him to safety!

He reached upwards; then something snapped, and a sucker from his wrist plunged down the cliffs into the raging sea beneath, leaving the Human Bat hanging helplessly to the face of the cliffs by one hand.

THE BAT'S LAIR.

Hanging by one hand to the face of the cliff, the Human Bat swayed at the mercy of the storm, which swept the cliff with unprecedented fury.

Caught by the gale, the Human Bat streamed from the cliff like a flowing pennon. A lull, and his body struck the rock with the force that well-nigh knocked the breath out of his body, and bruised him from head to foot.

Dislodged by the raging blast, a landslide from above clattered with a fearful roar seaward. A few stones struck the Human Bat's head and shoulder, but the great mass of dislodged soil swept harmlessly by.

"Gha-at!" shouted the Human Bat, in tones of fierce appeal; then gazed eagerly upwards.

There was no reply.

"Ghat! Help! Ghat, you dog!" he roared, scarce able to bear the strain upon arm and wrist.

It would be better to release the sucker, and plunged to his doom on the storm-tormented rocks below than to bear that fearful agony longer.

"Ghat, you cur, cannot you hear my voice?" shouted the Human Bat fiercely.

"Master! Oh, my master!" came in shrill, high-pitched tones from the cave.

With the sigh of a reprieved man, the Human Bat turned his electric eye upwards.

Peering down the cliff was a face that would have brought a thrill of fear to the stoutest heart.

Hideous though the face, it was the most welcome vision the Human Bat had ever seen.

"Quick, Ghat, a rope!" he gasped.

The face disappeared, and a minute later a stout hempen rope dangled by the Human Bat's side. Though only able to use one hand, the Human Bat had soon tied it beneath his armpits.

"Pull, Ghat! Pull, you misshapen dog!"

The rope tightened. He released his hold of the cliff, and a minute later the Human Bat lay panting and breathless inside the cave.

With a cry of dismay, Ghat sprang to his master's side. The dwarf's body matched his repulsive face. Barely four feet in height, his crooked back formed a bow with his misshapen legs; his long, hairy arms reached almost to his ankles, and his enormous splay feet struck the ground at every step with a horrible, flapping sound.

"Master, you are not dead? Speak to Ghat. Strike him! Anything to show you are not dead!" cried Ghat, wringing his hands as he bent, in a grotesque sorrow, over his dread master.

A swift blow across the dwarf's mouth answered his appeal.

"Cease, you whining dog! Think you the Human Bat can die—die?" snarled the Human Bat, struggling to a sitting position. And, picking himself up, Ghat crept to his master's side and timidly raised his hand to his lips.

"Ghat thanks you, master. Had you died, all the joy would have gone out of his life!" he said fawningly.

"Had I died! Ha, ha! Ghat, help me to my feet!" returned the Human Bat, in more kindly tones than he had yet used.

With an exclamation of delight, doglike in its eager forgiveness, Ghat placed one long, hairy arm round the Human Bat's waist, the other round his knees; and, with a strength of which his deformed body gave a little promise, carried him down a low, winding passage until further progress was stopped by a huge fallen rock.

"That will do, Ghat. I can walk now," said the Human Bat.

Staggering forward, he touched a concealed spring, and the rock disappeared.

Passing through the opening, the Human Bat entered a suite of brilliantly-lighted rooms—rooms fitted with every luxury that a soul could desire.

It had been but a bare, damp cavern when the Human Bat found it. Now walls, floor, and ceiling were boarded in, and it was as dry, warm, and cosy a retreat as any outlaw need have. Luxury, refinement, and good taste appeared on every hand in that unknown cave on the Yorkshire cliff that the Human Bat had selected as his lair.

A hall rich in tapestry, armour, and richly-carved oak furniture, drawn from the oldest houses in the British Isles, led into a magnificent dining-room, the walls of which bore pictures stolen from the famous galleries of Europe.

Taking the Titian, which had cost him so dear at the National Gallery, from his pocket, the Human Bat flung them to his servitor.

"Frame one and hang it between yonder pictures!" he ordered, pointing to a magnificent Turner and a priceless Morland.

The dwarf caught the picture, then awaited further orders.

"Dinner in ten minutes!" thundered the Human Bat.

Bowing low, Ghat hastened from the room. When the cooked repast Ghat had set before his master was finished, the Human Bat flung himself in a chair before the fireplace, piled high with a blazing fire of wood, whilst Ghat attended to his wounded shoulder.

As tenderly as a woman the dwarf removed his master's clothes, washed and bathed the wounds, then poured upon them some ointment, which eased the smarting pain, and gave the Human Bat immediate relief.

"Master, let me seek the man who did this, that I may tear him to pieces with my hands!" implored Ghat, his hideous face convulsed by a fierce, angry frown.

The Human Bat's cold, mirthless laugh echoed through the room.

"Do you think the man who did that lives, dog?" he asked contemptuously.

The wound dressed, Ghat set cigars and wine on a table by his master's side. Then he crouched like a dog on the hearth rug at the Human Bat's feet, who stroked his matted head, lost in deep-laid schemes for the future.

There was no room for love in the Human Bat's breast. Yet, strange to say, what affection his hard, mysterious nature could afford was bestowed upon the crouching creature at his feet.

Suddenly the Human Bat rose to his feet, and sent the dwarf reeling half way across the room with a vicious kick.

"To bed, you misshapen hound!" he cried.

Whimpering, Ghat crawled from the room, while his master entered a bed-room the most luxurious millionaire might have envied.

Many a lordly mansion had been ransacked to furnish the Human Bat's seldom-used bed-chamber. The carpet, of the thickest Turkey pile, had been taken from the state-room of a millionaire's yacht off Scarborough. The sheets were of the finest silk; the quilt from Hume Castle.[11]

Inviting though the couch was, the Human Bat could not even sleep like an ordinary human being. Throwing off his clothes, he sprang into one corner of the huge four-post bedstead; and, nose and knees together, fell into so deep a sleep that it might almost have been a trance.

Barely had he dropped off ere the door was slowly opened, and Ghat took up his accustomed place on the threshold. Here he remained on his guard, bright, faithful eyes fixed upon his master, without moving or allowing his drowsy lids to droop during the Human Bat's long forty-eight hours' sleep.

At the first sign of movement on his master's part Ghat hastened off, so that when the Human Bat arose he might find a breakfast, consisting of all the delicacies in season, awaiting him.

The meal over, the Human Bat entered a room, the floor of which no foot but his had ever trod. Even Ghat had never past its door.

Here he worked unceasingly for several hours. When he emerged his wings were mended, and fresh springs supplied two his hands and feet. He was once more ready to prey upon the human race.

THROUGH THE PORTHOLE.

It was night when the Human Bat sallied forth once more. Standing on the extreme edge of the cave, his eyes swept over the wide expanse of sea.

Far away to the south appeared the lights of a steamer forcing its way to some Northern, Scotch, or Continental port.

So silent, so motionless was the weird black form that a gull alighted close to his side. He moved, and the bird, spreading its white wings, flew away with a frightened cry.

His fearful, mirthless laugh startling the frozen air, the Human Bat spread wide his enormous wings, and, urged forward by the powerful springs in his heels, dashed in pursuit.

In vain the gull strove to escape its pursuer. A hundred yards from the cliffs the Human Bat overtook the shrieking bird, struck it down with a passing blow, then soared aloft, and, with a slow, regular beats of his enormous wings, glided in the direction of the oncoming steamer.

The Bat was in a playful mood, and what was joy to him was death to his victim. It was good to be on the wing once more. It was good to feel that he was again master of air, water, earth alike.

A loud unearthly shriek startled the watch on board the good ship Plover,

---

[11] Near Kelso in the Scottish borders.

bound from London to Granton.[12] Her captain looked fearfully in the direction from whence the sound came. A huge, shapeless, black form swept swiftly over the Plover's stern.

Even as those on board peered through the night, the Human Bat fastened his sucker-armed feet to the boat's side.

Drenched with spray, the Human Bat peered through the brilliantly-lighted portholes. Presently he came to a cabin in which lay a man tossing in uneasy slumber. His head had moved to the edge of the bunk, and beneath the displaced pillow the Human Bat saw a diamond-studded gold watch of enormous value, a roll of notes, and a well-filled purse.

From a canvas breastplate, not unlike a Cossack's bandolier, the Human Bat drew a small metal syringe, from which he injected a thick, milky liquid round the glass to soften it; then, with a glass-cutter's diamond, attacked the thick plate-glass.

A minute later the glass had been removed, and the plunder was almost his. Almost, but not quite! It lay six inches beyond his reach!

Withdrawing his arm, the Bat drew something that looked like a telescope without an object-glass or an eyepiece from his pocket. Into the smaller end of this simple but effective arrangement the Human Bat thrust a three-pronged hook, with which he speedily gained possession of the coveted jewels.

The purse, the role of notes, and the jewellery had already found a resting-place in the Human Bat's pocket, and he had just removed the three-pronged hook preparatory to flying off with his booty, when the cabin door opened, and a tall, evil-faced man crept to the sleeper's side.

"I would give much to wake him to let him know whose hand sends him to his doom!" muttered the coward, his hand poised in the air ready to strike. "But no; one cry for help, and I should buy my revenge with my life!"

Whilst the other delayed the blow, the Human Bat thrust the handle of a small blade into the tube, from which he had removed the three-pronged hook. Then, with all the strength of his sinewy arm, he struck at the coward. A wild, despairing cry rang through the ship, and the weapon, jerked from its owner's hold, flew past the Human Bat's head and settled in the wall of the cabin.

With a cry of terror the sleeper awoke, and sprang from his bunk on to the body of his still-breathing enemy.

But a moment sufficed for him to gather what had occurred. Dazed, confused, distracted, he started back, just as the captain, quarter-master, and steward burst into the cabin. Seeing two men on the floor, one of whom appeared intent on a grim and awful purpose, the captain and quartermaster flung themselves upon him.

In vain the man expostulated. Handcuffs were produced, and he was led a

---

12 Edinburgh.

prisoner from the cabin.

As the excited sailors entered the saloon, they were rooted to the floor of the cabin by a burst of wild, fiendish laughter that chilled all who heard it to the very marrow-bones.

Convulsed with hideous mirth, the Human Bat flew shorewards with his booty.

"Ha, ha, ha! Ho, ho, ho!" he roared. "Fine sport—grand sport!"

The officer on the bridge heard the weird laughter, but ere he could turn his eyes in the direction from whence the sound came, the Human Bat was half-way to the shore.

His lair reached, the Human Bat entered his bed-room, and, fastening himself on the ceiling, opened a trap door in the oak-panelled roof that gave admittance to his secret treasure-house.

It was a sight which would have brought a cry of wonder from any beholder's lips.

Above rose the jagged roof of the huge cave in which the Human Bat's luxurious house had been built. No attempt had been made to adorn the place. The floor was littered with gold and silver plate, ewers, dishes, etc., etc. watches, rings, jewels of all descriptions, gold coin of every denomination, were thrown about everywhere. Stirred by a draught from below, numberless banknotes fluttered like leaves in autumn, over the wealth-strewn floor.

The Human Bat might well have taken his place amongst the richest in the land. But he cared not for such things. It was the excitement of acquiring booty, not the value of the plunder itself, that appealed to him.

Nor was he a miser. He would scatter gold broadcast in his flight, laughing contemptuously when he saw men, women, and children fighting and scrambling for the yellow metal.

ONLY AN ANIMAL.

The snow lay deep upon the rugged moor. For miles around no human form could be seen; no human footprint disturbed the white covering Nature had spread over the earth.

Suddenly the Human Bat paused in his flight. A plaintiff bleating from below reached his ears. He looked down.

At first he could see nothing, but presently he detected a tiny black spot at the bottom of a deep, funnel-shaped hole.

Circling round the Human Bat dropped to earth. As he did so he discovered that the black spot was the head of a sheep which had fallen into some pit or hole, and was in momentary danger of being suffocated.

His stern face softened; a look of pity flashed from his eyes.

Careless of the fact that at any moment the side of the funnel-shaped opening might cave in and bury him in a tomb from which there could be no escape, this strange being, who an hour before had been moved to laughter by a man's fate, folded his wondrous wings and dropped slightly to the poor beast's side.

Stooping, he groped under the snow till he held the sheep's fleece. Exerting all his strength, he lifted the frightened animal from its perilous position. As he did so the snow beneath his feet gave way, and, dragged down by the weight of the bleating sheep, he found himself falling swiftly into the black unknown.

From above came a roar as of thunder; the snow on the side of the lonely mine caved in.

Intertwining his steel arms round the sheep—for the Bat would have accounted himself beaten had he allowed it to perish—he half spread his wings to check his fall; then, thrusting out his sucker-armed hands, struck out to right and left.

One hand touched the side of the mine, the other joined it; then his feet were stuck fast to the rocky soil, and he was safe. It needed no great discernment to guess what had happened.

The snow, falling upon a beam across the mine, had been partly frozen, then had become strong enough to bear the sheep's but not the Bat's weight.

Presently the dislodged snow from above ceased to fall. With the sheep clasped tightly to his breast, the Bat forced his way upwards, until at last he flung himself down on the snow, breathless but safe.

Finding itself in the upper air once more, the sheep struggled to get free; but the Bat never did anything by halves.

Far away to the northward smoke arose from a white mound that proclaimed a snowbound farm; and, rising, this strange being flew through the frosty air to carry the animal he had rescued to a place of safety.

Having dropped the sheep upon some snow-covered straw in the farmyard, the Bat had already recommenced his flight, when he was greeted by cries of terror from the windows of the house and from some half a dozen farm-hands engaged in a barn close at hand.

Suddenly the door of the farmhouse opened, and the farmer, gun in hand, rushed along a neatly-swept path in pursuit of the Bat.

Eager to secure so strange a bird, the farmer raised his weapon to his shoulder and pulled the trigger.

The Bat was too far off for the small shot to injure him, but the pellets, striking his unprotected hands and face, stung like whip lashes.

Like an eagle upon its prey, he swooped down upon the farmer, seized him in an iron grip, and, despite his terrified struggles, soared aloft with him, when the labourers, armed with scythes, flails, and pitchforks, dashed to the rescue.

Despite his struggles, the Human Bat soared aloft with him.

His wild, weird shriek echoing and re-echoing in the air, the Human Bat raised the half-throttled farmer high above his head and hurled him at the oncoming men.

Then, with a mocking laugh, he perched for a moment upon the snow-clad roof, and, opening his wings, flew swiftly over the moor.

SAVED FROM THE GALLOWS.

The Human Bat stood on the top of Edinburgh Castle. His hands rested upon Mons Meg, perhaps the oldest cannon in existence.[13] Rage, baffled greed, and bitter hatred against some person unknown filled his heart.

A respectable British tourist in the daytime, a remorseless spoiler during the night, the Bat, whilst watching the trial of James Grantison for the murder of his brother-in-law, Peter Danson, on board the Plover, had not been idle.

Money, plate, and jewels had rewarded his midnight efforts. Too astute to keep his plunder by him, the Bat had fixed upon a simple and, as he thought, a safe place for the stolen goods.

Wandering over Edinburgh Castle on the first night of his arrival, he had hit upon the monster cannon as a safe place for his plunder, and had thrust his booty down the gun's yawning mouth.

For once he had been mistaken. His ill-gotten gains had vanished, leaving no trace of the thief behind them.

---

13 Forged in Mons, Belgium in 1449 and given to James II of Scotland in 1457, this six-tonne siege cannon is now in the collection of the Royal Armouries and on loan to Edinburgh Castle.

His heart filled with bitter hatred against the whole human race, he gazed over the sleeping city. A fiendish desire to fly from house to house, or from mansion to mansion, and wreak vengeance for his loss filled his heart.

It was a blind wish, for he realised not how to carry it out. He had other work to do. James Grantison, the supposed murder of his brother-in-law, was a rich man. A rich man could pay well for an effort to save him, and would have to, too, if he would escape the shameful death that would be his on the morrow.

Twice the Human Bat had visited the condemned man in his cell. The first time he offered to set him free for £10,000; but Grantison loved his money almost more than life.

Again the Human Bat visited him. Twenty-five thousand pounds was the lowest he would now take to save his life. Still the miser refused to sign the necessary document.

This night the Human Bat intended to visit him for the third and last time.

On the parapet of the castle he spread his enormous wings, and, floating over Princes Street Gardens, made his way through the darkness to the embattlemented walls of the prison. Warders patrolled the prison yard, yet none saw the dark form alight from cloud-hidden skies.

Flying noiselessly in the direction of the grating from whence many a wretched prisoner has seen his last sun rise, the Human Bat approached the condemned cell.

"Grantison—come!" ordered the Human Bat, his face close to the bars that protected the small window.

"Ah, it is you! I knew you would not forsake me. My lawyer says nothing can save me!" whimpered the doomed man.

"He lies! He knows not of the Human Bat!" was the angry retort.

"But can you do what you say? It will ruin me, but I will give you the £25,000 if you can save me from the fearful fate that threatens me," agreed Grantison.

"Too late—£50,000, or you die!" came in low but fearful tones of menace from the Human Bat.

A wail of dismay burst from the money-grubber's lips.

"Where should I obtain so large an amount? Would you ruin me?" he cried.

"Farewell!" interrupted the Human Bat.

"No, no; do not leave me! I give in," wailed James Grantison piteously.

"Sign!"

The prisoner started back as the Human Bat's headlight filled the cell with its white, powerful beams.

"Sign!" repeated the Human Bat, thrusting a golden fountain-pen and a note of hand[14] for £50,000 pounds through the grating.

With evident reluctance James Grantison signed the note of hand.

---

[14] A promissory note, or promise to pay a specific amount.

"Here it is. Keep your word, or if I now go forth from here only to the scaffold you shall become a haunted man!"

"The Human Bat never betrays those who trust him," was the stern reply, as he snatched the paper from the other's trembling hands.

Mounting swiftly to the summit of the tower, the Human Bat spread his wings and flew swiftly to the open window of the chamber he occupied as an English tourist, in one of the best hotels.

*

A heavy mist had settled over Edinburgh as the passing-bell, ringing solemnly from the chapel tower, told the expected crowd thronging in the streets around the prison that James Grantison was being escorted from the condemned cell to the scaffold.

"He is not here! He has betrayed me!" moaned the trembling man, as, supported on either side by a warder, he followed close behind a white-robed clergyman, reading the Burial Service, to where the hangman awaited him.

One of the warders, touched by the man's constant moaning, whispered:

"Who did you expect to see? Who is it you want?"

"The Human Bat—the Human Bat!" repeated Grantison, clinging tightly to the man's arm.

Shrugging his shoulders, the warder looked significantly at his companion, and the two forced their helpless prisoner onto the trap.

A cry of terror burst from the condemned man's lips. Incapable of speech or action, he awaited the end.

As though miles away, he heard a voice nearing the fatal words in the Burial

Service which would be the signal for the hangman to pull the lever and to allow the doomed man to drop through the trapdoor.

Suddenly loud, startled cries rang in his ears. He felt a pair of steel arms cast round his body, and, with his tongue cleaving in terror to the roof of his mouth, felt himself carried rapidly skyward.

Not a sound escaped the horrified spectators as they saw the weird black form flying away with the condemned man, raising ever higher and higher.

"Ha, ha, ha! Ho, ho, ho!" laughed the Human Bat, his unearthly shouts striking terror into the hearts of all who heard him.

On the top of Burns' Monument he alighted. A few cuts of his keen knife set Grantison free.

"The Human Bat has kept his word," said that fearsome being, a ring of inexpressible triumph in his voice.

Unable to realise that it was not all some fearful dream, from which he would awake to find himself in the condemned cell, Grantison placed his trembling hands to his neck, wound round which he still seemed to feel the new hempen rope.

Loud shouts in the street below warned the Human Bat that he must not linger there.

"Come, we have no time to lose," he cried, dragging James Grantison to the parapet of the tower and pointing over the edge.

"No, no; we will be dashed to pieces!" moaned Grantison, drawing back.

With a contemptuous laugh, the Human Bat pushed him into space. Diving, he caught him ere he reached the earth; then, shielded from view by the fog, flew with him to his room at the hotel.

An hour later, Grantison, skilfully disguised as a lady, whose grey hair was nearly hidden by a black bonnet, and clad in a dress of the same colour, was being whirled by the Scotch express Londonwards.

IN THE GOVERNOR'S ROOM.

Chief Constable Bailie Macanna wiped large drops of cold perspiration from his forehead as he dropped into a chair in the governor's room.

"To think that such a thing could happen in a Christian country!" he gasped.

Sir Campbell Ayrley, governor of the prison, a tall, soldierly, grey-moustached veteran of a dozen wars, glanced angrily at the speaker.

"Confound it, man, pull yourself together! You will be going into hysterics in a minute!" he growled, tugging furiously at his moustache. "Well," he added, in more gentle tones, "perhaps I should not be too hard upon you, a mere civilian. I, Campbell Ayrley, who have faced death a score of times in every part of the Empire, knew what fear was when I saw James Grantison carried off by the—"

"Hush, man—Hush!" interrupted the other hastily. "Don't you know that when you pronounce his name he appears? Ugh!" he continued with a shudder.

"Come, come! Take a grip of yourself, man!" retorted the governor. "Whatever he was, he was interfering with officers in the execution of their duty, and you should have arrested him!"

"Me—me arrest the Human Bat!" ejaculated Bailie Macanna, aghast at the idea. "No, no, mon! You're responsible for the safe custody of the prisoners, and I am not one to thrust myself into another man's job!"

Sir Campbell was somewhat taken aback by this view of the case.

"I am not saying but what you have right on your side," he said slowly and thoughtfully; "but you will back me up when the authorities begin to ask impertinent questions? He came like a flash; he went like a flash. I wasn't ready for him. If he came now, fiend or no fiend, he should see the inside of a cell."

A loud crash, a mocking laugh, and the two men sprang swiftly apart.

The Human Bat stood before them!

"I am here," he said, looking mockingly from one pale, terror-stricken face to the other.

With a cry of terror the chief constable dived under the table.

Sir Campbell Ayrley was made of sterner stuff. He had, of course, been present at the interrupted execution, and a cross-hilted claymore without its basket guard, hung at his side.

"Man or demon, here's at you!" cried the gallant old warrior, as his keen blade flashed from its sheath.

The Human Bat remained, to all appearances, perfectly still, yet the old warrior was brought to an abrupt halt by the muzzle of a revolver in the Bat's hand that pointed straight at his heart.

"Stand back! I would not willingly kill so brave a man!" thundered the Human Bat.

Sir Campbell Ayrley lowered his sword.

"You are but flesh and blood, after all, then!" he cried, with a sigh of relief.

"That is as may be. Seek not to inquire into matters beyond your comprehension!" retorted the Human Bat. "Bid yonder trembling coward rise from the floor," he added. "Here is my confession, signed, sealed, and witnessed. Farewell!"

Throwing a rolled sheet of paper on the table, the Human Bat waved Sir Campbell aside.

"Stay!" roared the gallant old soldier, standing his ground, with a pale but very determined face. "On your own confession, you are an assassin! I arrest you in the King's name!"

"Ha, ha, ha!" came a loud peal of mocking laughter from the Bat's lips. "No mortal man could arrest me! The world in arms could not lay me low!"

Sir Campbell Ayrley's blade plunged swiftly forward; but it was not the

Human Bat he struck.

In the wall close by was the button of an electric bell. This the Baronet's sword struck, and a distant tinkling showed that the alarm had been given.

For a moment the governor's life hung in the balance; yet he gazed fearlessly, straight into the face of his enemy.

For several seconds neither moved. Then, as the sound of running footsteps proclaimed that assistance was at hand, the Human Bat thrust his weapon out of sight.

Simultaneously, determined to die fighting, rather than be shot down like a dog, Ayrley struck at him with his sword. The blow was wasted on the empty air. The Human Bat had disappeared.

"Take care! Be on your guard! He has vanished into thin air!" ejaculated the chief constable.

A mocking laugh caused both men to look up. The Human Bat was dangling from the ceiling immediately above their heads.

The next moment half a dozen policemen and warders burst into the room.

"Seize that man! Don't be afraid of him! He is but a Spring-heeled Jack from some travelling show!" ordered Sir Campbell Ayrley furiously. "Close the door and windows. He cannot escape us!" he added as the Human Bat moved towards one of the big casements.

A mocking peal of laughter echoed through the room. Yet no man faltered; but, stationed at doors and windows, looked to the governor for further orders.

"Call up warders with rifles!" commanded the governor. "Dead or alive, we will have him!"

Again that fearful laugh echoed through the room. As, detaching himself from the ceiling, the Bat swooped almost to the floor.

A shrill shriek of terror burst from the chief constable's lips. The Human Bat passed within an inch of his head ere, rising, he clung like a fly to the wall, near a large electric fan that ventilated the room.

Crash! The fan was shattered to a thousand pieces against a short iron bar the Human Bat had thrust into it.

His feet on either side of the opening, the Human Bat grasped the ironwork with both hands, put forth his enormous strength, and the iron rim, pulled bodily from the wall, clattered to the floor amidst a cloud of dust.

With loud cries of wonder the onlookers saw the Human Bat squeeze his long, thin body through the opening, pause for a moment on the opposite wall; then, opening his wide wings to the breeze, fly in the direction of Arthur's Seat.

But a few brief minutes later, and from the top of Salisbury Crags the Human Bat gazed over ancient Holyrood.

He saw a huge crowd running towards him through the streets. He saw signals flashing from the castle, and knew that telegraph and telephone were at work spreading a net from which he might find it difficult to escape. Yet his tall, black form, like that of some ill-omened bird, remained perched upon the crag.

A thousand pairs of eyes had witnessed the Human Bat's flight. A thousand tongues were eagerly detailing exaggerated accounts of his exploits. It seemed as though all Edinburgh had turned out to assist in the capture of this strange, unearthly being.

Yet, though every moment rendered escape more difficult, the black figure maintained its position on the elevated plateau.

Presently warders armed with rifles lined the base of Arthur's Seat. A company of kilted Highlanders swung at the double to the right, another to the left; wheeling, both encircled the huge hill that overshadows Edinburgh.

"Shoot him dead if he attempts to fly!" was the order that had been passed round to warders and soldiers alike.

The Human Bat had snatched a victim from the gallows; he had driven the chief constable almost mad with terror; he had flouted the governor of the prison, who himself led a mixed force of warders and soldiers up Salisbury Crags.

Amongst the warders were many ex-soldiers who had fought Britain's foes in every quarter of our mighty Empire; yet, so fearful was the reputation the Human Bat enjoyed, that there was not a man present who would not rather have stood in the broken square on Abu-Klea[15] than advance upon that strange being.

The Human Bat's very inaction struck terror to all hearts.

Nearer and nearer crept the advancing band. Yet the Human Bat made no signs of flight or resistance.

Within twenty feet of his quarry Sir Campbell Ayrley halted his men.

"Surrender! Human Bat, be you what you may, I arrest you! You are surrounded. Escape is useless—indeed, impossible!" he shouted.

There was no reply.

---

[15] A particularly fierce battle fought in Sudan in January 1885.

IN THE DEAD OF NIGHT.

"Have your rifles ready, man! Shoot him down if he tries to get away," ordered Sir Campbell, as, his sword shortened ready to strike, he laid his hand upon the motionless figure of the Human Bat.

As he did so the black form collapsed, leaving him to gaze in amazement upon an empty hat, a black coat, and a pair of crossed sticks stuck in the ground, which had supported the Human Bat's cloak and hat.

Whilst his enemies had sought to surround him the Human Bat had made good his escape, and was already seated, to all appearances an offensive traveller, in a first-class carriage attached to a south-bound train.

Later, disguised in a fresh mask that defied detection, the Human Bat entered the folding doors of the Manchester branch of the Midlands and Metropolitan Bank.

Approaching the polished counter, he presented the demand-note for £50,000 James Grantison had given him.

A cashier ran his eyes over the document; then, asking the Human Bat to wait, entered the manager's office.

A minute later the manager himself approached the Human Bat.

"There is some mistake here," he said politely, handing back the document. "Mr. James Grantison has stopped this note."

The Human Bat's eyes flashed ominously.

"Kindly retain it, sir," he said, in a hollow voice, in which lurked a menace. "On the 20th of March I will return for the money."

Turning on his heels, he left the building, and mingled with the pedestrians in the crowded streets without.

And that evening, as an express thundered across a bridge over the River Weaver, three out of four of the passengers seated in a first-class carriage in the centre of the train sprang to their feet, uttering exclamations of terror.

The fourth, the Human Bat, had flung open the door and plunged headlong into the night. Terror was upon every face. All believed the madman, as they deemed him, had rushed to his death.

But his faithful wings had carried the Human Bat safely to the ground, and, careless of the fact that the train had been stopped, that horrified searchers might seek for his body, he moved swiftly across country to where a tree-capped hill overlooked the village of Ackerton, and the ancient, battlemented mansion occupied by Mr. James Grantison.

It was a wild night. Heavy masses of broken clouds swept swiftly across the heavens, now obscuring the light of the moon, now allowing her bright beams to flood the landscape with silver rays.

Twenty minutes after his flight from the train the Human Bat landed upon the flat, leaded roof of Ackerton Church.

To the left nestled a cluster of thatched cottages; to the right rose Ackerton

Court; below lay a ghostly cluster of ancient tombstones. From his lofty eyrie the Human Bat watched the lights in the neighbouring cottages disappear one by one.

When the last light had vanished, he dropped noiselessly to the foot of the tower, then moved amongst the upright stones until he came to a magnificent marble tomb.

Drawing a mallet and chisel from his pocket, he approached this tomb, and, with the skill of a practised workman, began to cut letters on the smooth surface.

Chip, chip, chip! Never ceasing, never quickening, never changing time; the monotonous thud of the hammer, answered by the clear, crisp, metallic click of the chisel as it cut deep into the stone, continued unceasingly.

Chip! Chip! Chip! Letter after letter was cut deep in the stone.

A passing labourer, too terrified to run, stood for some minutes listening intently; then, curiosity overcoming terror, he crept cautiously in the direction whence the sound came.

Screened by the thick branches of a spreading yew, the yokel stood as though turned to stone, watching the shapeless black form clinging, as no mortal could have clung, to the side of the Grantison vault.

For some minutes the labourer stood fascinated by the fearful sight. Then a low moan of terror forced its way through his chattering teeth as the unknown moved its head, and he saw a fearful white, pallid face turned towards him.

A feeling as though the apparition was laying the innermost recesses of his heart bare filled him with terror as the fierce beam of light which flashed from the apparition's single eye fell upon him.

Then the Human Bat spoke.

"Fly for your life!" he ordered, in deep, rolling tones.

With a shriek the horrified labourer sped into the darkness. Tripped by a stone, he fell heavily, but, scarce conscious of his fall, picked himself up, sprang over a wall, crashed through a thick-set hedge, dashed over a plough, then rushed to the sexton's house in the centre of the village, and thundered wildly on the door.

Chip, chip, chip! Letter after letter, word after word, was cut deep in the yielding stone.

Presently the Human Bat's pointed ears quivered as the sound of excited voices and the tramp of many feet were brought to him on the wings of the gale.

Chip, chip, chip! Without turning he could tell that the dread place was swiftly filling with an excited crowd.

Yet he continued his task undisturbed.

Nearer and nearer crept the crowd, guided by the ghostly clicking of mallet and chisel.

Foremost, his rubicund face white with superstitious terror, came the sexton, backed up, though mostly unwillingly, by the village constable, who held a truncheon in one hand, a pair of clanking handcuffs in the other—why, he could not have explained to save his life.

Fascinated, yet terrified, by the fearful sight, the crowd clung trembling to each other. Suddenly the clicking ceased, the huddled shape straightened, and every man present drew back in panic-stricken alarm, as the Human Bat turned his glistening headlight and deathly-white face towards them.

With a low, wailing cry the Human Bat stretching out his long, talon-like hand, as though in menace to all within reach, soared aloft on his black, batlike pinions.

The sexton turned angrily towards the policeman.

"Jenkins, you have failed in your duty. Why didn't you arrest him?"

"What, arrest that? It's more than any mortal man would dare!" stammered the policeman.

To this the sexton could make no reply.

"After all, it could only have been some huge bird. Turn on your lantern, constable. See if there are any marks on the Grantison vault."

Very unwillingly the policeman approached the tombstone. Quivering with excitement, trembling with superstitious terror, a score of villagers pressed behind him.

At first his trembling fingers refused to move the slide of his bull's-eye lantern, but at length he turned the shutter, and a circle of light blazed full on the freshly-graven letters.

Exclamations of horror came from every lip. Beneath the lines that recorded the previous deaths in the family appeared, in large Roman characters, the words:

"James Grantison, died March 21st, 19—"

WORTHY OF HIS STEEL.

Whilst the events narrated above were taking place, the man whom they were most nearly concerned tossed uneasily on his bed, a prey to terror-haunted dreams. Everything about the room in which he slept showed its owner's miserly nature.

The furniture, though good, was out of repair, worm-eaten, and dirty.

Suddenly the moonbeams filtering through the diamond-paned window were obscured by a huge black form alighting on the sill without.

Cautiously opening the casement, the Human Bat entered the room.

James Grantison moved uneasily on the bed. The Bat stood as though carved in stone until the disturbed man quieted down once more. Then he stealthily crept about the room, placing tiny black cones on the mantelpiece, wardrobe, drawers, dressing-table, and chairs.

A roll of thunder reverberated through the room. With a cry of terror, James Grantison sat up in bed. As he did so his jaw dropped and his hair stood on end.

The cones the Human Bat had put about the room burst into red, green, and white flames, and by their ghastly light he saw, perched on the back of the tall, carved oak chair, the Human Bat leering at him.

For some moments neither spoke.

"What do you want with me?" stammered James Grantison.

"Payment of my bond," came in fearful, hollow towns from the Human Bat's lips.

"Mercy—mercy! I could not meet so big an account. Give me time—oh, give me time!" wailed the unfortunate man, torn 'twixt love of money and terror of his fearful visitant.

"Add not falsehood to your other sins!" thundered the Human Bat, standing with outstretched wings on the back of the chair. "Beware the 21st of March!"

Ere the master of Grantison Court could reply, the lights disappeared, the Human Bat vanished.

For several minutes James Grantison remained staring vacantly at the place where he had last seen his terrible visitant.

Suddenly he was startled by a thunderous summons on the front door of the Court.

Clad only in dressing-gown and slippers, Grantison rushed down the stairs and through open the door.

The sexton, almost as pale as the haunted man himself, stood on the upper step.

"Mr. Grantison, I have something urgent and important to communicate to you!"

"Come within," stuttered the miser. "I have just dreamt a dream so terrible it has unnerved me!"

Shutting the door on the excited villagers, the sexton told James Grantison of the fearful message cut on the slab in front of the family vault.

The old sexton did not like Grantison, yet at the latter's earnest entreaty he determined to do his best to save him from the fearful terror that overshadowed his life.

For some hours they sat in earnest conversation, and when he left the Court he had promised to travel to London that morning, and interview Danby Druce, the great detective.

Throughout the whole of that day the Human Bat remained hidden in a lumber-room immediately beneath the pointed spire of one of the old Court's many turrets.

Night fell.

Deep and loud the Court clock boomed out the midnight hour.

Like some wandering spirit the Human Bat glided over the gabled roof to wear a fire-alarm bell swayed on a mighty oaken beam from the summit of the Court's centre.

Entering the bell-loft, the Human Bat opened a trapdoor and descended to the pavement had court below.

The bell-rope, stained with age, trailed on the floor.

Seizing the rope, he looked around him.

He was standing in a semi-circular opening, some twenty feet in width, facing the large courtyard round which the house was built.

Clambering up the rope, he clung to it some half-dozen feet from the ground.

As he did so, a loud, deep clang startled the sleeping house.

Raising his body on his mighty wings, he allowed his weight to fall upon the rope once more.

Again the ominous peal rang out.

Suddenly every door giving admittance into the courtyard was thrown open, and a score of men, armed with pistols, each carrying bulls-eye lanterns, rushed in.

In a moment the Human Bat realised his danger.

Yet his fiercely-sparkling eyes glittering angrily upon his foes was the only outward sign of agitation he showed.

"Surrender! Your game is up!" cried a tall, slim, neatly-dressed man, advancing, pistol in hand, upon the Human Bat.

"Welcome, Detective Druce!" cried the Human Bat, careless of the weapon pointed at his heart as he clung to the swaying cord. "I am rejoiced to find a foeman worthy of my steel pitted against me."

"Drop to the ground, or I will fire!" insisted the detective.

A mocking laugh was the only answer the Human Bat vouchsafed.

Awaking a thousand echoes, the detective's weapon rang out. Druce was a dead shot, and the bullet sped true to its mark, but the Human Bat's steel breastplate saved his life.

Unwilling to risk another bullet, the Human Bat sped upwards. In mid-air he halted, then glided swiftly on one side, just in time to avoid the downward grip of a stalwart-policeman, whom Druce had sent to the turret to cut off his retreat.

Clinging to the wall, the Human Bat took in the situation at a glance. Capture seemed imminent.

On three sides were thick stone walls; above, the bell-tower; below, a courtyard filled with armed men. Yet, despite the odds against him, the Human Bat felt confident of escape.

A pistol-shot, followed by a fierce, angry, despairing yell, and, like a pheasant shot on its roost by a midnight poacher, the Human Bat fell earthwards.

With a cry of triumph, his foes dashed forward to seize him. But ere his body struck the stone slabs that covered the courtyard, his wings shot out, and, skimming over the detective's head, he reached the opposite wall of the court, and clambered swiftly up its steep sides.

Shot after shot rang forth. With vicious clicks, the bullets struck shivers from the wall right and left of him. The Human Bat's time had not yet come.

Up he went, ever up, until at last, with a wild, glad cry of triumph, he stood for a moment on the summit of the steep roof, then sprang into the black void before him. As he swept over the gravel drive, the swift beat of a motor-car fell upon his ears. He laughed mockingly to himself.

No car built by man could follow him through space. On he flew, heading straight for Nantwich, and one of his many secret layers.

Suddenly a bright light shot forth from below. Funnel-shaped, white, dazzling, it swept the heavens for a few seconds, then its blinding beams were focused on the Human Bat. In vain he tried to shake off this new and terrible foe.

Turn which way he might—soar to the clouds, drop to earth, cut the air in a zigzag path—that circle of light was ever with him. He could not see from whence it came, but knew that he was being chased, with the aid of a powerful searchlight, carried on the fore part of the motor.

The terror of that remorseless light got on his highly-strung nerves.

It clung to him, and would not be shaken off.

At last, unable longer to bear the strain, he hurled himself frantically to the earth, and plunged amongst the trees of a small wood.

A cry of triumph arose from Danby Druce's lips. He had driven his quarry to earth at last. The Human Bat was at his mercy!

°**ON THE AQUEDUCT.**

Revolver in hand, Danby Druce, the detective, sprang from the car, and, ordering his chauffeur to keep the searchlight full upon the wood, dashed to where he had last seen the Winged Man. But barely had he covered twenty yards ere an appalling shriek from the car brought him to an abrupt halt.

He wheeled round, and saw the chauffeur, evidently in the last stage of terror, leaning back in his seat, his eyes fixed upon something immediately above his head.

His heart filled with vague alarm, Danby Druce retraced his steps, but ere he reached the car the Winged Man enveloped the shrieking driver in his enormous wings.

Danby Druce had chosen the driver of his car for his reckless daring and iron nerve; but now he lay in the body of the car, whither the Winged Man had contemptuously thrown him, whimpering like a frightened child too terrified to move.

Not daring to fire, lest he should hit his man, Danby Druce, shouting to the Winged Man to stop, rushed from the wood. Too late!

Even as he reached the road, the car, with the Winged Man at the wheel, sped swiftly towards Nantwich. With a mighty effort Danby Druce caught the back of the car.

Wildly his fingers closed over the brass rim, and the next moment he was hanging by one hand to the back of the car. Gathering speed with every revolution of its wheels, the cart dashed down the long, wide road. In vain Danby Druce tried to reach the step. He must either abandon his weapon or his hold of the car. He chose the latter course, and the revolver dropped from his grasp.

Feeling as though his right arm would be dragged from its socket, the gallant detective clutched at the back of the car with his left hand. The tips of his fingers touched the brass rail. With a mighty effort he drew his body nearer; then a sigh of relief burst from his lips as both hands closed over the back of the car.

There was yet much to be done. With bulldog pluck he retained his hold of the car, though already the toe-caps of his boots had been frayed away ere he managed to get one knee on the step. Another breathless effort, and, panting but safe, he crouched on the step at the back of the car.

Cautiously he raised his head and looked forward. Brave though the detective was, a shadow of intense horror shook his frame as he saw the weird, aerial creature crouched over the steering-wheel, its headlight exceeding in brilliance the car's searchlight, sending forth its awesome beams ahead.

A minute's rest, to recover his panting breath; then, turning the handle, Danby Druce stepped into the body of the vehicle. An exclamation of terror rose to, but did not pass, his lips. At his feet lay the white, drawn face of the chauffeur.

° 25 JANUARY 1913.

PROLOGUE.

[The] Winged Man, a weird and wonderful being, suddenly appears from out of the un[known]. Who he is no one yet knows! Whence he came, no one can tell, but away up on the [York]shire coast in a subterranean, mysterious lair which he regards as his home, and a dwarf-like servant-man, Ghat, keeps [house] for him. Many are the tremendous [exploits] in which the Winged Man figures. [...] are his midnight exploits. In all parts of England and Scotland he scours [...] home. At one moment he is dis[...] amid the thunder and the lightning [...] the turrets of Edinburgh Castle, [...] a few hours he is constructing plotting [...] on the Underground River at Leeds, [...] on his bat-like pinions all the country over. Where he will rest next no one can tell! A thrilling moment in the record of this strange and weird career is when he rescues James Grantison from the felon's death on the scaffold, but James Grantison will not pay the sum the Winged Man demands, and has had the reckless daring to cheat the Winged Man of his due. He employs the assistance of Danby Druce, the famous London detective, who is the only person the Winged Man fears.

On the Aqueduct.

REVOLVER in hand, Danby Druce, the detective, sprang from the car, and, ordering his chauffeur to keep the searchlight full upon the wood, dashed to where he had last seen the Winged Man.

But barely had he covered twenty yards ere an appalling shriek from the car brought him to an abrupt halt.

He wheeled round, and saw the chauffeur, evidently in the last stage of terror, leaning back in his seat, his eyes fixed upon something immediately above his head.

His heart filled with vague alarm, Danby Druce retraced his steps, but ere he reached the car the Winged Man enveloped the shriek[ing] driver in his enormous wings.

Danby Druce had chosen the driver of his car for his reckless daring and iron nerve; but now he lay in the body of the car, whither the Winged Man had contemptuously thrown him, whimpering like a frightened child too terrified to move.

Not daring to fire, lest he should hit his man, Danby Druce, shouting to the Winged Man to stop, rushed from the wood. Too late! Even as he reached the road, the car, with the Winged Man at the wheel, sped swiftly towards Nantwich. With a mighty effort Danby Druce caught the back of the car.

Wildly his fingers closed over the brass rim, and the next moment he was hanging by one hand to the back of the car. Gathering speed with every revolution of its wheels, the car dashed down the long, wide road. In vain Danby Druce tried to reach the step. He must either abandon his weapon or his hold of the car. He chose the latter course, and the revolver dropped from his grasp.

Feeling as though his right arm would be dragged from its socket, the gallant detective

(Continued on the next page.)

Deeming his faithful comrade dead, Danby Druce's anger against the Winged Man, and his determination to hound him to justice, increased tenfold. Unarmed, he groped in the bottom of the car in search of some weapon to attack the motionless, weird form in the driver's seat. His nervous fingers closed over a heavy spanner.

As he rose to his feet, the clouds which had obscured the moon were torn apart, and her bright beams flooded the sleeping town of Nantwich.

At their feet flowed the Weaver, crossed by the Grand Junction Canal aqueduct.

Rising cautiously, Danby Druce crept close to the strange being. A hundred yards ahead the road turned, then dived beneath the aqueduct. After this was a straight run for several hundred yards.

Danby Druce withheld his hand.

At the fearful speed they were travelling, a straight road was indispensable if he would avert disaster to the car and its occupants.

Her off wheels revolving in the air, the magnificent vehicle whirled round the corner.

The time for action had come.

Trembling with suppressed excitement, Danby Druce grasped the back of the seat immediately behind the Winged Man.

At that moment the car plunged beneath the aqueduct.

A cry of baffled rage burst from the detective's lips as the heavy spanner descended.

His blow was wasted on empty air.

Like a flash, the Winged Man had risen as though shot from a mortar straight into the air.

"Confound it! He has escaped me after all!" ejaculated Druce, as, seizing the wheel, he brought the car's head back to the road just in time to save it from plunging into a deep ditch.

Shrill laughter rising in discordant peals from his lips, the Winged Man clung for a moment to the side of the aqueduct, then, clambering over the parapet, plunged into the cool, placid waters.

His flight from the Court, his fearful rush in the motor-car, had tired him out, so he was glad to float idly down the canal weaving plans for the eventual discomfiture of the man who had cheated him.

In Danby Druce he had met a foeman worthy of his steel.

Yet if James Grantison was guarded by a thousand Danby Druces, they could not save him from the Winged Man.

Deep in thought, he did not hear the beat of a horse's hooves, nor hear the swishing of disturbed water until something touched his head, and, looking up, he saw the rounded sides of a barge betwixt himself and the moonlight.

No time for thought.

Action alone could save him.

To the left of him towered the massive hull of the barge. To the right the stone-faced side of the canal.

It seemed as though nothing could save him from being literally crushed to pieces between the barge and the wall.

For a fraction of a second the man in charge of the horse saw what he believed to be a floating body. Then it disappeared as the Winged Man sank like a stone to the muddy bottom.

It was a desperate chance, but his only hope.

Soon he felt the keel of the barge pressing him down into the mud. Deeper and deeper he sank, heavier and heavier grew the moving weight upon his form, more fearful each moment the awful pressure.

One long, terror-laden minute, and the barge had passed by.

Stopping his horse, the driver hastened to the barge's stern, expecting to see a lifeless, inert body rise to the surface.

But there was nothing there, and, glad to escape further loss of time, he whipped up his horse, and the clumsy barge resumed its journey.

Held as though some ghostly, unseen arms to the canal's muddy bottom, the Winged Man, otherwise known as the Human Bat, fought for life.

At last his wondrous strength prevailed, and with a cry of terror the barge man threw himself face downwards on the ground to shut out the fearful vision, as, spreading his wings to the night breeze, the Winged Man flew slowly over his head.

Fierce anger filled the Winged Man's heart. Plastered with mud from head to foot, he dropped like a stone into the River Weaver, diving, rising to the surface, diving, and rising again, until he had washed every vestige of mud from his garments.

HOW THE WINGED MAN SAVED A LIFE.

Wet and cold, the Winged Man glanced down at the moonlit scene beneath. Immediately beneath him was a tiny, old, disused, and crumbling cottage, overshadowed by the enormous branches of a spreading chestnut-tree.

Alighting by the side of the ancient cottage, the Winged Man fumbled in the eaves for some minutes, then perched like some enormous bird of ill-omen upon the mighty branches of the chestnut-tree.

Presently a tiny spark glowed for a moment in the thatch, then it burst into flame, and in an incredibly short space of time the thatched cottage was ablaze.

Rendering the night hideous with horrible laughter, the Winged Man spread out his wings to the ever-increasing heat.

He needed fire and heat, and had, without a second thought, burnt down the cottage to dry his clothes.

Then swiftly a crowd gathered, and, forming a line, passed a chain of buckets from the river to the doomed house.

Ten minutes later loud cries of:

"Fire! Fire! Hi, hi, hi!" came from the direction of Nantwich, and soon a fire-engine was at work upon the blazing building.

Hidden from view by thick clouds of lurid smoke, the Winged Man surveyed the scene from his perch in the tall chestnut-tree, his pale lips parted in a fearful, gloating smile. He was dry and in comfort now.

Suddenly a terror-laden cry came from beneath a gable at the north end of the cottage.

Firemen, spectators, and villagers paused in their work to look at each other with pale, blanched faces.

"Great powers, there's some living person in the house!" cried the captain of the fire-brigade.

"That bain't no pusson, master, but it be our old puss on the roof. We shut him up in the ceiling to catch rats," returned one of the mob, ending with a loud, callous laugh.

Anger flashed from the Winged Man's eyes.

He who would have done so much without a moment's compunction, was stirred to fury at the thought of an animal being left to perish in the flames.

His wild, weird, mournful cry echoing above the roar of the fiery element, he sprang from the tree and alighted by the speaker's side.

Terror-stricken firemen and spectators alike shrank appalled from the pitiful apparition.

Grasping the terror-stricken cottage by both hands, he raised him above his head, as though to hurl him headlong into the burning building.

"Laugh now, if you like!" shrieked the Winged Man.

A low moan of horror arose from the terror-stricken spectators.

But the Winged Man let the trembling wretch fall to earth, and, with a contemptuous shrug, turned, and, snatching the nozzle of the hose from a trembling fireman's hand, sprang into the end of the cottage.

Clinging with his sucker-armed feet to a cross-beam, blackened with age, he brought the mighty stream to bear upon the lath and plaster just beneath the roof.

In an incredibly short time the shingle-studied plaster was swept away.

Dropping the hose, he told the laths apart with his bare hands.

Wonderingly the crowd watched the Winged Man.

A deep silence, broken only by the roar of the flames and the clang, thud, clang, thud of the engine, obtained over the scene.

A minute later, its green eyes shining fiercely with terror, scorched and burned in a dozen places, a huge black cat burst through the hole the Winged Man had made, and alighted upon his shoulder.

Rising at once in the air, the Bat hovered over the crowd.

"Brutes, who would have left this poor, dumb beast to perish in the flames, beware the Winged Man!" he cried, in loud, awe-inspiring tones.

A moan of horror answered the awesome threat, followed by a sigh of relief as his enormous wings carried the Winged Man in the direction of Nantwich.

A barn filled with barley served the Winged Man for a couch that night, and with the rescued cat sleeping peacefully on his breast, he slept soundly for several hours.

A WONDROUS ESCAPE.

He was awakened by the sound of many voices outside the barn. Rising, he crept to a small door or window used for ventilation in the gable end of the barn, and looked out.

The cat, as though fearful of being left behind, sprang upon his shoulder.

The barn was surrounded.

Some twenty yards away Danby Druce was talking with a police-inspector.

Cries of wonder and dismay greeted the Winged Man's appearance at the window.

"Ho, ho, Danby Druce, still on the trail, ay, old sleuth-hound!" cried the Winged Man, ere, rising from the threshold of the door, he flew rapidly over his would-be captors' heads.

But his wings, hardened by the water and the heat from the burning cottage, were stiff, and taxed even his iron muscles to move them.

By the time the outskirts of Nantwich were reached his arms ached, his legs tingled from fatigue, and he was glad to alight in a deserted street, and, draping his wings around him so that they appeared like a thick ulster, whilst a broad-brimmed soft felt hat hid his face from view, continued his flight on foot.

The Winged Man's wonderful influence extended over animals as well as men.

A word to the cat, and dropping to the ground, it followed at his heels like a well-trained dog.

Careless of the curious glances cast upon him by all he met, the Winged Man continued on his way, avoiding the heart of the town.

As yet, no man had ventured to molest him; but without daring to look behind him, he could tell from a shuffling of many feet and excited whispers, that a gathering crowd was following upon his heels.

Presently a policeman barred his path.

The constable's face was pale. Evidently the duty that confronted him was not to his taste.

"Stop! Are you the—" he began in trembling accents, then stopped, appalled by the wild, fierce cry the Winged Man gave tongue to as he sprang from the ground, and, clearing his head by a good three feet, alighted some twenty yards behind him.

Trembling with fear, the policemen put his whistle to his lips and blew a loud, shrill blast. Half a dozen constables, in response to their comrade's appeal for assistance, hastened on the scene. Yet though they moved towards the Winged Man, none cared to be the first to seize him.

With solemn strides the Winged Man moved forward. The police fell back, but the crowd, emboldened by the fact that the Winged Man's back was turned on them, quickened their steps. A man forced his way through their shrieking ranks to the front.

It was Danby Druce!

"Seize him! Mr. Grantison offers fifty pounds to the man who captures him!" he shouted, dashing eagerly forward.

The Winged Man hesitated.

Then a strange unfathomable smile on his white lips, he turned swiftly down a side street, and disappeared as though in flight.

With jeers, threats, and loud, angry cries, mob and police started in pursuit.

Presently the Winged Man turned down a narrow lane of low, disreputable-looking houses.

A cry of triumph arose from the mob.

They had him now, for a tall wall blocked up the only other exit from the lane.

As though to rob the Winged Man of the last hope of escape, Danby Druce and two constables who were well acquainted with the town hastened down a turning running parallel with the blind lane, and appeared on the top of the wall.

"Surrender! Escape is impossible!" cried Danby Druce, his voice shrill with triumph. "You are hemmed in on every side. If you attempt to fly, my men have orders to fire!"

A smile of amused contempt on his pale face, the Winged Man glanced at the speaker, then turned fiercely at bay.

Eager to share the promised reward, between forty and fifty stalwart men raced down the street towards him. A dozen feet from the Winged Man the mob came to an abrupt halt, spellbound when they saw the awful spectacle the Winged Man presented.

"Close on him! Seize him!" cried Danby Druce, alarmed by these strange preparations.

"Ha, ha! Ho, ho!"

A deep roll of mocking laughter chilled every heart. Fearing lest his quarry should escape him after all, Druce sprang forward.

Again that fearful laughter haunted the air.

Then the Winged Man raised his right foot and brought it heavily to the ground, and before the eyes of all the ground opened and the Winged Man disappeared.

For the first time, Danby Druce felt inclined to attribute supernatural powers to the Winged Man.

It is true Nantwich is honeycombed with salt mines and pits, from which the brine is being constantly pumped out. Into one of these pits the Winged Man had most probably disappeared. But if so, wonderful indeed must have been the chance which had brought him to bay over a possible lane of escape.

It was not chance which had led the Winged Man to that lane. Nantwich, its salt mines and its mysterious caverns, were as well known to this wondrous being as the Strand to a Londoner.

To be ready for some such danger as had recently threatened him, he had prepared the soil so that a heavy kick on a certain stone would loosen the earth and allow him to drop into the caves caused beneath Nantwich by the constant withdrawal of the salt from the earth. The fall of a dozen feet had brought the Winged Man to the floor of the cave.

His headlight, now clear and white, once more shining brightly before him, he turned towards where a round, tunnel-like passage, glistened with salt crystals, led apparently into the bosom of the earth.

Presently the Winged Man reached what looked like an enormous black subterranean sea.

It was one of the many lakes of brine that have supplied Nantwich with salt for over a thousand years.

Skimming lightly across the lake, the Winged Man squeezed through a crevasse in the rock, then stood gazing in rapture upon a sight that no eye but his had ever beheld.

He might have been standing in a magnificent cathedral, the walls of which were encrusted with gems of every description. Here were altars, pillars, chancel, choir, nave, and screen, carved into a thousand fantastic shapes by the hand of Nature.

As thoroughly at home here as in his lair on the Yorkshire cliffs, the Winged Man threaded his way through innumerable passages, and at length he paused beneath an uneven crack in the rocky ceiling above his head.

Into this crevasse he sprang, then entered a room full of crystal pendants, on the floor of which was spread, in reckless confusion, money, gold, gems of priceless value, for this was one of the Winged Man's many hiding-places, where he stored his plunder.

THE HAUNTED MIRROR.

James Grantison entered his dining-room at Ackerton Court.

He was nervous and ill at ease, for he had just received Danby Druce's description of the Winged Man's escape.

The story had struck terror into the miser's heart.

Before a large, old-fashioned wall glass, reaching from the ceiling to the top of a richly-carved oak dinner-waggon, he paused to note how the terror of the last few weeks had aged him.

Presently a strange, black object in the very centre of the glass riveted his attention.

So small was it that at first he believed it to be a tiny speck of dust, but has he gazed it grew bigger, until it grew to the size of a large bee.

Then he detected wings protruding from either side of a round, black body.

Paralysed with terror, yet unable to withdraw his eyes from the black, ever-moving object that seemed to exercise a hypnotic influence over him, James

Grantison stared with protruding eyes into the glass.

Nearer and nearer it came, growing larger and larger each moment.

From a bee it turned to the size of a swallow, a blackbird, a hawk, a falcon, an eagle.

Then—

James Grantison's heart almost ceased to beat, cold shivers ran up and down his back, he trembled as though in ague's awful grasp.

"The Winged Man—the Winged Man!" he groaned, reeling back to the table, yet unable to remove his eyes from the approaching figure.

Then would James Grantison have given every penny of his hoarded wealth to have been able to turn and fly.

But he was rooted to the ground with terror, his teeth chattering, his every limb trembling.

Nearer and nearer came that fearful reflection in the mirror, until now Grantison could distinguish every bending rib in those slowly-moving wings and sharp-pointed feet and the white, uncanny face.

Presently the Winged Man's reflection filled the entire mirror.

"Back! Come no further! I can bear no more!" The despairing cry ended in a shrill, terror-laden shriek, for a cold, icy hand was laid upon his shoulder as the awful never-to-be-forgotten voice of the Winged Man seemed from out of the mirror itself to hiss in his ears:

"I am here!"

Paralysed with superstitious terror, fearing the Winged Man's vengeance, James Grantison looked from the real Winged Man to his dread reflection in the glass.

Drawing the miser's note of hand from his pocket, the Winged Man tore it to shreds before his eyes.

"What, you forego your price! You forgive your debt?" cried Grantison, unable to conceal his satisfaction.

"The time for gold has passed. You must pay the price in another way," snarled the Winged Man.

Grantison turned a white, appealing face up to the Winged Man. There could be no mistake as to what the Winged Man meant by that other way.

"No, no! Have mercy! I will dismiss Druce! I will be your dog, your slave; only spare me!" he implored.

"Too late!" came the awful verdict from the Winged Man's lips.

His trembling legs refusing to support his body, Grantison dropped upon his knees, moaning out:

"Mercy—mercy!"

The scarce-formed words were forced by sheer terror from the trembling man's lips.

Once more the fearful replied: "too late!" filled the room.

Once more the hoarse whisper, that could scarcely be called a cry for mercy, broke the silence.

"James Grantison, twice have I saved your miserable life—once from an enemy's steel, once from a felon's end. How have you repaid me? By seeking my destruction, by pitting against me the only man in the world holds whose brain is worthy to contend with mine!" thundered the Winged Man.

The miserable wretch grovelled on the floor. Raising his head he would have spoken, but the Winged Man silenced him with an imperative gesture.

With wings outstretched, his face contorted with fearful rage, the Winged Man hovered over his victim.

"Fool, to think that you, a mere earthworm, without courage to hold the wealth you have acquired by knavery, could pit your puny brain against mine!" roared the Winged Man.

"Mercy—mercy!"

A dry, husky whisper was all Grantison could force from his parched throat.

Then even the power of speech left him as the Winged Man, rising from the floor, hovered over him with outstretched pinions, then descended with fearful deliberation, until but a few inches intervened between James Grantison's shrinking form and that of the avenger. He gave himself up for lost.

Twice he essayed to speak, twice words refused to come. At length, in so shrill a shriek that it seemed as though his very soul was being forced through his parched lips, he cried:

"All—all! Take all I have, but spare my life!"

Slowly the Winged Man's wings collapsed, and his feet dropping to the floor, he stood, with folded arms, gazing contemptuously upon his victim.

"Rise!" he commanded.

As one in a dream, James Grantison staggered to his feet.

"Lead the way!" ordered the Winged Man.

Surprise gave James Grantison the power of speech.

"Whither?"

"To the secret chamber, where, whilst Danby Druce was hunting me, as you fondly hoped, to my doom, you have hidden your gold to save it, as you thought—poor fool!—from me."

Terror gave place to blank amazement.

Lest the Winged Man should, after all, prevail, Grantison had withdrawn every penny he possessed from his various banks, leaving but a few thousands which he hoped, should the worst come to the worst, to foist upon the Winged Man as his total wealth.

Grantison trusted no one. With his own hands he had carried the gold into a secret room known only to himself, and yet this fearful being knew all about it.

The anger faded from the Winged Man's face.

Yet Grandison would rather have seen the most angry glare in his eyes than the fearful, blood-curdling smile that hovered on the Winged Man's lips.

Anger might cool, but the emotions that showed itself in that terrible smile was as merciless as the man-eating tiger of the Indian jungle.

With a gesture of impatience, the Winged Man pointed towards the door. Starting as one awakened from a dream, James Grantison led the way from the room.

Grantison Plays His Last Card.

Felt-hatted, long-cloaked—the draping of his wings made him seem garbed in an Inverness—the Winged Man followed his unwilling guide.

George Denning, Grantison's butler, who was in the hall, stared at the tall, dignified-looking stranger who followed his master with stately steps through the hall.

Denning had but an hour ago returned to Ackerton from a week's visit to a sick relative, and had not yet heard of the Winged Man's strange doings.

Yet he felt a feeling of helpless fear surge through his frame as the Winged Man glided by with noiseless steps.

His foot on the lowest step of the wide oak-balustraded staircase, James Grantison cast a swift glance of appeal for help behind him. The butler detected the signal, and followed.

Half-way up the staircase the Winged Man turned. Denning came to an abrupt halt, every vestige of colour flying from his round, well-fed face as he saw for the first time the Winged Man's coal-like eyes.

"Go!" thundered the Winged Man.

Then, as though confident his command would be obeyed, followed Grantison. Again he turned. The old man, anxious and trembling, still followed.

"Go!" thundered the Winged Man, stamping his foot angrily.

"No, no; let him come! Do not leave us, Denning," interposed James Grantison, in quivering tones, so different from his master's usually stern, decisive voice that Denning, though almost beside himself with terror, determined not to leave his old employer with this strange visitor to Grantison Court.

As though unconscious that his twice-repeated command was being disobeyed, the Winged Man waved James Grantison on, and the strange procession moved on.

The stairs terminated in a wide, domed-shaped arch, its woodwork supported by a grotesquely carved oaken figures.

As Denning stepped beneath this arch he paused, chilled to the heart by the Winged Man's weird, fearful, mournful cry. Then they Winged Man turned swiftly upon him. A cry of terror rose from Denning's lips.

Borrowing redoubled terrors from the dim light of the gallery, the Winged Man stood, his wings distended.

"Go!" thundered the Winged Man for the third time.

Clasping his hands to his eyes, Denning stepped back, missed the step, and, clutching wildly at the empty air, rolled headlong to the foot of the stairs, where he lay still.

"Thus is it with all who would disobey me!" cried the Winged Man, turning a significant glance upon James Grantison, who, moaning with terror, his shaking legs scarce able to bear the weight of his body, continued on his way until they came to what was known in Grantison Court as the Royal ball-room.

Here Queen Bess had tripped the light fantastic toe in the good old days, but for many years the floor had been declared unsafe, and even before the time of the Court's present occupier the ball-room had been disused. Still, ancient tapestry hung on the wall, and gilded furniture of a bygone age was strewn about the floor.

Ever since his butler's fall, leaving himself alone with the Winged Man, James Grantison seemed strangely changed. Before, he had proceeded with lagging, hesitating, unwilling steps; now a look of intense cunning shone from his eyes, and he moved across the ball-room with quickened steps.

Once more that dread smile crept into the Winged Man's eyes. Straight to the farther corner of the room Grantison led the way. Pressing himself tightly against the corner walls he drew his companion towards him. A shadow shook his frame as the weird being's garb brushed lightly by him.

Groping beneath the tapestry, Grantison touched what looked like a rusty nail, but was in reality the lever which put the machinery necessary to work this ingenious hiding-place into motion.

Immediately the whole corner walls and floor alike turned round, carrying Grantison and the Winged Man, until it formed the two sides of one of the four square towers which stood at each corner of Grantison Court.

Another secret spring caused the floor to sink to a large, vault like, subterranean chamber beneath the foundations of the old court, lighted by greetings hidden beneath the ivy that clung to the ancient wall.

"Fool that I am, I have forgotten a candle!" stammered Grantison, with a sidelong glance at the Winged Man. "No matter. We have not far to go. Follow me!"

As promptly as though he did not know that his treacherous guide was leading him to a fearful doom, the Winged Man obeyed, and Grantison led the way into one of the many dark passages that radiated from the vault like the spokes of a wheel.

Grantison Court had seen exciting times in the old days, and probably no place in England was so well fitted with secret hiding-places and subterranean passages.

"This way—this way!" cried Grantison eagerly as he moved swiftly down the tunnel, carefully counting each step as he walked. Presently he cried out: "One moment. I am uncertain which turning to take. Remain where you are until I call again."

Exulting as he heard the Winged Man's footsteps cease to follow, he dropped on his hands and knees. Presently his groping fingers closed over the edge of a narrow plank, across which he tremblingly crept.

He did not breathe freely until he stood upon the firm ground once more, for he had crossed on the plank a pit studded with long iron spikes, where, in days dead and gone, Grantisons had lured victims to their doom in this fearful tunnel.

The chasm crossed, Grantison whirled round a small wheel that protruded from the brickwork of the tunnel, and one end of the bridge dropped noiselessly into the chasm till it hung vertically down.

"All right—come!" he cried, wondering if the Winged Man could detect the tremor, which, do what he would, he could not keep from his voice.

He waited breathlessly. No sound from the Winged Man reached his ears. But what of that? He knew no tiger in its lair moved more noiselessly than the dreaded being into whose power he had fallen.

Scarce daring to breathe, Grantison listened for the terrified scream, the hurtling of a heavy body through the air, followed by a moan of agony at the bottom of the pit.

Nor was he disappointed. Suddenly an ejaculation of alarm reached his ears followed by a low, agony-laden moan, apparently from the bottom of the pit.

"Grantison, you treacherous hound, you have slain me!" cried the Winged Man's harsh voice.

"Ha, ha, ha!" laughed the triumphant man, scarce able to contain himself for joy and relief. "Who's the fool now?" he demanded.

"You!" cried a mocking voice behind him.

A flood of light filled the tunnel; and, turning, he beheld the same mysterious being he had sought to send to his death.

A loud, nerve-thrilling shriek escaped Grantison's lips. Then, urged by the hopeless despair that now filled his heart, he plunged headlong into the pit.

With a cry of rage the Winged Man dived after him. And ere Grantison's falling body reached the bottom the Winged Man had seized him by the arm, and a few flaps of his powerful wings carried them both in safety to the mouth of the pit.

"Not yet; your time has not come yet!" rolled in deep, sonorous accents from the Winged Man's lips.

"End me—kill me! I can bear no more!" moaned Grantison.

"Lead on! Those upon whom the Winged Man has set the seal of doom die only at his bidding!" was the response to his appeal.

RUINED!

There is a certain phase of extreme terror when, unable to bear more, courage—or, at least, calmness—comes to the rescue of the tormented one. Such a stage had James Grantison reached. As a walking machine, rather than a living being, he moved ahead of the Winged Man, until a few minutes later they had apparently reached the end of the tunnel.

Again James Grantison touched a concealed spring. A mighty slab of stone sunk into the earth, revealing a small door cut in the solid rock.

With trembling fingers Grantison removed a key from a chain he wore round his neck and unlocked the door. As he thrust it open the Winged Man's head light was extinguished and they passed through the doorway into a darkness that could be felt.

Not daring to address the Winged Man without being spoken to, Grantison was fumbling with nervous fingers for a matchbox, when suddenly the Winged Man's head light blazed forth.

A cry of dismay escaped James Grantison's lips. They were in a small apartment cut out of the solid rock. Around the walls stood a number of ancient, ironbound chests. A few hours before Grantison had left these chests closed, locked, and filled with rich, red gold. Now every lid rested against the wall; every coffer was empty.

"My gold—my gold—my precious gold!" cried Grantison, rushing from box to box.

"Robbed—betrayed—ruined!" he shrieked, a minute later, looking wildly around him, as he tore his hair with frenzied hands.

For a moment he had forgotten the Winged Man's presence. Suddenly the truth burst upon him. Beside himself with rage, he seized the Winged Man by the throat, crying:

"It is you—it is you who have robbed me! Scoffer and mocker, you lured me here, knowing that my gold had already passed from my possession into yours!"

James Grantison was no weakling, yet, though he grappled with the Winged Man with the vicious strength of a madman, he could not so much as shake that wondrously endowed being's firm stand.

Click! Icy-cold fingers touched Grantison's wrists; something harder and even colder than ice encircled his wrists. Sheer amazement robbed him of strength. He released his hold of the Winged Man and looked down in speechless surprise at his wrists. They were handcuffed. In vain he tried to speak. His tongue refused its office.

Paralysed with terror, unable to raise a finger to help himself, Grantison staggered back as the Winged Man laid his long index finger on the miser's breast, and thrust him, inch by inch, nearer the wall.

As Grantison's back touched the rocky side of the tunnel, the Winged Man reached above his head and pressed a peculiarly-shaped stone embedded in the rocky ceiling. The wall behind his victim gave way, and Grantison found himself staggering backwards, apparently into the very heart of the earth.

For hundreds of years the secret of the subterranean dungeons, vaults, and passages beneath Grantison Court had been handed down from father to son. Yet, numerous though the known secret hiding-places, there were as many more the secrets of which were known only to that mysterious being, the Winged Man.

Suddenly the earth opened beneath the terrified man. A deep roll of thunder struck upon his ears; red, lurid flames played around him; the scorching breath of an enormous fire swept across his body, and he remembered no more.

An hour later James Grantison awoke to consciousness. His eyes were closed, and for some time he dared not open them, lest he should see the livid horrors of that awful place. Presently the deathlike silence that obtained on every hand grew more than he could bear. Rising to a sitting position, he looked around him.

With a cry of relief, tears of joy rolling down his cheeks, he sprang from the couch upon which he found himself. He was alive, and, better still, in his own bedchamber.

Surely the appearance of the Winged Man in the glass, the terrible journey through the secret subterranean passages, the loss of his gold, and the fearful end of his adventures was all a dream?

No! His wondering eyes fell upon the wall immediately before him. Written in letters of crimson upon a square of white flame, appeared the words:

"Received of Mr. James Grantison, for services rendered, the sum of £117,421 7s 8d.—Signed, the Winged Man."

James Grantison remained staring at the writing on the wall until it disappeared; then, staggering to the fireplace, tugged at the bell-pull so furiously that it came away in his hands.

A white-faced servant answered his summons.

"Send Denning to me at once."

The girl burst into a flood of tears.

"Denning is dead, sir! He fell downstairs and broke his neck an hour ago!" she sobbed.

"Denning dead! Why was I not told?" demanded Grantison.

"We could not find you, sir. You were not in the house. I looked everywhere for you."

Grantison dismissed the weeping girl. Dropping into a chair, he buried his face in his hands.

It was all true then, and no dream. The Winged Man had indeed conquered. He was a ruined man!

DIGGERS BY NIGHT.

It was a wild night! Such a night as in the old days men believed witches revelled on bleak mountain-tops and demons rushed streaking through the air.

In fitful gusts, raising weird sounds and gibbering shrieks, the wind drove fiercely up Ixworth Street.

Not a soul was in sight. Who would be out on such a night unless impelled by duty—or some dark deed.

Presently a dark form stole from out a narrow lane.

Glancing fearfully around, he crossed the street. As he did so, a second form descended the steps leading to the pillared arch before the Pickerel, an ancient hostelry that had been famed in the old coaching days.

"That you, Sam?" whispered the new-comer.

"Yes, master," was the reply.

"I saw old Grogan, the policeman, go off Stanton way," declared the other. "He will be safe enough for the next hour, and before then you'll be safe in bed with fifty pounds in your pocket, and I will be on my way to London."

Whilst the above conversation was taking place, the two men had left Ixworth Street, and, skirting the wall round the churchyard, had crossed a small stream, to find themselves in the grounds of Ixworth Abbey.[16]

Both men knew every inch of the path they trod. Well for them they did so.

The night was as dark as a midnight cavern.

"Phew! The wind seems to drive through one," muttered Sam shifting the pickaxe and spade he carried from one shoulder to the other, and blowing on numb fingers to warm them.

"Just the night for our job, Sam," returned his companion encouragingly. "We'll be as safe from interruption as though on a desert island."

"Don't know nothing about no desert island, Master George Harman," growled the labourer; "but, as you say, it's just the night for a job like ours. Sakes alive, if it warn't for the fifty pounds you might do the job yourself! Mark my words, we aren't the only evil things about on such a night as this."

A low, contemptuous laugh escaped the other's lips.

"Then I pity the 'evil things' if they cross my path!" replied George Harman, balancing a thick, heavy bludgeon in his hand.

The next moment he jumped lightly over a ditch and forced his way through a quick set hedge.

Followed, though with evident reluctance, by his companion, Harman led the way to one corner of a ploughed field, from whence he strode along the ditch, counting every furrow as he walked until the fifth was reached, when he stopped and scrambled into the ditch.

"Turn on the lantern, Sam!" he commanded; adding angrily the next moment: "Keep its beams on me, you fool! Do you want to flash signals all over the country?"

Immediately the white circle of light fell upon the speaker, disclosing the features of one who, though still young, was aged by dissipation and evil passions unrestrained.

His well-fitting riding-breeches and cut-away coat contrasted strangely with the corduroy trousers, tied at the knees, rough coat, and skin waistcoat and cap of his low-browed, villainous-looking companion.

Straddling over the bottom of the ditch, Harman scraped aside the dead leaves with which it was more than half full. A terrible sight was revealed. From between the dead leaves appeared a pallid face.

---

[16] Augustinian Priory, not far from Bury St Edmunds, Suffolk.

"Keep the lantern still, you trembling fool!" growled Harman over his shoulder to the man who was holding the lantern to light his employer on his task.

"That'll do. Shut off the light!" he ordered after a while, scrambling out of the ditch with a dread and awesome burden, which, throwing over his shoulder, Harman led the way into the darkness that enveloped the field.

His companion, less hardened than himself, was almost beside himself with fear. He stumbled as he walked. His chattering teeth kept up a fearful accompaniment to that grim march.

"You pitiful coward!" growled Harman.

The choice he had made the place in which to hide the proof of his dark deed proved his daring and also his knowledge of human nature. Others might have buried the victim in one of the many woods about the ancient abbey, or in some hidden nook, but he would hide his burden where no one would think to look for its burying-place.

On the very top of a rise in the ground, too gentle to be called a hill, he threw his burden down upon some stubble as yet untouched by the plough. He would remove the upper crust of earth and stubble, replace it over the grave, then, on the morrow, the plough would pass over the spot, and all trace of what lay below would be effectually wiped out.

Soon the two men, Sam wielding a pick, Harman a spade, commenced their gruesome midnight task.

His blood warmed by work and by repeated application of Harman's brandy flask to his lips, Sam, with the thought of the fifty pounds before his eyes, worked as the lazy, hulking scoundrel had never worked before.

"Another foot and it will do," declared Harman at last, pausing to wipe the perspiration from his brow.

"It's shallow, master, but no plough shaft will ever reach it here," retorted Sam grimly; then, his face shining white and ghastly through the darkness, he cried: "Hush! What is that?"

From out the darkness came a peculiar noise, as if some huge bird flying overhead. Nearer and nearer came the mysterious, beating sounds. Instinctively the conscious-stricken men drew together.

"It is but a heron disturbed from the meadow," muttered Harman.

"No heron ever made that noise," returned the other, through his chattering teeth.

Then a loud cry of terror burst from his lips.

He would have sprung from the unfinished cavity had not Harman seized him by the neck, and pressing him against the earth, hissed in his ear:

"Silence, you fool! A word, and you are a dead man!"

Even as he spoke an unwonted terror filled his heart, for a dark form, like that of some enormous bat, was flying with huge, slowly-moving wings immediately over their heads.

"What can it be? Ugh! I'm trembling like a woman!" muttered Harman. "Come, coward! To work. It was only some big bird. Here, take a drink of this. It will put fresh courage into your milk-and-water heart," he added aloud, thrusting a flask into his accomplice's willing hand when the weird night-flyer had passed.

Sam raised the flask to his lips, and did not lower it until he had swallowed the last drop. Then, eager to get his task done and to feel the reward safely in his pocket, he drove his pick deep into the yielding soil.

A Vain Race.

So engrossed were the two men with their work, that they did not see the Winged Man himself alight within a dozen feet of them.

Suddenly Sam's pick gave out the musical ring of metal upon the metal.

Harman looked quickly up.

"What's that?" he demanded; then, pushing his accomplice aside, he scraped away the soil from the lid of a small iron box or chest.

George Harman knew that the field had at one time been part of the abbey, and, forgetful even of his terrible task, dug away the earth around the object and had soon drawn from the ground a small iron box, a foot long by six inches wide. The rusty hasp was easily broken, and within lay a small golden casket embossed with beautifully-executed classical subjects.

"What is it, master?" growled Sam curiously.

"Nothing; a mere trifle. I will pay you half what it fetches," returned Harman, slipping the gold box into his pocket. Once more they resumed their grim task.

"There, that will do. There's room for two here!" hissed Harman at last, resting on the handle of his spade.

Sam looked half fearfully at the speaker.

"Two! There aren't no other you've been and gone and made away with, be there?" he asked, in a low, awestricken voice.

"No; only that one there—and you!" cried Harman fiercely, as he brought his spade down with crushing force upon his comrade's head. "Dead men tell no tales."

With a low, gasping moan the unfortunate man fell at the scoundrel's feet.

"Fool! Did you think I have let you live to put a rope round my neck? No, no! George Harman is master of his own fate."

"You lie!"

The voice came from the foot of the grave. The next moment a fierce, blinding light flashed full in George Harman's eyes.

The fearful beams flooded the newly-made grave and the terror-stricken wretch, as well as the huddled shape at his feet, which a minute before had been a living man.

For some moments George Harman was too alarmed to move or speak. His heart almost ceased to beat. Icy fingers seemed to grip his spine. His hair stood on end. In speechless horror he gazed upon that black, threatening form.

"You lie!" repeated the Winged Man, stretching forth his fearful, talon-like hands as though to seize the guilty man. "You control your fate! You are mine—yes, mine!"

Still George Harman did not speak. Terror such as he had never before experienced had turned the very marrow in his bones to ice.

Gradually into his fear-dulled brain crept the remembrance of a report he had heard, and laughed at, of some strange, flying being known as the Winged Man.

Gradually his self-possession returned. Instinctively he knew that force would avail little against this wondrous being. Flight, and flight alone, would save him.

Turning quickly, he fled through the darkness as swiftly as his legs would carry him. A trained athlete, ever first in his college sports—he was a gentleman born—George Harman dashed across the field, cleared the intervening fence at a bound, and sped like a deer across the parklike grounds of the ancient abbey.

Presently he looked fearfully over his shoulders; the fearful beating of the Winged Man's wings fell like a knell upon his ears.

A dozen feet from the ground, the Winged Man was gliding through the air close behind him.

His courage rose as his peril increased. Straining every nerve he possessed, he reached the banks of the River Thet, then glanced over his shoulder once more.

The Winged Man had disappeared. For a moment he hesitated, then moved swiftly but silently along the shallow river until he reached the old bridge which carries the road from Ixworth to Bury St. Edmund's over the Thet.

A minute's delay beneath the arch, and he forced his way through the weeds until the low meadows which mark the course of the river were reached.

A triumphant laugh burst from his lips. He had baffled the Winged Man. Hark! Was that an echo that had replied to his laugh? No.

Hovering over the dark surface of the stream, he saw his relentless pursuer.

"The box!" demanded the Winged Man, holding his hand towards the trembling man.

"It is in—" began Harman, then checked himself. "I have dropped it; it is gone."

"Fool to think that a mere human worm like you could deceive the Winged Man! The box, or your life!" thundered the Winged Man.

"Never!" replied Harman ere he continued his mad flight across the meadows.

Vain would have been Harman's flight had the Winged Man chosen. But he preferred to play with him as a cat does with a mouse.

In vain Harman strove to dodge him. Each time the Winged Man turned him in the direction he would have him go. Presently a loud, deep, grinding noise fell upon the ears of pursuer and pursued alike.

Beyond the meadows arose a large water-mill. Thither the Winged Man was driving his victim. The mill reached, Harman put on a spurt, hoping to find shelter within.

Like a hawk swooping down on a flying partridge, the Winged Man descended, seized him by the collar of his coat, and bore him, paralysed with fear, from the ground.

Up flew the mysterious being, higher and higher. Too terrified even to cry for assistance, or to appeal for mercy, George Harman hung limp in the Winged Man's grasp.

A few strokes of his mighty wing carried him over the mill; then he released his hold, and with outstretched limbs the villain hurtled earthwards.

A loud splash proclaimed that he had fallen into the centre of the mill dam. Rising, grasping and struggling, to the surface, he looked fearfully around him again. The Winged Man had vanished.

Renewed hope springing to life in his heart, Harman struck out for the nearest bank. Another stroke, and the rest which he so much needed would be his.

But no! Even as with a frantic clutch he sought to seize the grass-lined bank, a dark form swept over the surface of the dam, a white, skeleton-like hand shot from out the darkness, and he was thrust back into deep water once more.

A WAKING NIGHTMARE.

Filled with a blind, unreasoning panic, Harman felt that fearful hand thrusting him further from the shore. The centre of the mill-dam reached, the Winged Man vanished.

Throwing himself on his back, George Harman drew long, cruel breaths of the night air into his exhausted lungs.

With clenched teeth, hard-set face, the obstinate courage of his race urging him to do or die, he turned and swam in the direction of the mill-garden.

Again he neared the shore. Again that fearful hand pressed him back. He dare not give way to the fearful dread that hammered at his heart, or he would have lost his reason.

Harman felt a hand grasp his own.

There was something grim and impish in the way the Winged Man allowed him to gain safety, only to thrust him back into the hungry depths.

A wild, fierce anger fired his heart. He would live! He dare not die! Rage lent him renewed strength. He must, he would, gain the shore.

With long, strong strokes he cleaved his way through the water. His hand closed over the grating of an overflow-pipe. Safe at last! No hand touched his shoulder. No fearful force drove him beneath the surface.

"Hurrah! Ah, what is that?"

Noiselessly and silently the Winged Man dropped on the wooden beam above his head. Icy-cold fingers tore his hand from its hold, and he was dragged with relentless force back to the centre of the mill-dam.

Mocking laughter filled the night air.

Nearly spent, his eyes dim, his heart beating like the piston of a steam-engine, Harman swam with dogged determination towards the nearest bank once more.

It was nearly over. His strength was spent, his courage well-nigh gone. It was only his indomitable will that, put to a good purpose, would have raised him to the top of any profession he might have chosen, which kept him afloat.

Slower, less regular, grew his strokes, quicker, fiercer, his laboured breathing. It was of no use. He was doomed.

Better the unknown, beyond the veil of doom, than that fearful, age-long struggle for life.

He ceased swimming, yet felt himself being borne swiftly onwards. The thunderous roar of the mill-wheel dinned in his ears. His end had come. A more fearful end than drowning would be his. He was being drawn with irresistible force towards the sluice beneath the water-wheel, over which the dark torrent poured.

The Winged Man had indeed proved the controller of his fate.

He closed his eyes, but the faces—faces engraved upon his brain and heart, faces of those who owed their ends to him—grinned at him from out the darkness.

With a shriek, he opened his eyes again.

Scarcely less awful was the sight of the revolving wheel moving slowly round and round, its broad blades striking the water with tremendous force.

"Help, help, help!" shouted George Harman frantically, as his exhausted body was pressed with the crushing force against the iron top of the sluice-gate.

He was doomed! Naught but miracle would save him. And the miracle happened. As though at the word of command, the mill-wheel ceased to revolve just as he pitched headforemost on to the slats.

For a moment he hung, clutching convulsively at the slime-covered woodwork. In vain! His fingers could not make good their hold upon those slippery paddles. Hope vanished, despair held him captive. Suddenly he was seized by a pair of strong arms and drawn within the wheel.

A glance at his preserver, and he struggled fiercely to break free. Better to be crushed beneath the mill-wheel's massive paddles than to fall alive into the Winged Man's hands.

Trembling in every limb, the wretched man looked into the cold face that towered above him. Then his nerves gave way. His oft-vaunted courage vanished like dew before the sun.

"Mercy—mercy! Man or ghost, which ever you be, have pity!" he whined.

"The mercy you gave to others shall be yours!" announced the Winged Man, in deep tones.

Trembling like one in a shivering fit, Harman felt cold fingers clasping his wrist, and he was led, cowed and beaten, on to the moss-grown stones at the foot of the wheel-pit.

As they reached the top of the worn stone steps, the miller, who was working all night to complete an important order for the next day, hastened towards them. One glance at the Winged Man's white face, and he fled, shrieking loudly for help.

Instead of following the terror-stricken miller, the Winged Man that his prisoner up two flights of wooden stairs, thick with flour-dust, to a square gable projecting over the road below, through which the miller's men raised the sacks of corn from the farmers' waggons.

Stooping, the Winged Man opened the double trap doors in the floor of the gable. Beneath them lay the white road.

"Jump!" ordered the Winged Man, pointing through the opening.

Harman covered his face with his hands.

"I dare not! Mercy upon me! I dare not!" he moaned.

The Winged Man looked at him, surprise and contempt in his eyes. Could this trembling wretch be the man who, though he knew him to be an unscrupulous villain, had, to a certain extent, redeemed his faults in the Winged Man's eyes by the gallant fight he had made against capture and death?

"Jump!" he thundered again, stamping his foot angrily upon the wooden floor.

It seemed to the terrified man that the very mill shook beneath the Winged Man's falling foot. One glance at the stern, white face of the mystic being who had become his master, and, dreading the hard road less than the Winged Man's anger, he uttered a wild, fearful cry, and sprang headlong through the opening.

Scarce more awesome was the Winged Man's long-drawn, mournful cry, as he plunged into space after his victim. Circling in the air, he pounced upon the fallen man, seized him by the arm, carried him up almost to the clouds, let go his hold of him once more, then again darted on him and stayed his downward flight, and lowered him gently to the road.

"To the place where you hid the golden box! March!" thundered the Winged Man.

His knees trembling so that they could scarce support his quivering body, his head bowed, his eyes fixed fearfully upon his companion, Harman obeyed the dread command.

Back across the meadows over which he had fled so swiftly, his breast filled with excitement, enjoyment of the wild race, anything but fear, Harman retraced his steps, a whimpering, cringing coward. Never again would he hold up his head before his fellow men. His nerve had gone for ever.

Once, when the Winged Man laughed aloud at his own thoughts, he almost fell to the ground through sheer terror. Passing beneath the bridge, Harman came to a halt. Thrusting his hand into a hole in the brickwork, he pulled out the box he had so strangely found, and handed it, submissively, to his conqueror.

For a moment the Winged Man's headlight blazed out, whilst he assured himself that it was indeed the golden box the other had so meekly surrendered to him. Then he flew slowly on.

Looking upwards, Harman saw the Winged Man rise on his fearful black pinions into the air, and disappear from view. He was alone.

Something seemed to snap within his head, and all was blank.

IN PERIL BY FIRE.

Within a bed-room in a large house some five hundred yards from Thurston Station, the Winged Man was examining the box he had taken from Harman.

A lover of the artistic and beautiful, the Winged Man was struck at once with the delicate workmanship on the lid of the golden box.

It was empty, but as, holding it to his ear, he shook it, something rattled inside.

Eagerly he searched amongst the raised work on its lid for some secret spring. No hidden mechanism could escape the Winged Man's keen eyes for long.

A tiny black mark, too dark for dirt, on the neck of one of the figures attracted his attention. Grasping the figure's head between his finger and thumb, the Winged Man moved it backwards and forwards until the lid flew in halves, and a closely-folded document dropped on his knees.

Thrusting the casket into his pocket, the Winged Man perused his find. It was Latin. Written in ancient English characters, yet the Winged Man read it off as though it had been a newly-printed newspaper of the present day. As he read his interest deepened.

"It must be something of great importance. A king's ransom—ay, more, an abbey's ransom!" he muttered, re-folding the paper.

In the act of replacing it in the golden box he paused.

"No, no! the Winged Man shares with none!" he muttered. "The wealth shall be mine; no other I shall gaze upon, no other fingers shall touch it!"

Thrusting the parchment into the grate, he applied a match to the precious document; then, as it burst into flame, sprang on to the bed, and, crouched on the pillows, was soon fast asleep.

Three days had passed since the Winged Man had last closed his eyes. An unwonted heaviness sealed his eyelids. Yet in two hours' time he would awake, as fresh and fit for work as though he had slept all night.

But barely a quarter of that time had passed ere a foe, against whom even he might fight in vain, stole upon the Winged Man. Fire—dreadful, all-denouncing fire—crept from out the darkness upon the sleeping being. Barely half the old parchment had blazed away ere it fell into the fender, and, opening, shot forth a tongue of flame, which licked some silken draperies hanging from an old-fashioned mantelboard.

Immediately the flame shot up, and a minute later the burning curtains, severed from the loops that held the silk, fell on to the half-rug. At first it seemed as though the flame might burn itself out without causing further damage. But, fanned by a draught from under the door, the smouldering fire grew bigger and brighter, until at last it burst into flame, and the room was doomed.

Fortunately for all within the house, Colonel Rote, the owner of the house, awoke, sniffed, detecting the smell of burning, and hastened on to the landing. Wreaths of smoke, pouring from behind the door, told that a fire had broken out in the empty guest-chamber.

Rushing to the door, he turned the handle. It was locked.

"Fire! Fire! Fire!" he yelled vociferously. Then hastening back to his room, he re-appeared a minute later armed with a heavy Army revolver, the muscle of which he placed against the lock, then pulled the trigger.

As the loud report echoed through the house a man and two frightened maidservants hastened upon the scene.

"The guest-chamber is on fire! How came the door locked. Sword and spurs, someone will have to suffer for it!" thundered the colonel, as he burst open the door.

Smoke, streaked with lurid flame, filled the room. On the threshold the colonel came to an abrupt halt.

"Powers above! What's that?" he gasped, staring with starting eyeballs at the Winged Man; who, half-suffocated, was standing with outspread wings, gazing in dazed consternation around the burning room.

His weird, wailing cry mingled with the roaring of the flames, the Winged Man made for the door. The colonel raised his pistol, but the Winged Man knocked up his arm, and the bullet crashed into the ceiling.

The next moment the old man was hurled roughly aside, whilst the butler and the frightened servants scattered in all directions, as, his mocking laugh echoing through the house, the Winged Man through up a landing window, paused on the sill to snarl defiance at the plucky old colonel, then, followed by wildly-aimed bullets, disappeared into the night.

DANBY DRUCE RESUMES THE SEARCH.

In quiet lodgings, in a quiet London Street, Danby Druce, the great detective, was carelessly turning over the leaves of an evening paper. Suddenly his eyes flashed, his face grew pale, his whole frame tautened, as he read a half-laughing, wholly-incredulous description of the strange events which had taken place at the little Suffolk villages of Ixworth and Thurston.

"Fools! They know not the Winged Man, or they would not dare to laugh!" he cried, bringing his hand down heavily upon the table.

His face hardened; a look of heroic determination crept into his eyes as he continued:

"Come, Danby Druce, be a man! Throw off this unnerving terror. Even were the impossible possible, and this winged scoundrel a being from another world, you would prove his match."

Sitting back in his chair, he touched the button of an electric bell. A man entered.

"Pack up our things, Bourne! Be ready to catch the nine-fifteen to Bury St. Edmunds!" he ordered. "You will go with me."

The man, an ex-policeman, who had been Danby Druce's companion in many a breathless adventure, saluted.

"Burglary?" he asked, leaning over his master's shoulder.

Suddenly his huge frame stiffened, his eyes flashed angrily.

"Is it the Flying Unknown we are after?" he demanded, laying a finger upon the paragraph referring to the Winged Man.

Danby Druce looked up in surprise.

"Do you know him?"

"Ay," replied the other fiercely. "It was my son who met his end through him in the National Gallery!"

"And you never told me," said Druce reproachfully.

"Why should I, sir?" replied Bourne. "What can you do against a being such as he?"

"I can catch him and hand him over to the police—and I will!" declared Danby Druce, with a bold, reckless, defiant laugh.

Half an hour later Danby Druce and his servant assistant were seated in an Ipswich express en route for Bury St. Edmunds, reaching that ancient borough about noon. Directly he alighted Danby Druce knew that he would soon hear news of the Winged Man.

Suppressed excitement was on every face. Women, pale and agitated, hastened from waiting-room to train, or clustered together as though for safety. Even the men seemed strangely ill at ease. At the slightest sound people would stop and gazed fearfully up in the air, or cast frightened glances over their shoulders.

It was as though a foreign foe had landed upon Britain's shores, or some fearful plague was approaching the doomed town.

Entering a fly,[17] Danby Druce was driven to the police-station. On the way he was struck by the absence of children in the streets. A few boys crept timidly from place to place, but that was all. As he entered the police-station and

---

[17] A low carriage driven by a single horse.

inspector hastened forward to greet him, relief depicted on his countenance.

"What lucky chance has brought you here, Mr. Druce?" he asked, shaking the great detective cordially by the hand.

"Why, what on earth is the matter, Wilson?" asked Druce in return. "The whole town seems mad with fright. You yourself look as though you had just seen the Winged Man."

The inspector started.

"The Winged Man is here!" he declared impressively.

SURROUNDED BY FOES.

"The Winged Man is here!" repeated the inspector, in low, awed tones. "Last night he appeared in the theatre during the last act. There was a rush for the doors; forty people were injured. He was seen afterwards flying about the town. Folk, in terror, shut and barred themselves in their houses. And his laugh! His horrible laugh! I am no coward. I was in the broken square at Abu Klea, and I'd rather hear the Fuzzie Wuzzies' fiercest yell than that awful, mocking, mirthless laugh ringing from the housetops in the dead of night."

"Courage, man! Take a grip of yourself!" interposed the detective. "I have had one tussle with the Winged Man, and came out second best. The next time we meet either he or I will go under now to business. the Winged Man is a public danger, and a menace to society such as has never been known before, and we must lay him by the heels."

For nearly an hour the two men discussed how best to capture the Winged Man, their deliberations assisted by the mayor, the officer in command of the barracks on the rising ground at the end of Northgate Street, and the colonel of the local Territorials.

Again and again their deliberations were interrupted by white-faced men arriving with the information that the Winged Man had been seen in various parts of the town. Now he was reported swinging on the cowl of the malt-house at the end of Southgate Street; again, clinging to a spire, and yet again in the hospital gardens.

The majority of these reports was simply groundless scares. the Winged Man had got on the nerves of the public. Every blackbird, every crow that flew over the old town was magnified by fear into the fearful, supernatural being.

A chop at the Suffolk Hotel, and then Danby Druce sallied forth to assure himself that his orders had been carried out. In the Butter Market, along Abbeygate Street, at every street-corner, were clusters of men armed with stout sticks, already to give the Winged Man a warm reception if he ventured to show himself in Bury St. Edmunds again.

"Good! The inspector has done his part well. Look to yourself, Winged Man, or your career will be ended!" muttered Danby Druce, well pleased with what he had seen during a brief tour round the town.

Every street-corner was guarded by three or more men, who, to protect their houses and families, were determined to capture the Winged Man or perish in the attempt.

Towards evening Danby Druce turned out of Risbygate Street into Eastgate Street. Suddenly he quickened his steps. A man, clad in dark, sombre clothes, a black felt hat drawn over his eyes, walked swiftly past him, but not before Danby Druce had seen a glimpse of a white face, and seen a flash of a pair of dark, piercing eyes.

Hurrah! His quarry was in sight. The Winged Man's course would soon be run. Yet Danby Druce made no sign, for the Winged Man was moving swiftly towards Angel Hill, and from that open space one so strangely endowed with powers of flight could easily escape.

Quickening his speed, Danby Druce followed the Winged Man across the hill. With a low, triumphant laugh, Danby Druce saw the mysterious being enter Abbeygate Street. The Winged Man was walking blindly into the trap prepared for him. Once in the narrow street, filled as it was with his own men, Danby Druce had little doubt that the Winged Man would soon be captured, for every other man was armed with small grappling-irons attached to light but strong cords.

These would be thrown at the Winged Man as he spread his pinions in flight, and would pull him to the ground, or, by tearing his wings, disable him so that he could not fly.

But that had reckoned without the Winged Man's almost supernatural intelligence. He also had recognised Danby Druce, and, eager to draw the detective's attention from the ruins in the Palace Gardens, where he was prosecuting his search for the abbot's treasure, he intended to lead his foe on a wild-goose chase towards the magnificent grounds of Ixworth House.

Suddenly Danby Druce blew a loud, shrill blast upon his whistle; then, springing forward, cried:

"Seize the man in black! It is the Winged Man!"

A score of men dashed upon the unknown; but, turning, the Winged Man faced his foes. His white face was convulsed with rage; the ruby light in the centre of his forehead blazed with a dull, red, sullen glow.

Uttering cries of terror, his would-be captors stood as though turned to stone around him.

"Seize him, cowards, or he will escape! Grapple with him, boys—grapple!" cried Danby Druce, forcing his way through the crowd.

The detective's words roused the special constables to action. Once more they advanced upon their weird foe.

With folded arms, a contemptuous smile on his thin lips, the Winged Man waited until the foremost man stretched forth his hand to seize him.

Then a cry of rage burst from his would-be captors, answered by peal upon peal of weird, unearthly laughter.

Springing from the ground, the Winged Man hovered on outstretched wings above their heads.

The men stationed on the hill had left their posts in response to the detective's whistle. Thither the Winged Man flew, and, alighting on the centre of the hill, walked with contemptuous indifference towards the Athenæum.

Suddenly a horseman dashed through the arched gate leading into the Angel yard. The rider was a wild, reckless young squire from one of the neighbouring villages, who had boasted that if the Winged Man crossed his path he would hunt him down as he would a fox.

Urged onward by spur and whip, the squire's horse clattered down the hill, its rider flourishing a stout hunting-crop above his head.

"Stop, you play-acting mountebank!" he cried. "Here is a man at last who's not afraid to meet you face to face!"

But he got no further. the Winged Man turned upon him, and the horse, whinnying with terror, came to so abrupt a halt as to hurl its rider over its head at the Winged Man's feet. Bruised and shaken, the young squire rose to his feet.

"Back to your kennel, dog—back!" cried the Winged Man, advancing threateningly upon the young man.

Rage, fear, and shame struggling for mastery within his breast, the young squire faced the Winged Man.

Spellbound, the mob watched the young man approach his strange adversary with clenched fists, and pale but determined face, to within three feet of where the Winged Man stood; then, to the amazement of all beholders, a loud cry of despair burst from his lips, and, throwing his hands above his head, he fled to the shelter of the Angel steps.

°DANBY DRUCE IS BAFFLED.

Casting a fierce, threatening glance upon the crowd, who shrank back in terror before that awful face, the Winged Man continued on his way, followed at a respectful distance by the mob.

Presently a stone hurtled past the Winged Man's head. Another and another followed, until a perfect storm of missiles darkened the air.

Like hail they thundered upon the roadway, crashed on to the pavement, or flew by overhead. Yet, without quickening his steps, the Winged Man strode majestically onwards.

A body of police, who had been lying in wait in readiness, barred the Winged Man's path.

"Halt, in the King's name!" demanded a sergeant, advancing, with evident reluctance, upon the weird being.

A mocking laugh was the only answer. Springing from the ground, he soared

---

° 1 FEBRUARY 1913.

high above the outstretched hands of the astounded constables, and a gasp of astonishment rose from the spectators as they saw him clinging like a fly on the wall to the Saxon Tower.

Up went the Winged Man, climbing the stonework as easily as though it had been level ground.

Higher and higher he clambered, until at last he stood with folded arms on the flat, square top, and gazed mockingly down on his baffled pursuers.

Summoned by the news that the Winged Man had again appeared, a mighty crowd collected round the base of the old tower, the finest specimen of Saxon architecture the world can show.

The Winged Man was in his glory. He loved to gather such a crowd as now filled the open space before the tower, throwing their hearts with his terror-inspiring form and fearful, long-drawn mournful cry.

Suddenly he rose in the air, waving his arms as though fighting off some unseen foe; then came a loud, thunderous report, a burst of flame, and the Winged Man had disappeared.

For several minutes a deep silence prevailed over the terror-stricken mob. Calling upon Bourne to follow, Danby Druce clambered over the rails, and dropped upon the flagstones round the sunken base of the old tower.

Throwing open a tiny door that gave admittance into the tower, the two men dashed up the winding stairs to the summit.

There was no one there. A heap of ashes alone marked the spot where the Winged Man had stood a few moments before.

Could this, then, be the end of the Winged Man? Was this handful of white ash all that was left of the fearful creature who had held Britain in a grip of awed terror so many months?"

Danby Druce could not say. In vain he searched the tower from top to bottom. No further trace of the Winged Man could he find. But barely had he taken his departure ere a stone in the wall of the tower moved aside, and the Winged Man, a sardonic smile hovering over his thin lips, stepped forth.

For several minutes he gazed through a narrow slit in the gaping crowd; then, rising, hung head downwards from the ceiling, draped his wings about his body, and slept.

THE SUBTERRANEAN PASSAGE.

It was midnight when the Winged Man awoke. Regaining the summit of the tower, he spread his wings to the night breeze, and reached the Abbey grounds. The streets were deserted; none dare venture out after dark.

Alighting at the bottom of the gravel walk which gives on to a stretch of fine lawn reaching to the banks of the River Larke, the Winged Man secured a pickaxe and spade from a shared by the side of an ivy-covered house, then perched on the jagged top of a stunted round tower in the centre of the lawn, watching the moon rise over the Abbot's Bridge.

As clear as print his wonderful memory retained the writing on the parchment in Ixworth House, according to which the rising moon would guide him to the treasure.

Nor was he disappointed. Leaving the top of the tower, the Winged Man flew to the ruins of the refectory, where the monks of old had ofttimes feasted, now half buried beneath mounds of earth.

As the moon rose higher in the heavens the shadow of a window formed a delicate tracery within the broken walls.

Presently a distant clock boomed forth the first hour of another day. Raising his pickaxe the Winged Man brought it down on the highest point of the window's shadow.

An ejaculation of satisfaction rose from the Winged Man's lips. The men of old never scamped their work.

Despite the many hundreds of years that had elapsed since the hidden machinery had last been used, it responded at once to the Winged Man's blow. The ground trembled; a strange, scraping noise filled the air.

Then a huge block of masonry weighing several tons glided to one side, leaving an opening just large enough for a well-grown man to pass through.

As the Winged Man dropped into the dark chasm a blast of poisonous gas met him; but he heeded it not.

His wondrous light shining from the centre of his forehead, he pressed on through a dark, noisome, secret tunnel, thick with fungi, deep with damp, moist, evil-smelling dust.

Toads, lizards, and enormous frogs scuttled away at every step. Snake-like eyes peered at him from holes in the broken walls.

Now and again the Winged Man would turn from his path to explore a side passage. In the majority of cases they ended in heaps of fallen masonry.

Another time he mounted a flight of fungi-covered stone steps and gazed from out a skilfully concealed hole in the Abbey gate upon the Angel Hill.

Presently the Winged Man found his way barred by an apparently immovable block of stone.

Groping over the right-hand wall, his fingers encountered a protruding stone. This he pressed, and the stone that obstructed his path moved aside, revealing a low crypt supported on what looked like an endless succession of short, squat pillars.

It was a dismal place. Hundreds of years had passed since human eye had seen its dark, forbidding walls.

In one corner of the crypt was a large furnace, adorned with rusty instruments of torture of every description.

Against the wall lay the mouldering woodwork of a rack, and a skeleton huddled against a pillar a short distance away. Passing a flight of steps leading to a secret opening in the extensive vaults known to exist beneath the Angel Hotel, the Winged Man strode swiftly through another long, subterranean passage on his strange and wondrous journey.

For nearly a mile the tunnel descended; then the Winged Man waded knee-deep in water that dripped from the sudden brickwork, and knew that he was passing beneath the River Larke.

A steep climb, as the subterranean passage tipped over the Southgate Hill, followed. Hour succeeded hour, yet the Winged Man had not reached the end of the tunnel.

Now and again he was compelled to stop and dig a path where the masonry had fallen in. Presently his way was blocked by yet another fall of earth. Vigorously he attacked this fresh obstruction.

Suddenly the earth gave to his assault. A blinding flash of daylight filled the tunnel. He stepped through a screen of training bushes on to the side of the steep hill in the centre of a wood, four miles from Bury St Edmunds.

The Winged Man's face was convulsed with rage. He ground his teeth; fierce exclamations escaped his lips.

He was in the open country, not within the four walls of an old house, as he had hoped to be.

Suddenly he started. The sound of a horn and the musical cry of hounds running to a breast-high scent fell on his ears.

Spreading his wide pinions, he soared to the branches of a huge oak, and, glancing in the direction from which the sounds came, saw a pack of hounds, followed by a long, straggling line of horsemen, approaching the wood.

Hundred yards ahead of the nearest hound, poor Reynard, his tongue hanging from his mouth, his brush draggled, was straining every nerve to reach the shelter of his earth, but in a broken, uneven gallop, which told that his strength was nearly exhausted.

Just as the fox reached the fence, the foremost hounds dashed forward to bury their fangs in its flank.

A loud yell, and the Winged Man had dropped between the flying, snarling hounds and their intended victim.

THE HAUNTED HOUSE.

It was a moment of tremendous excitement. Would the hounds come on and hurl themselves at the Winged Man, or would they retreat? The Winged Man faced them, with hands outstretched and his claw-like fingers working convulsively, and then on came the dogs, four or five springing at him at one and the same time.

The Winged Man uttered a hoarse cry of rage, and, seizing one of the hounds by the throat, he raised it, and hurled it thirty yards. Then up from the ground he rose in mid-air, with dogs clinging to his wings and sombre garb.

He twirled and darted and wheeled, uttering savage cries the while. Minutes had gone by before he could rid himself of the last of the dogs, which fell to the earth and crawled amongst its companions.

Whining with terror, trembling in every limb, the hair on their backs on end, the hounds snarlingly faced the Winged Man, until, extending his wings, he rushed towards them. With loud yelps of terror they turned and fled.

A quick forty minutes' run over stiff country had thinned out the hunt. At that moment there was no one within a field's length of the hounds.

The first to jump the hedge that hid the wood from view was the master, then came the whipper-in. Great was their amazement when they saw the whole pack, yelping with terror, rushed madly towards them. Why, they could not tell. The Winged Man had disappeared.

In the meantime, the Winged Man, retracing his steps, had regained the main tunnel, along which he strode until he came to a narrow, dusty staircase, ending in a secret passage lined with old oak wainscotting.

His goal was reached. He stood within Broughton Moat, an old building, half farmhouse, half mansion, where—though the parchment clue did not denote the exact spot—was hidden the abbot's buried treasure.

A pleasant smell of roasted meat reminded the Winged Man that he was hungry.

A crack in the oak panelling disclosed a large, well-furnished dining-room, in which a maid servant was putting a joint of roast beef upon the table.

Eagerly the Winged Man's hand swept the smooth surface of the panel. His fingers encountered a round knob.

Waiting until the servant had left the room, and the sound of a gong in the hall told that she was summoning the family to lunch, the Winged Man pressed the knob, and the panel opened. Stepping forth, he seized the beef, a loaf of bread, and a jug of beer, regaining the secret passage just as a lady and gentleman, followed by a grown-up son and daughter, entered the room.

Mr. Denton, the owner of Broughton Moat, looked angrily towards the table.

"Why on earth did you sound the gong before dinner was served?" he demanded.

The girl gazed in amazement at the place where, scarcely a minute before, she had deposited the smoking beef.

"It's gone, sir!" she gasped. "I put it there a moment ago with my own hands!"

Mr. Denton turned fiercely upon the girl.

"What on earth is the good of telling me that?" he demanded sternly. "If you had done so, there it would be now."

The bewildered girl began to cry.

"I don't know what has become of it, sir, unless the dogs have taken it!" she sobbed.

Mrs. Denton waived the girl angrily aside.

"Do dogs swallow dishes as well as joints of beef?"

"And where is the bread?" put in Julia Denton.

"I haven't taken them, sir—I declare I haven't! You may search my boxes, if you like!" sobbed the girl, too frightened to grasp the absurdity of her boxes being searched for a joint of hot beef in a dish full of gravy, a loaf of bread, and a quart of home-brewed beer.

"P'shaw!" said Mr. Denton. "You dreamt you brought them in. Ten to one they're in the kitchen all the while!"

An immediate search for the missing viands was commenced, needless to say, without result.

Under the table, over the table, under sofas and chairs, into every possible and impossible place they looked, little guessing that the smoking joint was rapidly disappearing down the Winged Man's throat, forty feet beneath the house.

Hastening along the passage with his booty, the Winged Man had come across a well-like opening down which he had dropped, to find himself in a square, paved room, admirably suited for a hiding-place whilst at Broughton Moat.

In the meantime, Mr. Denton, his wife, and family sat down to a cold, hastily-prepared lunch.

None felt inclined to eat. All were oppressed by a vague terror of some mysterious evil, the more terrifying from its very vagueness. Neither were their forebodings ill-founded.

This was the first of many strange manifestations destined to give the old house its name of the Haunted Moat.

That evening, just as it was growing dark, a scullery-maid, who had been to a lumber-room in the garret, rushed, shrieking, downstairs, and collapsed in a heap on the mat at Mrs. Denton's feet, who had hastened from the drawing-room to ascertain the cause of the uproar.

For several minutes she could get nothing from the frightened scullery-maid. At last she pointed up the stairs, crying:

"The lumber-room—the lumber-room! Oh, oh, oh!"

Then she burst into a loud, hysterical scream.

"Jim—Jim!" shrieked Mrs. Denton, rushing to meet her son, who entered the house at that moment. "Quick! The garret!"

Realising, from his mother's agitation, that something terrible must have taken place in the garret, Jim Denton sprang like lightning up the stairs. Presently his voice was heard calling from the top of the house:

"There's nothing here. Where do you—"

The sentence ended with an angry cry, followed by the fall of a heavy body.

More alarmed than ever, Mrs. Denton ran to the landing, to find her son sitting on a mat rubbing his ear, and half dazed by the violence of his fall.

"Good gracious, Jim, what has happened?" she demanded breathlessly.

"Hanged if I know, mother!" replied her son. "I found the garret empty, and was calling downstairs to reassure you, when somebody struck me on the side of the head. I staggered back, lost my balance, and fell. That is all. Anyhow, I am not going to rest until I find out who it was hit me, and have given him his own back."

Mrs. Denton would have called her son back, but the words were frozen on her lips, for her eyes were fixed upon a thin, white hand hovering immediately over her upturned face.

With a piercing shriek she fell senseless to the floor; whilst the Winged Man, closing the sliding panel, moved swiftly down the secret passage.

It was he who, sleeping head downwards in the garret, had frightened the scullery-maid almost out of her wits. It was he who had given young Denton the buffet on the side of the head which had sent him rolling down the stairs, for until the house was emptied of its occupants he could not hope to find the abbot's treasure. And he meant to make the occupants flee from Broughton Moat as from the plague.

A NIGHT OF TERROR.

It was late that night ere the occupants of Broughton Moat sought their beds. All felt unwilling to face the solitude of the bed-rooms until Mr. and Mrs. Denton retired to rest, and insisted upon the servants following their example.

But there was no sleep for anyone at Broughton Moat that night. All lay awake, expecting they knew not what. Nor were their fears groundless. Suddenly every ear was assailed by a loud, weird, nerve-thrilling shriek echoing and re-echoing through the winding passages and quaintly-shaped rooms of the old house.

Then came a series of tremendous thumps, as though the roof had fallen in.

White to the very lips, yet determined to discover the reason of the terrible noise which had drawn them from their beds, Mr. Denton and his son emerged from the various rooms.

"Merciful powers, father, what is it? What does it all mean?" asked the younger man, in an awestricken whisper.

"Goodness only knows, my boy! It seems as though some spirit of evil has taken possession of the old house," returned Mr. Denton solemnly, then moved towards the guest-chamber, a large apartment—oak-panelled, like every other room in the house—situated in the north wing, from whence, even as they spoke, came a fearful crash, as though a load of timber had been shot down inside it.

"Whatever it is, it's in the guest-chamber!" cried Jim Denton, quickening his steps.

Barely had they covered half the distance ere they were brought to a sudden halt by an indescribably weird and haunting shriek, followed by peal upon peal of mocking laughter, which increased in volume till it rose to a nerve-shattering, prolonged, fearful chuckle, then ended as suddenly as it had commenced.

"Dad, what can it be? Are they such things as ghosts, after all?" demanded Jim Denton, in low, trembling tones.

Twenty-four hours before Mr. Denton would have laughed the idea to scorn; now he could only shake his head in doubt, as, resisting an almost irresistible desire to flee, he laid his hand on the handle of the door, hesitated a moment, then dashed into the room. An exclamation of bewildered dismay rose from his lips.

The bright beams of the newly-risen moon revealed a scene of indescribable confusion and ruthless destruction.

The huge four-post bedstead had been dragged bodily into the centre of the room. Wardrobes, chests of drawers, wash stands were piled on the top of it. At the very carpet had been pulled up. Pictures torn from the wall lay smashed and trampled on about the room.

Even as the two men gazed upon the amazing sight, a loud crash from below reached their ears. Crash succeeded crash, interspersed by the rattling of falling china, and punctuated by the Winged Man's low, weird, mournful howl, which once heard could never be forgotten.

Swiftly father and son flew along the landing, dashed down the broad, open staircase, across the hall, through a short passage, into the kitchen, where they paused to gaze upon a scene of the most utter confusion. Plate-rack, dish-rack, even the dresser-pegs upon which the silver dish-covers had hung, were empty, and their contents hurled, broken, smashed, bruised, and bent, upon the floor. Nothing that could be moved remained in its original position.

The table had been overturned, the chairs smashed, the cupboard doors had been wrenched open, the very cover of the cooking-range had been torn off. The range itself was cracked and broken, as though by repeated blows from a blacksmith's sledge-hammer.

Even as anger at the destruction wrought struggled for mastery with ever-increasing terror, loud, fearful shrieks arose from the landing.

"Your mother! That was her voice, Jim!" gasped Mr. Denton.

To the foot of the open staircase they retraced their steps. Women servants, their unfastened hair flying behind their backs, men-servants with white faces, were fleeing precipitously from a fearful form, which hovered menacingly at the top of the stairs.

The spectre, clad from head to foot in white, trailing garments, bright with a fearful blue light, towered to the ceiling.

Raising its hand as though in warning, it disappeared, to the accompaniment of a crash which sounded to the terror-stricken spectators louder than the loudest thunder.

To the terror-stricken beholders it seemed as though the vision had vanished into the air. In reality, the Winged Man—for, of course, the spectre was that wondrous, awe-inspiring being—had turned his back to the terrified people, thus seeming to vanish from their sight.

The spectre hovered at the head of the stairs.

Chuckling with glee, the Winged Man stepped behind a sliding panel, and made his way to the subterranean chamber, wither he had already conveyed a store of wines, spirits, beer, tinned and fresh meats, and bread, from the larder. But not to rest.

He had yet much to do ere morning dawned. Laying aside the skull and phosphorus-covered sheet with which he had frightened Mr. Denton's household, the Winged Man left the house, and winged his way to Cambridge.

Like some dark bird of the night he issued forth from the window on the stairs of Broughton Moat, rose like a hawk into mid-air, and vanished.

DRIVEN FROM HOME.

By eight o'clock the following morning Danby Druce had heard of strange events that had taken place at Broughton Moat. His first impulse was to hasten to Broughton. Ere he could put his intention into execution, a telegram from Cambridge induced him to alter his plans. It ran as follows:

"Danby Druce, Angel Hotel,

"Bury St Edmunds.

"University Proctor assaulted on College Green by Winged Man. Come at once. Aylmer, Inspector of Police."

Ten minutes later the detective was travelling towards the old university town as fast as his magnificent car could carry him.

On his arrival at Cambridge, he was met by a score of witnesses who had seen the Winged Man.

The following evening Mr. Denton, his son, and Thomas Baker, a manservant who had elected to face the terrors of the house with his master, were alone in Broughton Moat, for Mrs. and Miss Denton was staying elsewhere.

Midnight boomed forth from the clock over the stable tower. Within the kitchen, a stout club on the table before him, sat Thomas Baker, fortifying his courage with an occasional sip from the jug of liquor by his side. In the dining-room James Denton, a revolver clutched in his right hand, awaited the coming night, whilst his father had thrown himself on his bed, a double-barrelled gun, loaded with buckshot, by his side.

Worn out with want of sleep—for, needless to say, he had not closed his eyes the previous night—Mr. Denton had just dozed off when he awoke to find his bed raised by some invisible agency; then it turned completely over, and he was hurled to the floor under both featherbed and mattress.

Hearing a commotion overhead, Jim Denton rushed upstairs, his revolver ready for immediate use. A light was burning in his father's room. At first he saw nothing but the overturned bed and a heap of clothes in the middle of the room.

"Father, father! Where are you?" he cried.

"Here!" came a muffled voice from beneath the bedclothes. "Help me out, quick!"

Thrusting his revolver into his pocket, Jim Denton was about to remove the featherbed which threatened to suffocate his father, when he felt his neck grasped from behind. Cold, clammy fingers encircled his throat.

In vain he strove to close with his unseen opponent.

Powerful athlete though he was, he was but as a child in the Winged Man's grasp. Soon his struggle ceased, the Winged Man's grasp relaxed, and Jim Denton fell, a huddled heap, at his weird assailant's feet.

The Winged Man strode in the direction from which he had heard a sound of approaching footsteps.

His cudgel grasped tightly in his right hand, Baker appeared on the top of the stairs. A shriek is so full of terror, so shrill, so hopeless, burst from his lips, that it pierced the semiconscious ears of Jim Denton, struggling back to life after his fearful encounter with the Winged Man.

Barring Baker's path was a fearful apparition such as, in his most awful dreams, he had never imagined could possibly exist. Save that it stood on two legs, the apparition bore but little semblance to a human being. Its arms were like two snakes, with tongues of living fire, its fearful face was surmounted by strands of glowing red flame.

Tom Baker was as brave as a man can well be, but the stoutest heart must have quailed before the fearful form the Winged Man had assumed.

Shrieking with terror, Baker clasped his hands over his eyes, dashed headlong into the hall, and, not daring to stop to open the door, plunged through the diamond-paned window into the night.

Aroused by the servant's terror-laden cry, Jim Denton sat up and looked around him.

Rising, he staggered to a chest of drawers on which was a flask of brandy, drank deeply of the contents; then, with dogged courage, returned to the task of releasing his father, whom he had soon set free.

Five minutes later Mr. Denton and his son were in the hall, looking in surprise at the broken window.

"Baker, Baker!" called the old man, raising his voice.

There was no response.

As he moved towards the kitchen his foot struck against something that rolled to the wall. It was Baker's cudgel, dropped in his hurried flight.

"Come, Jim! I've had enough of it! It's tempting Providence to fight the fearful being, or beings, who have taken possession of the old home," he said, in faltering tones.

Despite his fearful adventures, the young man's dogged courage rebelled against beating a retreat; but a glance at his father's haggard face warned him that the old man could stand no more, so, though reluctantly, he accompanied Mr. Denton out by the back door.

Passing through the paved courtyard, they came to a bridge over the wide moat which encircled the building.

To the left of the bridge was clear water, bounded, some twenty yards away, by a bed of rushes.

Suddenly Jim Denton laid his hand upon his father's shoulder.

"Listen! What is that?" he whispered.

"Help! Help! Help!"

The appeal for assistance came from the reeds.

"It is Baker. In his terror he has plunged into the moat. Come!" cried Jim Denton breathlessly.

Fear of the supernatural banished by the thought of a comrade's danger, the two men hastened along the side of the moat to the reeds. Again that fearful cry rang out.

"There, there! Near the duck's nest!" cried Mr. Denton, pointing, with trembling hands, to where the reeds reached to within some twelve feet of a tiny, bush-covered spit of land, on which the half-tamed wild ducks that haunted the moat were wont to build their nests.

Racing through an old-time orchard, the two men, eager to save human life, dashed through the bushes; then came to an abrupt halt, their eyes showing the fear which gripped their hearts. Through the reeds grinned a face that seemed to shine through the darkness.

For nearly a minute Jim Denton stood transfixed, motionless as a statue, whilst he tried in vain to draw his gaze from that awful face. Enframed in the reeds, it glared upon him for several minutes, then disappeared, not suddenly as it had come, but growing smaller each moment, until at last it appeared as a tiny black speck no larger than a penny.

A sigh of relief greeted its final disappearance. James Denton clasped his hands to his head.

"Merciful powers, can such things be? Or am I mad—mad—mad?"

"Is it gone?" came in a hushed, awed whisper from Mr. Denton.

The old man's iron-grey hair had turned as white as driven snow. With an effort Jim Denton pulled himself together. There was a look in his father's eyes which told that his over-wrought brain could bear no more.

"Yes, father, it has gone. Come, let us leave this haunted spot, never to return," he said.

Stooping, he half-carried, half-dragged his father to the high road. Twenty minutes later Jim Denton thundered loudly upon a friend's door, who, angry at being awakened at such an unreasonable hour, looked from out of an upstairs window.

He saw two huddled forms crouched on the doorstep. Candle in hand, he hastened downstairs, threw open the door, and found father and son senseless at his feet.

THE ABBOTT'S TREASURE.

But what cared the Winged Man? Even before Mr. Denton and his son had reached the high road, the Winged Man, flapping his inky pinions, had left the shelter of the reeds. Confident that none now remained to interrupt his search, he returned to the old house, only stopping to cut a wand from a clump of willows growing by the side of the moat.

Barring and barricading every door save one, the Winged Man moved from room to room, his head light shining brightly, his eyes fixed with intense eagerness upon the swaying stick in his hand. He stopped. The end of the wand was moving from side to side in a strange, weird way.

Gradually it swayed more and more to the left, until at last it pointed to a small, elaborately-carved chest that stood against a wall. Laying the wand aside, he drew a small but complete burglar's outfit from his pocket, and a minute later the Dentons' family plate was at his mercy.

Valuable though the find, in the Winged Man's eyes it was but dross. Nothing but gold or the rarest jewels would suit his fastidious taste.

A rapid search revealed a few valuable specimens of the silversmith's art. These the Winged Man took possession of ere he resumed his search for the abbot's treasure.

His divining wand held before him, he passed from chamber to chamber, from room to room, from attic to cellar, until at length he had traversed the whole house, yet the divining rod had not led him to the treasure he sought. His brow grew black as thunder; a wild spasm of fierce anger shook his frame.

Vain the long journey through the subterranean passage. Vain the wasted hours of toil with pick and spade. But he was not foiled in his search yet. He seized an old-time battle-axe from the wall of the entrance-wall, and struck at the beautiful oak panelling.

At the first blow, the head of the axe disappeared through the splintered oak. A cry of satisfaction escaped the Winged Man's lips. He had found a hitherto unexplored secret passage.

Grasping the sides of the splintered wood with both hands, the Winged Man tore the boards from the wall, revealing a dark, circular opening, into which he crept. Holding the divining rod as before, he moved cautiously along the freshly-discovered way. Presently the wand was again agitated; then pointed to what looked like the outlet of some drain or chimney flue immediately above his head.

Rising, the Winged Man forced his way up the slanting passage. A strong smell of soot warned him that he was approaching a smoke-chamber, such as is to be found in old houses.

Clouds of suffocating soot rose at every step, but the Winged Man noticed not the tiny black specks which clogged his nose and mouth, or dropped like flakes of black snow around him. His eyes were fixed upon the wand, which grew every moment more active. Presently it sprang from his grasp, and flew, as a needle to a magnet, to the soot-covered side of the smoke-chamber.

A weird, mournful cry, the Winged Man's sole outward show of emotion, echoed through the soot-clogged chamber as the weird wanderer attacked the covering of soot, six inches in depth, which hid the wall from view; with eager hands he scraped the black deposit away.

Nothing but the wall of the soot-chamber met his gaze. Eagerly he scanned the cement between the stones. A tiny square of rusty iron let into the wall rewarded his search. This he pressed with all his might, and a wild shout of joy issued from the Winged Man's lips, as the side of the chamber sank into the ground, revealing a tiny room littered with worn and rotten cloth, beneath which could be seen the glitter of gold! The gold the Winged Man worshipped! The gold he loved more than anything on earth!

Springing forward, he flung himself headlong upon the coarse sacking, and, hurling the dust of ages aside, plunged his arms elbow deep into a heap of gold coins. Presently he grew calmer, and commenced a systematic examination of that treasure he had been at such pains to secure.

Great had been his labours; great was his reward. Cups, chalices, platters of purest gold, all richly chased and some studded with the finest gems were before him. Piece by piece the Winged Man sorted out his find, putting the plates and cups in one heap, and the gold coins in another. With eager hands the Winged Man swept his find into sacks.

There was no time to lose. Daylight might bring back the dispossessed owners. Besides, ere long, Danby Druce would find that the Winged Man was not at Cambridge, and would undoubtedly hasten to Broughton Moat expecting to find him there. Not that the Winged Man feared Danby Druce. He only feared interruption before the treasure was secured.

His exploration of the subterranean passages in and around the old house had led him along one which ended in a small wood some half a mile from the house. Thither the Winged Man carried first the plate, which he buried beneath a blackberry bush in one corner of the wood; then the gold. Daylight was upon the Winged Man ere a hole deep enough for his sack full of golden coins was dug.

He could not resist the temptation of undoing the mouth of the sack and feasting his eyes once more upon its contents. With a joyous chuckle, he plunged his hands into the coins, laughing aloud as he felt the gold coins over his fists, and all unconscious that a face, almost rivalling his own in its weird pallor, was watching him through a knot-hole in the huge trunk of a hollow oak. A face stamped with every evil passion; a face marked from eyebrow to mouth with a livid scar.

An instinctive feeling that someone was near caused the Winged Man to spring to an upright position, his thin lips parted in a snarl like that of a wolf standing over its prey. The Winged Man's back was to the oak, and ere he turned round Black Jake was crouched in the bottom of the trunk, clenching his jaws lest his chattering teeth should betray him.

He had recognised the Winged Man. His cowed heart almost ceased to beat. He gave himself up for lost. Could even the thick, gnarled trunk hide him from the piercing eyes before which he had so often trembled?

Yet nothing happened, and the scraping noise made by a spade shovelling earth told that, for the present, he was safe. It was several minutes ere he screwed up sufficient courage to look through his peephole once more. He was just in time to see the Winged Man disappear into the secret passage which joined the wood to Broughton Moat.

Scrambling from the tree, the Man with the Scar fled as swiftly as his feet could carry him to the nearest village, where he did not recover his wonted self-possession until a mighty breakfast had instilled fresh courage into his heart. The Man with the Scar had nerves of steel.

Throughout that day terror and greed fought for mastery in Black Jake's breast. Greed triumphed.

Stealing a spade from a cottage tool-shed, he re-entered the wood, and, pausing now and again to look fearfully round, dug up the Winged Man's recently hidden gold.

THE RETURN OF DANBY DRUCE.

In the meantime, the Winged Man had returned to the smoke-chamber, fearful lest he had left a single golden coin amongst the rubbish on its floor. It was well for him he did so.

In one corner of the tiny, stone-lined room he saw what at first sight he took to be a heap of mouldy rags. Carelessly he threw them aside. His fingers touched something hard and round. Eagerly he drew the heap of rags towards him.

As he did so a rotten canvas bag hidden beneath the rags burst in pieces, and he stared for a moment transfixed with delight, his eyes dazzled by the brilliant reflection that came from a heap of diamonds, rubies, emeralds, and other precious stones lying at his feet.

"Ha, ha! It was well I returned. The smallest of these stones is worth all the rest of my booty put together!" cried the Winged Man, pouncing upon the gems and thrusting them into his pockets with both hands. First, having assured himself that he had secured the last precious stone, he returned to the entrance-hall.

As he did so the sound of excited voices from without reached his ears. Turning, he hastened to the dining-room, and passing through the sliding panel, strode through secret passages until he reached a spy hole which commanded a view of the hall.

Barely had he reached his post of vantage ere the village policeman, Baker, and a couple of farmers armed with shot-guns, entered and, each ready to run for his life at the first alarm, secure the plate chest and the wearing apparel of the owners of Broughton Moat.

The Winged Man made no sign. On the morrow the whole family might return if they wished. He had achieved his end.

To-day he would sleep. The following night he would remove his treasure to a more secure hiding-place, then leave Broughton Moat for ever. But even the Winged Man could not control Fate.

The men gone, the Winged Man retired to the bottom of his well. Suspended by his feet to the ceiling, he slept until sunset; then, eager to be up and doing, he sallied forth once more. Moving with his customary noiseless steps he passed through the dining-room, but even as he crossed the threshold he came to an abrupt halt. Before him stood Danby Druce.

"Ha! I was right, then. You are the ghost of Broughton Moat!" cried the detective.

"Well met, Danby Druce!" laughed the Winged Man. "Come, you and I have met before. In strength and wits you are but as a child compared with me. See if your legs will serve you better than your head. Follow. Catch me, and I yield without resistance. Fail, and your fate be on your own head."

Turning as the last word left his lips, the Winged Man reached the entrance to the sliding panel at a bound, and disappeared in the darkness beyond.

Thrusting his drawn revolver back in his pocket, Danby Druce followed.

"It's a sporting offer. I'll take it as a sportsman," he muttered.

The Winged Man could easily have outdistanced the detective had he wished. But it was the humiliation, and not the destruction of the detective the Winged Man craved. Again and again the Winged Man allowed Druce to approach almost within touch of his flowing garments; then, with a mocking laugh, dashed ahead. Presently the Winged Man vanished down a side turning.

"Hasten, Druce—hasten!" came in mocking tones out from out the darkness.

His teeth clenched, his heart filled with determination to capture the Winged Man, Danby Druce increased his speed, little suspecting that the Winged Man was clinging, like some bird of the night, to the edge of a circular opening in the roof of the secret passage.

Danby Druce passed beneath his foe. Then a noose dropped over his head, and the next moment the Winged Man had jerked him off his feet.

So sudden had been the descent of the rope, so fearful the strain, so awful the feeling that oppressed him, that, for a moment, Danby Druce almost choked, and writhed and struggled in a way which would very soon have ended his career had not his only chance of escape flashed through his brain.

Drawing a revolver from his pocket, he placed its muzzle against the cord just above his head and pulled the trigger. A flash, a reverberating roar echoed and re-echoed through the narrow passage, followed by a deep, awful thud as the detective fell heavily to the ground. Barely had he time to loosen the rope which was cutting into his flesh, ere a black object descended upon him.

The next moment he was lying on his back, the Winged Man on his chest, the dread being's fierce, glowing eyes gazing into his own.

"Ha, ha Danby Druce!" chuckled the Winged Man. "You ran well, as a man must who runs for his life, but it is I who have gained the prize! Thus I take it!"

As he spoke, the Winged Man snatched a long, keen stiletto from his girdle and raised it high above his head.

"What! No appeal for mercy! No wild promises of what you'll do if I let you go?" demanded the Winged Man, the stiletto poised above his prisoner's heart.

"Strike! I will not owe my life to you!" gasped the gallant detective, seeking to throw his fearful foe off.

In vain. "What, even though I am willing to reward you handsomely if you promise never to follow me again?" demanded the Winged Man.

"Strike!" almost implored Danby Druce. "Thing of evil that you are, I know mercy cannot dwell in your black heart."

Yet the blade remained poised in the air.

"Listen, Danby Druce!" said the Winged Man, in deep, impressive tones. "For a mere groundling, unable to soar through the air at will, or fly over the ground with speed-armed heels like myself, you have proved yourself a foeman worthy of my steel. Within this house I have found treasure worth an incalculable amount half of it shall be yours if you will join me in my warfare against mankind. It is fine sport. Feared by a nation that fears no earthly foes. Strong men grow weaklings, brave men cowards even at the mention of my name. Speak! Do you accept my terms?"

"Never! I would rather—" began Danby Druce, stealing his courage to receive the expected blow, when the Winged Man interrupted him, saying as he returned his weapon to his sheath:

"Your answer has saved your life. Rise! You are too brave a man to die!"

The Winged Man rose to his feet. As he did so his hands were seized from behind. Iron encircled his wrists. The Winged Man was handcuffed.

"Got him, sir! The Winged Man is ours at last!" cried Bourne, who, creeping behind the Winged Man, had thus skilfully secured him.

Danby Druce rose slowly to his feet. There was no exhortation on his pale face.

"Ten minutes ago I would have given all I possessed in the world to have the Winged Man helpless before me; now, Bourne, I wish you had been anywhere else then here. Duty compels me to hold him fast—yet he spared my life," he said solemnly.

"But I would not spare 'his!" Bourne shouted fiercely. "Ah, you flying freak, I'll see you standing over the trap yet!" he added, turning upon his prisoner.

The exhortation faded from out his eyes. There was a strange, mocking smile on the Winged Man's face which made him fear lest, after all, this wondrous being should escape.

"Fly now and welcome if you can!" laughed Bourne.

Yet the Winged Man said never a word, but allowed himself to be led from passage to passage until at length they stepped into the hall.

Danby Druce could not forget that the Winged Man had spared his life. As they emerged from the house, he turned to his prisoner.

"I wish to spare you humiliation. Give me your word of honour not to escape, and I will remove the handcuffs."

The Winged Man laughed in the speaker's face.

"Why should I?" he demanded.

A loud report, a single snap, and the cords, broken as though they had been threads, the thick steel links of the handcuffs wrenched asunder, the Winged Man, free once more, spread his pinions to the wind, and filling the air with mocking laughter rose to the roof of the many-gabled old house, leaving his supposed captors to gaze at each other in hopeless bewilderment.

GHAT'S SUMMONS

"Ha, ha, ha!" mocked the Winged Man. "The hemp is not yet grown, the iron still sleeps in the bosom of the earth, that will bind the Winged Man!"

Spreading his wide pinions, he dived from the pointed arch of the gable window, swooped down to within a dozen feet of Danby Druce and Bourne; then, rising, turned his head towards the tree-covered hill where he had saved the fox from the jaws of the hounds.

Crack, crack, crack! The shots rang out in quick succession, as Bourne, furious at the escape of the strange being who had slain his son, emptied three chambers of his revolver after him.

At the third shot the Winged Man rose like a stricken bird, turned a complete somersault; then, with folded pinions, fell towards the ground.

"He's down; I've wounded him!" shouted Bourne excitedly, running towards the falling black mass.

A mocking laugh—as, spreading his black pinions to the breeze, the Winged Man glided over a ploughed field—brought him to an abrupt halt, and ere the astounded man could fire again the Winged Man was out of range.

Doggedly determined to run their quarry down, the two men started on a hopeless cross-country chase, until, topping the timber, the Winged Man disappeared upon the other side of the tree-capped hill.

When, breathless with running, Danby Druce and Bourne reached the spot where they had lost sight of the Winged Man, he was nowhere to be seen.

"Perhaps he is hiding in the woods, sir," suggested Bourne.

"No, no; more likely we will find him amongst the abbey ruins," replied Danby Druce, setting off at a brisk walk towards Bury St. Edmunds.

An hour later the Winged Man entered the wood wherein his buried treasure was hidden. His sack of gold was gone!

Fearful was the Winged Man's rage. His face contorted with evil passion, he flung himself on the ground, writhing as though in the grasp of some fearful torture.

Within the Winged Man's many lairs were sums far larger than that which he had lost, but love of gold was this strange being's ruling passion. Yet, even for double the amount, the Winged Man would not have given way to the passion that consumed him had he known that human eyes were watching his every movement.

The Man with the Scar had hidden the hoard of ancient coins in the heart of the hollow tree, and, standing ankle-deep in gold, was watching the Winged Man through the knot-hole. His face was deathly white. Beads of cold perspiration bedewed his brow.

Yet, when the Winged Man dived into the subterranean passage, Black Jake followed, hoping to earn the reward offered for the Winged Man's capture that was placarded on the walls of every town in England. But, lost in the many turnings of the secret passages that honeycombed the old house, several hours elapsed before Black Jake, registering a vow that he would never venture into that dark, evil-smelling, subterranean maze again, crept stealthily through a sliding panel into the house.

In the meantime, the Winged Man had mounted to an attic. Standing at an open window facing north, he drew a cylindrical object, some eight inches long, from his pocket. It was covered with coils of wire, one end being fitted with a specially-prepared head, from which a number of thin wires and pieces of catgut converged.

It was a small instrument, yet, when pointing it through the window, the Winged Man tapped the drum-like end, it carried confusion to every wireless telegraph the station within a hundred miles.

Far away on the bleak Yorkshire coast, Ghat, the Winged Man's scarcely human servicer, slave, companion, call him what you will, was tending the furnace of that wondrous being's underground electric-power station.

Suddenly he dropped the long iron shovel he was wielding and hastened into an adjoining cave, from whence came a low, dull booming, like that of a distant drum. His eyes glistened with pleasure, for the sound came from the receiver of the Winged Man's yet imperfect wireless telephone.

Approaching the instrument, Ghat scanned it closely, then listened intently whilst the beating continued. When it ceased, he knew that his master wanted him, and also exactly where to look for him.

Filling the automatic stokers with sufficient coal to last for several days, Ghat closed up the cave, and, making his way to a huge rock that formed a black spot on the green surface of the moor, looked around to assure himself there was no one in sight; then thrust a piece of steel into a crack in the rock's side.

Immediately it opened, revealing a hollow receptacle, from which Ghat drew a motor-bicycle.

Leather overalls on his misshapen legs, a cape covering his deformed body, goggles and cap hiding his strangely-shaped head and hideous face, Ghat started on his southward journey.

ENTOMBED IN THE PIT.

Having summoned Ghat to assist him in removing the buried treasure, the Winged Man descended into the hall, and Black Jake, who had just reached the house, drew, trembling in every limb, beneath the shadow of a suit of armour standing on a pedestal at one side of the hall.

Fortunately for Black Jake, the Winged Man continued on his way to the dining-room without seeing him. Passing through the sliding panel, the Winged Man made his way towards the chamber at the bottom of the well, where he had left his jewels.

His heart beating like the piston of a steam-engine, the Man With the Scar, guided by the Winged Man's headlight, approached the pit's mouth.

Stretched on the flag-stoned floor of the secret passage, Black Jake thrust his head over the edge just as the Winged Man emptied the contents of a canvas bag on the floor.

The sight almost took Black Jake's breath away. A flood of avaricious desire swept through his heart. The smallest of those jewels was worth more than the paltry five hundred pounds offered for the Winged Man's capture, to say nothing of the fact that to claim it Black Jake would have to come into communication with the police, who might recognise him as an escaped convict with a reward out for his own arrest.

Fear vanished from his heart. He would face death a thousand times over to gain such a prize. A hundred plans flitted through his brain.

To drop a heavy weight on the Winged Man, crush him to the ground; then, obtaining a rope, or ladder, secure the spoil, was the first thought that entered his head. But he knew enough of the fearful flying being he contemplated robbing to convince him that the Winged Man could not be destroyed by ordinary means.

Ah, nothing that breathes the upper air can fight against starvation!

A cunning smile on his evil face, the Man With the Scar hastened from the vicinity of the pit, returning a few minutes later staggering beneath the weight of a pair of ironbound wooden shutters.

Noiselessly depositing his burden so that he could slide it to the mouth of the pit at any moment, Black Jake looked down upon his intended victim once more. Squatted on the ground, the Winged Man was gloating over his treasure. Fascinated by the glittering gems, Black Jake leaned so far forward that he was within an ace of falling headlong down the shaft. So imminent was his peril that he drew a suppressed cry of alarm from his lips.

Low though the ejaculation, it reached the Winged Man's ears. He looked up. Recognition in his eyes, he rose in the air.

Springing to his feet, Black Jake grasped one of the shutters and slid it swiftly over the mouth of the pit. Well he knew that once the Winged Man seized him in his iron grip his course was run. Terror gave him strength. With a mighty effort he threw the second shutter alongside the first.

A cry of rage proclaimed that the Winged Man was imprisoned in what might well prove a living tomb.

Heavy though the slabs of iron-covered wood were, but for the fact that the Winged Man had to grope for a foothold on the side of the pit ere he could put forth his full strength, he would have thrown them aside as easily as though they had been sheets of paper. That moment's delay proved Jake's salvation.

Close at hand a number of huge stones littered the floor of the passage. Working for his life, Black Jake piled stone after stone, rock after rock, upon the shutter, until at last even the Winged Man's enormous strength could not move them.

Dropping upon his knees, the Man With the Scar, almost beside himself with excitement and triumph, put his lips to the narrow opening between the shutters.

"Ha, ha Winged Man, I've got you now!" he cried exultantly. "You hidden gold is mine, and the diamonds and rubies that are in the pit will be mine when starvation has claimed you for its own."

"Fool! More than fool! Neither the gold of which you have robbed me nor the gems shall ever be yours. Nor will they purchase mercy from me when I have you in my power."

Black Jake laughed loud, but his laugh was forced and mirthless. The deep, rolling tones of the Winged Man's voice, the confidence with which he spoke, had already thrown cold water upon his hopes. Perhaps, after all, it would be wiser to take what he could get and let the Winged Man go.

"Hand me the stones through the chink, and you shall go free," he offered, adding: "Wolf don't eat wolf, you know!"

"Do you dare to class yourself—felon, thief, gaolbird that you are—with me, the Winged Man, who holds all England—ay, if I chose, who could hold the whole world—in the hollow of my hand? Get hence; you weary me! But, remember, the Winged Man never forgets, never forgives!" thundered the Winged Man.

Returning to the bottom of the shaft, he fastened himself to the ceiling of the chamber, and, draping his wings about him, was soon fast asleep.

Confident that the Winged Man could not escape, Black Jake strolled about the house, ransacking drawers, and thrusting anything of value he came across in his pockets.

"Let's see," muttered Jake, as he sat down to some cold meat, flanked by a bottle of brandy. "An ordinary man would be starved out in three days. If I give the Winged Man a week that will be sufficient. In the meantime, as this place is supposed to be haunted, and neither love nor money would induce the villagers to come near it, in daylight or dark, I can make myself very comfortable here."

By the time Black Jake had finished his meal the neck of the bottle had been applied so often to his lips that it was half empty, with the result that ere night came his brain was fuddled, his legs not quite under his control.

Presently he rose and looked stupidly about him. His eyes fell upon a large lamp in the centre of the table, the glass reservoir of which was nearly empty.

"This won't do; go out too soon. Where in thunder do they keep their oil?" he gurgled.

Pulling himself together, he made his way to a cupboard beneath the kitchen stairs, where during his wandering in search of plunder he had noticed a large drum of petroleum.

He looked round for some vessel in which to carry the liquid into the dining-room. His eye fell upon a housemaid's pail.

"That'll do," he muttered, tacking across the kitchen and securing the pail. This he placed beneath the drum, set the tap running, and was dozing off, when a splashing warned him that the pail was running over.

Without troubling to turn off the tap, he seized the bucket, and, spilling the petroleum at every step, made his way back to the dining-room.

Unscrewing the top of the lamp, he raised the pail with unsteady hands, and emptied part of its contents into the reservoir. By far the greater part flew over the cloth on to the floor.

"Seems as though I've spilt some," he murmured drowsily.

Then, the pail still clasped in his hand, he sank into a chair, and was soon buried in a heavy slumber.

BEGIRT BY FLAMES

About ten o'clock the Winged Man awoke. Dropping to the floor, he looked to right and left in alarm. Danger threatened. He knew, he felt it. A loud, unbroken roaring sounded on his ears.

At first he deemed it but the howling of arising gale as it hurled itself against the chimneys and gables of the old-time mansion. But soon and ominous, loud, cracking noise warned him of a much greater peril. The house was on fire!

Not for a moment did he under-estimate the danger of his situation. The wainscoting, the huge oak beams, all dry as tender, would burn like paper. Then the walls would fall in and entomb him beneath a mass of masonry from which there could be no escape.

Of outside help there was none. He alone knew the secret of the hidden well.

Fiercely he attacked the iron-cased boards which held him in with a short, thick jemmy he drew from his breast-pocket, until at last a strip of iron had been torn from right to left of the woodwork.

Then with a chisel as sharp as a razor he attacked the wood beneath, holding on to the shutter with his feet, whilst, bending his body upwards, he chipped off long splinters of dry wood.

Suddenly an ominous crack warned him to desist, lest he should bring the loose stones Black Jake had piled on the shutters down on him.

Wound round the Winged Man's waist was a length of thin but exceedingly strong rope, made of hair.

Poised immediately below the shutters, the Winged Man secured one end of the rope to his short but powerful jemmy; then, inserting the miniature crowbar between the shutters, dropped to the bottom of the shaft, and, putting forth the whole of his enormous strength, pulled on the rope.

With a loud, resounding crack the weakened shutter gave, and an avalanche of boulders fell with it to the bottom of the pit.

Sweeping the gems that had roused Black Jake's envy into his pocket, the Winged Man soared upwards, but only to find his way barred by an even more insurmountable obstacle.

The secret passage was full of suffocating, impenetrable smoke, before which even the Winged Man was forced to retreat.

In the meantime, a crowd of villagers, seeing lights in Broughton Moat, had gathered, at a respectful distance from the house, to watch the prodigy with gaping mouths and distended eyes.

Gradually the lights extended from window to window, then lurid masses of flames leaped against the window-panes. But no one yet realised that the old house was ablaze and already doomed to destruction.

The village policeman was the first to make the discovery. Calling upon the others to follow, he set the example, and a few minutes later the crowd was trampling over the flower-beds and well-kept lawn in front of the old house.

Suddenly a loud, fearful, piercing shriek fell upon their startled ears. The next moment a casement window was smashed to atoms, and a blazing figure, uttering loud cries of terror and pain, burst from the house.

"The Winged Man! The Winged Man!" he yelled.

The villagers sought safety in flight, all but the butcher, the constable, and Thomas Baker, who tried in vain to intercept the fleeing man.

Blinded by the flames, Black Jake, who had awakened from his slumber to find himself in the midst of the burning house, pitched headlong into the moat at the bottom of the lawn.

Death by drowning seemed to threaten the man who had so narrowly escaped being burned to a cinder. He had already sunk twice beneath the surface before the butcher sprang into the moat and pulled him out.

Although badly burned, a severe fright was the only other injury Black Jake had received, and a doctor who was called in to see him an hour or so later declared that he would soon be about again.

But ere that happened Black Jake was recognised as an escaped convict, and only returned to health to be escorted back to the prison from which he had escaped.

But to return to Broughton Moat.

It was evident from the first that the old house was doomed, yet, forming a line from the moat, the willing villages past buckets from hand to hand to try to save at least a portion of the building.

The West Wing had as yet escaped the flames, and upon that they directed their energies.

Suddenly a loud cry of:

"Back—back, for your lives!" rose from a man, who, mounting on a ladder placed against one of the windows, was hurling water on to the flames within.

Repeating his frenzied warning, he sprang from the ladder at the risk of his life and limb, then, followed by his alarmed comrades, dashed over the lawn.

Barely had they got out of danger, ere, with a crash, the whole front of the west wing collapsed, leaving a couple of bed-rooms, as yet untouched by the flames, exposed to view.

A loud gasp of terror escaped from every lip.

Standing in the centre of one of the rooms, his pinions outstretched, his headlight blazing fiercely, stood the Winged Man.

With bulging eyes they gazed upon that fearful being.

A fierce wave of flame swept over him.

Springing from the already tottering floor, he uttered a wild, weird cry, and dived headlong through the flames.

Dark masses of smoke pierced by spears of lurid flame hid the Winged Man from view.

A howl of terror, and the panic-stricken villagers fled, even the dauntless three who had witnessed, undismayed, Black Jake's exit from the burning building joining in the flight.

Well they might.

His clothes ablaze, wreathed in smoke, crowned in flame, the Winged Man looked as though he might well be the Fire King himself.

Choosing death by fire in preference to being suffocated, the Winged Man had forced his way along the smoke-filled passages.

At first it seemed as though his end had indeed come. Whichever way he turned flames hemmed him in. At last, blinded and scorched, he burst through a sliding panel into the bedroom in the west wing just as the outer wall collapsed. As it fell, a wave of air sent a thick curtain of flame surging heavenwards.

Through this mass of living fire the Winged Man dived.

Lurid tongues of flame clasped him in deadly embrace, and when at last the open air was reached he was ablaze from head to foot.

Then the Winged Man first felt pain.

Wildly beating the air with his flaming pinions, he swept backwards and forwards, up and down, until, unable to bear the fearful smart longer, he closed his wings and plunged headlong into the moat.

SNATCHED FROM HIS FOES.

Was the strange being human after all? It was this question which caused several of the crowd to hasten towards the spot where the Winged Man had disappeared.

Wondering, they gathered on the bank of the moat, talking in hushed, awed whispers of the fearful sights they had witnessed.

Suddenly the policeman darted forward, sprang into a clump of tall reeds, and raised a black, dripping form from out the water.

It was the Winged Man, limp, livid, pale.

Death—or, at least, the unconsciousness which precedes death—had marked him as its own.

So thought the wondering, yet triumphant, constable and his companions.

But the Winged Man was not dead, neither was he unconscious. In cases of injury by fire it is the shock that kills. No shock would ever harm the Winged Man. His burns caused him intense agony, otherwise he was as well, strong, and alert as ever.

But, alas! his wings were useless, and the wondrous springs, which enabled him to take such tremendous jumps, were weakened and out of order. Strong, fearless, agile though he was, he could not hope to overthrow the constantly increasing crowd which clustered round him, and his was not the nature to attempt an undignified struggle.

Presently, though with evident reluctance, the constable and the butcher raised the Winged Man from the ground and carried him down the gravel drive to the high-road.

News that the Winged Man had been captured spread like wild-fire, and the crowd increased so rapidly that by the time the procession entered the long, straggling village of Broughton, quite a number of people were trying to catch a glimpse of the fearful creature who had terrorised the country so long.

Toot! Toot! Toot!

The sound of a motor-horn in the rear of the crowd caused the hindmost to move to the side of the road.

Toot! Toot! Toot!

Louder and more insistent came the distant roar. With cries of indignation the crowd squeezed nearly into the ditch, as our powerful four-cylinder motor-cycle, its rider couched, nose and knees together, on the saddle, came with lightning speed towards them.

"Take his number, some of you!" yelled the policeman. "He is travelling at a hundred miles—"

He ended the sentence in the ditch.

The Winged Man's legs had struck him full in the back, sending him plunging heavily forward.

Astounded by this unexpected sign of life in one whom he had believed would not live another hour, the butcher dropped the Winged Man's head and shoulders.

In a moment the Winged Man was on his feet. Seizing the butcher by the middle, he hurled him on to the struggling constable, then placed himself in the track of the on-coming cyclist.

Without slackening speed, Ghat, for the motor-cyclist was he, thrust out a long, brawny arm as he passed, seized the Winged Man round the waist, swung him, as likely as though he had been a child, onto the handle-bars before him, and, ere the villagers realised that a rescue was taking place before their very eyes, disappeared in a cloud of dust down the road.

"Is the master pleased?" asked Ghat over the Winged Man's shoulder.

"You have done well," replied the Winged Man, perhaps the greatest commendation the faithful Ghat had ever heard from his master's lips.

All chance of pursuit, even if the idea of such a thing had entered the villagers' heads, over, Ghat stopped the machine, and when they resumed their journey a few minutes later, the Winged Man wearing Ghat's cap and goggles, was in the saddle, with the dwarf, a huddled, shapeless, grotesque bundle, on the carrier behind him.

A wild ride ensued. Roughly speaking, one hundred and fifty miles lay between themselves and the Winged Man's Yorkshire lair, yet barely had three hours passed since Ghat snatched his master from his captors' grasp ere the Winged Man was stretched on a couch in his luck curiously-furnished cave overlooking the wild North Sea, whilst Ghat attended to his wounds.

Food and rest, and the Winged Man was himself once more.

Springing from a pedestal in one corner of his room on which he had slept in preference to bed, the Winged Man strode through endless tunnels, where the unceasing thud, thud, of pickaxe and spade told that Ghat, who required as little sleep as his master, was filling in his spare moments by excavating fresh caves for the Winged Man's use.

Rewarding Ghat's industry with a cuff and a kick, the Winged Man proceeded to his laboratory. For three days and nights, without rest, without food, the Winged Man toiled in his magnificently-appointed workshop and laboratory.

When at length he emerged, he was provided with new winged garments which would resist the fiercest flames. He had no wish to repeat the experiment of Broughton Moat.

Refreshed, and ready to resume his warfare on the human race, the Winged Man sallied forth once more.

°

FROM PRESTON SPIRE.

From the summit of a spire towering high above the clock-tower of the town-hall, the Winged Man gazed upon the sleeping town of Preston, in Lancashire.

It was a clear, starlit night. The tall shafts of various cotton mills piercing the air were dwarfed by the spire of St. Walberg's built by the inventor of hansom cabs.

Suddenly his attention was attracted by a huge, round object swaying to the breeze near some gas-works on the outskirts of the town.

Rising, he spread his pinions, and flew towards the gas-works to examine the balloon. As he glided through the air he drew a long, sharp knife from his belt and gazed at its keen edge with evident satisfaction.

"I am Lord of the Air, and allow no man to share my dominion," he murmured grimly, as he alighted upon the balloon's yielding surface.

He raised the knife to plunge it into the silk outer covering; but, changing his mind, dropped to the side of the car. Presently he glided beneath the shadow of a loaded coke-waggon as a man stole noiselessly into the yard, glanced at the balloon, then crossed to a small door marked "Office" near the Winged Man's hiding-place.

The new-comer shook the office door.

"Hallo! Who's there?" demanded a sleepy voice from within.

"It is I—Ranger," was the low-voiced reply.

The sound of a bolt being shoved back in its socket, and the door opened. A man holding a candle above his head appeared in the doorway. Ranger blew the candle out.

"There's no need to call attention to the fact that we are just off, Pearce," he

---

° 8 FEBRUARY 1913.

said angrily.

"Off! It still wants an hour to the time you named," objected Pearce.

"What of that? The job is done. You could leave a note on your desk saying we took advantage of a favourable wind to try to cross the Irish Channel. Come on, if you are ready. We'll be freer from possible eavesdroppers in the balloon. It's a perfect night for an ascent," replied the other.

Five minutes later the balloon rose steadily and majestically into the night air.

"What's that?" cried Ranger, as, when about a dozen feet from the ground, the balloon's ascent was checked.

The next moment it had recovered from the slight jerk caused by the Winged Man springing from the ground and fastening himself on to the bottom of the car.

But the jerk, slight though it was, had been sufficient to put the two men within the car in serious jeopardy; indeed, for a moment, even the Winged Man was in peril. Fortunately, he continued to glance westward, and saw in time that they were travelling in a straight line for a tall mill shaft.

Never did the Winged Man lose his presence of mind. Grasping the side of the car, he allowed his weight to fall on his wings, and the balloon shooting upwards, cleared a huge chimney by a couple of feet.

Danger over, the Winged Man fastened himself securely to the edge of the car and prepared to listen. Up went the balloon, higher and higher, until the River Ribble, Preston, its parks, and cotton mills, appeared like toys beneath them.

Five thousand feet above the earth, the balloon's ascent was checked, and she moved at some twenty miles an hour in the direction of the sea.

"You've done it?" asked the man who had been addressed as Pearce.

"Yes. There is sufficient of the new explosive beneath Peterson's mill to blow it to pieces were it twice as big."

"Phew! What a stick-at-nothing villain you are, Ranger!" ejaculated Pearce. "It seems to me that you would have ruined your rival as much by destroying the mill when it was empty, as when some five hundred innocent human beings were at work within. They are doomed!"

"Doomed!" returned Ranger. "Ay, doomed!"

HURLED THROUGH SPACE.

"I pay; all you have got to do is to obey orders!" returned Ranger sullenly. "After all, they're only common factory workers, and if the whole lot are wiped out of existence it won't matter."

Though he knew it not, Ranger had pronounced his own doom. By this time the lights of Preston had faded from view, and tiny specks, like stars, showed that they were about halfway between Southport and St Anne's-on-Sea.

"Well, have it as you will," agreed Pearce.

A half-triumphant, wholly cruel laugh escaped Ranger's lips.

"I always do; and, as long as I wield the power of gold, always will!" he boasted.

"Liar!"

The deep bass voice seemed to come from immediately beneath their very feet, where no human being could possibly be. Simultaneously the two men rushed to the side and looked. There was nothing there. They could not see the Winged Man clinging to the bottom of the car immediately beneath them.

"It was only a screaming gull!" cried Ranger.

"Idiot!" came the same deep, bass voice from below.

"Great Scott! Who is it with us?" declared Pearce, his teeth chattering, his hair rising from his head in terror.

Both men clutched at the rim of the car, as they gazed, with starting eyeballs, in the direction from which arose a loud burst of goblin-like laughter.

Slowly a white face, awful in its pallor, appeared above the edge of the car!

"Villains, who would doom the innocent to a terrible end, prepared to meet your fate!" came in low, solemn accents from the Winged Man.

For nearly five minutes the Winged Man gazed at his victims, enjoying the terror depicted upon their countenances.

"Ha, ha villains who know not mercy! Behold!"

A quick flash of steel, and one of the ropes that held the car to the balloon was severed. Again the knife was raised; again the loose end of a severed cord fell against the basket-work of the car.

"Hold, man or demon, which ever you be; it is our doom you seek!" gasped Pearce.

"Doom! You talk of doom?" retorted the Winged Man contemptuously.

He severed yet another cord. Nerved by the imminence of his danger, Ranger snatched a heavy stick from the bottom of the car, and struck viciously at the mocking, white face.

He was too late. The Winged Man had disappeared. Eagerly Ranger peered over the edge of the car, but even as he did so a cry of terror rose from Pearce's lips; for, reappearing on the other side of the wickerwork construction, the Winged Man seized him by the back of the neck, and, hurling him to the bottom of the car, cut two more cords ere a hand could be raised to prevent him.

Frantically Ranger clutched at the cord of the safety-valve. The Winged Man was before him, and the end of the severed cord came away in his hands. Helpless, hopeless despair claimed Ranger and Pearce as its own.

A snap; as yet another cord gave way before the Winged Man's sharp blade, recalling them to the imminent peril of their position. Then another and another cord was severed.

Shrieking with fear, they clung to the side of the car as it gave beneath their feet. A louder, shriller, more despairing cry than any that had preceded it burst from Pearce's lips as he plunged headlong into the hungry sea below, leaving Ranger clinging for dear life to the basket, held to the balloon by but four thin cords.

Relieved of Pearce's weight, the balloon rose at a terrible rate.

Ho, ho! Look up, you trembling coward! The king of the air welcomes you to his domain!" shouted the Winged Man in the doomed man's ears.

Peal upon peal of awful laughter rent the air. One by one the remaining cords were severed, until, his eyes bulging from their sockets Ranger held on by the one remaining cord. Cutting the cord immediately beneath Ranger's hands, the Winged Man allowed the car to fall into the sea. Suddenly a wild, weird peal of laughter burst from Ranger's lips.

"I die, but not alone!" he cried, drawing a revolver from his pocket.

Clinging by one arm to the slender cord, he fired straight into the mouth of the balloon. A terrific burst of flame, a loud, deafening explosion, and the balloon disappeared in a ball of fire. Blinded by the flash, deafened by the roar of the explosion, knocked breathless by the concussion, the Winged Man fell like a stone some fifty feet ere his open pinions checked his descent.

He looked around him. Impenetrable darkness below, a star-spangled sky above, alone met his gaze. With a blinding glare, the Winged Man's head light flashed forth its powerful beams. Some fifty feet beneath him was a dark, swiftly-falling mass.

As a swimmer, with clasped hands, plunges towards the water, so the Winged Man dived through space in pursuit of Ranger's falling body. With arms and legs outstretched, his white, ashen face fixed with fear, the unfortunate man fixed his terror-laden eyes, with a look of hopeless appeal, upon the Winged Man's white, pallid face.

Each moment the impetus of his fall increased. Ere half the distance between where the balloon had exploded and the sea had been accomplished, nature herself would release him from his sufferings. He feared to die.

For the first time the full enormity of the deed he had contemplated tore into his heart.

"Help!" came in a low, gasping cry from his parched and pallid lips.

Then his last hope disappeared, for the Winged Man, flashing by, disappeared into the void beneath. Terror-stricken, Ranger awaited the end. Moments like hours past; then it gradually dawned on him that, had his fall continued as it had begun, he would ere this have been no more.

A wild hope, full of possibilities, flashed through his brain. For a fraction of a second he closed his eyes in semi-unconsciousness. When he opened them again the air had ceased to whistle past his ears; the feeling of suffocation which had brought him so near death was gone.

Yes; in some wondrous way his speed was checked, though he was still falling, headforemost, and, with outstretched arms, seaward—falling, but so gradually that the sensation was pleasant rather than the reverse.

ON THE PUMP BEAM.

Screwing back his head, Ranger looked up. A black mass hovered overhead. It was the Winged Man, who, with outstretched wings, was bearing him gently to earth. Even in that perilous moment, Ranger looked curiously for the means by which the Winged Man had arrested his fall, but in vain. The feeling of joy which had swept through his heart at the prospect of a respite from death passed almost as quickly as it had come. Terror of the unknown, fearful apparition hovered so threateningly overhead chilled his heart with new-found dread.

What if he was destined to be for ever the prey of that fearful, menacing form? As though in answer to his unspoken thought, deep, resonant, yet clear as the booming note of a passing bell, came in hollow tones from the Winged Man's lips.

"I am the king of doom!"

The sailors upon an outward-bound ship heard Ranger's bitter, despairing cry, and shuddered as they gazed into the blackness above.

A faint light glowed for a moment like a falling star, then all was blackness once more, and the ship continued on her voyage under a cloud of superstitious dread, for there was scarce a man on board who did not believe that they had received a supernatural warning of approaching doom.

With the cry, Ranger's consciousness fled and all was blank.

*

Plang! Plong! Plang! Plong!

Monotonous, insistent, the metallic yet dull thuds seemed like blows rained on Ranger's head as he slowly awoke to consciousness. He felt very ill, as though in the throes of seasickness.

Plong! His head dropped.

Plang! It rose again.

Surely he was at sea? The monotonous noise, intermixed as it was with the whir and roar of machinery, and the heat of engines, all seemed to speak of a steamer's deck.

Plong! Plang!

He looked around him. An arched wall above his head; a wall to the right; another wall, pierced by a narrow window, to his left. He tried to raise his hand to his aching head. In vain; it was bound tightly to his side. A cautious movement of his legs revealed the fact that they were also tightly secured. Then he became conscious that his body was lying upon some flat, hard surface, barely three inches in width.

This, then, was the punishment the Winged Man had decreed should be his. Was he on earth or—A fearful shadow shook his frame. He closed his eyes. He dare not think. The whir of machinery grew more distinct as his brain grew clearer. The truth burst upon him. He was in, or close to, a cotton-mill in full work. Up and down, up and down he was carried.

"Where am I? What has happened?" he thought. "Ah, I recognise the thudding sound at last! It is the beating of an ever-moving pump. Why have I been brought here?"

A trembling seized him. He dare not pursue the subject further. Slowly he turned his head, and, as the top part of his body rose, shot a quick glance through the window.

The sight which met his gaze struck terror to his heart.

"No, no; it cannot be! I dare not—" he began; then, as the end of the beam to which he was fixed rose once more he glanced through the window again.

A low, fear-laden groan burst from his lips. The glimpse of a distant country he had seen from the window had revealed his position all too plainly. He was in the very cotton-mill he had undermined with a new and terrible explosive.

What was the hour? It seemed as though the beam would never rise again, but at length his head rose level with the opening, and, peering through the narrow window, he gazed into the heavens. Alas! Clouds covered the sky.

"Help—help—help! Here, in the pump-house! Help!" he yelled at the top of his voice.

The maddening plong-plang of the pump was the only answer to his frenzied cry.

Again he shrieked aloud for help; again the whir of machinery drowned his voice. He tried to shout again, but his parched lips refused to utter a sound. A dogged, sullen resignation settled on his heart. Where now were all his carefully-worked-out schemes for the destruction of his rival? They could only end in one way. He himself would be overwhelmed in the destruction he had planned.

Suddenly a voice sounded from below. It was the sweetest music he had ever heard.

"Hallo! What on earth are you doing there?" came in a man's voice from almost immediately beneath him.

With difficulty turning his head, Ranger looked down.

A man in the blue overalls of an engineer was standing, oil-can in hand, regarding him with open-mouthed astonishment.

"Quick! Cut me down! For your own sake, for the sake of hundreds of your comrades, cut me down!" shrieked Ranger.

The man ran off without reply.

A bitter groan of despair burst from Rangers lips. He believed himself deserted. But no! The rise and fall of the iron beam ceased. Then a ladder was placed against the piston-rod; and a few minutes later, Ranger, tingling in every limb as his bonds were released, lay in the centre of an astonished crowd of operators and engineers.

"Hallo! Why have you stopped the looms?" demanded the mill manager, thrusting his way through the crowd. "Why, Mr. Ranger, what are you doing here?" he added, recognising the prostrate man.

"The time—quick—the time!" gasped Ranger, his white, scared face looking eagerly into that of the new-comer.

"Steady, Mr. Ranger! Take a grip of yourself, man!" expostulated the other.

"The time—the time!" interrupted Ranger, stamping his foot impatiently. "James Freeman, whilst we are talking here, death is creeping upon all within this building!"

The manager looked significantly at the engineer.

"No, no; I am not mad!" continued Ranger, interpreting the glance aright. "I tell you we might as well be in the crater of an erupting volcano as in this building. At eleven o'clock there will not be a single wall of this mill standing!"

Ranger spoke with such earnestness that, despite his belief that terror had driven the rival cotton-spinner mad, the manager of Peterson's Mills was impressed.

"Then we will soon know whether your fears are well-founded or not, Mr. Ranger," he said, with a smile, "for it wants but five minutes to eleven now."

With a bitter cry Ranger clasped his hand to his head.

"What shall I do? What can I do?" he moaned. Suddenly, as one who shakes off some unnerving terror, he cried: "Quick! Follow me! We may yet be in time!" He led the way to a staircase leading to the first floor.

"Pull up the third board to the right," he directed, adding fiercely to the crowd of workers who hastened forward to see the cause of the stoppage of work: "Get out! On your lives, leave this place!"

They stared at the speaker in amazement. Then a girl giggled, and the others, frightened for the moment, joined in her laughter.

A grunt of astonishment from the engineer greeted the discovery that the board he had seized had come up without trouble, showing that it had been previously loosened. Beneath the board he found a small box, which, in obedience to a sign from the manager, he flung out of the window.

Mr. Freeman stooped to examine the place where the box had lain. Under the floor in the centre of the room was what looked like a number of small cubes, bound with coarse canvas. Ere he could speak, for terror bound his tongue, Ranger sped swiftly up the stairs, tore up a loose board from the floor, and, seizing a similar box, hold it from the window.

Just then a distant clock boomed out the hour of eleven.

"Thank Providence!" came fervently from Ranger's lips. "Is Mr. Peterson in his office?" he added, turning to the manager.

"He will be by this time," replied the other.

"Then take me to him."

"But the explosive," demanded Freeman—"that is, if explosives they are," he added, correcting himself.

"They are all right. The machinery which alone would have exploded them has been removed," replied Ranger.

And, followed by the manager, he entered the mill-owner's office just as that gentleman drove up in a motor-car.

RANGER'S DOOM.

Breathlessly the manager related to the cotton magnate all that had occurred.

"Good gracious! It reads like a scene from a melodrama!" ejaculated Mr. Peterson. "What light can you throw on the strange occurrence, Mr. Ranger?" he added, turning to the man whom he knew to be his enemy.

When his end had seemed so near, Ranger had made up his mind to make a clean breast of everything, if he lived. The danger past, more prudent counsels guided his words.

"You and I have not always been friends, Peterson," he began, with pretended frankness, "but I am not your only enemy. Last night a man called upon me. He said he had deposited a quantity of explosive under the floors of your mill. He asked me to assist him. Of course, I refused, and in revenge he and his comrades seized and bound me to the beam of the pumping-engine, where your man found me just in time to frustrate one of the most atrocious schemes ever invented."

"It sounds impossible," declared Mr. Peterson. "Who was this man—the unknown enemy?"

Ranger hesitated; then, looking fearfully round the room, said:

"The Winged Man!"

Mr. Peterson and his manager exchanged glances.

"My dear sir," objected Peterson, "you are surely not one of those foolish persons who believe in the Winged Man! I have never yet ceased to wonder that the police should have taken the idle tales that are going about seriously enough to issue a reward for his arrest."

"They are not idle tales," retorted Ranger eagerly. "I know they are true, for I have seen him. The Winged Man is a danger to the State. No man is safe, no mill is safe, while he is at liberty. He intended to destroy your mill. It may be my turn to-morrow. I will add another five hundred pounds to the reward. You will surely do the same."

"I would gladly make it five thousand pounds if I believed it possible that so wonderful being existed. My dear sir, I am grateful for what you have done. Take my advice. Go home, rest; then you, like myself, will feel inclined to laugh at this Winged Man. Winged Man, indeed! Where is he now?"

"The Winged Man is here!"

The three men turned as the deep, rolling tones fell upon their ears.

With a cry of horror, Ranger shrank back into the furthermost corner of the office. Mr. Peterson dropped into a chair, gazing with starting eyes upon the unexpected apparition. Mr. Freeman, pale to the very lips, trembling in every limb, retreated towards the window.

A sardonic smile on his thin, bloodless lips, the Winged Man stood, with folded arms, surveying the three men.

"The Winged Man is here!" he repeated mockingly. Then, his eyes blazing with anger, he turned upon the shrinking man in the corner, and, pointing a long, talon-like finger towards him, cried: "Liar, scoundrel, fool! Despite last night's experience you would dare to saddle the Winged Man with your crime? Look at him! See the cringing, frightened wretch! It was he who is black heart planned the outrage, then thought to avert suspicion by a midnight flight in his balloon to Ireland."

"It is false! I—" began Ranger.

Rising a few inches from the floor the Winged Man glided towards him.

His hands clutched against the bare wall, his legs scarce able to support his body, his face white and livid, Ranger watched the fearful being approach.

When within four feet of where his victim stood the Winged Man stopped, and with slow, solemn movements glided back, beckoning Ranger to follow.

Ranger trembled, and gave a look of piteous terror at the Winged Man's white, expressionless face; whilst the mill-owner and manager watched, to astounded, too terrified, to speak or move. In the centre of the room Ranger came to an abrupt halt, and stood as motionless as though death had already laid its chilling finger upon his heart.

"Speak!" thundered the Winged Man.

Ranger trembled, a look of piteous terror flashed from his eyes; he swayed backwards and forwards, waving his arms wildly above his head, as though striving to flee, but unable to move his lower limbs.

"Speak!" thundered the Winged Man.

A moment's silence; then, in the dull, expressionless tones of one talking in his sleep, Ranger made his confession:

"I hate you, Peterson! I hated you when we were boys at school. I hated to hear you spoken of as a kindly and humane employer. I hated you most when the girl I loved chose you instead of me. Again and again I have tried to ruin you, but in vain. To that end I determined to destroy your mill in such a way that even if insurance cover the loss it would be swallowed up by compensation to the injured. I bought the explosives. With my own hand I deposited them between the floor and the ceiling, where, as the manager knows, I found them. The Winged Man, who intercepted my flight, saved me from a mercifully sudden death, too good for such a wholesale murder as myself, and time to be to the beams of the pumping-engine. Here, should you require it, is proof of what I say."

As he spoke he hurled a bundle of letters at the astounded mill-owner's feet; then, with a cry of such bitter despair that it lingered in the hearers' ears for months, Ranger clasped his hands to his head and rushed from the room.

"Great providence! Save that I have been more successful than he, I don't think I have ever done that man the slightest wrong!" ejaculated the mill-owner, turning to where his strange visitor had been standing a moment before. The Winged Man had disappeared. How, neither man could say. Half an hour later the Winged Man pushed open the door of a palatial mansion, standing in its own grounds on the banks of the Ribble, a few miles from Preston.

A manservant, indignant at the intrusion of the stranger, came forward to enquire his business. With a wave of his hand the Winged Man motioned him back. Trembling in every limb, the footman retreated before the strangely-garbed, white-faced figure.

"I have business with your master. See to it that we are not interrupted!" commanded the Winged Man, pausing with his hand on the handle of a door that opened into the hall.

A dull, muffled report came from beyond the door. With an exclamation of alarm the footman darted forward; then stopped, as though turned to stone before the strange being's upraised hand

"Go! Summon a doctor!" ordered the Winged Man. "Tell him the Winged

Man is here!"

Ere the astounded man could speak he passed through the thick, oak-grained door into a splendidly-furnished library. Turning the key in the lock, the Winged Man strode to a table in the centre of the room.

A few thin wreaths of smoke hovered over a man's head and shoulders as they lay across the table; one arm was stretched out, the other bent; his hand grasped the butt of a still-smoking revolver. A small wound in the victim's forehead proclaimed that Ranger had paid the penalty of his crime at his own hands.

For nearly a minute the Human Bat gazed at the man who was no more, a look of contempt upon his thin lips, then turned to the side of the fireplace, where a safe had been let into the wall. On the writing-table lay a bunch of keys. These the human bat seized, and, opening the safe, swept into his pockets everything of value it contained; then, opening the window, spread his wings and flew towards the ruins of a distant tower, on the summit of which he overhauled his recently-acquired booty.

THE WILL.

It was a wild, bleak, dreary night. The wind howled fitfully amongst the chimneys of a small village a few miles from Bristol, rising now and again to such fury that it set the bells swaying in the old abbey tower, bringing forth a dull, muffled clang that filled the hearts of the sleepless dwellers in that old hamlet with superstitious terror.

So fierce was the storm that some of the inhabitants had not gone to bed at all, as lights in many windows betokened. At one house, protected from the road by a high wall, a tiny flickering light showed a solitary watcher.

Within, an old, bent, decrepit man poured over a number of papers which lifted the writing-table before him. Presently he looked up, and, gathering the majority of the papers together in a number of little parcels, secured them by pieces of red tape ere he put them back, neatly labelled, into a drawer by his side. Only two were left. One a large, blue document; the other a tiny slip of paper, yellow with age.

"No, no; they shall never have it! I hated him as a boy. I hated him as a man. I hate him even now that he has gone. Now that he has gone his children shall not inherit the property in Bristol which is theirs by right. The sins of the fathers—ay, the sins of the fathers!" he mumbled through his toothless gums, as he grasped the larger document, upon which he had inscribed in a round, legal hand:

"The last will and testament of Robert Ayres, merchant, Bristol."

"Ha, ha, ha! Ho, ho, ho!" chuckled the old man. "The lawyers want to see the papers of John Ayres that I hold, do they? They shall see them—all but the will of the present Ayres' grandfather, and his marriage certificate; without which they claim upon the Ayres's estate must fall to the ground."

He rubbed his hands in unholy glee.

"I wonder if it's true, as some believe, that the spirits of those gone before can see that which goes on around them? I hope so! I hope that Robert Ayres can see me now—can see me take this document and consign it to the flames!"

Thus mumbled the old man who sought to spite one who now lay silent and cold in the wind-swept grounds of the abbey, a quarter of a mile away. He knelt by the side of the grate, in which a few coals flickered; for Nathaniel Hyam grudged even sufficient fire to warm his aged body.

"Come, Robert Ayres, if you can; behold the destruction of your hopes!" he went on. And the room re-echoed to his fiendish chuckle.

But even as the paper touched the glowing cinders he drew it back, and, rising to his feet, burst into peals of almost maniacal laughter.

"Aha, aha! This is better! Robert Ayres expended the greater part of his life, and spent his entire fortune to trace his descendent from the original owner of Ayers Court. Death stopped the work, but ere he died he entrusted his secret and his papers to me. I will be faithful to my trust; all but two shall go to his lawyer, and these he shall have himself."

Chuckling, the old man placed the smaller paper within the larger, and, thrusting them both into his pocket, hobbled from the room, where, by the light of a fluttering candle-end, he arrayed himself in an old, worn overcoat, wrapped a faded woollen scarf round his neck, and put a gamekeeper's fur cap upon his head.

Thus arrayed he sallied forth. Passing through the carefully-barred gate which pierced the wall of the neglected old-time garden, Hyam stood for a moment in the village street, looking cautiously to right and left.

There was no one about; so, pausing now and again to steady himself against wall, tree, or fence, he forced his way against the gale until the gates of the old abbey was reached.

Boom! The sound, hollow, threatening, unnerving, came from the old abbey tower.

"Pshaw! It is but the wind!" muttered Nathaniel Hyam; yet his aged limbs carried him less quickly, and he glanced now and again apprehensively over his shoulder as he advanced towards his goal.

An exclamation of anger burst from his lips. He had forgotten the necessary tools to excavate the atrociously ingenious hiding-place in which he intended depositing the deeds. But luck favoured him. Close at hand lay a spade, which had been left behind that afternoon.

Depositing his lantern on a flat-topped stone, the old man seized the spade. Wielding it with a strength his aged limbs gave a little promise of, he had soon dug a hole a foot deep in the spot where he had planned. Fearful were the old man's chuckles as he carefully thrust the papers into the hole. The secret was safe there. The dead man's lawyers might search the world through, they would never find now the resting-place of the missing-link which alone held the orphaned children from their heritage.

"Oho, oho!" laughed the old man mockingly.

"Oho, oho!" came back the answer.

"Strange echoes—strange echoes!" muttered the old man aloud.

"Strange echoes—strange echoes!" came back in mocking tones from immediately behind him.

THE MISER'S FATE.

Nathaniel Hyam started. Livid with fear, he grasped his spade as though prepared to face some unseen enemy. Then he turned. The spade fell from his nerveless grasp. His lower jaw dropped on to his faded scarf.

Its legs tucked up beneath it, its pallid face showing white through the darkness, its fierce eyes fixed with a fearful, concentrated glare, a strange, black, motionless form was seated on a slab of stone.

"Who—who are you?" gasped the old man, his voice rising to a shriek of terror.

Gradually the figure rose to its feet, stood with wide, distended wings; then, leaning slightly forward, it seemed as though about to fall upon the terror-stricken old man, who, uttering a piercing shriek, dropped with uplifted hands upon his knees.

"Mercy, mercy!" he shrieked. "I cannot die; I am not ready to die! Spare me, spare me!"

Then his hands dropped to his eyes that they might shut out the blinding glare of the Winged Man's headlight.

For some minutes neither spoke. The silence became unbearable. Looking timidly up, the old man said:

"Who are you? Speak!"

"I am the Winged Man, the scourge of such as you, robber of orphaned children that you are. Since I overheard the lawyer demand the papers belonging to the man who lies buried here, I have watched you unseen."

Nathaniel Hyam rose tottering to his feet.

"Have mercy! I will make amends!" he cried.

"Give me the buried papers and you shall live," promised the Winged Man.

Eagerly the old man thrust his hand into the loose soil, and groped about beneath the stones.

Nothing but damp, freshly-turned earth rewarded his efforts. Frantically he grasped the spade, and commenced re-digging the hole.

It was in vain. The papers had disappeared. Trembling he turned. The Winged Man was gone.

A moment's hesitation, then through his fear-stricken brain crept the thought that, come what might, he must replace the earth, and leave the place as he had found it.

Working frantically, he restored the place to its former condition; then, hurling the spade from him, hastened from the abbey grounds.

The wind blew him to right and left. Again and again he was rolled in the muddy road, yet each time he arose.

He felt not his bruises; his only wish, his only hope, was to gain the shelter of his house.

At length, with a sigh of relief, he burst into the room in which we first saw him, and, dropping into a chair, laid his elbow on the table, and buried his face in his hands.

Presently a thought struck him. He looked down at the drawers in which he had placed the Ayres documents.

The draw was open, the contents gone! A breath of cold, biting wind fanned his cheek. He turned to find the door, which not even the old hag who acted as his housekeeper had ever seen unclosed, wide open.

A greater terror than that to which the Winged Man's awful form had given birth filled his heart.

"My gold—my gold!" he muttered.

Snatching up the candle, he tottered through the open door, down a flight of damp, moss-grown steps to an arched cellar, stretching far away beneath the old house. A sigh of relief escaped his lips.

Upon a shelf along one side of the cellar they intact the dozen canvas bags in which the old miser kept the results of many years' pinching and saving.

"My gold, my gold, my precious gold!" he crooned, fondling the canvas bags.

With trembling fingers he undid the mouth of the nearest bag, and plunged his hand inside.

A loud, piercing, despairing shriek burst from his lips. Instead of rich, red gold his fingers closed over damp, moist earth from a newly-made grave.

"Not all gone—not all gone!" he muttered passing rapidly from bag to bag.

His hope was groundless. Bag after bag he opened and cast aside, revealing only fresh earth.

As the last bag dropped with a dull, heavy thud upon the damp flagstones, the old man clutching wildly in the air, fell beside it. The cellar was bathed in light. The Winged Man stepped to the old man's side.

Nathaniel Hyam raised himself on his elbow and opened his eyes.

His eyes, filled with unspeakable misery, looked into the Winged Man's white face.

"All gone—gold, vengeance—all gone!" he moaned. Then his face stiffened, and all was over.

Suddenly the Winged Man started, then rapidly replaced the bags on the shelf, and re-tied them.

Barely was the last bag in its place ere a shrill woman's voice was heard in the room above, calling:

"Nathaniel Hyam, what's wrong wi' ye that ye goes squealin' out like that, wakin' honest bodies in the middle o' the night?"

There was, of course, no answer. Presently a shuffling of slip-shod feet told that the speaker was approaching the door leading to the cellar.

"Huh! Something must be wrong, or the old miser would never leave this door open!" continued the voice, in tones of one who, living much alone, was accustomed to speak her thoughts aloud.

An old woman, holding a light above her head, shuffled into the cellar. She was clad in rags, wrinkled, grey-headed, and bent.

Her eyes fell upon the prostrate form of her master.

"Gone at last, have ye, you old money-grub?" was her heartless comment.

Then, her eyes glistening with greed, she turned towards the shelf on which the gold lay, and, without another thought of the dead man, lying untended and uncared for on the cellar floor, seized a bag.

"An' left the gold behind yer, too! Aha, it's mine—all mine!" muttered the old hag, working her toothless gums horribly.

"You lie, woman; it is mine!" cried the Winged Man, in deep, hollow tones, as his light, blazing forth, rendered the cellar light as day.

For a moment the old woman glared, terror-stricken, at the fearful apparition that confronted her; then, turning swiftly, ran quicker than she had run for years up the stone steps, through the study, out of the house, screeching at the top of her voice.

Barely had the old woman left the vault ere the Winged Man followed, carrying a sack he had picked up in the cellar, containing the stolen gold.

Passing through a dirty neglected hall, that yet showed traces of former grandeur, and mounting a magnificently oak, balustraded staircase, he reached a gallery, rich with pictures, now neglected and almost ruined, but once of priceless value.

In a room filled with worm-eaten furniture and moth-destroyed hangings, he threw open the shutters of a large window and gazed out into the night.

Already the sound of excited voices in the village street told that the old housekeeper's shrieks had aroused a number of villagers.

Assuring himself that his bag of gold was safe, the Winged Man stepped through the window and, poising himself on the sill for a few moments, spread out his black pinions, and soared into the night.

A hush fell on the excited crowd as the regular beatings of those fearful wings struck upon their ears.

Paralysed with terror, all gazed upwards, striving to pierce the blackness of night that obtained around.

Presently a low moan of horror burst from a score of lips, as, looking more weird and awful than ever in the uncertain light, the Winged Man came in sight.

Too terror-stricken to move, the crowd watched the fearful apparition as it hovered, almost motionless, overhead.

A moan of terror responded to the Winged Man's weird, awful cry, followed immediately by the musical clink of gold striking stone. A shower of gold had fallen upon the astounded onlookers.

Greed conquered, fear was forgotten. With loud cries, the crowd sprawled on the ground, fighting furiously for the coveted coins which had dropped, as it were, from the very heavens into their midst.

Even the Winged Man's cry of rage when he discovered that the rotten sack to which he had entrusted his precious horde had paid him false, could not strike terror into the gold-hunters' hearts.

Furious at the sight of the gold disappearing into the yokels' greedy pockets, the Winged Man fell like a meteor into the midst of the struggling, fighting, scrambling mob. Seizing a burly labourer by the legs, he used him as a flail with which to beat his comrades off.

The Winged Man's black form, his fearful, pallid face, the sight of their comrades whirled by the heels as easily as though he were a child in that relentless grip, brought back the terror greed had banished from the villagers' hearts.

They fled in all directions, whilst the Winged Man, throwing his flesh-and-blood cudgel from him, secured as much as he could find of the scattered gold;

then, rising swiftly, flew in the direction of Bristol City.

THE REWARD OF TREACHERY.

In an old house in Wine Street, Bristol, Horace Denver, the later Robert Ayres' solicitor, slept the sound sleep which always follows a well-spent day.

He awoke with an uneasy feeling that someone beside himself was in the room. Opening his eyes, an ejaculation of terror burst from his lips.

Standing at the foot of the bed, his arms folded, the Winged Man surveyed him thoughtfully.

"You are Horace Denver?" demanded the strange being.

"I am. What do you want with me?" replied the lawyer, striving to fight against the nerve-chilling terror which was quickly over-mastering him.

"I come to tell you Nathaniel Hyam is dead, and that the papers which will give your client possession of the Ayres estate are in my possession!" announced the Winged Man.

"Who are you? How do you know that Nathaniel Hyam is dead? What have you to do with the Ayres papers?" demanded the wondering attorney.

"I am the Winged Man! Let that suffice!"

"And the Ayres papers?" asked the lawyer, professional instinct overcoming even terror.

"Listen! The clock strikes three. Meet me in the council-house at this hour to-morrow morning. Bring with you a thousand pounds in gold, and they are yours!" promised the Winged Man impressively. "Refuse, or attempt to play me false, and they are lost to you for ever! Farewell!"

As the last words left the spectral visitor's lips Denver sprang from his bed.

The Winged Man had vanished!

He rushed to the door. It was locked on the inside. He flew to the windows. They were as tightly clasped as when he retired to rest.

with wide, distended wings; then, leaning
slightly forward, seemed as though about t
fall upon the terror-stricken old man, who
uttering a piercing shriek, dropped with up
lifted hands upon his knees.

"Mercy, mercy!" he shrieked. "I canno
die; I am not ready to die! Spare me, spar
me!"

Then his hands dropped to his eyes that th

"It was a dream—a vivid, lifelike dream!" murmured Denver.

"It was no dream. I am here!" cried a voice at his elbow.

And, turning, he saw the Winged Man standing by his side. Terror held the lawyer paralysed, and ere he could recover, the Winged Man had again vanished.

Punctually at the hour appointed, Horace Denver entered Bristol's ancient council-house. He was alone, but concealed at various points close at hand were a number of policemen, who, as Denver entered the old place, silently and noiselessly surrounded the building, for it had been arranged that as soon as Horace Denver emerged with the document safe in his possession, they would rush in and secure the Winged Man.

Eagerly Bristol's Chief Constable crouched in a doorway, waiting Denver's reappearance.

Not a light appeared at any of the windows, not a sound had come from the ancient building, since Denver had entered.

An hour passed; then, fearing lest their townsmen had met with foul play, the chief constable gave the signal, and the police rushed into the place.

"Mr. Denver, where are you? Speak!" cried the chief constable anxiously.

All was silent as death, save for the noise made by the policeman's boots.

Their bullseye lanterns flashing hither and thither, each holding his breath in dread of, they scarcely knew what, the constables pressed forward until they reached the old council-chamber.

Suddenly the chief constable dashed forward. Crouched in a corner, shielding his face with his hands, was Horace Denver.

His hair, which, when he entered the building, was scarce tinged with grey, was now as white as driven snow.

His face was ashen, his eyes fixed with a haunting terror which never again quite left them.

"Where is he—where is the Winged Man?" demanded the chief constable.

"Hush! Do not mention that fearful name! I hope he is gone!" shuddered Denver.

"Gone! Impossible! He could not have disappeared without my men seeing him!" declared the officer.

"He has gone—I tell you he has gone!" persisted Denver.

"And the Ayres papers?"

"He knew—how, none can tell—that I had betrayed his secret, and they are lost for ever!" whispered the lawyer. "Take me away, take me home; I dare not stay! Surely no mortal man has gone through what I have experienced this night and has lived!" he added, looking fearfully around him.

The chief constable laid his hand upon the solicitor's shoulder.

"What has the brute done to you, Denver?" he asked.

"Oh, no; I may not—I dare not! I must never mention it to a soul!" almost whispered the other.

"And the money?"

"That is gone, too! The Winged Man said my breach of faith justified his taking it!"

"Beg pardon, sir," interrupted a policeman, in loud, excited tones, "the Lord Vesney—"

"What of the Lord Vesney?" demanded the chief constable, turning abruptly, for it was one of Vandyck's masterpieces, and the greatest prize Bristol possessed.

"It has been cut from the frame!" was the alarming reply.

It was true. The present Lord Vesney had offered to cover the canvas with guineas if the Council would sell it. They had refused, and now the Winged Man had taken it!

In a moment Horace Denver was forgotten. Next to their charter itself, the inhabitants of Bristol prized the "Vesney" portrait more than anything else they possessed.

"Quick! Search the building from top to bottom! It shall be—it must be—recovered!" shouted the chief constable, paling as he thought of the unpleasant things the Town Council would have to say to him about the loss of the picture.

Immediately the police scattered in every direction. Not a nook or cranny of the old building escaped their scrutiny. But in vain! Least of superstitious men though he was, the chief constable experienced an uneasy gripping at his heart.

Who was this fearful foe that had visited Bristol?

Locks and bars seemed alike unable to keep him out, or to keep him in.

A MIDNIGHT CHASE.

The chief constable strode up and down the room, waiting impatiently the sound of strife which would proclaim that the Winged Man's hiding-place had been discovered.

But ere long the sound of heavy footsteps converging on the council-chamber warned him that the search had been of no avail.

"Well, inspector," said the chief constable brusquely, as that officer entered the room, accompanied by his subordinates, "where is the Winged Man?"

"I am here!"

All started and turned in the direction from whence the voice came.

Enframed in the broad gilt frame from which the picture had been cut crouched the Winged Man, his fearful face contorted in a mocking grin, his hand grasping the uppermost corners of the frame.

An appalling silence fell upon the astounded constables.

"The Winged Man—the Winged Man!" arose in a hushed, awed whisper from every lip.

"What want you with the Winged Man?" thundered the mysterious being, remaining poised inside the picture-frame.

"Villain or Phantom, whichever you be, you shall give an account of yourself! Forward, men! Seize him!" cried the chief constable, as he attempted to close with the weird apparition.

With a bewildered, terrified cry, the chief constable came to a halt within a couple of feet of the frame.

The Winged Man had disappeared. Naught but the bare wall and the vacant frame met his gaze. A mocking laugh overhead caused all to look up.

Suspended by his feet, the Winged Man hung from the ceiling. The next moment his headlight blazed forth in a baleful, yellow glare. Spreading out his wide pinions, he swooped headforemost upon the astounded policeman.

They were brave men, as brave men as could be found in all the broad realms under King George's sway; yet how could mere human beings hope to contender against so fearful a foe?

Uttering loud cries of terror, they turned and fled, leaving the Winged Man master of the scene. But not for long.

Driven with shame at the unworthy panic which had drawn him from the room, the chief constable gathered his men together, and was about to renew his attack on their fearful foe, when loud shouts from without proclaimed that the Winged Man had again evaded them.

Hastening into the street, he looked up just in time to see the Winged Man flying in the direction of Broad Quay.

"A hundred pounds to the first man who lays hands upon him!" came in ringing tones from the chief constable's lips.

"A thousand pounds to the man who captures me!" was the Winged Man's mocking response.

"Thief, scoundrel, we will have you yet!" retorted the chief constable, furious at being flouted before his men.

at being flouted before his men.

Then commenced a chase the inhabitants of Bristol will never forget.

At first it seems that they would be frustrated at the very commencement, for, flying over the northern branch of the harbour, the Winged Man flew slowly towards the cathedral, upon one of the pointed spires of which he perched, illuminated by the wondrous light which came from the centre of his forehead.

Waiting until his pursuers poured into the open space before the cathedral from Trinity Street and College Green, the Winged Man uttered his weird, nerve-chilling cry, and flew in the direction of Brandon Hill.

The crowd—for by this time hundreds of awakened citizens had joined the police in their endeavour to arrest the daring Winged Man—followed swiftly on his track.

Upon the summit of Brandon Hill the Winged Man gazed, apparently oblivious of his danger, over the city, whilst, emboldened by the confidence that numbers ever give, the crowd and police, armed with all manner of weapons, commenced scaling the hill's precipitous sides.

Yet the dark form perched upon the extreme edge of the hill did not move.

There was something so threatening in the very quietude with which the Winged Man watched their approach that as his would-be captors drew nearer their steps grew slower.

Hemmed in on all sides, it seemed impossible that the Winged Man could escape.

Still, the crowd halted some twenty feet from the fearful being.

The chief constable pushed his way to the front.

"In the King's name, I call upon you to surrender!" he cried.

But barely had he taken a single step forward ere the black form vanished in a ball of fire, and those nearest staggered back, clasping their hands to their scorched faces.

For nearly a minute no one ventured to move, and when at last they crept cautiously forward they saw but a patch of scorched, burned, blackened grass to show the spot on which the Winged Man had stood.

In speechless astonishment they crowded round the ill-omened spot.

Even as they did so cries of fear arose from every lip. A sudden flash of light, accompanied by a mocking laugh, attracted their attention. Looking upwards, they saw the Winged Man hovering over their heads.

"I am here!" thundered the Winged Man, sweeping down within a few feet of their heads. "Follow who dare!" he added, as he rose slowly in the air.

But none ventured to renew the chase.

A mocking smile on his lips, the Winged Man circled in the air, and the crowd at the southernmost extremity of Brandon Hill fell back as he alighted in their midst.

His head raised defiantly, his wings folded close to his side, his arms crossed over his breast, the Winged Man passed slowly through the ranks of those who had sworn to capture him.

Not a hand was outstretched to seize the strange being. With low moans of terror all recoiled as the Winged Man approached until, when the furthermost ridge of Brandon Hill was reached, he spread his wings and disappeared in the darkness.

THE ABDUCTION OF THE COLONEL.

A mild spring morning had tempted the inhabitants of Clifton to enjoy the health-giving breezes on the tall ridge above the Avon; but instead of strolling up and down the promenade, as was their wont, they were gathered in groups discussing the strange events which had electrified Bristol in the early hours of that morning.

"Nonsense, my dear sir—nonsense!" fumed Roger Richbrooke, a retired colonel. "Winged Man, indeed! Who ever heard of such a thing? Nonsense! What's that—chief constable reliable witness? Bah! He had been dining with the mayor!"

"And nearly all the police force of Bristol as well, I suppose?" interposed his companion sarcastically.

"Undoubtedly they had been following their chief's example elsewhere," persisted the colonel, as he paused upon Clifton Suspension Bridge to look down upon the boats and shipping which dotted the water.

"When I see the Winged Man I'll believe in him, not before!" he declared emphatically.

"Behold, I am here!"

"Carbines and cartouche boxes!" yelled Colonel Richbrooke, springing back, as, stepping from behind one of the enormous girders, the Winged Man stood before him.

The colonel took a quick grip on his nerves; then, somewhat fiercely, though not quite so confidently as he had spoken to his companion, who, throwing appearances to the wind, had beat a hasty retreat, he said:

"So you're the scoundrel who has been playing pranks on Bristol, are you? Take off that fancy dress, wipe the white paint of your face, and go home, or it will be the worse for you!

"Jack boots and bandoliers!" he added, as, apparently without the slightest effort, the Winged Man rose to an iron support high above his head, then crept along the sloping rail like a fly on a twig, pausing now and again to beckon the colonel to follow.

The colonel hesitated; then, clutching his malacca-cane in his right hand, strode angrily after the Winged Man.

"The Afghans never frightened me, and they are a precious sight uglier than this mountebank!" he murmured. "Now, my man," he added aloud, as the Winged Man came to a halt in the centre of the bridge, "what are you going to do—take yourself off, and play your pranks elsewhere, or must I give you in charge?"

To the colonel's indignation the Winged Man laughed in his face; yet there was a certain amount of admiration in that strange being's eyes as he said, pointing to Hotwells, nestling at the foot of the precipitous cliff:

"See, there is a policeman yonder. We will go to him, then you may give me in charge, if you wish!"

"Oh, I may, may I? I'll see you hanged before I climb up and down the cliff! You will come with me!"

"On the contrary you will come with me!" repeated the Winged Man, as, grasping the astounded colonel round the waist, he sprang on to the parapet of the bridge, then plunged headlong into space.

Down they sank—down, down, down!

Just as the water was reached the Winged Man spread his pinions and floated gracefully over the surface.

Immediately before them was a pleasure boat occupied by three young man.

One glance at the Winged Man and his astounded, terror-stricken burden was sufficient for them.

Uttering loud cries of terror, they plunged into the river and swam ashore.

Checking his onward flight, the Winged Man threw his burden into the bottom of the boat; then, taking the sculls, pulled, in a way which showed that he was an accomplished oarsman, down stream.

Shaken, breathless, yet unsubdued, Colonel Richbrooke struggled into the stern seat.

"By my sword, the Trinity stroke!" he ejaculated.

A strange smile, laden with pain rather than mirth, crossed the Winged Man's lips; then he settled himself to his task once more.

Leaning well forward, he dipped his sculls as cleverly as a Putney waterman, the boat flying ahead at a wondrous rate.

Already a dozen boats, armed by spectators and watermen, were in swift pursuit of the Winged Man.

Presently they rounded a jutting point, and came to a miniature bay, in which were a number of boats laden with holiday folk.

"Ahead!" shouted the colonel, as the Winged Man's boat bore down upon a flimsy skiff containing a young man and woman.

But the Winged Man paid no attention, and, without reducing the length of his stroke an iota, continued on his way.

A loud crash, followed by a woman's terrified scream for help, and the heavier boat, crashing through the lighter vessel, swept on, leaving the young man and girl struggling in the water.

"Confound you, sir, stop! You'll drown them and ourselves too!" thundered the colonel, half rising from the stern seat.

"Silence!" thundered the Winged Man; and, used to command rather than obey though he was, the colonel sank back in his seat.

A minute later he leaned quickly forward.

"Back water! You'll ram the cliff in a minute!" he cried, pointing to where a tiny stream forced its way through the base of the cliff into the water.

"It's the Winged Man! Close round him! Stop him!" came in excited shouts from behind.

The Winged Man looked up. The entrance to the tiny bay was crowded with boats, all ready to cut off his retreat.

"Stop, madman, phantom, or whatever you are! We—" began Colonel Richbrooke, then ceased speaking abruptly, for even as the last sentence left his lips the prow of the boat pierced the base of the cliff.

But no shock followed.

It looked to the astounded spectators in the pursuing boats as though the solid cliff opened at the weird being's command, for its walls moved to the right and left, and the Winged Man's boat, with its two occupants, shot into the darkness beyond.

A STRANGE RECOGNITION.

As the Winged Man's boat entered the base of the cliff, secret doors, carefully painted to resemble rock, closed on their own accord, and when the pursuers arrived upon the scene, a hot stream—one of the many which has given Hotwells its name—was trickling into the waters of the Avon, on the spot where the boat had vanished, and many present believed that what they had witnessed had been the creation of their own excited fancy.

Clutching the sides of the boat, the colonel sat in the stern seat gazing fixedly before him. Intense darkness hid everything, save the white, pallid face of the strange boatman, from view. Colonel Richbrooke gave himself up for lost. But he had borne his King's commission. He was a British soldier, with the reputation of the British Army to maintain, even though no one was present to behold how he bore himself, save the strange, and, as he now believed, supernatural being, who was pulling him apparently into the very bowels of the earth.

"Welcome to my home on the banks of the Avon!"

Colonel Richbrooke started.

It was the Winged Man who spoke, for the words had come from his mouth, and his lips had moved, yet that voice took the gallant old Colonel back twenty years.

By the beams of the Winged Man's headlight he gazed into the white, stern face before him, but ere he could speak the softened expression with which the Winged Man had regarded him vanished, and his face became expressionless, forbidding, pallid as before.

Wondering, awestruck, Colonel Richbrooke gazed around him. They were floating on a dark, apparently limitless, subterranean lake; the massive roof above their heads was supported on thick pillars of roughly-hewn stone.

Presently the boat's bows grated against a rocky platform.

Springing ashore, the Winged Man beckoned Colonel Richbrooke to follow, and led the way up a flight of mossgrown, stone steps.

An exclamation of admiration burst from the colonel's lips. He gazed in astonishment round a large cave, the walls of which were hidden by exquisite draperies, dotted here and there with priceless pictures, foremost amongst them being the unframed canvas the Winged Man had taken from the Council Chamber of Bristol.

"Where are we? What is this place?" demanded Richbrooke.

"We are in one of my many resting-places," declared the Winged Man. "One which till now no foot but mine has trod."

"Why reveal it to me?" asked Colonel Richbrooke bluntly.

"Question me no further. It is the Winged Man's will; that is enough," was the proud rejoinder.

"No, it is not enough. I am a soldier; it will be my duty to lead the police to your lair."

The Winged Man shrugged his shoulders; then, signing his unwillingness to remain where he was, moved aside a curtain and disappeared into an adjoining cave.

Approaching an irregular aperture that gave light to the cave, the colonel looked out. To right and left stretched the broad, craft-covered River Avon; immediately opposite a steep bank, and some distance to the left, the suburb of New Clifton.

Five minutes later the Winged Man, clad in the ordinary garments of every-day life, stood before him.

White to the very lips went the old colonel. Gazing straight before him, like one in a dream, he advanced slowly and unsteadily towards the Winged Man.

"It is you, you—" he began.

With a gesture of command the Winged Man raised his hand.

"The past is dead!" he cried, in low, sombre tones. "Come, tell me of the world I have left for ever! How go those we knew in the old days before I died? But, on the peril of my displeasure, mention not the name that was once mine."

Dropping on his knees, the white-head veteran raised the Winged Man's hand to his lips, then regained his feet, and, standing at attention, saluted.

It was noon when they entered the Winged Man's hidden subterranean palace. Evening fell, yet the two were so engrossed in the past as to be careless of the flight of time. Presently the Winged Man arose, and, approaching the wall of the cave, touched a secret spring. The jagged, uneven rock opened, revealing a hiding-place, in which was stored wine worth its weight in gold. Carefully removing a quaintly-shaped bottle, the Winged Man produced glasses, and, filling them to the brim, courteously handed one to his companion.

A sweet, fragrant aroma filled the room. An excited, eager light flashed from Colonel Richbrooke's eyes.

"To the loyal, true-hearted past!" he said reverently, as he raised the glass aloft.

"To the happy ones gone before us!" responded the Winged Man. Then each raised the brimming glass to his lips.

"Ah, this is wine! It's thirty years since I tasted it last, yet I know I am not mistaken in its origin!" he cried enthusiastically.

"You are right. It is from the Imperial cellars. There are about seventeen bottles of this wine left in the world. I have sixteen in my various retreats," replied the Winged Man, as he refilled his guest's glass; then, though neither spoke, each drank a toast in silence, the nature of which none but themselves might know.

With a sigh, the colonel sank back in his chair, his head dropped on to his breast, and a minute later he was fast asleep.

When Colonel Richbrooke awoke, the morning sun was shining brightly into his bed-room, where he lay stretched, fully dressed, on a couch beneath the window. For some minutes he remained prostrate, slowly recalling the events of the previous night; then he glanced round the bed-room, with its solid, well-chosen furniture.

"Surely it was a dream, but a dream so vivid, so——"

He ceased speaking, and, raising his left hand, gazed at a superb ring upon the third finger, a ring that had not been there the previous evening. Wonderingly he drew the wide, gold band from his finger. Writing within met his gaze. It ran as follows:

"To Colonel Richbrooke, in memory of a past friend."

As the colonel rose from his couch, his eyes fell upon a bundle of banknotes, and a slip of paper, on which was written:

"He of whom we spoke last night is cruising incognito round the British Isles. He will be in the Bristol Channel to-morrow. Seek him out and say: 'Beware! Lest the doomed return to life and hurl you from the throne you have usurped.'"

There was no signature, but none was needed. The bold, firm handwriting was as familiar to the colonel as his own.

THE SONG OF THE SYREN.

In the meantime, having disposed of his sleeping visitor, the Winged Man returned to his cave, and traversing an apparently endless number of subterranean passages, entered a large cavern, one end of which was occupied by a small but exquisitely-toned organ.

Throwing back his wings, the Winged Man seated himself before the instrument. For a moment his fingers wandered aimlessly over the firm, strong touch, drew out notes vibrating with almost every human feeling.

A deep undercurrent of unspeakable melancholy pervaded his playing. Yet so sweet, so new, so entrancing was it, that a man stretched on the green sward immediately above the cave raised himself on his elbow and looked in astonishment around.

To the right, left, and rear was a wide stretch of open plain—no houses, no wood, no place from whence the sounds could come.

Before him stretched the sunlit, ever-moving sea. Far away in the distance appeared the brown sails of a fishing-boat and the whole of a homeward-bound steamer.

No living thing was in sight, save the circling gulls overhead, yet those wondrous, entrancing notes continued to charm the ear of the recumbent man. Wonder, surprise, and intense delight beamed from his eyes.

Claude Mann, a musician of no mean repute, who had come down to breathe the strength-renewing air of the Bristol Channel, deemed that it was no earthly music he was listening to, but an inspiration straight from the spheres.[18]

To him was known the music of all who had ever charmed the earth with sweet tones, yet even the greatest masters of songs had never produced such a sweet succession of perfect sounds as those to which he was listening entranced.

There was unfolded the whole story of human wrong, human love, human despair. Every note seemed a word which told of sorrow, yet the sorrow of a strong, proud man who would eat out his heart in solitude rather than let another share his grief.

Instinctively Claude Mann drew a notebook from his pocket, and not daring to trust so great a musical treasure to memory, dotted down the strains as the rose from the earth to his listening ear.

Suddenly the music ceased. The Winged Man, the agitation which had convulsed his soul soothed by the power of music, left the organ, and, floating to the ceiling, clung tightly to the uneven roof, and was soon fast asleep.

Claude Mann rose as one awakened from a trance to his feet. A great happiness filled his soul. Fortune and fame were assuredly his.

That evening Claude Mann set out for London. Within a week "The Song of the Syren," as he had named the Winged Man's piece, had taken a foremost place amongst the great musical compositions of the world.

IN A TYRANT'S POWER.

Obedience to orders was Colonel Richbrooke's creed. Accordingly, without loss of time, he set out to intercept the mysterious yacht of which the Winged Man had spoken.

Late that evening the pilot cutter he had engaged for the purpose met a magnificent steam-yacht flying the burgee of the Thames Yacht Club steaming up the Bristol Channel.

Probably Colonel Richbrooke would have allowed the yacht to pass without inquiry, but in a deck-chair on its poop he detected a tall, stern-faced, dark-haired man, who, though he had not seen him for more than twenty years, he recognised as the man he sought.

"Yacht ahoy!" healed the pilot.

---

[18] The Music of the Spheres is the ethereal sound created as the celestial bodies orbit and rotate in the heavens.

"Hallo! What you want?" came in broken English from the yacht's bridge.

"Is Count Ixier on board?" demanded the colonel.

"He is. Who wants him?" cried the dark man, leaning over the side.

"I have an important message to deliver, count," replied Colonel Richbrooke.

Count Ixier turned to an officer standing by his side. Immediately the yacht was stopped, an accommodation-ladder lowered, and a few minutes later the colonel stepped from the cutter on to the grating. As he clambered up the brass-bound steps he noted that, though evidently a pleasure yacht, her crew bore the unmistakable impress of trained men of war. There was a puzzled frown on the count's brow.

"You have a message for me, sir?" he said courteously. "Have I not seen your face before?"

"Twenty years ago, count," returned the old man. "Perhaps you will remember me better if I explain that the date was March 20th. A stormy evening. A certain house in a certain Continental town. A brother who had sought to seize a brother's throne was preparing to leave his native land, glad to escape with the life he owed to his brother's clemency."

Black as thunder grew Count Ixier's brow.

"Follow me!" he said, turning on his heel and leading the way. "Well, Colonel Richbrooke, for I remember you now, what is your business with me?" demanded the count, pacing in the centre of a small, elegantly-furnished cabin near a splendidly-appointed saloon.

Colonel Richbrooke repeated the Winged Man's message. Pale to the very lips went the count.

"Back from the grave? No, no! Is he living?" came in a terror-stricken whisper from his parched and pallid lips.

"I have nothing to add to my message nor any explanation to give," replied the colonel coldly.

"You know who I am. You know that I am not one to be defied with impunity. I demand the meaning of your strange warning!" cried the count.

"And I can only repeat the statement that I have none to give!" retorted Colonel Richbrooke.

Count Ixier struck a gong upon a table. Twice its reverberating notes rang through the cabin. The door opened. A petty officer and a couple of seamen entered the room.

"Seize that man!" ordered the count.

"Do so at your peril! I am a British subject, the yacht is in British waters, and I defy you!" cried Colonel Richbrooke.

With an evil laugh the count made a sign to the sailors, and Colonel Richbrooke was borne, struggling fiercely, to the floor. A minute later he was handcuffed, gagged, and bound.

"Give the pilot this. Tell him that Colonel Richbrooke will be my guest for the next few days," said the count, throwing a couple of sovereigns on the table.

As the petty officer left the cabin Count Ixier turned upon his prisoner.

"Unbind him," he ordered.

Immediately his well-trained men obeyed.

"Remain on guard without. Be ready to return if I call."

With folded arms the colonel awaited his capture's will.

"You speak of a March 20th many years ago. It would have been well for you had you remembered that date ere you set foot on this yacht," began Count Ixier ominously.

He waited for a reply, but the old Colonel did not speak.

"Of all the men who witnessed my downfall, you alone remain alive. My arm is long, my vengeance sure," continued the count. "From the moment you set foot on this vessel your fate was sealed."

Colonel Richbrooke shrugged his shoulders.

"It will be but one more black deed to add to the many you have already committed," he declared, his lip curling with contempt.

"Call it what you will, the fact remains the same. Ere another sun has risen you shall join the rest of my foes in the dark unknown, unless—"

Brave, ready to face death though he was, Colonel Richbrooke could not repress a start of renewed hope as the last word fell upon his ears. Count Ixier smiled grimly.

"Unless you tell me where I can lay hands upon he who has dared to send the message you have all too faithfully delivered."

"That I will never do," returned Colonel Richbrooke firmly. "Nor if you knew him as I know him would you want to see him again. Be warned in time. Mobilise your army, surround yourself with police, double the vigilance of your fleet, he will laugh your precautions to scorn."

A scornful laugh escaped Count Ixier's lips.

"I know how to defend myself, and to protect my friends. The man you mention can do neither."

"Fool!"

The word, loud, penetrating, shrill with scorn, seemed to fill the entire cabin. Both men started. Count Ixier's heart for the moment was filled with fear, Colonel Richbrooke's with rising hope.

"Fool!" was repeated in stentorian tones once more.

The eyes of both men turned towards the round plate-glass glazed porthole from whence the sound came.

"The Winged Man!" burst instinctively from Colonel Richbrooke's lips.

"It is he!" gasped Count Ixier, as he gazed with starting eyes upon the fearful, white, frowning face of the Winged Man enframed in the brightly polished brass work of the porthole.

Quick as lightning Count Ixier drew a revolver from his pocket, and the men on guard without rushed in, to find their commander, the still smoking weapon in hand, gazing with white, blanched face at the shattered porthole.

Then every heart was chilled by a fearful, deep, mocking peal of laughter which came from without. The sound roused Count Ixier to fury.

"By the powers, he shall mock me no more! Arm every man! A thousand marks to the one who shoots the jeering demon!" shouted the count, as, leaving his prisoner in the cabin, he rushed up the companion-way.

Immediately the yacht's searchlight blazed forth, scouring sea and sky alike, whilst, rifle in hand, the crew searched the whole vessel from deck to keel. But their search was in vain, for none had thought to look beneath the stern windows, where, riding at ease upon the rudder chain, sat the Winged Man.

Shaken to the very soul, yet more determined to vengeance than ever the count descended, to find his prisoner awaiting him as calmly as though no danger threatened.

°**AN ACT OF VENGEANCE.**

Shortly after midnight, just as the rising moon shed her beams over the sleeping sea, the yacht lay-to off a tiny islet of the Devonshire coast. At the foot of her accommodation-ladder a petrol launch filled with armed men rocked to the gentle swell. At the top of the accommodation-ladder two Marines saluted as Count Ixier, in the full uniform of an Admiral of a foreign navy, took his place in the stern of the launch.

Heralded by the slow tapping of a muffled drum, regarded on either side by armed sailors, Colonel Richbrooke took his place in the centre of the launch, which put off from the yacht's side, and flew swiftly over the waves. The tiny island was but half a mile in length by some three hundred yards in width, with a jagged, precipitous rock some thirty feet above highwater mark, at the northern end.

The island reached, Colonel Richbrooke, escorted by his armed guard, was marched to the base of the rock. Then the rest of the launch's crew having landed, Count Ixier issued a few sharp, short orders, and, performing in line, the men advanced until within a dozen paces of the prisoner. Count Ixier advanced towards Colonel Richbrooke.

"You have yet time to save your life. Lead me to him I seek, and you shall go free. I swear it!" he cried.

"Why waste further time? I have faced death too often in my country's service to fear it now," was the brave response.

A look of unwilling admiration swept into Count Ixier's eyes. Then he made a sign to a non-commissioned officer standing near, who stepped forward with a handkerchief to bind the prisoner's eyes.

° 15 FEBRUARY 1913.

"No, thank you, friend; bullets have no terror for me," said the colonel, waving him aside. And the man, saluting, stepped back.

"Load with ball ammunition!" ordered Count Ixier, who was himself in command of the firing-party.

A series of sharp clicks fell ominously upon the prisoner's ears as the men told off to shoot him opened the breeches of their rifles, and thrusting in cartridges, closed them again.

"Ready! Present! Fire!"

The twelve rifles rang out simultaneously, but ere the last word of the fatal order left the count's lips, a dark form dropped from the summit of the rock, and stealthily drawing the colonel swiftly aside, allowed the bullets to patter harmlessly against the granite surface of the rock.

A shout of rage from Count Ixier was echoed by cries of terror from the firing-party, as rising on his awful pinions, his baleful headlight blazing from the centre of his forehead, the Winged Man soared towards them.

A moment's breathless suspense; then, throwing down their arms, the firing-party fled towards the launch.

His weird, mournful cry rending the air, the Winged Man swept back on his black, fearful pinions over the heads of the fleeing sailors, and alighting on the brink of the waves, cut off their retreat from the launch.

"Back! Your work is not completed! Back! The Winged Man commands!" he thundered.

A tremor shook the sailors' stalwart frames. One—the officer in command of the boat—with rare courage, rose to his feet, crying:

"Who are you who dares to order about the sailors of the King?"

"I am the Winged Man, his master and yours!" came the immediate response.

A brave but mirthless laugh rose from the officer's lips.

"Let this test your lordship over us!" he cried, snatching a revolver from his pocket and aiming it at the Winged Man.

Not a muscle of that strange being moved, not a lid quivered; but, facing his would-be slayer with folded arms, he transfixed him with his fierce, burning eyes.

A look of stony horror crept over the young officer's face, the revolver dropped from his nerveless grasp, and, striking the side of the boat, exploded as it fell into the shallow water.

Entranced, fascinated, the sailors watched the strange scene.

"Fall in!" commanded the Winged Man, turning suddenly upon them.

As men obeying some irresistible influence, the sailors stood to their arms.

"You will march your men back to the spot from whence they fled, Lieutenant," directed the Winged Man.

The officer tried to resist, but in vain; a will-power greater than his own enforced obedience. Mechanically saluting, he placed himself at the head of his men.

With slow-moving pinions, the Winged Man soared a few feet above the marching men.

Trembling, unnerved, terror-laden, Count Ixier awaited the outcome of his strange experience.

Dropping to earth, the Winged Man strode slowly and solemnly towards the count, and laid the two first fingers of his left hand on the man's breast.

Count Ixier started. A shadow convulsed his frame. Then, his face colourless as marble, his eyes fixed in a stony stare, he followed the Winged Man to the spot where Colonel Richbrooke had so nobly faced death a short time before.

Colonel Richbrooke watched the proceedings in astonishment.

"Firing-party, resume arms!" came in mechanical tones from the officer's bloodless lips. "Attention!"

Colonel Richbrooke looked from the white, statue-like figure standing with its back to the wall of rock, to the firing-party that confronted him. Then his gaze wandered to the tall, upright form of this the stern-faced Winged Man. In a flash the meaning of it all burst upon him.

"Great powers, this cannot be!" he cried, turning to the Winged Man. "What has this man done to deserve death?"

"Let a people groaning under unjust taxation, let prisons filled with innocent men, let the graves of countless innocent victims answer!" was the fearful reply.

"But you—you above all men, must not be his executioner!"

"It is not I, but Fate! Speak!" added the Winged Man, turning upon the doomed man. "From your own lips shall you be judged. Are you worthy of mercy or of death?"

A fearful convulsion shook Count Ixier's frame. Twice he attempted to speak; twice in his tongue refused its office. Then, clear and distinct, the awful word "Death!" came from his pale, bloodless lips.

Scarcely less pale than the doomed man, the firing-party hung upon the Winged Man's every movement—and abject terror, an unspeakable horror dilating every eye.

The Winged Man waved his hand.

"Attention! Ready! Present! Fire!" came in dull, lifeless tones from the officer's lips.

Once more the sharp, whip-like crack of the rifles scared the gulls flitting around the island. No hand was stretched forth to save the guilty man. Pierced by half a dozen bullets, he sank, dying, to the ground.

Striding to the prostrate man's side, the Winged Man knelt and whispered something in his ear. What it was, none may ever know. Struggling on one elbow, he struck fiercely at the Winged Man, then fell heavily back.

The Winged Man beckoned Colonel Richbrooke to him.

"Lieutenant, march your men back to the launch!" ordered the Winged Man.

Mechanically the officer turned to his men.

"Firing-party, right-about turn! Quick march!" he ordered.

Barely had the sailors taken a dozen steps towards the boat ere the Lieutenant felt as though a fearful weight had been lifted from his heart, as though a cloud which had hemmed it him in, impalpable yet irresistible, had vanished.

He remembered that the weird horror who had encompassed his King's death yet lived. A wild desire for vengeance took possession of his heart.

"Men of the King's yacht, halt! By some superhuman power we have been forced to slay our lord! Let all who would avenge him follow me!" he cried, wheeling round, sword in hand.

"Death to the slayer of our King!" cried the sailors; then burst into a loud cheer, which was stifled ere it found utterance, whilst all gazed in amazement at the spot they had just left.

The Winged Man, Colonel Richbrooke, and the slain man had disappeared!

A few stunted shrubs was the only vegetation the little island boasted. Scarcely a rat could have found a hiding-place upon its bare, wind-swept surface, yet to living men and a dead one had disappeared as completely as though the earth had opened and swallowed them up.

Awed and wondering, the lieutenant led his men back to the launch, and, the launch regained, sailed from Britain's shore, the bearer of news which would bring public sorrow and private rejoicings to an oppressed and downtrodden land.

Barely had the yacht's sails disappeared beneath the horizon, ere two large rocks moved slowly apart, and the Winged Man, followed by Colonel Richbrooke, emerged, the stones closing automatically when the two had passed through.

"His is an awful fate. A sudden death, and nameless grave," said the old Colonel, baring his grey locks as he stood gazing sorrowfully on the spot they had just left.

"A King's best monument is that left by noble deeds," said the Winged Man solemnly. "This man lies in a fitting tomb. Come, your boat awaits you."

"My boat?" repeated Colonel Richbrooke, looking around him.

"Yes; yonder she lies!" declared the Winged Man, pointing to a fisherman's float, rising and falling to the gentle swell a dozen yards from shore.

Skimming over the waves, the Winged Man seized the cork, and raised it from the water, disclosing a thin wire cable. Drawing the cable to land, the Winged Man hauled it in until a round, glistening object, not unlike a torpedo, rose to the surface.

This the Winged Man drew ashore. Touching a spring in the bows, the upper half of the steel object, it opened to right and left, forming a small but serviceable canoe.

"Farewell! Yonder lies your path!" cried the Winged Man, pointing to the distant shore.

With a farewell wave of the hand the Winged Man sprang from the ground. Up he went, borne aloft on his mighty pinions. Up, up, until at last he appeared but a tiny speck in the cloudless heavens.

With a frowning brow and a sorrowful heart Colonel Richbrooke entered the canoe and paddled slowly towards the mainland.

A RECORD RUN.

Backwards and forwards, from the tiny copse adjoining Broughton Moat to the coast, the Winged Man had flown, working with untiring energy to convey the abbot's treasure from the place in which he had hidden it to the wind-swept walls of an ancient ruin on the East Coast, beneath which was yet another of his numerous, luxuriously-furnished lairs.

The Winged Man had made his last journey, and had only returned to Broughton to make sure that all his spoil was gathered in, when his attention was attracted by the baying of hounds close to a large house, half mansion, half farmhouse, known as Broughton Rookery.

The hunting season was over, for violets and other wildflowers filled the woods and hedgerows, destroying the scent, rendering hunting well-nigh impossible.

But though foxes were left alone, an occasional drag, when newly-sown land could be avoided and a line chosen, was occasionally indulged in.

It was from Broughton Rookery, where lived James Dyson, the young squire, whose boast that he would capture the Winged Man single-handed had brought such ridicule upon him in Bury St. Edmunds, that the baying of the hounds had come. An informal meet was being held there to wind up the season with a last drag.

Capped, booted, and spurred, Squire Dyson, accompanied by a score of sporting friends, whom he had entertained to an early breakfast, emerged from the rookery door.

A loud baying of hounds welcomed him.

"Down, Tyler! Whoa, Nimrod! Steady, Conqueror! Back, Flamer! Ah, Rifleman, would you!" cried the squire, addressing his favourite hounds as they clustered around him.

"Hallo, captain!" he went on, turning to a military-looking man who cantered up the gravel-drive at that moment. "Are you going to give us a good run to-day?"

Captain Dewing shook his head.

"I'll do my best, but Cicero is not quite himself this morning!" he cried, patting the horse's head. "I walked Southgate Hill, and came at a gentle canter the rest of the way, but, see, he is covered with lather already!"

A look of vexation crossed the young squire's face.

"That's a pity, for this run may be my last, certainly it will be the last of the season," he replied.

"Nonsense, old chap! We'll have many a good run yet, I hope," returned the captain, looking somewhat pityingly upon the young squire.

It was an open secret that, owing to agricultural depression, Dyson had for many years found it difficult to make both ends meet.

Dewing, leaning over his saddle, addressed his host:

"Who on earth is that chap on the grey horse?" he asked, indicating with an almost imperceptible flourish of his crop an ill-dressed, coarse-looking man, apparently far from ease, on a tall, raw-boned grey mare.

Squire Dyson flushed and bit his lip.

"Don't tell the other chaps, Dewing," he replied. "It's a bailiff. His mate, dressed as a groom, is in the kitchen. He would not let me ride my own horse, confound him, unless he accompanied me in the field!"

"If old Cicero had only been in fettle, I'd have taken him across a line of country that would have made him sorry he had ventured on horseback," replied Captain Dewing, looking vindictively at the bailiff. "What's the debt, old chap?" he asked.

"Seven thousand odd," returned the squire despairingly.

Captain Dewing shrugged his shoulders.

It was more than he dared think of advancing, even if the proud, though reckless young squire, would have accepted the loan.

James Dyson looked at his friends' mounts. The ground was already getting hard, and none had brought out their best hunters.

"There's not a horse here that could give us a proper drag, and I feel just in the mood for a hard ride," he grumbled. "I'd follow the Winged Man himself if he was here."

"The Winged Man is here!"

The joyous baying of the hounds sank to a low, frightened whimper, as, with drooped sterns and lowered muzzles, they crept for protection close to the master and whipper-in, whilst the jests and laughter of the hunters ceased, as at the word of command.

"The Winged Man is here!" came a loud, thunderous voice.

"The Winged Man is here!" repeated that weird, unconquerable being, smiling, as he noted the consternation his presence caused.

"Back, you mountebank!" stammered the squire, his rubicund lips as white as his neatly-tied cravat. "What want you here?"

Dogs, horses, men trembled, as the Winged Man's weird, fearful laugh fell upon their startled ears.

"A wager—a wager!" cried the Winged Man. "I'll be your drag afoot. Seven thousand pounds if your hounds pull me down in less than forty minutes!"

"Have nothing to do with him, Dyson. You know the alternative with such as he," whispered Captain Dewing.

Again the Winged Man's weird mocking laughter broke the almost deathly silence that obtained over the field. The young squire shook off his well-meaning adviser.

"And if I lose?" he demanded, turning to the Winged Man.

"Then for five years you shall be my slave, my dog, to order at my will!" was the awful reply.

An indignant refusal rose to the young squire's lips, but as he did so his eyes fell upon the bailiff, who was trembling with terror.

"It is the exact amount I am in debt for," thought the squire.

"It's a bet. Tom, draw off the hounds!" he said aloud.

Only too pleased to get away from the vicinity of that awful black form, the hunt withdrew to a corner of the park-like meadow.

Drawing a phial from his pocket, the Winged Man poured its contents over the soles of his feet; then, with a cry of:

"A minute's grace is all I ask!" bounded across the level sward with long, loping strides, that covered twenty feet at each leap, yet with an ease that brought cries of mingled admiration and amazement from the spectators' lips. The minute over, the huntsmen brought the hounds to the spot where the Winged Man had recently stood.

Immediately the hounds took up the scent with a loud, prolonged burst of music. It was not the usual deep-chested bay of excitement and delight, with which hounds announced that they have struck a fox's sent, but deeper, louder, with an underlying current of fierce anger, such as Tom, the old Huntsman, in all his forty years' experience, had never heard.

Carefully selected, almost as large as stag-hounds, the pack swept forward at a pace which promised soon to leave the field behind. A furze hedge, growing on either side a low, railed fence, was the first obstacle over which the hounds forced their way, then a plough, then an, as yet, unturned stubble.

For most of all, filled, it seemed with the same fiery madness as the hounds, James Dyson road that day as he had never ridden before.

Crossing the high-road to Bury St. Edmunds, the Winged Man flew swiftly over the park surrounding Broughton Hall, down the gorse-lined drive, past an old windmill; then, turning to his right, flew over hedge, ditch, gate, and style, in long, easy lopes. The labourers working in the fields fled from the Winged Man, whilst the hounds, quiet as they ever are when running to a breast-high scent, raced half a field behind him.

The hounds had not gained, on the other hand they had not lost ground. Taking ditch and hedge in fine style the bailiff claimed second place of honour in the strange, unique hunt, not because he wished it, but because he couldn't help himself.

Chuckling at his own cleverness, he had tied himself on to the saddle of the old grey, as "hard" an old hunter as ever followed the hunt and the wise old mare had, from the very first, taken the bit in her teeth and bolted with her miserable rider.

As they raced through Bayton Village, a number of men, women, and children, roused by the clatter, rushed from their houses, to stand gasping as the Winged Man sped by.

Shaken, bruised, breathless, the bailiff by this time had had enough of it. Squire Dyson might ride his horse to death for all he cared, the creditors might be as angry as they liked, all he wanted was a moment's breathing space, a moment's respite from the jog, jog of his ever-moving, apparently tireless steed.

"Help! Help! Help! A crown to the man who'll stop this beast of an animal!" he shrieked, but ere the words had well left his lips, Bayton was left behind.

Leaving the highway near the mill, the Winged Man sped in the direction of Tostock. Never before had the hounds run at such a pace.

Squire Dyson was leading, the bailiff following, the huntsmen next, then came that whipper-in, Captain Dewing, and two of the best-mounted men, racing in a bunch, with the others trailing in the rear.

Fiercely the bailiff tugged at his reins, as, again turning to the right, the Winged Man headed in the direction of Hesset. The grey was beginning to have had enough of it by this time, so allowed her rider to guide her to a slight extent.

Had the bailiff known the A B C of riding, he could have got the mastery of the mare long before; but, frightened out of his life, worn, weary, feeling as though every bone in his body had been shaken out of place, and would never come in again, he lost his head, and tugged first at one rein and then the other, and with the result that, realising she had a perfect idiot in the saddle, and had better take charge of affairs herself again, the mare dashed over a low fence into the road.

Laying back her ears, she charged blindly at a tall thorn-fence, some twelve or fifteen feet in height, totally ignoring her rider's efforts to steer her towards a gate.

Crash! The mare had forced herself and her rider through the fence, the stout thorns tearing his clothes, scratching his face and hands, and mauling him everywhere within reach.

"Phew! This is awful! I feel just as if I had been ridden over by a bush-barrow!" moaned the unfortunate bailiff. "Oh, mercy, this is the very end!" he added, frozen with horror at the sight of a wide stretch of water, apparently reaching from one tall hedge to another, in his immediate path.

"I'm doomed!" thought the unfortunate man. "That there Winged Man ain't playing the game. No mortal horse could jump that water."

But the bailiff had done the Winged Man an injustice. Screened by bushes was a narrow earthen causeway at one extremity of the water, and over this the Winged Man had rushed.

"Whoa, you beast! Stop, can't ye? Turn round, or I'll be—Ugh!"

The last ejaculation was torn from his lips as the cunning old mare parted her forefeet firmly on the loose soil, and sent the unfortunate bailiff forward with such a jerk that the rope which bound him to the saddle broke, and he was hurled head-over-heels into one foot of water and three of mud.

Plastered from head to foot with the black, evil-smelling mud, the bailiff rose like an ill-dressed Neptune from the water.

"That's right, my man; have a bath; you want it!" cried Captain Dewing as he galloped past the struggling, spluttering man. Each one of the hunt had a laughing remark or some unsolicited advice to give the bailiff; but as he was in no danger of drowning, no one stopped to help him.

Eventually, after many unsuccessful attempts, he drew himself to dry land, muttering vengeance against the man who had lent him the horse.

Choosing his path, the Winged Man headed straight for the Rookery.

Bending over his saddle, Squire Dyson followed, with faltering hopes. It wanted but three minutes to the stipulated time, and, though the hounds had gained upon the quarry until they were racing within a dozen yards of him, it seemed hopeless that the Winged Man could be overtaken in the short time that was yet left.

Presently a cry of delight burst from his lips. Either intentionally or by accident the Winged Man had ended a field surrounded on three sides by a wood. He had given his word not to fly. The hounds must surely have him!

Even as the thought flashed through Dyson's mind the Winged Man swung round; but the momentary hesitation had proved fatal, and the hounds were upon him. One buried its fangs in the loose cloth that enswathed his right leg.

Opening his wings, the Winged Man sprang from the ground, but even as he did so a second hound seized a loose fold of his partially extended pinions. Borne down by the struggling animals, it needed the whole of the Winged Man's enormous strength to rise from the ground again. Slowly he soared aloft, three hounds hanging like leeches to his garments.

"Back, Nimrod! Let go, Tyler! Steady, boys—steady!" cried the squire, plying his whip amongst the hounds who were springing up to seize the Winged Man.

Stooping in mid-air, the Winged Man tore the clinging dogs from their hold; then, rising above the trees, disappeared from view.

It was not until the Winged Man had vanished from sight that Squire Dyson remembered the wager. The Winged Man had gone, and it was unlikely that he would ever return to redeem his word with the seven thousand pounds. Dejectedly Dyson called off his hounds.

"Whoa, Homer! Whoa, Nimrod! Get along, Tyler!" he cried, making the covert resound with the cracks of his whip.

But the hounds heeded not his cry. Snarling, fighting, bristling with rage, they were scraping at a rabbit's borrow on the brow of the ditch near which the Winged Man had fallen, as though they were terriers enjoying a rat hunt.

Old Nimrod, the steadiest and wisest of hounds, seemed to have lost his head as completely as the youngest couple there.

"Get away, for'ard—for'ard! Leave it! 'ware rabbit!" cried Dyson, edging his horse amongst the hounds, and slashing at them with his whip, just as Tom, the old huntsman, rode up.

"Here, Tom, the hounds have gone mad!" ordered the M.F.H. "Get them out of the rabbit-hunting business before anyone sees them. Look at old Nimrod. To think that a staid old hound like him should disgrace himself so!"

Old Tom shook his head.

"What can you expect, sir," he cried, "when such a thing as this takes the drag? Whoa, you brutes!" he added, throwing himself off his horse in the midst of the pack.

But whip, lash, and butt-end alike failed to quiet the raging pack.

Suddenly old Nimrod, slashing at a kennel companion's shoulder with his fangs, thrust his head deep into the hole, and drew out what looked like a fur cap. Tyler tried to snatch it from him; but Nimrod swung round, and in doing so brought his muzzle in collision with Homer's head. The latter hound's teeth closed upon the other end of the fur. Bracing their forefeet to the ground, the two hounds tugged at the prize until, with a suddenness which sent them back on their haunches, the fur was torn in half, and a brightly-shining, glistening object dropped on the ground.

Old Tom gazed with superstitious terror at the valuable object so strangely flung at his feet.

With a loud shout, Squire Dyson hustled the old huntsman aside, and snatched up a diamond-studded golden snuff-box. With trembling hands he opened it; then, with a wild shout of joy and relief, waved above his head a batch of one-hundred-pound notes.

The Winged Man had paid his wager, and Squire Dyson was saved from ruin. Was this the purpose of the Winged Man? Who could fathom the mysterious purposes of this strange being?

A SPELLBOUND AUDIENCE.

The Albert Hall was crowded from stalls to gallery by an eager audience, assembled to hear what the musical critics declared to be the finest musical composition that had ever been given in the world.

In a corner seat in one of the upper galleries sat a figure clad in sombre black. None had even seen him enter; none knew whence he came.

Flushed with anticipated triumph, Claude Mann took his place, baton in hand, at the conductor's desk. An outburst of tumultuous applause greeted his appearance.

A wave of patriotic ardour swept through the mighty audience, for if what the papers said was true, England had at last produced a composer far ahead of her Continental neighbours.

At the first tap of the baton every tongue was hushed, and the black-robed figure, the look of anticipation of one who loves music with his whole heart and soul on his face, leaned breathlessly forward.

Turning his back to the main body of the hall, Claude Mann raised his long, thin hands above his head; then the tapering point of his ivory batten dropped, and the listening music-lovers were thrilled by the low, soft, entrancing strains which flowed from the stringed instruments before them.

As the first note fell upon his ears the dark figure started; his piercing eyes flashed angrily, his white, almost freshness hands clenched convulsively.

Louder and louder group the wondrous, almost unearthly strains, thrilling the hearts of the audience with the joy and delight of life. The dullest there knew that he was listening to a wordless tale of a strong man's life. Very soon, scarcely perceptible at first, but growing more pronounced at every bar, an underlying current of deepening sorrow swept through the music, until even that was drowned in a crash of majestic, triumphant harmony.

The audience seemed to see a king mounting his throne, surrounded by the pomp and majesty of a mighty nation. Rendered by the force of a full band, the triumphant strains carried the audience into the life of one who was a king among his fellows.

As sadness had crept into joy, so now a vague feeling that something was wrong with the supposed hero of the theme rendered the audience uneasy. The rolling drum seemed to tell of a man roused to fight cunning, unseen, unscrupulous foes.

Louder and more oft-repeated came the discordant note, until that in turn gave place to the crash of arms, ending in the despairing unveiling of a strong heart bowed to the dust; yet, said though the tones, there was still an inexpressible ring of majesty throughout the hall.

Suddenly every instrument was silenced. A minute's anxious waiting, then the theme was taken up in a loud, wild, weird burst of discord—discord which set the listener's teeth on edge, yet through it all round the harmony of a mighty tune.

Again the notes softened to the sweetest strains. Again they rose in a wild fierce blast of melody. Now a deep, unspeakable fear found its way into the melody—fear relieved by a moment of triumph—fear that spoke of terrified men and women—of wild, fiercely-joyous flights through earth and air, until the whole mighty audience turned pale, and every mind was full of thoughts of the strange, weird being who is doing is had thrilled all England with foreboding and superstitious fear.

Now and again the strains would hush to the softest and most touching pathos, only to break out a moment later more fierce, more thrilling, more full of dark forebodings than before. At length, with one final, weird crash, the music ceased, and Claude Mann, pale, exhausted, but with the light of a great triumph in his eyes, stood bowing like a king upon his throne to the multitude he had held entranced so long.

Suddenly a man, the foremost critic of his age, arose in his seat.

"Three cheers for Claude Mann, the greatest composer of all time!" he cried, hoarse with emotion and excitement.

Never, even when Patti[19] sang "Home, Sweet Home" before the Queen, had the walls of Albert Hall echoed with such a burst of applause as that which replied to the critic's appeal.

But, as though some black spirit had appeared in their midst, every tongue was hushed as, with a prolonged, weird, mournful cry, which echoed through the domed hall like the dread voice of Fate, the Winged Man—for the man in black was he—sprang upon the ledge before him, and, stretching wide his pinions, swooped down upon the orchestra.

---

[19] Adelina Patti (1843–1919), celebrated opera singer who performed in Europe and America.

"It is mine! The glory of this hour is mine!" he cried. "Wretch, eavesdropper, you have stolen the very secret of my soul!" he added, turning furiously upon the conductor.

With a cry of terror Claude Mann stepped back. Yet the fame he believed was his by right was too great prize to be relinquished without a struggle.

"Avaunt, whoever or whatever you be! The fame is mine. While stretched upon a moor, near Bristol, the 'Siren's Song' came to me," arose in gasping accents from between his chattering teeth.

The Winged Man looked searchingly at him.

"I believe you, and forgive. Few men could have set my piece to music as you have done," he admitted generously.

With an abrupt movement the Winged Man took a violin from the leader of the orchestra, then pressing it beneath his chin, drew the bow across the strings.

A few minutes before there was not one in the audience but would have said that the music they had been listening to was perfection, but none had ever listened to such enchanting yet strangely weird notes as arose in response to the Winged Man's delicate touch. The silence, broken only by the murmurs of suppressed delight, filled the mighty hall.

For ten minutes the Winged Man held the audience spellbound; then, still playing, he rose on extended pinions from the conductor's rostrum, and, soaring to the domed ceiling, disappeared through one of the windows.

ABOVE A SEA OF FACES.

An inspector of police on duty within the building rushed to a telephone, and rang up Scotland Yard.

"Send help at once! The Winged Man is in the Albert Hall!" he cried.

Then the instrument fell from his nerveless grasp, for "The Winged Man is here!" came in quick response from over the wires.

He held the audience spellbound.

Silent, bewildered, awed, the huge audience poured from the building.

Already the police were on the alert, and, guided by the staring upwards of passers-by, was soon following the Winged Man in the direction of Knightsbridge. Awestricken crowds filled the streets.

A sea of faces was' turned upwards as the Winged Man glided over the housetops. A loud crash came from immediately beneath him. A motor-'bus driver, leaning sideways from his seat, eager to catch a glimpse of the wondrous being whose name was on everyone's lips, had sent the bonnet of his engine crashing into the side of a horse-drawn 'bus.

A loud, nerve-chilling, mocking laugh burst from the Winged Man's lips as he noted the wreckage he had occasioned.

On he flew, the regular beats of his black, fearful pinions carrying him slowly eastwards. Cries of wonder, tinged with fear, arose as incense to his ears. What cared he that, with lightning swiftness, messages were passing from police-station to police-station, whilst every available man was being sent forth to secure one whom the authorities had come to look upon as a national danger?

Common-sense told him that it was so, yet the knowledge only served to send a thrill of pride through his veins. He was apart from the human race. His hand was against every man, every man's hand against his.

Policemen on horseback, policemen on bicycles, policemen in motor-cars, congregated beneath him.

It was evident that the authorities were determined that this time he should not escape them. Yet he only laughed louder.

Now clinging for a moment to the side of a shop, now skimming to within a few feet of the terrified spectators' heads, sending 'bus and cab horses rearing, plunging, kicking in all directions, he continued along Knightsbridge.

On the way he passed a huge emporium, the first floor of which was glazed with plate-glass. A score of customers and assistants, hearing the outcry in the street, had rushed to the window to see what was wrong.

Swerving in his flight, the Winged Man fastened himself upon the glass. His fearful headlight blazed like living coal, he thrust his white, pallid, awful face against the smooth surface. Once more his loud, mocking, mirthless laugh chilled every heart.

Before a jeweller's shop, some fifty yards ahead, protruded a large electric clock. The constantly-increasing crowd, spellbound, yet unable to withdraw their eyes from the weird flying form, saw the Winged Man rise to the top of a building on the opposite side of the road, and tear off the parapet a cone-shaped stone.

What cared he that a huge lump of masonry, torn from beneath the cone, had struck a man senseless to the pavement? None noticed the sufferer's fall. All were watching with breathless interest the Winged Man's strange manœuvres.

Bearing the stone cone aloft, the Winged Man retraced his flight some twenty yards. Then, urged forward by two flaps of his mighty pinions, he flew at a terrific pace, the point of the cone aimed straight at the centre of the clock.

Crash! A loud, prolonged ejaculation of wonder from the crowd, and the Winged Man, having cut through the face of the clock as an acrobat cuts through a paper hoop, continued on his flight.

CUT CLEAN THROUGH THE CLOCK!

151

On the magnificent gateway near Achilles' statue[20] the Winged Man alighted, and, with folded arms, scornfully surveyed police and public, who, like baying hounds around a hunted stag, encircled him.

"Surrender! You cannot escape. We have orders to capture you, dead or alive!" cried a police superintendent, standing up on the front seat of the motor-car in which he had pursued the Winged Man from the Albert Hall.

"The Winged Man is here. Capture him who can!" came back the defiant answer, as, spreading his pinions to the breeze, the Winged Man sped over the sea of faces which filled Grosvenor Place.

A deathly silence had taken the place of the loud exclamations of terror and amazement which had hitherto greeted the Winged Man. Suddenly the silence was broken by the notes of a bugle sounding the "Assembly" from the direction of the Wellington Barracks.

The Winged Man heard and understood its message. Danger was as this strange being's very life-blood. He could not have lived without the breathless excitement which accompanied almost every hour of his life. Even when soaring over Buckingham Palace he saw a company of white-jacketed Guards, their rifles at the trail, hastening at the double to cut off his retreat, he continued his flight as slowly and deliberately as before, with the result that by the time he reached the open space before Victoria Station the Guards were drawn up ready to receive him.

An officer in undress called upon him to surrender. The Winged Man hovered motionless in the air.

"Men of his Majesty's Guards, fire!" he ordered, a tinge of mockery in his tones.

"Your doom be upon your own head!" cried the officer. "Ready! Present—"

Like clockwork the rifles of the best disciplined company of the finest battalion in the world were pointed at the Winged Man. Borne forwards by a gentle breeze, the Winged Man drew momentarily nearer the line of rifles.

"Fire!" burst from the officer's lips.

ON THE UNDERGROUND.

Even as the order to fire left the officer's lips the Winged Man, folding his wings to his side, sped with lightning speed straight at the line of soldiers. Bullets hissed, shrieked, or whistled viciously past him. One flattened itself against his bullet-proof breast-plate. Yet, unhurt, unscathed, he sped like a shell from a quick-firer over the soldiers' heads, and ere they could turn round had disappeared into the door of the Underground Railway.

Hiding his flight with marvellous precision, the Winged Man swept down the staircase to the platform.

---

[20] The Achilles statue was a memorial to the Duke of Wellington for his victories in the Peninsula and Napoleonic Wars, situated at the Park Lane end of Hyde Park.

To right and left flew the frightened crowd, tumbling over each other, yelling with horror, as that terrible being swept so close over their heads that their hats flew in all directions as he brushed by.

An east-bound electric train had a moment before it left the platform. Striking terror into every heart, the Winged Man attached himself to the rear carriage as it disappeared into the tunnel.

A detective, who had been a horrified spectator of the Winged Man's flight, rushed into the signal-box, and soon a telegraphic message had shot ahead of the Winged Man—a message which caused the signalman in the box at St James's Park to stop the train to which the Winged Man clung ere it reached the station.

A number of police and civilians, entering the St James's Park end of the tunnel, stood on the alert, ready to capture the Winged Man when he emerged.

At the same time the soldiers, forcing their way through the terrified, excited crowd, had entered the Underground station at Victoria, with orders to shoot the Winged Man on sight.

Lighted by the yellow beams of many lanterns, the company of Guards marched slowly up the tunnel.

"If the other end of the tunnel is as strongly held as this, we are bound to have him. He cannot escape us," said the officer in command of the Guards, turning to the detective who had despatched the message from the signal-box.

The detective smiled, and rubbed his hands.

"I already feel the reward in my pocket, sir," he declared confidently.

In the meantime, half-way between Victoria and St James's Park the Winged Man had dropped from the end carriage, and, with the aid of his glowing headlight, commenced a careful examination of the up rails.

Presently he dropped on his knees and wiped the dust from an iron chair. A mark which might have been an accidental scratch upon its iron jaw rewarded his search.

Turning towards the wall, he made his way to one of the many refuges cut to allow the workmen employed on the line to stand clear of passing trains.

Pressing his hands against the arched roof of the manhole, he thrust upwards with all his might.

The roof yielded to his touch. A black opening appeared, the further end of which the light blaring from the centre of his forehead failed to pierce.

Leaving the cunningly concealed trap door open, the Winged Man stepped back on to the line.

A grim smile parted his bloodless lips. The patter of many feet, the sound of excited voices came from both ends of the tunnel.

DEFYING AN ARMY.

Within that confined space sounds travelled far, and the detective's boast came clear and distinct to his keen, listening ear.

Nearer and nearer drew the double line of his pursuers, broken only by the live rails on the centre of the double track.

It was a weird sight. At one end a dark mass of porters, policemen, civilians; at the other the flickering lanterns shed their light over the white fatigue-jackets and the glittering bayonets of the soldiers.

Suddenly the detective's voice was heard. There was a ring of anxiety in it, very different to the confident tones in which he had last spoken.

"Close up. Don't let him pass. Whatever you do, don't let him pass!" he cried appealingly.

"That's all right. You see to your end; we'll see to hours," came back from the distance.

Shielded by the darkness, the Winged Man awaited the approach of his foes. Nearer and nearer they came, yet though but a dozen yards separated them from the Winged Man, they had not yet seen him. More uneasy than ever grew the detective.

"Where is he? Where is the Winged Man?" he shouted through the tunnel.

"The Winged Man is here!" came in a deep, thunderous roll from immediately between the two search-parties. Cries of terror, moans of fear burst from every lip.

"Steady, man! Stand fast! For the credit of the Guards, steady!" cried the officer.

Never before was an appeal more needed. Never, perhaps, in their long and glorious history have men of the British Army been called upon to face so fearful a foe.

As the words, "The Winged Man is here," issued from his lips that weird being took his stand deliberately on the live rails.

An elephant might easily have been scorched and slain by the fierce current which flashed through the Winged Man's body. Unscathed, that strange being bore the fierce shock that turned his living form into a fountain of electric fire, for from every feature of him fierce flashes, like forked lightning, shot into the darkness.

The Guards, pale-faced, but determined, with bayonets at the charge, advanced boldly upon this weird, this fearful, this awful apparition. In vain. The Winged Man had vanished.

Ten minutes later, from the crowded platform of Victoria Station, arose the beginning of a loud cheer, as from out the darkness marched the white-jacketed company of guards; but as the soldiers stepped into the full daylight of the station, the cheering was hushed as though by magic.

Silence reigned throughout the enormous crowd.

Could these men be the stalwart, healthy soldiers who had gone in pursuit of the Winged Man a short half-hour before? It seemed impossible.

They looked like walking automatons rather than men, so white and haggard with a, such a look of fear was impressed on every face.

Yet discipline and force of habit prevailed, and it was with the old swinging Guards' stride that the company returned to barracks.

*

In the meantime, the Winged Man having regained the manhole, rose through the open trapdoor, and entered a long, narrow passage, constructed a year or so before by his faithful servitor Ghat. The passage terminated in a large, commodious cave immediately beneath Westminster Abbey.

Here the Winged Man was quite at home. Such as though his other retreats, few could equal in comfort, luxury, or convenience, this unsuspected, undreamed of, refuge in the heart of London. It was like the centre of a spider's web, from which radiated long since forgotten passages, to right and left, to north and south.

It is a well-known fact that builders in London demolishing old houses, or laying the foundations of new ones, have discovered subterranean passages, caves, and cellars no one has ever ventured to explore.

No one, that is to say, save the Winged Man, to whom the secret underground ways of London are as familiar as the streets above.

It was past midnight, yet the Union Jack flying from the Victoria Tower proclaimed that Parliament was still sitting.

A question of national importance was being thrashed out, and a heated discussion had just terminated, when a Member rose in his seat and demanded that orders should at once be given for the destruction, by fair means or foul, of the weird creature known as the Winged Man.

Loud roars of laughter greeted the speaker, for there were still many people who did not believe in his existence.

The Member glared angrily around the august assembly.

"The honourable gentlemen would not be so ready to laugh have they seen this terrible, this fearsome—ay, I do not hesitate to add—supernatural being, flying over the heads of the crowd which filled our streets this afternoon, had they seen him pass unscathed through a volley fired by a company of Guards, to disappear amidst a blaze of lightning in the centre of the tunnel of the underground railway, I tell you, gentlemen, we have that in our midst which is a greater danger to our metropolis than a foreign foe landed on our shores would be. I ask you, sir, he added, turning to the Home Secretary, "to put all the forces of the Crown to work, until this creature, this Winged Man, is secured, or wiped off the face of the earth."

A smile upon his face, calm, staid as ever, the Home Secretary rose in his place.

"I am afraid the Honourable Member has given me a somewhat difficult task," he began. "We are aware that a creature, endowed with powers of flight, has terrorised various parts of England during the past few months—that the police throughout the country are straining every nerve to capture him; yet, according to the honourable gentleman's own statement, this being has already solved the difficulty for us by an act of voluntary cremation; therefore, gentlemen, until the Winged Man condescend is to appear on earth again—"

"The Winged Man is here!" came in loud, thunderous, reverberating terms from the roof.

Like a stone the Winged Man dropped towards the centre of the floor, then, checking his flight with outstretched wings, flew to the Speaker's chair—for the House had gone into committee—and sat with folded arms, surveying the astounded and bewildered Members.

Never before had the august seat had so strange an occupant. The Members gazed at the fearful intruder, scarce able to believe the evidence of their senses.

With a quick forward movement, the Winged Man rose to his feet.

"Gentlemen of the British House of Commons, the subject I have listened to to-night has been a virtual declaration of war on the part of this mighty kingdom against he who now stands in your midst!" he cried, in deep, ringing tones. "You have thrown down the gauntlet; I accept the challenge. Here, before the majesty of the Commons, I defy you. From henceforth it shall be war—war to the knife. War, war, war!"

"War, war, war!" came a hundred echoes from every part of that magnificent chamber.

With a disdainful glance around, the Winged Man strode to the centre of the House.

The bulging eyes and white faces of the Members of Parliament showed how terribly the Winged Man's threat had affected them.

Suddenly a tall, dignified man rose in his place on the Opposition benches.

"Gentlemen—men of Briton! What! Are we all cowards? Will no man raise a hand to seize this self-convicted, boasting braggart?" he cried.

His words roused the Members of Parliament from the stupor of terror into which they had fallen. Every man rose to his feet.

The benches became a sea of angry, determined faces.

"Call the police! Guard the doors! See to the windows! The Winged Man is here! Seize him! Seize him!" came from every side at once, as with one accord they sprang forward to secure the being who had dared to flout the oldest Parliamentary assembly in the world within its own walls.

Like a rock in the centre of a raging sea, the Winged Man stood unmoved amidst the turmoil.

Calmly he waited until the foremost of his would-be captors was within touch of his flowing garments; then stamped angrily on the floor.

To the utter amazement of the thunder-stricken spectators, the floor opened, and the Winged Man disappeared down a yawning cavern. But the Winged Man had now no superstitious countrymen to deal with, but level-headed, clever men of affairs.

Ever to the front, the aforesaid Member directed the actions of his fellow-members. Pickaxes and crowbars were produced, and soon the entrance to the subterranean tunnel in which the Winged Man had taken refuge was laid bare.

Truncheon-armed, two policeman dropped into the opening. The Member of Parliament himself would have gone, but his friends held him back. His life was too valuable to be risked in such a cause.

The beams of their bullseyes thrown well ahead, the policemen cautiously advanced down the winding tunnel, to find themselves amongst the rounded pillars and fluted arches of an old-time crypt.

Here their search ended, for no outlet through which the strange being could have escaped was to be seen.

Now and again they were alarmed by bursts of mocking laughter rising apparently from roof, walls, and floor, until at last, unable to face the weird, unseen terrors which surrounded them, they returned to where the Members of Parliament, clustered round the yawning hole, awaited them.

Unable to believe the policemen's statement, a number of Members entered the crypt, tapping the walls in search of secret hiding-places, but in vain.

None noticed a tiny crack in one of the pillars into which the Winged Man had thrust the blade of his knife, causing the entire mass of stone to revolve, revealing a circular opening immediately beneath where the base of the pillar had been.

THE CAVES OF LONDON.

Down this opening the Winged Man had clambered. He walked rapidly along winding passages, through dark cellars, and low-roofed crypts, until suddenly he came to an abrupt halt, a dark, angry frown upon his brow.

"What's this? Men here! Who dares to trespass on my domain? The earth belongs to earth-worms, but the air and the secret caves beneath the surface are mine alone," he muttered, his face ablaze with fury then stole cautiously towards where the flickering light of many fires illuminated the crypt.

Presently he came to a standstill, and remained for several moments surveying the curious scene spread out before him.

It was as though he had come upon the outpost of a small army.

At this point the subterranean caves opened into a long succession of cellars and crypts, as each filled with the yellow glare of a fire, burning upon stone or earthen floor, as the case might be. Each fire seemed to have its own particular group.

Here were gathered the wastrels, the unfortunate, the starving of that part of London.

Near one fire a man, whose flabby face and shabby frock-coat told that drink had been the cause of his downfall, was sleeping. By his side crouched a tiny waif, a late edition of an evening paper still clutched in his white, cold hand. Next to him and aged woman, with grey, tattered locks, muttered and mumbled in her sleep. On the opposite side of the fire, her pillow a basket, slept a flower-girl.

Their presence there told the Winged Man that building operations were in progress in the vicinity of Piccadilly. It is only at such times that these forgotten storehouses—in which the merchants of London used to hide their wealth from the Kings and Barons, or to pressure them from the devouring preserve them from the devouring fires which in olden days swept away whole streets at a time—are, as it were, thrown open to the night-roving public.

At other times the police see to it that the inlets into the subterranean passages are closed, or they would constitute a serious and ever-present danger to the occupants of the surrounding houses.

Deep snores proclaimed that sleep had sealed almost every eye; yet some were awake, for the sound of voices came from where the dancing lights of a fire shone through a gap in the broken wall.

Opening wide his broad pinions, the Winged Man skimmed silently and noiselessly over the sleeping groups. Clinging to the brickwork, he peered over the jagged, broken masonry into a cave—or, to be more correct, a tiny cellar—in which two men were squatting before a small pile of brightly-burning logs.

An odour of strong shag came from their short clay-pipes. A bottle, which they now and again applied to their lips, stood on the floor between them. The first words the Winged Man heard caused him to lean eagerly forward.

"I suppose there isn't any chance of its being a trick of Black Jake's to induce us to get him out of quod?"[21] asked one, a tall, respectably-dressed man, with a decidedly Jewish cast of countenance.

His companion was short and squat, with burglar and villain indicated clearly on every line of his coarse, brutal face. He laughed significantly.

"You may bet your life on that!" he said confidently. "Black Jake knows that his life would not be worth a moment's purchase if he tried his tricks on old Bill. Why, I'd do it for him as soon as look at him, and he knows it!"

"You'll be doing folks in once too often, Bill," growled the other, half fearfully, half enviously. "It'll end in a dance in air for you, if you don't mind."

"Let it! It won't bring the dead back to life!" was the rejoinder. "Now, Saul, what are you going to do? Join me in getting Black Jake out of Dartmoor, or not?"

"How much will it cost?" asked the other cautiously.

"A pal of mine as is doing a stretch for bashing a cop sounded one of the warders. He'll make things easy for Jacob for fifty quid. He won't do the job a penny under," replied Bill.

"How much did you say Black Jake nabbed from the Winged Man's pile?" asked Saul Myers.

"Bless ye, he couldn't stop to count it!" laughed Bill. "He was in too much of a fright all the time left old Fly-by-night[22] should pop on him, but he says that there was well over a bushel and a half of the shiners."

---

[21] Prison.

[22] Normally meaning untrustworthy or unreliable. This is also the name of a horse ridden by Spring-Heeled Jack for the Holderness Plate in *The Human Bat* (volume 4 in this series).

The Jew's eyes glittered avariciously.

"And what do I get out of it?" he demanded.

"A third of the boodle,[23] whatever it is," promised Bill.

"All right; it's a bit out of my line, but I'll risk it," assented the Jew.

"Good on you, Saul! Jake's a pal, and I'm allus eager to oblige a pal, especially when it will put half a bushel of shiners into my pocket," chuckled Bill. "Hand over the flimsies."[24]

A cunning smile shone in the other's eyes.

"Not being exactly tired of life, I don't bring money to such a place as this. Come to my office to sell a dog—anything you like—to-morrow morning at ten o'clock," he replied, rising.

The Winged Man glided silently away, leaving the two men to make their way towards where a tiny shaft of light came through a narrow opening, which had given the wastrels of the night, who sheltered in the caves, admittance to their warm and dry retreat.

The Winged Man's eyes flashed with delight as he strode softly from cellar to cellar, from crypt to crypt. He had been sore troubled by his inability to discover where Black Jake had hidden the coin he had stolen from the abbot's treasure. Now he was on the scent, he did not intend that the gold should slip from his grasp a second time.

Little had the pressures pair suspected how near the Winged Man had been to them. Little did they reckon how they had given their secret away. But the Winged Man knew now, and what he once knew he never forgot.

AN ACT OF REPARATION.

It was not until he was conscious of a slight difficulty in breathing that the Winged Man realised that, lost in thought, he was traversing unknown parts. With an ejaculation of surprise, he looked around.

Yes it was true. Fate had directed his steps to a part of the caves in which he had never been before. Thoughtfully he recalled every step he had taken. A few minutes' reflection told him that he must be somewhere in the neighbourhood of the network of poor streets off Shaftesbury Avenue.

Congratulating himself on his good fortune in having discovered this extension of his underground domain, the Winged Man strode outward, pausing now and again to scratch some hieroglyphics upon the wall for Ghat's benefit, should it suit the Winged Man's purpose to send him thither at any future time.

Presently he found himself in what had evidently been a large cellar. Crumbling wine-bins lined the walls. It seemed that his wanderings must end here, for the short flight of dust-covered stone steps that formed the only means of egress from the cellar had long since been bricked up.

------

23 Illegally gained money.
24 Bank notes.

Drawing a small but exceedingly powerful jemmy from the breastplate of tools he always carried, the Winged Man struck once or twice upon the brickwork on the summit of the flight of steps. It gave back a hollow sound, and a few minutes later the Winged Man was hard at work removing the bricks.

An opening made, he found himself in a large cellar, down one side of which lay a number of huge casks, each pierced by a leaden pipe, showing the Winged Man that he was in the cellar of an hotel.

It was yet early morning; so, only stopping to replace the bricks over the opening through which he had passed, and making a mental note that he would order Ghat to turn the brickwork into a secret door at the first opportunity, he mounted a second flight of steps, to find his way barred by an ordinary modern door.

It is true it was locked, but under the skilful manipulation of the Winged Man's burglars' outfit, it flew open, and he found himself in a narrow passage behind the counter of a large public-house. Passing through the bar, he glided noiselessly up the staircase, and, leaving the publican's living rooms and a large dining-room unexplored, made his way to the top of the house, intending to take his flight from the roof.

Suddenly he came to an abrupt halt, and listened intently. Above him was a sloping roof, which showed that he had reached the attics of the public-house. Before him was a door, from behind which came a series of strange sobs.

The Winged Man had heard similar sounds before; and knew the meaning of them. Springing to the door, he thrust it open. A terrible sight met his gaze.

With one blow of his keen knife, the Winged Man severed a rope, and a man fell, limp, into his arms.

"Kindness or cruelty? Probably the last I was a fool to baulk his wish," muttered the Winged Man.

Then his eye fell upon an addressed envelope lying in the centre of the table. "Miss Rivers, Arringer Street, Bristol," he read.

Glancing towards the young man, who was slowly fighting his way back to life, the Winged Man tore open the envelope, and, by the light of his head-lamp, scanned its contents.

"My poor Elsie," it began, "forgive this added sorrow which I am bringing upon you. When the Winged Man stole the papers—to secure which my father had spent his entire fortune, and thus reduced myself and sisters to beggary—I offered to free you from the promise you had made to marry me.

"Nobly you refused, begging me to go out into the world, and make a home for you. I have tried, Elsie. No tongue can tell the rebuffs, the bitter disappointments, the long, weary tramps in search of employment I have endured. And now, dear, farewell! I can fight no longer. For three days no food has passed my lips.

"I know that while I live you will never take your freedom. When I am gone, you will choose a worthy object. May Heaven grant you a long and happy life."

Then followed expressions of love and the messages to dear ones; with this the unhappy young man had concluded. Slowly and deliberately the Winged

Man tore the letter into a thousand pieces.

Then, warned by the increasing light penetrating through the uncurtained window that day was upon him, he extinguished his headlight, and, after leaning for some minutes over the table, opened the window, and launched himself upon the murky London air.

Slowly John Ayres fought his way back to life. His wondering eyes flew about the room.

"Am I—can I—be yet alive?" he muttered disjointedly. "No, no! I remember the fearful sensation; I remember the vivid sparks flitting about my eyes, the one last, awful pang, then oblivion. Yet I am not dead. I draw in the morning air; my eyes see the familiar walls of the bear, comfortless garret which has been my home so long. It was a dream. I dream to that, in despair, I determined to rid the world of a useless encumbrance.

"It was no dream. It was true!" he almost shrieked, springing from the bed on which the Winged Man had laid him. "I was found, cut down, and they have left me, thinking me dead," he continued. "But when they find that I am still alive, what awaits me? Shame, exposure, and the police-court. To have the finger of scorn pointed at me as one who attempted to kill himself and failed. I dare not, I will not face it! I have bidden farewell to the world. The window yet remains. What the cord failed to do, the hard pavement below will accomplish."

Rising unsteadily to his feet, for he was still weak after his late fearful experience, he made for the window. A loud, mirthless laugh burst from his lips.

"No, no; I am still dreaming! A mocking dream follows me even in my waking hours! There is—there can be—no gold, no papers!" he cried aloud, pointing with trembling hands to the table. "Yes, it's real, rich, yellow gold!" he shouted, clutching frantically at a heap of sovereigns lying upon the table. "Gold means food, shelter, more fitting clothes to seek the employment my heart desires!"

His eyes fell upon the papers on the table. They were addressed in strong, wonderfully clear characters, to "John Ayres, Esq., On the brink of the unknown."

In a moment his nervous fingers had torn off the wrapper; then a wild, joyful shout burst from his lips. He held the Ayres papers which would restore his birthright to him. Then, his weakened frame able to bear no more, he sank down on the table, and, his head resting on the time-stained documents, burst into tears.

John Ayres was saved.

The Winged Man had made reparation.

SNATCHED FROM THEIR GRASP.

It was night. Swaying from a branch of a twisted and gnarled ancient oak, by the side of the country road, the Winged Man swung to the night air. Resting, after a seventy-mile flight, he watched the long, white road which had disappeared into the darkness beneath him.

Suddenly the swaying ceased. Opening his wide pinions, the Winged Man swooped almost to the ground; then, rising above the tree-tops, remained motionless in the air, as a cart containing three men advanced at a swift trot down the road.

When immediately beneath him, the horse swerved swiftly to the right, nearly throwing the occupants of the cart into a ditch; then, bounding forward, dashed clattering down the road.

"Whoa, you beast!" came a hoarse voice from the cart "what has scared you now, I wonder? I don't see anything! Do you, Saul?" asked Bill the Burglar, with difficulty regaining control of the frightened horse.

"A rabbit dashing across the road—anything is enough to frighten a horse at night," returned his companion in quavering tones, which showed he was not quite so thoroughly at his ease as he wished to appear.

"It isn't! It couldn't have been! Great powers that be, if it was the Winged Man!" came in horse, trembling tones from the third occupant of the trap.

A loud burst of contemptuous laughter arose from Bill's lips.

"Skilly[25] and 'white wine' seems to have taken all the pluck out of you, Jake!" he said contemptuously. "You never used to be frightened at shadows!"

"I hadn't encountered the Winged Man then," replied the Man with the Scar, in low, hushed tones, as he gazed fearfully over his shoulder, little guessing that the weird being he had half expected to see leering upon him from the back of the cart was at that moment hovering noiselessly within a few feet of his head. But a louder laugh than ever burst from the burglar's lips.

"Blessed if the whole wide world don't seem to be scared to death of this here Winged Man," he said scornfully. "Let 'em! If the Flying Jigger is wise he'll keep out of my reach, I can tell him, a-spoiling trade as he does. Why, there ain't a house as isn't locked up twice as careful since he has been about!"

"Hush, Bill; he may be listening at this very moment!" whispered the Man with the Scar.

"Oh, stow it, Jake; you make me tired! Anyhow, he ain't so mighty smart as you make out, or he wouldn't have let you diddle him out of the gold as you did!" asserted Bill.

"Hang the gold! I wish I'd never seen it! I wish you had left me in prison! At any rate, I was safe from him there!" retorted Jake.

A snort of contempt was the only answer, for Bill the Burglar, who was driving, had all he could do to control the trembling, frightened horse.

It was not a young horse by any means, merely a livery stable-keeper's hack, hired by the three men to take them to a supposed dying relative in the country, yet it seemed endowed with the strength of a dozen, as, now swerving to the right and left, now nearly throwing the men out of the cart by coming to an abrupt halt, and refusing to go until it had been unmercifully thrashed. Never did horse act so curiously as this one.

By the time the roadside copse where Jake had hidden his stolen gold was

---

[25] A thin oatmeal broth flavoured with meat.

reached, the horse's terror had, to a certain extent, communicated itself to the men in the cart.

Their destination reached, the three men alighted, and with difficulty hitched the horse to a convenient gate. Plunging into the wood, Jake led the way, though with evident reluctance, until at last the hollow oak was reached.

Clambering on one of the spreading branches, Jake gained the trunk, and, dropping to the leaf-covered bottom, forgot his fears in the delight he felt when he found his gold untouched.

"Hi, Bill!" he cried, his face at the knot-hole through which he had watched the Winged Man's disappearance into the subterranean passage, which connected the copse with the moat.

"Well, is it there?" asked the burglar eagerly.

"Yes; safe enough!" was the reassuring reply, as the Man with the Scar scraped the yellow gold and fallen leaves together into three small bags which he had brought for the purpose.

Ten minutes later the three men, each carrying a bag of gold, made their way back to the cart.

The horse was trembling in every limb, and bathed in lather. But, so far, their journey had been successful, and, having deposited their precious loads in the bottom of the vehicle, they scrambled headlong into the cart and turned the horse's head towards Bury St. Edmunds.

"Phew! You may laugh if you like, but I'm glad we have left that wicked wood! Each moment I expected the Winged Man to swooped down and claim his gold," said Black Jake, glancing across Myers to the burglar.

"Dry up about the Winged Man! You seem to have got the Winged Man on the brain. He knows better than to come falling about where I am!" boasted bill. "Besides," he added, with a loud laugh, "dog don't eat dog! The Winged Man himself ain't no worse than old Saul Myers, quiet old dog that he is! Cheer up, Saul! You haven't spoken for this last—"

He ceased speaking, his dark, evil face turned ashen grey, for Saul Myers had disappeared, and in his place sat the Winged Man.

"Here, stop the cart! Who are you? What are you doing there? Where's Saul?" Bill the Burglar cried, in a series of ejaculations.

"I am the Winged Man!" cried that strange being. "Your accomplice is flying for his life back to the copse."

A loud, piercing shriek of terror burst from Black Jake's lips. Throwing down the reins, he strove to fling himself from the cart, but the Winged Man's iron grip held him tightly.

The Winged Man turned upon Bill the Burglar.

"Well, you wish to see me—I am here!" he said mockingly.

With a mighty effort the burglar conquered the rising terror which gripped his heart. Stealthily he drew a concealed knife from beneath his coat. Raising it swiftly above his head, he brought it down to within an inch of the Winged

Man's breast, when a cry of terror burst from his lips, for the blade fell clattering to the bottom of the cart, splintered into a score of pieces.

"Poor fool, to think that a weapon made by human hands could injure the Winged Man! Go!" cried the Winged Man, as, seizing the burglar by the belt, he lifted him by one hand and threw him bodily into a ditch by the side of the road.

Whilst all this was taking place the frightened horse was cluttering down the road at break-neck speed, the swaying cart jolting and bumping over the stones, threatening each moment to hurl its occupant into the road.

Had not the Winged Man held him down, Black Jake, who was crouching against the back seat, limp as a sack, would have been precipitated from the cart.

The burglar disposed of, the Winged Man turned upon the Man with the Scar.

"Who sent you to Dartmoor? Speak, dog!" thundered the Winged Man.

"The judge at the assizes," came in a hoarse whisper from Black Jake's lips.

"You lie!" thundered his awful companion. "It was I—the Winged Man—who ordained that you should return to prison for daring to rob me of my gold!"

"I found it. I didn't know it was yours," Jake summoned up sufficient courage to reply.

"All plunder is mine! To such as you belong what the Winged Man disdains," was the answer. "Come, your prison-cell awaits you!"

"Mercy! Don't send me back to that awful place! I'll be your dog, your slave! I'll do your every bidding! Give a man a chance!" pleaded the Man with the Scar.

He had scarce had time to taste the joy of his recently acquired liberty, and now to be hauled back to the confinement of a convict's cell seemed more than he could bear.

"Your sentence was ten years. Within ten weeks you shall be at liberty," promised the Winged Man.

Then, rising, he blew a loud, shrill blast on a golden whistle.

Immediately a new terror was added to the many which convulsed the Man with the Scar's very soul. A dark, misshapen, goblin-like form sprang from the roadside, and, seizing the fleeing horse by the bridle, drew it back on to the road, just in time to save the cart from being dashed against a tree.

With a wild, weird, awful yell the misshapen apparition sprang upon the terrified animal's back; then, turning, leered into his master's face, for it was Ghat, the Winged Man's ill-shapen, brutal, yet ever faithful servant.

Twisting the reins round his wrist, Ghat got the animal well in hand, and, forcing it forward, by drumming his heels upon it side, they sped on at a gallop.

"Come!" thundered the Winged Man.

Black Jake started as one aroused from a terrible dream. A wild hope coursed through his heart. The seat the Winged Man had occupied was vacant.

"Come!"

The voice came from immediately above his head. He looked up. Hovering within a few feet of his head, on his awful, widely-distended pinions, was the

Winged Man.

"Mercy!" came in a low moan from the unfortunate man's lips.

He shuddered as his appeal was echoed by a terrible burst of laughter from the bunched-up form clinging to the horse's withers.

"Come!"

The word seemed to reverberate over the adjoining night-covered fields, so loud, so fierce, so laden with evil was it.

The Man with the Scar, moved by an impulse he could not resist, rose to his feet. Immediately a stifled moan burst from his lips. Icy-cold fingers grasped him by the neck and he was borne, limp and terror-stricken, from the cart. Up, up, up, until, a thousand feet above the earth, the Winged Man hovered in mid-air, his victim clasped in his strong, remorseless grasp.

"Are you not mine—mind, body and soul? Will you ever dare to rob me again? Will you not obey my slightest wish in future?" thundered the Winged Man.

"Kill me—kill me! I can bear no more! This terror will drive me mad!" came in gasping accents from trembling man's white, pallid lips.

"Oh-o! You have not yet learned the lesson of obedience! I require an answer, not an appeal!" thundered forth the Winged Man, as, opening his fingers, he allowed Black Jake to slip from his grasp.

Down dropped the shrieking man, until, just as the rapid rush through the air was about to prove fatal, the Winged Man swooped down upon him, and, checking his flight, held him motionless in the air.

For the next ten minutes the Winged Man played with Black Jake as a cat plays with the mouse. Now he would let him for almost to earth, now bear him aloft, as though he would leave the earth for ever behind, until even Black Jake's stolid, unimaginative brain could stand no more, and all was blank.

°IN HIS MAJESTY'S PRISON.

Within a long, narrow passage, with iron doors thick with heavy rivets, opening into it, a warder—a bundle of keys dangling on his belt—passed from cell to cell, listening at one cell, thrusting back the cover from the observation-hole of another, until suddenly he started, as the loud tinkling of an electric bell echoed and re-echoed through the sleeping prison.

A look of amazement crept over the warder's face.

"No. 29? Why, that was Black Jake's cell, and it's empty now!" he muttered, his eyes fixed upon the indicator over the cell door.

As though in answer to his thoughts, the bell's shrill summons rang out once more.

There was no mistake this time. The gong of the bell was a little loose, and he could see it yet vibrating.

The warder moved towards the cell. With trembling hands, he inserted a key in the lock, and, flinging the door open, touched a switch which flooded the cell with light.

Enframed in the door, he stood gazing upon a low prison cot, on which, clad in the hideous grey, black-arrow dotted uniform he had worn before his escape, was Black Jake, whose escape some weeks before had puzzled the prison authorities.

But, astonishing though Black Jake's escape, it was nothing to his return.

"No. 842!" cried the warder, addressing the prisoner by the only designation by which convicts are known.

But Black Jake never moved. He was breathing heavily. His face, as white as a sheet, was contorted into a look of such fearful horror that the beholder shuddered.

The warder was as brave a man as any on the staff of that big prison, yet he stood enframed within the doorway, not daring to approach nearer to that prostrate, motionless form.

Twice he tried to advance into the cell; twice an overmastering terror forced him back.

At last, white to the very lips, he closed the door behind him with a clang, and, his hair standing on end with terror, made his way to a bell-push at the further end of the gallery.

What it was filled his soul with such fear he could not have said, yet never again did he recall Black Jake's face to mind without a shudder.

The warder was trembling from head to foot. Twice he endeavoured to push the button home, twice he failed. At length he succeeded, and a loud, deep clang came from somewhere without.

A minute later the doors at both ends of the gallery were flung open, and half a dozen armed warders, buckling on their belts as they ran, entered the gallery.

° 22 FEBRUARY 1913.

Instead of finding their comrades fighting for life against the attack of one or more desperate convicts, intent upon escape—for it is a strict regulation of the prison that the alarm shall not be given except for a good cause—they found the warder standing in the centre of the gallery, his face white and blanched with terror.

"What is it, Masters? Why did you give the alarm?" asked a first-class warder.

"Black Jake—842—" stammered the frightened man.

"Well, what of that? 842 has made good his escape, as you know well enough!" was the angry retort.

"I know—I know!" stammered the bewildered warder. "But he has returned!"

The chief warder gazed searchingly at the speaker.

"You have either been sleeping on duty, or you're intoxicated! In either case, I will arrest you for giving a false alarm!" declared the first-class warder, angry at being disturbed for nothing.

"Oh, no, it is neither! Go to No. 29; he is there!"

"Take away his revolver, lest he does some mischief to someone! I'll see into this!" thundered the warder angrily, as he strode in the direction of No. 29, and, throwing the door open, entered.

Like Masters, he stood paralysed with astonishment on the threshold.

In the same position as when Masters had discovered him, Black Jake lay upon his cot.

"By the powers, Masters was right!" muttered the chief warder; then, beckoning one of his men to follow, strode to the side of the cot.

Pinned to the convict's cot was a slip of paper. Wonderingly the chief warder bent down and read:

"Returned to the custody of his Majesty's prison for ten weeks by the Winged Man."

"The Winged Man!" repeated the chief warder, springing to an upright position.

"The Winged Man!" came like an echo from behind him.

The chief warder wheeled round.

Standing, enframed by steel, in the open doorway of a cell immediately opposite No. 29 was a dark, awful form, with white, or-inspiring face, and deep, black, shining eyes.

Snatching his sword from its scabbard, the chief warder sprang forward. Even as he did so the door of the cell closed with a resounding clang, followed by a wild, fearful yell, as of a man in the grasp of some overmastering terror.

"Quick, Masters! Your keys—quick!" cried the chief warder.

Aroused by his superior's voice, the warder hastened forward.

With trembling hands, the chief warder thrust the key into the lock then uttered an exclamation of astonishment for the bolted lock had been slipped back!

A cold chill of supernatural dread was beginning to creep over the chief warder's frame; yet he determined to probe this mystery to the bottom. Flinging the door open, he entered.

On the bare, coverless cot a man cowered, the coarse blankets drawn tightly over his head.

Striding to the side of the cot, the chief warder tore the blanket aside, revealing the frightened face of No. 811—a brutal wife-beater, who had killed his wife with an unlucky blow, and had narrowly escaped the gallows for his crime.

With a cry of joy, the cowed wretch sprang from the bed and clasped the chief warder's hand.

"There—there!" he cried. "I saw him. A ghost, or perhaps"—he trembled so that his teeth clattered—"the prince of darkness himself!"

As he spoke he pointed with shaking hand to the farther corner of the cell.

The warder switched on the electric light. Its white beams filled the narrow cell, revealing the fact that, save for the prisoner and himself, the cell was empty.

For several minutes the chief warder stood gazing about him in blank amazement. A hard-headed Scotsman, he had no room in his common-sense brain for belief in ghosts or spirits, yet what he had seen that night had certainly shaken his disbelief in the supernatural.

Suddenly the clamour of a hundred electric bells, all ringing at once, fell upon his startled ear. Then, with a loud boom! boom! boom! the alarm-bell of the prison rang out.

Immediately the silence which had obtained throughout the sleeping prison was turned into a pandemonium of shrieks and yells, as the awakened convicts, believing the prison to be on fire, thundered at the doors of their cells, and begged piteously to be set at liberty.

A white-haired, military-looking man, his sword-belt buckled hastily around the outside of a dressing-gown, hastened upon the scene.

"What's all this uproar about? Fire, or mutiny?" he demanded angrily, as he entered the gallery.

Saluting, the chief warder poured into the governor's ears a brief account of the incredible events which had happened.

"Good gracious! Have my whole staff gone mad?" fumed the governor. "I only wish the Winged Man was here! I'd see that he didn't escape!"

"The Winged Man is here!"

All are turned in the direction from whence the deep, sonorous tones had come.

Floating midway between the ceiling and the floor was the weird form which had struck such terror into the chief warder's heart.

A moment's terror-stricken silence, then:

"Close in on him, men! Seize him! Shoot him without mercy if he resists!" came from the gallant old warrior's lips as, darting forward with drawn sword, he made a furious pass at the Winged Man.

So unexpected was the governor's attack that it was only by throwing his body forward, and skimming like a fish in the water through the air close above the old man's head, that the Winged Man escaped unwounded.

Then the deep roar of Service revolvers echoed through the narrow confines of the gallery, as shot after shot was fired at the fleeing figure. At length the firing ceased, for the Winged Man disappeared through a doorway at the end of the gallery.

THE GOVERNOR'S OATH.

But there was yet another danger for the weird being to face.

As, with long, strong beats of his black pinions, he made his way towards the door that gave admittance into the courtyard, it was to find an armed warder hastening towards the scene of the disturbance barring the way.

Up went the warder's weapon to his shoulder as he aimed straight at the Winged Man's only vulnerable point—his head.

But a fraction of a second intervened between the time the butt of the rifle touched the warder's shoulder and the moment his finger pulled the trigger, yet that fraction of a second sufficed for the Winged Man to blaze his powerful searchlight full into the warder's face.

Dazzled, blinded, frightened, the man jerked up the muzzle of his rifle, and the bullet sped harmlessly on its way down the gallery, missing the Winged Man's head by but an eighth of an inch.

The next moment the warder felt his rifle snatched from his grasp, a strong hand seized him by the belt, and, calling loudly for help, he was carried, struggling violently, into the courtyard and up the precipitous walls of the building.

The courtyard was filled with warders, and a score of rifles were levelled at the strange unearthly form that—their comrades clasped in his arms—scaled the building as easily as though the sheer height had been level ground; yet, fearing to harm their comrade, not a trigger was pulled, until at last the Winged Man disappeared from view behind a stone parapet running around the buildings.

A moment later the dark form reappeared; then, uttering his weird, wild, mournful cry, spread his pinions to the breeze and glided slowly towards the ground.

"Shoot him! I'll be responsible!" roared the governor.

"No, no! Don't fire! Don't fire!" came from above.

A score of warders had raised their rifles to their shoulders, but as the appeal reached their ears they lowered their threatening muzzles.

"Shoot, you fools, or the treacherous dog will make you rue your mercy! Fire—fire!" shouted the governor.

Setting the example, he raised his revolver and fired straight at the white faced immediately beneath the balloon-like arrangement that supported it. A howl of terror, and a heavy body fell with a thud to his feet.

"Hurrah! Got you at last, Winged Man!" cried the elated governor. "On him, lads! Bind him, handcuff him, put him in irons! He is in our power, and shall only leave it for the scaffold!"

A loud, mocking peal of laughter from the black sky immediately above their heads greeted the governor's words.

"Bah! The fellow's ventriloquial tricks' won't frighten me!" declared the governor contemptuously. "Bring him along! We'll see how he likes the punishment cell and a dose of the cat!"

Again that weird, mocking laughter startled the night air. The governor looked at the huddled form, which offered no resistance, though four warders were kneeling upon him to hold him down. Suddenly one of the warders released his hold.

"Hanged if it isn't Dick Whipper!" he cried.

"Who?" ejaculated the governor.

"Dick Whipper, sir, the man the Winged Man carried off," explained the warder.

Beside himself with rage, the governor hurled the men to right and left, then, snatching a lantern from a warder's hand, held it close to the fallen man's pallid face. It was true!

Instead of the Winged Man, the governor had captured one of his own men, who lay half enveloped by a spreading cloth which, being ingenuously secured by cords to his body, had formed a parachute that had checked his fall to the earth. Again that mocking laugh rang through the night.

"By the powers, man or demon you must come to earth some time, and I will have you! I swear by my oath to the King never to rest, day or night, until I have laid you by the heels!" swore Colonel Grimshank.

Snatching a rifle from a warder's hand, the governor fired it haphazard in the direction from whence the laugh had come. The next moment, warned by some strange instinct, he stepped back.

A slab of masonry, torn from the stone coping, fell from a hundred feet above his head, crashed on to the pavement within a few inches of where he stood, and, bursting like a shell, hurled its jagged fragments around.

Then stone after stone dropped into the courtyard. The splinters bruising or severely injuring the majority of those present. At last, unable to bear the fusillade, the warders snatched up the bodies of their wounded comrades and ran for shelter within the building.

But not for long. The governor's words had been no empty threat.

"Fire the alarm-gun! Turn out every man!" he ordered. "We'll have this Winged Man, let him strive his best to evade us!"

A warder hastened off to where the signal-gun, a mortar, was secured to the flat roof of an adjacent building. Thrusting a blank cartridge into the gun, the warder rammed it home, then applied a match to the touch-hole. A reverberating roar, and a stream of flame, bursting into a cloud of smoke, shot from the huge weapon's mouth. Then the warder, uttering a cry of terror, turned and fled.

Stone after stone dropped into the courtyard.

The cloud of smoke was torn asunder, disclosing within it the hideous form of the Winged Man. Cries of wonder and alarm from the courtyard proclaimed that others beside the fleeing warder had witnessed the phenomenon. A silence like that of night hung over the prison. Even Colonel Grimshank was for the moment awed and subdued. A feeling of despair chilled even his gallant old heart. How could mortal man hope to fight so awful, so terrible a foe.

Slowly recovering from the stupor of amazement which had held him helpless in its chilly grasp, he looked around upon his white-faced, anxious men. Shaking himself, as one who throws an unbearable weight from off his shoulders, the governor drew himself up to his full height.

"Men of his Majesty's prison guard," he thundered, "the more difficult the task the greater the glory! We have no ordinary foe to contender against. I want no cowards. Those who are prepared to risk all, to dare all, in an attempt to capture this fearful being, step to the front!"

A moment's hesitation, then as one man the body of warders advanced.

"It is well," continued the governor, well pleased at the response of his appeal. "We will scour the country. Let every armed warder who can be spared from the guard be ready in ten minutes' time; but, mind, there must be no summons to surrender; we fire on sight."

It was in a large room opening into the courtyard that the order was issued, and, hastening to his own apartments, the gallant old soldier reappeared about ten minutes later clad in full uniform, a revolver in its scabbard at his sword-belt. By the time he emerged from his house all were ready to commence their fierce struggle against the Winged Man.

A warder held the governor's charger at the door of his residence. Mounting, he issued a few rapid, concise orders to the chief warder, then, putting himself at the head of his men, rode through the folding gates, which were flung open to allow his exit, and, when the last of the search-party had passed through, closed with a sonorous clang behind them.

IN THE MORASS.

Though determined to leave no stone unturned to achieve the capture or destruction of the flying menace which terrorised the country, the colonel rode forth with no plans made, safe to scatter his men in all directions, in the hope that the Winged Man, dropping to the ground, would be captured.

Nature itself seemed on the governor's side, for as the armed party emerged from the gates, the wind blew aside the clouds which had obscured the undulating stench of more around the prison, lightened by the silvery beams of the moon.

Though in an ever-increasing circle the avengers searched the country around the grim stone prison, their eyes were more often distracted towards the starlit heaven than to the dreary moorland.

As the country grew wider the intervals between the searches became farther apart, until at length, when Colonel Grimshank wrote his horse to the summit of a hill, the warders to right and left were but dots in the distance.

Taking his night-glass from its case, the old veteran swept the horizon. Presently he uttered an exclamation of delight. Far away in the distance, a tiny speck was speeding over the moor.

Even as he gazed wings shot from either side of the distant figure, and Colonel Grimshank knew that the Winged Man was in sight. A blast from a silver whistle warned the warders that the hunt was afoot, the quarry sighted.

Sticking spurs into his horse, the governor flew over the level sward in swift pursuit of the Winged Man. His reins lying loose on his arm, Colonel Grimshank assured himself that every chamber of his revolver was loaded, then, thrusting the weapon back into its scabbard, he settled down to ride his hardest.

In grim silence he galloped over the moor. There would be no question of summoning the Winged Man to surrender. Death by shot or steel should be the flying hawk's lot if once the gallant old veteran got to close quarters with him.

On he sped, decreasing the distance at every stride, though the Winged Man, with closely-folded wings, was moving over the ground in long loops which covered twenty yards at a stride.

Those who had once seen the Winged Man moving swiftly, noiselessly across country, would have known at once that he was purposely allowing himself to be overtaken. Scarce touching the ground, the Winged Man sped onward, his keen, flashing eyes peering through the darkness to right and left.

A slight tinge of colour relieved the livid pallor which usually marked his face. His eyes flashed with excitement and enjoyment. Presently, when Colonel Grimshank was within a score yards of him, the Winged Man turned sharply to the left, then to the right, then continued straight ahead once more.

Lightly though he tried, his padded feet sank deeply into the yielding soil. Colonel Grimshank's horse, a magnificent grey, trembled, snorted, and would have stopped; but, carried away by the excitement of the chase, filled with a determination to conquer or die, Colonel Grimshank held him on his course.

Warned by instinct of the terrible danger which menaced him, the horse swerved to right and left. Already the noble animal was a fetlock deep in the yielding soil. Presently, with an abruptness which would have unseated a less skilful rider, the grey came to a halt.

"On, you brute—on!" almost shrieked the governor, striking the horse on the flank with his sword.

Maddened by pain, the noble beast uttered a shrill neigh of remonstrance, then sprang frantically towards where the Winged Man hovered a foot from the ground.

"Scoundrel I have you now!" cried the old warrior, standing up in his stirrups, and raising his sword high above his head.

The next moment his confident cry was changed to a shout of alarm, as his horse, alighting in the centre of a bottomless morass, sank to its girth in the slime-carpet, treacherous marsh.

Too late Colonel Grimshank realised his peril.

A fearful death, such as might well have appalled the bravest heart, threatened him, but the old soldier faced his foe unsubdued, unconquerable to the end.

Allowing his sword to swing by its sword-knot, he snatched his revolver from its sheath.

Crack—crack—crack! Three shots in rapid succession hastened the steps of the warders, who were moving to their commander's assistance.

Despite his awful danger, Colonel Grimshank's nerves were like iron, his hand and steady as a rock.

Two bullets struck the Winged Man on his impenetrable breastplate, the third hissed by close to his ears.

Crack, crack, crack! Three more shots rang out, yet the Winged Man stood as before, his hands clasped behind him, a look of contemptuous indifference upon his pale, awful face.

Then arose perhaps the most awful, nerve thrilling sound that can fall upon the human ear.

The terrified shriek of a dying horse. The noble beast, struggling vainly to burst from its living tomb, had sunk till naught but its head remained above the surface.

Even its rider, buried to the waist, was thinking swiftly to his doom.

One more fearful shriek, and the horse had disappeared from view.

Gliding towards his victim, the Winged Man held out his hand.

"Never; I will not owe my life to you!" gasped the old man, as he aimed a furious cut with his sword at the outstretched hand; but the sweeping cut was intercepted by the Winged Man's leg.

Then came the ring of steel on iron, and the highly-tempered blade, shattered into a score of pieces, fell on to the green, deceptive surface of the bog.

Again the Winged Man approached. Evading the other's wildly grasping hands, he seized the governor by the collar of his tunic, tore him from the clinging mud, and glided swiftly over the trackless, treacherous waste.

Four warders, not daring to venture into the bog, stood, horror-stricken witnesses to these wondrous events.

"Fire—never mind me—fire!" gasped the governor.

The warders hesitated, then one raised his rifle to his shoulder. The next moment he dropped its butt on to the ground.

"I can't do it! If my bullet struck the old chief had never know another moment's happiness!" he cried.

"Gatling, shoot! If I have at any time earned your gratitude and respect, shoot!" pleaded the old man, as the Winged Man, and slowly beating pinions, bore him straight up into the air.

"I cannot, sir—great powers, I cannot!"

"Dawson, Robbins, Phillips, don't let me be carried away alive by this demon!" came in imploring tones, rendered faint by distance, from their chief.

"He is right, lads; fire!" cried one of the warders.

And the next moment four rifles hurled their deadly missiles towards the flying form of the Winged Man.

"He is hit—he is hit!" came in exultant tones from every voice at once, as they saw the Winged Man's upward progress checked.

Then, gathering the struggling form of their chief in a close embrace, the Winged Man folded his pinions around him, and dropped like a stone towards the earth.

"They are killed! They are dead men!" came in awestricken whispers from the four men, as, with a loud, fearful, crashing sound, the descending bodies struck a slime-covered, stagnant pool of water and disappeared beneath the surface.

It seemed as if they had gone for ever.

PRISONERS OF WAR.

Retaining his senses with the dogged persistency of his race, Colonel Grimshank felt the waters close above his head, then, struggling wildly, he found himself being dragged along beneath the surface for a short distance ere they rose again.

Spluttering and choking, Colonel Grimshank drew in a long breath, and looked in amazement around him.

The moonlight landscape, the star-bespangled sky had vanished. A deep, impenetrable darkness obtained on every side.

Suddenly a brilliant light shone out.

They were standing knee deep in water in a low, dark tunnel. On a sluggish subterranean stream floated a shallow, flat-bottomed boat.

All this the governor took in at a glance, then his eyes alighted upon the source from whence the light had come.

Even his iron will could not subdue an ejaculation of superstitious terror when he discovered that the powerful beams protruded from the centre of his capture's forehead.

As easily as though he had been a child the Winged Man laid the governor of the prison in the bottom of the boat; then, entering, drew a short pole from its loop at the sight, and proceeded to punt the frail craft along the slowly-flowing river.

At times the rough roof of the natural tunnel through which the subterranean river flowed almost touched the Winged Man's stooping head. At others, the walls of the rock narrowed so that the boat could scarce pass, then widened again, until they seemed to be floating through some unknown underground lake.

Presently the bottom of the boat grated upon the shingle the bed of the subterranean river.

"Rise; our journey ends here!" ordered the Winged Man.

Wonderingly Colonel Grimshank obeyed; fearfully he looked around him.

A little way from where they had disembarked the river sank into the earth, leaving a stretch of yellow shining gravel, along which the Winged Man escorted his prisoner, until at last they reached a large cavern furnished with rough articles of furniture.

In the centre of the cavern was a large stone. Laying his hand upon the stone, the Winged Man pressed it gently to one side, and the huge mass, weighing several tons, slid easily aside, revealing a small, well-like aperture some four feet squared, into which, too proud to remonstrate, Colonel Grimshank was lowered.

Then the mass of rock moved over him, and all was dark.

Rising to the roof of the cave, the Winged Man crept along it until he reached what looked like a crack in the earth above him. Up this he crept, and passing between two huge rocks, emerged inside one of those strange, old-time erections, consisting of three broad, upright stones, into which a fourth formed a rough roof, with which the moor is dotted.

In long-forgotten, prehistoric times, when England was inhabited by a race of savages, it is probable that the upper slab had been used as an altar for human sacrifice. There were dark stains still upon it.

However, whatever its former use, it now marked the entrance to one of the Winged Man's secret lairs.

Rising, the Winged Man moved across the marsh to where a group of warders stood, their eyes fixed upon the spot where their chief had disappeared.

They saw not the Winged Man soaring above their heads. Suddenly one, of sharper hearing than his comrades, started back in alarm.

Too late!

As men will when confronted by some fearful unknown peril, they were grouped together, talking in low, awe-stricken whispers, and, consequently, were unable to avoid the sweep of the enormous casting net the Winged Man through over them.

Entangled in the thick meshes of the net, the warders strove in vain to break free. Their struggles only served to entangle them worse than ever in the net.

"A fine catch!" came in mocking accents from above, as, hauling upon a rope in the centre of the net, the Winged Man dragged them across the bog, then plunged them into the waters of the stagnant pool, through which he had led his first prisoner.

Twenty minutes later the four warders had joined their chief in the black hole beneath the Winged Man's secret lair.

Then he sallied forth once more.

The broad tongue of solid land protruded into the bog from the hill beneath which warders and chief were imprisoned. Along this narrow path some half-hour later for mounted warders dashed in pursuit of the Winged Man.

The summit of the hill reached, they flung themselves from the horses, and, firing as they ran, rushed headlong beneath the massive stone.

Even as they did so the Winged Man shot forth his net once more, and four more prisoners were added to his haul.

From time to time he sallied forth. Not once did he return empty-handed. Ere day broke every warder who had gone forth in search of the Winged Man was imprisoned beneath the grass-covered hill.

BLACK JAKE TO THE RESCUE.

In the centre of the uppermost slab of stone on the summit of the hill the Winged Man sat, his elbow on his knee, his chin in his hand, watching the sunrise, a round, red ball, on the eastern horizon.

Suddenly he started to his feet. Loud, deep, ominous came the roar of the alarm-gun from the prison; then a rifle-shot rang out, followed by another, and yet another.

The Winged Man sprang from the slab of stone, and cleaving the air with swift beats of his mighty pinions, made his way towards the forbidding walls of the prison.

Hovering over the slate roofs of the massive building, he looked down. Shrieks, execrations, yells of rage, punctuated by volleys of musketry, greeted his ears.

A fearful sight met his gaze. Disorganised by the terror at the Winged Man's presence, the warders had allowed the convicts to break loose. Seizing iron bars, spades, tools from the work-shed, anything that hate and vengeance could turn into a weapon, two hundred desperate convicts were attacking the few warders left on duty. Others were seeking to better their way to liberty through iron doors.

A huge ruffian, in convict's garb, had just thrown a warder, and was kneeling upon the prostrate man's breast.

Like a thunderbolt the Winged Man dropped from the heavens on to the would-be assassin. Strong ruffian though the convict was, he was but as a child in the Winged Man's grasp.

Tearing the ruffian off his victim, the Winged Man hurled him with fearful force on to the flagstones, where he lay, stunned and helpless.

"Back to your holes, dogs, back!" thundered the Winged Man.

A deep silence succeeded the pandemonium of sound which had hitherto obtained in the prison-yard.

"Dogs, scum of the earth, scoundrels, do you hear me?" repeated the Winged Man. "Back to your cells, I say, back!"

Cowed, trembling, overawed by that awful, threatening face, and the baleful red light shining with supernatural lustre from the centre of the strange being's forehead, the convicts slowly gave ground.

Scourging them with words sharp as a scorpion's sting, the Winged Man drew a short, many-thonged wire-whip from his girdle, and, slashing out to right and left, slowly drove the convicts back.

Wondering, awe-stricken, yet bound to their posts by a sense of duty, the warders, assisted by the Winged Man, gradually recovered their lost ground, and soon the convicts, having been first formed in a line along one side of the courtyard, were being marched back to their cells in batches.

Ill would it have gone with the warders but for the Winged Man's timely appearance. Ill would it have fared with them even now but for the Winged Man's fearful scourge. Yet the public reward, and the governor's handsome promise to the man who secured the Winged Man, drove all thoughts of gratitude from their hearts.

A whispered consultation, and two of the warders crept upon the Winged Man from behind.

Deeming that he had earned a temporary truce from his foes, the Winged Man was off his guard. It was not until a sharp blow on the hamstrings sent him rolling on the flagstones. And he felt the warders pinning him down, that he realised the treacherous nature of the attack that was being made upon him.

"Shame—shame!" ran like wildfire from the ranks of the astounded convicts.

"Bust me if there is a lag amongst us as 'ud turn upon a pal like that!" declared a burly convict.

The Winged Man exerted his enormous strength to throw off his foes. Accustomed to deal with refractory convicts, a warder, in a rough-and-tumble like the present, was equal to four ordinary men.

The Winged Man was just beginning to realise that he was indeed fighting now for his life and liberty, when a grey form sprang from the convicts' ranks, seized the warder kneeling upon the Winged Man's chest by the collar of his tunic and sword-belt, drew him from off his victim by main force, and held him against his comrades.

So swift, so unexpected was the attack that the second man also released his hold, and the next moment the Winged Man had regained his feet.

"You—you do this for me?" he asked, fixing his eyes upon the Man with the Scar.

Black Jake shifted his feet uneasily.

"Perhaps I am a bit of a fool! Anyhow, I may be a bad 'un, but I plays the game!" he replied sullenly.

Almost ere the reply had left Black Jake's lips the Winged Man had shot like a rocket into the air. So sudden and unexpected was his flight that two warders, who had rushed forward to seize him, came in a violent collision, and rolled on the flagstones, to the delight of the grinning convicts.

Once more the Winged Man had escaped, but had left Black Jake to bear the brunt of his gallant rescue.

An Interrupted Interview.

The Man With the Scar was standing where the Winged Man had left him, gazing at the clump of chimneys beyond which the flying being had disappeared, a look of utter disgust on his face, when three warders flung themselves upon him, and with blows and kicks bore him to the ground.

With loud shouts of rage, the convicts stepped forward to the rescue of their comrade, but only to recoil from before the warders' threatening rifles.

Uttering terrible exclamations of rage and despair, Black Jake was dragged to his feet, handcuffed, and escorted by a brace of warders towards the punishment cell.

Their prisoner was unarmed and handcuffed, yet, furious at the escape of the Winged Man, the warders, whom he had robbed of the anticipated reward, clapped a broad leather belt, to which was attached a pair of iron staples that encircled his arms, round his waist.

Opening the door of a dark punishment cell, they shoved him in headlong. Unable to protect himself in any way, Black Jake's face came in violent collision with the opposite wall. Terrified by the pain and the darkness, the Man With the Scar cried to the warders to return.

The clanging of a heavy iron door, a brutal, mocking laugh, was the sole reply to his appeal.

*

Three hours later, a wet, mud-bedaubed, bedraggled procession, in torn uniforms, entered the prison gate.

Foremost of all marched the governor, his brow black as thunder, more determined than ever to try conclusions once more with the Winged Man.

Heavy news met him. Despite the Winged Man's assistance, the revolt of the convicts had not been put down without loss.

Two warders and seven convicts lay seriously wounded in the prison infirmary.

Nor was that the worst. The Winged Man, who had misled him, duped him, fooled him, and had got the better of him in every way, was still at liberty.

Yet, owing to the great assistance he had rendered the warders, the governor felt reluctant to proceed against him further.

In calmer moments he might have allowed the dictates of gratitude to prevail; but he had been made a laughing-stock before his men, and that is an injury no one in authority can afford to give.

At the first outbreak of the mutiny a warder had telegraphed to the nearest garrison town for reinforcements, and shortly after the governor's return a company of infantry arrived and bivouacked in the prison yard.

It was a strange tale Colonel Grimshank had to tell Captain Steel, the officer in command of the soldiers—a tale which brought an incredulous smile to the captain's lips.

"Then, Colonel Grimshank, I am to believe, on the unimpeachable authority of your word, that the Winged Man really exists?" asked the officer.

"Twenty-four hours ago I would not have believed my own brother had he told me what I have just narrated. I have not only seen this weird, this fearful being, but I have experienced his power," returned the governor solemnly.

Captain Steel, of the Newshire Regiment, looked in bewilderment at the speaker.

"If that is so—and I feel sure now that this weird being has an actual existence—it behoves us to strain every nerve to capture or destroy the Winged Man," he said impressively.

"You are right," admitted the governor. "So far as we know, he is alone at present; but he has solved the secret of aerial flight. Soon he will gather other scoundrels as evil as himself to his side, and the whole of England will be at their mercy. Yet, to give the fellow his due, he is not entirely against law and order. Without him, the warders I had left in charge of the prison would have been massacred to a man, and three hundred of the worst scoundrels I have ever had under my charge would have let been let loose upon the country. Therefore, I am glad you have come. With a clear conscience I can leave the pursuit to you."

Captain Steel looked rather blank at this.

"That is all very well, but my men are infantry, not aeronauts," he objected. "We'll deal with him if he comes to earth, but we cannot follow him through the air. Where is he now?"

"The Winged Man is here!"

The voice came from the top left-hand corner of the large room in which the above conversation had taken place, and there, clinging to the wall like a spider, his white, livid face turned mockingly upon Colonel Grimshank and Captain Steel, hung the Winged Man.

For several minutes the governor and captain stood gazing in speechless amazement at the weird, unearthly form.

"The Winged Man is here!" repeated the awful apparition. "Come, your courtyard is full of soldiers, warders guard every door and wall! Seize me, if you can!"

Still neither man spoke. Releasing his hold of the wall, the Winged Man alighted, and, folding his arms, regard them with a look of amused contempt.

"Well, the Winged Man is here!" he repeated. "Call in your soldiers. Take him, if you can!"

With a low, fierce cry of fury, Captain Steel drew his sword, and lunged fiercely at the strange being.

It was a shrewd thrust, aimed straight for the centre of the breast, yet the Winged Man scarce reeled beneath the blow; but the highly-tempered steel bent, then broke in half, upon his bullet-proof breastplate.

"Aha, aho!" came a chilling, mocking laugh from the Winged Man's lips. "Steel cannot touch me, neither can bullets harm!" he cried, as, stepping back, the captain looked from the hilt of his broken sword to the being who, indeed, seemed impervious to shot or steel alike.

"Colonel Grimshank, you have been my guest, now I am yours. Have you nothing to say—no word of greeting or farewell to give?" continued the Winged Man, addressing the governor.

"Neither; but go!" was the tremulous reply. "Thanks to you, the mutiny, which but for you would never have taken place, has been quelled. I owe you consideration for that; otherwise you should never leave this place alive!"

"Thanks for your clemency!" retorted the Winged Man, with a laugh. "I go; but remember, he whom his comrades know as Black Jake must be set at liberty to-morrow morning. Obey, and all will be well. Refuse, and the world shall learn how the Winged Man pays his debts!"

Sweeping the two men aside, the Winged Man strode down the long corridor outside the room, and, throwing open a big window, seized the thick iron bars that protected it, and bent them as easily as though they had been straws; then passing through the opening, flew over the wide expanse of wind-swept moor.

SAVED FROM THE TRIANGLE.

Captain Steel and Colonel Grimshank remained for several minutes looking into each other's white, terror-stricken features.

"Great powers!" ejaculated Captain Steel at last. "What is he—man or spirit?"

"If he was the Dread One himself, he should not save No. 842 from punishment!" declared Colonel Grimshank determinedly. "He was the ringleader in the recent mutiny; but for him the Winged Man would now be a prisoner."

Captain Steel shook his head.

"I know, Colonel Grimshank, you will do what you think right, whatever the consequences may be, yet, personally, I'd rather face a battery of enemies' artillery than incur that fearful being's wrath!" he declared emphatically.

"Not if it was your duty to do so, Captain Steel," replied the governor. "And it is my duty to punish No. 842. To-morrow morning he shall publicly receive twenty strokes of the cat."

Was it fancy, or did a deep, rolling sonorous laugh, in truth, fall upon the startled ears of the two men, causing them to look hastily around, then into each other's eyes, in which, brave though they were, each detected a lurking, latent terror.

Another day dawned over the grim, forbidding prison.

Two and two the convicts were escorted from their cells, and formed up along one side of the prison yard.

At the further end the warders not actually on duty were posted.

Opposite the convicts stood the red-coated infantry, their captain on their left flank.

At the bottom of the prison yard a wooden triangle had been erected, hanging from the top of which were two noose-ended ropes.

A deathly silence obtained on every hand, broken at last by Captain Steel giving the order:

"Load with ball-cartridge!"

A subdued murmur arose from the convicts' ranks. Why had they been summoned thither? Why were the soldiers present? Why had the order to load with ball-cartridges be given?

Uneasily they shifted from foot to foot, glancing now and again from the warders and soldiers to the iron door which gave exit from the corridor in which the dreaded punishment cells were situated.

An air of dreadful expectancy hung over the crowded prison yard.

A single tap on the drum caused all present to start nervously.

"Attention!" shouted the captain.

The next moment the iron door was flung open, and, preceded by the governor and a couple of warders, Black Jake, closely guarded, his broad-arrow-dotted jacket thrown across his bare shoulders, emerged.

Drawing a document from its blue envelope, the governor read the order of the day, which sentenced No. 842 to twenty strokes of the cat.

A look of heart-racking, unnerving terror flashed from the convict's eyes. Beneath his beetling brows he cast a swift glance upon his fellow-prisoners, and the stern, hard-set faces of warders and soldiers, then he glanced upwards.

Naught but the cloud-dotted sky met his gaze, and, with hard-set face, he moved slowly towards the fearful triangle.

A low-voiced order from the governor, and a burly warder bared his arms, and removed from a black-cloth case, hanging to one of the supports of the triangle, the cat-o'-nine-tails, the many lashes of which he ran through his fingers.

At a touch from one of the warders Black Jake started; then, without a word, took his stand before the triangle.

With evident unwillingness a warder secured the ropes round the prisoner's wrists, whilst a second warder removed the convict's coat from his bare shoulders.

Swinging his cruel scourge, the warder looked towards the governor. For a moment Colonel Grimshank hesitated.

It went against the grain of us to reduce a fellow-creature to the level of a disobedient beast. Yet discipline must be maintained. It was his duty to carry out the sentence the prison regulations ordered should be the lot of a man who lifted his hand against a warder.

Setting his teeth, the governor lifted his hand.

Immediately the many-thronged whip was whirled above the convict's head. But even as it hissed through the air a missile struck the flagstones in the prison yard.

A loud explosion, and them next moment convicts, warders, and soldiers alike reeled back with a fearful, pungent odour, which made all who inhaled it staggered back, sick and faint, and which ascended from the fallen bomb.

Then those who were not too terrified to look saw a dark form dropped like a stone to the side of the prisoner, caught a brief glimpse of flashing steel as the weird form cut Black Jake loose from the triangle, and the next moment, borne upwards in the grasp of the Winged Man, Black Jake was snatched up from beneath the governor's very nose.

Cries of terror and howls of fear arose as the Winged Man, bearing the rescued convict in his arms, flew over the prison wall; then, with long, sweeping beats of his huge black pinions, vanished in the clouds over the distant sea.

IN THE WATER TOWER.

Endowed with almost superhuman strength though he was, the Winged Man found Black Jake no lightweight. Yet his mighty pinions forced him swiftly onwards, each long, sweeping beat carrying him nearer the distant sea.

Already the sonorous boom of the alarm gun had aroused the country-side. Once more men on horseback and on foot, armed guards and civilians, each eager to earn the reward offered for the recapture of the escaped convict, were afoot scouring the country-side.

Beaten, crushed, terrified, subdued, the Man with the Scar hung limp and helpless in his weird rescuer's arms.

Black Jake's eyes were tightly closed.

Once he had ventured to look down, but the sight of the earth gliding by so far beneath had struck such awful terror into his heart that he did not dare to repeat the experiment.

Poised on outstretched wings, the Winged Man flew in a circle whilst he looked around for some place of rest.

Upon some rising ground three miles ahead he saw a large mansion.

A glance in the direction of the prison, now lost in the distance, disclosed a number of tiny dark specks, which the Winged Man knew to be horsemen spurring over the plain.

Unburdened by the convict's weight, the Winged Man would have laughed pursuit to scorn; but, laden as he was, it would be impossible to reach the sea ahead of his pursuers.

Not for a moment did the idea of abandoning the man he had rescued enter his head.

Whatever his motive, Black Jake had come to his assistance when in peril, and the Winged Man no more forgot a service rendered then he did insult offered or injury received.

Once more resuming his flight, the Winged Man mounted higher and higher. He rose until he appeared to the astonished eyes of the spectators but a mere speck in the distance.

As the rarefied air ten thousand feet above the earth's surface was reached, Black Jake opened his eyes. A wild, piercing shriek of intense dread burst from his lips.

"Fear nothing. You are as safe as though on the solid ground," declared the Winged Man reassuringly.

"Release me! Let me go to my death! Every moment at this awful height is unendurable agony! If I rendered you a service in the prison, repay me by the boon of immediate death," pleaded the fear-maddened man.

Loud laughed the Winged Man.

"Whose dog are you?" he demanded, in deep, thunderous tones.

"Yours, sir," came in trembling accents from the white lips of the Man with the Scar.

"Then obey. Hold your tongue, and fear nothing," commanded his captor.

Poised on outstretched wings, the Winged Man measured the distance between the castle and the spot in the sunlit heavens where he hovered.

Then, with a suddenness which brought a shuddering moan from Black Jake's lips, he sped head downwards in a slanting direction towards a large, square-turreted tower which rose high above the house to which he directed his flight.

A loud, piercing cry of fear burst from the convict's lips.

A faint tinge of colour upon his pale face, his eyes flashing brightly with excitement, the Winged Man enjoyed this lightning-like glissade through the air, the more because of the terror which chilled his companion's heart.

Wild adventure, hairbreadth escapes were to the Winged Man as the very breath of life. To snatch a victim from the authorities, to beat, baffled, and to defy them, was the greatest joy this strange, weird, unearthly being could enjoy.

Even as, on outstretched pinions, he dropped from the dizzy height to which he had flown, his pursuers clattered over the gravel drive leading to the mansion immediately beneath him.

Already the inmates of the house were alarmed. Male and female servants, Sir Jasper Canby and his guests, hastened on to the lawn in front of the house to watch the terrible black figure, that like some ill-omened bird of prey was sweeping earthwards.

Soon the Winged Man's fearful form and white, pallid face—the limp, motionless body of the convict dangling from his iron auxiliary arms—flashed into full view.

So fearful, even in broad daylight, was the apparition, that strong men turned pale, women sank fainting to the ground.

His unconscious wife lying in his arms, so Jasper Canby turned to face the foremost horseman just as the Winged Man landed on the summit of the large, square water-tower.

"What is it?" was the question which arose from his pale lips.

A Dragoon, one of a squad who had been hastily summoned to join in the pursuit, saluted.

"It is the Winged Man, Sir Jasper. He has been playing pranks at the prison, and has carried away one of the convicts. But he cannot escape us now. We have received orders to capture him dead or alive!"

Perched on the coping-stone at one corner of the tower, the Dragoon's words were carried to the Winged Man's ears.

A shadow shook every frame as a wild, weird, nerve-chilling yell, in which was a note of defiance, fell upon the listeners' ears.

Swift as lightning, the Dragoon drew his carbine from its bucket, clapped it to his shoulder, and pulled the trigger.

With a wild, despairing cry the Winged Man sprang a dozen feet into the air, then disappeared from view behind the tower's wide stone parapet.

"Well done, Trooper! You shall be the richer by a five-pound note if you have winged him!" panted Colonel Grimshank, as he reigned in his horse by the Dragoon's side.

Then he turned to Sir Jasper Canby.

"The Winged Man has fallen upon your water-tower, Sir Jasper. Is the tank full?" he asked.

"It is supplied by an artesian well,[26] and fills automatically," was the reply.

"Good! Then have I your permission to enter and secure this flying demon?"

"Certainly, Colonel," returned the baronet. "With your permission, I will lead the way."

Ordering his warders, revolvers in hand, to accompany him, Colonel Grimshank followed Sir Jasper through the entrance hall to a square room at the base of the tower.

FACE TO FACE.

A revolver in his left hand, his sword in his right, Colonel Grimshank thrust his way past the baronet, eager to be the first to lay hands upon the Winged Man.

Higher and higher up the winding stair leading to the summit of the tower they mounted, the warders following two and two behind their dauntless old leader, until when within the smaller chamber immediately beneath the tank, all were brought to a standstill by a deep, sonorous order to halt.

They looked around, but could see no one.

"It must be at the Winged Man who spoke," whispered Sir Jasper Canby.

It was his first encounter with the Winged Man, yet already the strange awe which with which all regarded that terrible creature was turning the blood in his veins to ice.

"It was the Winged Man," came from somewhere immediately above their heads. "What seek ye with him?"

"That you will know if once again I get within shot or sword-thrust of you!" shouted Colonel Grimshank fiercely.

A mocking laugh answered the threat.

"The time for my alightment has come! Behold!" came back the ominous answer.

Glancing upwards at the tank immediately above his head, the veteran governor uttered an ejaculation of amazement, for, glowering upon him from the bottom of the tank that formed the roof of the small room into which the armed party had crowded, he seemed to see the white, mocking, threatening face of the Winged Man.

Awed, yet unconquered, Colonel Grimshank raised his pistol until its muzzle was within some eighteen inches of that fearful face, and pulled the trigger.

The loud, a reverberating report of the exploding weapon was succeeded by a deep, sullen roar, as, fired by the concussion of the bullet, a bomb fastened by the Winged Man to the bottom of the tank exploded, tearing a huge, gaping wound in the tank, through which a torrent of water rushed in a fierce, resistless flood.

Down it poured, straight upon so Jasper Canby, the governor, and the warders, an irresistible, apparently unending cascade.

---

[26] A well from which water flows without the need for pumping.

Uttering wild shouts of terror, officers and men alike made for the staircase.

Too late! The flood was already upon them, and, borne off their feet, they were carried, struggling, shouting heap of humanity to the bottom of the tower, where they lay, a confused mass of writhing bodies and madly-waving legs and arms.

By chance the door of the small room in the base of the tower was closed, and the water, unable to find an outlet, rose with fearful rapidity, threatening to drown the wet and draggled men beneath its surging flood.

Suddenly all cries were hushed, as what looked like a huge, round ball, floating like a cork on the surface of the foaming water, was swept into the room.

Opening, it disclosed to their terror-stricken gaze the fearful form of the Winged Man.

"Fools, to think to capture one who is unconquerable, invincible! Even now you are at my mercy; but the Winged Man seeks not your lives."

As he spoke the King of Mystery seized the handle of the door and pulled it open, despite the enormous weight of water against it, just as, alarmed by the cries of the attacking-party, a number of their comrades rushed to the rescue.

The water, tearing through the handsomely-furnished hall, bore the new-comers off their feet, and, sweeping by, left them wet, draggled, and humiliated, on the floor.

A deep cut in his forehead, Colonel Grimshank rose to his feet.

"The Winged Man—where is he?" he cried, looking wildly around.

None could say, for the moment he had opened the door the Winged Man had disappeared.

Rushing out of the house, the governor demanded of those on guard without if they had seen the Winged Man pass.

"He has not been this way, sir," declared a warder, looking in astonishment at the wet, dragged figure of his chief.

"Then he must have retreated up the water-tower. Follow me!" cried Colonel Grimshank.

Disaster, defeat, humiliation only made him more determined than ever to wreak his vengeance upon the Winged Man. No one responded to his call. Sir Jasper was stretched upon a sodden couch with a broken leg, and the warders were too thoroughly frightened to volunteer.

"What? Will none accompany me? Then I go alone!" cried the brave old man.

And, scorning further comment he retraced his steps up the stairs down which he had been hurled so ignominiously a few minutes ago.

Five minutes went by, yet no sound came from above. Those who had refused to accompany their chief looked shamefacedly at each other. Another five minutes of breathless anxiety, then Sir Jasper struggled from off the couch.

"Some accident has befallen the governor. If none of you fellows dare go to seek him I will go myself, though I have to crawl up the sodden steps upon two hands and a knee," he declared.

Shamed by the contempt in the baronet's tones, the warders moved in a body towards the stairs. They were no cowards. Ten times their number of human beings would not have pulled them, but what could mortal man do against one so wondrously endowed as the Winged Man? It was tempting Fate to pit their puny strength against that awful being.

In fear and trembling, the warders mounted the stairs, expecting every moment to be confronted by that fearful being whom steel could not touch nor bullets pierce. At last they stood in the tiny compartment beneath the tank.

"Colonel Grimshank! Are you here, sir?" shouted a warder, after a few minutes' hesitation.

A low, indistinct murmur from above responded to his call.

Close at hand a ladder of iron bars, driven into the wall, led to the tank that occupied almost the whole of the roof of the water-tower. Forcing his way upwards, the warder who had last spoken stood on the narrow leads that surrounded the enormous tank. The wooden trap door that gave access to the interior of the tank was open. Cautiously he peeped within, then sprang into the tank.

Lying bound and gagged in the bottom of the iron receptacle was a figure clad in convict's garb. Visions of the reward he could claim floated before the warder's eyes.

"Got you, No. 842!" he cried bending down over the prostrate figure. Then the note of triumph died from his voice.

Lying gagged and bound, his limbs encased in the hideous grey, marked with broad arrows, was the governor of the prison.

Raising his superior in his arms, the warder thrust him through the opening where he was seized by a comrade, who rapidly released his chief.

"Quick! The Winged Man and No. 842 are hidden behind the tank!" cried Colonel Grimshank, as soon as he could speak. "Courage, lads! He is only human, after all. Seize him!"

Encouraged by the gallant old chief's words, four warders dashed round the tank. Disappointment awaited them. There was not a hole or cranny in which even a wounded sparrow could have hidden or escaped, yet no sign of the two they sought met their gaze.

°THE CAVE BY THE SEA

Loud cries of astonishment and dismay from below caused them to rush to the parapet and looked down. They were just in time to see the Winged Man emerged from the window on the first floor, and, with Black Jake clinging tightly to his neck, spring on to the governor's horse. The frightened stable-boy holding the reins released his hold.

Peal upon peal of mocking laughter bursting from his lips, the Winged Man drummed his heels into the frightened horse's side, and charged straight towards

---

° 1 MARCH 1913.

where some half a dozen warders lined a low wall at the bottom of the magnificently-kept lawn.

An irregular fire greeted the Winged Man, but every bullet flew wide of its mark. Raising his horse to jump with a masterly touch of the rein and heel, the Winged Man cleared warders and wall with a good twelve inches to spare. Now came a mad rush down hill, which, despite his double burden, the horse performed in safety.

"Hurrah! We have beaten them! I said I would save you, Black Jake, and I have done so!" cried the Winged Man triumphantly.

Black Jake, clinging desperately to the Winged Man, did not share his weird companion's triumph.

"Speak, man! Has it not been a glorious struggle against overwhelming odds?" demanded the Winged Man.

"Yes, sir, certainly, sir," came from between the ex-convict's chattering teeth. "But if it's all the same to you, please don't do it again."

"Bah! You cowardly cur, I doubt if you were worth the trouble of saving, after all!" retorted the Winged Man contemptuously.

A minute later an ejaculation of anger burst from his lips.

Dashing from a wood a cavalry patrol was riding its hardest to cut off the Winged Man's retreat to the sea. For ten minutes the soldiers hung closely on the Winged Man's heels; then, finding that they were losing ground, they dismounted and opened fire upon both horse and man as they dashed by, some fifty yards away.

A bullet sent the stolen governor's cap whirling from Black Jake's head; a second raised the horse's flank; a third, too truly aimed, struck the noble beast just behind the ear, and, springing into the air like a wounded rabbit, he rolled on the ground.

A shout of triumph from the soldiers hailed the shot; but it died away ere it found utterance, for, borne aloft on his sable pinions, the Winged Man skimmed lightly over the ground; then, rising, continued his flight towards a precipitous cliff which overhung the sea a mile ahead. Remounting, the patrol resumed the chase.

The edge of the cliff reached, the Man with the Scar looked apprehensively down to where the sea was beating fiercely upon the iron-bound rock more than three hundred feet beneath.

"Where are you taking me, sir? We'll be drowned. You cannot fly across the Atlantic."

"Whose dog are you?" demanded the Winged Man once more.

And, moistening his parched lips with his tongue, Black Jake held his peace.

On they flew until the jagged rocks rising above the surf had been left behind. Then a cry of terror from Black Jake's lips was echoed by shouts of amazement and horror from the soldiers lining the top of the cliff; for, enfolding his companion in his wings, the Winged Man fell like a stone towards the sea.

Down he went—down and down, until at last, with a deep, sullen splash, he disappeared beneath the waves.

"Come on, lads! He must come ashore somewhere. Unless he is as much of a fish as he seems a bird, we'll have him!" cried the corporal, leading the way down a rugged path that descended the cliff.

With carbines at the ready, the soldiers followed the corporal, reaching the base of the cliff just in time to see the Winged Man and Black Jake disappear into a narrow opening in the base of the cliff.

Half a dozen bullets flattened themselves against the rocky wall of the cave; but the Winged Man seemed to bear a charmed life.

"What are you going to do, corporal? Go in after him?" asked a trooper, with an uneasy laugh, as the soldiers came to a halt twenty yards from the entrance to the cave.

"Not much!" returned the corporal decidedly. "Go back and ask for orders, Denning. We'll see that he doesn't leave the cave."

Wheeling round, Denning had covered half the distance up the cliff, when Colonel Grimshank, pale and worn, but as determined as ever, appeared upon the scene.

"Where is he? Where is the Winged Man?" he demanded breathlessly.

"In yonder cave, sir. The corporal will see that he doesn't get out," explained the trooper.

"But we can't wait till he chooses to reappear. I, for one, am going in to haul him forth, if I have to do it with my naked hands!" declared the colonel emphatically.

"I don't think you will, sir, if I may be so bold as to say so," said a voice at his elbow.

And, looking round, he saw an old fisherman, summoned on the scene by the firing, standing beside him.

"Why not?" demanded the governor irascibly.

"'Because there won't be no need. The tide is coming in," was the reply.

It was true. Already the rising tide was driving the soldiers from before the cave.

Colonel Grimshank took in the situation at a glance. In a few minutes now the mouth of the cave would be covered, then the Winged Man must either come out or perish miserably within the rock.

Soon, in response to Colonel Grimshank's orders, warders and soldiers lined the base of the cliffs, their rifles pointed straight towards the half-covered mouth of the cave. In vain they waited, expecting each moment to see the dark, weird form of the Winged Man emerge.

Not a report from within showed that aught was moving in the cave. Higher and higher mounted the waves, until at last the low opening was completely closed.

"Poor souls! Poor souls! They'll never leave that place alive!" cried the fisherman compassionately. "They won't be the first, by a long way, who have been caught in that death-trap. Only last summer a couple of children took refuge in there from a storm, and were drowned."

"Is there no exit?" asked the colonel.

"'Tain't likely. Why, that cave is a good three hundred feet underground," replied the fisherman.

"Well, well, perhaps it is better so. They would have had scant mercy when we captured them," declared the governor, unable to repress a feeling of disappointment that he himself had not had a hand in the Winged Man's destruction.

CUT OFF FROM HIS KIND.

The fisherman's sympathy had been misplaced. The Winged Man would never have entered that cave had he not been assured of escape. Not so Black Jake. As the waters poured through the mouth of the cave he would have fled, but the Winged Man held him fast.

"Move at your peril!" thundered the Winged Man, pressing the Man with the Scar against the rocky wall of the cave.

Reaching up to the lower roof of the cave, the Winged Man released a large object from the iron hooks that secured it, and a raft fell with a splash into the water.

Shuddering, Black Jake, in obedience to a sign from his captor, clambered upon the raft which floated immediately beneath a chimney-like shaft directly above their heads. As the tide rose it carried the raft and its two occupants upwards, until they reached an upper cave lighted by a crack in the face of the cliff.

Without a word the Winged Man signed to the Man with the Scar to land. He did so in fear and trembling. On one side of the cave was a ship's bunk, torn complete from some sunken vessel. On either side of the bunk were curtains of seaweed. Shells formed a carpet for the floor. The walls were ornamented with stuffed and dried sea monsters.

Here, as though about to enfold them, was an enormous stuffed octopus. Hanging from the ceiling, as though floating in its native element, was a dried sunfish. Huge crabs peered through crevices in the rocky wall. Enormous sea-snakes wound their slimy lengths over the projecting crags.

Obedient to the Winged Man's whim, Ghat had transformed the cave into a miniature mermaid's haunt.

Scarce believing but that the things he saw were alive, the Man with the Scar seemed to shrink into half his former size. Suddenly he started, and looked fearfully at the Winged Man, as that weird being thundered at him the oft repeated question:

"Whose dog are you?"

"Yours—yours!" came in a gasping cry from Black Jake's lips.

"From your own lips your doom is pronounced," came in a sonorous roll from the Winged Man's lips. "Body and soul you are mine; your whole being is mine. Henceforth you shall live as I command, die when I order. Kneel!"

Trembling violently, the wretched man sank upon his knees.

"Lower, dog—lower! Crouch at my feet!" commanded the Winged Man.

Subdued, robbed of all power to resist, the Man with the Scar prostrated himself at the Winged Man's feet, his head upon his outstretched arms.

For a moment the Winged Man stood gazing with a look of unutterable contempt upon the writhing form at his feet. Suddenly he bade him rise with a contemptuous kick.

"Bah! Dog and slave you are; dog and slave you shall remain!" he announced. "Had you shown the slightest spark of manly spirit, reward, not punishment, would have been your portion. Listen! Nine days of the ten I sentenced you to remain unexpired. For nine days you will remain here. By that time pursuit will have slackened, and you may return to the outer world once more. But be sure of this, from henceforth you are mine. At the slightest sign, you shall be ready to obey my summons."

Black Jake moved his head slowly round, his eyes almost starting from his head, his cheeks ashen, his lips pallid, his frame shaking like a quivering aspen.

"Not alone—not in this terrible place alone!" came in agonised appeal from his lips.

"Alone; for such is my will," was the inexorable reply.

Disdaining further discussion, the Winged Man led his prisoner from store-room to store-room, showing him ample food and drink to have lasted twenty men the time of Black Jake's incarceration; then, as the raft began to sink as the tide went, the Winged Man moved towards it.

"No, no! If you have a grain of mercy you will not leave me here alone!" pleaded Black Jake.

Beside himself with terror, he grasped the Winged Man's hand. As though the suppliant was some obnoxious reptile, the Winged Man cast him off.

"Whose dog are you?" he demanded; his awful tones echoing and re-echoing through the vaulted roof.

"Yours, but—" began Black Jake; when the Winged Man, turning fiercely upon him, cried:

"Then obey, or expect a dog's doom!"

So fierce the gesture, so threatening the look which accompanied these words, that Black Jake recoiled to the further end of the cave and crouched on the floor, well-nigh mad with fear; whilst, motionless as a statue, the Winged Man stood on the centre of the raft, his arms folded, his glowing eyes fixed upon his prisoner, while the raft sank lower and lower.

Twice Black Jake strove to move forward, intent upon jumping upon the raft, no matter what the consequences to himself might be; but each time terror of the weird, unearthly being into whose power he had fallen prevented him.

But when naught but the Winged Man's face remained above the level of the cave's floor, fear of being alone over mastered his awe-stricken terror, and, with a loud, appealing cry, he sprang forward. Even as he did so a loud, rushing noise, followed by a ringing, metallic clang, filled the cave, as an iron shutter, dropping from the roof, cut him off entirely from the only entrance to the Winged Man's wondrous lair.

Beside himself with terror, the Man with the Scar drummed upon the iron plate, shrieking, yelling, imploring to be let out, in turn. In vain; not a sound answered his appealing cry. He was alone, cut off from his kind by an impenetrable barrier of rock and iron.

With a deep sigh, the Man with the Scar reeled back against the wall. The next moment he had sprung forward with an exclamation of horror. A fearful cold hand had touched him on the back of his neck. Fearfully he glanced over his shoulder, then stood as though turned to stone, gazing at the hideous form of the octopus, against one of the feelers of which he had inadvertently leaned.

Trembling with terror, Black Jake stood staring at the octopus.

Trembling, he retreated and stood with his back to the iron shutter, his groping fingers clawing at its rivets, his eyes fixed upon the octopus until it seemed as if the dead monster was advancing slowly, stealthily, irresistibly upon him.

For nearly five minutes he remained confronting that unspeakable horror. Slowly his courage returned when he realised that the Winged Man had spoken truly, and that the monsters by which he was surrounded were unable to harm him.

Staggering like a drunken man, the Man with the Scar made his way to a cupboard in a small cave set apart for a larder. Seizing the first bottle he came to, he knocked the neck off against the wall. Careless of cut lips, he put the jagged glass to his mouth and drank deeply of the contents. The ardent spirit, which at any other time would have rendered him hopelessly intoxicated, served only to infuse fresh courage into his heart, and he was enabled to examine the succession of caves which would be his home for so many days.

On their tour through the caves the Winged Man had pointed to one door through which Black Jake might not pass. Two or three times the Man with the Scar approached it. Beyond it, perhaps, lay liberty, and the blessed light of the sun! Yet he dare not disobey the Winged Man's explicit command.

As hour succeeded hour a burning curiosity, an overpowering desire to escape, drew him once more to the fatal door. His hand upon the door-latch, the Man with the Scar stood irresolute for some minutes. At length, pulling himself together with a mighty effort, he flung the door wide open. A breath of cool, fresh air fanned his heated brow.

Beyond lay freedom. Yet the Man with the Scar took no forward step. He stood as though turned to stone, his foot half lifted, his body inclined slightly forward, his hands raised to a level with his shoulders, a look of abject, nerve-shattering terror upon his face. His eyes fixed in a stony stare, as well they might, for of all the horrid spectacles he had seen, that before him was the most awful, the most terrible!

A darkness which could almost be felt lay before the Man with the Scar, from the centre of which appeared a white, glistening skull, rendered doubly hideous by a pair of fearful, crimson eyes.

Even as Black Jake gazed, the skull moved grotesquely from side to side, then opened and closed its freshness jaws; whilst, like a lurid tongue, a spear of flame shot from between its teeth. With a low, shuddering moan Black Jake dropped unconscious upon the floor of the cave.

FOOLED BY DEATH.

About the time that Black Jake first approached the forbidden door, Colonel Grimshank, Captain Steel, and a body of warders descended the rock on the brink of the outgoing tide, and rushed to the entrance of the cave.

Every man stood, revolver and rifle advanced, ready to fire directly the Winged Man appeared.

Lower and lower sank the tide, until at last but some two feet of salt water remained beneath the dome-shaped entrance to the cave.

Turning took Colonel Grimshank, Captain Steele had just suggested an advance into the dread opening before them, when a cry of astonishment, triumph, and awe burst from the watchers. Borne swiftly towards them by the out flowing tide came a dark, huddled mass of clothes, from whence protruded a pair of strangely-shaped feet, and two limp, life-less, white hands.

"It is the Winged Man!" cried Colonel Grimshank. "Imprisoned in the cave by the rising tide, he has been drowned," he added, pointing with trembling hands to wear, its further progress checked by a piece of wave-worn stone, the Winged Man's body rose and fell to the gentle movement of the waves, some six feet from the entrance to the cave.

Yes, it was certainly their dread foe. Bullet nor steel could touch him, but the mighty ocean had done what man could not achieve. The Winged Man was dead.

There he lay, powerless to wreak further mischief. His wild, fearful course was run.

Several minutes elapsed ere any present ventured to approach.

Moved by a common impulse, both Captain Steel and Colonel Grimshank stepped forward. Grasping the prostrate figure by the arm, the former rolled it over on to its back.

His shoulder resting against upon a piece of rock, the black-capped head had fallen back, disclosing a white, colourless neck, open almost to the chest.

Fearful though he looked in life, the Winged Man appeared even more terrible now.

Water glistened on his white, pallid face, his eyes were fixed in a stony stare, his lips were parted in a snarling grin of defiance, that showed his white teeth, his long, thin, attenuated body, crossed and recrossed by countless straps, which looked strangely like the narrow bands with which the ancients bound their dead.

A solemn hush fell upon the spectators. Awe and wonder filled the hearts.

Reverently Captain Steel removed his cap, those standing round followed his example—all save Colonel Grimshank, and he was looking at the Human Bat's face, a troubled look of awakening recognition in his eyes.

Suddenly the governor dropped upon his knees by the side of the still, motionless figure.

Bending down, so that none could follow his actions, he drew aside the bottom of the tight-fitting heard which enveloped the Winged Man's head and shoulders. A strangely-shaped, red mark met his gaze. As one in a dream, he rose to his feet.

"It is he," came an involuntary whisper from his lips.

"Who? Do you know him?" asked Captain Steel looking at his friend's white face with a way amazement.

"Yes, yes!" returned Colonel Grimshank. "I thought when first I saw that fearful face I had known him in the past. May his body rest in the peace he has never known on earth! Greatest of a great race, there lies all that is left of—"

Loud cries of amazement and horror drowned the conclusion of a sentence which might have told so much, for the Winged Man had risen to his feet.

"Silence! By the memory of the past, I command your silence! Betray not the secrets of the grave!" came in loud, sonorous awe-inspiring tones from the Winged Man's lips.

Then, with a gesture of inexpressible dignity and command, the Winged Man rose in the air, and propelled by long, slow sweeps of his mighty pinions, soared above the heads of the astonished crowd.

"He has fooled us! Fire! Bring him down at any cost!" cried Captain Steel, awakening from the stupor of amazement into which the strange events which had just taken place had thrown him.

A score of rifles were clapped to as many shoulders; but, ere a trigger could be pulled, the Winged Man, dwindling as he soared into the clear, cloudless heavens, disappeared from their ken.

GHAT'S ASSISTANT.

The ninth day of Black Jake's incarceration—the day on which the Winged Man had promised him escape from the tide-bound cave—had come.

A man of greater intelligence, and stronger imagination, would have been driven mad by this the horrors that surrounded him, but Black Jake had almost grown accustomed to his strange surroundings, and by the time the day of his liberation arrived, perfect rest and good food had improved him, both in body and mind.

It is true that, now and again, he had glanced with a shudder at the forbidden door, but never again did he risk facing the horror which lay beyond its threshold.

As to the dried monsters, etc., by which he was surrounded, the Man with the Scar had scarcely given them a single thought after the first scare.

Tired of watching the ships pass by, through the fissure in the rock that lighted the cave, Black Jake had just turned to a table, strewn with the remains of many feasts, in the centre of the cave, when he started violently, as a loud knocking reverberated through the cave.

He was clad in a blue serge suit, from the Winged Man's store, his hair had grown, and he had no fear of detection if once he got clear from the immediate neighbourhood of the prison, yet his first thought was that the warders had at length discovered his retreat.

His next—and his hair began to rise on end—that the Winged Man had returned.

The knocking was repeated.

Whence came it? Hastening to the iron shutters which protected the shaft leading to the lower cave, he demanded:

"Who is there?"

Even as he spoke, the sound was repeated to his right.

Turning, he moved wonderingly towards the innermost part of the cave.

Again he started, again a tremor shook his frame. More impatient than before—angry, prolonged, insistent—the knocking fell like the boom of a passing bell on his ear.

The sounds came from behind the forbidden door. Motionless, terrified, the Man with the Scar stood staring at the fatal portal.

Again the knocking was resumed, accompanied by a violent shaking of the door. Screwing up his courage to the sticking-point, Black Jake drew near the door.

"Who is there?" he demanded at length.

"Oh, you're alive, are you?" came in muffled tones to his ear. "Open! I bear a message from the Winged Man!"

A moment's hesitation, and, turning the key in the lock, the Man with the Scar flung the door open. As he did so, he staggered back with a cry of dismay.

Standing on the threshold was the most extraordinary figure he had ever seen. So ugly, so squat, so fearful to gaze upon was the new-comer, that Black Jake could but believe him to be a being from another world.

It was the Winged Man's misshapen servitor.

"Well, what are you looking at? Admiring my beauty—eh?" came in mocking tones from Ghat's lips.

"Who are you? Whence do you come?" demanded the Man with the Scar.

"I am Ghat, the Winged Man's confident, friend, and slave," was the reply. "I have been sent to summon you to your toil. Disobey me at your peril!"

Black Jake laughed loud and long.

"Obey you! A thing like you!" he cried contemptuously.

"Yes, and keep a civil tongue in your head, or it will be the worse for you!" returned Ghat fiercely.

For answer, the Man with the Scar shot out a brawny fist, and, seizing the dwarf by his long, shaggy beard, pulled him mercilessly backwards and forwards.

Taken by surprise, the dwarf could not resist at first; but when he did Black Jake received the surprise of his life.

His first intimation that he had undertaken a larger contract than he could fulfil was Ghat's fist, planted scientifically between the eyes. He staggered back.

For the next few minutes the Man with the Scar had a confused vision of a too broad body, on short, misshapen legs, and a pair of long, muscular arms, whirling before his eyes, striking over his guard and through his guard, blows which it was impossible to ward off.

At length—bruised, bleeding, conquered—he lay, howling for mercy, on the floor.

Springing on to the back of a large stuffed crocodile that swung from the roof, at a bound the Winged Man himself might have envied, Ghat leered contemptuously upon his beaten foe.

"Get up!" snarled Ghat at last.

The Man with the Scar rolled on to his hands and knees, then raised himself painfully to his feet. A sullen frown darkened his bruised face.

"There's a pretty state to leave my compartment in," commented Ghat, pointing to the broken victuals on the table. "Anyone could see a pig had been living here for over a week. Set to work and clear it up! Look lively!"

"Who in thunder are you ordering about? I ain't your dog, anyhow!" growled Black Jake.

"What, not had enough of it yet? Want a little more—eh?" said Ghat. "If you're the Winged Man's dog, you're my puppy!"

"Who said so?" demanded Black Jake.

"The Winged Man," was the reply.

"Got any writing, or sign to show?" asked Black Jake.

Ghat nodded.

"Like to see it?" he asked.

The Man with the Scar made a gesture of assent.

Without a word, the leering dwarf dropped from the stuffed crocodile to the floor, then stripped to his waist.

His body was covered with a network of wounds, some old, white, and healed; others, recently inflicted—red, angry, and livid.

"That's the Winged Man's signature. He has written it on my back often enough for me to know. You'll be just as familiar with it as I am before long, my fine fellow!" promised Ghat.

"Never! I'll throttle him with my naked hands first!" hissed the man with the scar, between his clenched teeth.

With a shrill cry of rage, Ghat seized him by the throat.

"What! You would kill the Winged Man? You'd rob me of the only friend I've got in the world?" he cried, in fierce angry tones. "Oh, if my master had not need of you—if he had not work for you to do! Mind this, if there is any throttling to be done, I'll do it. I'd tear you limb from limb, and throw your body to the winds, if I dare, wretch and scoundrel that you are!"

Carried away by the paroxysm of rage, it seemed to the alarmed Jake that the dwarf intended putting his threat into execution then and there. His thick, stubby knotted fingers were pressed so deeply into Black Jake's windpipe that soon the wretched man's struggles grew faint, his face turned from ashen grey to purple, his tongue showed black through his open teeth. Reluctantly, as a tiger would leave its prey, Ghat allowed the new assistant the Winged Man had given him to drop half-unconscious to the floor.

"Oh, if my master had not taken you under his protection I'd kill you as I would any who come between the Winged Man and the only being in the world who loves him!" he panted.

A few minutes later the Man with the Scar, of his own accord, rose, and, staggering to the overladen table, commenced to clear it.

A hundred times during the next few months, whilst working for his new master under Ghat's unsleeping eye, did Black Jake wish himself back in the convicts' prison.

A thousand times did he execrate the hour in which he had rescued the Winged Man from the warders' grasp.

THE RAILWAY COLLISION.

Crouched on the bogey-engine attached to an express train, his back against the smoke-box, his eyes staring unblinkingly along the stretch of rail before him, the Winged Man was being borne along at fifty miles an hour towards Burton-on-Trent.

Lulled by the swaying of the engine, enjoying the fierce rush of the air, the Winged Man drew a diamond-studded chronometer from his pocket, and, with the aid of his brilliant headlight, looked at the time. It yet wanted eighteen minutes ere the train was due at Burton, and, confident of his power to awaken at any moment, the Winged Man closed his eyes, and dropped off to sleep.

With a rush and a roar the express dashed through a station. A signalman, his hand upon a lever with which he had just cleared the line for the express, started and rubbed his eyes in amazement, for he had caught a fleeting glance of the Winged Man's shapeless form huddled together on the engine's bogey.

A porter hailed him from the platform.

"What was it, Tom?" he demanded. "Did you see his white, fearful face, his long, bony hands?"

"Yes; some poor fellow has been caught on the line, thrown into the air, to fall back across the bogey," replied the signalman, leaning out of his window.

"No; it was the Winged Man," interposed a postman, stopping on his way to collect the mail-bags that had been thrown into the net of a catcher.

"The Winged Man!" repeated both men.

"Yes; I saw him in Leeds, and I'll never forget the sight. It was awful, fearful," replied the postman, with a shudder.

Having secured an audience, the postman launched into a long description of the Winged Man's flight across the great Midland town.

His hearers listened breathlessly. Suddenly an ejaculation of dismay burst from the signalman's lips.

"Heaven help me, I have forgotten the 10.40 local!" he cried, as, staggering to his instruments, he hurriedly gave the belated signal which should have sent the local at the next station on to a siding until the express had passed.

Adhering to the bogey-plate, all unconscious of the fearful danger which threatened the train, the Winged Man's sleeping form was carried at lightning speed over the metals. The trembling of the mighty engine, the loud, shrill blast of a whistle, the shaking caused by the hand-brakes being put hard on, as the Westinghouse was applied, a dull, crashing roar, aroused him from a dreamless slumber. He glanced ahead. Before him, almost within touch of his hand, appeared the tail-lights of a stationary train.

A moment's, nay, a fraction of a second's hesitation, and the Winged Man's wondrous career would have been brought to a fearful termination. With lightning rapidity he thrust out his long, muscular legs, and sprang upwards.

The Winged Man was but just in time. Even as he cleared the engine's chimney the mighty engine plunged into the guard's van of the slow local with a sickening crash. Splinters of wood and huge masses of iron flew in all directions. A blinding cloud of steam hid the Winged Man from view, as, hovering a dozen feet above the ground, he surveyed a scene which brought a shudder of horror even to his hardened frame.

Warned but a minute before their danger, many of the passengers from the slow local had rushed headlong on to the platform. Their flight availed them little. Ere they could reach a place of safety, the guard's van and two carriages were hurled by the force of the collision on to them.

A moment's fearful silence, then a deafening roar. The boiler of the engine had burst.

A pain-laden exclamation forced itself from the Winged Man's lips. A fountain of boiling water had been hurled upon his right hand. Yet that cry passed unheeded. All eyes were fixed upon the fearful scene that wrecked trains present.

Following close upon the explosion came loud shrieks of terror, moans of agony—above which now and again could be heard the strained, awe-stricken, yet calm, brave voice of the station-master, begging the panic-stricken people to keep calm, and issuing orders for the rescue of the imperilled passengers. It was indeed a fearful sight, one which dwelt long in the Winged Man's memory. Things which a minute before had been living men and women were scattered, dismembered, mutilated masses of humanity over the lines and platform.

Closing his eyes to shut out the fearful scene, the Winged Man flew round in a circle, then darted off towards where a number of lights proclaimed a distant village. A red light on a wrought-iron arch surmounted a large gateway showed where a doctor resided.

The Winged Man alighted at the front door of the medical man's house, and rapped furiously upon the panels, whilst at the same time he tugged at a big iron bell-pull that hung beside the door. A distant clang from somewhere within the house reached his ears.

A minute later the door opened and a tall, clean-shaven man of about forty, clad only in trousers, dressing-gown, and slippers, and holding a candle above his head, appeared on the threshold.

He started with an ejaculation of alarm as his eyes fell upon the Winged Man's forbidding face.

"Who are you? What do you want?" he demanded.

"Come!" was the only explanation the Winged Man vouchsafed.

Then, seizing the astounded man round the waist, he clasped him tightly to his breast, and, springing from the doorstep, flew, despite his heavy load, almost as swiftly as he had come, back to the scene of the disaster.

So quickly did he fly, that almost ere the doctor had recovered sufficiently to question him, they had reached the scene of the accident. Then the brave medical man forgot his fearful, unnerving experience, forgot the wonder with which he had greeted the appearance of his strange captor, forgot everything, save that before him were a number of men and women in need of help.

Strangely enough, though the Winged Man had set the doctor down in the midst of the excited crowd, scarce a voice was raised in astonishment or terror.

Death, before whom even fear of the Winged Man vanished, was gathering in a rich harvest that night. As one nail drives out another, so the fearful horror of the scene had overcome their horror of the Winged Man.

But the Winged Man did not remain amongst the crowd long. His keen eye had detected a discarded ulster and a cloth cap in one of the carriages that yet kept to the metals.

These he secured, and a few minutes later, the collar of the ulster turned up over his ears, the cloth cap drawn down over his eyes, the Winged Man forced his way through the crowd to the immediate vicinity of the piled-up carriages.

At once those seeking to rescue the injured realised that a master spirit was in their midst.

Calm, cool, decisive, the Winged Man rang out orders. Instinctively all obeyed him, as one used to command, whilst the doctor saw how skilful the strange unknown bound up the wound of this sufferer, stopped the bleeding artery of another, without for a moment withdrawing his vigilance from those whose humane endeavours he was directing.

A hundred men, each trusting to his own unaided intelligence, could not have done half so much in double the time as the forty willing workers who obeyed the Winged Man's instructions.

Nor was he content with verbal help alone. Once three men were vainly attempting to lift a huge beam of wood from off an imprisoned man when the Winged Man, moving swiftly from place to place, paused amidst them.

Without a word he seized the end of the beam, and, exerting his enormous strength to the utmost, held it until, with tender care, the rescuers had pulled the imprisoned man from his perilous position.

Again, when, working with greater energy than discretion, a porter had raised a splintered bar aside, and the whole of a third class carriage, leaning over, threatened to bury half a dozen workers beneath its enormous bulk, it was the Winged Man who sprang forward, and, checking its descent, held it as though his frame had been turned into an iron pillar until the imperilled ones were in safety.

THE WINGED MAN'S VOW.

Shortly after the accident, carts and carriages of all descriptions had arrived from the village.

Lifted into the vehicles by tender hands, the wounded were soon being despatched to the houses of the kind-hearted villagers.

For two hours the Winged Man, and those who were voluntarily obeying his commands, worked unceasingly, until at last every human being that could be saved had been rescued from peril.

A crowd standing around the flat-topped, closed-up newspaper stall attracted the Winged Man's attention. Thrusting the people aside, he looked down upon the still living, but fearfully crushed and mutilated engine-driver.

The engine-driver's face was drawn with agony, huge drops of perspiration stood upon his forehead, and from his lips came one continual cry:

"Maisie, my motherless bairn! Oh, Heaven, let me see her once more before I die!"

The doctor looked up as the Winged Man approached. His eyes were filled with tears. Used to the sight of suffering though he was, he was a father himself, and the constant cry of the engine-driver for his daughter pierced his heart.

"Poor fellow, would it be possible to bring his child to him!" he whispered.

"Do you know where he lives?" asked the Winged Man, in the same tone.

"Trenton Street, Derby," was the reply.

"Will he live an hour?" demanded the Winged Man.

The doctor shook his head.

"Impossible! Death may come at any moment!" was his verdict.

"Yet he will live to see his child!" declared the Winged Man confidently.

Bending over the dying man, he said, slowly and distinctly:

"Listen! What is it you desire most of all at the present moment?"

"To see my daughter—my golden-haired little Maisie," came in laboured accents from the dying man's lips.

"Then you shall see her! Fight against Death with all your might, with all your soul, and with all your strength. Keep him off, and Maisie shall be in your arms within an hour," promised the Winged Man.

A glad light of hope shone from the engine-driver's eyes, but died almost as quickly.

"You are a very kind, strange being. You mean well, but you can't do it. She is in Derby, and I—I am here. An express engine could not go there and back in a day," he gasped.

For a moment the Winged Man hesitated. The experiment he was about to try might have fatal results to the man he wished to serve, the shock might slay him.

Slowly he removed the cap from off his head and threw aside the borrowed ulster. The Winged Man stood revealed.

With cries of terror the crowd shrank from him. But not so the engine-driver. Again the light of hope gleamed in his eyes.

"You are the Winged Man. They speak of you as one without heart, without mercy, incapable of kindly thought towards us human beings!" he exclaimed. "But your eyes are true, your face bears the mark of great sorrows long endured. I trust you! I will live—ay, enough I know Death itself is standing over me—I will live!"

Rising from the midst of the shrinking crowd the Winged Man spread wide his pinions to the breeze, and vanished like a meteor from the gaze of the astounded spectators.

Maintaining his strength by constant sips of brandy, yet owing his grasp of life more to a dogged determination to await the Winged Man's return, the engine-driver lay, his head propped on his folded coat, careless of the almost unendurable agony he suffered, buoyed up by the hope of seeing his loved child once more before he died.

But when fifty minutes had passed, and the Winged Man had not returned, a look of anxiety crept into his glazed eyes.

"Oh, doctor, will he fail me?" he cried piteously.

"I cannot tell. I hope not. Yet this I will say. I, like yourself, saw that in his face which gave me confidence that, whatever mortal—or should I say more than mortal—man can achieve, the Winged Man will do," replied the doctor confidently.

"The Winged Man is here!"

There was a ring of triumph in the deep, sonorous announcement, as, dropping like a stone from skies lightened by the first rays of the rising sun, the Winged Man alighted by the dying man's side.

Wrapped in a blanket, shielded from the keen morning air with tender care, its head upon the Winged Man's shoulder, a lovely golden-haired child little child of about six years was sleeping as peacefully as though still in the cot from which the Winged Man had taken her.

THE WINGED MAN'S WARD.

"The Winged Man has kept his word!" ejaculated the doctor.

"Maisie dear—my own, my poor little bairn!" cried the engine-driver, holding his hands longingly towards his child.

"Dada—dada! Why are you lying there? Why am I here? What is the matter, dada? How pale and white you look!" cried the child, as, with almost womanly tenderness, the Winged Man laid her in her father's arms.

"Maisie dear, you must be brave. Be dada's own little girl! Dada is going away, Maisie! You won't forget him—promise me you won't forget him!" gasped the dying man.

The child looked up, scared, white-faced, and trembling. Her eyes met those of the Winged Man.

"Oh, dada, I can't spare you! We are all the world to each other! Don't leave me! We have been so happy, and we do love each other so!" implored the child.

And, sobbing as though her little heart was breaking, she allowed her head to drop upon her father's breast.

The engine-driver seemed unconscious of his daughter's presence; not even her soft cheek pressing his own, her golden strands falling upon his pallid face, seemed to have power to rouse him now.

Yet he heard the child's infant pleading. His eyelids had clouded over his glazing eyeballs, but, with a last flickering access of strength he clasped the child to his heart; then, struggling on to the elbow of his disengaged arm, looked appealingly, but with strange confidence at the Winged Man.

As though he read the dying man's thoughts, the Winged Man bowed his head in assent.

"Maisie, listen! Your dada must go—but—there is—one here who will watch over you—who will protect you—who will be more to you than I could ever have been!" cried the stricken father, in laboured, gasping tones.

"Sir," he added, turning to the Winged Man, "I will give my child into your keeping. As you do by her, so may Providence do by you."

"As I do by her, so may Providence do by me!" repeated the Winged Man solemnly.

Those around, moved by an impulse they could never afterwards explain, removed their hats and stood bareheaded, as though witnessing the Winged

Man's promise to the dying man.

For several minutes a deathly silence, broken only by the low sobbing of the child, obtained over that wreck bestrewn platform.

Presently the Winged Man stooped and drew a handkerchief reverently over the engine-driver's face. The end had come. His brave spirit had passed into the unknown.

Very gently the Winged Man took the child from her father's arms, and those who had only heard the Winged Man spoken of as a monster, without a single redeeming quality, noted, with amazement, how trustingly the child put its little arms round his neck, and buried its tear-stained face against his black, tight-fitting jacket.

Suddenly a man who had a moment before entered the station hastened forward. A look of surprise flashed into his face as he saw the Winged Man's burden; yet, without a moment's hesitation, he stepped to the weird being's side, and, clapping a revolver to his forehead, said:

"Winged Man, you are my prisoner!"

It was Danby Druce, the famous detective! Duty had called him to a neighbouring town. Hearing of the railway accident, he had hastened to offer his services. To his amazement, he beheld the Winged Man standing amidst a respectful and admiring crowd on the platform of the station.

He knew nothing of what had taken place; he cared nothing. All he knew was that the Winged Man was before him, and that he would not let him escape this time.

But he reckoned without the strange insight into his true nature the Winged Man had allowed the crowd to see.

With the child in his arms the Winged Man could scarcely have resisted, but help from an unexpected quarter was at hand. A huge navvy, channels where tears had flowed down his grimy cheeks, seized the detective by the hand which held the revolver.

"No, no, lad!" he cried. "I don't know who or what you are, but if ye were the Prime Minister, Scotland Yarder, and the Houses of Parliament all rolled into one, you shouldn't lay a hand upon the Winged Man whilst I am near to prevent you!"

"Unhand me, you fool! In the name of the King I call upon all present to assist me to secure this public scourge!" cried Danby Druce, looking fiercely round. "You are losing the chance of your lives!"

"You'll get ducked in the horse-pond if you don't look out!" declared a burly farmer standing by.

"Ay, duck him!" came from every side at once.

"Fool, you will have him escape!" cried Danby Druce, struggling to break free from the navvy's grasp.

"Hold your tongue, you blithering idiot!" began the navvy, with more energy than politeness. Then he ceased speaking. A broad grin parted his lips, and he released his hold of the detective.

Eagerly Danby Druce turned round. An exclamation of baffled rage burst from his lips. The Winged Man had disappeared.

Rising as gently as a butterfly on the wing, lest he should frighten the clinging child, the Winged Man was already a mere speck in the distant sky.

In a tiny cottage on the outskirts of Burton a gentlewoman and invalid daughter lived, or, rather, starved, on a small annuity scarce large enough for one. It was to the cottage occupied by these ladies the Winged Man directed his flight.

It was during that darkest hour which precedes the dawn that the widow and her daughter were alarmed by a strange knocking in a room adjoining their own.

Fear for a moment held them paralysed. Then, on the knocking being followed by the plaintive cry of a child in distress, they sprang from their beds, and, after a moment's hesitation, rushed into the room. Sitting in the middle of the unmade bed was little Maisie.

"Why, you pretty little mite, how did you come here?" asked the old lady, her motherly heart going out at once to the tiny child.

"Dada's dead, and a man with wings brought me here—he is coming again one day. Please will you be good to Maisie?" lisped the babe.

"What ever does the child mean?" asked the old lady, turning to her delicate, white-faced daughter.

"What is that you have in your hand, dear?" asked the girl, without answering her mother's question.

"For Mrs. Drew, from man with wings," replied the child, holding a sealed and directed envelope to the speaker.

Wondering who the man with wings could be, the lady opened the envelope, then stood gazing in astonishment at four fifty-pound Bank of England notes which she held in her hand. A piece of paper fluttered to the floor. She picked it up.

"A similar amount will be paid each year for the maintenance and education of this orphan child," she read aloud.

Even had there been no remuneration it is probable that Mrs. Drew would have taken Maisie to her kindly old heart, yet the sight of the notes, the promise contained in the letter, meant freedom from the hard, bitter struggles to make two ends meet which had rendered their lives miserable so long.

Willingly she undertook the charge, and thus became foster-mother to the Winged Man's ward.

IN THE CELLARS.

Peering from between a couple of enormous vats, a number of which formed an avenue down the centre of a large, dimly-lighted cellar, the Winged Man listened with a frown to the idle chatter of a group of sightseers who were being shown over one of Burton's famous breweries.

They had already visited the Maltings, and viewed with astonishment the thousands of bushels of sweet-smelling malt with which their low-ceilinged floors were covered, and were now about true traverse the huge storing-vaults ere ascending to taste the "Barley Wine," as Burton's strongest beer is called.

The vats were enormous, strongly-hooped casks, each containing several hundred gallons of beer.

To avenge a slight, the Winged Man had placed an explosive beneath each cask, intending to destroy the vats, and allow their contents to flood the floor.

As the party approached, the look of evil satisfaction on the Winged Man's face deepened. He clutched tightly at a string, a pull on which would explode his carefully-placed bombs.

Little recking of the danger that threatened, the gay party drew nearer.

A lady on either side of him, the owner, Sir Verity Vanner, approached, and the Winged Man's face darkened as his eyes alighted upon the corpulent form of the wealthy brewer, and he rubbed his long, thin, transparent hands in glee as he prepared to pull the fatal cord.

No thought of mercy entered his heart.

Tightening his grasp on the cord, the Winged Man leaned forward the better to see the effect of the explosion, when his whole frame grew stiff and rigid, a look of wondering admiration softened the fiery glare of his keen, piercing eyes, as they followed a tall, dark, beautiful girl, who walked, like a queen surrounded by her court, in the centre of the little group.

The fatal cord dropped from the Winged Man's grasp. Instinctively he drew back, lest a chance glance should discover his white face between the enormous vats. All thoughts of vengeance vanished from his heart. He would have died himself rather than inflict a moment's pain upon so beauteous a woman.

Even as he watched the lovely vision, she withdrew from the centre of the crowd, a slight, almost imperceptible motion of her hand summoning a tall, handsome, military-looking man to her side.

"You are coming to the ball at Sir Verity's to-night, Captain Roland?" the Winged Man heard her ask.

"Do you think I could keep away?" asked the captain, in a low voice.

"If you tried very hard, I dare say it is just possible you might," replied the girl, laughing.

"Ah, you under-estimate the power of love!" whispered the other.

A pang of fierce, wild, jealous hate swept through the Winged Man's heart, and he felt inclined to cry aloud with joy when the girl with an impatient shrug, hastened after the little party, which by this time had almost reached the end of the vault.

In his eagerness to get another glimpse of the lovely vision which had so entranced him, the Winged Man stepped from his place of concealment, and was gazing after the party with folded arms, when he felt himself seized from behind, and a hoarse voice roared in his ears:

"Hallo! Where did you spring from? What are you doing here?"

The next moment a loud shriek of terror burst from the vatman, for the Winged Man turned, and he saw for the first time that awful, white, nerve-thrilling face.

At his cry the visitors had come to an abrupt halt. Loud cries of terror greeted the Winged Man as, borne on his black pinions, he soared to the top of one of the enormous vats.

Captain Roland was the first to regain his courage.

"It is the Winged Man!" he cried. "Seize him!"

The appeal was in vain; the hardiest there did not dare face the Winged Man.

"Cowardly hounds!" muttered Captain Roland contemptuously. "As you all seem in such mortal terror of the mountebank, I will capture him with my own hands!"

As he spoke he placed his foot upon the bottom rung of an iron ladder leading to the top of the vat.

Then how it happened none can ever tell.

Probably Captain Roland stepped upon the cord the Winged Man had dropped. But be that as it may, the hidden bomb exploded, a dozen vats were torn in pieces, and a flood of nut-brown ale swapped the floor of the vault.

Fortunately, the visitors were standing near a flight of steps leading to the ground floor of the big brewery, up which, led by the host, the brewer's guests fled in panic-stricken flight.

All save Annette Royle, and she, paralysed with terror, was unable to flee. With a cry of horror, Captain Roland strove to reach the side of the girl he loved. Reeling from side to side like a drunken man, he was but half-way towards her, when, swooping forward on outstretched pinions, the Winged

Man glided over the frothing sea, and, snatching up the fallen girl in his arms, bore her over the heads of the visitors into the open.

A loud shriek of terror burst forth from Miss Royle's white lips.

"Fear nothing, lady! Not a hair of your head shall be injured!" promised the Winged Man.

But, mad with terror, the girl struggled to break free from that awful grasp. A sigh of regret burst from the Winged Man's lips, as, depositing her gently on the ground, he crashed through the second window, and flew, followed by a yelling and excited mob, who, however, were speedily left behind, for the streets of Burton are blocked by more than thirty railway level crossings.

A WEIRD DANCE.

It was night. Vanner Hall, the residence of Sir Verity Vanner, seemed on fire, so brilliantly illuminated without and within it was, for the great brewer was giving a ball in honour of his silver wedding, to which some two hundred guests had been invited.

The ball-room, big though it was, was crammed to its utmost capacity. From a gallery at the north end the Black Hungarian Band, which had been brought down from London at enormous expense, was playing a dreamy waltz.

Presently a violinist, seated near a pair of spreading palms, felt a light touch resting on his shoulder. Without ceasing to play he looked up, then remained, his bow half drawn across the fearful strings, gazing in terror at the fearful apparition which was grinning upon him from beneath the spreading leaves of the palm.

A cry of horror arose to his lips—a cry frozen ere it could find utterance by the fierce, forbidding glare which shone from the Winged Man's eyes.

"Beware!" came in low, fearful accents from that strange being's lips. "I am the Winged Man, to disobey whom is doom!"

Without a word the musician, moved by some unseen but irresistible influence, glided from his seat, and retreated behind the palm.

Drawing the violin from its owner's paralysed grasp, the Winged Man seated himself in his empty chair; then, falling in with the music, drew his bow over the strings.

The tune was the same, the time was the same, yet every member of the orchestra felt that some new power, some unknown, irresistible influence was at work amongst them. New life, new energy, new force was placed into the old refrain. Turning, the conductor looked in the direction from whence the weird, entrancing sounds had come.

For a moment his baton ceased to wave, and a few discordant notes burst from the orchestra. But the next moment, loud, clear, and wondrous sweet, the Winged Man's violin rose above all the other instruments, calling them to follow.

Terrified, wondering, yet unable to obey the impulse to fly which filled every heart, the twenty odd men continued to play the waltz. Their bows moved in unison, but they no longer paid attention to the conductor's baton.

Every eye was fixed upon the Winged Man, following every movement of his bow, and keeping wondrous time.

Suddenly the Winged Man sprang to his feet. Instinctively the orchestra followed his example. As though possessed by a spirit of mad rage, the Winged Man's bow flew over the strings of his violin. Faster and faster, louder and louder, yet wondrously sweet, the music swelled forth, and the dancers, filled with the same wild recklessness as the orchestra, whirled round and round on the highly-polished floor in a way that surely no fashionable ball-room had ever witnessed before.

"Swifter, you dogs—swifter! Quicker, you alien scum!" screamed the Winged Man, his eyes glowing like a living coal, as he fixed them upon the orchestra.

Wilder and wilder grew the strains, and one by one the players' instruments dropped from their nerveless fingers. Yet the volume of sound decreased not. The Winged Man's single violin filled the whole of that enormous room with wondrous melody.

Approaching the front of the orchestra, he stood, a fearful, black, ominous vision, upon the carved oak balustrade immediately before the conductor's seat.

The floor of the ball-room looked like a battlefield. It was littered with the panting and breathless forms of the dancers, who, exhausted by their vain endeavours to keep up with the music, had sunk, worn out or unconscious, on the floor.

A single couple alone kept up the dance. Annette Royle was the woman, the owner of a brewery adjoining the large Vanner establishment the man.

Suddenly a loud, hoarse, mad laugh issued from the lips of the girl's partner, as, releasing his hold of her slim waist, he flung up his arms and sank unconscious on the floor.

The music ceased.

White, panting, but with a look of wild exhilaration in her eyes, Annette Royle stood in the centre of the ball-room.

"To your instruments, dogs!" cried the Winged Man, turning upon the white-faced, astounded orchestra. "Play as you have never played before, or the Winged Man's vengeance shall descend like a thunderbolt upon you."

With one accord the orchestra resumed their instruments. Turning his back for a moment upon the ball-room, the Winged Man raised both hands above his head, then brought them swiftly down. The orchestra crashed forth with a wild, weird dance. What it was they never knew. None had seen or heard it before, yet, in response to the Winged Man's wondrous power, they played on, without falter, without a mistake.

THE BETROTHAL.

Turning, the Winged Man lent eagerly forward, fixing his dark, piercing eyes upon the panting woman, whose lithe, graceful form swayed from side to side in response to the music.

Slowly she stretched her beautiful, white arms towards the Winged Man, who, gliding gracefully through the air, paused immediately above Annette Royle, and, entwining his fingers in those of the beautiful girl, bowed his head and kissed her on the lips.

A cry of horror, rage, and dismay rang through the ball-room.

Darting out from a curtained doorway, Captain Roland sprang forward to snatch the girl he loved from the Winged Man's grasp.

Ignoring the enraged officer's approach, the Winged Man dropped to his feet, clasped the willing girl round the waist, and the next moment to the weird, fearful, yet entrancing strains of the orchestra the two whirled round and round in a mad, wild dance.

At first the girl was very pale, but as they swept round and round the room, so fast that the bewildered spectators could scarce follow their movements, Annette Royle's cheeks flushed, a light of intense enjoyment glowed from her eyes, and her lips parted in a happy smile, showing two rows of white, pearly teeth.

Louder and louder played the band, swifter and swifter revolved the dancing couple.

"Brave girl, you at least do not fear the Winged Man?" whispered that weird being in his partner's ear.

"Fear! Why should I fear? Never have I enjoyed a dance like this!" came pantingly from the girl's lips.

"Then you do not wish to stop?" asked the Winged Man, evidently well pleased at the reply.

"Stop? No! Oh, that it could go on for ever!" was the enthusiastic reply.

"Nothing is so fleeting as happiness," replied the Winged Man, somewhat sadly. "One more turn round the room, and we must part."

"No, no! Not yet—not yet!" panted Annette.

"It must be. You do not realise the fearful prostration[27] which would follow this dance if I allowed you to keep it up too long. It might, indeed, prove a dance of death for you.

"Then let death come. I fear it not, so that it does not part us," returned the girl, her voice blending with the music as though she sang the words instead of speaking them.

"You mean it? They call me the enemy of mankind, a scoundrel against whom every honest man's hand is raised. And would you dare to share the Winged Man's lot?"

"Ay, his lot and his power!" returned Annette Royle, a look of eager ambition flashing from her beautiful eyes as she spoke.

The Winged Man shot a commanding glance towards the orchestra. In a

---

27 Exhaustion.

moment, in the twinkling of an eye, as though some unseen power had paralysed their very nerves, the musicians' play ceased.

Drawing a gold-tipped, ebony baton from his pocket, the Winged Man faced the orchestra.

One arm encircled Annette Royle's slender waist, the other rose and fell as he beat time for the band. So low were the first notes that arose from the orchestra that it seemed to the spellbound listeners as though it was but an echo from a distance. Gradually it grew louder, until the strains filled the room.

Surely never before had mortal ear listened to such music. All the evil, all the sorrow, all the pain, all the suffering the human race has endured throughout countless ages was expressed in those low, tremulous tones.

"Listen! Listen to the warning of the music. Sorrows unspeakable must be the lot of her whom the Winged Man weds. Speak! Are you still prepared to link your fate with his?" inquired the flying horror.

The tremulous notes of the music ringing in her ears, Annette Royle seemed to feel the Winged Man's eyes tearing the secrets of her very soul from her bosom.

A reply which would have revealed her very soul in all its revolting nakedness arose to her lips, formed thereto by the Winged Man's wondrous power. But ere she could speak, Captain Roland, love conquering the terror which had caused him to stand as though turned to stone within a few feet of the couple upon whom all eyes were directed, sprang forward and grasped the Winged Man by the throat.

"Scoundrel! Spirit of Evil that you are! I will die rather than this noble girl shall fall into your power!" he hissed.

Then a strange thing happened. None saw the Winged Man move, yet Captain Roland's fingers, which a fraction of a second before had gripped warm, living flesh, closed on empty air, and the Winged Man was standing by his side regarding him with a mocking, scornful smile.

For nearly a minute Captain Roland remained as motionless as a marble statue, gazing with incredulous eyes at his hands, which were still uplifted as though grasping the Winged Man's throat; then, with a cry of despairing rage, he turned upon his foe once more.

But the short respite from the fascinating stare of the Winged Man's eyes had given Annette Royle time to recover her wonted self-command. She was no ordinary woman. Endowed with a rare courage, boundless ambition, and a strength of will which had raised her from a very low station in life to rank as an equal with the proudest leaders of society.

The Winged Man's weird personality attracted and interested whilst it repulsed her, but her quick wit had realised how greatly an alliance with a being so wondrously endowed would assist her ambitious plans.

To think with Annette Royle was to act. As Captain Roland approached the Winged Man with upraised fist, she flung herself before her weird lover.

"You forget yourself, Captain Roland. I am not aware that I have ever given you cause to consider yourself my champion," she cried coldly.

Captain Roland started back, amazement depicted in every line of his countenance.

"Annette! Miss Royle! You cannot—you surely do not mean to say that you are willing to form this alliance?" he gasped.

Annette Royle drew herself up to her full height. Tall, faultlessly made, beautiful as a Greek statue, she looked a very queen, as, waving Roland aside, she extended her white, shapely hand to the Winged Man.

The action was accompanied by a look so full of love and devotion that the Winged Man felt his heart beat as it had never done before as his hand closed upon the woman's fingers. Dropping upon one knee, he pressed her shapely hand to his lips; then, rising, stretched his pinions to their full width.

"Farewell! Ere long I will return to claim you!" he cried.

Rising, he flew to the gallery, where, as men in a trance, the musicians were playing, at the Winged Man's unspoken command, a low, soothing lullaby.

Snatching a violin from one of the players, the Winged Man pressed it against his chin. Immediately every part of that magnificent ball-room was filled with an indescribably grand melody of triumph.

It was scene those who witnessed could never forget. The enormous ball-room dotted with kneeling, standing, or prostrate figures. Even the latter had raised themselves on their elbows to gaze, fascinated, at the weird form of that awful musician.

Gradually a murmur, it could not be called a cry, of amazement arose from every lip. Slowly, almost imperceptibly, the Winged Man's weird, awful form grew shadowy and indistinct, whilst the volume of sound drawn by the lightning-like strokes of his bow across the violin-strings grew less, until, just as the Winged Man faded entirely from view, the sound died away.

MISTRESS AND MAID.

Her arms straight down by her side, her faced turned towards the spot where the Winged Man had stood a moment before, Annette Royle appeared to the spectators like some enchanted princess in a fairy-tale, who was slowly turning to stone before their eyes.

Yet, in truth, Annette Royle's brain was as clear as it had ever been. She was playing a deep, a desperate game; perhaps she did not quite realise how desperate it was herself. Gold was her idol, and, if report spoke true, wealth beyond the dreams of avarice was the Winged Man's.

As men waking from some awful dream, Sir Verity Vanner's guests edged slowly towards where Annette Royle held the centre of the room. Gradually Annette's hands rose until they covered her face. Then, with a gesture as though tearing a bandage from off her eyes, she threw her hands above her head, and glanced fearfully around.

Staggering towards Captain Roland, she clung tightly to him, sobbing convulsively as she did so.

"Take me from this haunted spot! Tell me it's all some awful, some fearful dream!" she cried imploringly.

Captain Roland's honest heart was filled with relief and reawakened hope.

"Yes, yes, Annette. It was but a dream. I will not believe that such things can be possible," declared the captain, clasping the trembling girl round the waist, and feeling as though he would gladly fight a score of the Winged Men for the sake of the woman he loved so dearly.

"You are sure it is not true—that I did not pledge myself to that fearful, that awful being?" persisted Annette.

"No, no. Do not alarm yourself," stammered Captain Roland, scarce knowing what to say—for had he not heard Annette plight her troth with his own ears? "Whatever you said, what have you pledged yourself to do, cannot be binding, for it was forced from you by some more than human agency."

A loud, piercing shriek of despair escaped Annette's lips.

"Then I am pledged to him, and he will demand me as his wife. Oh, save—save me!" she cried. Then her beautiful head fell upon the young soldier's shoulder, and consciousness fled.

Amidst a scene of the utmost confusion—for the guests at the interrupted ball were talking excitedly, and magnifying the Winged Man's exploits a thousandfold—Captain Roland carried Annette Royle from the room, and, her bed-chamber reached, left her in charge of her maid—and olive-skinned brunette, in whose veins flowed the fiery blood of a Spanish gipsy.

Barely had Captain Roland, after begging Miss Royle's maid to call him directly Annette recovered consciousness, left the room, ere, with a low, mocking, musical laughed, the supposed fainting girl arose and sat on the side of the bed.

Nina looked at her mistress without surprise.

Evidently a good understanding existed between mistress and maid. In fact, when alone they were accomplices and equals, save Annette Royle, as the master-mind, led where the other gladly followed.

"Well, what is the joke, Annette?" asked Nina, in a low voice; for it was more than probable that Captain Roland's anxiety would keep him close to his loved one's door. "I thought you didn't intend to accept that English captain?"

"Good gracious no, Nina! Of course I don't," replied Annette, with a scornful laugh.

"Then, why faint in his arms?" insisted the lady's maid. "It is an old trick, but I know you are a past mistress in the art of working upon men's feelings."

"To throw dust in the eyes of the fools downstairs, Nina. I am betrothed."

"Then all the fools have not been left downstairs, that's all I can say," returned the other angrily. "Why spoil our career at the outset? We are continually climbing higher and higher in the social scale, and you could marry a great deal better than anyone in this old titled snob's house. Who is it? Not the brewer's son, I hope."

A mischievous smile hovered over Annette Royle's red lips.

"Who holds the whole of England in the palm of his hand? Whose power is the greatest in the land?" she asked.

"Have done with your conundrums," growled Nina angrily. "Who is it, tell me?"

"Nina, my lover is greater even than the rulers of the people. It is the Winged Man!" laughed Annette.

THE THEFT OF THE DIAMOND COLLAR.

Nina, Miss Annette Royle's maid, looked at her mistress as though unable to believe the evidence of her ears.

"The Winged Man! The Winged Man here, and I never knew it!" she almost screamed. "Surely you must have been mad to have allowed such a chance to escape!"

"I think I made make a pretty good use of the chance," retorted Annette. "He has fallen head over ears in love with me, and if I don't make something out of it I am not Annette Royle."

"A bird in the hand is worth two in the bush," growled Nina excitedly. "The rooms will be empty. Now's our chance. Whatever is missed will be put down to your new master, the Winged Man."

"I was thinking of that, but I am afraid it is too late," replied Annette thoughtfully. "You have never seen the Winged Man, Nina. Even I had difficulty in keeping myself-possession in his presence. In fact, I am not at all sure that I am wise to attempt any games with him."

"That is your look-out," replied the maid indifferently. "Mine is to make hay while the sun shines. So here's off!"

Discarding the neat black dress which, as Annette Royle's lady's- maid, she wore indoors, Nina donned a threadbare suit of blue serge.

Over this disguise she drew a long, dark cloak, and crept noiselessly on to the landing. A perfect pandemonium of shouts, hysterical shrieks, and cries of anger came from below; but, paying no heed, Nina glided swiftly from room to room.

She was scarce gone ten minutes, but when she returned it was to throw down on the coverlet of the bed a heap of glittering jewels and money.

Barely had she exposed her booty to Annette's delighted gaze ere both women were startled by a loud rapping on the door.

Scarcely had Annette time to fling a loose skirt over her accomplice's recently-acquired plunder ere, without waiting for an invitation, the door was thrust open, and Lady Vanner burst into the room.

"Oh, my dear Miss Royle, I am so glad you have recovered!" cried her hostess. "I am in such a state of bewilderment, I don't know what to do. That fearful Winged Man has driven all the servants crazy. I cannot get anything done, and my daughter Nelly is in hysterics in my room. I hate to take her from you—you must be nervous, after your recent fearful experience—but can you spare Nina a little while? She is so good, so clever, and Nelly is so fond of her."

WHO WAS THE THIEF?"

A quick glance passed between mistress and maid. Nina yet wore her disguise beneath her cloak, and discovery seemed certain; but at any cost Lady Vanner must be got out of the room.

"Certainly, my lady; I will come at once," agreed the lady's-maid.

A few minutes later Nina, her eyes fixed upon a magnificent diamond, worn by the brewer's wife, followed Lady Vanner to her room.

Miss Nelly Vanner was stretched upon a couch, sobbing and laughing in turn. In a moment Nina was by her side.

Lady Vanner had not exaggerated the lady's-maid's capabilities. With cool, firm hand she smoothed back the thick tresses from Nelly Vanner's white forehead. Immediately the girl's hysterical struggles ceased. Nina's quick eyes swept over the bottles arranged on the dressing-table.

"A little sal volatile,[28] quick, my lady! Tell me where I can find it!" she cried, noticing that there was none of that useful drug in sight.

"In the next room—in the ornamental cupboard to the left of the bed. Shall I get it?" replied the mother.

The next moment she had disappeared through the door, whilst the anxious mother, leaning over her daughter, tried to comfort her.

Suddenly her ladyship was startled by feeling a gloved hand laid upon her shoulder. Terror froze her heart.

Her starting eyes gazed straight into the muzzle of a small revolver.

"Not a word, as you value your life!" said the robber, in a hoarse voice. "Quick, unclasped that collar! Obey, or you die!" he added, more fiercely than ever, as an expostulation rose to Lady Vanner's lips.

Cowed by the threat, the terrified lady undid the diamond collar with trembling fingers.

"Your rings, your bracelets! I hear steps. If I am discovered, you shall not live to give evidence against me!" came in a whisper from the burglar.

Believing that each moment might be her last, Lady Vanner obeyed the masked intruder.

"Kneel! Look round, on your peril!" was the next command, obeyed almost ere the words had left the burglar's lips.

With noiseless tread the burglar retreated, pausing for a moment at the door through which Nina had disappeared to look back at the bedside which he had just left.

What he saw there filled his heart with dismay. Nelly Vanner lay, her face turned to the door, a look of terror, amazement, and surprise in her widely-distended eyes.

The next moment the burglar had disappeared. Then came a loud piercing

---

[28] Smelling salts.

shriek of terror, followed by a crash of glass, and the next moment Nina rushed into the room, crying:

"Help! A burglar! He has jumped through the window!"

With an agility the stately lady seldom showed, Lady Vanner rose to her feet.

"Why did you not stop him?" she demanded. "He has got my diamond collar and rings!"

"Me? Me stop an armed desperado like that? Surely Lady Vanner, you are joking!" replied the lady's-maid. "How did he get into the room? He must have come from the corridor."

"No, no!" interrupted Nelly Vanner. "He came from mother's boudoir."

With difficulty Nina repressed a start. Who could tell whether the girl she had believed unconscious would give the clue to the detectives—who would undoubtedly be employed—that would lead to her capture?"

"Then he must have been standing behind the door ready to enter. I—" began Nina, then paused, and pretended to be listening intently ere, with a cry of, "Miss Royle, my mistress—I hear her calling!" darted from the room.

"Come back, Nina! Do not leave me alone!" shrieked Lady Vanner.

Nelly laid a restraining hand on her mother's arm.

"Mother, let her go! The burglar had Nina's eyes!" she said.

Lady Vanner looked with undisguised astonishment at her daughter.

"My dear child, that is folly. It was a man—a man in blue serge. I saw him myself," she declared.

"It was no man; it was a woman," insisted Nelly Vanner.

"It was neither. It was the Human Bat!"[29] came in deep tones from the window, the thick curtains shading which were thrust aside.

Lady Vanner dropped like a stone across her daughter's bed; but Nelly looked unflinchingly into the Winged Man's glittering orbs.

"Who or what you may be mine know not, yet truth must prevail. It was Annette Royle's made Nina, who, disguised as a man, rubbed my mother of her jewels," she declared.

Hard, stern as ever was the Winged Man's white, livid face, yet from his eyes there flashed a momentary gleam of admiration and respect.

"What, child, you dare to contradict the Winged Man? Beware! Repeat your suspicion to a soul, and, as true as the stars shine above the earth, you shall meet with your reward!" he cried threateningly ere he disappeared from view.

Nelly Vanner's loud cries for assistance brought guests, servants, and her father into the room.

In vain Nelly Vanner declared that she had seen Nina, dressed in men's clothes, seize her mother by the throat.

---

[29] Again, the title "The Human Bat" is used here; however if this was what he actually said without the link to the earlier series, the characters would not have known who he was.

None believed her. More acceptable to the astounded household was Lady Vanner's tale that the Winged Man himself had confessed to the robbery.

°THE TRUTH IN SPITE OF ALL.

Eight o'clock the following morning a motor-car dashed up to the baronet's mansion. A clean-shaven, sharp-featured man, the light of battle in his eyes, alighted.

It was Danby Druce, summoned by wire to the baronet's assistance. Eagerly he had obeyed the summons, for had not the telegram mentioned that the Winged Man was there? And Danby Druce only lived to capture the weird, supernatural being who had baffled and defeated him so many times.

Nelly Vanner was too ill to see the famed detective when he arrived, and neither Sir Verity nor Lady Vanner had thought it worth while to mention what they deemed her idle fancy.

Neither, considering the extraordinary adventures of the previous day, it is to be wondered at if Annette Royle was also confined to her bed.

In other cases Danby Druce's first care would have been to search for clues, to try to follow the movements of the perpetrator of the crime: but such modes were of no use against the Winged Man.

Clues were not wanted, for it was seldom that the Winged Man deigned to hide his handiwork; and as for tracking, who could follow the flight of a bird in the air, a fish in the sea, or a mole burrowing beneath the earth?

Often had Danby Druce stood baffled, furious, and dismayed, watching the Winged Man soar high over his head.

Once he had seen him disappear into the earth, and once plunge into the water, like a flying-fish returning to its native element.

To capture so elusive a quarry seemed a hopeless task, yet it was its apparent impossibility which made the quest of the Winged Man the one absorbing passion of Danby Druce's life.

There were a dozen men staying with Sir Verity Vanner. Each of these dozen had a different plan for catching the Winged Man, which he was anxious for Danby Druce to try, all, needless to say, equally hopeless.

They badgered him with useless and idiotic questions to such an extent that, but for the certainty he felt of the Winged Man's return to the Hall, Danby Druce would have fled from his well-intentioned advisers.

Sullen anger filled his heart. Successful detective that he was, failure played upon his nerves.

Until the present time he had despaired of ever securing his elusive foe, but now a new element had come into the scene.

Eagerly he had listened to the baronet's account of the Winged Man's strange

---

incident with Annette Royle. Once let the Winged Man fall into a woman's toil, and half his cunning, half his strength would forsake him.

Whilst Annette Royle was at the Hall the detective felt convinced that, sooner or later, the Winged Man would return.

Consequently, though having to be constantly on the alert against the many amateur detectives staying at the house, he remained in or about the mansion, ostensibly unwilling to leave until Annette Royle was sufficiently recovered to see him.

This the young lady in question and was determined should not be for several days. Truth to tell, there was that in her past—a gambling incident—which would mean social ruin if discovered.

To her knowledge she had not come in contact with Danby Druce, yet the great detective had a wonderful memory, and if he took it into his head to discover her antecedents—well, the ladder of social success she had climbed so painfully would be thrown down, and she would never be able to take the position in society she had already gained again.

Nina, as we have before said, had been born in Spain, and the New York police would have been able to have given Danby Druce interesting particulars regarding her past; but so far as she had escaped attracting the attention of Scotland Yard.

For two days and two nights Danby Druce kept constant watch over the suite of rooms occupied by Annette Royle.

In vain. The Winged Man did not put an in an appearance. It was the night of the third day after the ball the Danby Druce, muffled from head to foot in dark clothes, the better to remain invisible in the shadows of the sleeping house, leaned thoughtfully against the mantelpiece of Sir Verity's magnificent library.

Suddenly he started, every nerve athrill, as the door of the library opened slowly. A momentary shiver of fear shot through the detective's veins, as a form clad in white, with golden hair hanging below her waist, a lighted candle in her hand, glided so noiselessly into the room that she seemed treading on air.

The next moment he saw it was a young lady clad in a white silk dressing-gown.

He had not yet seen Nelly Vanner; yet from the likeness she bore to his hostess he recognised her as Lady Vanner's daughter. In the centre of the room she came to an abrupt halt. Raising her candle above her head, she looked searchingly round the room.

Fearing to discover himself lest the shock should injure the frail-looking girl, Danby Druce kept perfectly still.

Suddenly she started, and, leaning forward, peered with dilated eyes to where he stood: then she shrank back.

"Are you the Winged Man?" she demanded, in low, trembling accents.

With a reassuring laugh Danby Druce stepped forward.

"On the contrary young lady, I am Danby Druce," he replied. "Surely Sir

Verity Vanner's daughter seeks not that evil, weird individual?"

"I seek him?" replied the girl, with a shudder. "Why, the very thought of him makes me tremble! Heaven grant I may never see him again!"

"Amen to that!" laughed Danby Druce. "Are you looking for anything? Can I be of any assistance?" he continued.

"I was looking for you, Mr. Druce. Have they told you the truth?" cried the girl, laying a trembling hand on his arm.

"In what way?" demanded the detective, astonished at the question.

"With regard to the thief who stole my mother's diamond collar," was the reply.

"There seems little doubt about that, Miss Vanner, for I presume you are Sir Verity's daughter?"

The girl bowed assent.

"It was the Winged Man," declared Druce confidently.

"No, no!" almost shrieked Nelly Vanner excitedly. "A thousand times no! It was—"

"Beware!"

Both started as the deep, warning tones reverberated through the silent house. With a stifled shriek of terror the girl shrank close to the detective. Danby Druce laid his hand reassuringly upon his companion's arm.

"Fear nothing I will protect you even from the Winged Man!"

"Ha, ha, ha! Ho, ho, ho!"

A loud, mocking peal of laughter, which seemed to come from every corner of the room at once, answered the detective's confident assertion.

Drawing an electric torch from his pocket with his left hand, Danby Druce stood, a cocked revolver in his right, by the girl's side.

For a moment he hesitated. The Winged Man was close at hand, and he was handicapped by the presence of this weak, frail girl.

"Miss Vanner, be brave. Return to your room alone, and leave me to face this fearful being," requested Danby Druce.

"Not till I have spoken. Not till I have told the truth," returned the girl almost fiercely.

"What, in the face of my express order to the contrary, daring all, risking everything, you will yet speak?" came apparently from immediately behind the detective.

Danby Druce flashed his brilliant searchlight round. Save for himself and the upright form of the pail-faced girl, the room was empty.

"Yes, despite everything. I will speak," asserted Nelly Vanner. "It was—"

Again she was interrupted. This time by Danby Druce.

"Silence, young lady! Though I see you possess a secret which would give me a great advantage over the Winged Man, for your own sake I beg you to remain silent," he said earnestly. "Great Powers! You cannot know the fearful power of the monster of iniquity whose anger you are about to bring upon your own head!"

"I cannot!" replied Nelly Vanner desperately. "Rather than the guilty should escape punishment I will risk all. Annette Royle's maid, Nina, disguised in men's clothes, stole my mother's diamond collar!"

An ejaculation of amazement burst from Danby Druce's lips—amazement tinged with triumph. If he could lay his hand upon the Winged Man's accomplice, next to the arrest of the weird being himself, it would be his greatest triumph. Few men knew the Winged Man's capabilities better than he, and he feared each moment to see the fearful, dark, horror-inspiring form swoop down upon the lovely girl and strike her dead at his feet or carry her away captive.

It was hard to have to leave the room with the knowledge that ere he returned the Winged Man might be miles away; yet until he had seen Nelly Vanner safe with those who would protect her, he dared not leave her.

"Miss Vanner, you have behaved nobly," he declared; "yet I would be wrong if I did not warn you of the terrible risk you have run. Let me put you in charge of your father. To-morrow you shall repeat what you have said to-night."

The girl's trembling hand rested on his arm. Danby Druce moved towards the door, but barely had he taken a couple of steps ere he was seized by the neck in an iron grasp, lifted from the floor, and hurled across the room.

"Nelly Vanner, despite my express orders, despite the punishment you feared, you have dared to speak the truth. I promised you your reward. Behold, it is yours!" announced the Winged Man.

As the deep, sonorous tones fell upon her ears, a heart-chilling wave of terror swept through the unhappy girl's veins. She felt something, cold as ice, clasped her throat, her senses fled, she reeled, and with a loud, piercing, desperate shriek, which echoed and re-echoed throughout the building, fell heavily to the ground.

With a piercing shriek the girl fell heavily to the ground.

Bruised and breathless by his fall, but otherwise uninjured, Danby Druce sprang to his feet, and rushed to Nelly Vanner's assistance. He had dropped his electric torch, but groping in the dark, he soon found the girl's unconscious form, raised it in his arms, and groped his way to the electric switches near the door. Another moment and the library was plunged in light.

"Miss Vanner, fear nothing. He has gone. I—"

Danby Druce ceased speaking. A look of absolute amazement crept into his eyes. He stared as though fascinated upon the girl's white throat on which, reflecting back the beams of the electric light in a thousand dazzling colours, was the diamond collar, which, from the description he had received, he recognised as that stolen from Lady Vanner!

AN ACCEPTED CHALLENGE.

Danby Druce was more puzzled than he had ever been before. All his life he had been too accustomed to divide the truth from falsehood, and could not for a moment doubt but that Nelly Vanner's tale was true.

If so, it pointed to the fact that the Winged Man had an accomplice. Never for a moment did the detective believe it possible that the Winged Man would take on his own shoulders the blame for a crime committed by another.

Raising Nelly Vanner's unconscious form in his arms, Danby Druce carried her into a dressing-room adjoining her mother's. Knocking at the door which connected the two apartments, he glided from the room, leaving Lady Vanner to discover her daughter stretched upon a couch with the missing diamond collar round her neck.

A feeling of absolute despair seized Danby Druce in its grasp. He had set his heart upon capturing the Winged Man, yet it seemed as though he might as well try to arrest the wind, or the fleeting shadows of night, as that weird, awful, mysterious being. Yet with every failure, his determination to conquer the Winged Man or perish in the attempt was strengthened.

As he stood by the side of an old weather-stained sundial in the centre of Sir Verity Vanner's magnificently laid-out garden, he raised his hand aloft, saying:

"By all that I hold dear in the world; by all my hopes in this world and hereafter, I swear to devote the rest of my life to the capture of the Winged Man. Death alone shall end the chase!"

A loud, mocking laugh responded to the oath. It seemed to come from immediately behind him. Danby Druce turned. There was no one there. It was a clear, star-lit night, yet between himself and the house no moving body intervened. Again that laughter rang out. Again the detective turned, then started back in horror.

Crouched on the top of the sundial, his wings draped close to his body, his fearful face shining like marble through the darkness, his headlight, baleful, lurid, sat the Winged Man!"

"I accept the challenge, Danby Druce!" cried the awful being. "Your wit against mine! You, with all the forces of law and order behind you; I alone, unaided. As you have spoken, so shall it be!"

For a moment a shiver of superstitious terror held the detective motionless, then with a cry of rage he sprang at the sundial. The pedestal was empty. The Winged Man had gone!

"Merciful powers! Am I going mad? Am I dreaming, or can such things really be?" gasped Danby Druce, staggering back, his hand to his forehead. "Surely this man is more than mortal?"

"Ay, more than mortal is the Winged Man!" came in clear, dignified tones from behind the sundial, as with a triumphant, almost contemptuous smile upon his lips, the Winged Man stepped into full view of the astounded detective.

"Come on, Danby Druce. You have sworn to take me. I am here!" he added mockingly.

The detective sprang at him once more, but half-striding, half-flying, he glided towards the laurel-hedge which divided the flowers from the kitchen garden. Straining every nerve to overtake his retreating foe, Danby Druce dashed on. The Winged Man disappeared through a gap in the hedge, and Danby Druce, forgetting his superstitious terror of a few minutes before, followed close behind.

Suddenly an exclamation of triumph burst from his lips. Before him stood a tall, dark form. Dashing forward, he seized the figure in both hands and bore it heavily to the earth.

"Aha! Winged Man, the chase ends here!" he cried.

"You lie, Danby Druce, it but begins!" retorted the Winged Man.

Looking up, Danby Druce saw the Winged Man hovering, like a hawk over its prey, a dozen feet above his head.

"Then who are you?" cried the detective, rolling his captive over on his back.

Then, with a cry of horror, he sprang to his feet. White as chalk itself, motionless as a corpse, one of his own men, whom he had planted at the Hall to intercept the Winged Man's flight, lay before him.

At first he thought the man was dead. But even as he poured a few drops of brandy from his flask between his clenched teeth he opened his eyes and looked, frantic with fear, around him, muttering:

"The Winged Man—the Winged Man!" then lapsed into unconsciousness once more.

The man had caught but one glimpse of that weird terror's awful face, and looked into those unfathomable eyes but for one second, yet terror had for the moment still the beating of his heart, and he remained motionless, as though turned to stone, whilst Danby Druce, taking him for the Winged Man, flung himself upon him.

Summoning another man to his side with a low whistle, Danby Druce left the unconscious man in his charge; then plunging into the intricate maze of paths leading from the north side of the house, strove to think out some plan by which to capture the Winged Man.

Suddenly he started back. His whole frame grew tense and stiff. The light fall of feet and the frou- frou of a woman's garments beating against the side of the path fell upon his ears. Instinctively he drew back beneath the shade of a flowering shrub. Nearer and nearer came the footsteps, then dim, and as yet indistinct in the darkness, he saw two women approaching. The shorter of the two he recognised at once as Nina, the taller, he guessed, would be Annette Royle. Nor was his supposition incorrect. Fearing discovery, Annette Royle had determined to leave the house, taking with her the plunder she had already secured, confident that the power of her beauty would draw the Winged Man to her where ever she might be.

"Good-morning, Miss Royle! Early hours for a young lady and her maid to be abroad." said Danby Druce, stepping forward as the girls drew alongside him.

With a stifled shriek, Annette started back.

"Who are you?"

"Danby Druce, very much at your service. The keen air is bad for you, I'm am afraid, Miss Royle. You will kindly oblige me by returning with me to the house. I wish to have a few minutes' conversation with you."

Nina, taking advantage of Danby Druce's attention being centred upon her mistress, slipped noiselessly by. But nothing escaped Danby Druce's eagle eye. A low whistle, and ere Nina had taken a dozen steps, she found one of Danby Druce's men confronting her.

Escape was hopeless, and with as good grace as possible, the two women followed their captor back to the house, Danby Druce himself taking charge of a fair-sized brown bag Annette carried, declaring, with mock politeness, that he could not think of allowing so beautiful a young lady to carry her own luggage.

In sullen silence, Annette and Nina allowed themselves to be escorted into an ante-room adjoining Sir Verity's library, where the bag was opened, revealing a considerable portion of the jewellery which had been stolen the previous night.

Delighted though he was at the recovery of so many of the stolen jewels, Danby Druce was far from content. He knew that the Winged Man had taken Annette Royle as a confederate, and his one great anxiety at the present moment was to hand the two women over to the police, where the Winged Man could not rescue them.

Fearing lest, if he called Sir Verity, the baronet, to save a scandal, should refuse to prosecute, Danby Druce determined to take the law into his own hands.

Awaking a sleepy groom, he indulged him to harness a pair of horses to a brougham and drive them into Burton. Outwardly overcome with dismay and shame, but a raging volcano within, Annette Royle allowed herself to be escorted to where the brougham awaited them. Eagerly she looked around, scanning the grey heavens which were being lightened by the first beams of the coming day.

Some instinct seemed to warn her that the dread being to whom she had become a confederate was not far off, and would ere long sweep from the skies to her rescue.

A FEARFUL RIDE.

But there was no response to Annette Royle's appealing glance upward at the skies.

Warned by some occult instinct that the woman in whom he took so great an interest was in danger, the Winged Man was winging his way back from Burton to the Hall as quickly as his wings could force him through the air.

Seated by the side of Annette Royle, whilst Nina was closely guarded by one of the detective's men on the front seat, Danby Druce, with every nerve on the alert, remained, revolver in hand, as the carriage rolled through the early morning light in the direction of Burton.

Ere he had encountered the Winged Man, Danby Druce had looked a man in the prime of life. Now his face was wrinkled with care, grey threads appeared amongst his dark-brown hair, and his heart beat wildly with elation.

There was a feeling of disappointment in Danby Druce's heart that the Winged Man should have an accomplice. He had deemed him to strong a man to trust his fate in a woman's hand; but, as the reader knows, Danby Druce did the Winged Man an injustice.

Alone the Winged Man lived. Alone he worked.

Annette Royle interrupted Danby Druce's train of thought.

"Now, sir, perhaps you will kindly explain the meaning of this outrage. Why am I arrested?" she demanded, turning angrily upon the detective.

"Not arrested, Miss Royle; merely detained while inquiries are being made. Had you not attempted to leave the Hall in so stealthy a manner you might still have retained your liberty, though under surveillance."

"Cannot a lady and her maid go for an early morning walk without incurring suspicion?" demanded Annette.

"I will be in a better position to give an answer to your question when you have been through the hands of the female searcher at Burton police-station," retorted Danby Druce.

Annette Royle turned pale. Hidden in various parts of the clothes worn by the two women was the greater part of the plunder Nina had secured the previous night. Yet Annette was absolutely fearless. A mocking laugh rose to her lips, but ere it could find utterance it was choked by a fearful terror that met her eyes.

A steel blade, six inches long, pierced the cover of the brougham immediately above her head. As though drawn by some giant's hand, it ripped the top of the brougham open from end to end. The next moment two long, white hands were thrust through the orifice, the light cover was torn aside with fearful force, and the Winged Man glowered down on the occupants of the carriage through the opening.

The groom, alarmed by the noise behind him, turned, saw the Winged Man, and, uttering a long, piercing shriek of terror, sprang headlong into a hedge by the side of the road.

Even as he did so, Danby Druce, taking swift aim at the Winged Man's ghastly face, pulled the trigger of his revolver. The bullet sped wide of its mark. The report alarmed the startled horses. Snorting with terror they galloped swiftly down the road.

All this had taken place in the suburbs of Burton, and the streets were filled with men and women going to work in one or other of the enormous breweries.

All stood aghast at the runaway horses and the swaying brougham dashed down the street. Not a hand was raised to check the frightened animals, for the Winged Man, clinging with outstretched wings to the top of the brougham, struck terror into all who saw him as, with frenzied strength, he tore fiercely to enlarge the opening he had already made.

Soon, beneath his ceaseless efforts, the hole widened. Again a shot rang forth, a shot followed by mocking laughter, as the bullet buried itself in the Winged Man's breastplate.

The door opened. Overcome with terror, Danby Druce's assistant forsook his chief and leapt out of the vehicle, alighting with crushing force upon the pavement, where he lay, stunned and fearfully injured.

Scarce knowing what she did, for a single glance at the Winged Man's fearful face had robbed her of every particle of her wonted courage, Nina followed her custodian's example.

Fortunately for her, a countryman, who gazed with gaping mouth at the fleeing carriage and its fearful occupant, received her in his arms.

On sped the terrified horses, their terror increased tenfold by the frightened shouts of the spectators.

Presently the panic-stricken witnesses of this weird incident uttered cries of warning and fear. The horses were drawing the carriage each moment nearer to a level crossing, between the closed gates of which a light engine was puffing slowly over the rails.

Barely had the work people realised the peril which beset the occupants of the carriage, ere the maddened horses, their shrill neighs of terror piercing the air, struck the gate just as the engine passed between them.

The brougham was seen to rise from the ground, balance itself for a moment upon the overthrown horses, then fall with a crash upon the engine.

A shuddering moan burst from the terror-stricken spectators; then, astonishment conquering horror, the crowd uttered cries of amazement, for out from the shattered top of the brougham rose the black, forbidding form of the Winged Man. In his arms he held a woman's fainting form.

His weird, nerve-thrilling cry, shrill now with triumph struck terror into every heart as the Winged Man soared aloft with his prize.

For a moment the crowd stood paralysed with horror; then, with one accord, rushed forward to rescue the other occupant of the brougham.

But their assistance was not required. Bruised and dazed by the fall, but otherwise uninjured, Danby Druce had been hurled from the brougham on to the permanent way by the side of the engine.

Staggering to his feet, he looked wildly around. Drawn up close to the broken gate of the level crossing was a 24-h.p. motor-car. With a cry of joy Danby Druce clambered over the gate.

"I proved your innocence; I saved your life. If you have any call upon your gratitude, help me to capture yonder flying demon!" he cried, pointing with extended arm to where the Winged Man, rising high above the roofs of the houses, was flying off in a westerly direction.

Neil Holmes, the driver of the car, to whom the detective had appealed, looked in amazement at the speaker. Then a look of recognition flashed into his eyes.

"Mr. Danby Druce!" ejaculated, adding immediately: "Tell me how I can serve you. Even though I gave my life for you, sir, I would still be in your debt."

"Thank you," replied the detective simply. "I knew I would not appeal in vain. After him—after him!"

Neil Holmes turned his car around, and a minute later Danby Druce was once more in pursuit of the Winged Man.

THE BURNING HUT.

As we have before mentioned, the streets of Burton are crossed and recrossed by countless railways, and by the time Neil Holmes's car had passed the great trunk canal, the Winged Man, but a mere speck in the distance, was flying in the direction of Hanbury.

Ere Oxiter was reached the car had gained considerably on the Winged Man. Some half a dozen miles further on a cry of triumph came from both men as they saw their quarry drop to earth amongst the trees of a large wood.

"We have got him now!" said Neil Holmes joyfully.

"You do not know the Winged Man," retorted the detective bitterly. "If he was alone we might as well be in the midst of the desert of the Sahara as here, for all chance we would have of capturing him unaided. However, it is the woman we want. If we can capture her, we may be able to lure him to his doom."

As Danby Druce spoke he alighted from the car, which had come to a standstill close to the spot where he had last seen the Winged Man. Barely had the words left his lips ere a loud, shrill cry for help in a woman's voice, apparently coming from a little distance to the right, reached their ears.

Both men plunged into the wood. Cry after cry arose to guide them in their search. Presently they reached a dilapidated hut, every door and window of which was closely barricaded. Revolver in hand, Danby Druce approached the hut and subjected both doors and windows to a close scrutiny. Then he returned to where he had left his companion against a tree some twenty feet away.

"They are in the hut. The windows and doors have been recently blocked up," he declared.

"What do you intend doing?" inquired Holmes.

Ere Danby Druce could reply, four labourers, who had been at work in an adjoining field, and had heard the woman's cry for help, dashed upon the scene; whilst from an opposite direction two gamekeepers, their guns under their arms, and a woodman, his axe on his shoulder, hastened up.

Danby Druce's face brightened.

"Luck is on my side for once!" he cried, as he advanced to meet these unexpected reinforcements.

A few words put the new-comers in possession of the facts of the case. All had heard of the Winged Man, and all knew of the handsome rewards that were out for his capture. Besides, none of those present had ever seen the weird terror, consequently they had no idea of the awful appearance of he whom they were so eager to capture.

Acting under Danby Druce's orders, one of the keepers was stationed at either side of the house, with orders to shoot the Winged Man down without a moment's hesitation if he attempted to escape by flight.

Then a man mounted guard over each window and the back door; whilst Danby Druce, armed with the woodman's axe, proceeded to attack the front entrance.

"Are you all ready?" asked Danby Druce.

"Ay, ay, sir!" came back the ready response.

"Then, mind, seize him at once. Don't give him a second to prepare for flight or fight, or we are done. Now!"

Swinging the axe high above his head, Danby Druce brought it down upon the panel of the door. The axe head crashed through the wooden panels as though they had been made of paper.

The next moment the detective staggered back, a cry of alarm on his lips. Wreaths of black, choking smoke forced their way through the opening he had just made.

"Quick, lads! The hut is on fire! Attack both doors and windows! Down with the barricades! We must take him prisoner before he is burned to ashes within the hut!" shouted Danby Druce.

Immediately the labourers fell to work on the barricades, all but the gamekeepers, and they stood prepared to protect the workers should the Winged Man attempt to attack them.

Suddenly, with cries of alarm, the would-be rescuers staggered back before a sudden outburst of lurid flame. The interior of the hut was a perfect furnace. It had been used to store faggots, and they, as dry as tinder, were blazing fiercely.

That the conflagration was the result of an accident Danby Druce did not for a moment doubt.

FROM OUT THE FLAMES.

Even the Winged Man, master of the elements though he appeared to be, dared not have kindled that fire himself.

So fierce was the blaze, so long, red, and threatening the serpentine tongues of flame, that, bursting from the doors and windows, they forbade the would-be rescuers' approach.

There was no elation in Danby Druce's heart as he watched what he believed to be the end of the Winged Man. Though that weird terror had baffled, beaten, and held him up to ridicule on a score of different occasions, he had grown to respect him, and, had he been able, would have dashed into the flames to his enemy's assistance, even though it had been but to have arrested him the next moment.

"Seems to me, sir, as how the Winged Man will never trouble us again. I suppose we'll get the reward?" asked one of the gamekeepers.

"Hang the reward!" retorted Danby Druce angrily. "Poor beggar! I would not have doomed a mad dog to such a fearful end!"

"Good-bye to the Winged Man!" said Neil Holmes solemnly. "He is dead!"

"You lie! He lives!" rose in deep, loud tones above the roar of the devouring element.

Then as the roof fell in with a crash, sending a shower of sparks flying heavenward, his wide wings extended, his face wreathed in a mocking smile, the Winged Man soared through the flames, straight into a cloud of smoke which hung above the trees.

For nearly a minute Danby Druce and his companions looked at each other in awe-stricken amazement.

"Great powers! He cannot be of this earth! No human being could have emerged alive from so pitiless a furnace!" ejaculated Neil Holmes at last.

Then he came to an abrupt halt, gazing with white, blanched cheeks and his companion.

"The woman! The callous, cold-hearted wretch, has left her to perish in the flames!"

"You lie!" came the Winged Man's sonorous denial.

And, peering through the smoke, they saw him, a dark-muffled form clasped in his arms, hovering above their heads.

"Fire! Fire!" cried Danby Druce. "Aim at his legs and face; they are his only vulnerable points!"

Out of the flames rose the Winged Man.

The keepers raised their guns to their shoulders; but ere they could pull a trigger the Winged Man, diving into the thickest of the smoke, disappeared from view.

Presently they saw him once more, but he was flying with slow-beating wings in the direction of Dovetail, far beyond the reach of gun or pistol.

"Quick—to the car! After him—after him!" cried Danby Druce.

Though his one object in life now was the destruction of the Winged Man, he was a sportsman from the sole of his feet to the tips of his fingers, and a load seemed lifted off his heart now that he knew the Winged Man had not perished in the flames.

A word of farewell to the labourers and gamekeepers, and Danby Druce and Neil Holmes raced back to the car.

BAFFLED ONCE MORE.

Resuming his goggles, which he had thrown down upon the indiarubber sheet, covering the body of the car, Neil Holmes sprang to the driver's seat. Danby Druce took his place beside him, and the chase was resumed.

Along the course of the winding Dove the car flew, now almost overtaking the Winged Man, now being left far behind as he crossed or recrossed the river where there was no bridge.

His foe's tactics puzzled Danby Druce. The Winged Man was playing with them, leading them a long, hopeless chase, when, by choosing one of the many trackless paths on the picturesque banks of the river, he could have easily evaded them. Unless, indeed, he was in practically unknown country, and hunting for some place of refuge.

Now and again, whenever they came within pistol-shot, Danby Druce, hoping that a lucky bullet might lay the Winged Man low, opened fire upon him. He did so on a part of the picturesque road, where huge rocks rose perpendicularly on either side of the narrow road they were traversing.

In response to one-shot came a cry of pain and rage from the Winged Man. Fluttering like a badly-wounded bird, he, with difficulty, reached the summit of one of the rocks we have mentioned, then sank in a saddled heap on its top.

Neil Holmes brought the car to a halt.

"Your last shot did for him," he declared.

His heart beating wildly with hope and triumph, Danby Druce sprang from the car, and clambered up the uneven base of the rock. At length success had crowned his efforts. Not burned in despair, not slain by accident, but brought down after a long, patient chase, the Winged Man lay wounded, perchance dying, on the summit of that rock. It was a difficult climb, yet eagerness to secure the Winged Man urged him on, and a few minutes later the summit was reached.

The glow faded from Danby Druce's heart, the light of triumph from his eyes. There, upon the moss-grown rock lay an empty cloak, but the Winged Man had vanished. Danby Druce rubbed his eyes, unable to believe the evidence of his senses. He had made so certain that the Winged Man was stricken down that the disappointment was almost more than he could bear.

A loud ejaculation of amazement, followed by a cry of terror from below, caused him to look in the direction of the car.

Sweeping like an eagle upon its prey, the Winged Man had darted upon Neil Holmes. Twining his long, sinewy hands round the fear-paralysed man's collar, he bore him swiftly to the summit of the second rocky pillar, upon which he placed him ere he flew back to the car.

So swiftly had all this taken place that air Danby Druce could attempt to go to his friend's assistance, the Winged Man had returned to the car.

Instead of driving off as the detective confidently expected he would do, the Winged Man tore off the India rubber sheet from the body of the car.

Cries of baffled rage and astonishment rose from Danby Druce's and Neil Holmes's lips, as, her beautiful face wreathed in mocking smile as, Annette Royle, who had been hidden in the body of the car ever since the burning hut had been left, suddenly appeared at the side of the Winged Man.

"Farewell, Danby Druce! You would have parted two true, loving hearts, but I bear you no malice!" came in mocking tones from the Winged Man's lips, as, rising, he flew swiftly to where, in full view of the astonishment-paralysed men on the rock, the swift waters of the Dove float down a miniature rapid, towards where the narrow river deepened, ere it fell between two rocks into what is locally known as the "Devil's Cauldron."

Hovering a moment over the river, the Winged Man suddenly closed his wings, and dropped like a stone into the water.

With scarcely beating hearts and starting eyes the two men watched the Winged Man, the girl clasped in his arms, borne by the swift torrent towards the "Devil's Cauldron," at the bottom of which, whirling round and round, foaming, seething, fearful even to gaze upon, was a circular basin into which no human being might fall and live.

For a moment the Winged Man and his burden remained poised on the edge of this basin, then, with a loud, mocking cry, Annette Royle's white arms clasped round his neck, the Winged Man flung up his hands and disappeared into the cauldron.

Ten minutes later, white-faced and trembling, Danby Druce and Neil Holmes were stretched full-length on the edge of the cliff, gazing into the swirling whirlpool below, seeking in vain for some trace of those who had disappeared within it.

"Surely this is the end of the Winged Man!" shuddered Neil Holmes.

Danby Druce shook his head.

"Neither fire, water, bullet, nor steel can slay him. Depend upon it he is close at hand. Perhaps even now laughing in his wild, weird way at our amazement!" he declared, as he rose, and walked slowly back to the car.

A SUBTERRANEAN PALACE.

Neither was the detective far out.

Had the Winged Man plunged into that fearful whirlpool naught could have saved him. His asbestos garments had brought him safely from out the fire, but even his superhuman strength would have availed him little against those constantly revolving waters.

At the very edge of the cup-like basin was a hole in the rock big enough for a man to creep through. Thither the Winged Man had borne Annette Royle, then through constantly winding passages, which led to one of his haunts in the heart of the Peak District.

A fearful journey. A nerve-racking scramble through the bowels of the earth followed. Now borne in the Winged Man's arms as he skimmed lightly over the surface of a subterranean lake, now stumbling onward in the darkness, supported by the weird being's arms, the rays from his blazing head-light showing Nature's grotesque handiwork on the walls of the several caves, now creeping through holes scarcely big enough to admit her slender body, now dropping down well-like chasms, now rising up mighty chimneys like shafts in the living rock.

Again and again the terrified girl paused, gasping for breath, to lean upon the Winged Man's arm. Accustomed to breathe the gas-tainted air beneath the surface, it had little or no effect upon the Winged Man, although painful, and at times dangerous to others.

"Is it far? Is it far?" moaned Annette.

"Courage, beautiful one! A few minutes longer and we shall have reached our destination," returned the Winged Man encouragingly.

Once more Annette, with wondrous courage, though almost unconscious from sheer weariness and terror, pressed on by her weird conductor's side.

Suddenly she paused. Her heart almost ceased to beat. From out of the darkness, immediately on her right, came an ominous, fearful sound.

It was like nothing the beautiful adventuress had ever heard before.

It was a cry such as might have been wrung from a being in torture. It was the last straw.

With a hysterical shriek, Annette threw herself on her knees.

"Dread being—man, monster, fiend whatever you are—have mercy! Take me to the upper air, give me to the police—anything; but let me see the light of day once more!" she implored.

"What? Leave the man whom you have sworn to love?" demanded the Winged Man.

Annette remained silent. A wave of horror and repulsion, almost hatred, for the calm, fearful, demonish-looking form by her side swept through her heart.

THE CELLS OF THE DOOMED.

With a deep sigh, as though he could read her inmost thoughts the Winged Man laid his hand upon her smooth, white forehead. The effect was magical.

As though some black curtain had been lifted from her soul the terrible fear which had gripped her heart departed, and she became the cool self-contained, calculating adventress once more.

It is true, horror of the Winged Man remained, but above all was the desire to possess herself of his gold by fair means or foul.

Again that fearful cry rang out.

A stifled shriek burst from Annette's lips, but she was better prepared for it this time, and, though deadly pale, met the unknown horror dauntless.

"Brave girl, worthy even to be the Winged Man's bride!" said that weird being, laying his hand upon her arm. "Fear nothing. The cry came from my gaolers— ay, trustee gaolers, whom neither promise nor gold could buy!"

"Are there such men?" asked Annette, with a cynical smile.

The Winged Man drew her to wear a faint light shone through a crevice in the rocky wall.

"Behold the only absolutely unbribable warders in the world, guarding the cells of the doomed!" said the Winged Man.

Peering through the opening, Annette Royle saw a strange sight.

The fissure in the rock opened into a long narrow corridor, cut out of the solid rock, lighted by a number of irregularly-shaped holes in the face of the bosom of the hill, in which they then were.

Opposite these holes were a number of smaller caves, evidently chiselled by the hand of man, from out the living rock.

Before each cave was a thick door, or gate, of iron bars; and Annette shuddered as she saw a wretched being, with thin wasted hands, grasping the bars of his prison, his white, misery-laden face staring straight at one of the light holes, through which he could catch a glimpse of the blue, unclouded heaven above.

A glimpse of arms and legs in the other caves told that they, too, were occupied by similar unhappy creatures.

"Who are they? Why are they imprisoned here?" she demanded, not daring to look at her companion lest he should read horror and loathing of him in her eyes.

"Men who have dared to cross the Winged Man's path!" explained the Winged Man, in deep, solemn tones. "Men who have persecuted the orphaned and friendless; men, who, as a prison-warders or policeman, have tyrannised over the wretched criminals in their power, and are now tasting the punishment they themselves inflicted! Men speak evil of the Winged Man, but yonder scoundrels bear witness to his justice."

"And it was from those cells that the fearful cries arose?" demanded Annette.

The Winged Man whistled.

A cry, something between a human shriek and a dog's bark reverberated through both ends of the corridor.

The next moment Annette started from the crevice, as two hideous gorillas sprang into view, stood mouthing with their huge, white-fanged chops, and turning their heads from side to side in a listening attitude.

"Those are the warders who cannot be bribed!" said the Winged Man, with a smile. "Trained by my own hand, they attend my prisoners, let them out for exercise, and return them to their cells at sunrise and sunset. Woe to the unhappy wretch who attempts to escape! Torn limb from limb by my warders, their bodies are thrown down into a crevasse, which even I have never yet been able to fathom. What think you of my warders, Annette?"

The girl did not answer.

It had been with difficulty even whilst moving that she had kept her heavy lids open. Standing still, sleep had overcome her, and, her head leaning upon her shapely arm that was pressed against the rocky side of the fissure, she slept.

Taking the lovely form in his arms, the Winged Man sped swiftly through the winding passages until at length he reached a dark, yawning chasm, down which he dropped.

His descent ceased in a long, brilliantly-lighted cave, the walls of which were hung with tapestry, torn from a castle on the Rhine.

Soft couches, beautifully upholstered chairs, magnificently inlaid tables, went to make up the furniture of the room.

The Winged Man whistled shrilly. Like a pantomime demon, Ghat sprang through the concealed a concealed trap door in one corner of the cave.

"Master, my dear Master, returned at last!" he cried, approaching the Winged Man with ungainly strides.

Then, for the first time, he noticed Annette in her semi-conscious state.

He came to an abrupt halt. A fierce, angry frown contorted his hideous features.

"Who is she? Why do you bring her here? Away with her!" he cried petulantly.

"Silence, cur amongst dogs that you are! Behold your queen and mine!" thundered the Winged Man.

A look of wild, fierce, jealous hatred blazed for a moment from Ghat's eyes; then, as Annette Royle, moving uneasily in her sleep, turned, so that he could see her face, a swift change came over his features, and a look of wild, dazed admiration appeared as he stood gazing as though fascinated by the girl's wondrous beauty.

Then, his eyes fixed depreciatingly upon his master, he crept forward, and, raising a fold of Annette's skirt to his lips, kissed it, repeating as he did so:

"Your queen and mine, master—or, yes; your queen and mine!"

With a contemptuous laughed, the Winged Man kicked Ghat aside; then, carrying his fair burden into an apartment adjoining the larger room, laid her upon a couch of cloth of gold, covered her with rich, rare furs; then, drawing an embroidered Persian rug over her fair form, left her to sleep off her weariness.

Annette disposed of, the Winged Man soared to the dome-shaped ceiling of the larger apartment, and hung head downwards, his wings draped around him, and was soon fast asleep.

THE SLAVE.

Three hours later, Ghat's trap door opened, and the misshapen Ghat thrust forth his huge, ungainly head. A half-terrified glance above showed him the Winged Man suspended from the ceiling. Slowly he drew his body on to the floor of the cave, then crept noiselessly to the curtained archway leading into the room where Annette Royle slept.

Swiftly drawing aside the curtain, he peeped in. As he did so every vestige of colour fled from his face, leaving it a peculiarly repulsive and corpse-like yellow.

Step-by-step Ghat drew himself rather than walked into the room, his eyes fixed upon the girl's perfect profile. Despite his hideous form, Ghat possessed a loyal, loving nature. It is true the ill-treatment and contempt of the only being on earth he had hitherto loved had soured his nature. Yet the sight of the beautiful woman stretched in sleep before him brought to life all that was good in his nature.

For the first and only time in his life, Ghat was in love. Not the dispassionate way of men accustomed to meet their fellow-creatures on equal terms, but with the wild, mad, irresistible devotion of a being who knew not what to be loved meant. His heart beating wildly, as it had never beaten before, his whole frame tingling from the top of his shaggy head to the soles of his enormous splay feet, Ghat approached the couch.

For some minutes he stood pale and trembling as he looked upon those lovely features, then Annette Royle awoke, her lovely face rendered ten times more beautiful by the happy dream-smile upon her lips.

Then her eyes opened, and Ghat recoiled, as though she had plunged a knife into his heart, before the look of repulsive terror which swept across her face.

"The gorilla, the gorilla!" she shrieked. "Help, help, help!"

Standing on a pedestal in one corner of the room was an enormous wide-mouthed vase, ornamented with the green five-toed dragon, which showed that it had been looted from the Imperial Palace in Peking, for none but the Emperors of China are allowed to possess anything with the five-toed monster delineated upon it.

A single bound carried him half-way to the vase, the next he had disappeared within it, just as the Winged Man, consternation on his face, swept in full flight into the room. Seated on the edge of the couch where he had left her, Annette Royle was gazing around the room with fear-dilated eyes. Courteously the Winged Man approached and grasped her trembling hand.

"What is it that has alarmed you, sweet one? Tell me?" he asked.

"The gorilla, the gorilla!" was all Annette Royle could say.

The Winged Man looked swiftly to the right and left, then, with an indulgent laugh, replied:

"You have been dreaming, Annette. The gorillas could never reach this place."

"No, no; I am certain I was not dreaming. I opened my eyes, my heart filled with happiness, and then—and then—"

The girl paused, and she lowered her eyelids to hide the agitation and terror that possessed her soul.

The Winged Man seized her hand. Awakening love had lolled the Winged Man's keen senses to sleep, or he would have known that what he believed to be a tremble of delight that shook Annette Royle's frame was, in reality a scarcely-suppressed shudder of horror and loathing.

It had been a fearful shock to awake from a dream of Peter Armstrong, the only man who had ever called forth a responding throb from her heart, to find first the hunchback bending over her, then the Winged Man.

It was too much; she could not bear it, and her body fell limp. Restoring the girl to the couch, the Winged Man hastened from the room, returning shortly afterwards with a draught which he poured between Annette's lips.

Annette Royle opened her eyes, smiled faintly then pretended to drop into a deep slumber. The Winged Man stole noiselessly from the room, little guessing that it had been no dream, but reality, which had struck such panic at Annette's heart.

Crouched in the vase, his face contorted with diabolical rage, trembling so that he feared he would attract the Winged Man's attention, Ghat raged and fumed. Had Annette Royle tried her best to find some phrase, some word, by which to pierce Ghat's heart and insult him beyond forgiveness, she could not have hit upon anything better calculated to do so than to liken him to a gorilla.

Ever since the Winged Man had trained his watchful warders Ghat regarded them with the greatest repugnance; as well he might, for scarce a day past but the Winged Man compared Ghat unfavourably with his brute fellow-servitors.

Slain by a carelessly-spoken word, Ghat's love was dead. A great undying hatred for the woman who had scorned him took its place. Hearing no sound but the heavy breathing of the sleeper, Ghat thrust his hideous head, covered with tangled elf-locks, from the mouth of the vase, and gazed at the sleeper.

Wondrous indeed was the change that had taken place within him. The thought that she would be his mistress and he her slave was more than he could bear.

Stealing cautiously from the vase, he once more approached the couch. Through her long, dark, silken eyelids, Annette Royle watched the fearful, misshapen, scarce-human form approach. Fear gripped her heart. With burning eyes Ghat paused by her side, and drew from the loose folds of his ragged coat a small but exceedingly sharp, broad-bladed dagger.

A cry of alarm rose to Annette's lips, but terror held her down. Leaning over her, the dwarf pressed the hilt of the dagger against the back of the couch, then left it with the point resting against her shoulder, in such a way that on awaking and turning, as she naturally would do, on to her back, the deadly little instrument would pierce her heart.

His fearful object achieved, Ghat stole silently from the room and disappeared down his trapdoor. Squatting cross-legged before a fire of smouldering charcoal in the cold, bare cave which formed his living-room, he chuckled fiendishly and maliciously to himself.

Annette Royle had seen the dwarf's hand withdrawn from her back without the dagger which it had previously clasped, and, without moving her body, she groped behind her. Her fingers touched the coal cold steel blade. With a shudder she drew it from its place. Rising, she walked to a wall-mirror, and with her fingers concealed the weapon amidst the thick plaits of her long, silken, raven tresses.

THE GREED OF GOLD.

Annette Royle had entered the Winged Man's subterranean retreat with the determination that if she could not obtain a hold on his wealth by trickery, to become his wife. But the memory of Peter Armstrong restrained her. He was the one love of her life.

Thus it happened that though the Winged Man wooed her as he had never wooed woman before, she refused to become his queen. Yet she dared not leave it this subterranean resort for the Winged Man brought news from outside that Danby Druce and a bevy of detectives were still in the neighbourhood searching everywhere for her.

Then one day the Winged Man led Annette Royle through several caves until at last he paused before a huge rock, which apparently blocked up the natural tunnel through which they had been walking.

"Annette Royle, will you be my wife?" he asked. "Think not that I wish you to be an outlaw's bride. I have wealth, and in another country we can lead a life of luxury and happiness."

The girl shrank back.

"Not yet—do not ask me yet! I have not yet learned to love you!" she stammered.

A melancholy smile crept into the Winged Man's eyes. Still holding her shoulder with the right hand, he laid the palm of his left upon her brow, and with the first and third fingers pressed down her eyelids.

"Annette Royle, will you be my wife?" he demanded a second time.

The girl trembled from head to foot; her face grew ashen white. In vain she tried to utter the words she had before spoken, but instead came from her unwilling lips:

"If it is your will, I will become your wife."

"I know that if it were my will that you should become my bride, you would," he said coldly. "But is it your will?"

By his wondrous will-power he had forced assent from the girl's lips. But he would not take a bride so won.

Removing his hand from her forehead, he said:

"No—no! Nature intended me to be alone in the world. Better that than an unwilling partner. Come!"

Turning abruptly, the Winged Man pressed a concealed spring.

A loud, thundering sound reverberated through the tunnel, as, like a gate upon its hinges, the huge rock, weighing several tons sank into the earth, disclosing a large iron door, which the Winged Man unlocked with a key he had taken from a golden chain that encircled his neck.

As the door swung noiselessly open, the Winged Man shut off the electric torch that had guided them through the tunnel.

Grasping Annette Royle by the arm he led her through the doorway.

Suddenly, the beams of his torch illuminated the scene.

With a cry of wonder and delight, Annette Royle clasped her hands to her eyes, half-blinded by the dazzling glitter which surrounded her on every side.

Surely never before had human eyes gazed upon such an accumulation of wealth.

°THE BRIDE OF THE WINGED MAN.

Arranged on sloping shelves of velvet were countless diamonds, rubies, pearls, necklaces, brooches, bracelets, watches, tiaras; in fact, every ornament in which the heart of man or woman rejoices; whilst littered on the floor, as though things of no worth, were gold and silver cups, intermixed with heaps of glittering sovereigns.

Annette Royle could scarce credit the evidence of her senses.

Millions could not have bought the contents of this room, and yet she knew it was but a portion of the Winged Man's hidden wealth.

The Winged Man touched her on the shoulder.

She started violently, and looked towards him.

A dark frown clouded his brow.

It was an evil light that glittered from Annette Royle's eyes. The light of avarice and greed. A light which showed that gold, diamonds, and gems were the things most to be desired of all the good life can give in Annette Royle's eyes.

The Winged Man swept his hand round the room.

"Should I ever marry, the contents of this room shall be my wife's dowry. Annette Royle, will you be my wife?" he asked, in deep, sonorous tones.

"And it will be mine—all mine, to do what I like with, to spend as I like?" demanded Annette breathlessly.

"I have said it shall be my wife's dowry," replied the Winged Man coldly. "You have not answered my question."

"Yes—yes! A thousand times yes! What is love compared with gold like this?"

° 15 MARCH 1913.

cried Annette Royle, dropping upon her knees and plunging her arms up to the elbow in a heap of gold.

Almost roughly the Winged Man drew her to her feet.

"Then you consent? I would rather you had been won by love of me than love of gold. Yet perhaps it is better so. Come!" he commanded.

Annette Royle was unwilling to leave the treasure vault, and when she did so, with the Winged Man's permission, she carried with her gems worth a fabulous amount.

LOVE TRIUMPHANT.

Very moodily, considering he had just been accepted by the woman he loved, the Winged Man led the way from the treasure chamber to wear four paths crossed each other.

He paused.

"You have not yet visited my present!" he declared. "Come, you shall see how the Winged Man punishes those who are false to, or who thwart him."

There was an undercurrent of ominous threat in the Winged Man's tones which sent a shudder of horror through Annette's frame.

A cold, metallic laugh burst from her lips.

The Winged Man looked searchingly at her, yet did not speak.

He led the way down a dark, gloomy passage, until at length they found their way barred by a snarling, grinning gorilla, crouched ready to spring.

Annette clung in terror to the Winged Man's arm.

Thrusting the gorilla away, the Winged Man pointed to a cell door.

Hobbling forward, the man-ape flung it open, and darting in, drew out by the scruff of his neck, a miserable-looking, half-famished being.

"You would not think, Annette, that that cringing hound was once one of the first lawyers in the north of England, and mayor of his town. Even now the police are searching for him throughout South America on a charge of having used the funds of orphans and widows entrusted to him. He fled with his ill-gotten gains, but the Winged Man had marked him as his own. See what he is now."

"Serves him right!" declared Annette. "But what of the gold?"

"In the dead of the night I flew round to the various happy homes that the scoundrel had plunged into misery and poverty, and left a portion of the stolen gold at each," explained the Winged Man.

A look of contemptuous discontent flashed into Annette's eyes, but she held her peace.

The next man the Winged Man showed her was a warder from a convict establishment, who had cruelly abused his authority.

Then came a key part of a public lunatic asylum, who had beaten one of his patients to death, and only escaped imprisonment from want of evidence against him.

Man after man the Winged Man produced, relating the history of each as the wretch was drawn from his cage.

"Here is the pride of my collection. A swell mobsman, a clever and unscrupulous rogue, known as Peter Armstrong, who discovered one of my hidden haunts, and tried to rob me," said the Winged Man, pausing before one of the cells.

The gorilla went in as before to pull out the prisoner.

"Get off, you beast! Keep your hands off me!" cried a voice from within; and his little eyes flashing fiercely, the gorilla retreated before the tall, handsome man who emerged from the cells. "It is well, Winged Man, that you are always protected by these unholy beasts, or I would—"

He got no further.

A low, moaning cry burst from Annette Royle's lips.

White as death she staggered forward with outstretched arms, crying:

"Peter! Is it—can it be you?"

"Annette, my darling, it has been the thought of you alone that has enabled me to bear the treatment of the heartless demon into whose power I have fallen!" he cried, and the next moment the two were locked in each other's arms.

Ashen hued went the Winged Man.

He staggered back as though stabbed when he saw the girl he loved clasped in the arms of his despised prisoner.

Suddenly the Winged Man took a step forward, and grasped Annette fiercely by the shoulder.

"Girl! Who is that man? Speak!" he demanded.

"A friend—a dear friend. One whom I thought dead," replied Annette Royle.

"And you love him?" demanded the Winged Man.

Annette Royle hesitated.

"Ay, I love him! But Heaven help me, I have promised to marry you!" she cried.

"Annette, what are you saying? It cannot be—it shall not be! You marry a being of another world—accursed fiend, hated by the whole creation. I repeat, it cannot—it shall not be!" thundered the prisoner.

A loud, mocking laugh burst from the Winged Man's lips.

"It shall—it must be! Who dares gainsay the Winged Man?" he cried.

"I do!" cried Peter Armstrong. And his eyes falling upon the dagger in Annette's hair, he snatched it from out her raven tresses, and, wheeling it above his head, with a wild, almost mad cries, hurled himself upon the Winged Man.

Straight to the heart sped the steel, but the Winged Man raised not so much as a finger to ward off the blow, yet the weapon shattered against his bullet-proof breastplate.

Peter Armstrong dropped the jewelled handle of his useless weapon on the floor; then, beside himself with fury, clutched desperately at the Winged Man's throat.

But ere he could reach his foe the gorillas were upon him.

Strong, well-built man though he was, Peter Armstrong was but a child in those long, hairy, muscular arms.

In vain he struggled, in vain he strove to fling the brutes off.

Almost ere Annette could turn with a cry for mercy for her sweetheart to the Winged Man, the gorillas had borne their prey down. One huge route, its huge forepaws upon the miserable man's forehead, was snapping its teeth before his face, as though longing to bury its huge, white fangs in his throat.

The sight roused Annette from the stupor of despair into which the fearful sight had thrown her.

"Have mercy—have mercy! Kill us both, or spare him. Take back your gold and your jewels—take back all you have given me, but spare my lover's life!" she cried, dropping on her knees at the Winged Man's feet.

With folded arms the Winged Man looked sternly down upon her.

"Be mine without the dowry, and I spare yonder man's life!" he cried, in cold, sonorous tones.

"Yes—yes! Spare him—spare him!" pleaded the girl.

"No, no, Annette! I would rather die ten thousand deaths than see you wedded to yonder inhuman wretch!" interposed Peter, in accents of horrified despair.

A sign from the Winged Man, and, rising reluctantly from their prisoner, the gorillas thrust him back into his cage-like cell and drew the bars upon him.

"Annette," said the Winged Man, leaning over the still kneeling girl, who, her face hidden in her hands, was sobbing bitterly. "Choose! A prison life with him, or a life lightened by all that wealth can give, with me. Choose!"

Slowly the girl rose to her feet.

For a moment she stood glancing from one to the other, from the wondrous being endowed with more than human power, to the miserable wretch who had fallen under the ban of the Winged Man's displeasure.

Love fought with avarice for domination over her heart. Suddenly, with a gesture of one who abandons all that life holds dear, she turned towards the prison cell. A look of baffled rage and bitter disappointment swept across the Winged Man's face.

"Stop!" He thundered. "Your choice, when made, is irrevocable. Move or speak at your peril!"

A stride carried him to the nearest wall of rock. He touched a secret spring. Shutters flew over the cracks in the rocks, through which the daylight penetrated, plunging the whole place into a darkness that might almost be felt.

THE FINAL CHOICE.

A low, terror-stricken moan burst from Annette Royle's lips. The low, deep, breathing of the gorillas seemed to fill the whole place; yet she dared not move—dared not attempt to fly from the unseen horrors that surrounded her.

Never before had Annette Royle known what real terror was. She was brave, braver than the majority of women, yet that awful darkness, the companionship of those fearful beasts, the knowledge of the irresistible power wielded by the man against whom she had pitted her wit and beauty, all combined to fill her with a nerve-shattering terror.

Slowly she raised her hand to her face. A low, shuddering moan escaped her lips.

"Annette, my betrothed, though iron bars divide us, yet I am here!" cried Peter Armstrong roused to madness by the sound of his loved one's distress.

The thought of her lover's presence gave Annette Royle renewed courage.

"The feeling of fear is gone, Harry.[30] I am brave once more!" she cried resolutely.

"Good girl! Brave girl! Courage all may yet be well!" came back the answer through the darkness.

Then followed age-long minutes of utter silence. Suddenly Annette Royle noticed that the darkness was being relieved by a low, mysterious light. Whither it had come she could not tell.

Slowly it permeated the long prison gallery. A whimper of fear arose from the gorillas. A prolonged whistle echoed from rock to rock, followed by loud, staccato cries.

Evidently it was a signal the apes understood, for, without a moment's hesitation, they flung open the bars, and drew Peter Armstrong from his cell; then a shaggy paw on each of their prisoner's shoulders held him tight.

As slowly as it had come, the light faded until Annette could see naught but the shadowy form of her lover and his grim custodians. Suddenly she started, and a terrified shriek burst from her lips, as, with a roar like distant thunder, one side of the gallery was torn asunder, and a fierce, bright light flooded sombre scene.

So dazzling was its beam that at first Annette Royle could see nothing; then, as her eyes grew accustomed to the glare, she breathed a prolonged sigh, in which adoration and delight predominated over astonishment and fear. She dropped upon her knees in homage.

Where a few seconds before had been an apparently solid mass of rock, stood the Winged Man. No European monarch, no Turkish Sultan, no Eastern potentate in India's most palmy days had ever presented so splendid an appearance as did the weird, wondrous creature, whom Annette Royle realised,

---

[30] Later, the narrator refers to Peter Armstrong as "Handsome Harry". There is no explanation for this, unless it is describing his physique, as, when it is used later Armstrong begins a boxing match.

with a flush of pride and triumph, was ready to lay his wealth at her feet.

He still wore his close-fitting clothes of sombre black, but on his head flashed a crown rich with the finest gems the world has ever seen. Diamonds formed a breastplate over his chest. His arms were encircled by bands of gold. A belt of rubies, pearls, and diamonds encircled his waist, and a cloak of gold, embroidered with pearls, hung gracefully from one shoulder.

His head proudly raised, his tall form set off to advantage by the magnificent apparel, the Winged Man looked every inch a king. Slowly the Winged Man raised his arm, and pointed to where Peter Armstrong, lost in amazement, was standing betwixt his guard.

He was clad in filthy rags, his face bearing marks of his recent struggle with the gorillas, his hair matted and unkempt; his face half hidden in a stubbly beard.

"Annette Royle, you stand between the lowest step to which a man can fall, and the highest point to which a being such as I can rise! Either lot may be yours. Choose!" cried the Winged Man.

Slowly Annette Royle turned from the glittering figure that addressed her, and fixed her eyes upon her lover. Then she turned to the Winged Man once more.

"Annette, beware! Trust not yonder demon!" cried Peter Armstrong, in tones of agonised entreaty. "He will lure you to destruction!"

His words fell unheeded upon Annette Royle's ear. Slowly, as one walking in her sleep, she moved over the smoothly-trodden, rocky floor, and grasped the Winged Man's outstretched hand.

A wild cry of bitter rage and despair burst from Peter Armstrong as he strove to dash forward, seeking death at the Winged Man's hand rather than life with the knowledge that the girl he loved had proved false to him.

But ere he had taken a single step the gorillas were upon him, and, in obedience to a glance from the Winged Man, thrust him back into his cell.

"By my right hand, Annette Royle, you shall never regret your choice!" cried the Winged Man.

Annette Royle fled down the corridor. The gorillas stepped forward to intercept her, but at a sign from their master they retreated.

With folded arms, the Winged Man watched Annette Royle reach the cell, and, thrusting her face through the bars, impress upon her his prisoner's lips the salute she had refused him, her promised husband.

"Trust me, dear one," whispered the girl. "It is for your sake I am acting thus. I will be true to you—true till death!"

Then aloud, for the Winged Man to hear, she cried:

"Think of me, as I shall think of you, as one belonging only to the happy past—the past which can never be recalled!"

Without a word, she returned, with bowed head and faltering steps, to where the Winged Man awaited her.

IN PERIL OF EVICTION.

"My good woman, it is nothing to me if your husband is out of work, and that your only child is dying for want of the medical attendance you cannot afford to give her. Of course, I am sorry for you, Mrs. Tribbet, and all the rest of it, but I must have my money. I'll give you until this time to-morrow to pay the three weeks' rent due, or I'll distrain upon your goods."

The pale-faced, emaciated woman glanced appealingly at the big, prosperous-looking landlord who had just pronounced her doom, and she knew but too well the doom of her sick child.

"Oh, sir, I cannot pay you yet. Have you no heart, no compassion? Where can I go, what can I do, if you turn me out of doors?" she sobbed.

"Why, there's the workhouse! You and your brat will be much better off there!" was the brutal reply. "As to your husband, probably the lazy, hulking scoundrel is in prison by this time!"

A pained flush dyed the woman's white face. Drawing herself up, her eyes flashing with the proud anger of an injured queen, she said:

"Woman never had a better husband than mine has ever been to me. It is through no fault of his he is out of employment. No matter. By this time to-morrow we will be gone, though it be to die in a ditch. And I pray that Heaven's vengeance may descend on you, and that the same mercy you have shown to me may be shown to you in your hour of need."

The brutal laugh that rose to the landlord's lips was changed to a cry of terror as a sepulchre role voice from the door of the tiny cottage cried:

"Amen to that! Sleek, money-grubbing vampire that you are, this woman has pronounced your doom!"

"Who are you?" gasped the landlord, his bloated cheeks quivering like a jelly with terror.

"I am the Winged Man! Go! But be sure the curse of the stricken and helpless will follow you to your grave!"

In vain the landlord tried to speak. Overawed by the Winged Man's awful personality, he slunk, cowed and trembling, from the cottage.

White-faced, speechless, the woman clutched the side of a plain deal table to keep herself from falling as she gazed with terror-stricken eyes at her fearful visitor.

"Fear nothing. I am a terror only to evil-doers. To yourself I am the bearer of freedom from such scenes as that I have just witnessed. Listen," he continued, holding up his hand as the woman was about to speak. "What ails your child?"

In low, trembling tones the woman named a complaint which naught but good feeding and constant attention could cure.

Without a word the Winged Man took a bundle of banknotes from his pocket and laid them on the table.

"Take your child to the nearest hospital. Give these to the matron in charge. Money buys all things; she will attend to your child. Then return hither. I have need of your services," he ordered.

"Is it true—can it be true?" murmured the woman, passing her hand wearily across her brow.

Then her fingers closed upon the rustling banknotes, and she would have flung herself at the Winged Man's feet had he not stopped her.

"Mind, this money is not a gift, but a payment in advance for services to be rendered. For a period not exceeding three months I require your help. Beneath the bowels of the earth, closer at hand then perhaps you deem possible, awaits my future bride. She has no maid to attend upon her once. Wait upon her, and a similar amount to that in your hand shall be yours."

The woman hesitated. She saw her child restored to health, her husband unhampered during his first months of work by having to support home, but paying off his debts.

A few questions satisfactorily answered by the Winged Man, and she consented.

"It is well!" said the Winged Man. "Be at the Marble Rock at midnight. Fail on your peril! The Winged Man knows how to reward and how to punish!"

Turning on his heel, the Winged Man strode from the cottage. Rising, he skimmed the ground behind a tall hedge which bordered the road along which the landlord was hastening. Flying on ahead, he alighted immediately before his intended victim. With a cry of terror the landlord came to an abrupt halt.

"Don't hurt me! I am an old man. Have mercy! I cannot bear ill-treatment!"

"Then that should have made you more considerate for those in your power!" thundered the Winged Man. "You are rich."

"No, no! You have been misinformed. I am poor—very poor. A few houses and cottages in this district is all I have to live upon!"

"Seek not to deceive me!" thundered the Winged Man. "But yet you tell the truth. You are poor—poor in comparison with what you may be. See, this stone is worth fifty thousand pounds. If you would earn it, be at the Giant's Marble at twelve o'clock to-night. Farewell!"

As the last words left his lips the Winged Man sprang into the air and vanished beyond black storm-clouds which hung heavily over the earth.

As he pierced the clouds a bright flash of lightning illuminated the scene. The lightning was followed by a loud, reverberating roar of heaven's artillery. To the frightened landlord it seemed a fitting sequel to his fearful adventure, and he believed that the weird being who had just left him was the Evil One in person.

Yet, fiend or man, the supernatural being had offered him wealth such as in his wildest moments he had never dreamt of possessing, and already the landlord had made up his mind to be at the Giant's Marble at the appointed time.

It was a thick, heavy, oppressive night. Now and again the moon, bursting from the heavy masses of storm-clouds, shone over a scene rendered sombre by a threatening thunderstorm.

Two people approached the Giant's Marble from different opposite directions. One, a woman, advanced with hesitating, shrinking steps; the other, a man, pressed eagerly forward towards his fearful trysting-place. They were Mrs. Tribbet and her brutal landlord.

The woman reached the rock, and stood gazing abstractly about her until a grunt of terror at his side caused her to look round.

It was her landlord, who, coming suddenly upon the dark, veiled figure, had well-nigh fallen to the ground in the extremity of his terror.

The next moment he recognised the woman whom he had believed to be a ghost.

"Oh, it's you, is it? What are you doing here?" he growled fearfully.

A loud roar of thunder drowned the young woman's reply, and a bright sheet of dazzling light swept over the scene.

The light came not from the electricity-charged clouds above their heads, but from the Marble Rock, as it opened, disclosing within its heart the fearful form of the Winged Man.

With a cry of terror the woman dropped senseless to the ground. The man would have given all his ill-gained wealth to have been able to have fled; but terror held him in its icy chain—a terror that increased tenfold as the grotesque, misshapen form of Ghat darted past the Winged Man, and, seizing the woman, bore her inside the rock.

"You would have wealth," cried the Winged Man, soaring above the panic-stricken man's head. "Enter, and behold riches such as even you, worshipper of gold though you are, have never dreamt off!"

"No, no! I dare not—I cannot!" gasped the landlord. "Avaunt, foul fiend!" he added, in a rising shriek, as the Winged Man seized him in his grasp and carried him within the rock, with which a loud report closed behind them.

Sheer terror robbed the wretched man of consciousness. When he awakened he was a prisoner within the gorilla-guarded cells, whilst the woman who had been his companion through the fearful ordeal was comfortably installed as Annette Royle's companion in the Winged Man's luxurious apartments.

RICH AND RARE WERE THE GEMS SHE WORE.

The Bulton Assembly Rooms were a blaze of light as carriage after carriage discharged its burden of wealth and beauty.

Presently a common hackney carriage drove up to the carpeted entrance, and a woman, whose opera-cloak and priceless furs added fresh charm to her partially-hidden beauty, tripped lightly into the house and presented her card of invitation to the servant stationed at the door.

Ten minutes later, whilst festivities were in full swing, Annette Royle entered the ball-room amidst ill-repressed ejaculations of admiration from the men, and low-voiced whispers of envy from the women—the first brought forth by her wondrous beauty, the second by the rich jewels she wore.

Rich and rare indeed they were. Priceless diamonds flashed from a tiara an Empress might well have coveted. Strings of pearls of great price adorned her white throat. A girdle of diamonds encircled her shapely waist.

A million pounds could not have purchased the jewels with which the Winged Man had adorned the woman he hoped to make his wife.

A crowd immediately surrounded the wondrous unknown. Twice over might her program have been filled, but barely had two gilded youths scribbled their names upon the highly ornamented cardboard, ere a thin, clean-shaven man lounged through the crowd, at the sight of whom the colour faded from Annette Royle's cheeks, the light of happiness from her eyes, the assurance from her face.

"Delighted to renew our acquaintance, Miss Royle. Dare I venture that you have saved a dance for me?" he asked.

Instinctively the girl held out her program. The stranger ticked down three dances, alongside which he had written the name of Danby Druce.

"Fear not. It is not you I seek, but another," he whispered.

With a deep sigh of relief Annette Royle turned to the first partner who had claimed her hand, and soon fears of the present and doubts of the future were alike forgotten in the intoxication of a dreamy waltz. At length Danby Druce's turn came.

Annette Royle, a vague feeling of terror gripping her heart, bowed an assent.

"And now, young lady, to business. I need not ask whence you obtained the priceless jewels that adorn your person. None but the Winged Man could have provided them," said Danby Druce, as he seated himself by her side in a fern-hidden recess. "It is at his bidding you are here. Am I right or wrong in my supposing that you have already made up your mind not to return to the Winged Man?"

Annette Royle hesitated.

"Mr. Druce, I will be open with you. I wear these jewels as the Winged Man's promised wife," she declared.

The fronds of an enormous hothouse plant immediately behind the two were moved silently aside, and the white face of the Winged Man peeped between them, his eyes aglow with satisfaction at the girl's reply.

Danby Druce was about to make some remark, when Annette Royle checked him with upraised hand.

"But that will never be. Within a rocky cave the Winged Man holds, a tortured prisoner, the man I love. He bade me choose between love and gold. To gain time to think out some plan by which to achieve my lover's liberty, I pretended to choose his gold—his hated gold, accursed, as all must be that is touched by his hand!"

An expression of almost unbearable agony swept over the Winged Man's face. The next moment it had disappeared, leaving it cold, hard, impassive as usual. The Winged Man was in hiding and had heard all.

"How can I, a weak woman, fight against so fearfully-endowed a being?" continued Annette Royle, in low, quick, eager tones. "But you are—you are a man—fearless, quick-witted. I will make a bargain with you, Danby Druce. The Winged Man trusts me. I will lead that weird terror into your hands if you will swear to release Peter Armstrong."

Danby Druce held out his hand.

"Agreed!" he cried eagerly. "Once the Winged Man it in my power, you and your lover shall be free to go where you will."

The luxurious vegetation behind the unconscious pair closed once more, and the Winged Man's white, frowning visage disappeared from view.

TRAPPED!

Half an hour later Danby Druce left the Assembly Rooms, lit a cigar, and strolled slowly down the street. Presently he was joined by Annette Royle, who had appropriated another's tam-o'-shanter[31] and long-sleeved coat, which completely hid her ball-dress from view, in lieu of her opera-cloak.

For half an hour the two walked rapidly over hill and dale, until at last they struck a footpath which carried them in a rocky glen, through which a miniature mountain torrent roared and foamed.

Leaving the path, Annette Royle led the way to the brink of a tiny chasm some ten feet across. Moving aside some twigs, a hidden ladder was disclosed to view.

This, at a touch on hidden spring, fell to the bottom of the chasm on the opposite side of the stream.

Without a word Annette Royle led the way, then clambered along a narrow ledge by the side of the tiny torrent, and, to Danby Druce's astonished eyes,

---

[31] A traditional Scotch bonnet usually worn by men.

seemed to disappear into the heart of the rock.

He followed, to find a small opening, beyond which came Annette Royle's voice calling upon him to follow.

He did so, and found himself in a tunnel sloping downwards at an angle which rendered walking in the dark dangerous. Presently Annette stopped.

"Have you a match? I am not quite sure of my way," she whispered.

"I have something better—an electric torch," replied the detective, drawing a small, leather-covered box from his pocket.

The next moment a brilliant light showed that they had reached a large, irregularly-shaped cavern, pierced by several tunnel-like exits and entrances. Through the centre of the cave ran a fair-sized stream.

"Which way now?" asked Danby Druce.

"The third tunnel to the left of the river," said Annette Royle, as though repeating some well-conned task.

"And the Winged Man?" asked the detective.

"I will conceal you in his private apartments. You must do the rest. His capture should be easy, as he will never dream of an enemy in this, his favourite haunt," replied Annette; then turned and clasped Danby Druce's arm in terror, for a peal of malicious laughter rang out through the vaulted cave.

"What was that?" she cried.

"It was the Winged Man," came back in stentorian tones from immediately above their heads.

In a moment Danby Druce's pistol was out, whilst the electric beams of his lamp flashed in the direction from whence the words had come. There was nothing overhead save a jagged ceiling of rock.

"We are discovered! We must fly—fly for our lives!" cried Annette Royle, in terror-stricken accents.

Danby Druce hesitated. He had not come so far to go back empty-handed; yet, on the other hand, he could fight better, and, if need be, lay down his life with an easier conscience if the woman who had risked so much to serve him was in a place of safety.

Rapidly they retraced their steps. Alas! the tunnel through which they had entered the cave had disappeared—or, to be more correct, was blocked by a huge slab of rock.

With growing alarm they dashed from tunnel to tunnel. In vain. All were closed by huge rocks more firmly than by iron doors. They were imprisoned in that fearful cave.

"No matter," hissed Danby Druce. "It is his life or mine!" he said, cocking his revolver and backing against the nearest wall; whilst Annette Royle, her brave spirit for the moment subdued by the unexpected ending to their attempt to secure the Winged Man, sank, cowed, to his feet.

Presently she raised her head, then, half rising, clung with frenzied grip to the detective's arm.

"See, the water is rising!" she gasped.

"Aha, aho! Aho, aho! Thus perish all who would betray the Winged Man!" cried a voice to the right of the detective.

He turned. A warning scream burst from Annette Royle's lips. Too late! Seized by an iron grip from behind, the revolver was torn from his grasp and hurled into the centre of the stream.

Then Danby Druce was released, to find the Winged Man gazing at them.

The Winged Man's whole frame seemed bursting with rage, hate, and despair.

"With you, Danby Druce, I would have fought on equal terms, but she, the false's-hearted adventurous, shall perish, and it is written that you must share her doom!" thundered the Winged Man. "Hour by hour yonder waters shall arise, driving you from ledge to ledge, until at last, weakened by starvation, you seek death beneath the flood."

As he spoke the Winged Man pointed to a number of platforms cut in the rock almost to the top of the cave.

Rising to the top of the cave, the Winged Man uttered his melancholy, long-drawn, weird cry, plunged, and, dropping like a stone into the stream, vanished beneath its surface.

GHAT'S VENGEANCE.

Passing through a cleverly-contrived trap in the bed of the subterranean river, the Winged Man gained his living-apartments. A cringing form crossed his path. It was Black Jake, reduced by ill-treatment to the Winged Man's most abject slave. With a fierce, mad shriek of rage, the Winged Man sprang upon Black Jake's shrinking form, and thrashed him unmercifully.

Attracted by the unfortunate wretch's cries, Ghat came upon the scene, his hideous face contorted into a malicious grin. But the Winged Man sprang upon him also, and soon his cries arose louder even than those of his fellow-servitor.

With long, angry strides the Winged Man traversed passage after passage, tunnel after tunnel, until at length he stood within his prison gallery.

His face contorted with rage, he surveyed the man, who, despite his rags, Annette Royle had preferred before him.

"No, you shall live—at least, long enough to know that Annette Royle has passed away!" cried the Winged Man, shaking his fist at his helpless prisoner.

A cry of rage and despair burst from Peter Armstrong's lips. Seizing the solid bars, he shook them with almost superhuman strength in a vain attempt to get at his taunting captor. Then, turning on his heel, the Winged Man returned to his luxurious living-apartments once more.

Presently he paused before a large ebony door, beyond which none but he had ever penetrated. For a few moments he stood steadfastly regarding the door. Then, passing his hand wearily over his brow, seized the handle, and pulled it open.

As he did so, he was met by a current of scent-laden air; whilst, so low as to be scarcely audible, the sweet strains of music greeted his ears.

Hour after hour passed, yet the Winged Man remained beyond the black door; whilst, as he had said, driven from ledge to ledge, Annette Royle and Danby Druce mounted before the rising waters towards the top of the cave.

Suddenly the black door was swung outwards, and a figure emerged. Could this be the Winged Man?

It was, but changed in a way none would have deemed possible. The hard, cruel, revengeful light of one whose hand is against all men, and who knows that all men are against him, had left his eyes. A smile parted his lips; his face was calm, peaceful, almost happy.

In times of mental agony, when his lot seemed greater than he could bear, the Winged Man was wont to plunge into this wondrous room, from which he always emerged as we see him now.

Striding to the mat, he stamped with his foot three times. Three sonorous clangs from a hidden gong came floating into the room. A moment later Ghat appeared.

"Annette Royle and Danby Druce are imprisoned in the water cave. I doomed them to death. I have relented. Open the sluice."

At the first words a gleam of fearful joy had shone from the dwarf's eyes; but as the Winged Man proclaimed his softening mood it was followed by a look of sullen disappointment.

"Go! Why do you hesitate? Quick, or it may be too late!" added the Winged Man, as Ghat appeared unwilling to depart.

Yet the dwarf did not move until, with an impatient ejaculation, the Winged Man moved towards him, when he hastened with ludicrous haste from the room.

From tunnel to tunnel he sped, until at last he came to where a machine, like the steam winch of a ship, occupied the centre of a small apartment.

Attached to the winch was a chain passed through the floor of the cave to the sluice-gate that held up the water that inundated the cave.

His hand upon the starting-lever, Ghat hesitated; then, with a fiendish chuckle, thrust a bar of iron into the largest cog-wheel of the winch. This done, the malicious little dwarf opened the throttle-valve to its fullest extent. The steam rushed into the cylinder, the wheel moved, then, encountering the iron bar, was smashed into a dozen pieces, whilst the machine came to an abrupt halt.

"Aho, aho! Aha, aha! The deed is done. Naught can save the woman who called me a gorilla from death!" he cried, in tones of evil joy.

"You lie, dog of evil that you are!" roared a hoarse voice at his elbow.

And Ghat, filling the cave with shrill cries of terror, fled from before the angry visage of the Winged Man. A couple of strides, and the Winged Man had overtaken his fleeing servitor.

Seizing him by his streaming hair he swung him over his head; then, striding to the centre of the vault, beneath the floor of which he could hear the deep roar of many waters, struck the ground with his foot.

Immediately a trap door opened, revealing the cavern in which Danby Druce and Annette Royle stood upon the topmost platform of rock. The waters already flowed over their shivering shoulders.

"Live or die, sink or swim! Take your chance, you spiteful dog!" shouted the Winged Man, as he flung Ghat into the seething flood.

Then Danby Druce, supporting the half-fitting form of Annette Royle in his arms, saw him plunge headlong into the water, as though intent upon rescuing his faithful servitor.

WITHIN THE WHIRLPOOL.

But such was not the Winged Man's intention. As relentless in mercy as in rage, he dived to the bottom of the flooded cavern until at length of broken chain guided him to the sluice by which alone the cavern could be emptied. Seizing the iron ring to which the chain was attached, he tugged at it with a giant's strength. For a moment it resisted his efforts; then, as with bursting lungs he tugged at it again, it gave a little.

Frantically the Winged Man strove to open the sluice ere the necessity of breathing forced him to the surface. A weird spectacle he would have presented had there been anyone in those depths to have seen him, as, his feet braced against the rock, he pulled with all his might at the iron ring.

Suddenly the sluices opened, and, releasing his hold, the Winged Man made a spring to the surface. But he had reckoned without the vortex caused by the imprisoned water running through the narrow opening. The most expert swimmer must have given in before that fearful danger, but the Winged Man fought against the rushing waters, which seemed to be closing around him like the core of some enormous fish, pulling him down to the lowest bed of the subterranean river.

Suddenly, though yet many feet beneath the surface, he felt the cool air playing round his heated forehead, and his body being whirled swiftly round and round. It was a fearful struggle; but, refreshed by a deep breath of air, the Winged Man resumed his fight against the water. A spurt, and, though being carried constantly backwards, he managed to mount higher and higher the tunnel of water, until at length even his great strength seemed to be giving out.

From their rock of refuge on the wall of the cavern, Annette Royle and Danby Druce watched, as though fascinated, the awful scene that was being enacted beneath them.

More than once Danby Druce thought the Winged Man's course was run, but ever and again that wondrous being, recovering the ground he had lost, pressed higher and higher up a funnel of swiftly-revolving water.

Suddenly the Winged Man saw that which caused a cry, drowned in the roaring of the waters, to escape his lips.

Clinging like some huge, misshapen spider to the dripping walls of the cave, his eyes shining fiercely through the darkness, his matted hair hanging in wet, draggled masses around his hideous face, a naked knife between his teeth, Ghat clambered unseen over the rocky wall of the cavern to where the rescued ones, all unconscious of the new danger that threatened them, watched with breathless interest the Winged Man's struggle with the whirlpool.

Nearer and nearer crept the enraged dwarf. The Winged Man himself could not have clung with more steady hold to the rock then did this creature his slave, his dog.

Instinct caused Annette Royle to turn her head. Two fierce, leering eyes glared at her from the gloom. Ghat she could not see; darkness hit his fearful form from view. But the Winged Man saw him, guessed his purpose, and strained every nerve to avert the intended murder, yet he was held by the waters, which whirled round him with a rapidity which would have rendered any but himself giddy and dazed.

He struggled to mount his liquid path. In vain. A momentary glance assured him that ere he could reach the ledge Ghat's foul end would be achieved. A desperate resolve entered the Winged Man's heart.

His wings, enfolded, protected by their outer covering, were dry. Could he but open them within the circles of water that towered above his head he might yet be in time. To think was to act, to dare was to achieve, with the Winged Man.

Forcing his body through the glistening wall of water, the Winged Man spread his wings. For a moment he was whirled round as the rushing water caught his extended pinions, but one despairing, strong beat of his wings carried him to the centre of the whirlpool.

Half a minute later a cry of rage burst from Ghat's lips as the weapon he was about to plunge into Annette Royle's heart was snatched from his grasp, and the

Winged Man, holding him by the throat, hurled him into the terrible vortex below.

A wild yell of baffled rage and despair burst from Ghat's lips; then the waters closed above his head, and he was swept towards the tunnel, through which the river was pouring with fearful violence.

The terror of death gripped Ghat's heart as the roar of the rushing waters sounded in his ears. He gave himself up for lost. Shielding his head with his arm, he was carried at a tremendous rate onwards, until, just as the necessity of breathing had caused him to open his mouth, he was thrown over the edge of a low precipice into a swirling basin beneath.

More dead than alive, Ghat crawled ashore, vowing vengeance upon the Winged Man.

A FEARFUL FIGHT FOR ALL A MAN HOLDS DEAR.

To return to the water cave.

Poised on outstretched wings, the Winged Man hovered before the platform on which the shivering pair stood.

"Why have you done this thing, Annette Royle?" he demanded, in a cold, stern voice. "I trusted you. I sent you forth with jewels a queen might have worn with pride. For your sake I was ready to abandon this wild, free life, and become an inhabitant of the outer world once more. All I have, my past, my future, I would have laid at your feet. And you have betrayed me. Why have you done this thing, Annette Royle?"

"Because a woman's heart cannot be bought, Winged Man," replied the girl, raising her white, frightened face proudly to his. "You tempted me with wealth incalculable, but my heart swerved not from its allegiance to my lover. I pretended to accept your wealth, and your jewels rare, but it was only to secure his liberty."

The Winged Man bowed his head.

"Annette Royle, your boldness has saved your life."

"A useless gift, unless shared by him I love," returned the girl, in accents of despair.

"He for whom you have done so much will surely do some trifle to assist himself," retorted the Winged Man, adding, as he turned to the detective: "Danby Druce, you came an uninvited guest, you will remain an uninvited one. Let there be a truce between us for a few hours, then you shall return to the open air and resumed the chase, if you will. Come!"

Without waiting for an answer, the Winged Man caught Annette Royle and Danby Druce up in his strong arms and bore them through many passages to the prison gallery, pretending not to notice that Annette Royle had picked up Ghat's knife, which had fallen on the rocky ledge at her feet, and had concealed it in her dress.

Before Peter Armstrong's cell the Winged Man released the unwilling companions of his flight.

A whistle brought the gorillas on the scene.

At a sign from the Winged Man, the faithful custodians released their prisoner.

"Peter Armstrong, ere you were fool enough to embark upon the dishonest career which brought you hither, you had made your mark as a light-weight boxer. Perchance you lack training; but freedom from dissipation will make up for it. Yonder gorillas obey my slightest word, and why? Because with no other weapon than my fists I reduced them to submission, and filled their hearts with fear of their master. Do the same with one, and life, liberty, and sufficient capital to purchase a thousand acres of land in Canada shall be yours. If you were defeated, your body shall be hurled through yonder crevice."

"Would that it were you I had to fight, Winged Man, rather than this blind instrument of your cruelty. I accept the ordeal," agreed the prisoner.

"Bravely spoken," replied the Winged Man. "But brave words are not always accompanied by brave deeds. Follow me!"

Laying his hand upon a gorilla's shaggy arm, the Winged Man led the way to a large, circular cave lighted by a concealed opening in the roof.

With a clang a pair of iron doors closed, apparently of their own accord.

Raising Annette Royle and Danby Druce in his strong arms as easily as though they had been children, the Winged Man bore them to a narrow platform of rock some twelve feet from the floor, and, pointing to Peter Armstrong, uttered a loud, shrill, piercing whistle.

Immediately the gorilla sprang into the centre of the rocky arena, its huge, shaggy chest rising and falling, its hair on end, its fierce, brutal eyes glistening with rage.

For some moments brute and man faced each other in silence; then, with a bloodcurdling shriek of rage, the gorilla launched itself like a thunderbolt upon the unprepared man.

But Peter Armstrong had not forgotten the tactics of the prize ring.

Throwing himself on the ground, he allowed the huge brown body to shoot over him; then, springing nimbly to his feet, got home a crushing blow on the side of the gorilla's face.

A howl of pain and rage burst from the surprised beast. Then it rushed at its opponent once more.

This time Handsome Harry did not attempt to avoid the onslaught, but, springing lightly forward, brought his fist with crushing force into the centre of the gorilla's enormous frame.

Throwing up its arms, the brute staggered back.

Loud cries of admiration from the Winged Man and Danby Druce joined Annette Royle's shrill cry of triumph, as the beast seemed about to fall. But, rapidly recovering from the blow, which would have knocked a strong man out, the gorilla, its teeth chattering like castanets as it opened and closed its jaws with vicious snaps the enormous ape sought to close with its nimble foe.

But in vain.

Warming up to his work, Peter Armstrong seemed to move on springs. Now here, now there he darted, making a furious rush at one moment, closing in and delivering double blows with fearful precision the next, Peter Armstrong fought as he had never fought before.

And well he might.

Upon this battle depended all that a man holds dear—life, love, and liberty.

Even Danby Druce, who had at first looked upon the unequal contest with horror and disgust, now forgot everything save the excitement of the moment, and cheered to the echo each well-struck blow that thudded home on the gorilla's bony frame.

Annette Royle, her face flushed, her eyes sparkling, watched every move as though her life—as perchance it did—hung upon the issue of the fight.

Two tiny spots of red upon the Winged Man's pale face betrayed the excitement under which he also laboured.

Ten minutes of ceaseless strife, and though Peter Armstrong's breath came in short thick gasps, his blows growing less assured, less frequent, the gorilla was in even a worse state.

The foam which bubbled from its lips was tinged with blood, its hideous face swollen and bleeding.

At last, unable to face its triumphant foe, the gorilla uttered a low, jabbering cry of terror, and, fleeing to the furthermost corner of the cavern, crouched to the earth terror-stricken and beaten.

Without a word, the Winged Man bore Annette Royle to the centre of this strange arena, where, panting, breathless, but triumphant, Peter Armstrong gazed proudly around him.

"Well have you fought. The prize is yours. Annette, I had hoped—no matter, that dream is past. Peter Armstrong, she is yours. Guard her as the apple of your eye, or fear the Winged Man's wrath. Your future is in my hands. Ere you leave this cave, the money I have promised shall be yours."

As he spoke, the Winged Man released his hold of Annette Royle, who, with a glad cry of joy, flung herself into her lover's arms.

As she did so, Ghat's murderous knife dropped from the folds of her dress, and fell with a clang upon the rocky floor.

The Winged Man picked it up.

"For whom it was this knife intended, Annette Royle?" he demanded.

"For your heart, had Peter Armstrong been slain," returned Annette Royle, turning from her lover and facing the Winged Man, without a quiver on her beautiful lips.

A strange, unfathomable smile crossed the Winged Man's lips.

"Brave men and women are not so plentiful in the world that I dare risk the loss of either," he replied, then clapped his hands.

Like a stone Ghat fell from the roof, alighted on his feet, and stood expectant before his master.

"The deed of gift and tickets," demanded the Winged Man.

Ghat handed the Winged Man a long, blue envelope, which he in turn passed to Annette Royle.

Wondering, she opened the envelope, to find within the title-deeds of a one-thousand-acre farm in Canada, made out in favour of Peter Armstrong, and two first-class tickets to their destination.

Annette Royle and her lover bent eagerly over the papers, whilst Danby Druce, his curiosity aroused, glanced over their shoulders.

With a puzzled frown, the great detective turned to the Winged Man.

"These papers were prepared before the fight commenced," he said eagerly.

The Winged Man produced a loaded revolver.

"I was prepared to kill the gorilla should my prisoner have been in danger," he explained; then, turning to Annette Royle, continued: "You have your chance, as your future husband has his. See you avail yourself of it. Farewell."

He made as though he would move off, but Annette Royle, her beautiful face aglow with grateful joy, stopped him.

"Forgive me, Winged Man. From the moment we first met, Peter Armstrong and I have been all in all to each other!" she cried.

"Tut, tut, child!" replied the Winged Man, laying his hands in a fatherly manner upon her glossy curls. "We were both acting a part, but I rang down the curtain."

Then, beckoning Danby Druce to follow, he led the way towards his living apartments.

THE OPPRESSOR'S DOOM.

Within a cave so sumptuously furnished that it might have been a room in an Eastern monarch's palace, the Winged Man came to an abrupt halt, and, folding his arms, gazed fixedly at the great detective.

Danby Druce met those awful eyes without a tremor.

"When you stole like a thief in the night into my domain beneath the earth, your life was forfeited to me!" he thundered at last. "You are in my power. A foe to be swept from my path. Do you know what holds my hand?"

Danby Druce affected to yawn.

"A lingering remnant of what at one time did duty as your conscience, I presume," he replied.

The Winged Man laughed sarcastically.

"You have answered my question without intending to," he said. "If I killed you, there would be no one left on earth brave enough, clever enough, to cope with me. Yet it is not my will that you should leave these caves unscathed. I leave you now for a time. Amuse yourself in this room and the adjoining; you may find a few trifles worthy your attention. Soon I will return, then for the next few hours you shall be my guest. After that your skill, nerve, and ingenuity alone may save you."

Not once whilst his captor was speaking did Danby Druce remove his eyes from the Winged Man's dark, inscrutable orbs; then, carefully choosing a cigarette, he tapped it with steady fingers upon the silver lid of his case, saying calmly:

"Have your permission to smoke?"

The Winged Man's eyes kindled with admiration and the respect which one brave heart never fails to accord another, but he said nothing, and, bowing ascent, glided from the room.

Arriving in a cave fitted with shelves bearing priceless volumes and rare editions, the Winged Man touched a bell.

A door opened, and, twisted into a ball, Ghat rolled to his master's side; then, disentangling his legs and arms from the complex knots into which he had twisted them, sprang to his feet.

"Send Mrs. Tribbet hither."

Ghat saluted, and departed. A minute later the evicted woman entered the room.

"The reason I brought you here that no longer exists, yet your ready obedience shall be rewarded. Ghat will pay you what I promised. Go!" he directed.

Scarce able to believe her good fortune, Mrs. Tribbet would have stammered out a few words of grateful thanks, but the Winged Man dismissed her with an imperious wave of the hand.

Again the Winged Man touched an electric bell. This time there was no need for Ghat to appear. He had previously received his instructions, and with the scant ceremony Jabez Rice, the cruel and miserly landlord, was ushered into the Winged Man's presence.

Rice was deathly pale, and trembled so that his huge, overfed body seems a mass of jelly, as he stood gazing with bulging eyes at the Winged Man.

"You look pale perhaps you are hungry?" was the Winged Man's unexpected question.

"No, no! I could not eat a morsel here. I repent your bargain. Let me go hence," came in a series of panting shrieks from the landlord's lips.

A loud, mocking laugh greeted the appeal.

"Never more!" came in thunderous tones from the hard landlord's weird host. "You have had your choice; it is made for ever. Follow me!"

Despite his terror, despite his tottering legs, the landlord impelled by a power he could not resist, moved heavily through passage after passage in the rear of the Winged Man.

Presently his guide came to an abrupt halt before a pair of enormous iron doors, set in the living rock.

"Listen, oppressor of those whose misery and destitution have so often appealed to you in vain! Wealth untold lies before you, behind you a loaf of bread, a pitcher of water. Choose which you like."

"It is a joke, or perchance a dream—a ghastly dream!" murmured the terror-stricken man.

"It is no dream, but stern reality. Bread or gold—choose!" thundered the

Winged Man.

For a moment Rice hesitated; then, the light of cupidity shining from his eyes, he moved in the direction of the iron doors, crying:

"There is naught gold cannot buy, naught evil it cannot alleviate. Gold—rich, red, precious gold! Give me gold!"

His voice rose with every word he spoke, until it ended in a shriek of blind avarice.

A strange, unfathomable smile upon his thin, bloodless lips, the Winged Man touched a hidden spring. A loud crash like thunder shook the air, the doors swung noiselessly back upon their hinges, revealing a large room literally paved with gold, for the floor was ankle-deep in coin.

Frightened by the noise, the landlord had stepped back; but as his eyes fell upon the heaped-up wealth, he uttered a loud shriek of joy, and, flinging himself on his knees, commenced drawing the gold by handfuls towards him, as though he feared it should be snatched from him.

A repetition of the thunderous report forced itself upon Jabez Rice's gold-maddened intellect. He turned. A momentary spasm of fear swept through his brain. The iron doors had closed upon him, and he was alone.

Yet the sight of the wealth lying around him in uncounted quantities drove the passing fear from his heart. With eager hands he clasped the minted coin, thrusting handful after handful into his pockets until they were full to overflowing with the glittering metal.

Even when he had secured so much of the coveted fold that he could scarcely stagger beneath its weight, he was not satisfied. Tearing off his shirt, he tied it into a bag, and swept yet more treasure into it.

This done, he looked around him, his face black with discontent that he could secure no more of the coveted treasure. A door to the left attracted his attention. He moved towards it, but unable to leave the Winged Man's store behind him, he sank to the floor and, crooning like a child, piled the gold in little heaps around him.

Hour succeeded hour, until at last greed of gold was shared by constantly increasing pangs of hunger. Shouldering his extemporised bag, he again moved towards the door, and flung it open. A dark tunnel lay before him.

With many a backward glance at the treasure-house he was leaving, Jabez Rice threaded his way down an intricate passage. suddenly he came to an upright halt, as a loud, reverberating roar immediately before him fell upon his astounded ears.

Breathlessly he listened, then, as the ominous sound was not repeated, moved forward once more. As he did so a glimmer of daylight caused him to quicken his steps.

"Daylight at last!" he muttered, tightening his grasp upon the load of gold he carried.

Then a cry of joy burst from his lips. Far away in the distance he saw a small, brilliantly-lighted room, in the centre of which stood a table piled with every luxury the heart of man could desire.

"I believe—I really believe I'd have given a pocket full of my gold for such a feast," he cried aloud, then staggered back.

A huge yellow form sprang from out the darkness, and he found himself face to face with an enormous lion, held in check by a stout iron chain.

It was some minutes ere the miserable man realised what the lion's presence meant, for chained though it was, it could easily reach from side to side of the narrow passage, and the food he so greatly needed might as well have been a thousand miles from him, for all chance he had of ever reaching it alive.

Furious of being baulked of its prey, the lion filled the cave with loud, deafening roars as it strained and tugged at its chain in a way which made the unfortunate landlord rush back in the treasure-chamber, and bolt and bar the door behind him.

Hungry though he was, the sight of the gold consoled his avaricious heart. For several hours he remained seated on the floor, with the yellow sovereigns piled up around him, trying to evolve some scheme by which he might become possessed of the whole of it.

At length hunger drove him to action once more. There was yet another door he had not tried. Through this he passed, only to find that the rock-lined cavern ended near a deep crack in the rocky face of a precipitous cliff, through which he could discern the smiling Derbyshire landscape, the beauties of which he had never appreciated as he did now that he found himself unable to reach the sunlight in which it was bathed.

Slowly he drew himself back to the treasure-chamber; then, as, famished and starving, despair seized him in its grasp, he thundered with his naked fists upon the iron doors, crying to be let out.

In vain! Entombed in the heart of one of Derbyshire's hills, none knew, or, had they known, could have rescued Jabez Rice from the fate to which his soul craved.

Gladly would he have given double the quantity of gold he had secured for a single crust of bread, a drop of water to moisten his parched lips. At last there came a time when nature could stand no more, and he sank unconscious upon the golden bait which had proved his undoing.

That evening a bowed, stricken, attenuated form, which none would have recognised as the cruel, heartless owner of so many of the poorer houses around Buxton, crept to the house in which his family, having searched the countryside in vain for their head, were assembled, exhibiting an outward show of grief they could not really feel.

But the landlord returned home an altered man. Never again did the distressed, miserable, and hopeless appeal to him in vain. The Winged Man's lesson bore fruit which carried joy to many a poverty-stricken household.

°Calm Before the Storm.

No sooner had Danby Druce found himself alone then he moved stealthily about from room to room, noting with wondering admiration the exquisite taste, wealth, and luxury with which every cave was furnished.

But all the time he was searching for some opening by which he could escape; or, at least, bear in mind for use as occasion offered.

In vain he tapped the panelled walls, or, moving aside the rich hangings, closely examined the rock walls behind them. He could find no means of egress from what he soon realised was nothing more or less than a splendid prison.

Danby Druce laboured under no delusions as to the terrible danger into which he had so recklessly plunged. He had staked his all when he had invaded the Winged Man's hidden retreat, and had lost.

"Well, so let it be! A man can die but once, and what matters the mode of death, so long that it be swift and painless," he muttered.

A braver man than Danby Druce did not exist, and, realising that probably he had but little time to live, he resolved to make the time yet left him pass as pleasantly as possible.

Neither had he any lack of amusement. In each room he found priceless works of art and vertu which delighted his heart.

One room in particular awakened his interest.

Never outside a public museum had he seen so fine a collection of arms and armour as the Winged Man had gathered here. There were weapons of almost every kind, from the stone axe of prehistoric man to the magnificent rifle with which the British Army is now armed.

But it was the whole suits of armour, representing almost every stage of history and every country in Europe, that attracted his attention the most.

He had been twice round the room, carefully examining each article it contained, when suddenly he came to an abrupt halt before a magnificent suit of armour inlaid with gold. It had evidently belonged to some powerful noble, or perhaps a crowned king. Its visor was down, and in its clenched hand the dummy figure held a magnificent battle-axe.

"Strange that I should have overlooked this, the gem of the whole collection!" he muttered, bending forward the better to examine the gold work on the highly-polished breastplate.

As he did so the figure moved. The mail-clad hand that grasped the battle-axe was raised above its head as though about to strike him down.

But, though too astounded to move, the descending axe struck him not, but, passing above his head, alighted with a resounding crash upon the panels immediately behind the pedestal on which it stood.

° 22 March 1913.

As it did so the wall flew open, revealing a table groaning beneath plates and dishes of pure gold from which smoking viands sent a savoury odour through the apartment. At the head of the table sat the Winged Man, his white face lightened by an hospitable smile of welcome.

"Enter, Danby Druce! Dinner is served, and I await my guest!" said the Winged Man, rising and indicating by a courteous wave of his hand an empty seat opposite him.

Without a moment's hesitation the detective accepted the invitation of the Winged Man, and was soon discussing one of the best-cooked meals it had ever been his lot to taste, though he had often sat, an honoured guest, at the tables of the highest in the land.

Nor was the excellent repast, the rich golden service upon which it was served, the priceless wines, the only things the detective had to wonder at.

In the black-coated servitor, who, with the noiseless movements of a well-trained servant, waited upon them, he was astonished to recognise Black Jake.

The Winged Man proved a perfect host, keeping his guest interested with anecdote after anecdote, which showed that at one time or another he had moved as an equal amongst the world's greatest men.

The meal over, the Winged Man rose, saying:

"We will have coffee in the library," and led the way towards a large wall-glass, which occupied the entire end of the room from the floor of the cave to the ceiling.

To Danby Druce's astonishment, the Winged Man seemed to pass entirely through the glass, but, following, he found that what he had taken to be a-looking-glass was in reality nothing more nor less than an ingeniously contrived reflection from several glasses on either side of passage which led him into a small cave surrounded by bookshelves.

The Winged Man apparently walked right through the glass.

With the change of room, the Winged Man seemed to change his nature.

He was no longer the genial, courteous host, but became once more the impassioned, cold-blooded being Danby Druce had ever known him to be.

In the centre of the room was a chess-table, the pieces already set out, and by its side another table upon which lay a large black pistol.

"I have heard, Danby Druce, that you are considered the fourth best player in England," said the Winged Man.

"I certainly play a little," replied the detective modestly.

"I trust you play more than a little," replied the Winged Man, with a cold, relentless smile, "for on your skill at chess this evening depends your life! Beat me, you live; lose the game, you die!"

"And if I refuse to play?" demanded Danby Druce, facing his captor.

"Need we discussed what will happen in that case? You are a man after my own heart, Danby Druce, and I would be sorry if you forced me to extremities!" was the Winged Man's ominous reply.

"In other words, if I win, I gain nothing; if I lose you murder me?" cried Danby Druce, in tones of mocking contempt.

"No; I propose a more sporting offer than that," explained the Winged Man. "Beat me at yonder table, and I give you the word of honour of one whose word has ever been his bond to deliver myself to you a prisoner at any spot, at any time you like to name."

An eager light flashed into the detective's eyes. With flushed cheeks he seated himself at the table, crying:

"Agreed! I play with the white men!"

"Good! I play with the black!" The door opened, and Ghat entered the room.

Standing respectfully by his master's side, he began to speak in a tongue Danby Druce could not understand.

"There is no need for concealment, Ghat!" said the Winged Man. "Say what you have to say in English. Mr. Druce will not live to avail himself of the information!"

Despite his iron nerve, a shiver of dread shook the detective's frame as the ominous words fell upon his ears. Yet not for a moment did his heart fail him, and he determined, if cool, daring skill could achieve his liberty, he would yet live to claim the fulfilment of the Winged Man's promise, and bear him in triumph to prison.

"Information has just been received, my master," began Ghat, in English, "that the mail steamer Licanda will land £50,000 at Liverpool to-morrow for transhipment by special train to Hull."

"Good! Find out the time the train leaves Liverpool, and the hour at which it is timed to pass the various important stations en route. Go!" ordered the Winged Man; then, rising from his seat, stood lost in thought so long that at length Danby Druce interrupted his train of thought by saying:

"Pardon me, my host. I am eager to get this game over. I have made first move."

"I have already done so, too," replied the Winged Man, pointing at the king's pawn, which was advanced two squares.

A puzzled frown contracted Danby Druce's forehead. He could have sworn that the piece had been in its original place when he spoke; yet, without a word, he responded with a similar move.

Barely had his fingers left the pace ere he started back, with a cry of astonishment.

The queen's pawn had moved forward one square of its own accord, although the Winged Man still stood four or five feet from the table.

"I play you, not the powers of darkness!" cried the detective, with a forced laugh, as he moved a piece.

"Perhaps it is the same thing," retorted the Winged Man, as a knight sprang, apparently of its own accord over a row of pawns on to an advanced square.

The mysterious movement of the pieces, apparently, of their own accord, startled the detective; but his thin, determined lips were only pressed more closely together, as riveting his whole attention on the board, he played a game such as he had never played before, striving his utmost to keep his eyes off the Winged Man's white, cold, emotionless face the while.

For nearly an hour nothing was heard but the subdued thud of the pieces as they rose and fell upon the board and the heavy breathing of the detective.

It was uncanny and supernatural, this game against a man who moved his pieces without touching them, yet even as he played he was conscious of a thrill of keen delight in the contest.

Never had he played so brilliantly; never, even on that great occasion when he had beaten the foremost chess player of the day, had he met so skilled an opponent.

Piece after piece was taken and removed from the board, until at length Danby Druce, his fingers trembling with excitement, saw what he believed a chance of securing a victorious termination to the game.

The Winged Man's queen lay at his mercy.

"Your queen is gone, the game is mine!" he cried triumphantly, as he snatched his opponent's queen from the board.

"On the contrary, you have fallen into a trap from which there is no escape!" cried the Winged Man, moving up his castle.

White to the very lips went Danby Druce. By taking his opponent's principal piece he had blocked up the square by which alone his king could have escaped.

In vain he exerted his utmost skill.

Slowly and relentlessly the moving pieces closed around his king, and at length he leaned back in his chair, cold drops of perspiration rolling down his livid face, the terror of death in his heart, as cold, calm, yet fearful in the intensity of its evil triumph came the single word:

"Checkmate!" from the Winged Man's lips.

A STRANGE AWAKENING.

"I have lost—lost!" murmured Danby Druce, moistening his parched lips with his tongue.

Without a word the Winged Man leaned forward and raised the black pistol from the table.

"You have staked your life, Danby Druce, and lost. Your hour has come!" he cried, aiming the pistol full in the centre of the detective's forehead.

The immanence of death restored the great detective's wonted courage.

"Yes, Winged Man, I have lost. Take the forfeit; it is yours!" he cried, fearlessly facing his inveterate foe.

Yet the Winged Man's finger did not press the ready trigger.

"Fire! Keep me no longer in suspense! Fire!" cried Danby Druce, fearing lest his overstrained nerves should give way, and he should disgrace himself by a cry of terror, or perhaps even an appeal for mercy.

"The distance is too short. I wish to kill, not to butcher you!" cried the Winged Man, moving slowly backwards.

Within a dozen feet of the doomed man he paused.

"Thus do I claim payment of our wager, Danby Druce!" he cried, pulling the trigger.

There was a loud report, thick, black smoke burst from the muzzle of the pistol, for a moment enveloping the detective's head. Clasping his hands to his brow, Danby Druce staggered back.

There was no pain, yet he felt unconsciousness stealing over him. He had heard that those stricken by a bullet in the brain feel no shock, for their nerves are paralysed by the contact, yet he could think no more. His reeling senses fled, and he dropped unconscious on the floor.

Twenty-four hours later, Danby Druce opened his eyes and gazed—scarce crediting his senses—around him. Surely he was dreaming, or, perchance, his soul freed from its body, had returned to the habitation it knew so well.

The hangings of the bed upon which he lay, the wall-paper, pictures, even the play of sunlight on the floor, were all familiar to him. He was in his bed-room in his own chambers in London!

He remembered the whole scene, the Winged Man's luxurious subterranean dwelling, the fearful game of chess against such awful odds, the steady weapon levelled at his head, and the succeeding unconsciousness.

For several minutes he lay wrapt in thought. He knew the Winged Man to be a murderer, yet one who never killed save when justice demanded the victim's death. A robber, yet one who distributed his stolen wealth with a lavish hand on all in distress and poverty. He knew him to be unscrupulous in his methods.

Despite all this, there was a certain feeling of awe and respect, almost amounting to reverence, in Danby Druce's heart when he thought of the Winged Man.

At least the Winged Man's thoughts were magnificent ones. There was nothing petty, mean, or sordid about the weird terror of the air.

Suddenly Danby Druce sprang from his bed, his face clouded with anxious thought, an almost frightened light in his eyes. Rushing to an electric bell, he pressed the push home.

No immediate response being forthcoming, he rang again and again. Presently from the landing came the sound of low, agitated voices. Yet no knock upon the panel of his door told that his summons was being attended to.

His small stock of patience exhausted, Danby Druce threw open the door, crying:

"Confound it, Seymour, why are you stopping gossiping there? I have rung three times—"

He ceased speaking, for his voice was drowned in a chorus of loud shrieks as a number of female servants, the lift attendant, and the hall porter, who had been standing in an affrighted crowd on the landing outside his flat, turned and fled as though for their lives.

"What ails the fools, Seymour? Have you also gone stark, staring mad?" demanded Danby Druce of his valet, the only one who had held his ground, who was gazing at the great detective, his eyes and mouth wide open, as one who cannot believe the evidence of his senses.

For a moment Danby Druce awaited a reply; then, struck by the comical expression of utter bewilderment upon his manservant's face, burst into a loud laugh.

Turning on his heel, he beckoned Seymour to follow.

"Now, you open-eyed ass, explain yourself! What is it all about? What has frightened that pack of fools outside?" he demanded.

"Beg your pardon, sir, what is wrong with you, sir?" stammered Seymour.

"Me! What is wrong with me?" asked the detective, surveying his reflection in a large wall mirror. "Anyhow, what time did I reach home last night?"

"That is it, sir," interposed Seymour eagerly. "That is what frightened us all so. You know you told me you would not require my services until to-morrow. When I went away last night, I locked the outer door as usual, and came back this morning. Whilst having a chat with the housekeeper in the domestic offices, your bell rang."

Danby Druce nodded.

"I see; you thought the flat was haunted—eh?" he asked.

"Well, sir, I didn't know what to think. Both the lift keeper and the hall porter declared you had not returned. When we went to the door of the flat it was still locked, yet we heard your bell ring again, and I was about to burst open the door when you burst out upon us."

"The door was locked?" asked the detective, striding thoughtfully up and down the room.

"Yes, sir. Beg your pardon, sir, I always lock it when you are out. Besides, I put a thread in a chink of the door in such a way that it must fall out if anyone passes through. That thread was there this morning, sir," declared Seymour impressively.

Almost as perplexed as his servant, Danby Druce dismissed the man with an order to call at the City offices of Messrs. Harmand & Hodder and ask them for the running time of the special train which they were about to despatch from Liverpool to Hull.

HOT ON THE TRAIL.

Left to himself, Danby Druce stood for several moments twirling an unlighted cigarette between his finger and thumb, lost in deep thought.

Last night he had witnessed that fearful game of chess, the memory of which would linger in his mind as long as he lived. Midnight had seen him stretched senseless upon the floor of the Winged Man's subterranean palace in Derbyshire. This morning he had awakened in his own room, safe, unharmed, none the worse for his fearful experience.

He remembered the mysterious way in which chessmen had been moved upon the board during the never-to-be-forgotten game he had played with the Winged Man.

Could it be possible that in some similar way he had been transferred to the room in which he stood?

The idea was abandoned as quickly as it had sprung to life in his mind. There must be some other explanation of the mystery.

He had seen the Winged Man raise heavy men from the ground; in fact, he himself had but shortly before experienced the awful sensation of being borne through space in the Winged Man's strong arms.

Yet it seemed impossible, in spite of his almost supernatural strength, that the Winged Man could have carried him so far in so short a time.

That he had been brought to his flat ere the rising sun shed its light upon the earth was certain.

His chambers overlooked a busy street. A locked door intervened betwixt himself and the back of the building. If the Winged Man had borne him hither in daylight he must have been seen by some policeman patrolling the streets or labourer going to his daily toil.

Returning to the bed upon which he had found himself on awakening, Danby Druce, like a hound picking up the scent, examined the couch and the carpet around it.

Magnifying-glass in his hand, he passed slowly across the room to the window, his eyes within a few inches of the carpet.

As he did so his movements became more abrupt and alert. Presently he raised his head and looked around him. Had Seymour been present he would have known that his master was hot on the trail of some baffling mystery.

The window reached, Danby Druce continued his investigations. Upon the brass hasp was a tiny scratch showing where it had been clasped by some small, but strong instrument which had thrust it back and had also re-closed it.

Suddenly he started forward, and stood for nearly three minutes closely examining the woodwork to the right of the window. So indistinct that it would probably have escaped the observation of a less keen and patient investigator, the impress of a thick thumb was imprinted upon the white enamelled paint.

Before the mind's eye of the detective arose the long, delicately-formed, yet wondrously strong hand of the Winged Man.

"I am right. He has ceased to fly alone, and shares with another the secret of his flight," muttered Danby Druce. "Ah, I have it! It was his drudge, the misshapen dwarf, Ghat, who helped bring me hither last night."

There was no need to carry investigation further. Even Danby Druce could not follow the flight of the Winged Man through trackless space.

Yet, hoping to find confirmation in his belief that two people had been employed to bring him hither, Danby Druce flung up the sash and anxiously examined the window-sill.

It had been a cloudy morning, but now the sun, piercing through the clouds, poured with terrific force full upon the front of the house.

Danby Druce glanced down at the window-sill, started back, rubbed his eyes, then looked down again.

Yes, his vision had not paid him false. Drawn from the stonework by the heat of the sun's beams, faint and indistinct at first, but growing clearer each moment, a number of letters, gradually forming themselves into words, appeared in view:

"Remember the special train. It leaves Liverpool at 8.30 this evening. But the specie van in which the gold travels will never reach Hull.

(Signed)   WINGED MAN."

Again and again the detective read over the challenge—for such indeed it was. Even as he did so the letters grew fainter and fainter, until at length they disappeared for ever.

All traces of awe and amazement had passed from the detective's face as he turned towards the centre of the room. Save for the keen, eager look in his face, Danby Druce was as cool and implacable as ever.

"He knew that I would leave nothing to chance, that I would not lose the slightest opportunity of gathering all the information I could respecting his movements, and would therefore try to find some trace of himself and his assistant on the window-sill," muttered Danby Druce, as, applying a match to his unlighted cigarette, he threw himself back into a chair and commenced to revolve in his mind some plan by which he might thwart the intended robbery.

There was no anger in his heart, no feeling of hatred against the Winged Man. On the contrary, the respect with which he had ever regarded him was increased tenfold. Here was a foeman worthy indeed of his steel. Inch by inch, step-by-step, he would fight him with his own weapon.

He respected his foe, but their fight, all the same, should be to the death!

"Beg your pardon, sir," said the well-trained Seymour, entering. "Count Mazipah is without with a private letter from the King of Italy."

"Admit him," ordered Danby Druce.

Seymour bowed, and retired. A dapper, lightly-built man, faultlessly groomed and attired, was ushered into the room.

"Mr. Danby Druce, I believe?" began the visitor.

The great detective bowed.

"My master the King of Italy, has commanded me to secure your services—"

Danby Druce held up his hand.

"I beg your pardon, count, tell me nothing further. It is quite impossible that I should accept any further commissions," he declared.

The count looked at Danby Druce in astonishment.

"But it is a Royal command!" he insisted. "Besides, here is an open draft upon the Royal Treasury. Fill it up to any figure you like; it shall be honoured. But we must secure the services of the greatest detective the world has ever seen."

Without a moment's hesitation Danby Druce waived the document aside.

"It is useless. Convey my sincere regret to your Royal master. Tell him there is no occupant of a European throne I would sooner serve than he, save his Majesty King George V., yet my every minute, my every thought, every drop of blood in my body is from this moment devoted to one object, and to one object only."

The count bit his lips with vexation, yet curiosity prevailed.

"Is it permitted that I inquire who this client may be whom you prefer even before my Royal master?" he asked.

"To a certain extent my client is his Majesty's Government," replied Danby Druce. Then, drawing himself up to his full height, a look of proud, unalterable determination upon his face, he added: "But in this matter I work for my own hand, and by my own hand. I have sworn to capture the Winged Man, and not rest day or night until I have laid him low!"

Count Mazipah was much too politic and polite to say what was in his thoughts, but after many vain attempts to induce Danby Druce to alter his determination he took his leave, with the firm conviction that much study had driven the great detective mad.

Barely had Count Mazipah taken his departure air a closely-veiled lady entered the room.

She refused her name, but an antique ring, of enormous value, upon her finger told Danby Druce, as she also left the room unsatisfied, that he had sent away one of the richest duchesses in the British peerage.

PROFESSOR HEXMIDER.

Telephonic messages, personal applicants, all imploring the great detective's aid, received replies in the negative, until at last Danby Druce was about to order Seymour not to admit any more visitors, when he heard that faithful servitor's voice raised in remonstrance.

The next moment the outer door was flung open, and a huge, black-bearded man strode into the room, dragging Seymour after him, as the latter made frantic efforts to hold him back.

The new-comer was it all man of enormous physique, with the pale face and absent-minded expression of one who passes his days in study.

The visitor's clothes, though of good quality, were thick with dust, stained with chemicals, and torn in a dozen places. His soft felt hat was battered out of shape, his beard untrimmed, his long-haired matted and unkempt.

"You are Danby Druce!" said the strange visitor, panting before the detective.

His host bowed.

"I am; but, as my man has doubtless told you, I have for the time being abandoned all public practice," he replied."

"So he said; but I told him that was nothing to me, unless"—a look of consternation for the moment flashed into the stranger's dark, piercing eyes—"unless you have relinquished your pursuit of the Winged Man."

Danby Druce looked searchingly at the other.

"Seymour, you may go," he said.

The valet, bowing, left the room.

"You are, I presume, one of that wondrous being's victims?" asked the detective.

The visitor threw back his head and a scornful laugh burst from his lips.

"I? No. I fear him not. It is he that ere long shall fear me. I am Professor Hexmider," he announced.

The detective looked at his visitor with awakened interest. Before him stood one whose attempts to solve the problem of aerial flight had made him in turn the laughing-stock and the admiration of the whole world.

"Glad to meet you, Professor—at least, would have been at any other time," Danby Druce began. "Now, unfortunately, my every moment is occupied. On another occasion—"

The Professor's deep, bass voice ruthlessly interrupted the detective's excuses.

"Look here, Danby Druce, if you go on pitting your limited capabilities against such a grand chap as the Winged Man, you'll find yourself knocked out in no time," he declared. "What's the good of trying to catch a being who can fly and leave you looking like a fool on earth any time he likes?"

"True enough," retorted Danby Druce good-humouredly; "but we must take our limited capabilities as they are. Earth-bound though I am, there must come a time when the Winged Man will be at my mercy; then it will not be my fault if he escapes."

"It will be his if he is caught," growled the professor. "But to business. You know me, you know what I have done, and what I have attempted to do. I also am a busy man. Come down to my place at Dartmoor, and I'll lend you a pair of wings which will put you on level terms with your great opponent. Not that I have any animosity against him," added the professor. "On the contrary, I admire him for what he has done. But he has dared to call himself King of the Air. He shall find that his sovereignty shall not go long undisputed."

"I am afraid—" began Danby Druce when the professor interrupted him by saying quickly:

"So am I. I am afraid that you are not so smart as you pretend to be, or you would jump at an opportunity like this in a moment."

"May I ask why you made this offer?"

"Because, in spite of what I said just now, I think you are the smartest detective in England. That is not saying much, mind. The majority of you are a set of fools. However, you are about as good a one as I can get hold of. Just think of the advertisement it will be if, with the aid of my apparatus, you destroy or capture the Winged Man!"

"Agreed. I will be at your place by three o'clock the morning after to-morrow."

"Three a.m.!" roared the professor.

"Yes, three a.m.," repeated Danby Druce with a smile. "It is above all things necessary that the Winged Man should know nothing about our alliance. Good-bye!"

And, shaking hands with the professor, whose grasp showed, at any rate, that study had not weakened his muscles, Danby Druce prepared to defeat the Winged Man's attempt on the special train.

ON THE FOOTPLATE.

It had been Danby Druce's intention to enter the specie car and keep watch himself over its precious contents; but he had reckoned without the very simple precaution taken by the officials at Liverpool, who had placed a special lock on the van, and had sent the key, earlier in the day, to the firm to whom the precious freight was consigned at Hull.

Blaming his stupidity in not having taken this possibility into his calculations, Danby Druce elected to ride on the engine, and, having taken his station on the footplate, the special resumed its journey.

A few miles outside Manchester, Danby Druce had unmistakable proof that the Winged Man was at work.

A fresh supply of coal on the furnace had sent a thick cloud of smoke, enlivened by dancing sparks, pouring from the funnel, when suddenly he heard the stoker's shovel clatter on the footplate, and a grimy hand grasped him by the arm; whilst, with chattering teeth, the stoker pointed through the look-out to where, leaning forward at right-angles from the funnel, could be seen, enveloped in wreaths of smoke, the indistinct form of the Winged Man.

The next moment the weird horror, bursting through the smoke, shot by. Leaning from out the engine's cab, Danby Druce saw that the Winged Man, though apparently straining every nerve to keep up with the swiftly-flying train, was being gradually left behind.

Now he hovered over the specie van, and a sigh of relief escaped from the detective's lips as he saw the car draw away, as it were, from beneath the fearful night-flying apparition.

At that moment the engine-driver seized him by the waist and pulled him back on the footplate, just in time to save his brains from being dashed out against the brickwork of the tunnel, into which the engine, with a loud, mournful whistle, plunged.

The roar as the locomotive rushed through the tunnel drowned all further conversation, and when at length the train emerged into the open Danby Druce peered down the line of carriages through the starlit night.

"It's no good looking after that there flying terror, sir!" expostulated the engine-driver. "He can't have followed us through the tunnel, he was clinging to the sides of one of the carriages so he has been swept off long before this. I would not stick my head out like that, if I were you. You have had one narrow escape, and I may not be so lucky as to pull you back quick enough next time," he added.

Danby Druce acknowledged the wisdom of the engine-driver's advice; yet, though he hoped that the speed of the train had baffled the Winged Man's flight, an instinctive feeling that all was not as it seemed caused him to risk his life again and again by looking towards the rear of the train.

Besides the specie car there was a passenger coach and a guard's van. Reassured by the sight of the brightly-shining lamps of the latter, Danby Druce concentrated his attention upon the metals, fearing lest the Winged Man had put some obstacle on the line to throw the train off the rails.

As mile after mile was covered and nothing happened Danby Druce's spirits rose. Presently the railway crossed a wide stretch of broken moorland, dotted with tall shafts and the spider-like erections which proclaimed the presence of numerous coal-pits. Now and again the wheels rattled and clanked as the engine tore over points leading to various private sidings. Then came a wider stretch of moorland; then, as they crossed the border into Yorkshire, they plunged into thickly populated country once more.

"The most dangerous part of our journey is over, driver," said Danby Druce, with a sigh of relief. "Had the Winged Man, whom you saw shortly after leaving Manchester, intended evil against us, it would assuredly have been on the desolate track of country through which we have just come."

"You needn't worry about that, sir," declared the engine-driver. "Winged Man or no Winged Man, a man is not going to play tricks with a train going at sixty miles an hour."

Danby Druce shook his head.

"I don't think you quite appreciate the Winged Man's wondrous powers," was all he said, as he glanced out of the cab towards the tail-lights of the train.

Danby Druce was right, save that he himself did not even yet realise the wondrous power wielded by the Winged Man.

THE TRAIN ROBBERY.

Suddenly the engine-driver shut off steam and jammed on the break.

"What is the matter?" shouted Danby Druce, trying to make himself heard above the thunder of the gripping wheels.

"Signal against us," was the short reply.

As, groaning and shrieking, the engine glided past a sentry-box, a man, leaning out of the window, bawled at the top of his voice.

"Good heavens!" ejaculated the driver. "Impossible!"

"What's that?" demanded Danby Druce.

"He says we have left part of our train behind us," replied the engine-driver.

In a moment Danby Druce had sprung on to the permanent way. Even as he did so, with a shriek, a rush, and a roar, a night express flashed into view.

Warning shouts from the engine-driver, fireman, and signalman was the first intimation Danby Druce had of his danger. A glance over his shoulder showed an engine's brightly-burning lamps, fire issuing from the ash pan like the fiery teeth of some old-time fable dragon, almost upon him. On his left rose a solid wall of coal; on his right the stationary train he had just left.

But one chance of escape was left. Flinging himself to one side, he struck the rail, and rolled over on the six-foot-way just as the express dashed by. A fraction of a second later and he must have been ground to pieces beneath the merciless iron wheels.

White with terror, the fireman of the special train dropped from the footplate, expecting to find Danby Druce cut to pieces, and breathed a sigh of relief as Danby Druce sprang to his feet, and hastily assuring the gallant fireman that he was unharmed, rushed to the rear of the special. As he expected, the guard's van and the van containing the gold were both missing.

"It's a coupling broke away. We will soon fix that up again!" cried the fireman, who had followed the detective along the line.

"It will be too late," replied Danby Druce. "That is no accident. See the vacuum tube has been ingenuously blocked up! It was the Winged Man's doings!"

Then, ere the fireman could reply, he set off running to where a tiny red spark in the distance appeared—the tail-lights of the express.

The driver, having witnessed the accident, was backing to pick up what they feared would be the mutilated remains of the train's victim.

"Is he killed?" asked the guard, who, with swaying a lantern, was proceeding the retreating train.

"No; I am all right. But a van containing fifty thousand pounds, attached to a special train, is missing. I want you to carry me until we come to the van. There is little chance of our being in time to prevent the robbery, but we may yet track the scoundrel down."

The guard demurred; but, upon Danby Druce producing his credentials, consented, and shortly afterwards the express moved on, with Danby Druce on the footplate of the engine.

Some half-hour later the express slowed down sufficiently to allow Danby Druce to drop on to the permanent way alongside the lost guard's van.

As the express moved on, Danby Druce started forward, with a cry of astonishment. There was only one van upon the rails. The specie van had disappeared. Scarce able to believe the evidence of his senses, Danby Druce rubbed his eyes, and gazed in amazement around him.

"Yes, I have not been mistaken. There is only one carriage there," he declared aloud.

Taking an electric torch from his pocket, he carefully searched the rails. Presently, in a gutter by the side of the permanent way, he saw the print of a man's foot. Evidently the man whose footsteps Danby Druce was following had been running down the line, for the marks were wide apart, and now and again he came to places where broken bushes showed that the unknown had fallen in his haste.

Some half-mile from the van Danby Druce picked up the rounded peak-cap of the guard, and knew that the man he was following was the guard of the special train.

For a few yards further he continued following the fleeing man's track, expecting every moment to see the specie van derailed by the side of the track. Presently he paused where, the grass growing between the rusty iron metals, a sliding branched off from the main line.

Danby Druce was about to pass on when he noticed what looked like a splash of wet upon one of the rails. Bringing his electric torch to bear upon the mark, he found that it had been caused by grass crushed beneath some heavy weight.

With a low ejaculation of delight, Danby Druce, leaving the line he had been following, crashed through the rank weeds which almost hid the abandoned siding from view. Again and again broken vegetation told him that he was on the right track, until at length the track ended in what had evidently been at one time a busy yard. But now, save for the usual debris of such a place, all was quiet, silent, and deserted.

Danby Druce gazed around him in dismay. The van had vanished as entirely as though it had melted into thin air.

THE DESERTED MINE.

To return to the Winged Man.

The Winged Man had not been baffled by the tunnel, as the engine-driver suggested; but, clinging tightly to the rear of the guard's van, had been carried safely through it.

Keeping a sharp look-out ahead for tunnels and bridges, the Winged Man crept over the guard's van, across the top of the strong, iron-bound specie car, then dropped between the last-named vehicle and a box car, which, together with a low truck, intervened betwixt himself and the engine, where, swaying to the movement of the train, he remained perched until the line commenced a sharp downward grade.

Clambering down, he seated himself astride the buffers of the specie car, and, taking a small, vice-like instrument from his pocket, clasped it round the tube of the vacuum pipe, on the side of the joint nearest the engine.

This done, he uncoupled the cars, and, with a few rapid movements of his strong fingers, disconnected the tube of the vacuum brake.

Immediately the air rushed out, and the brake, closing on the wheels of the two vans, gradually slowed them down, whilst the engine and two trucks continued on their way, the driver, fireman, and Danby Druce all unconscious of what had happened behind them.

Rising swiftly in the air, for there was yet much to be done, the Winged Man flew to the rear, then dropped between the guard's van and specie car.

As he did so he caught a glimpse of the white, frightened face of the guard, pressed close against a pane of glass at the end of the guard's van, who, too terrified to spring from his van, as he had intended, staggered back, and, ere he could recover his self-control sufficiently to leave his van, the Winged Man had disconnected the two vans, the foremost of which, carried forward by its own weight, started running with constantly-increasing speed down the steep gradient, leaving the guard's van, its brake still on, standing on the rails.

A deep-drawn, mournful cry, tinged with triumph, arose from the Winged Man's lips, as, soaring aloft, he flew swiftly ahead of the run-away van.

Presently he alighted by the side of a grass-grown track, and, grasping a rusty switch, turned the van into a siding; then, replacing the switch, followed the van, as, carried forward by its own momentum, it dashed over the grass-grown track.

Suddenly, with a fearful crash, the van plunged headlong through a dark opening in the earth. The Winged Man's scheme had succeeded in every particular. The van, with its enormous treasure, lay crushed and broken at the bottom of a disused coal-pit.

Even before the sound of the crash had died away a dark form swept through the air and alighted by the Winged Man's side.

Without wasting time in words, Ghat—for the new flying creature was he— set to work replacing the rotten baulks of timber which protected the mouth of the pit, until but a small hole was left, down which the Winged Man dropped; whilst Ghat, having closed up the last hole, spread his pinions and disappeared into the starlit sky.

Five hundred feet beneath the earth's surface the Winged Man stood upon the wreckage of the specie car, gazing with triumphant eyes at a yellow stream of gold, that flowed like some wondrous river, from out the torn, distorted, and broken sides of the van.

"It is mine—it is mine! The spoils of war once more are garnered by the Winged Man!" he cried exultantly.

Then, using a piece of wood as a lever, he wrenched open the already broken door and gained the interior of the shattered van.

Many of the strong boxes containing the gold had been torn in pieces, but the majority, each as much as a strong man could well lift, lay thrown about the interior of the van in all directions.

Grasping one of the latter, he bore it down a long-since-abandoned working. Swiftly he strode with his booty through the tainted air. At times he had to bend almost double in the narrow seam, at others to crawl painfully over heaps of fallen rock yet ever pressing onwards, further and deeper into the bowels of the earth, to where Ghat had constructed a passage that led through some natural caves in the side of the hill to the outer world.

But the Winged Man was not destined to reap the fruit of his skilfully-planned plot.

Presently he came to a lake of inky-black water, above which was a roof, supported by countless pillars of coal, left by the miners ere the mineral gave out, and the working of the vein no longer paid.

Up to his waist in the inky flat, the Winged Man pressed on. Suddenly he came to an abrupt halt. A distant, thunderous roar assailed his ears. The ground shook as though in the throes of a mighty earthquake; whilst the water agitated as though by some mighty storm, rolled hither and thither, breaking in foaming waves against the side of the working.

Suddenly the Winged Man clapped a mask over his nose and mouth. He was not a moment too soon. From the uneven floor of the excavations arose a seething, boiling mass of water, followed by a tremendous outburst of flame. Then report succeeded report as the gases in the disused mine exploded. Like a feather blown by the wind the Winged Man was hurled to and fro by the repeated explosions.

Fortunately for the Winged Man, it was all over in a minute, and, bruised by violent contact with the sides of the roof of the working, he rose painfully to his feet, he was conscious of a loud, deep, continuous roar, as of many waters, and discovered, to his astonishment, that the lake through which he had been wading was rapidly disappearing.

It was a fearful position for any living creature; yet above the roar of the waters arose the Winged Man's fearful laughter, as, flinging his hands above his head, he gazed around him, as though defying Fate to do her worst.

He loved, and he lived for danger, and here he was, surrounded by dangers such as would have slain any living creature but himself. Well he knew that the whole place was filled by the dreaded after-damp, that fearful gas which has taken toll of so many thousands of lives in our British collieries.

Suddenly his laughter ceased. An eager, listening expression on his face, he leaned forward. To the Winged Man's listening ears came the alarmed cries of men in deadly peril.

THE FIGHT WITH THE FLAMES.

The Winged Man glanced reluctantly in the direction from whence he had just come. He knew that Danby Druce would ere this be upon the track of the missing van, and he had little doubt but that the detective would in time find the pit into which he had plunged the van. Then the recovery of the gold would be but a question of time.

What though if human beings were perishing within a few yards of him? Let them perish. He had not taken all this trouble to secure so enormous a haul, and then to lose it for the sake of a little sickly sentimentality.

At his feet, embedded in the mud, lay the gold-chest he had dropped. Turning a deaf ear to the cries for assistance, he stooped to raise it, but even as he did so a cry of "Help—help! Father, where are you? Help! I am dying!" in a boy's voice, reached his ears.

Like a stone the partly-raised chest dropped from the Winged Man's grasp. Turning, he made his way swiftly towards a huge hole torn by the explosion in the floor of the pit.

Beyond, perchance, lay perils too great even for him, wondrously endowed though he was to overcome. Yet, with the boy's cry ringing in his ears, he turned his back upon his recently-acquired treasure, and plunged headlong through the jagged hole. Spikes of rock bruised his body and limbs, jagged pieces of stone tore his flesh, yet the Winged Man pressed on, guided by the cries of the entombed men.

Speeding in the direction from whence the cries arose, the Winged Man came upon a gallery filled with suffocating smoke, and illuminated by the brilliant flames of lurid hue.

Safe in his fireproof clothes, guarded from the deadliest gases by his mask, the Winged Man plunged into the flames. The heat was awful, blistering, scorching, yet the Winged Man pressed on, until at length he reached a distant working, where four men and a boy were retreating before the constantly-advancing flame.

A cry of hope arose from the entombed miners' lips, changed to an ejaculation of dismay, despair, and terror as the eyes fell upon the fearful form of the Winged Man.

"It is the Evil One, the demon of the mine!" shrieked an old, grey-haired miner, shrinking back as the Winged Man approached.

"Silence, coward!" thundered that weird being. "Fear nothing! I will save you. I am the Winged Man!"

A cold shiver of dread passed through the veins of those upon whose ears fell the name of the one they had been taught to regard as a weird, supernatural, heartless monster.

"Approach at your peril! Go! We want nothing at your hands, not even life!" cried a brawny miner, facing the Winged Man with uplifted pick.

"Stand aside, fool!" commanded the Winged Man. "This is no time for superstitious folly. I have sworn to save you, and for my word's sake I will do so!"

Raising the boy in his arms, he covered him with his flame-proof wings, and plunged once more into the fire. A moment's fierce struggle against the overwhelming flames and the Winged Man had reached a band of gallant rescuers, who had descended, determined to rescue their comrades or die.

The cry of horror which burst from the miners' lips as the Winged Man flashed from the flame into their midst was stifled ere it well found birth by ejaculations of surprise as the weird apparition thrust the half-unconscious boy into the arms of the nearest miner, then plunged fearlessly back into the wall of fire that barred their path.

Man after man the Winged Man bore safely through the flames until the last of the little party had been rescued from immediate peril.

But there yet remained much to be done. Even as the rescued ones turned to gain the shaft a second explosion, louder, fiercer, and more terrible than the first, seemed to shake the very earth itself.

With shrieks of terror the miners flung themselves upon the floor.

A foreman grasped the Winged Man's arm to draw him down; but, with a scornful laugh, he shook himself free, crying:

"Neither fire-damp nor fire can harm the Winged Man!"

And a cold shiver of dread shook every frame as a half-mocking, half-triumphant, death-defying laugh rang through that confined space.

"Up, men! The after-damp has passed us," cried the Winged Man, a minute later.

And, his dazzling head light burning brightly, he led the way along the gallery, until at length further progress was stopped by a fall of rock from the roof which lay across their path.

Even as the miners stood, with pale, blanched faces, regarding this obstacle to their further progress, a white-faced, frantic man dashed forward, crying:

"Quick! The waters are on us! Flee for your lives!"

A moan of despair, rather than terror, burst from the imprisoned ones. Whither could they fly? Tons upon tons of fallen rock forbade further progress. Behind them was the blazing mine, creeping upon them from somewhere in the darkness—a more dreaded enemy still rising water.

Instinctively every eye was turned upon the Winged Man. Anger and dismay imprinted upon every face, the miners started back as a weird laugh escaped the lips of their guide.

"Ho, ho, ho!" he shrieked.

"Ho, ho, ho!" came back the answer.

"What are you, fiend or man, that you can give tongue to such ill-mirth at such a fearful time?" demanded the grey beard.

"Both, or neither, as the future may prove," was the Winged Man's enigmatical reply.

Then that fearful, nerve-chilling laugh rang out again, replied to by the same broken echo.

"By James, you white-faced fiend, do you dare to mock our misery?" demanded a miner.

"Down with him! He has lured us here to our death!" cried a dozen voices.

With one accord the infuriated miners advanced upon the Winged Man, then, with a loud, indignant "No, no lads! Do not forget he saved us from the fire!" a small form staggered from the ground, and the boy whose appeal had drawn the Winged Man into the pit placed himself before the Winged Man as though to protect him against the angry mob.

A soft light shone for a moment in the Winged Man's eyes.

"I thank you, youngster, but the Winged Man needs no champion," he said, in gentle, yet thrilling tones.

"Fools!" he added, in his old, stern, cold, commanding tones, addressing the miners. "Have you not heard that brave men laugh in the face of death? Death is on you now. To right, to left, in front, behind, turn where you may, he lurks, ready to claim you as his own. Death is near, I say, but life is nearer. Follow me!"

Grasping the boy beneath the armpits, the Winged Man disappeared into what looks like the solid rock on the top of the fallen debris.

For a moment a deathly silence ensued. Then an ejaculation of amusement arose from those who had been standing nearest the Winged Man when he had disappeared, as the flying horror's headlight illuminated the cutting once more, and a shout of joy arose from the miners when they saw that it came from a hole in the rock to the left-hand corner of the fallen rock.

"Come, men! Stands not gaping there like wonder-stricken fools!" cried the Winged Man.

And, the man who had expressed his determination of killing the weird horror leading the way, they clambered up the fallen rock. Five minutes later the rescued miners stood in the main gallery of a large, deserted mine.

An almost imperceptible ray of light on their right showed the direction of the ill-covered, deserted shaft; but, to the miners' astonishment, the Winged Man, turning his back upon the daylight, led the way, apparently, into the bowels of the earth. For a moment the miners hesitated.

"Where are you leading us? This is not the way to safety!" cried one.

"Ask no questions, but follow!" ordered the Winged Man.

"Come on, lads! He has led us to safety so far, and I for one will follow him to the end," said the oldest of the party. And the next moment the miners were treading heavily in the rear of their strange leader.

As though he followed some well-known path, the Winged Man, the rescued boy clinging tightly to his folded wings, led the way through gallery after gallery, tunnel after tunnel, until at last, with loud cries of joy, the miners dashed forward, to find themselves in a large cave on the side of a precipitous hill.

DEATH ABOVE, DEATH BELOW.
In the meantime Danby Druce, having lowered a lighted candle into the shaft

into which the specie-van had been plunged, saw sufficient to justify the belief that his search was ended, the treasure found.

Rapidly hastening back to the main line, he connected a pocket telephonic apparatus with the wires, calling up a large town, secured the services of a travelling-crane and breakdown gang, then hastened back to the pit-head to guard the missing treasure he had so skilfully tracked.

Even as he reached the pit-head a loud explosion and a burst of flame told of disaster in a neighbouring coal-mine. Though the scene of the explosion lay half a mile away, he could hear the loud, excited voices of men mingling after a little while with the despairing shrieks of women bereaved of their dear ones.

Half an hour later a breakdown train arrived. Under Danby Druce's skilful direction, the men drew aside the baulks of timber that covered the pit's mouth, and a bo's'n' chair[32] having been rigged to a wire rope, Danby Druce descended.

He found the van a hopeless wreck, but the treasure, to all appearances, intact. Securing one of the gold-chests, Danby Druce fastened it to the rope, and, sitting astride it, gave the signal to be hauled to the surface.

His every nerve on the alert, working both legs and arms to keep his swaying body from coming into collision with the rugged side of the shaft, Danby Druce was drawn to within some six feet of the surface, when loud cries of alarm from above proceeded the stopping of the crane, and he was left swinging above the dark, deep abyss.

Wondering at the cause of the commotion, he looked up. The sunlight was darkened. A pang of terror pierced the brave detective's heart. Descending like a sweeping hawk from the as your sky, came a fearful, winged figure.

"Pull me up! Don't you hear? What are you stopping for?" he cried, with angry vehemence.

There was no response. Evidently those in charge of the crane had fled before the weird horror hovering overhead.

A glance into the black depths beneath, and, setting his teeth, Danby Druce drew his revolver.

Half-way across the opening above his head the iron arm on the crane pierced the air. With scarcely beating heart Danby Druce glanced upward. His aerial foe was in the act of alighting with outstretched wings on the head of the crane.

Drawing an axe from his belt, the flying terror prepared to sever the wire rope, at the end of which Danby Druce swung, helpless and at his mercy.

Yet not for a moment did the great detective's courage failed him. Raising the pistol, he took swift aim at the descending arm, and pulled the trigger.

A loud, piercing shriek told that the well-aimed bullet had sped true to its mark, and Danby Druce leaned swiftly to one side as the falling axe whizzed by his head.

A feeling of inexpressible relief, he saw the mighty wings unfolded and bear their

---

[32] A wooden board slung by a rope.

owner, swaying like a stricken bird, from out the detective's line of vision.

Five minutes past by—the longest five minutes of Danby Druce's life. Presently a white face peered over the edge of the pit's mouth.

"Thank Heaven, sir, you are alive!" gasped the engineer in charge of the crane—for it was he.

"No thanks to you if I am! Pull me up, quick! I must be after the Winged Man!" retorted Danby Druce angrily.

A minute later Danby Druce stood once more upon the solid earth he had never hoped to reach again, save as a shattered corpse.

Rapidly explaining the position of the destroyed van, Danby Druce left one of the railway officials in charge, and, reloading the empty chamber of his revolver, he hastened towards where the rapidly dwindling form of the flying man was moving slowly over the tops of some distant trees.

The Winged Man was wounded, perhaps severely. His chance had come at last, and he did not mean to let it slip.

But by the time Danby Druce had reached the wood his quarry had disappeared, and, search though he might, he could find no trace of him.

SAVED FROM THE MOB.

The sound of excited voices mingled with the gasping cries of sobbing women led Danby Druce to the pit-head, around which a pale-faced crowd were clustered, eagerly scanning the faces of those brought up by the ascending cages from the harvest of death below.

His card gained him admittance through the cordon of police, and ere long he was proffering his services to the white-faced, agitated pit-owner, who at the first alarm had hastened upon the scene.

"It is very kind of you, Mr. Druce, but I am afraid there is little hope of saving any more lives," he said, in unsteady tones. "A party of gallant rescuers descended half an hour ago. Since then another explosion has taken place, and we fear the worst."

Even as he spoke there was the tinkle of a bell, and the big rope over the wheel at the head of the pit began rising rapidly ascending.

"Well, Peters?" asked the owner despondently.

The man addressed, a brawny miner, shook his head.

"It's no use, sir. A fall of rock some twenty feet in thickness has cut off the retreat of the poor fellows at work below, and the brave chaps who went to their assistance."

A despairing shriek greeted the announcement, and a bereaved wife burst through the cordon of police, and would have flung herself headlong down the pit had not Danby Druce seized her in his arms.

"Let me go! My Jack is below. Let me die with him!" she pleaded, struggling to break free.

"Do not despair," said the owner, in kindly tones. "You may depend upon it that all that men can do will be done to save your husband and his comrades in misfortune."

"Yes, yes, I know! British workers in British mines never leave their comrades in peril. Yet, oh, sir, I cannot live alone!" moaned the woman, as she allowed herself to be led to where her aged mother was sitting upon an overturned truck, rocking herself to and fro in the extremity of her grief.

Twice eager volunteers descended, twice they returned, each time with the news that further falls of rock had occurred, that the fire below was burning fiercer than ever, and that now huge volumes of scalding steam showed that in places fire and water had met.

This unable to render assistance, Danby Druce was about to return to the deserted mine in which the specie-van lay, when loud bursts of cheering from the outskirts of the crowd reached his ears.

"They are safe—they are safe! Heaven be praised, they are safe!" cried five hundred voices in one mighty, almost hysteric cry.

Forcing his way in the direction from whence the joyful sounds came, Danby Druce saw a body of men surrounded by their wildly gesticulating, shouting comrades approaching the mine.

At their head, a grim smile parting his bloodless lips as he noted how even the cheering men shrank from him, marched the Winged Man, showing no trace of Danby Druce's well-aimed bullet.

Surprise robbed the detective of power to move or speak, as the Winged Man came to a halt before him.

"Well, Danby Druce, we meet again, you see!" was the Winged Man's greeting.

Danby Druce shot a quick glance towards the inspector in charge of the police.

"Inspector, that man is the Winged Man! Arrest him!" he cried, ignoring the other's greeting.

The inspector moved forward as though to obey, then came to an abrupt halt as a howl of rage burst from the rescued miners.

"Hands off the Winged Man!" cried one of the rescued man. "But for him we would have perished in the pit. He saved our lives, and the police of the whole of England shall not touch him!"

The inspector glanced inquiringly at Danby Druce.

"No matter. The Government's instructions must be obeyed. Seize him!" cried Danby Druce, laying his hand upon the Winged Man's shoulder.

At a sign from the inspector three policemen stationed themselves at his side; but a hundred miners dashed forward, and, hurling the police to right and left as though they had been but children, seized Danby Druce, and would have torn him to pieces had not the Winged Man snatched him from their grasp, and, rising in the air, flew away with him, followed by the astounded cries of the amazed miners.

A hundred feet above the miners' heads, the Winged Man, Danby Druce clasped tightly in his arms, hovered in the air.

"My lads, I thank you!" rang out his deep, sonorous tones. "I saved your lives. You have saved my liberty. The account is even, save that perchance when men speak evil of the Winged Man you will tell them how he abandoned fifty thousand pounds to render service to gallant men. Farewell!"

Five miles from the pit's mouth the Winged Man alighted on the summit of a tall, barren hill. Releasing his captive, he seated himself on a huge rock which jutted from the bare, brown soil.

"The honours are divided, Danby Druce. I secured the treasure, you have regained it. Farewell until we meet again!"

Danby Druce smiled bitterly.

"Yet whenever we meet you leave me your debtor," he cried despondently. "But for you the mob would have told me to pieces, and I, despite what you have done, would have arrested you."

"And rightly. It was your duty. The Winged Man complains not of those who do their duty," came back the answer, as he sprang from the rock, and with swift beats of his huge wings and flew swiftly away.

°THE HOUSE ON THE MOOR.

It was a wild night as Danby Druce, his head bowed to the fierce blast, forced his way over the deserted waste of Dartmoor. Half an hour before he had been dashing along the road in his magnificent 40-h.p. car—a car which had never paid him false before. Yet suddenly, and for no apparent reason, it had come to a sudden halt in the bleakest part of the great Western moor.

In vain, Danby Druce and his chauffeur sought to find out what was amiss with the magnificent engines which had propelled them so swiftly and so easily from London.

Sparking plug, engine gear, all seemed in perfect order, yet, though again and again the starting-handle was moved, the engine failed to respond, until at last Danby Druce had alighted, and instructing his chauffeur to remain with the car till morning, set stolidly forth on his fight against the wind and storm, determined, if human endeavour could accomplish it, to reach Professor Hexmider's house by the appointed hour.

Danby Druce was strangely nervous. Not the nervousness borne of fear, but that strange sensation we all feel, yet can never account for, of impending misfortune.

"Strange," muttered Danby Druce to himself, as he stopped for a moment to press his cap closer on his head ere he faced the gale once more. "I feel as I have never done but in the presence of the Winged Man. Can that weird being be near?"

° 29 MARCH 1913.

He looked half-fearfully around him.

The bleak more, crossed by the black shadows of the flying cloud as it swept across the moonlit sky, alone met his gaze. Yet in the very howling of the wind, he seemed to hear the Winged Man's fearful cry.

"This will never do, Danby Druce. If the Winged Man is by, then ought I to rejoice rather than fear him. Fear him? No! Danby Druce fears not that treads the earth orbits the air with sable wings!" he cried aloud.

Was it fancy, was it the wind whistling through the trees, or did, indeed, the Winged Man's fearful laugh respond to his boast? With an irrepressible shiver, Danby Druce continued on his way.

Presently a twinkling light attracted his attention. Close at hand a rambling old house loomed on the horizon.

"That ought to be the place," muttered Danby Druce; "indeed, it must be, for Hexmider himself told me that his nearest neighbour lived five miles away."

Despite the blast which now and again assailed him with such fury as to almost tear him off his legs, Danby Druce soon reached the Professor's house.

As he grasped a huge iron knocker, he was jerked almost off his feet, for the door swung inwards, drawing him into a large entrance-hall, which as though by magic, became bathed in the beams of a score of an electric arc-lamps. With a clang the front door closed behind him.

Danby Druce looked around in surprise, not altogether unmixed with alarm, for on either side of him stood to mail-clad forms, one holding aloft a double-headed battle-axe, the other pointing directly towards where he stood with his shortened spear.

The next moment there was a bird-like flutter of wings, and the great detective looked up in amazement as a tiny model of the Winged Man, guided by some unseen agency, flew directly towards where he stood, then, placing a letter in his hand, soared upwards and attached itself to the ceiling.

The missive was about the size of an ordinary visiting-card.

"Welcome, Mr. Danby Druce. Hang your coat on the fourth peg to the right, then follow the direction of the outstretched hand."

Wonderingly, Danby Druce did as directed. Barely had his coat touched the peg ere two many jointed iron arms sprang from a concealed cavity in the wall, brushed his coat, shook it, folded it neatly, then seemed almost to swallow it, so quickly was it thrust behind a sliding panel.

HAWKSHAW OF SCOTLAND YARD! PAUL SLEUTH, PRIVATE DETECTIVE!
The Wonder 1ᴰ
Dramas of the Breadwinners of Britain.
THE Wonder 1ᴰ
The Star Story Paper
EVERY TUESDAY.
[Week ending March 29, 1913.
A MASTERPIECE OF MYSTERY.
The Most Thrilling Story-Drama Ever Penned!
THE WINGED MAN, or 'Twixt Midnight and Dawn!
The Story of a Strange Genius who, Possessed of Wonderful Powers of Invention, sets forth to deal out Justice to the Evildoers of the Modern World.
THE DUEL IN MID-AIR BETWEEN THE WINGED MAN AND HIS RIVAL!

At the same time an exquisitely formed clay hand sprang from out the wall a little distance away, its fingers opening and shutting as they beckoned him onward. Hand succeeded hand guided Danby Druce through corridor after corridor, room after room, the doors opening and shutting of their own accord, and by their action flooding the apartment through which he passed in light, until at last they guided him to the great inventor, who approached to greet his guest with outstretched hand.

"Welcome, Mr. Danby Druce! What do you think of my staff of servants? Do they not serve me well, and guard their master faithfully?" he asked.

"Splendidly!" laughed Danby Druce, as he returned the other's hearty grip. "Yet I was thinking as I came along that probably ordinary human help would come less expensive. You must employ a whole staff of engineers."

"On the contrary, one man who attends the machinery is the only person in this house besides myself. Everything—cooking, waiting, cleaning—is done by electricity. That reminds me. You have had a long journey, and would doubtless like to have something to eat. It is early for breakfast, yet too late for supper. Come with me."

But Danby Druce refused the other's proffered hospitality.

"A whiskey-and- soda and a couple of biscuits is all I require," he declared.

Without moving from an adjustable chair into which he had thrown himself, Professor Hexmider touched a button. Immediately a table arose from a trapdoor close to Danby Druce's elbow, on which stood a decanter of whiskey, a siphon of soda, a cabinet of cigars, and a biscuit-tin.

As he sipped the refreshing beverage thus cleverly provided, Danby Druce described how he had been delayed on the road, then, eager to get to business, asked Professor Hexmider to show him the flying apparatus he had travelled down to Dartmoor to see.

THE PROFESSOR'S WINGS.

Ten minutes later, the two men stood in a large workshop, fitted with furnace, retorts—in fact, everything a scientist and inventor could require.

Danby Druce had seen some of the finest workshops in the world, yet never had he seen one raised to such a pitch of perfection as the one in which he then stood. Passing through the shop, they entered a large, lofty, covered-in shed with a movable roof. As they passed through the doorway, Danby Druce came to an abrupt halt.

"I was a fool to think that I could hide aught from him. See, the Winged Man awaits us!" he said, pointing to where, standing on a pedestal in the centre of the shed, was a tall, black-winged figure.

Professor Hexmider's strident laugh reverberated through the apartment.

"I thought you would be deceived by the likeness. Approach, it is but a dummy figure!" he cried.

Thus abjured, Danby Druce entered the room. As his host had said, the form on the pedestal was but a cleverly-constructed imitation of the Winged Man. Eagerly, Danby Druce examined the model whilst Professor Hexmider explained how it worked.

Great minds often work unconsciously in the same groove, and, although Professor Hexmider and the Winged Man had never, so far as the former knew, come in contact, yet Danby Druce found himself examining with minute care an exact representation of the Winged Man's wondrous flying apparatus. Exact save in one particular.

Whereas, the ribs which supported the Winged Man's extended wings were of some light and unknown material Professor Hexmider had used small tubes of highly-tempered steel. Danby pointed this fact out, adding:

"It does not matter. If your invention acts as well as it looks, the Winged Man's career is ended."

"Try it and see. You must not expect to be able to fly at first. Even young birds, to whom flight is an instinct, have to learn from their feathered parents," returned the professor.

A delightful sensation of excitement thrilling his frame, Danby Druce donned the close fitting garment to which the flying apparatus was attached, then mounting some steps at the further end of the long building, launched himself bodily into the air.

A few yards he flapped clumsily onward, then, losing his balance, fell ignominiously to the ground.

"Ha, ha, ha! Ho, ho, ho!" roared the professor.

"Ha, ha, ha! Ho, ho, ho!" came as an echo from immediately above their heads.

Quickly the Professor looked towards the glazed skylight from whence the sound had come. Naught but the blackness of night met his gaze.

"It was only an echo—what else could it have been?" said the professor half-doubtfully, as he picked Danby Druce up and set him on his feet once more.

Again and again the detective essayed to fly, at first with anything but satisfactory results. But he persevered, all unconscious that a mocking, half-contemptuous smile upon his lips, the Winged Man was watching his every movement through the skylight.

Daylight found Danby Druce still striving to master the art of aerial flight, and ere the professor announced that the lesson had lasted long enough for one night, he had succeeded in flying half the length of the shed without disaster.

A few hours' sleep, and Danby Druce, confident that at length he had acquired a weapon by the aid of which he could meet the Winged Man on equal terms, returned with grim persistency to the task of mastering the use of the wings.

A bright summer's day had succeeded the previous night's storm, yet, though large beads of perspiration rolled down his cheeks, Danby Druce persevered in his self-imposed task.

At first the strain upon his arms and legs had been almost more than he could bear, but for two days he practised, an hour on and an hour off, until at length he was able to turn to right or left, up or down, backwards and forwards, remain poised in the air, or swoop like a hawk to the ground at will.

At dinner on the second evening, Danby Druce announced his intention of taking his first flight in the open at twelve o'clock that night.

The day had been hot and oppressive. Though it was evident that a storm was hanging about, both the professor and the detective agreed that the absence of wind would be the best possible condition for Danby Druce to attempt a flight of any height upon his newly-acquired mode of propulsion.

With almost a father's tenderness, Professor Hexmider gave the last few finishing touches to the wings which were to bear the detective aloft. Then, accompanied by the detective, went to the front door, where Danby Druce's motor-car, in which, by the aid of a powerful searchlight, the professor intended following the first flight of his great invention, awaited him.

"You are sure you can put on the wings alone?" asked the professor, as Danby Druce stood on the threshold of the door.

"Yes; thank you! I'd rather do everything myself. I cannot have you always with me to see that all is right, you know," said Danby Druce.

"All right; but be sure that every strap is tight, every buckle secure, every nut screwed well home," insisted Professor Hexmider, as the car moved in the direction of an adjoining hill, towards which Danby Druce was to wend his first flight.

THE CHALLENGE.

Watching until the car was out of sight, the detective hastened back to the shed. As he entered the lofty room, the same strange feeling of vague awe and easiness he had so often experienced before, when in close proximity to the Winged Man, filled his heart.

Anxiously he gazed around him, half expecting to see the flying horror's white, weird face, gazing with a mocking smile upon him, from some lofty corner, or to see his fearful frame suspended, bat-like, from one of the iron girders which supported the movable roof, a portion of which was now open. But though he gazed searchingly around, no sign of the dreaded being met his gaze.

Standing as the Professor had left it, in the centre of the apartment, was the life-like model of the being whom he was so shortly to meet on equal terms in his native element.

From a box reposing at one end of the shed, Danby Druce removed a closely folded net. Save for his revolver, this net—made of the finest silk—was the only weapon with which Danby Druce had armed himself to encounter his great foe.

It was like a fisherman's casting-net, round, and edged with small weights. When hurled in the air it opened, and, having reached the extremity of the cord, closed automatically round anything it struck.

"Aha, Winged Man! Once I get you within reach of this net, your skill, your wondrous strength, will avail you little, and the victory will be mine!" cried Danby Druce triumphantly, as, gathering the net up, he threw it with practised hand at a large chest a little way from the bench.

Noiselessly the net closed over the wooden receptacle as the detective jerked the centre-cord.

"Aha! Ho, ho, ho!"

Danby Druce sprang to an upright position, glancing with fear-laden eyes around. From whence had come that fearful laugh?

Eagerly he peered through the open roof, expecting to see the Winged Man's fearful form hovering in the starlit sky.

There was nothing there, nor, though rushing swiftly from end to end, from side to side of the shed, he searched every available hole and corner, could he see aught of his fearful foe.

Again and again that mocking laugh rang out, rousing Danby Druce to fury. Once he glanced apprehensively at the winged model standing on the pedestal. Waxen face was as set and solid as when he had last seen it, in Professor Hexmider's company.

"The Winged Man is near. Well, it is better so! It will save me a long search for him," muttered the detective, fastening his casting-net to the belt holding his revolver.

Even as the words left his lips, loud, clear, and resonant, the professor's electric clock boomed forth the hour of twelve.

"By Jove! I must hasten, or, thinking something has gone wrong, the Professor will return," thought Danby Druce, as he laid his hand upon the top button of the closely fitting tunic, intending to strip it from the model, and don it without delay.

Even as he did so, he started back with a cry of alarm.

Instead of a cold, wax throat, his fingers had encountered human flesh. So sudden, so unexpected was the discovery, that for the moment, robbed of power to move, the detective gazed with starting eyes upon the Winged Man, who had taken the dummy's place upon the pedestal.

Slowly the Winged Man extended his wings, then, with his white hand held half-clenched above his head, gave tongue to peal upon peal of mocking laughter.

"Ha, ha, Danby Druce. You would meet the Winged Man on equal terms— eh? Come. A thousand feet above the earth we will fight for the mastery of the air. Your poor imitation of my wondrous work is in yonder room. Follow if you dare. It is I, the Winged Man, who challenges you to combat."

With an ease and grace which, despite his chagrin and annoyance, Danby Druce could but admire, the Winged Man glided almost imperceptibly from the ground, rising higher, until at last, his weird, mournful cry piercing the air, he disappeared in the blackness of night without.

For nearly a minute Danby Druce stood gazing, with gaping mouth and staring eyes, through the aperture, then sprang forward with a loud cry of:

"I accept the challenge, Winged Man. Either you or I shall never reach the ground alive."

From high above his head, the Winged Man's mocking laughter replied to the accepted challenge.

Rushing to the room the Winged Man had indicated, Danby Druce saw the dummy figure standing, untouched and injured, in the centre of the floor.

There was no need to ask if the wings had been tampered with. Whatever his faults the Winged Man was a sportsman to the back bone, and would not, he knew, avail himself of a mean, or unworthy advantage.

Twice Danby Druce paced the room, his brow contracted, his fists clenched, then turned once more to the dummy figure. All the excitement had gone from his heart. He was as cool and determined as the Winged Man himself could be.

Five minutes after the Winged Man's disappearance, Danby Druce followed his foe in his aerial track.

What though he was about to enter upon the most fearful, most dangerous task he had ever yet attempted. The greater the danger, the greater the glory should he succeed; the less the shame should he fail.

WILL O' THE WISP.

In the meantime, Professor Hexmider, his huge frame trembling with excitement, was seated in Danby Druce's car, scanning the workshop through a pair of night-glasses.

Presently an ejaculation of delight escaped his lips as the powerful glass revealed a tiny black speck shooting upwards from the roof of the workshop. Closer and closer came the flying figure.

"Look, my man! Congratulate yourself that yours are the first eyes to behold the triumph of my invention!" he cried excitedly, turning to the chauffeur. "See how easily he moves through the air. A bird could not fly more gracefully. My name will go down as the first to solve the problem of aerial flight."

"After the Winged Man, sir," interrupted the chauffeur.

"The Winged Man? That for the Winged Man!" cried the Professor, snapping his fingers triumphantly. "His invention is but a clumsy parachute, compared to my wings."

But even as he spoke it seemed as though something had gone wrong with the wings, for as the flyer glided by overhead, he swerved to the right, fell a score of feet, checked his downward flight, then glided off some two hundred feet above the roadway.

"Confound the fellow; he has lost his nerve! Did you see how deathly white he was?" added Hexmider.

But the chauffeur did not reply. He was trembling in every limb.

"Why, man., What ails you? You, too, look as though you'd seen a ghost."

"That was not my master, sir!" gasped the chauffeur. "It was the Winged Man!"

"The Winged Man!" repeated incredulously. "Nonsense, man! He knows better than to come near me. I tell you, it was Mr. Danby Druce. I recognised him plainly."

"And I recognised the Winged Man," insisted the other. "Heavens above, sir, a man who has once seen that fearful face never forgets it!"

"Winged Man, or no Winged Man, he has got my wings, and I am after him!" growled Hexmider irritably. "Full speed ahead, chauffeur."

For a moment the man hesitated, then the car sped noiselessly in the wake of the flying figure. As they did so the chauffeur's courage returned. Again and again he had been a terrified witness of the Winged Man's flight, but never had he seen him fly so erratic a course as he was doing this night.

Now rising, now falling, now swaying, as though he was about to plunge headlong to the ground, whilst a low groan, as though of terror, reached their ears from his lips.

Presently, still following the aerial figure, the car left the road, and, bumping over the unequal ground, continued its way across the moor.

"We had better slowdown, sir, or we'll shake her to pieces," expostulated the driver.

"No, no! On, on!" was all Hexmider could say. "He will fall in a minute. Why doesn't the fool alight?"

Wonderingly he shouted the question.

"I cannot—I cannot! Keep near me—for Heaven's sake, keep near me!" came back the appealing response.

Then as the ground sloped downwards to what looked, in the starlight, like a level meadow, the flying figure quickened its speed, and, the chauffeur increasing his sparking, the cart flying at nearly twenty miles an hour down the hill.

Presently an ejaculation of horror burst from both men as the flying figure fell headlong into a clump of rank, coarse grass.

"He is down! Heavens, from such a height he must have smashed every bone in his body!" cried the chauffeur.

"Yes, and the apparatus which has cost me years of work into the bargain!" growled Hexmider.

Quicker and quicker flew the car, till suddenly it seemed to be dropping into space. A fearful squashing sound came from behind it, and it swiftly-revolving wheels through up thousands of mud and water.

"Good gracious! We are bogged!" ejaculated Hexmider.

"Ha, ha, ha! Ho, ho, ho!" laughed a fearful voice immediately before him.

With a cry of horror the chauffeur covered his face with his hands. Professor Hexmider, cold chills chasing each other up and down his spine, sat gazing with staring eyes to where, floating a few feet above the treacherous surface into which he had lured them, was the Winged Man.

"Ha, ha! Ho, ho! The learned Hexmider, the greatest scientist of his age, fooled, duped, led to his death in the pitiless bog!" shrieked the Winged Man, in fiendish glee. "See how your car sinks beneath your feet! Look round. The black void of night hems you in, a fitting prelude to the black void of the death which awaits you!"

As the Winged Man held his last awful taunt at his would-be rival's head he flew tantalisingly to within three feet of the giant professor's head.

Without a word of warning, without a cry of rage to announce his deadly purpose, Hexmider sprang upwards and seized the Winged Man by the ankle. Taken by surprise, the Winged Man allowed his wings to drop for a moment, but only for a moment. The next, with a mighty effort, he soared heavenwards, drawing Hexmider, big man though he was, upwards as easily as though he had been a child.

Twenty feet above a stagnant pool on the outskirts of the bog the Winged Man paused in his flight. Then a howl of pain was drawn from the professor's lips. A fearful, unbearable tingling shot from hand to elbow as the Winged Man touched Hexmider's wrist with wires from the powerful battery that provided electricity for his wondrous headlight.

Convulsed by the fearful current shooting through his body, blue electric sparks flashing from toes and fingers, the professor writhed and twisted in a vain attempt to release his hold. But the electric current held him fast until the Winged Man turned it off; then, his nerveless fingers releasing their hold, Hexmider have plunged headlong into the stagnant pool.

There was but eighteen inches of water in the pond, yet, numbed and paralysed with terror as he was, Hexmider might would undoubtedly have drowned had not the Winged Man, flying with lightning speed, swooped down upon the chauffeur and bore him, too terrified even to cry out, to the edge of the pond, and left him to rescue his master's friend as best he might.

"Now to assert my sovereignty over the starlit heavens!" cried the Winged Man in loud, thrilling accents, as, like an arrow shot from a bow, he soared upwards.

A thousand feet from the earth he paused, and gazed earnestly in the direction of the House on the Moor.

As yet but a tiny speck in the starlit heavens appeared the flying form of Danby Druce.

"By my sovereignty of the skies, he flies well!" cried the Winged Man admiringly. "It is good! He has ever been a foeman worthy of my steel. I would not take him at a disadvantage usurper though he be. Now for the signal for battle!"

Thrice in quick succession the Winged Man's powerful headlight blazed forth into the darkness; and Danby Druce, his whole being thrilled with the delightful sensation of his bird-like flight through the air, responded to the challenge with a loud, defiant shout.

Slowly the Winged Man soared heavenwards.

"Hasten, Danby Druce! See, a storm arises! We must soar above the clouds, or fight in the dark. Choose which you will. Night or day is alike to me," shouted the Winged Man, his voice carried through the clear, silent air to Danby Druce's ears as plainly as though he had been close at hand.

"Lead where you will. I will follow, Winged Man. At least I meet you on equal terms!" cried Danby Druce exultantly, as, increasing the beat of his sweeping wings, he rose above the gathering clouds.

Up they went, up and up, until two north, south, east, and west twinkling lights showed the proximity of moorland villages.

A loud clap of thunder startled the sleeping air; a flash of sheet-lightning tore the heavens from east to west; yet neither noticed the warring of the elements. Majestic though Nature's strife, it could be nothing to men nerved for combat which must end in the total annihilation of one or the other.

His eyes fixed upon the Winged Man's glowing headlight, Danby Druce sought to close with his ever-mounting foe.

"Behold our field of honour!" cried the Winged Man, as with a sweep of his arm he indicated surrounding space. "Surely never before has a duel been fought in this clear ether."

Some twenty feet from his foe Danby Druce halted, on outstretched wings, to gather breath for the coming struggle. Awe, amazement, keen delight thrilled his frame. His had been no ordinary life, and should he be defeated his would-be no ordinary death.

"Gaze well around you, for this scene will be the last your mortal eyes will ever behold! Is not so mighty and Empire well worth fighting for? Emperor of earth, air, and sea, I brooked no rival!" thundered the Winged Man.

It was indeed a wonderful, awesome, and magnificent spectacle upon which Danby Druce gazed, scarce hearing his antagonist's vaunts.[33] Miles overhead, undimmed by clouds of vapour, shone countless stars. Beneath him—and a momentary shudder shook his frame as he gazed—a seething inky sea of clouds.

Even as Danby Druce drank in the awful beauty of the scene a resonant roar seemed to shake the very heavens, as the thunder crashed from out the black, electricity-charged clouds. The next moment the clouds seemed turned into an enormous wall of livid fire, from whence a million flashes of forked lightning shot out in all directions. Then came a deathly stillness, broken by a clap of thunder louder than any which had preceded it.

The very presence of the Winged Man was forgotten in admiration of the magnificent yet terrible war of the elements that was being waged at his feet. Danby Druce remained poised five hundred feet above one of the fiercest

---

[33] Boasting.

storms which had raged over Dartmoor for many years.

Suddenly the clouds were rent in twain, revealing for a second the rugged Dartmoor, lighted by the fires of the fearful storm.

A hand laid upon his shoulder caused Danby Druce to look round.

The Winged Man's pale, fearful face was close to his own, gazing triumphantly, mockingly at him.

With a momentary tightening of the heart-strings Danby Druce saw the play of the lightning below reflected from the head of a broad-bladed spear, which the Winged Man held aloft as though about to plunge into his back.

"Now who is King of the Air, poor mortal?" cried the Winged Man exultantly.

Fearful though his danger, terrible though the proximity of death, Danby Druce's I encourage did not slacken.

"I accepted your challenge to fight, trusting to honourable treatment, and you would murder me!" he cried, a ring of contempt in his tone.

"You lie, Danby Druce! In your heart you know you lie! The Winged Man takes no mean advantage of the one he will yet conquer with the unaided strength of his own right arm. Had I been a murderer, as you call me, you would have been dead ere this!" cried the Winged Man, releasing his hold of the other, and soaring aloft; whilst Danby Druce, disengaging his casting-net from his belt, mounted after him towards the starlit heavens.

An instinct seemed to warn Danby Druce, the detective, that he was even now winging his way to doom.

That mysterious and dread being in advance of him seemed so self-reliant, so sure of victory, that the heart of Druce sank in despair; but, like the bulldog he was, the detective resolved to die game.

He would fight to the finish. At any rate, he would die a hero's death.

He was sailing through the thunder-cloud, when suddenly the Winged Man turned and came at him with a terrific rush.

Ere Druce could defend himself, ere he could manoeuvre an inch out of his foe's way, the Winged Man had him by the throat.

"Gaze for the last time around you!" cried the Winged Man, "for in two seconds more you will have ceased to live!"

THE FIGHT ABOVE THE CLOUDS.

But as quickly as he had gripped Druce, the Winged Man let go his hold again.

"No, we will fight it out!" he cried. "Come, follow me!" And he mounted into the heavens. Casting-net in hand, Danby Druce, beating the air with his huge wings, mounted in circling flight towards where the Winged Man paused and awaited him.

Wondrous though Hexmider's wings, their wearer lacked the long practice, almost super-human strength, and perchance the knowledge of the unknown, possessed by the Winged Man, and Danby Druce's brave heart sank for a moment as he saw the Winged Man drop on one knee, if such an expression may be used where there was naught but empty air to stand upon, and, poised on half-spread wings, raise his spear aloft.

Despite a control of his wings, which was a little short of wonderful considering his lack of experience, Danby Druce realised the great advantage the Winged Man had over him in the air. Yet he was not one to decline a conflict, no matter how hopeless the outcome of it might seem.

Taking care to keep beyond the deadly thrust of the Winged Man's weapon, Danby Druce, his net held ready for immediate flight, circled round and round the statuesque figure, striving to get above him that he might make his task more sure. But though he put forth all his strength, Danby Druce was unable to soar above his opponent.

It seemed as though the Winged Man's scarce-moving wings could do but little then keep him from falling headlong to the earth; yet so wondrously where they made, so skilfully used, that the nearly imperceptible movement sufficed to render all Danby Druce's attempts to get above him in vain.

"Ho, ho, hawk! Why do you not strike at your quarry?" demanded the Winged Man mockingly.

"My time will yet come!" panted Danby Druce, his breath coming in short, quick gasps, not so much from the exertion of flying as by reason of the rarefied upper strata of air they had reached.

Upon every side arose an arc of the deepest blue, beneath them vivid, lightning-torn clouds, whilst the almost inaudible roar of the striving elements at their feet told more than aught else to what an enormous height their wings had carried them.

Upward they soared, higher and higher each moment, until suddenly Danby Druce shot forth his wings to their fullest extent and remained poised in mid-air. He could do no more. He had reached the highest point to which one not gifted with power of breathing the thin air thousands of feet above the earth's surface might hope to attain. Slowly he began to fall towards the earth. A contemptuous, mocking laugh from the Winged Man's lips followed him in his downward flight.

"Aha, poor earthworm! See how imperfect, how weak, your apparatus! Follow, Danby Druce—follow if you can!"

As he spoke, the Winged Man assumed the attitude of one about to jump from the solid earth; then, speechless amazement mixed with admiring envy, Danby Druce saw him soar higher and higher, swifter and swifter, up into space, until but a tiny speck high above his head; yet so clearly seen in the clear, cloudless atmosphere, that every line of his body, even the contour of his white face could easily be discerned.

Then he saw him place his hands above his head, and, like a swimmer about to plunge into the sea, descend headforemost towards the earth. Down he came, growing larger and larger each moment, but at such tremendous speed that Danby Druce remained gazing in horror at his foe's descent, until with a sudden movement of his wings, he shot in a swift circle above the detective's head, and remained poised with outstretched wings and folded arms within six feet of his astounded rival.

In a moment Danby Druce forgot the Winged Man's almost supernatural exhibition of skill, forgot everything save the fact that at last his foe was within reach of his casting-net.

A swift movement of his arm, a jerk of the wrist, and the net, opening as it flew, sped towards the Winged Man. A cry of triumph arose from the detective's lips, drowned in a peal of mocking laughter, as, dropping like a stone, the Winged Man evaded the treacherous meshes.

She grinned at his failure, conscious that until he could refold his net he was at his foe's mercy, Danby Druce, sweeping as a pigeon moves in its flight from the lofty branches of some mighty oak, flew through the clear, invigorating air, drawing in the cord by which his now useless net was suspended as he flew.

A quick glance over his shoulder showed that the Winged Man was following in quick pursuit.

Exerting his muscles to the utmost, Danby Druce swept on, careless whither he went, so that he had time to arrange his net ere the Winged Man overtook him. On he dashed, sloping downwards, whilst on his startled ears fell the swishing sweep of his pursuer's mighty pinions.

Presently a glance over his shoulder showed him the Winged Man poised in the air, his spear grasped, javelin-like by the middle, as he prepared to hurl the fearful weapon into Danby Druce's heart.

Even as he gazed the spear left the Winged Man's hand. Instinct rather than reason warned the detective to check his downward flight by extending his huge wings.

The ruse succeeded, and the Winged Man's weapon, its bright blade dyed a ruby-red by the reflection of the storm-clouds beneath, swept harmlessly by within a few inches of his outstretched legs.

"Now, Winged Man, you are weaponless, and at my mercy!" cried Danby Druce, pouncing upon him as a hawk pounces upon its prey.

The net was not ready for throwing, but he cared little for that. His one and only desire was to come to the death-grips with his foe and bear him earthward, even if they were both dashed to pieces on the ground beneath. But failure again awaited him.

Even as his outstretched hand touched the Winged Man's arm, the other, dropping earthward, eluded his grasp, then, diving through the air, sped in swift pursuit of his falling spear.

Wrapt in amazement, Danby Druce watched the strange race. It seemed impossible that the Winged Man could overtake the heavy weapon, yet, just as its glistening point pierced the upper strata of rolling thunder-clouds, the

Winged Man grasped it by the haft, and, waving it triumphantly overhead, rose to resume the interrupted flight.

The ease with which the Winged Man had recovered his weapon, his swift, and laboured flight through the air, sent a wave of disappointment, almost amounting to despair, through the detective's heart, yet is not for a moment did the idea of relinquishing the strife and seeking safety in ignoble flight into his head.

Experience had taught him that the higher they went the less resistance did the wind offer to his wings, and consequently the greater the advantage the more experienced Winged Man had over him.

Therefore, as his fearful antagonist appeared on a level with him, instead of mounting, he uttered a loud cry of pretended terror and turned to flee, hoping for us to draw the Winged Man within reach of his casting-net.

Then commenced a chase which must have thrilled the heart of the least emotional of spectators, could any have been present to watch that fearful flight.

Turning now to right, now to left, now diving, now rising a hundred feet with a single beat of his huge wings, Danby Druce flew hither and thither, again and again avoiding the fierce thrusts of the Winged Man's deadly weapon—deadly insomuch that the broad-headed blade need only cut the membrane of which his wings were composed, to send him hurtling earthward to his doom.

Easily though his wings worked, clear, pure, invigorating though the air he breathed, Danby Druce ere long became conscious that he was tiring, whilst the swallow-like movements of his remorseless foe told that the Winged Man's iron frame was as tireless as ever.

Presently there came a time when Danby Druce must gain a moment's respite, or acknowledge defeat. Scorning the latter, and to gain the former, Danby Druce swooped downward towards the storm-clouds, from whence flashed fiercer, more brilliant, more awful sheets of lightning than before, as the storm devastating the countryside reached its climax.

Down he went, glorying in the swift rush through the air, and gaining fresh strength with each moment's rest, until twenty feet above the red, threatening, lurid clouds, a tingling thrill sweeping from head to foot, warned him against the condensed mass of heaven's electricity towards which he was plunging.

Numbed by the constantly increasing series of shocks, it was as much as Danby Druce could do to rise from the vicinity of that fearful storm-cloud, whilst, as though to show his superiority, the Winged Man remained poised within a few inches of the lightning-charged clouds, revelling in the fierce electric shocks which coursed through his frame.

THE END OF THE FIGHT.

A hundred feet above the clouds, Danby Druce turned and gazed upon his opponent. The Winged Man presented a truly awful spectacle. His pale face flushed with pride; he stood clad from head to foot in a garment of electric sparks which flashed from every portion of his frame.

"Speak, presumptuous earthworm!" shouted the Winged Man, shaking his extended hand and sending a cascade of electric sparks flying from his open fingers. "Do you still venture to dispute the sovereignty of the air with me?"

"To the death!" came back the bold defiance. "Waste not time in useless words! There is not room enough on earth, nor even in space itself, for you and I, Winged Man!"

"So be it! With your own lips you have pronounced your doom!" came in thunderous, resonant tones from the dread being's lips.

Seeming to spurn the living thunder-clouds with his heel, the Winged Man sprang straight at his foe.

By this time Danby Druce had got his net once more in hand, and as the Winged Man approached hurled it over him; but, with a mocking laugh, the flying terror dashed out of reach, then, soaring high above Danby Druce's head, gathered his spear under his right arm, turned a partial somersault in the air, and the spear-head, projecting a few feet from out his folded wings, hurtled, like some fearful missile shot from a giant's bow, straight to where Danby Druce was poised upon partially-open wings, his net held ready to throw, waiting at what he knew the Winged Man intended should be the final attack.

But Danby Druce was not yet conquered.

By but a few inches he avoided the Winged Man's deadly swoop, then, as with a cry of baffled rage his fearful foe dashed by, he copied his foe's tactics, and dashed downwards in swift pursuit. For the first time the Winged Man was taken by surprise.

He had not deemed it possible that Danby Druce could escape his unerring aim, and when he found the detective still an injured he looked up, expecting to see him a hundred feet away flying for dear life.

Instead of which, to his utter amazement, almost dismay, the gallant detective, whom nothing could daunt, was literally close upon his heels.

Then the Winged Man turned. Too late! Already the fatal net had descended upon him. As, with a jerk, it reached the end of the cord awaited circle closed over him, pressing his wings to his side. Meshed in the strong, unbreakable net, the Winged Man, for the first time since his wings had beaten the untraversed parts of the air, felt himself a helpless, hopeless prisoner.

Unable to do aught to check his descent, the Winged Man fell a dead weight upon the cord, snatched it out of Danby Druce's grasp, and the next moment, bundled ignominiously into a ball, the net-enslaved figure fell into the very heart of the lightning-charged clouds.

A feeling of almost unbearable elation thrilled Danby Druce's heart as he saw the fire-clouds open to receive the Winged Man, then closed over his head.

"Hurrah! Victory! Victory!" shouted Danby Druce.

As though in echo to his cry, a deafening role as if of a thousand thunders fell upon his stunned ears; whilst a thousand thoughts of flame shot to east, to west, to north, to south from the spot where the Winged Man had disappeared.

Blinded, stunned, Danby Druce covered his face with his hands as, with swift beats of his mighty wings, he soared from his perilous position. A familiar swishing noise close at hand caused him to look up. He could scarce believe his eyes. Floating calmly by his side, a mocking smile upon his lips, was the Winged Man.

No trace of the net remained, save a few charred ends which had become entangled in the Winged Man's wings, to show how he had regained his liberty. Doubtless the fierce electric fire in the centre of the storm-cloud had burnt the silken strands of the net as easily as though they had been of paper.

If further evidence of the terrific heat through which the Winged Man had passed was needed, it was shown in the blackened haft of his spear; whilst its head, which when Danby Druce had last seen it had shone like silver, was dimmed with the bluish glare which intense heat gives to highly-tempered steel.

"Are you, then, indeed more than human?" demanded the detective. "No living man could have borne that heat unscathed."

For a few minutes the Winged Man gazed into the other's face without speaking, his flashing eyes showing how greatly he appreciated his foe's involuntary homage.

"I am the Winged Man!" was the only answer he vouchsafed.

"But come, Danby Druce, prepare to meet the doom you have so oft invited!" he continued. "And I am loth to slay you, but you have staked your life, and lost. Die!"

As the Winged Man spoke he shifted his grasp of his spear from the butt to near the head, and raised the heavy haft aloft.

"I die, Winged Man, but not alone!" shrieked Danby Druce, as, throwing all his strength into one final beat of his wings, he hurled himself towards his foe.

But the Winged Man was ready for him. Darting backwards, he brought the heavy handle of his spear with crushing force upon Danby Druce's head.

Had that blow reached its mark, the great detective's career would have ended then and there, but, fortunately for Danby Druce and the world at large, he received the full force of the blow on his extended arm; then, sick, faint, and well-nigh unconscious, spread out his wings, thus checking his descent, and allowed himself to fall towards the earth.

Poised in mid-air, the Winged Man gazed, half triumphantly, half disdainfully, at his falling foe.

"He brought it on himself; yet he was a brave man, and I regret being obliged to slay him," he muttered.

Stunned and confused, Danby Druce felt himself falling with constantly increasing speed towards the terrible masses of rolling, lurid clouds which covered the earth like a fearful curtain.

A shadow shook his frame. So the end had come. He died, and died in vain, for the Winged Man yet trod the earth—or, rather, flew the heavens.

Suddenly renewed hope sprang to birth in his heart. As though opening an avenue of escape, the storm-clouds immediately in his path divided to right and left, revealing to the apparently doomed man a glimpse of the earth he never expected to reach alive.

With one final effort Danby Druce guided himself towards this opening. But he was too weak to judge his distance correctly, and, though his body and left wing escaped the clouds, the tip of his right pinion penetrated the rolling mass of condensed electricity.

A fearful, unbearable spasm of pain swept through his veins as the electricity, running along the steel framework of his wings, sent shock after shock flashing through his tortured body.

So terrible was the agony that it was more than even his dauntless spirit could endure, and a loud, despairing shriek, which thrilled even the Winged Man's heart with pity, pierced the air.

Yet a moment before, seeing his intended victim had a chance to escape, the Winged Man had poised his spear ready to hurl it through the man's descending body; but as the detective disappeared in a sheet of blue, electric flame he held his hand and watched his victim roll over, then plunge with constantly-increasing speed earthward until the clouds, meeting together once more, shut out the falling man from view.

"Lord of earth and sea and sky, I reign supreme!" came in deep, loud vibrating tones of triumph from the Winged Man's lips as, spreading his wide wings, he flew swiftly northwards.

Terrible indeed were Danby Druce's thoughts as, his body still tingling with the fearful electric current which had run through his limbs, he felt himself hurtling t through space.

His one wing served to check his flight, but well he knew it was not sufficient to save his body from being dashed to pieces when it struck the earth. Down—down he went.

A fearful feeling of sickness crept over him, and all was blank. Presently he opened his eyes.

His every limb ached as though a thousand fiends were tearing at his muscles. Cold, clammy waters closed in above him.

Presently he was conscious that an iron grip had encircled his wrist.

"Leave me, Winged Man! May I not even die in peace?" he gasped, defiant to the end.

"Die in peace! Who is talking about dying? You have had a narrow escape; but, then, if you will try to fly through a thunder-storm, what can you expect?" cried a loud, breezy voice.

And, looking up, he saw, with a feeling of delight almost too great to be borne, Professor Hexmider gazing down upon him.

Then Professor Hexmider's face grew dreamt dim and indistinct, and he lost consciousness once more.

GHAT'S DOWNFALL.[34]

For three days Danby Druce lay in Professor Hexmider's house, hovering between life and death. Then, owing principally to the big-hearted inventor's nursing, he recovered sufficiently to relate what had occurred during that terrible struggle above the clouds.

"Make me another pair of wings, and I will take up the chase again," he added, undaunted by the fearful experience he had undergone.

Professor Hexmider shook his head.

"That will be difficult, if not impossible. When we reached home, after I had pulled you out of the pond into which you fell and saved your life, I found that the Winged Man had visited my laboratory. Not only had he destroyed all my working models, but the specifications of my wings upon which I have spent so many laborious years."

A sigh of bitter regret escaped Danby Druce's lips.

"But don't despair. We will not yet relinquish the sovereignty of the air to the Winged Man. What wings could not do, an airship may yet accomplish. As soon as I get you off my hands I will set about constructing one, in which you and I together will hunt the Winged Man down. But I am a pretty nurse to allow my patient to excite himself like this. I won't speak another word. Lie here, and try not to think of the Winged Man until we are ready to take the field against him once more."

Evidently to avoid further discussion the good-natured Professor hastened from the room.

Left to himself, Danby Druce's thoughts reverted to the fearful conflict in the air, which was to return again and again in many a fevered dream, and thus thinking he dozed off.

Night had fallen ere he awoke again, but a table, bearing medicine bottles, that stood by his bedside, and a dim light burning on the washstand, told that Hexmider had not neglected his professional duties whilst he slept.

For some minutes he lay in a semi—conscious state, gazing around him, then he gradually realised that a strange numbness had seized his legs, which was mounting every moment higher and higher upwards.

Amongst other things, Danby Druce possessed a smattering of surgical knowledge, and cold drops of perspiration bedewed his brow as he realised the

---

[34] This is the chapter heading as it appears in the original, although the chapter actually dealing with 'Ghat's Downfall' is in the next issue.

fearful truth.

Paralysis was setting in; a fate worse than death threatened him. He, the most energetic and active of men, would be doomed to pass the rest of his life a hopeless, helpless invalid, confined to his bed, whilst others moved about happy in the full possession of their limbs.

"Heaven protect me! Anything but this!" he cried aloud. "Better—a thousand times better—to have perished at the Winged Man's hand!"

"Who calls the Winged Man?"

The deep, rolling, sepulchral tones came from the foot of the bed. His hands by his side, Danby Druce raised himself with difficulty to a sitting position.

The bed upon which the detective has been placed was an old-fashioned four-poster; standing at the foot of which, holding apart the curtains with extended hands, stood the white-faced, fearful form of the Winged Man!"

Holding apart the curtains with extended hands was the fearful form of the Winged Man.

KILL OR CURE.

For nearly five minutes Danby Druce remained gazing with staring eyes at the weird horror leering at him from between the curtains, too dumbfounded even to think connectedly. At length, with a mighty effort of will, he recovered his shattered faculties, and, scorning to show the terror which consumed his heart, gazed back at the Winged Man as haughtily as though he did not know that he was at his fearful foe's mercy, and did not feel convinced that the Winged Man had come to kill him.

"Congratulation, Danby Druce!" cried the Winged Man, breaking the lengthy silence. "I begin to think that, like myself, you bear a charmed life. None have ever met the Winged Man in deadly strife and lived to tell the tale."

"Lived—ay, lived to wish that I had died!" retorted the detective bitterly.

"What! Danby Druce, whose heart I have ever deemed the bravest in the world, save my own, a puling, despairing coward?"

"I am no coward," returned the detective. "It is not death I fear, but life. Would that your spear had pierced my heart, or that I had been dashed to pieces on some out-cropping rock, rather than end my days, as I must now do, a broken, paralysed, bed-ridden wretch?"

For a moment the Winged Man lost his wonted self-possession. A look of infinite pity flashed from his eyes.

"Paralysed, did you say?" he asked, in a low voice. "You—paralysed? No, no, man. It shall not—it must not be!"

"But it must be, because it is. Not even you, wondrously endowed though I acknowledge you to be, cannot restore strength to my lifeless limbs."

"How do you know that?" inquired the Winged Man suddenly. "Listen! I not only can, but will give you back the use of your limbs."

Danby Druce could not repress an exclamation of delight, which died away in a half-contemptuous, half despairing moan as the Winged Man continued:

"Yes; I will restore your dead limbs. I will render you strong and fit for work as ever, but on that you acknowledge me as sovereign of earth and air alike, and will be my dog, my slave, until it pleases me to release you from your servitude."

"Winged Man, I begin to think that what men say of you must be true—that you are the King of evil himself, or you would never propose such terms to one so completely at your mercy as myself," was the contemptuous reply.

"Then you refuse?" demanded the Winged Man.

"Ay, once and for all, and for ever. I refuse!" returned Danby Druce, glaring fiercely at his foe.

"And if I restore your strength, will you yet continue to track me down?" persisted the Winged Man.

Danby Druce hesitated.

To relinquish the pursuit of the Winged Man was tearing the great desire which had dominated him so long from his heart; yet if he received so great a benefit from his hands, how could he treat him as the deadly enemy he undoubtedly was? But the fearful horror which had struck a cold chill to his heart when he was first discovered in his helpless position was yet strong upon him.

Bowing his head, whilst a flash of shame dyed his pale, bloodless cheeks, Danby Druce replied in a low voice:

"Gratitude would forbid my injuring a benefactor."

It cost the great detective much, this renunciation of all his hopes and ambitions. The Winged Man shook his head.

"No; it cannot be. I said there was only one condition upon which I would cure you. That one condition you have refused, fortunately for yourself. A Russian prisoner, slaving in the silver mines of bleak Siberia, has a happier lot than he who serves the Winged Man. Therefore, without condition, repudiating the slightest claim upon your gratitude, I will set your legs free of the numbing paralysis which holds them prisoner."

As he spoke, the Winged Man bent down, and, thrusting his hand beneath the bedclothes at the foot of the bed, grasped Danby Druce by the ankles.

A loud cry of pain burst from the detective's lips. A fierce current of electricity had said his body tingling, though the legs, through which it passed, still remained devoid of feeling.

Tighter and tighter grew the Winged Man's grasp upon Danby Druce's ankles; fiercer and more oft repeated shocks shook the detective's frame; whilst, his teeth and hard set, his eyes staring, his fists clenched, he bore the torture without another murmur.

Presently his pain was forgotten in a flood of joy, as a slight tingling in his toes told that the power to feel, which must precede the power to move in the paralysed, was returning to his legs.

For a moment the Winged Man released his grasp, and, as the electric current from the dread being's quivering flesh ceased for a moment, Danby Druce sank back on the pillow with a sigh of relief.

But the respite was short. Once more the Winged Man's long, deathlike fingers closed over his ankles.

"Listen, Danby Druce! Your danger has been greater than I suppose. I find my personal store of electricity will not avail to cure you. Can you bear more, or must I leave you to your fate?"

With an irrepressible shadow, Danby Druce recalled to mind the fearful agony of those fearful shocks; yet to be hale and strong once more was all he craved.

"On your word, which, unscrupulous though I know you to be, you have never yet broken, will it cure me?" he demanded earnestly, adding, with a frenzied motion of appeal: "If not, let me die in peace."

"It will cure or kill. When you brave the ordeal?" was the reply.

"Ay; a man's body half dead and half alive is of little use to him," returned Danby Druce, with a bitter, mirthless laugh. "Proceed; let the consequences be what they may, I trust you."

Without a word the Winged Man strode to the window, where he stood, with arms outstretched, gazing into the black night without. Was it fancy, or did Danby Druce see pale, almost invisible streams of bluish flame shooting out from the black storm-clouds which hovered over the house, concentrating their almost invisible glare upon the black, weird, motionless figure of the Winged Man?

He did not know—he could not tell—and ere he could find an answer to his unspoken question, the Winged Man, his face hard set, stern, in a look of concentrated thoughts such as Danby Druce had never seen there before, returned to the foot of the bed.

"Farewell, Danby Druce, if your weakened frame is unable to bear that which I must call upon you to endure," were his ominous words, as he once more seized Danby Druce by his ankles. Then, leaning forward, his fierce, blazing eyes riveted those of the detective.

A fearful electric shock swept through Danby Druce's veins; but, almost unbearable though it was, the detective was scarce conscious of it.

His whole being, his whole soul seemed to be in his eyes, as he gazed in a species of terror less fear at the Winged Man, whose black-clad form seemed growing larger and larger each moment, whilst blue, snake-like coils of flame shot out, like a thousand fluttering ribbons, from every part of his body.

Larger and larger the Winged Man seemed to grow to the awe-stricken detective; more terrible his dark, fathomless eyes; deeper the pallor of his deathlike face; more frequent, more nerve-shattering the terrible thrills caused by the electricity shooting through the patient's body.

As though moved by some outside influence he could neither see nor control, Danby Druce felt the upper part of his body raise itself from the bed.

Then, as he saw the Winged Man's fearful form towering from the ground to the top of the tall four-postered above his head, he was conscious of a spasm of a fierce, awful shock, as the electricity flowed irresistibly through his every nerve; then something seemed to snap in his brain, and all was blank.

THE WINGED MAN'S FAREWELL.

When Danby Druce recovered consciousness, the storm-clouds, which had hung like a black curtain over the earth the previous night had disappeared, and the sun was shining brightly into his room. A strange feeling of elation succeeded the depression that had overwhelmed him the previous evening.

For a few moments he lay, gazing at the canopy over the huge bed, until his eyes were riveted upon what at first he took to be a dark-brown skin, but, as he regarded it more closely, he saw that the material had been scorched by some fearful heat.

Like a flash, the terrible events that had occupied the hours of darkness returned to his mind. With a low moan, he covered his face with his hands, and turned over on to his side. The next moment joy succeeded despair. He could move his legs.

The Winged Man had kept his word—nay, more, not only had the paralysis left his legs, but his body was no longer wracked with the pain of the countless bruises he had sustained from the fearful fall.

With a glad cry, he sprang from the bed, and moved swiftly up and down the room. Yes; it was true. He was cured—cured!

"Would that the Winged Man was here that I might thank the most dangerous of foes!" cried Danby Druce aloud.

"The Winged Man is here!"

As the loud, well-known tones thrilled through the room, the double doors of a large wardrobe between the fireplace and the window were thrown open, and the Winged Man, his wings draped about his majestic frame, stepped on to the floor. Following a sudden impulse, Danby Druce stretched forth his hands.

"Let there be peace between us, Winged Man. After what has happened, how can I look upon you as a foe?" he said earnestly.

"Because it is my will," returned that strange, wondrous being. "No, Danby Druce; a feeling of regret, such as I thought myself no longer capable of, swept through my frame when I saw you hurtling through the air to your doom. Willingly would I then have given the richest of my hidden stores of wealth to have called you back to life. You are a man! As a man I respect you and welcome you as the only living human being worthy to do battle with the Winged Man. Willingly I clasped hands with a noble foe."

"In friendship?" asked Danby Druce eagerly, for he had ever felt himself drawn towards this strange being.

Sadly the Winged Man shook his head.

"It may not be. The Winged Man must never know a human friend. As foes we have contended, Danby Druce; as foes we will content to the end. Listen! No man gifted as you are gifted may live for himself alone. You belong to the human race, and it is your duty to serve your clients. I hate and defy every human being save yourself. Farewell! When next we meet it will be as deadly foes!"

Once more the Winged Man and Danby Druce clasped hands. Suddenly withdrawing his fingers from the other's grasp, the Winged Man stamped upon the floor. The polished boards, dividing to right and left, allowed him to pass through; then closed over his head, whilst Danby Druce, scarce able to credit the evidence of his senses, stood gazing with starting eyes at the spot upon which the Winged Man had stood a moment before.

Presently he awoke to the knowledge that he held some hard, round substance in his clenched fist. Opening his hand, he looked down. Reposing in his palm was a magnificent diamond ring, the Winged Man's farewell gift, and at the same time his gauge of battle.

Slipping the valuable gem on to his finger, Danby Druce—fear, wonder, and amazement banished by his professional instinct—dropped upon his knees on the spot through which the Winged Man had disappeared. He had followed the weird terror too long, and had tracked his every movement too closely, to believe with the common herd that the wondrous being was endued with supernatural powers.

The Winged Man had disappeared through the floor; there must, therefore, be some means of exit from the room, unknown probably to Professor Hexmider himself. But search though he might, no sign of a trapdoor met his gaze.

°DANBY DRUCE HIMSELF AGAIN.

Danby Druce, after a turn or two about the room, stood as nearly as he could guess upon the same spot as the Winged Man, and, copying the weird terror's movements as close as possible, stamped his foot.

The results exceeded the detective's most sanguine expectations. As a matter of fact, his experiment proved rather too successful, for, the floor opening, he found himself rolling head over heels down a narrow but steep flight of stairs, built in the wall dividing two of the lower rooms.

Down he went, bumping his head, arms, legs, and shoulders, clutching vainly against the stone wall to check his descent, until at length he plunged head over heels into what he at first believed to be a shallow well, but which, as shivering with cold—for he was clad only in pyjamas—he rose to his feet and groped about in the darkness, he found was a square, dungeon-like cellar about eight square feet.

Despite his discomfiture, Danby Druce laughed heartily at his mishap.

"This is a nice predicament for an invalid almost miraculously raised from a sickbed to find himself in," he muttered. "And that reminds me that I must find my way out as well as in."

But this Danby Druce did not find so easy as he had expected. It is true he found a doorway, but when he had passed through it, groping in vain for the stairs down which he had fallen, he realised that he had wandered into an adjoining cell.

Curiosity prompted him to discover the dimensions of this second subterranean retreat. It was much larger than the first, and by the time he had drawn his fingers along the wall for some minutes it suddenly flashed upon him that he had lost the direction of the door through which he had entered.

Hastily retracing his steps, he at length found an opening in the wall, passed through, and ran against a stone pillar, evidently one of many, which told him that instead of retracing his steps he had lost himself still further in another vault.

Thus he wandered on, probably going over the same ground again and again,

---

° 5 APRIL 1913.

until he began to think he would never reach the upper air again.

In the meantime, Professor Hexmider, who, fearing his patient should become delirious during the night, had barred the door ere he left him, hastened into Danby Druce's room. To his amazement, the bed was empty.

Alarmed by his friend's disappearance, he hastened to the window. It was closed, and the hasp shot back. With the could Danby Druce have gone?

"Locked doors, barred windows! He must have melted into thin air!" soliloquised Hexmider.

Thoroughly alarmed, the professor searched under the bed, threw open the doors of the big wardrobe, calling his friend by name as he did so. Then, more bewildered than ever, he rushed on to the landing, and soon his strident tones had brought his old housekeeper, his solitary assistant, and Danby Druce's chauffeur upon the scene.

In accents of utter bewilderment Professor Hexmider announced that though the door was locked on the outside, the window barred on the inside, his guest had vanished.

"The Winged Man has taken my master!" moaned the chauffeur, in trembling accents.

"The Winged Man? Heaven defend us! I know I'd go mad with terror if I saw him!" ejaculated the housekeeper.

Then, with a loud shriek and a thud which seemed to shake the old house to its foundations, she sat down on the floor; whilst the chauffeur and the assistant, panic-stricken, dashed headlong from the room. Even Professor Hexmider, brave though he was, staggered back in a fright as the doors of the wardrobe opened, and a black, troubled figure emerged, then, to Hexmider's amazement, threw himself into a chair and burst into a hearty roar of laughter.

It was Danby Druce, who, finding at length a narrow door giving admittance to a flight of stairs, had mounted them, and emerged from the wardrobe through which the Winged Man had first appeared.

As soon as the Professor had recovered from his alarm, and the old housekeeper, scrambling on all fours, had fled precipitously from the room, he gave his astounded host a full account of all that had happened.

At first the Professor was inclined to believe that the detective was suffering from delirium; but there was no denying the fact that Danby Druce, whom he had left the previous night a helpless invalid, was, through some mysterious agency for which he could not account, restored almost, if not quite, to his former health.

GHAT'S DOWNFALL.

A week later Danby Druce and Professor Hexmider were discussing the details of the proposed airship as they strolled through a small, park-like wood attached to the House on the Moor, when their attention was attracted by the chattering of innumerable starlings and a loud cawing of rooks.

"A hawk?" suggested Professor Hexmider, breaking off the conversation.

Danby Druce shook his head. A knowledge of woodcraft and a lifelong study of Nature had helped to make him the great detective he was.

"More likely an owl driven from its refuge into the bright glare of the sun, or, perhaps, some strange bird escaped from an aviary," he corrected. "Whatever it is, it must be something very much out of the common, for I never heard birds make such a noise in my life."

"And no wonder, for, see, it is the Winged Man!" ejaculated Professor Hexmider, pointing to where, about fifty feet above the trees, a huge, flying figure, mobbed by countless swarms of rooks and starlings, darted hither and thither.

To right and left, up and down flew the figure, striving in vain to escape from the horde of birds which surrounded him on every side. Now and again a strong-beaked rook would dart in and inflict painful wounds with its beak upon the flying figure's unprotected hands or face.

Then a wild cry of rage and pain would reach the astounded spectators' ears, as, abandoning flight, the Winged Man would dash into the midst of his foes, scattering them to right and left, yet for the most part wasting his blows on air, though now and again a stunned or broken-winged bird fluttering to the earth announced that he had got a blow home.

His face beaming with smiles, Professor Hexmider seated himself upon the trunk of a fallen tree, and, holding his sides, sent his deep-chested laughter echoing amongst the trees.

"Look at him! Look at the Lord of the Air now! Mobbed by crows! The very birds have risen in rebellion against the arrogant usurper. Ha, ha, ha! Ho, ho, ho! Is that the fearful being even you are afraid of, Danby Druce? Is that the Winged Man?"

"It is not the Winged Man!"

Professor Hexmider turned swiftly round, then sprang to his feet with a yell of terror.

Standing in the cleft of a hollow tree immediately behind the log on which the professor had been seated, was the Winged Man, an angry frown adding tenfold to the terrors of his stern, fearful face.

His arms folded, his wings draped in funereal folds around his spare, though well-built frame, anger flashing from his eyes, he strode forward; whilst Hexmider, every bit of colour fading from his face, retreated before him.

"I am the Winged Man!" continued that weird being, in deep, sonorous tones. "To me alone belongs the empire of the air! As for yonder miserable clown," he added, pointing to where the flying figure, all unconscious that his master's eyes were upon him, was trying to wreak fruitless vengeance upon his feathered assailants, "he is but my dog—my slave. I furnished him with wings that he might exalt his master's honour; instead of which"—and the Winged Man's face became convulsed with wrath—"he has brought me—me, the Winged Man—to contempt!"

Turning on his heels, he strode to an open space betwixt the trees, followed at a respectable distance by Danby Druce and Professor Hexmider.

Coming to an abrupt halt, the Winged Man turned his white face upwards to where Ghat, hemmed in by rooks and starlings, was striking furiously to right and left, filling the air with shrill, animal-like shrieks of rage, until, forgetting that he was in the unsubstantial air instead of upon the solid ground, he neglected to keep his wings moving, and fell swiftly earthwards.

Realising his mistake, he extended his wings. Too late! Ere he could check his downward flight he fell amongst the branches, and the next moment was hanging ignominiously head downwards from the jutting branches of a mighty oak; whilst his feathered foes, chattering and cawing with triumph, descended upon him like a black cloud, pecking at him with their beaks and clawing at him with their sharp talons.

For some minutes the unfortunate dwarf hung helpless in the midst of his foes; then, glancing downwards, his eyes fell upon the Winged Man.

"Master—master, help me! They will claw my eyes out! They will peck me to pieces like an overripe cherry!" he cried.

"And richly have you deserved your fate, fool!" retorted the Winged Man, making no effort to release his servitor.

For ten minutes Danby Druce and Professor Hexmider watched the strange scene, until suddenly the Winged Man put an end to the fight by rising from the ground and soaring above the black mass clinging like a swarm of bees to Ghat's struggling form.

A score feet above the suspended dwarf, the Winged Man uttered a loud, shrill, piercing shriek. The effect was magical. Cawing and chattering, the birds flew in all directions, whilst, sweeping upon the trembling Ghat, the Winged Man bore him to the ground.

Grasping the dwarf by the shoulder with both hands, he looked with so fierce a glance of concentrated hatred and rage upon his trembling servitor that Professor Hexmider and Danby Druce moved forward under the impression that the weird horror was about to tear the cringing dwarf to pieces.

Such indeed seemed the Winged Man's intention, for his long, thin, talon-like fingers closed around Ghat's throat until the dwarf's hideous face turned purple, his starting eyes seemed bulging out from his head, his tongue protruded from his blackening lips.

"Hold, awful terror! Would you kill the poor wretch?" ejaculated Hexmider, springing forward.

"Back! The Winged Man brooks not interference from mortal man. Speak!" he added releasing his hold of Ghat's throat. "Whose dog are you?"

The poor wretch's eyes rolled for a moment in his head, he held a deep breath; then, moistening his parched lips with his tongue, moaned pitifully:

"Yours, most mighty master! Yours to do what you will with—to spare or to kill!"

"You hear?" cried the Winged Man, turning triumphantly towards his companions. "Those who serve the Winged Man own neither will nor the right to live."

Once more he seized Ghat in his iron grasp; then, dragging large strips of leather-like material from his body and limbs, hurled them furiously to the ground, until at length, trembling with terror, Ghat stood stripped of his wings.

"Go! Taste no food, let no water pass your lips, accept no hospitality by the way, until you reach my refuge on the Yorkshire coast!" thundered the Winged Man.

Only pausing to cast an appealing glance, full of undying affection, upon the Winged Man, who, badly though he treated him, was the only thing the wretched dwarf loved in all the world, Ghat set forth upon his long, weary, foodless tramp across England.

"Let what you have seen sink into your mind, Professor Hexmider. Naught destitute of feathers shall soar above the earth save I, the King of Space, the Winged Man. Sole Lord of the Air, none shall tread its trackless paths save myself!"

"And I," interposed Professor Hexmider bravely—"I dispute your right to the title you usurp."

The Winged Man gazed at the huge, big-boned Professor, with the good-humoured contempt one might regard a wayward child.

"You? Tut-tut! You are drunk with rage and envy. Why, even on earth, on equal terms, you could not hold your own against me."

"Stripped of your wings you would be but a babe in my hand," boasted the professor. "I'd like to try a wrestling bout with you for any sum you like to name."

"Come—for a thousand pounds!" cried the Winged Man.

As he spoke he tugged sharply at a tag hanging over his left shoulder. Immediately his mighty wings dropped to the ground, and Danby Druce, for the first time, saw the Winged Man without his draped wings.

Fearful, weird, awe-inspiring looked the Winged Man furnished with his mighty wings, but now, his spare, well-knit frame clad in tight-fitting black clothes, upright as a lance, the detective was obliged to own his great foe looked every inch a king.

A puzzled expression appeared upon the professor's face, and he glanced wonderingly at Danby Druce, whose countenance showed rising interest, but there was no eager light in his eyes as the professor expected to see, now that the Winged Man had placed himself voluntarily in his power.

The Winged Man read the professor's thoughts.

"Mr. Danby Druce and I understand each other. There are times when truce is proclaimed between us," he said; adding, as he turned to his huge opponent: "Come, Professor, your fame as a wrestler has reached my ears. Surely you will not decline the contest!"

"Not if you with the Evil One himself!" shouted Hexmider. "Catch-as-catch-can—for a thousand pounds!"

AS MAN TO MAN.

The Winged Man looked admiringly upon the magnificent proportion of the man with whom he was about to wrestle. His rare smile changing for a moment the entire expression of his face, he grasped Hexmider's hand, saying:

"Agreed! The first two falls out of three. Mr. Danby Druce shall be referee."

The detective nodded, and pointed out a grassy plot in the centre of a ring of magnificent oaks as a suitable spot for the trial of strength.

The two appeared ill-matched, for, well-built though the Winged Man, Professor Hexmider was a perfect Hercules—big boned, deep-chested, without an ounce of superfluous flesh about his body, yet, as Danby Druce took his stand mid-way between the combatants, he felt confident that the Winged Man would prove the victor.

Yet, even he was not prepared for the exhibition of strength and skill he was about to behold.

Stripped to the waist, Professor Hexmider took his stand opposite the Winged Man, who, his hands advanced, his body slightly bent, awaited the signal to commence.

"Go!" cried Danby Druce.

Like some huge projectile Professor Hexmider flung himself towards the Winged Man, who, finding that the skilful Cornishman gave no opening for a grip, contented himself by ducking under his arm, appearing, calm, cool, and ready for a second attack, immediately behind him.

Professor Hexmider at looked at his opponent in amazement.

"I thought the man did not live who could avoid my grip!" he ejaculated.

"Perhaps the man does not live," responded the Winged Man calmly.

"Man or fiend, once you are in my clutch the victory is mine!" returned Hexmider boastfully.

Well he might feel confident of victory. A Cornishman, reared in a Cornish village, he had been a wrestler since earliest childhood, and though he had met the foremost wrestlers of the West of England, he had never yet found his match.

Save for a quiet, almost contemptuous smile, the Winged Man made no response, and once more Hexmider advanced to the attack. This time the Winged Man did not refuse close quarters, and Danby Druce saw, with rising excitement, his host's mighty arms clasped round the Winged Man's lithe, supple form.

With a mighty heave of shoulders, loins, and legs, Hexmider strove to raise the Winged Man from the ground. He might as well have striven to have uprooted a forest oak, so firmly were the Winged Man's feet planted on the ground.

As though possessed of arms of triple steel, the Winged Man enfolded the Cornishman's bulky frame in a remorseless iron grip, and Hexmider, feeling his mighty ribs bending beneath the pressure, gasped for breath.

His muscles standing out like the gnarled knots of a mighty branch, Hexmider strove his utmost to throw the Winged Man, until, suddenly—how it happened he could never quite understand—he was lifted off his feet, whirled round, and the next moment found himself flat on his back, with the Winged Man kneeling on him.

"First-round!" shouted Danby Druce.

Relieved of his conqueror's weight, Hexmider rose, dazed, puzzled, and somewhat shamefacedly, from his ignominious position.

Three minutes' respite, sorely needed by the panting and well-nigh exhausted Professor, though the Winged Man's pulse was not quickened by a single beat, and they faced each other once more.

Warned by the results of the previous bout, that he would need all his strength, all his skill, all his knowledge of the thousand-and-one tricks a lifetime of wrestling had taught him, Professor Hexmider, his feet planted well apart, his elbows crooked, his arms hanging lightly by his sides, prepared to become the attacked instead of the attacker.

His whole body seeming to move on well-oiled springs, the Winged Man glided slowly round and round Professor Hexmider, watching for an opportunity to close.

Nor had he long to wait. Tired of being compelled to keep ever face to face with the Winged Man, Hexmider was about to resume the offensive, and had just shifted his feet for the purpose, when, like a flash of lightning, the Winged Man was upon him.

Once more Hexmider experienced the irresistible, almost supernatural, strength of the Winged Man's mighty arms. Then he found himself lifted from the ground, whirled at arm's length above the Winged Man's head, and hurled, breathless, panting, and defeated, on the grass.

So severe had been the shock that it was some moments ere Professor Hexmider could recover his shattered faculties, and when at length he rose slowly and painfully to his feet, the Winged Man had refixed his mighty wings, and, floating a few feet from the ground, was surveying his conquered foe with a smile of triumph.

Rubbing his aching limbs with both hands, Professor Hexmider looked ruefully at his conqueror.

"It was a fair fall, and I am proud to have been beaten by such an opponent," he said generously. "I gladly pay the thousand pounds. Well you have earned it. I have never before met my match."

Resuming his coat, the professor produced a cheque-book and a stylographic pen, with which he filled in a cheque for the agreed amount, and handed it to the Winged Man, it must be confessed with a sigh, for the professor was not a rich man, and the loss of the thousand pounds would mean delay in the construction of the airship upon which his heart was fixed.

Thrusting the cheque into a pouch at his belt, the Winged Man, with a gesture of farewell, disappeared above the tops of the surrounding trees, leaving Hexmider and the detective to discuss the strange being who had just left them, as they walked home to lunch.

It was at this meal that the professor confessed his inability to continue to work upon the airship for want of funds, and Danby Druce was about to place his own banking account at his friend's disposal, when Hexmider, who had dipped his ladle into a soup-tureen which had been brought up by an electric lift to the table, uttered an ejaculation of astonishment.

No brown, appetising fluid filled the spoon, and, wonderingly, the professor glanced inside. The tureen was empty, except for a piece of folded paper lying in the bottom.

A puzzled frown upon his brow, Professor Hexmider secured the paper, opened it, then leaned back in his chair, gasping as though unable to believe the evidence of his senses.

"Hallo, Professor, what have you got there? You seem surprised at something!"

"Surprised! Surprised is not the word for it, I am simply astounded! Look here!" returned Hexmider, handing the paper to Danby Druce.

It was the cheque the professor had given the Winged Man shortly before. Across it was written the words:

"Kindly accept this as a contribution towards the airship you are building. Do not refuse; it is only fair I should help pay for an invention which I will destroy when complete.

"The Winged Man."

THE LIVING STATUE.

His huge pinions beating the still night air, the Winged Man flew over the darkened enshrouded town of Birmingham.

So close to the tops of the houses did he fly that belated travellers, and policeman on their beats, gazed fearfully into the black void above their heads as the awe-inspiring sounds fell upon their ears.

Recking little of the wonder he was producing below, the Winged Man continued on his way. Presently he paused in his flight, and bathed with a momentary flash of his brilliant headlight a huge tarpaulin-enshrouded figure, which stood beneath scaffolding on the summit of a small hill just outside the great Midland town.

There was no one near save a solitary night watchman, and he, careless of his charge, was sound asleep in his little wooden hut.

Dropping to earth before the scaffolding, the Winged Man allowed the beams of his headlight to illumine the pedestal upon which the covered statute stood.

Engraved in letters of gold were the words:

"To James Tyler,[35] the first to earn the title of King of the Air."

His eyes flashing like twin stars, the Winged Man read and re-read the chiselled words.

"It lies—the marble lies!" he hissed angrily. "I alone am King of the Air!"

Drawing aside the tarpaulin, the Winged Man stood for several minutes contemplating the beautiful piece of sculpture the citizens of Birmingham had erected in honour of the man who had made the first ascent in a balloon from British ground.

A paroxysm of rage shook his frame. Exerting to the full his superhuman strength, he tore the statue from its pedestal; then replacing the tarpaulin, carried the marble effigy with slow, strong beats of his wings across some fields, and dropped it into the middle of the river Thame.

"King of the Air forsooth! It is King of the Mud I crown you!" he cried, as, with a low, contemptuous laugh, he flew away.

The following afternoon a special train from London brought several members of the British Aeronautical Society to Birmingham, there to witness the unveiling of the statue to James Tyler, who can rightly be called the father of British ballooning.

Birmingham was en fete that day. The streets were gay with streamers. Nearly every house flew its flag as a procession, formed by the local Volunteers, several fire brigades, and numerous carriages containing the mayor and corporation, past towards the hill on which the statue had been erected.

The procession, credit to the town though it was, yet lacked its principal attraction, for Horace Trinkerton, R.A., the famous sculptor to whom the statue

---

[35] James Tyler (1745–1804) Scottish aviator, the first person to fly in a hot air balloon in Britain in 1784. It is ironic that he is hailed as the "father of English aeronautics" as his pioneering flight was in Edinburgh, The first person to fly over England was an Italian, Vincenzo Lunardi.

owed is its existence, was absent, and though telegrams, and even special messengers, had been sent to summon him to take part in the day's proceedings, he had not put in an appearance.

Horace Trinkerton had disappeared, whether of his own accord or spirited away by some envious rival none could guess, any more than they imagined that the very moment the procession left the town-hall Horace Trinkerton was sleeping off the effects of a drug the Winged Man had poured down his throat in the early hours of the morning, in one of that weird being's secret haunts.

An enormous crowd had gathered to witness the unveiling of the statue of James Tyler, and as they opened to let the procession by, cheer after cheer rent the air.

Alighting from the motorcar in which he had travelled from Birmingham, the mayor, preceded by his mace bearer, and surrounded by the panoply of civic greatness, made his way bowing courteously to right and left, in the railed-in space immediately in front of the tarpaulin-draped statue.

KING OF THE AIR.

We will not tire the reader with a detailed account of the somewhat tedious ceremonial with which the authorities thought fit to embellish the proceedings. Suffice it to say that at length a well-known aeronaut, who had consented to perform the final ceremony, stepped forward and launched into a long description of aeronautics, until the majority of those present wondered why on earth they had not stopped at home and read an account of the proceedings in the local paper, comfortably seated before a fire.

But all things, even a faddist's[36] speech, must have an end, and a sigh of relief burst from his listeners when the speaker, ending his speech with a final outburst of poetic fervour, grasped the cord which would undo the fastening securing the tarpaulin to the top of the scaffolding, and cried:

"Hail to the father of English aeronautics. Hail, thrice hail, to the rightly styled King of the air!"

As the last words left his lips he jerked the cord, and the enswathing tarpaulin fell to the ground.

The half-raised cheer died away until a dead silence held all present in its grip, as discrediting the evidence of their senses, the crowd gazed upon the Winged Man, who, with partially-extended wings and folded arms, a half-triumphant smile upon his lips, gazed contemptuously around him.

Owing to the well-chosen position of the statue, there was scarcely a man present who could not see the weird terror's jet black form mounted on the pedestal. The mayor was the first to break the silence.

"I—I think I'll go home," he stammered.

---

[36] Enthusiast.

And, despite their terror, the citizens laughed aloud as the weak expression of fear passed his lips.

His worship had moved towards the waiting car, when the whole vast crowd was thrilled, and the mayor himself brought to an abrupt halt by a sonorous "Stop!" from the Winged Man's lips.

"Stop!" continued that fearful being. "Let none dare to move hand or foot, on pain of instant punishment! What, you creeping earthworms, your heads covered in the presence of he whom you have this moment hailed as King of the air!! Hats off! Hats off, I say, to the Winged Man, whose sway in the trackless realms of space is undisputed, undisputable! On your knees, dogs that you are, lest—"

He left the sentence unfinished, and, to the terror-stricken eyes of the huge crowd, seemed to grow larger and larger as he stood for a moment towering above their heads, his wings extended, brilliant electric flashes shooting in a thousand bluish points from every line of his wondrous form.

A low, reverberating moan of terror swept through the seething crowd, as, obeying an impulse they could neither understand nor resist, everyone present dropped upon their knees.

Blame them not. Perchance braver man could not have been found, search the world through, yet the fearful powers of the Winged Man by his great knowledge had wrung from Nature forced them to obey.

It was an impressive scene—a scene none present are ever likely to forget. The kneeling thousands, the gold-lettered marble pedestal, upon which the black-winged form of the Winged Man towered with kingly dignity.

Again the mayor was the first to break the silence, not by word, but by actions. He is usually rubicund face as white as extreme terror could make it, he cast one fearful, despairing glance around; then, dropping on hands and knees, sought to crawl beneath the motorcar which had brought him on to the scene.

Suddenly the horror which gripped his soul found vent in a loud, piercing scream, as, like a hawk upon its prey, the Winged Man swooped down upon him, seized the valuable chain of office by its massive gold links, snatched it from his shoulders; then, waving it triumphantly in the air, remained poised some twenty feet above the earth, shouting in stentorian tones:

"The King of the Air claims tribute from his slaves!"

Whether it was the epithet "slaves," which never can, and never may be applied to free born Britains, or whether the insult to the city, in the person of their mayor, stirred the crowd to action, it is impossible to say: certain it is that the spell was broken, and a mighty roar of indignant rage rent the air like a thunder-clap as the crowd surged like an angry sea beneath the Winged Man, who, filling the air with mocking, taunting laughter, dangled the chain just out of reach of their wildly-grasping hands as he flew, in an ever-increasing circle, round and round, until at length the outskirts of the crowd was reached.

There he remained poised, on swiftly moving pinions as though the unsubstantial air beneath him was solid ground.

"Beware, men of Birmingham!" he cried, in knell-like tones. "To you belongs the earth, to me the air. Seek not to crown another sovereign of my domain, lest worse befall you.

A FEARFUL SANCTUARY.

Ere the last words had left his lips a horseman, mounted on a magnificent bay charger, jumped from out the hedge-hidden road on to the soft green sward of the meadow surrounding the hill. With a single glance he took in the situation.

Digging spurs deeply into his horse's flank he galloped noiselessly to where the Winged Man, enjoying the sensation his words had created, remained poised some eighteen inches above the outstretched hands of the nearest man. It was not until he felt a strong grip close round his ankles, and heard a triumphant voice ring in his ears, crying, "Not yet, Winged Man, is the victory yours! Yield! You are my prisoner!" that he realised his danger.

"Not yet, Danby Druce!" cried the Winged Man, in mocking tones, as ere the other could guess his purpose, he dropped upon him, enfolding the gallant detective in his huge wings.

"To me, friends! Seize him! Let him not rise again, or he will escape!" shouted Danby Druce.

Muffled in the Winged Man's leathery wings though he was, the detective's voice reached the astonished spectators' ears.

In a moment a hundred pairs of hands were stretched forth to seize the weird, fearful being who had brought disgrace upon their town. But ere they could seize him the frightened horse, neighing shrilly with terror, plunged forward and, taking the bit between his teeth, galloped swiftly down the hill, bearing the Winged Man and Danby Druce, so mixed up together that the spectators saw nothing but a huge black mass, from which now and again shot a hand or arm as it swayed to and fro, like a ship at sea, upon the horse's back, which flew at a speed borne of mad panic towards the River Thame.

Low, breathless cries of horror burst from the astonished spectators when they saw that the maddened beast was bearing its double burden nearer the river-bank at each stride, cries which accumulated in a loud shout of despair as they saw the horse, as though striving to clear the wide river at a bound, gather itself together, rise from the ground, and fly a score feet, with front and hind feet outstretched, ere it plunged, neighing shrilly, into the gently-flowing river.

But, ere touched the water, the Winged Man, seizing Danby Druce by the throat, tore him from the saddle and bore him upwards.

The great detective was indeed worthy to contend against so fearful a foe. Terrible though the odds against him, terrific though the strife, not for a moment had his dauntless heart failed him.

A consummate horseman, his grip had defied even the Winged Man's almost irresistible attempts to drag him from the saddle, but when he felt, rather than saw, the horse bound into the river, he had allowed himself to be plucked from the saddle, for well he knew that in the water the Winged Man could easily thrust him beneath the surface and hold him there till life was extinct.

"Again, Danby Druce, I triumph!" hissed the Winged Man in his great foe's ears.

"You lie, accursed being!" retorted Danby Druce, snatching a knife that reposed on his hip from its sheath and striking wildly at his foe.

In vain. The keen blade glided off the Winged Man's bullet-proof cuirass.[37] Yet the blow was not entirely wasted, for the keen blade cut through the Winged Man's wings, it, passing downwards, severed his left pinion almost from his body.

So unexpected was Danby Druce's thrust that for a moment the Winged Man lost control of his wings, and the two, after rolling over and over in the air, crashed with considerable force through a clump of willows growing close to the water's edge on the further bank of the river.

TO CAPTURE THE WINGED MAN.

For a moment the Winged Man relaxed his hold. Shaking himself free, Danby Druce struggled to his feet, and, gaining the solid ground, stood on the defensive.

Panting and breathless, for even the Winged Man's iron frame had felt the strain, the two faced each other. Danby Druce, his every muscle strained to its highest tension, awaited the Winged Man's charge.

But it never came. Draping his wings around him, the Winged Man surveyed his opponent with admiring, almost friendly eyes.

"Well done, Danby Druce!" with the unexpected words which came from his lips. "I am grateful to the lucky star which preserved your life, when you fell, scorched and paralysed, from the thundercloud. I would rather the whole human race perish than that you should cease to live!"

Then, turning, the Winged Man sped swiftly over the fields, just as some five hundred men, filling the air with shouts of rage, plunged into the river, and, wading, scrambling, swimming, hastened to where Danby Druce was standing.

Rage filled every heart. In a moment Danby Druce realised the advantage the Winged Man's injured pinion and the just rage of the crowd would give him.

Stepping forward, he put himself at their head.

"Follow me, lads!" he cried in ringing tones. "The Winged Man is chained to the earth with an injured wing! Now or never we will capture him!"

"Hurrah! Forward—forward! Death to the Winged Man!" came in one loud, fierce, determined roar from the crowd. The next moment the Winged Man, glancing over his shoulder, saw the fields covered with a constantly increasing crowd of pursuers.

---

[37] Breastplate.

Flinging back mocking laughter in response to the mob's vengeful cries, the Winged Man, covering the ground in a series of enormous bounds, turned his face northwards.

As a fox to its earth, so the Winged Man was fleeing to one of his many subterranean haunts, there to repair his injured wing. But he had reckoned without the anger his action had aroused.

The whole countryside was up in arms against him. Soon he found his way barred by a second crowd, summoned to the assistance of the first.

With a snarl like that of a hunted wolf, the Winged Man turned in the direction of Birmingham, but only to be headed off again and again, until at length he realised that he had become the centre of a momentarily contracting circle of relentless foes.

"Bay, dogs, bay!" hissed the Winged Man through his clenched teeth, as he shook his fists angrily at the foes who hemmed him in. "You think you have me; but the Winged Man will yet read you a lesson you will never forget!"

Then he dashed straight at the nearest foeman. As a captured tiger speeds round and round the circling fence of bamboos with which the Indian huntsmen have hemmed him in, so the Winged Man circled round the shrieking ranks of his pursuers, looking for some loophole of escape, some weak spot through which, with one final, despairing effort, he might break free.

But none presented itself, until at last the unpleasant thought that, after all, humiliating capture might be his fate, entered his head.

The next moment he dismissed the thought with a fearful, defiant, mocking laugh, which chilled the hearts of all who heard it. His face convulsed with fury, he sprang to a hedgerow, grasped a sapling by its tender top boughs, and pulled it up by its roots.

The yielding top gave to his frenzied grasp, as did the tender branches, until soon his extemporised club was ready for its work of death.

But quickly though he worked, ere this strange weapon was finished his foes were all but upon him. Before he had looked for the weakest spot in the line, now the fire of battle scorched in his veins, and he made straight for where the crowd was thickest. Uttering a loud, blood-curdling scream of defiance, he made the stout sapling circle round his head, as, urged forward by his mighty springs, he dashed upon his foes.

A huge navvy, one of the true Midland sort, who fear neither man nor ghost, barred his path. But that moment taught the navvy what fear was, for, wielding the sapling in both hands, the Winged Man bore down upon him.

In vain he turned to flee. Too late! The descending roots, clogged by a hundredweight of earth, struck him between the shoulders, and he plunged headlong to the ground.

Loud, deep, and resonant arose the Winged Man's terrible laugh; then from his lips came a strange, weird battle-song in an unknown tongue.

Those who saw the mighty deeds the Winged Man performed that day speak of them still with bated breath, but those who saw his face carried the fearful memory with them to the grave.

An angry Prince of the Nether World flogging his rebel subjects into submission could not have looked more terrible. Pale ever, at that hour the Winged Man's countenance was the colour of the newly dead.

His eyes seemed like flaming pits the fire; his lips were parted in a snarling grin, which showed, glistening like ivory, his tightly clenched teeth.

Brave men recoiled before that fearful apparition; strong men gazed upon him, and sank senseless to the ground. Yet all were of the good old British Bulldog breed, and though none doubted but what a forward movement meant instant death, they closed around him, terror-stricken, but determined to conquer or die.

His wild, weird song, rising high above the shouts of the combatants, his huge club hissing like a rising storm, it hurled through the air, the Winged Man cut a lane through his swarming foes.

Yet, despite his mighty club, despite his fearful presence, the men of Birmingham closed in a relentless throng upon the Winged Man's rear. Little cared he for that.

The impossible had been made possible. With his unaided arm he had cut his way through five hundred inveterate foeman.

Turning, he hurled the sapling at his nearest foes, laughing as he saw a dozen rolled over like ninepins when the fearful missile struck them.

Then his battle-song, changing to a pæan of triumph,[38] he dashed over the field towards where, some five hundred yards away, arose a tall wall, beyond which appeared the shaft of some works, foundry or manufactory.

But even as he neared the wall a cry of exhortation arose from his panting pursuers. Summoned by a messenger who had scorched into Birmingham by the mayor's motor, a squadron of cavalry dashed upon the scene.

---

[38] Triumphant song.

WITHIN THE POWDER FACTORY.

As the soldiers galloped with drawn swords after the Winged Man, there was not a man amongst the pursuers but thought the weird being's course was run at last.

"The soldiers have come! Hip, hip, hurray! Now we'll have him! Hurrah!" they panted, cheering wildly, yet not ceasing in their efforts to overtake the fugitive.

"Fools!" snarled the Winged Man over his shoulder, as, without pausing in his flight, he dashed headlong at a solid brick structure before him.

A gasp of incredulous wonder arose from the crowd.

"Would he dash out his brains against the solid wall?" they asked.

Then every man, save Danby Druce, came to an abrupt halt; even the soldiers reined in their horses, and gazed in amazement at the Winged Man.

Six feet from the wall he sprang up, and, attaching himself to its perpendicular surface, where neither foothold nor handhold could be obtained, sped, as swiftly as he had sprang over the ground, to the top.

On the narrow coping he remained poised, maddening the baffled crowd with mocking laughter.

"To the gates—to the gates! He cannot, he shall not escape now!" cried Danby Druce, hastening to wear a pair of huge gates, some hundred yards away, gave admittance to the largest Powder Mills in the Midlands.

In vain the gatekeeper forbade their entrance, explaining the danger of unauthorised persons, shod with steel-nailed boots, moving amongst the drying-houses and magazines, where a large quantity of powder, that had been prepared for a Government contract, was either packed, ready to be sent off, or in process of manufacture.

But the well-meant expostulations passed unheeded, as, in a mighty, irresistible wave, the crowd swept through the gates.

As calmly as though an uninterested spectator, the Winged Man watched his foes approach, then, as they drew near, sprang on to the roof of a large, low building, the walls of which were composed of mounds of solid earth, and, tearing off the road, disappeared within.

It was the magazine. Within, fifty tons of mylanite, and two hundred tons of the coarse, black, octagonal tubes of explosives, used in the largest naval guns, was stored.

Ten minutes later, Danby Druce, the manager of the factory, and inspector of the police, and the officer in command of the soldiers, passed along the covered way, which gave admittance to into the magazine, and, as the manager unlocked the door, crowded into the dimly-lighted storehouse.

They were brave men, or they would never have attempted to enter that place so long as the Winged Man was there; but, brave though they were, terror gripped their hearts, when, as though turned to stone, they gazed through the brilliant light which suffused the low, wooden-pillared vault at the Winged Man.

The Winged Man was seated, as though upon a throne, on a huge pile of boxes, filled with mylanite, around him a thousand powder casks. Like a carpet beneath his feet, was what looked like pale, yellow dust, but which all new was fine-grained sporting powder, of so high an explosive power that the slightest spark would set it ablaze, and commenced an explosion such as the annals of England's gunpowder factories could not equal.

But though they gazed upon the accumulation of powder, which might well be designated as the very embodiment of death, it was upon the Winged Man their thoughts were concentrated.

Seated, as we have said, upon piles of boxes containing the deadliest explosive known to science, his back resting against some powder kegs, his legs crossed, his whole attitude betokening careless case, he puffed nonchalantly at a cigar, the aroma of which filled the place.

The fall of an ash, an almost invisible spark dropping from the Winged Man's glowing weed, and the factory, and all within five hundred yards of it would be wiped off the face of the earth.

"Welcome, gentlemen. Make yourselves at home. The accommodation is limited, but never has a king granted audience amidst more impressive surroundings," was the Winged Man's mocking greeting.

"For Heaven's sake be careful! If that cigar fell from your fingers a thousand lives would be placed to your account," pleaded the white-faced manager.

"What's that to me? What care I if thousands of your accursed kind perish?" snarled back the Winged Man.

Paying no further heed to the dumbfounded men, he produced a richly-jammed cigar-holder, and placed the cigar in it, took from his breast a case of tools, and, as calmly as though in one of his own subterranean caves, proceeded to repair the injury to his wing caused by Danby Druce's knife.

Presently he looked up.

"What, still here?" he said mockingly. "As Shakespeare says, 'What fools you mortals be.' If you were not unintelligent asses, you would long, ere this, have placed a mile of open country betwixt yourself and me. You must be longing for death, to linger so long in this antechamber. Go; for by my head, I swear, that when this cigar is finished, I will drop the lighted end amongst the powder!"

The men looked from each other to the glowing end of the half-finished cigar, then whispered excitedly together, whilst the Winged Man, his wing repaired, leaned back upon his terrible throne, apparently unconscious of their presence, and smoking quietly upon the mount of death, lapsed into deep thought. Once more he looked up.

A NOBLE DEED.

His visitors had gone, all save Danby Druce; and he, his pale face lined with anxiety, was leaning with folding arms against a pile of boxes.

"So your friends have taken my well-meant hint. Why do you not follow their example, Danby Druce?" demanded the Winged Man.

"Because I have sworn never to leave you as long as it be in my power to keep you in sight, until I see you expiate your crimes on the scaffold," was the bold reply.

"Danby Druce, you know me better than any living man. Have you ever known the Winged Man false to his word?" thundered the Weird Horror.

"Never!" truth forced Danby Druce to reply.

"Then go; for that which I have sworn I will perform!" asserted the Winged Man.

The detective's sole reply was a contemptuous shrug of his shoulders, and for some minutes he surveyed the Winged Man in a deathly, unbroken silence, unbroken within that infernal magazine as without, for the manager and the inspector of police had carried the Winged Man's message to the crowd who were running to death, and at that moment, except for these two, there was no living soul within half a mile of the factory.

Whilst the events above recorded had been taking place, night had gradually spread her sable mantle over the scene.

"Danby Druce, beware!" came in deep sonorous tones from the Winged Man. "The glowing end of my cigar approaches the rim of the holder."

Danby Druce cast a longing glance at the star-spangled sky, showing through the gaping hole by which the Winged Man had entered.

"Go!" repeated the Winged Man, rising, and pointing to the door.

"Not unless you come with me as my prisoner," declared the detective firmly.

"Your fate be upon your own head!" thundered the Winged Man; and the next moment the magazine glowed like a fiery furnace, as the beams from his brilliant headlight turned from white to red.

"Farewell, Danby Druce, farewell for ever!" came in loud, awful tones from the

Winged Man's lips, as, opening his wings, he soared heavenwards into the night.

In a single bound Danby Druce reached the throne the Winged Man had just vacated, and, his heart beating wildly, followed with eager eyes the dark form, turned to an image of blood by the baleful red beams of his headlight.

Suddenly a gasp, half of relief, half of dread, burst from the detective's parched lips. The Winged Man had kept his word. A tiny spark was descending straight to the hole in the roof of the magazine, beneath which Danby Druce had taken his stand.

Glowing fiercer and brighter, as it fell swiftly through the air, the cigar end descended. Swift was its fall; but to Danby Druce it seemed as though it was held back by some unseen hand, so intensely was his every sense concentrated upon it.

Nearer and nearer it came to where Danby Druce, with outstretched hands, awaited it.

Cold drops of perspiration bedewed his brow, an irresistible impulse to shriek aloud tore at his heart-strings.

He knew the chances were a hundred to one against him. Should he fail to catch the falling spark—death! Even should his hands close upon it, a tiny piece of tobacco-leaf might fall upon the powder, and the result would be the same—death!

Quicker than the swiftest lightning-flash, a thousand dashing thoughts swept through the detective's brain.

Thank heaven, the glowing end is at length within his reach. A loud, piercing shriek burst from his lips as it struck the palm of his hand; then, as his fingers closed over it, a dark curtain seemed to descend upon his brain, and he remembered no more.

An hour later, the three who had first accompanied him re-entered the magazine. They found the great detective stretched senseless over that fearful heap of explosives, clasping in his burnt and blistered hand the extinguished end of the Winged Man's cigar.

AT THE LLEWELLYN ARMS.

Twynford is a small village nestling in Cwamba Valley, on the borders of Wales.

At one time the road through Twynford had led northward to Montgomery, some twenty miles distant, but a few years ago the northern extremity of the beauteous valley had been blocked up by double mounds of soil and huge walls of solid concrete, to form a reservoir to supply the West of England towns as far as Birmingham with water.

Attached to the Llewellyn Arms was a large room, the floor of which was sunk four feet below the surface of the road, it stunted windows secured by iron bars, the door high up in the wall at one end, by which alone admittance could be gained. Although it formed as secure a meeting-place for conspirators as could be desired.

Within this room at fifty men were assembled, listening to one of their number, who was explaining to his eager listeners a simple but effective plan to lay the Winged Man by the heels, and make those present the richer by a hundred pounds apiece, for the reward for the Winged Man's capture had advanced by leaps and bounds, until now it stood at £5,000.

"Now, lads, as far as I can see, there is nothing further we can do to-night. What will be a fortune to many here awaits us for the taking, if we can only stick together and hold our tongues," concluded the speaker.

"We'll hold our tongues right enough!" growled a stalwart labourer. "It's a chance as don't come to the likes of us twice in a lifetime!"

"But what if the Winged Man does not fly across the Valley to-morrow night, as he has done every night for the last week?" interposed another.

"That's the only weak point in our scheme, and that we must risk," declared the leader. "Now, lads, our business done, let's have a few quarts of mulled ale to celebrate the occasion."

"You can have the ale right enough," growled a stalwart individual whose soiled apron proclaimed him the public, "but if you wanted mulled you'll have to do it yourselves down here. The kitchen fire is out, and the missus won't lighted again for anyone, you know that as well as I do."

A murmur of sympathy arose from the conspirators, for it was a well-known fact that if their host held the licence, Mrs. Turnbull held him in the hollow of her hand.

"That won't take us long, Jim," declared the leader. "There's plenty of old wood and boxes littering about. You get the beer and a saucepan, we'll soon have a fire."

Taking care to collect the money ere he left the room, the publican climbed up the rickety, wooden stairs leading to the door, and tapping upon it, was let through by a man on guard without.

By the time he returned with the saucepan a bright fire was blazing on the open hearth, and soon the enticing fumes of the steaming ale stole through the apartment, as with skilled hands, the public and added the necessary condiments.

"Hark! What is that? I thought I heard somebody moaning!" cried the village blacksmith, who, shortly before, had exhibited to the admiring gaze of his fellow-conspirators an ingenious arrangement of chain, anklets, and bars, with which they intended to rivet upon the Winged Man, once they got him into their power.

An immediate hush fell upon all within the room. All started, as upon their listening ears fell a hollow moan.

"It is the wind," declared Tim Davis, the leader.

"There aren't no wind," growled the publican.

"Then what on earth can it be?" queried the village clerk, looking fearfully around him.

The answer came with unexpected promptitude. A rumbling in the chimney, a heavy fall of soot, and the next moment, a large, black form fell into the midst of the fire, then with wild, almost unearthly shrieks of pain, sprang into the apartment.

"The Winged Man! The Winged Man!" arose in a terror-stricken chorus from fifty pairs of lips, as the gallant conspirators, dividing to right and left, crouched trembling in the four corners of the room.

"It aren't the Winged Man; it's his brother, the King of Evil himself!" stammered the village clerk.

"No, it is not the Winged Man, or you would all have been struck dead ere this!" came in a fierce, hissing shriek from Ghat's lips, for it was the Winged Man's deformed but faithful servant who had been instructed by his master to find out the reason of the nightly gatherings at the Llewellyn Arms.

As the words left his lips, Ghat, baring his yellow teeth in an angry snarl, sprang to the long, narrow window, and, seizing the iron bars, strove to drag them from their place, but the bars were embedded deeply in the masonry, and ere he could bring his full force to bear upon them, the conspirators, risk covering from their sudden panic, flung themselves upon him.

Ghat fought like a wild-cat, biting, kicking, hitting, struggling, and putting forth such enormous strength, that even when they had him on the floor, it took half a dozen strong, able-bodied men to hold him down.

"Clap the irons on him, quick, Trotter!" cried Tim Davis, who was sitting on Ghat's head.

The next moment he sprang to his feet with a loud, shrill yell of pain, as Ghat, beaten, but not subdued, made his teeth meet in his leg.

"Oh, he's bitten me! I shall go mad, and die flying through the air, just as if I was the Winged Man!" moaned the unfortunate man. "Can't you look slippy with those irons, Trotter?" he added impatiently, for the blacksmith showed no sign of obeying the order.

"No, I can't!" retorted Trotter determinedly. "These here irons were made for the Winged Man, and no one else but the Winged Man shall wear them!"

"Then no one else will wear them!" shrieked Ghat, foaming with impotent rage. "Fools, to think that clodhoppers like you will ever succeed in capturing my master! Be wise, let me go, and abandon your absurd attempt to do what even the great Danby Druce has failed to accomplish!"

But the West of England breeds stubborn natures.

"Not much, master!" jeered Davis. "You don't escape, anyhow, and before twenty-four hours are past you will have the Winged Man as a companion in prison. What were you doing up that chimney?"

But Ghat refuse to answer; and though his captors tried their utmost to induce him to speak, he maintained a dogged silence.

At length, angered by his obstinacy, they thrust him, head and heels together, into a rough deal box, and not wishing to divide the reward into smaller portions, as they would have been compelled to have done had more people been taken into their confidence, for the room was used for other purposes during the day, they carried him, box and all, into a hey-loft over an adjoining stable, where, after gagging him, lest his cries should attract attention, they left him.

IN THE DEVIL'S HEEL MARK.

About two hundred yards below the last house in Twynford's straggling, village is a rugged gorge, marked by a deep indentation, some six feet deep, known as the Devil's Heel Mark. Tradition had it that a holy hermit once dwelt within this gorge, to whom appeared his Satanic Majesty, who expressed his willingness to make the hermit king of all Wales in exchange for his soul.

But the hermit was not a seller of souls just then, and as a gentle hint that he considered his Satanic Majesty's room preferable to his company, he sprinkled him with holy water. Whereupon, the Father of Lies, furious at finding the hermit a little too wide-awake to fall into his trap, stamped so angrily upon the ground that his heel sank six inches into the solid rock. Around the Heel Mark grew, in wild luxuriance, shrubs, weeds, and various kinds of creepers.

Crouched in a small copse close at hand whether fifty men who had sworn to capture the Winged Man, whilst, as a bleating kid is secured by Indian hunters to lure the monarch of the jungle to his doom, so a child, snatched from its unwilling mother's arms by her husband, who formed one of the band, was seated in the centre of the depression.

Unable to see the hidden men, and believing himself deserted in a spot which, even the grown-ups of Twynford avoided after dark, the boy filled the air with cries and calls for its mother.

The conspirators had abated their trap well. All new that the Winged Man had a particularly soft place in his heart for little children, and no other earthly sound would be so sure to lure him from his aerial path.

Regularly at ten o'clock for the past three weeks had the Winged Man flown over this spot, and it had become a regular custom for the inhabitants of Twynford to stand, awe-stricken, on the outskirts of the village, listening with bated breath to the hissing beat of his huge pinions, or shuddering with terror as they caught a momentary glimpse of the fearful, flying form hurtling like some monster bird of ill and through the air.

This night the crowd at the end of the long village street was composed principally of old men, women, and children, the adult males for the most part being conspicuous by their absence. None knew, for the secret had been well kept, of the proposed attack upon the Winged Man.

Presently Davis, who, as leader, had been, not entirely to his satisfaction, elected to the most prominent, and therefore most dangerous position, felt a cold shiver of dread sweep through his veins. Distant as yet, but wondrously distinct, like no other sound he had ever heard, came the beat of the Winged Man's wings.

Louder and louder grew that awe-inspiring sound, intermixed now with the shuddering cries of the unfortunate child at the bottom of the pit. Presently the huge, dark form swept upon the scene.

The child, whose sharp ears had warned it of the Winged Man's presence, now uttered louder and more frenzied shrieks for its mother as its startled eyes saw the Winged Man's awful form hovering overhead.

Immediately the Winged Man paused in his flight and circled round the pit; then, in wondrously sweet, soothing tones, cried:

"What is it, little one, lost—eh? Do not be afraid. I will carry you to your mother!"

Immediately the child's cries ceased, and, on his charitable errand intent, the Winged Man dropped, in spiral descent, to its side. But even as he stooped to raise the sobbing infant in his arms the starlit heavens above the jagged rim of the pit became darkened, and the next moment the Winged Man was borne struggling to the ground beneath the heavy folds of a huge tarpaulin.

"Hurrah, lads, we have got him! Quick, into the pit, or he may yet escape us!" cried Davis.

The Winged Man realised that he had fallen into a cunningly-contrived trap.

Suddenly his whole frame quivered with rage as he felt a heavy hand laid upon his ankle, another seized his wrist, others his arms, neck, and body, whilst, enveloped in the skilfully cast tarpaulin, he was unable to make an effectual resistance.

"Scoundrels, by whose cunning the Winged Man has at last been trapped, beware! It is not for myself I appeal—a thousand such as you could not prevail against me! Relieve me of this child, then do your worst!" came in short, angry, staccato sentences from the Winged Man, who, fearful lest the little one should be injured, allowed the iron anklets to be slipped round his legs without resistance.

Another second and he felt a belt of the same material clasped round his waist. Yet he made no attempt to resist.

A minute later the child was snatched from his grasp, then, like lightning, the blacksmith and his fellow-conspirators thrust the Winged Man's arms into iron staples prepared for them and his wrists into handcuffs.

"Now, Winged Man, who is beaten? A thousand could not capture you—eh? Less than fifty have done the trick!" cried Davis triumphantly.

THE WINGED MAN'S WARNING.

Weighed down by close upon half a hundredweight of iron—for Trotter, the Twynford blacksmith, was determined that the Winged Man should not easily burst his bonds once they were fitted upon him—the triumphant villagers hauled the Winged Man with unnecessary violence from the pit; then, the usual reserve broken, the whole fifty, wild with excitement, performed a species of war-dance around their captive, whilst a wondering crowd from the village hastened upon the scene as the astounding intelligence that the Winged Man was at last captured passed from lip to lip.

But, as their excitement cooled down, more than one present felt their joy clouded over by a premonition of impending disappointment.

Why or wherefore they could not tell, save that, instead of anger, dismay, or fear the Winged Man's stern features were relieved by a quiet smile of amusement, much the same as a grown-up person might regard the weak attempts of a child to accomplish something much beyond its powers.

Suddenly those nearest the Winged Man noticed his muscles contract as though about to make a great, and, it seemed, a despairing burst for liberty.

With a cry of alarm Davis, Trotter, and half a dozen others flung themselves upon him, some seizing his arms, but the majority hanging on to the thick chains of the iron belt which secured him. Then, as though in a single voice, a shrill, astonished yell of agony burst from six pairs of lips, as the men who had seized the Winged Man writhed and strained to break free, their white, ashen faces contorted with fear, as electric shock after shock was sent coursing from the Winged Man's hidden storage-battery through their veins.

Shrieking with terror, howling for mercy, the six formed a circle of writhing forms around the Winged Man. In vain they tried to disengage their hands. The fierce current which racked there every nerve held them fast prisoners.

For a moment the Winged Man hesitated. Another shock, and each living form would be a lifeless corpse. But he held his hand, and, switching off the current, allowed the men to drop, limp and half unconscious, to the ground, where they lay, their twitching bodies and low moans alone showing that they lived.

Glaring contemptuously down upon the men who would have held him, his iron chains clanking at every step, the Winged Man moved towards where the remainder of the conspirators were crowded together for protection, not daring to face their fearful foe, yet unable to fly.

"Fools! Madmen! Imbeciles!" cried the Winged Man, in fierce, intense tones. "Ignorance alone could have deemed it possible to hold the Winged Man in iron bonds."

As he spoke, his frame seemed to expand to the awe-stricken beholders' starting eyes, his outspread pinions bore him from the ground, his legs and arms shot out spread-eagle fashion, and five loud, pistol-like snaps caused the trembling spectators to start violently, as anklets, wristlets, and body-belt fell clattering to the ground, whilst the Winged Man, freed from his bonds, soared above their heads.

Low moans of terror rose from those who had witnessed this proof of the Winged Man's wondrous strength, silenced when they saw his headlight blaze forth a baleful red.

"Woe to the Vale of Cwamba!" came in thrilling tones from the Winged Man's lips. "Ere another son has risen and sunk again it shall be a barren waste of water. Thus shall men learn to fear the Winged Man!"

Whilst speaking he had risen slowly and majestically, and when the last words left his lips naught could be seen but his baleful headlight glowing from out the heavens.

°THE MIDNIGHT WATCH.

It was just in time to hear the Winged Man's fearful warning that Danby Druce, to whose ears had come news of his life-long foe's presence in the Cwamba Valley, arrived upon the scene.

He knew the valley well; he knew the mighty mass of water held in check by an artificial dam at the further end of the valley, and, even ere the Winged Man had finished speaking, knew that he meant to destroy the dam, and let that fearful flood sweep over the peaceful scene.

Only pausing to gather from the beaten and dejected conspirators an account of their attempt to secure the Winged Man and its disastrous failure, Danby Druce entered his car and drove swiftly away.

From town to town he went, enlisting the service of the police in every borough. By the time the sun rose on the peaceful valley once more, the enormous reservoir was guarded by close upon two hundred constables; whilst in the centre of the dam, Danby Druce saw that an alert and unfaltering watch was kept.

The sun swept majestically through the heavens until it rested upon the western horizon, and yet the Winged Man made no sign.

Little the great detective suspected that, boring like a mole beneath the surface, the Winged Man was at work with pick and shovel in the very heart of the dam, weakening the defences by numberless tunnels, and chipping holes in the solid concrete in which he inserted cartridge after cartridge loaded with a high-power explosive.

An hour passed, darkness reigned over the scene. In the centre of the embankment Danby Druce stood, buried in a deep reverie. To right and left the rounding sides of the valley, behind him the grass-grown slope of the great dam, above him the starlet heavens, before him the deep, dark waters of the mighty

---

reservoir, reflecting back, like glittering points of golden spears, the stars above.

There was scarce a breath of wind to cause a ripple on the lake's glassy surface. It seemed as though all Nature breathlessly awaited the Winged Man's vengeance.

Although two hundred men were about the dam, no sound broke the silence of the night save the deep booming of a heron, or the grating cry of some wandering night-jay.

As Danby Druce gazed upon the water at his feet, and involuntary shudder shook his frame as he realised the mighty force that was only held in check by the enormous embankment upon which he stood.

Then, just as the moon shed its first beams upon the sylvan scene, he turned on his heel and gazed down the valley. His elevated position commanded a view of many of the villages which had taken refuge from the clear, westerly breezes in the Cwamba Valley. Here and there a light betokened that all the population had not fled, but the majority of the houses were deserted.

The Winged Man's warning had sunk deeply into the people's hearts, and those who remained were only those who, not having seen the Winged Man, could not understand the terror his name inspired in those who had once stood face-to-face with that weird horror.

Suddenly Danby Druce faced the reservoir once more.

That same fearful, indescribable feeling, neither fear nor horror, but akin to both, which he had ever experienced when the Winged Man was near, swept through his frame.

Yet, if anything, a deeper, more perfect, peace, reigned over the apparently sleeping scene.

Eagerly Danby Druce strained his ears, listening for the first swish of those awful wings which would herald his flying foe's advance, whilst, with upturned face, he searched the heavens, his every nerve strung to its utmost tension, his brave heart beating steadily and true, as he awaited the coming conflict.

At that moment, low and solemn, came the deep boom of a distant clock striking the midnight hour.

As the last echoing notes died away, Danby Druce clasped one hand over his eyes as he staggered back half-blinded by a bright, dazzling light which appeared with startling suddenness from the water some twenty feet from where he stood.

His hand shading his eyes, Danby Druce peered into the heart of what seemed a ball of red-hot, glowing metal, then, as his contracting pupils grew accustomed to the bright glare, he saw awful, awe-inspiring, inexpressibly horrible, the Winged Man, floating in the centre of the ball of light, his wings extended, his hands stretched out over the valley in a gesture of awful denunciation.

In loud, sonorous tones, that reverberated like rolling thunder from one side of the valley to the other, striking terror into every hero's heart, the Winged Man sang:

OR, 'TWIXT MIDNIGHT AND DAWN

333

"From air's dizzy height
Down to the realms of night,
Fire flashing left and right,
Death to my foes.
I am the Winged Man,
I am the Air King,
I am conqueror."

As he spoke, from out of the blaze of light in which he stood a thousand writhing tongues of many-coloured flame, each disappearing with a crack as of a pistol-shot, whilst, by the glare of the central illuminant, police and watchers could be seen gathered about the reservoir and along the steep summit of the dam.

"To the hills! Fly for your lives!" continued the Winged Man, in deep, sepulchral tones. "The dogs of death are upon you! Fly, ere it be too late!"

As the thunderous echoes of his voice died away, the watchers, stricken with sudden panic, fled, some rolling down the side of the dam in their mad terror. But the majority, remembering the Winged Man's words, sort the high ground on either side of the valley.

All fled, all but Danby Druce, and he, with devoted courage, sublime in its refusal to yield, faced his fearful foe, alone—unsupported.

"Fly, Danby Druce; though you are my deadly enemy. The world cannot afford to lose such men as you," adjured the Winged Man.

"Never!" came in hard, determined tones from betwixt Danby Druce's clenched teeth. "My game is afoot. I will not turn back from the chase."

"Then follow if you dare!" cried the Winged Man, as he plunged head-foremost into the reservoir.

With a shudder, Danby Druce noticed a thick cloud, accompanied by a hissing noise as of water poured on a red-hot iron, as the Winged Man dived beneath the surface.

Yet he hesitated not a moment. The challenge had been thrown out. It must be accepted, for like some fearful luminous marine monster, the Winged Man's diving form could be seen cutting its way through the placid liquid. Throwing his hands above his head, Danby Druce dived forward in headlong pursuit.

DEATH DEFIED.

Barely had the water closed over his head ere Danby Druce was conscious of a fearful upheaval of the waters around him, a dull, muffled roar burst on his ears, and the next moment he was hurled with fearful violence back to the surface, to fall, breathless and panting, but with every sense on the alert, into the reservoir.

Fighting his way back to the surface Danby Druce looked around him.

Shrieks of terror and cries of "The dam has burst!" fell upon his ears, until they were drowned in the loud, ever-increasing roar of the waters.

Wonderingly he gazed at the dam, expecting to see it riven in twain, but to his astonishment the long line cutting the horizon, which marked the summit of the reservoir bank, was unbroken. Yet the roar of an escaping flood told that a breach had been made, and that the Winged Man's vengeance had commenced.

The next moment the mystery was solved in a way which struck a chill of dread to Danby Druce's heart, brave and dauntless though he was.

Some invisible, intangible hand seemed drawing him slowly beneath the surface.

He cast a swift glance into the waters, expecting to see the Winged Man's glowing form beneath him, but the waters were as black as night itself, yet the downward pull continued, whilst he felt himself being carried round and round in a circle.

For five precious minutes wonder and curiosity held the detective motionless, then, as he realised that the breach had been rent in the bottom of the dam bank, he and he was being drawn irresistibly into the vortex, he threw his body forward and struck out for the nearest bank with all his might.

Too late! The downward pull was greater than the utmost efforts of his frenzied strength.

Round and round he was carried, until at last he found himself being whirled swiftly round the outer rim of what seemed to be an enormous tunnel.

Let the reader watch the water pouring from a bath-room basin, and he will realise how Danby Druce was carried to the bottom of the reservoir.

Round and round he was whirled, until his senses reeled, his head seemed swelling as though it would burst, and with one long, last despairing cry he found himself being drawn to where, with fearful force, the water was hurtling through the hole the Winged Man had blasted in the base of the dam.

Suddenly that weird being shot like a falling star down the centre of the whirlpool, seized the panting detective from its deadly grip, bore him half unconscious to land, deposited him on a mossy bank, then, wheeling, hovered once more over the centre of the vortex.

Fearful, indeed, was the sight he presented to the white faced spectators who had paused on the side of the valley to watch with horror-stricken eyes the water pouring as though from an enormous hose, from the base of the reservoir.

Rendered distinct by the fierce, searching glare, every line, every mark, of the Winged Man's face could be seen by those on land. Fearful, indeed, it looked in its scarcely human, malignant triumph, as the Winged Man gloated over the mischief he had done.

Yet, great though the work of destruction he had accomplished, and was accomplishing, the Winged Man was not entirely satisfied.

Though an impression was growing in the minds of men that the Winged Man was immortal, the weird being himself knew different. He knew that one day death must claim him as his own, yet he would not, if he could, have had it otherwise.

He had gained much, he had lost more. Life was the only stake he could play for, which had power to thrill his heart.

As he had again and again saved Danby Druce that he might have some foe worthy of his steel, so again and again he had apparently thrown himself into the very clutches of death to burst from the grim terror at the last moment.

As he hovered above the whirlpool the black void at the tapering point of the vortex seemed to possess a peculiar fascination for him.

He could not say how wide the passage cut through the concrete wall by his skilfully-laid cartridges would be, yet the uncertainty led him to gamble once more with the dread king of terrors.

His wild, weird, mournful cry piercing the night air, he folded his wings close to his body and dived head-foremost into the centre of the vortex.

Down he fell, deafened by the roar of the escaping flood; then, striking the slanting bottom, glided off, as a bullet flies off steel, into the midst of the whirling mass of water.

Immediately he became like a helpless log tossing in the whirlpool at the foot of the mighty Niagara.

Great though his strength, wondrous though his power, he could do nothing but allow himself to be whirled at express speed in the black, water-filled the tunnel he had cut with his own hands.

The idea that perchance, whilst working unsuspected beneath the closely-guarded dam bank, he had been digging his own grave, flashed through his brain, but he greeted the thought with mocking, death-defying laughter, as he was whirled round and round between the rocky, jagged walls.

Presently, with a suddenness that brought an ejaculation of pain even from his iron soul, the Winged Man's further progress was stopped, and his arms were pinned to his side by jutting crags. He was hemmed in on every side.

Had he braved death once too often?

The passage was narrower than he thought, and he was stuck fast within a few feet of the washed-out tunnel.

Despair could have no place in the Winged Man's breast, but consciousness of defeat, for a moment weighed him down.

The next he drew in a long, deep breath of the cool night air, as his body, blocking up the tunnel, kept the water from flowing through, and caused it to flow rapidly to the foot of the dam.

"Aha, Death. I will beat you yet!" shouted the Winged Man, struggling to break free.

Defiant though his words, the Winged Man knew he was still in fearful danger.

The weight of water behind him was more than the strongest mortal could have borne. It seemed to be crushing even the Winged Man's strong lower limbs to pulp, until suddenly the rock against which his sides were pressed gave way, and, like a shot from a gun, he was ejected into the valley.

For a few yards he shot straight forward; then, as the air got beneath his opening wings, he glided slowly upward, until at length his swiftly-moving pinions bore him some fifty feet above the earth.

"Victory, victory! Once more the Winged Man escapes unscathed! He lives to watch the confirmation of his vengeance!"

A FLOATING TOMB.

Little the Winged Man knew what a great deal had hung upon his precarious position in the tunnel. Short though the time he had held the water back, it had sufficed to allow many men, women, and children, who, incredulous of his warning, had remained in Twynford, to escape.

Yet one human being remained in the doomed village. Forgotten, gagged and bound, his deformed limbs cramps in their narrow quarters, Ghat still lay in the box into which his captors had thrown him.

Parched with thirst, his vitals gnawed with hunger, Ghat endured unspeakable torments, the greatest of all being that the master, whom despite the systematic cruelty with which he ever treated him, he loved with blind, doglike affection, was in danger of falling into his foes' hands.

"Oh, my master, my master, perhaps even now your glorious career is ended, and, like me, you are a bound, helpless prisoner!" was the cry which rose again and again to Ghat's lips.

At length, about the time the Winged Man appeared to Danby Druce on the waters of the reservoir, the unfortunate dwarf dropped into a sound, half-unconscious sleep. He was awakened by strange sounds beneath him.

At first he thought he was back in the Winged Man's favourite haunt on the Yorkshire coast, with the ocean billows breaking at the foot of the cliff, yet he missed the familiar roar of the restless waves.

Wonderingly he gazed at the rafters above his head, listening for he knew not what. Gradually it dawned upon him that the sound which had so perplexed him was the lapping of constantly rising water against the side of his prison.

Despite his own awful position a feeling of elation caused Ghat's blood to course swiftly through his veins.

He, who knew the Winged Man so well, recognised his master's handiwork in the disaster which had overtaken the village. He knew, as well as though he had been an eye-witness of the events of the past twenty-four hours, that the Winged Man had escaped his foes, and had wreaked his fearful vengeance upon them.

A minute before the terrors of death had gripped his soul, now he cared not if Fate willed that he should die. The Winged Man, his revered master, was alive, and it pleased to Ghat to think that additional vengeance would fall upon the people of the valley when the Winged Man discovered his useful servant's end.

Nearer and nearer came the roar, quicker the tremors which shook the building followed upon the other, whilst now and again a fearful crash told that some less substantially built house had been swept away.

Presently Ghat felt the box in which he was imprisoned tremble, then sway slightly from side to side. Ten minutes later it was afloat, and Ghat, new-found hope springing to life in his breast, found that it was watertight.

Once or twice he feared the end had come, as the strange craft which bore him was hurled by the flood against the wall. But each time it rebounded and righted itself again, until at last Fate guided it to an open, unglazed window, and a minute later it was being swept swiftly along by the flood on a level with the eaves of the houses.

A sudden jar told that the box had come in contact with some stationary body, and a moan of terror burst from Ghat's lips as he felt it heel almost on its side. Fear lent him strength, and, with almost superhuman force, he drew himself over to the other side.

He was but just in time, in another second the water would have flowed in, and his strange craft would have foundered.

As it was, the sudden movement not only saved his life, but also loosened his bonds sufficiently to enable him to sit up.

Wonderingly Ghat gazed around him. Where before he had been accustomed to see smiling fields, well-kept gardens, and trim cottages, was a wide expanse of rapidly-flowing, foaming water, dotted here and there with wooden buildings that look strangely like badly-constructed arks.

Ghat's first care was to free his limbs of the sodden bonds which bound them.

This was a work of time, for his fingers were numbed with long immersion in the water, and the ropes seemed as though they would never come apart. But at length he succeeded, and, with a sigh of relief, raised his arms above his head, as far as the swaying craft would allow, stretched himself.

As he did so a strange and awful bellowing immediately in his rear caused him to look round. A cry of terror burst from his lips. A herd of bullocks, their wide-staring eyes and distended nostrils proclaiming the terror-stricken panic which possessed them, was swimming with the irresistible current.

Their horned heads thrust above the surface of the water, they looked far more terrible than indeed they were. Perhaps Ghat's fear was not entirely unfounded.

One move of the long, straight horns, even an eddy caused by their huge bodies as they swam past, would, he knew, wreck his strange boat.

A piece of wood torn from the side of a barn floated by. As a drowning man catches at a straw so Ghat seized the plank, and, turning it into an extemporised paddle, commenced working for dear life, striving, with little success, to turn his boat-box from out the path of the terrified animals.

The frightened bellowing of the bullocks growing nearer and nearer each moment, Ghat laboured at the paddle, working as he had never worked before, whilst the perspiration rolled in huge drops down his wrinkled cheeks.

Now and again he would cast a swift, frightened glance over his shoulder, each time to find that the herd, borne swiftly forward by the full force of the escaping flood, which slowly but surely overtaking him.

On he dashed, his reckless strokes causing his keelless boat to rock ominously from side to side. His whole frame trembled beneath the fearful strain upon his muscles.

Soon short, quick gasps told of breath exhausted, strength well-nigh gone. Yet he persevered, though the rough edges of the plank tore his hands.

Suddenly the end came. Swimming onward in blind terror, the foremost bullock blundered into the stern of Ghat's frail craft; then, in a sudden access of terror, forced its fore legs and shoulders well out of the water, and the next moment sank beneath the surface, with Ghat clinging to the long, coarse hair covering the frontal bone between its horns.

Ghat gave himself up for lost, yet he clung frantically to the swimming beast, and the two rolled over and over beneath the surface, until at last Ghat uttered a wild, piercing shriek of joy as his head emerged from the covering flood and he breathed the refreshing air once more.

To right and left of him were the horned heads of the swimming oxen.

To leave his hold of his unwilling charge's head would be madness. Gored by the oxen's long, sharp horns, or struck senseless beneath their wildly pawing feet, he would be struck down ere he had swum a dozen strokes.

No; unpleasant though his position, his only hope would be to remain where he was. Changing his grip from the hair to the thick butt-end of the horn, Ghat allowed his bowed legs to encircle the beast's throat. Thus strangely mounted, he was carried swiftly past houses, the rooms of which were crowded with their late unfortunate occupants, who uttered loud shrieks of terror when they saw the dwarf's fearful face peering from between the bullock's wide-spreading horns.

Although Ghat was safe for the moment, he only looked upon it as a respite from death. Already he could feel the strokes with which the beast beat the water growing fainter, wilder, and more irregular. Instinctively he scanned the blue heavens.

"Master, my master, come to Ghat's help, or he dies!" he shrieked, in despairing tones.

"Fear not, the Winged Man is here!" said a deep, sepulchral voice at his left hand.

With a cry of joy, Ghat turned. Used to his master's vagaries though he was, Ghat could not repress an ejaculation of astonishment as he saw the dread being whom he called Lord standing, his feet planted between the horns of the swimming oxen, as a performer in a circus rides to bare-backed steeds.

"Oho, oho! 'Tis fine, 'tis grand, 'tis glorious! See the Winged Man's revenge!" he cried, indicating, with a sweep of his hand, the scene of desolation through which he floated.

With an exultant cry Ghat glanced back over his shoulder towards the now distant village of Twynford.

"What, my master, are they all dead? Washed like rats from out their holes? All those who struck me, tortured me and left me bound and helpless to die in yonder box!" cried Ghat, pointing to where the water-logged craft which had brought him in safety so far still floated.

"What is that?" demanded the Winged Man, turning swiftly upon him. "Have they dared to ill-treat a servant of mine? Hounds, dogs, that they are! Had I known it before not one should have escaped! Yet perchance, Ghat, even you will allow that you have been well avenged!" he added indicating the foaming flood around them.

But Ghat did not answer, for at that moment, with a low, moaning bellow, his ox sank beneath the surface, and sent him rolling head over heels into the foaming waters.

The next moment the dwarf's hideous head appeared above the surface. Like a hawk on a basking fish, the Winged Man swept down upon his faithful servitor, seized him in one hand by his long, matted, red hair, and bore him, kicking, struggling, and howling with pain to a small hill which formed a tiny island in the desert of waters close at hand, where he left him to get off as best he might, or wait until the waters subsided; then skimmed, with long, strong beats of his mighty wings over the agitated waters.

On he flew, until at length he hovered over where, like the lower part of an enormous plough, the ever-advancing water rushed forward on its errand of destruction.

FOR THE CHILDREN'S SAKE.

It was a fearful night, the sloping bank, the ever-moving water hurtling at tremendous speed down that erstwhile peaceful valley; but more awful than aught else was the weird, awe-inspiring figure that, like the Spirit of the Flood, seemed to be leading an army of water to the charge.

Suddenly the Winged Man shot heavenward. A hundred feet above the earth he remained poised, shading his eyes with his hand as he gazed, with a dark frown, towards where, and eye-sore on that beautiful landscape, an ugly red building stood on the summit of a small hill in the centre of the valley. At the windows of the building a number of school children looked, with pale, frightened faces, upon the advancing waters.

"Fools! Cowards! They have fled and left the schools unwarned!" muttered the Winged Man.

But in this he did the fugitives of Twynford an injustice. The schoolmistress had had due warning of the flood's approach; but, trusting that the waters would not reached the house, and also fearing lest the children, sent home alone, should be swept away in the swiftly-moving flood, had elected to remain where she was.

It was an error of judgement, a well-nigh fatal error, for the Winged Man knew that the waters would rise to the eaves of the school-house.

Quickening the beats of his mighty pinions, the Winged Man swept swiftly forward. A prolonged shriek from half a hundred children proclaimed that the weird horror had been seen.

Forgotten was the terror of the approaching flood, forgotten everything, as their little hearts palpitating with terror, their eyes distended with fear, the children, many clinging to their teachers' skirts, watched the Winged Man's approach.

Half-way betwixt the flood and the house he paused in his flight; then, with a wild, weird cry, dropped like a stone earthward. So swift his descent, so fearful the cry which burst from his lips, that children and teachers alike looked to the spot upon which he had descended, half expecting to see him lying a mangled corpse on the grass.

But fear was soon changed to wonder, for the ground seemed to open, and the next moment the Winged Man had vanished apparently into the very bowels of the earth.

A moment's hesitation, then the wonder they had witnessed was forgotten as a girl of twelve, pointing with trembling hand towards the approaching flood, cried:

"Look, the waters are upon us! We shall be drowned!"

The teacher uttered a cry of despair.

"And I kept you here when you might have escaped! Heaven help me, I have brought about your deaths!" she shrieked.

But even as the words left her lips a loud explosion rent the air, the schoolhouse trembled to its very foundations, and a wall of fire shot across the path of the flood, hurling a huge masses of rock and earth heavenward, to fall with a deep thud into the raging waters.

One piercing cry of terror, then silence, broken by loud cries of astonishment as children and teachers alike watched, scarce able to credit the evidence of their eyes, the wondrous scene taking place within two hundred yards of them.

The swiftly-moving wall of water had been turning into a foaming, tossing, roaring whirlpool; yet its progress seemed checked, for though they could see portions of houses, floating furniture, and the bodies of drowned animals being swiftly borne towards them, they were all swallowed up in the foam-capped line which formed a barrier between the school and the flood.

Hour succeeded hour, yet, though thousands of tonnes of water swept upon the line of foam, none reached the schoolhouse, from whence, as well as from the sides of the valley, wondering eyes watched the phenomenon.

When the water subsided a partial explanation of the mystery was found in a wide, yawning chasm which cut the valley almost from side to side. Down this chasm the waters had poured through a countless succession of caverns, on to an unoccupied stretch of moorland half a mile away.

All knew that the Winged Man had caused the explosion which had let the water into the cavern, thus saving the schoolchildren, but none knew at how tremendous a cost. The cavern, one of his secret hiding-places, had been filled with the plunder of years. Without a moment's hesitation he had sacrificed it lest the children's lives should be endangered.

When Danby Druce heard that gold plate stolen from a ducal mansion, and priceless silverware stolen from various public collections, had been found on the water-swept common when the flood sank into the sandy earth, he, at least, guessed the sacrifice the Winged Man had made.

A FRIENDLY MEETING.

"Even though the Winged Man remains uncaptured, a man must dine," muttered Danby Druce, as he came to a halt before the brilliantly-lighted entrance to one of London's most expensive restaurants.

A slight indisposition, which would have been severe illness to one less inured to hardship than the great detective, had followed his fearful experience in the Cwamba Valley, and it needed no doctor to tell him that he must take a short respite from his labours if he wished to maintain his vigour of mind and body unimpaired.

Some take their holidays abroad, others fly to the seaside, or to the country, for rest; but Danby Druce found sufficient distraction in the busiest haunts of fashionable London.

As he entered the restaurant he threw back his black cloth cape, and tenderly raised the petals of a magnificent orchid, which he wore just above the red button of the Legion of Honour, presented to him a year or so before by the French Government.

Although, had he chosen, Danby Druce could have covered his coat with decorations bestowed upon him by various Continental Governments, he seldom wore anything except the little red button; for it reminded him of one of the most stirring episodes of his life, when he unearthed a vile conspiracy against the French Republic and saved that gallant nation from a disastrous war.

Passing down the long line of tables, he made his way to where he could observe without being observed; for, although on pleasure bent, detection had become second nature to Danby Druce, and he knew, none better, how often Fate throws a good thing into a man's hand when he least expects it.

Formerly Danby Druce used to be able to distract his thoughts entirely from whatever work he might have on hand, but now the Winged Man was ever present in his mind.

Do what he would, try though he might, schemes to capture the dread being, who was rapidly becoming a scourge to the law-abiding British public, occupied his thoughts until they were interrupted by the approach of a waiter.

He had just dismissed the man with an order for the soup and fish with which he intended to begin his repast, when he looked quickly up as a low, well-modulated voice said:

"Mr. Danby Druce, I believe?"

"That is my name, sir; but I am ashamed to own I do not recognise you, though your features certainly seem familiar," replied the detective, scanning the somewhat pale, but exceedingly handsome features of the well-dressed, aristocratic-looking stranger who had addressed him.

"Probably so," returned the other, with a strange smile; adding, as he motioned to a chair opposite Danby Druce; "But if you are not expecting friends, may I have the pleasure of dining with you?"

"Delighted, I am sure!" returned Danby Druce, wondering at the strange thrill that ran through his veins as the other spoke.

"So, Mr. Druce," continued the stranger, seating himself, "you do not recognise me, yet it is not long since we parted. Save for my headgear, I am wearing practically the same clothes, though, perchance, put on somewhat differently."

As the stranger spoke he raised his right hand and checked it twice. For a moment it seemed as though the sleeve was attached to the body of the well-fitting dress-suit the stranger wore; the genial smile vanished from his face, a stern, melancholy light sprang into his eyes.

Danby Druce sprang from his chair.

"The Winged Man!" he gasped.

Of all the surprises his weird antagonist had given him, probably this was the greatest.

The Winged Man bowed.

"Yes, it is I; but unless you want to spoil these good people's dinners, you will keep the knowledge to yourself. Though we become deadly enemies again to-morrow, let us be friends for to-night," he suggested.

"So let it be," cried the detective, grasping the other's hand, "as I am on holiday!"

But Danby Druce scarce knew what he was eating, for the Winged Man proved himself a brilliant talker and kept his companion interested from first to last.

Course succeeded course, until at length, dinner over, the Winged Man suggested a visit to the theatre.

Arm in arm the detective and the Winged Man left the building, the best of friends. Little either of them guessed that a new element was about to enter their lives, and element destined to turn what had been almost friendly rivalry into dead, grim earnest.

A FACE IN THE CROWD.

"And now a little supper at the Cecil, to end up one of the most enjoyable evenings I ever remember having spent," said Danby Druce, as the two emerged from the theatre.

"With pleasure," agreed the Winged Man, "I did not think that it was possible for time to fly so quickly. If I did not fear that with use these pleasures would cloy, the Winged Man should disappear from public notice, and——"

He broke off abruptly; a deep sigh full of infinite regret escaped his lips as he added:

"No, it is a dream of the past; the past that can never be recalled. Death alone can give the Winged Man rest or happiness."

A wave of sympathy shot through Danby Druce's heart; yet to offer a pity to the Winged Man would be an impertinence. So, signing his companion to enter the taxi he had just hailed, he stood aside to let him pass.

As he did so a girl suddenly sprang from a narrow passage near where they were standing, for the two had walked some little distance from the theatre to get out of the crush.

"Oh, gentlemen, save me from him!" she cried, gazing with large, fear-laden eyes from Danby Druce to the Winged Man.

"Who, little one? Don't be afraid; he shall not hurt you," began Danby Druce, an emotion like nothing else he had ever experienced before thrilling his heart as he looked into a face more beautiful then he believed it possible for any woman to be.

But the next moment, with a frightened glance over her shoulder, the girl glided swiftly away, and was lost in the throng of people pouring out of the theatre.

Both the Winged Man and Danby Druce made a step forward as though to follow her, but they checked themselves, and stood on the pavement looking at each other, with a light in their eyes which had not been there a moment before.

Grasping Danby Druce by the arm, the Winged Man let him back to the taxi. Not a word was exchanged. Yet each knew the thoughts that occupied the other's heart.

The Cecil reached, the detective and the Winged Man alighted. Drawing Danby Druce aside, the Winged Man led him into a deserted corner of the huge courtyard.

"Ten minutes ago, Danby Druce, I would have said that the woman did not live who could again stir this heart to love," he whispered. "I find that I am human still. Beware how you cross my path!"

Danby Druce shuddered. A flood of anger surged up in his heart.

"That lovely, dainty child—she was little more—bound for life to a scarce human, crime-tainted monster like the Winged Man!" he thought. "Never shall you link a pure, innocent woman's fate to yours!" he cried aloud, pale-faced, but determined.

"Fool! Look back upon the past. Remember that I, the Winged Man, hold your life, your very existence, in the hollow of my hand!" thundered his fearful antagonist. "Better seek to stay the tempest from its path than the Winged Man from the course he chooses to follow!"

Then, so swiftly that Danby Druce could scarce believe it was the same man speaking, he continued:

"But enough of this. Let's not this pleasant evening be ended in strife. If Fate will that we must be foes, let us complete the night's programme we have commenced first."

Without waiting for the detective's answer, the Winged Man led the way into the hotel.

But the pleasure of the night had gone. The glamour[39] the Winged Man had thrown over Danby Druce was no more.

The conversation during supper was forced and unnatural, and both were glad when, the meal over, they left the hotel and strolled down a by-street towards the Embankment.

It was midnight. From the Strand came the roll of wheels, as taxis bore late theatre-goers homewards. In the middle of the street the Winged Man came to an abrupt halt.

"Danby Druce, it is useless for you and I to deceive each other," he cried. "Neither saw that girl for more than half a minute, yet we are both prepared to wreck our careers, and, if need be, perish for her sake. I am determined that she shall be mine. Choose. Will you surrender her to me, and thus earn the Winged Man's undying friendship, with all that it must mean to any mortal man, or risk

---

[39] Enchantment, illusion/

incurring my deadly hatred?"

Almost instinctively, so quickly came the answer from the detective's lips:

"I refuse—utterly, entirely refuse!" he declared emphatically. "I love her too dearly not to save her from the Hades upon earth which would become her lot if she became your wife—ay, at the cost of my life!"

For a moment Danby Druce recoiled before the hate-contorted face of the Winged Man, as, raising his talon-like hands above his head, he allowed his wondrous wings to grow, as it were, from his sides; then, his wild, weird, melancholy cry startling the night air, he soared heavenwards.

FROM THE RIVER'S ICY GRASP.

Thoughtfully Danby Druce wended his way down the street. The Embankment reached, he turned towards Blackfriars Bridge. It was a dark, oppressive night. Even as Danby Druce reached the riverside, a loud, deep resonant thunderclap spoke of the coming storm. But Danby Druce heeded it not.

Before his eyes floated the lovely face which, though seen for but one brief second, had been stamped on his heart for ever.

A dazzling streak of lightning flashed from the electricity-charged clouds. Straight from the heavens it fell, then seemed to burst into a ball of fire around Cleopatra's Needle.

An ejaculation of wonder on his lips, Danby Druce stood as though riveted to the ground, for the Winged Man stood with outstretched pinions on the top of the huge stone.

The next moment darkness blotted out the scene, and Danby Druce—why, he could not tell, unless with some mad idea of scaling the obelisk and coming to death-grips with his foe upon its pointed summit—rushed forward.

But ere the Sphinx-guarded monument was reached, a loud cry for help in a woman's voice brought him to an abrupt halt. Immediately the Winged Man was forgotten.

Dashing passed Cleopatra's Needle, he ran at full speed in the direction from whence the cry had come.

Again the appeal arose. This time echoed by a shriek of terror in a man's voice, and the next moment Danby Druce came upon a fearful sight.

Within the ring of light cast round an electric light standard, the Winged Man was struggling fiercely with a tall, dark, pallid-faced man.

Struggling scarce expresses what Danby Druce saw, for, big-boned, large-framed man though the stranger was, he was but as a child in the Winged Man's iron grip.

As he thrust him backwards to the ground, gripping him as though he would tear him limb from limb, a woman who had been crouched beneath the parapet wall of the Embankment sprang, with a loud, bitter cry of despair, or terror—the detective could not tell which—on to the parapet, where she stood poised, her long, silken tresses, loosened in the struggle with the man who was receiving his punishment at the Winged Man's hands, trailing like golden streamers down her back.

Then, her hands clasped to her eyes, she plunged headlong into the river. Danby Druce had not seen her face, yet he knew that she whose rash act he had just witnessed was the one who had killed the rising friendship betwixt himself and the Winged Man.

Without a moment's hesitation Danby Druce vaulted over the low stone wall. The tide was running out with fearful rapidity when, after sinking almost to the muddy bottom of the Thames, Danby Druce rose to the surface.

He looked around him. All was black as ink, save where, like twinkling stars, the lamps of the Embankment marked the river's course. Treading water, Danby Druce waited and listened, hoping to hear a frenzied cry for help, or, at least, some despairing sob, as the waters closed over the unfortunate girl's head.

None came, and, not daring to waste further time—for every second might mean the difference between life and death to the girl he already loved so dearly—Danby Druce flung himself forward, and forced his way downstream.

She could not be far away. So quickly had he sprung after her that she must already be within reach. Yet his heart felt like lead in his bosom.

In the fearful darkness which obtained he might pass almost within touch of the drowning girl, and not see her. But fortune befriended him. A dozen strokes, and his outstretched hand touched sodden cloth.

In a moment his fingers had closed over the floating garments, and the next he had seized the girl round the waist, and, treading water, drew her unconscious form towards him, whilst a loud cry for help burst from his lips; but the appeal was drowned in a loud clap of reverberating thunder.

Suddenly he started, and drew the girl closer to him as though to place his body betwixt her and harm, for a bright white light casting its final-shaped rays backwards and forwards over the water, was approaching from down the stream.

The Winged Man was searching for them with his keen eyes.

Throwing himself on his back, Danby Druce let go the girl's body for a second; then, clasping her under his chin, forced his way through the water in the direction of the shore.

In vain. A blaze of light from the Winged Man's headlight fell upon him, and the next moment, with cries of mingled triumph and rage, the Winged Man, like some foul bird of night, swooped down upon him.

"What, you would rob the Winged Man of her he swears to make his own?" he demanded mockingly.

And the next moment Danby Druce felt the Winged Man's long, talon-like fingers clasp his throat. In vain he strove to beat of the grisly horror. He was thrust below the surface, and, compelled to release his hold lest he should draw the girl down with him, a pang of unutterable despair rent his heart as he felt her yielding form snatched from his grasp.

In another second he was on the surface once more, just as a dazzling ribbon of electric flame skimmed over the river, and he caught a momentary glimpse of the Winged Man bearing the girl shoreward in his arms.

ON THE EMBANKMENT.

Once more Fate befriended Danby Druce. Carried down-stream by the tide, he struck against the side of a pier. His groping fingers closed over an iron chain, by the aid of which he drew himself on to the platform. A moment to regain his breath, and Danby Druce dashed up the sloping gangway.

An iron gate barred his progress, but, spurred by the thought of the unknown girl in the Winged Man's power, he scaled it with ease, then glanced swiftly up and down the deserted pavement.

Even as he did so the swish of wings above his head caused him to look up. It was the Winged Man flying past, and alone.

Despair and relief struggled for mastery in Danby Druce's breast—despair lest the Winged Man should have allowed the girl to drop back into the hungry river; relief that, at any cost, she was not in the weird horror's power.

The next moment he was running in the direction from whence the Winged Man had come. Presently a cry of joy burst from him.

Before him lay the beauteous unknown. She was stretched upon a seat, her shapely head resting upon its iron arm.

"Why has the Winged Man deserted her?" he wondered.

Without pausing to answer the unspoken question, determined, at any rate, to make the most of his opportunity, he seized her in his arms, and, reaching the centre of the road, sped westward, not pausing until he reached the statue to Brunel near the public gardens.

Then for the first time he paused to look around him and try to determine what was best to be done.

He dare not take the unconscious girl home. He would not take her to the police-station or hospital lest questions should be asked which would lead to her being charged with attempted suicide.

On the other hand, he dare not carry her through the streets. Late though the hour, the sight of a man carrying an unconscious woman would be sure to attract attention, and probably lead the Winged Man on his track.

Oh, that a taxi would come past! Then he could drive to some place where she might find shelter for the night.

But taxi-drivers know better than to look for fares in the early hours of the morning on the Embankment.

He was about to try to reach some more frequented thoroughfare, when a glance down the road showed him a white light flashing to and fro some twenty feet above the ground, and he knew that the Winged Man had returned, and, like a hound casting for the scent of the fox, was searching for the missing girl.

Flight was hopeless. Only one chance remained.

Pressed close to the statue, the girl's white face hidden beneath the lappets of his coat, Danby Druce awaited in breathless suspense the Winged Man's approach.

GONE!

His headlight searching roadway and pavement, the Winged Man drew nearer and nearer Danby Druce's place of concealment.

Before the weird horror's advance clattered a hansom cab, drawn by a snorting, panic-stricken horse, his nostrils dilated with terror, whilst the driver, casting terror-stricken glances over his shoulder at the fearful apparition, scarce attempted to check his mad career.

On the pavement, his white face evincing utter astonishment, ran a man whom Danby Druce took, and rightly, to be a doctor, whilst a policeman, blowing frantically on his whistle, when he was not calling upon the Winged Man, "in the King's name," to stop, panted behind, now and again making frantic efforts to drag the weird horror down.

Very gently Danby Druce laid the beautiful unknown on the pedestal behind the statute; then, with every nerve strung to its highest tension, prepared to do battle for what was dearer to him than life. It seemed impossible but that the Winged Man should discover his hiding-place.

Never had minutes seemed so long as those which intervened between the time Danby Druce first saw the Winged Man, and that when the beams flashed backwards and forwards across the road alongside the statue.

Over they went until they bathed the trees by the side of the river with their silvery beams.

Then the white disc of light swept back.

Nearer and nearer it came, until the outer circle lit up lettering on the pedestal.

Another inch, and the Winged Man must have detected his foe's hiding-place.

But it was not to be. The beams retreated to the centre of the road, and shortly afterwards the Winged Man passed by.

Suddenly the light was extinguished, and Danby Druce knew that the Winged Man had flown off.

Not for a moment did he think that the weird horror had relinquished his search. He knew the Winged Man too well for that.

In vain Danby Druce stepped into the road, looking up and down for the lights of an approaching taxi.

Suddenly he muttered an exclamation of impatience.

"Fool that I am not to have thought of it before!" he muttered. "There is a cab-rank close at hand!"

Stooping, he pressed a kiss upon the girl's unconscious lips, then, turning, sped, at the top of his speed, to the rank.

It was vacant. Even the shelter was locked up for the night.

With flying feet Danby Druce dashed up Norfolk Street, reaching the Strand just as a taximeter cab, its red flag showing that it was not engaged, sped by.

"Stop!" shouted Danby Druce, as he dashed into the middle of the roadway. "You are disengaged?"

"Yes, sir," replied the man; "but—"

"No excuses or objections," interrupted the detective. "I know the hour is late, yet you'll do your best night's work you ever did in your life if you drive me to Ham."

The man picked up his ears.

"It's worth a fiver, sir!" he growled, adding hastily: "I am late as it is, and will get into a row anyhow."

"I'll give you ten pounds if you do exactly as you're bid, and keep a still tongue in your head afterwards," promised Danby Druce.

"It's a bargain!" cried the man, and the next moment Danby Druce sprang into the body of the vehicle with a lighter heart than he had felt since the Winged Man had snatched the beautiful unknown from him in the river.

He had discovered a way by which he might baffle the Winged Man at last.

At Ham dwelt an old valet and his wife whom the great detective had helped many a time with money. These good people would look upon the girl as a sacred charge, and, if need be, guard her with their lives.

It did not take the taxi long to reach the Embankment and pull up alongside the Brunel statue.

Springing from the vehicle, Danby Druce ran to where he had left his charge on the pedestal.

The now-found joy fled from his heart.

The hiding place was empty—the girl was gone!

If the chauffeur had thought his generous employer drunk when he offered him so large a fare, he certainly thought he was mad now, for Danby Druce rushed hither and thither like one demented, whilst the chauffeur, fearful of losing his fare, drove backwards and forwards up and down after him.

The first effects of his despair wore off, Danby Druce, deeming the unknown in the Winged Man's hands, gave up the chase, and was driven to his own rooms, where he paid the driver the stipulated sum, much to that worthy's joy.

A DECLARATION OF WAR.

Too miserable to sleep, Danby Druce paced up and down his library, haunted by thoughts of the fate which he knew must await any girl who linked her life with that of the Winged Man.

Suddenly there was a loud crash. A thousand splinters of glass flew into the room, and Danby Druce sprang aside, just in time to save himself from the Winged Man's frenzied grasp.

Twice had the Winged Man hovered outside the detective's room that night, but each time to find it wrapped in darkness.

The third time he had seen a light shining from the library, and, too mad with rage and baffled hate to gain admittance in the usual way, has plunged head foremost through window and blind alike.

Dropping upon the floor the Winged Man strode angrily towards the startled detective.

"Where is she? Where is the girl whose life I saved—of whom you have robbed me? Speak, or I will tear you limb from limb!" he cried, in a hoarse, fierce whisper.

Danby Druce faced the Winged Man, undaunted and unafraid.

"It is I who should ask that question. Where is the girl I, not you, saved from a watery grave?" he demanded.

"Isn't she here?" asked the Winged Man anxiously. "It was you who removed her from the seat on which I had placed her, whilst I went to summon medical aid, for I tracked your sodden footsteps from the river. Fool that I was not to kill you when I had you at my mercy!"

"It was I," admitted the detective. "Hidden behind the Brunel statue we escaped your search." The Winged Man gnashed his teeth with rage as he heard how near he had been to success and yet missed it. "After you had passed I left her to fetch a conveyance in which to take her to a place of safety. When I returned she was gone. Therefore, I ask you, the Winged Man, what have you done with the girl whom, despite you, I will make my wife."

The Winged Man took one step forward, his hand raised in fearful menace, then paused.

"Fool, treble fool, to defy me, whom you know is unconquered, unconquerable. I would kill you where you stand, but I spare you for your gallant attempt to rescue my future bride."

"I neither ask, nor will receive, mercy at your hands!" retorted Danby Druce contemptuously. "Go! When the beauteous one is found, when she is placed beyond the power of her unknown enemy; then, Winged Man, we will meet again, never to part till you or I shall cease to live."

°A Strange Meeting.

"So be it, Danby Druce!" exclaimed the Winged Man, standing with folded arms before his foe. "I have loved and I have hated. Never have I loved as I love now. Never have I hated as I hate you, oh, my enemy!"

Then, without a word, the Winged Man disappeared through the broken window into the darkness without.

Little either the Winged Man or Danby Druce knew that all this time Mary Evanson, the girl they sought, was within five minutes' walk from the spot where Danby Druce had left her.

Just off the Strand is the street that seems to have been forgotten, so old and dilapidated are its houses.

In one of these houses Mary Evanson lay stretched upon a low iron bedstead. Her lovely face was marred by a look of sorrow nearly akin to despair; her sunken eyes, her wasted cheeks, told of privation and starvation.

The sting of poverty cuts deep. It seemed to take all the hope and courage from her heart, and, returning to her miserable lodgings, she had laid down, not caring if she never got up again.

Besides, she feared each moment to come across a man who had persecuted her so with his unwelcome attentions, until at last she had come to fear and hate him.

And with good cause. More than once he had sworn, his eyes glistening with a fearful light of dawning madness, that if he could not win her, no one else should.

Consequently, it was only to procure the necessities of life that she ventured out, and then to hasten back as quickly as she could.

Thus it happened that earth and air were searched in vain by Danby Druce and the Winged Man.

And now Mary's resources had come to an end. Her last penny had been spent on food. On the morrow her landlady would turn her out to starve in the streets.

No wonder she had sobbed herself to sleep, bathed in the beams of the full summer moon, which poured through uncurtained windows into her miserable attic.

Though she knew it not, help was near.

His outstretched pinions beating the air with slow, languid strokes, very different from the strong, fierce beats with which he generally hurled himself through space, the Winged Man, shielded by darkness, sailed slowly through the night.

He also, as far as his supernaturally strong constitution would allow, was weak and ill. Scarce a morsel of food had passed his lips since Mary Evanson's

---

° 19 April 1913.

disappearance.

The old-time red roofs of the street in which Mary Evanson lived attracted his attention. Circling in the air, he alighted near a shack of chimneys, opposite the sleeping girl's room.

A great weariness oppressed his soul. His whole being craved for sleep.

The moonbeams reflected from a gable window opposite attracted his attention.

Launching himself into space, he crossed the street, and a minute later had alighted noiselessly upon the crumbling parapet, hoping to find an empty room in which he might snatch a few hours' sleep ere resuming his search.

Peering through the window, he saw a woman's form stretched upon a bed within the room.

Even as he gazed the woman moved uneasily in her sleep.

The Winged Man's eyes flashed a pity but very rarely seen in them.

His search was ended.

Before him lay sleeping the beautiful unknown.

Then a great wave of pity swept through his heart as his practiced eye told him of the suffering and privation the woman he loved with such all-devouring passion must have undergone.

The shabbily-furnished room and told of the struggle the lovely girl must have had for her existence.

Noiselessly he inserted the blade of a long knife between the window-sashes, pushed back the clasp, and crept cautiously into the room.

In the centre of the tiny, low-ceilinged apartment he paused while his eyes rested upon the pinched, but still lovely features of Mary Evanson.

Another step or two forward, then he came to an abrupt halt.

"No, no; she must not see me thus, or she will hate me for ever!" he muttered.

Drawing back, he thrust his hand into his breast-pocket.

It was empty, and he remembered how, alighting amongst the watermen by the side of the river, he had lavished gold and silver upon them, in the hope of gaining some information of the one he sought.

The Winged Man, who had almost unlimited treasure concealed in the bowels of the earth, was, for the moment, penniless.

Yet not quite. In the black scarf he wore twisted round his neck was a diamond of the finest water[40] surrounded by magnificent rubies.

This he snatched from his throat, and, stooping, thrust it lightly into the coverlet of the girl's bed, in such a position that it must attract the sleeper's eyes directly she awoke.

Then, stealing softly from the room, he closed the window behind him, and with his heart full of joy, for he had found her he sought, flew towards Westminster Bridge, where suspended from the centre arch, he slept soundly

---

[40] The degree of brilliance in a diamond.

until awakened by the first beams of coming day.

The Fatal Gift.

With a weary sigh Mary Evanson opened her eyes. Her gaze fell upon the bare walls that hemmed her in, then wandered through the window, and, rising, she surveyed the vista of roofs and chimney-tops before her, until, through an open space where two streets met, she caught a glimpse of the Thames.

Very different the sun-kissed waters looked now to what they had done the preceding night when, overwhelmed by a sudden accession of despair, she had flung herself into their cold embrace. As the events of the preceding night crossed her mind, a puzzled frown settled upon her brow.

Thrown across the solitary chair the room possessed were her sodden clothes.

She remembered her mad plunge from the Embankment—she remembered the dark waters closing over her head.

Then, so dimly that it might be but the fading recollection of a passing dream, she seemed to feel herself snatched from death by a pair of strong arms, and to see a handsome, clean-shaven face gazing earnestly into her own.

But even as her brain conjured up this vision of the recent past, it was blurred and rendered indistinct by another face—a fearful, pallid, deathlike visage, which glowered at her from out of the darkness, its eyes flashing with unbridled love.

Then all was blank, until she awakened to find herself lying, in a huddled heap, behind a statue on the Embankment, whence she had crawled, with swift, though uncertain, steps, back to the only home she knew—the attic from whence she would be driven with reproaches and perhaps blows on the morrow, when her landlady found she could not pay her rent.

With a half-stifled sob, Mary Evanson turned from the window, despair depicted upon her beautiful face.

Suddenly she uttered an exclamation of joy. Flashing white and crimson in the bright sunlight, the Winged Man's priceless present lay where he had placed it upon the coverlet of the bed.

"How did it come here? I have never seen it before. Can anybody have entered the room whilst I slept?" she asked, her face suffused with colour at the thought.

A loud, insistent knocking at the door caused her to turn round, as her landlady, without waiting permission, bounced into the room.

"What's the meaning of this, Miss Evanson?" began the woman, without giving her lodger time to speak. "Ain't it bad enough to keep out till all hours of the night, without turning the stairs into a perfect waterfall, as you did last night? I won't have any more of it; pay your rent, and go!"

"I am very sorry—" began the girl, when the irate dame interrupted her with a snort of contempt.

"Oh, yes, I dare say! You needn't go on, I know what's coming! You all begin like that when you are going to do a poor, hard-working woman out of a week's rent. But it won't wash with me! You might—"

She ceased abruptly, her small, beadlike eyes twinkling avariciously as she gazed at the valuable pin Mary held in her hand.

"Ho, ho! That's the meaning of it, is it?" she sneered. "I always thought you were no better than you should be, and now I know you are just a common thief!"

Mary looked at the speaker, anger struggling with amazement in her bosom.

"How dare you?" she cried at last, stamping her little foot angrily.

"Hoity, toity! Aren't we put out!" sneered Mrs. Porson. "Only think of a milk-and-watery-goody-goody girl like you being a thief!"

"I am not a thief," retorted Mary indignantly. "I have no idea how this pin came into my room. I had only just found it lying on my counterpane as you came in!"

"You won't get a magistrate to believe that, nor the police, either!" snorted Mrs. Porson.

"The police!" gasped Mary, white to the very lips.

"You might as well give me notice at once, for you won't want my room any longer. His Majesty will pay for your next night's lodging," was the brutal reply.

Mary looked incredulously at the speaker.

"I tell you I have no idea where this pin came from! I found it on my counterpane," she repeated.

"And I tell you that you'll never get anybody to believe such an unlikely tale. Look here, I am an honest woman, and can't afford to lose my character by having such as you under my roof. I am going for the police."

With her hand upon the door latch she paused, and looked back at the white-faced, amazed girl, standing, as though turned to stone, in the centre of the room.

"Well, well, I don't want to be hard on you. Give me the pin, and I'll say no more about it."

"How can I? It is not mine to give," objected Mary, drawing the pin back from the other's eager, outstretched hand.

"Of course it isn't! All the same, it is in your possession, and that is nine points of the law, anyway," replied Mrs. Porson. "Come, come, give it to me. I'll sell it, and we'll go halves," she added persuasively. "If you don't, as an honest woman, there will be nothing for me to do but to call in the police."

Then, as Mary made a gesture of dissent, she strove to snatch the valuable gem from her hand.

For some minutes the two struggled, and Mary, who stood little chance against her burly assailant, was on the point of giving in, when Mrs. Porson uttered a loud cry of pain, and, releasing her hold of the trembling girl, staggered back, clasping a hand to her bleeding cheek, along which was a thin red scar caused by the point of the pin accidentally coming in contact with her face.

"Oh, you murderous little vixen, you shall suffer for this!" she muttered between her clenched teeth.

Then, avarice conquered by a desire for vengeance, she rushed from the room, slamming the door behind her.

Panting and breathless, Mary Evanson sank back on the solitary chair. Raising the pin to a level with her eyes, she gazed fixedly at it.

It was a magnificent jewel worth sufficient to keep her in comfort, almost in luxury, for many weeks.

Whence had it come? Who had brought it?

She could not tell. Still, certain was it that her mysterious visitor intended it for her.

Food she must have, or die.

She would not sell, only pawn it, and keep an exact account of the money she spent; then, should its unknown owner turn up, make restitution as best she might.

Rapidly throwing on her half-dried clothes, she stole downstairs and out into the street.

Turning down a side street running parallel with the Strand, she made her way to that busiest of all London arteries.

AT THE PAWNBROKER'S.

Presently she paused before a shop over which hung three golden balls, then stopped to look shamefacedly up and down the street.

It was her first visit to a pawnshop. It seemed as though every passer-by knew her errand, and was sneering at her in their hearts.

Yet hunger and fear lest Mrs. Porson, pouncing upon her, should haul her off to the police-station, caused her to take her courage in both hands, and, entering the side door over which the pawnbroker's sign hung, she moved timidly towards the counter.

"Well, Miss?" demanded a sharp-eyed, hatchet-faced assistant, as Mary entered.

"I want you to lend me some money—a very little—please, on this," stammered Mary, handing the pin.

The young man's studied indifference vanished as he held the pin up to the light.

"Is this yours?" he demanded suspiciously.

"No—that is to say, yes," stammered poor Mary, all unprepared for the question.

The assistant cast a quick, comprehensive glance at the flashed, trembling girl.

Her beauty touched even his callous heart.

She did not look a thief. Indeed, no one accustomed to stealing would be thrown into such confusion by so simple a question; yet he knew—none better, for few see the seamy side of life so thoroughly as the pawnbroker—what hunger and distress will drive any man or woman to do.

"How did you get it? Who sent you here?" he asked abruptly, yet in more kindly tones.

"I—I found it," was Mary's condemning confession.

"Look here, my girl, you should take lost property to Scotland Yard, not to a pawnbroker's," said the assistant, making as though to hand the pin back, then paused, looked compassionately upon the trembling, confused girl, then, with a shrug of his shoulders, turned towards a distant part of the shop, saying:

"All right. Stop a minute. I won't keep you long."

"Please don't. I am so hungry," wailed poor Mary as she sank, half fainting, on to a chair.

The assistant heard the appeal.

"Confound it, I am not a blessed cop!" he muttered, and was about to hand the jewel back to the girl, when the door was burst open, and a policeman, closely followed by Mrs. Porson, entered the box.

"There she is! That's her, constable, just in the act of pawning my poor dead husband's property!" cried the landlady triumphantly.

Turning to Mary, she pretended to wipe tears from her eyes as she cried:

"Oh, Mary, Mary, how could you treat me so, after all I have done for you? After the many weeks I have let you occupy my room without seeing a penny-piece of my rent, how could you steal my poor dead husband's pin from my dressing-table? Even that I might have forgiven if you had not flown at me like a tiger-cat when I walked, accidental, like, into the room."

Poor Mary, staggering to her feet, gazed at the woman, despair, horror, and incredulity on her face, as the flood of lies burst upon her ears.

Denial rose to her lips; but ere the words could find utterance the wooden walls of the narrow box swam round, and she would have fallen heavily to the floor had not the policeman caught her in his arms.

When she came to herself, she was in a cell in Bow Street, with a stern-faced but kindly female warder bending over her.

"WHERE IS THE GIRL?"

Three hours later Mrs. Porson returned home in triumph.

Unable to refute the false evidence of her accuser, or to explain whence the pin came, and obliged to acknowledge that she had been detected in the act of trying to pawn it, Mary Evanson had been committed for trial, whilst the pin, at her accuser's earnest request, was returned to its pretended owner.

No feeling of compunction for the beautiful, unhappy girl entered Mrs. Porson's heart as she mounted the flight of stairs which led to the room Mary Evanson had recently occupied.

To do her justice, she believed that her late lodger had really stolen the pin, and she had returned home intent upon searching Mary's scanty wardrobe for further hidden plunder, or, for the matter of that, for anything of value she could lay her hand upon.

To her disappointment, shabby though neatly-mended clothes, a few valueless trinkets, a well-thumbed book or two, was all that rewarded her search.

Yet she was well content, for even to her unaccustomed eyes it was evident that the jewel was of considerable value.

Indeed, at one time she was inclined to wish it had not been quite so valuable, for the police asked how her husband had been able to afford so valuable a pin.

Fortunately for her, Mrs. Porson's husband had been a bookmaker, and, like others of his class, was accustomed to invest a portion of his winnings in jewellery, as being easily carried about and easily converted into money.

Rising from her lodger's poor box, she stood feasting her eyes upon the sparkling gem which had so unexpectedly come into her possession.

"It's worth a hundred pounds if it's worth a penny," she muttered. "I wonder where the little fool got hold of it? Anyhow, it's mine now, and she may rot in prison for the rest of her life for all I care," she muttered viciously; then uttered a loud shriek of terror and dismay as a long, white, talon-like hand was thrust over her shoulder, and the coveted pin was snatched from her grasp.

"Help! Thieves! Thie—" she shrieked, then ceased to cry out, but gazed with ashen face and starting eyeballs at the fearful form and stern, threatening visage of the Winged Man.

Swift as lightning the weird horror's disengaged hand seized her by the throat.

"Where is the girl who occupied this room? Speak, woman, or die!" thundered the Winged Man, his fearful visage contorted with fury.

Twice Mrs. Porson essayed to answer the Winged Man's question, but each time terror, and the weird monster's cold, clammy fingers, checked her utterance.

"Please, sir, I didn't know!" she gasped at last.

"Didn't know what?" roared the Winged Man, in thunderous tones.

"That she was a friend of yours, sir, or I would never have let her go to prison."

"Prison! That frail, beautiful girl in prison! Speak, lest I tear you limb from limb! Tell me, wither have the vile minions of the law carried her? Name the place, that I may tear it stone from stone!" he demanded fiercely, releasing his hold, and allowing the woman to drop upon the floor, where she knelt, quivering in every limb with the fearful terror that assailed her soul.

FROM INFORMATION RECEIVED.

The Winged Man stood towering over the wretched Mrs. Porson like some fearful thing of evil, glaring at her with fierce, kindling eyes which seemed to read the inmost recesses of her soul.

"Speak, woman! How much longer are you going to keep me waiting here?" thundered her fearful visitant. "On what charge was this beautiful, friendless, unhappy girl arrested?"

Mrs. Porson plucked up sufficient courage to look the Winged Man full in the face.

"I don't think it can be the same young lady you are thinking of, sir," she began glibly. "Miss Evanson wasn't beautiful; she wasn't more unhappy than she ought to be; and, as to being good, why, there, she was the wickedest, slyest, deceitfulest hussy that ever walked!"

"Silence!" thundered the Winged Man.

And Mrs. Porson, who had partly risen in her excitement, dropped tremblingly on to her knees again.

"Silence, I say!" repeated the Winged Man. "For the third and last time, why was she arrested?"

Finding it impossible to evade the question longer, Mrs. Porson repeated the tale she had told, with such success, before the magistrate.

Emboldened by the Winged Man's silence, the woman ventured to look him in the face; then started to her feet, and retreated slowly to the furthermost corner of the room, watching with dilated eyes the fearful form of the Winged Man a growing larger and larger, until his fearful frame seemed to fill the whole attic.

"Perjured traitress, shame to your sex!" he thundered. "I say, what reason is there that I should let you cumber the earth? Heartless monster of iniquity that you are, I, the Winged Man, with my own hands fastened this pin to the coverlet of Miss Everson's bed whilst she slept!"

Twice the wretched woman essayed to speak, but each time no words passed her parched lips.

"You promised not to hurt me, sir," she stammered at last.

"Nor will I," came back, in low, ominous accents from the Winged Man, "if you obey my commands. Fail me, and I will carry you a thousand feet above the earth and let you fall to the doom you so richly deserve!"

"Mercy—mercy! I will do anything, everything, you require!" sobbed Mrs. Porson.

"Then go without a moment's delay, back to Bow Street. There make a full confession of what you have done," commanded the Winged Man. "Remember, naught will save your life but Mary Evanson being set free without a stain upon her character. Go! Fail me at your peril, even though you have to take her place in the prison cell for perjury!"

Careless of what she promised, careless of what she did, so long as she escaped from the presence of the fearful being who seemed to read her every thought, Mrs. Porson swore on her knees to obey him to the letter.

"No more words, woman! Actions alone can save you. Go! Unless Miss Evanson is here within an hour I will follow; then pray for mercy to the stones in the street, not to me!"

Trembling so that she could scarcely descend the stairs, Mrs. Porson, too terrified even to resume the bonnet she had thrown aside on her return from the police-court, hastily left the house.

The Strand reached, she almost ran into the arms of an inspector of police. A means of escape from the Winged Man flashed into her mind. Darting forward, she seized the inspector by the arm, crying:

"Help! He is there—he is in my house! Come!"

"Who?" ejaculated the inspector, trying to throw off Mrs. Porson's grasp upon his arm.

"The Winged Man!" replied the woman excitedly. "Don't stop talking here. Get a policeman—get a hundred policemen—and come at once, or he may escape!"

The inspector looked searchingly at the excited woman. Evidently her terror was very real; and also, what he doubted first of all, she was perfectly sober.

"You are certain of what you say?" he demanded sternly.

"I will stake my soul upon the truth!" said the woman emphatically. "See, the marks of his fingers are still round my throat," she added, turning down the lace which encircled her neck, and showing for red marks where the Winged Man had gripped her.

Already the two were surrounded by a gaping crowd. From lip to lip passed in hushed, awed tones, the fearful words: "The Winged Man!"

At that moment above the heads of the crowd appeared the helmet of a policeman hastening to discover the cause of the obstruction.

The inspector beckoned to him, and, tearing a leaf out of his notebook, scribbled a few lines upon it, then ordered him to hasten to Bow Street as quickly as he could.

Whilst the policeman was gone on his errand, the inspector, escorting Mrs. Porson into a shop, drew from her all she thought it wise to tell of her interview with the Winged Man. Visions of promotion dancing before his eyes, the inspector listened.

It would indeed be a feather in his cap if he could arrest the weird horror who had terrorised over the people of England all too long, to say nothing of the enormous reward offered for the Winged Man's capture.

A sergeant entered with the report that every available man on duty and in reserve at Bow Street was awaiting orders without.

Having given Mrs. Porson in charge of an officer, with instructions to detain her at Bow Street until his return, the inspector set off, as quickly as the enormous crowd which had gathered would allow him, to the address Mary's landlady had given him.

A DELUSIVE CAPTURE.

As, at the head of his men, with a huge crowd blocking up the entrance to the street behind him, the inspector reached the door of Mrs. Porson's house, he was met by shrieking, hysterical women, and pale-faced, frightened men, who, casting fearful glances behind them, dashed headlong down the stone steps into the street.

"Now, then, steady, my man! What's the matter? Have you all gone mad?" inquired the inspector, shaking a fat German musician, one of Mrs. Porson's lodgers, by the hand.

"Mad? You, mad, also, if into that house you go! How you call him? The Man who is Winged is there!" gasped the trembling Teuton.

"Glad to hear it. I thought perhaps I might have been sent on a fool's errand," replied the inspector grimly.

Yet he did not seem in any hurry to enter the building. Giving his men orders to keep the crowd back, he glanced down the street as though expecting something; then, stepping to the other side of the road, carefully surveyed every window.

One belonging to an empty room on the third floor was veiled by a thick blind; but even as the inspector looked this blind was rent from top to bottom, and the fearful, black form of the Winged Man appeared, a malicious, mocking smile on his almost bloodless lips. Angry contempt flashed from his eyes.

A shudder of horror swept through the mighty throng. Many had seen the Winged Man before, but the majority now saw him for the first time.

"The Winged Man! It is the Winged Man!" came in an awe-stricken whisper— it could scarcely be called a shout—from the crowd.

"Ay, dogs, earthworms, contemptible crawlers on the earth, I am the Winged Man!" thundered the weird being.

The inspector was a brave man, yet his cheeks grew pale as he glanced upwards at the Winged Man's fearful form. Nevertheless, he stepped boldly into the middle of the road.

"In the King's name, I order you to give yourself up!" he commanded. "Resistance is useless. We are here in force. You are cornered at last, Winged Man; you cannot escape!"

With a mocking laugh the Winged Man turned upon his heel and disappeared from the window, just as a subdued cheer from the breathless crowd greeted the appearance of three policeman, who, emerging from the skylight of an adjacent house, crept stealthily towards the open attic window by which the Winged Man had gained admittance into the house.

With an angry frown the inspector silenced the expectant crowd. He had no wish to warn the Winged Man that his only means of escape was cut off.

Then, with a jingle of bells, and hoarse shouts of "Hoy, Hoy, hoy!" three horse fire-escapes dashed through the dividing crowd, and, in obedience to the inspector's orders, were reared against the window.

Barely had they touched the wall ere nimble, axe-armed firemen sprang up, and stationed themselves at the windows.

Then a loud, shrill whistle from the back of the house told the inspector that the rear was equally well guarded. Drawing a revolver from his coat, he signed a score of constables to follow, and dashed swiftly into the house, followed by deafening cheers from the admiring crowd.

Scattering to right and left the police searched the lower rooms and basement, leaving not so much as a cupboard, in which the Winged Man could have taken shelter, and investigated.

But no sign of their weird quarry could be seen, save, perhaps—though none connected it with the Winged Man—a strange, pungent odour filled the house.

Leaving his most reliable men to guard the staircase, the inspector led the way to the first floor; but here, also, disappointment awaited them.

"Come on, lads, there's the second and third floor, and the attics to be searched. He must be in one of them. He cannot possibly have escaped!" cried the inspector, leading the way upstairs, his revolver advanced ready to fire, for the order had gone forth that, dead or alive, the Winged Man's crime-stained career must be cut short.

Higher and higher they mounted. The whole house resounded with the policeman's heavy tread.

Every room, every cupboard, even chests, were overhauled in vain. Gnawing his moustache in disappointment, the inspector rushed from attic to basement, from window to window, eagerly questioning his men; but only to receive the same standing answer, that the Winged Man had not been seen.

Perplexed and baffled, the inspector paused at the head of the third flight of stairs, and passed his hand wearily across his brow. The feeling of utter helplessness was gradually creeping over him. An experienced officer, of many years' service, never before had he been so hopelessly baffled. By his side stood a grizzled old sergeant.

For nearly a minute the two looked at each other without speaking.

"It is useless, sir! No human being will ever lay hands upon the Winged Man!" asserted the sergeant in hushed, awed tones.

"Nonsense, Hemingway!" retorted the inspector irritably. "He is but an improved edition of the Spring-heeled Jack of forty years ago. Surely, man, you don't believe the tales which are spread abroad, which make him a superhuman, flying spirit?"

The sergeant shook his head.

"I don't know what to think, sir!" he replied. "You and I both saw him at the window. Since then, every possible exit from the house has been guarded, and we have searched the house so thoroughly that even a rat could not have escaped us. Unless he can vanish into thin air, he must still be in the house, somewhere, and, if so, where is he?"

"The Winged Man is here!"

The voice came from immediately behind the two men. Turning, they found themselves face to face with the Winged Man.

Up flew the inspector's arms, crack went his ready pistol, but the bullet, though aimed straight at the Winged Man's heart, rebounded from his bullet-proof breast-plate. Then, ere the astounded inspector could pull the trigger once more, the Winged Man, leaning forward, stamped violently on the floor.

As though the action liberated the fires which scientists tell us burn constantly beneath the earth, dazzling flame flashed from top to bottom of the house, and the next minute the stairs and banisters, saturated with an inflammable liquid by the Winged Man, burst into flame.

Loud cries of alarm from the various rooms told that the flames had already extended to other parts of the house.

His dark, fearful pinions reflecting the lurid glare like polished ebony, the Winged Man soared up the staircase above the inspector's head, who, firing one last, despairing shot after his wondrous foe, fled to the window, to find the fire-escape already crowded with escaping men.

As the spectators saw flames burst from every window at once, a loud shriek—it could scarcely be called a shout—found its way from every lip. Then, anxious to render every aid they could, they swept aside the cordon of police, and crowded round the front of the burning house, cheering almost hysterically, as policeman after policeman, fireman after fireman, descended from the blazing building.

So thoroughly had the Winged Man done his fearful work, that almost ere the last policeman had left the building the house was a raging furnace from top to bottom.

For several minutes the crowd stood spellbound, watching the devouring element doing the Winged Man's fearful work. Then a low, shuddering moan of terror burst from their closely-packed ranks. The centre of a thousand serpentine tongues of flame, the Winged Man burst from the roof of the doomed building, and, standing poised with outstretched wings upon its stone parapet, raised his hand, as though commanding silence.

In a moment every tongue was hushed. Loud, clear, resonant, the fearful words: "Beware of the Winged Man! Let not so much as a hair of Mary Evanson perish, or the whole of London shall burn even as this house!" fell upon their listening ears.

Then his long, weird, fearful cry, echoing far and wide through the darkened air—for night was casting her stable mantle over the scene—the Winged Man spread his wings to the breeze, and glided swiftly over the tops of the intervening houses towards Bow Street.

MASTER OF BOW STREET.

So speechless with horror, so overwhelmed with the Winged Man's last warning threat with those who had heard his words and witnessed his flight, that, of all that vast crowd, but one man realised whither Winged Man was flying, or what his errand, and he, springing from out the motor-car which had just dashed upon the scene, reached the outskirts of the crowd just in time to see the Winged Man's awful form, dim in the uncertain light, speeding across the Strand.

It was Danby Druce, summoned by telephone upon the scene. In a moment he turned, and, thrusting aside all who barred his path, he strained every nerve to reach Bow Street Police Station before the Winged Man.

But, swiftly though he ran, he was only just in time to see the Winged Man dropped, like a meteor from heaven, upon the policeman on duty before the door, and, seizing the astounded officer by the belt, hurl him breathless, bruised and bleeding into the middle of the street, then dashed into the building, slamming the heavy door to behind him.

A sergeant, seeing a dark form swiftly shoot to the bolts of the door sprang, with a warning cry to put his comrades on the alert, upon the intruder.

But ere his hands could seize the Winged Man, that weird horror struck him to the ground with a fearful below between the eyes, which would have felled an ox.

Turning, the Winged Man dashed into the charge-room, seized the officer on duty ere he could flee or fight, and carried him, struggling, kicking, and calling vainly for assistance, to an open cell, into which he flung him, slamming to the door, and, turning the key, thrust it through the observation-hole in its centre.

There was now but one foe left for the Winged Man to meet. It was the policeman who acted as warder over the cells, where prisoners were kept until their cases could be tried, or they could be conveyed to Pentonville. The warder, a stalwart, young North-countryman, who feared neither man nor fiend, seized an iron bar in both hands, and, swinging it above his head, rushed furiously upon his fearful foe.

Round swung the heavy iron, but just as it seemed about to fall upon his head, the Winged Man sprang up to the ceiling, and, as the huge bar whizzed beneath his feet, dropped onto the shoulders of his assailant.

Seizing the warder by the neck, he gripped his throat with his knees. In vain the policeman dashed from wall to wall, seeking to rid himself of the fearful being, who, like Sinbad's Old Man of the Sea, clung with his hands and legs around his neck. Presently his struggles grew fainter, and at last, with a deep moan of rage and agony, he sank beaten to the floor.

Snatching a bunch of keys from the policeman's belt, the Winged Man rushed frantically from cell to cell, in one of which a woman rose, uttered a piercing shriek, then fell heavily to the ground in a dead faint.

It was Mrs. Porson, but the Winged Man gave her no second glance. To find Mary Evanson, to bear her from that fearful place, was his only thought, his only hope.

But though he opened cell after cell, it was in vain, for no sign of Mary Evanson greeted his longing eyes.

With a cry of baffled rage he turned towards where a female searcher lay huddled up at the further end of the long passage.

In a moment he was by her side.

"Speak, woman! What have they done with Mary Evanson?" he cried.

The female warder looked with terror-starting eyes at the weird horror.

"She is not here—upon my word of honour she is not here!" she gasped at length.

"Tell me, whether has she been taken?" demanded the Winged Man.

"To Pentonville!" came the reply.

"When? How long ago?"

"The prison-van could scarcely have left the door when you entered the station," came in hurried, trembling accents from the woman's pallid lips.

Waiting to hear no more, the Winged Man dashed to the door, flung it open, and, soaring above the heads of the crowd of civilians and police who were striving to gain entry, foremost among whom was Danby Druce, flew northward, his blood-curdling cries of rage striking terror to the hearts of all who heard them.

"She shall burn—London, the mistress of the world, shall be reduced to a heap of ashes if aught of evil befall is the woman I love!" muttered the Winged Man, then flew on in silence, glancing eagerly into the crowded streets below in search of the black, ominous vehicle known as the "Black Maria."

SNATCHED FROM HIS GRASP.

It was at the entrance to Caledonian Road that the Winged Man overtook the "Black Maria."

The first intimation the guardians of the vehicle had of the terrible danger that menaced them was the Winged Man sweeping down, like a hawk upon its prey, on to the driver, and hurling him from his seat.

Throwing the reins on to the frightened horses' backs, the Winged Man uttered a loud, unearthly shriek that caused them to bound swiftly forward; then, rising, allowed the vehicle to pass under him, and fastened himself on its back just as, alarmed by the swaying of the vehicle as the frightened horses dashed madly along the crowded streets, the policeman riding by the side of the door flung it open to find out what was wrong.

The next moment he also was rolling in the road, hurled forth by the Winged Man's resistless arm.

For a moment the Winged Man stood motionless as a statue, despite the rolling of the vehicle, listening with delight to the cries of terror from the narrow cells in which the prisoners were confined during their journey from Bow Street to the great central remand prison.

Soon his keen ear detected a cry for help in frightened, girlish tones.

In another moment he was at the narrow door from behind which the cry had come.

It was locked; but, seizing the padlock, he exerted his fearful strength and tore the bolt from its hasp.

The next moment a loud, frenzied cry of terror burst from Mary Evanson's lips as the Winged Man, seizing her in his arms, bore her from the narrow cell.

Knowing that a catastrophe must soon occur, the Winged Man rushed to the open door, and a cry of amazement arose from pedestrians and travellers on tram and 'bus alike as they saw the Winged Man, a girl's form clasped in his arms, rise from the vehicle, just as it came in violet contact with a lamppost, and fell heavily over on to its side.

The crash was accompanied by a loud, bloodcurdling shriek of rage, as the door of the van, swinging to, caught the Winged Man a fearful blow on the side, that sent him headlong into the centre of the road, where he narrowly escaped being trampled beneath the feet of the eager crowd rushing to the assistance of those imprisoned in the van.

So severe was the blow, so unexpected his fall, that to save his precious burden from injury, he was fain to let her go.

Mad with terror, the girl sprang wildly to her feet, and, careless of everything, save that at any cost, she must escape from the weird horror who had drawn her from the cell, threaded her way through the crowd, and sped down the street.

Too terrified to see where she was going, it was not until she found herself almost against the bonnet of a car that she realised her danger.

Too late she turned to flee.

Despite hastily-applied brakes, the mudguard of the vehicle struck her in the back, she was thrown hastily to the ground, whilst Danby Druce, who, seated by his chauffeur's side, had driven in pursuit of the Winged Man, sprang from the vehicle and raised her in his arms.

Without a moment's hesitation he lifted her into the body of the vehicle, whilst, in response to his master's orders, the chauffeur wheeled round the car, and drove, as swiftly as the traffic would allow, back whence he had come.

A FUTILE CHASE.

And what of the Winged Man? How came it that he had allowed the girl, to achieve whose rescue he had made such herculean efforts, to be snatched from his grasp by his deadly foe?

The reason shows that even the Winged Man's wondrous power had its limits.

Free, with untrammelled wings, or even thanks to his giant strength, upright on the earth, he could laugh at all attempts to capture him; but even as he rolled to the ground, a plain-clothed policeman recognised him, and, springing forward, pinned him to the ground, calling loudly upon the standers-by to help in the King's name.

A score of men from the crowd sprang to his side, but only to start back appalled by the wild, frantic, almost maniacal cry of rage which burst from the Winged Man's lips.

"May every disease that afflicts man light on your bodies! May your lost souls wander for ever through space!" shrieked the weird horror, his fierce, intense tones curdling the blood of all who heard him as he cursed those who held him prisoner.

Yet the policeman, kneeling upon the Winged Man's body, held his prisoner to the ground by outstretched wrists.

"Fool, release me, or perish!" hissed the Winged Man.

"Not much! If you're the Evil One himself, I won't leave go of you until you are safely handcuffed!" replied the triumphant constable.

The Winged Man made no reply; his pale face was hard and set, and there was a look which baffles description upon his clean-cut features.

Suddenly the circle round the Winged Man and his would-be captor widened, whilst the spectators looked on in dumbfounded amazement, saw the Winged Man's body lifted by some unseen agency, bearing the policeman from the ground.

Higher and higher the Winged Man rose from the earth. Yet his rigid arms remained stretched out as though they still rested upon the earth.

His eyes fixed as though fascinated upon the Winged Man's white, deathly face, it was not until the two were some ten feet above the earth that the policeman was conscious of the incredible events in which he was an active participant.

Terrible must have been that gallant officer's terror, when, looking past the Winged Man's recumbent head, he saw empty air where he thought to see solid earth, and to find himself being gradually carried higher and higher above people's heads.

It was more than even his brave heart could stand.

Releasing his hold of the Winged Man, he flung himself headlong from off the weird horror's body, and fell heavily to the earth, where he lay in a state of collapse from which he was destined to awaken a nerve-shattered, prematurely-aged man.

In the meantime, the Winged Man, bending his body forward, extended his wings, and, rising to a level with the upper story windows of the tall houses on either side of the road, shot quick, searching glances over the long street.

He was just in time to see Mary Evanson's unconscious form lifted into the covered-in body of Danby Druce's motor-car.

Like an arrow from a bow, the Winged Man cleaved through the air in pursuit, but just as he was about to swoop down upon the car, a crowded motor-'bus accidentally intervened betwixt the Winged Man and his prey.

So swiftly was the winged horror flying, so intent was he upon the deadly vengeance he intended to wreak upon the detective who had reaped the fruit of his work, that the Winged Man plunged into the midst of the crowded garden seats ere he could stop himself.

The scene which followed baffles description.

The passengers had seen the weird horror pounce like an eagle amongst a flock of doves into their midst, and, screaming with terror, shrieking wildly in frenzied horror, men and women, girls and boys, rushed for the staircase, or, careless of broken limbs or not, flung themselves over the sides of the swiftly moving 'bus in all directions, leaving the Winged Man in sole possession of the bus's upper deck.

As, with a grinding and creaking of brakes, the 'bus came to a halt, the Winged Man rose in the air, and looking about him, was just in time to see a car sweep round a corner some fifty yards ahead.

He darted in swift pursuit.

Immediately over the car he fluttered as though about to swoop down upon his prey, then hesitated, glanced around, saw that the street was partially deserted, and dropped noiselessly upon the top of the car, and curled himself up on a canvas-covered spare tyre, chuckling at the thought of how little Danby Druce guessed that his deadly foe was so near him.

On dashed the car, heading in the direction of Epping, until at last the comparatively deserted road ran over Wanstead Common.

The Winged Man's time for action had come.

Crawling like some black, loathsome insect down the side of the swiftly-moving vehicle, he thrust his hand unseen into a small box by the driver's side, and laid his fingers upon the electric battery attached by wires to the car's four sparking-plugs.

A fearful shock, which would have floored an ordinary man, but was scarcely noticed by the Winged Man, shot through his frame as his body absorbed all the electricity in the battery.

Immediately the engines ceased to work, and the compressed gas, no longer ignited, acting as a brake, pulled the car up short.

Springing into the road, the Winged Man flung open the door, seized a man from off the seat nearest him, and, hurling him into the roadway, cried:

"Lie there, Danby Druce, dog that you are! At present the Winged Man has other work to do. But be sure the time will come when he will crush you like corn betwixt the upper and nether millstone!"

Then, amidst loud shrieks of terror from the other occupant of the car, the Winged Man seized her muffled form in his arms, and soared triumphantly into the dark, cloud-covered the sky.

Very tenderly the Winged Man pressed the limp, lifeless form of the terrified woman to his heart. Bending his stately head, he impressed a long, lingering, loving kiss upon her pale, bloodless lips.

Even as he did so, his keen eyes detected something which made him pause in his flight, and flash his head light full on the woman's face.

"Fooled! Foiled!" he hissed, as he found that the woman he had captured was beautiful, it is true, but not Mary Evanson.

It was well a blessed unconsciousness had closed the woman's eyes, for none could have seen that fearful, rage-contorted face and have retained their reason.

Disappointment and rage blazed from his eyes.

Every evil passion the human heart can feel seemed concentrated in his face as, his huge black pinions stretched to the night breeze, the Winged Man swung the girl's unconscious form twice round his head, then hurled her, with a mocking, bitter, exultant laugh into space.

But even as, obeying the instinct of blind, unreasoning passion, the Winged Man hurled that beauteous woman to her death, he realised what a foul, heinous crime he was committing, and, with an ejaculation of remorse, dived after her falling form.

But even as he glided through the hissing air he realised that it would be too late.

He could, it is true, overtake her ere she touched the earth, but would then be too close to the ground to save her from injury.

There was but one course left—a course which might leave him wounded, stunned, helpless, at the mercy of his earth-bound foes.

Yet not for a moment did the Winged Man hesitate.

A single beat of his enormous pinions doubled the speed at which he fell, and the male occupant of the car, looking in horror upwards, beheld, with a groan of anguish, his young wife falling as it were from Heaven itself, whilst the black, fearful form of the Winged Man hurtled through the air as though in pursuit.

Swift as a falling meteor, the two dropped earthwards.

Then a cry of "Thank Heaven, he has missed her!" burst from the husband's lips as he saw the Winged Man glided by.

When the girl was but ten feet from the earth, the Winged Man checked his flight, passed under her, and the next moment was borne with crushing force to the ground as the girl's body alighted between his shoulders.

A fearful spasm of pain swept through the Winged Man's frame, but he recked little of that.

He, who had never failed, had once more achieved an apparently impossible task.

Though jarred and bruised, her fall had been broken by the Winged Man's self sacrifice, and the woman he had hurled to her death was saved.

With a loud cry at the husband raised his wife in his arms; then, her unconscious head resting upon his shoulders, stood, ready to give up his life, if need be, in her defence against the Winged Man.

But, to his relief, instead of attacking him, the Winged Man crawled painfully down the road; then, rising unsteadily to his feet, extended his wings and flew, swaying from side to side like a wounded bird, towards Epping Forest, where, clinging to the branch of a mighty oak, he hung for nearly an hour to recover from the effects of his fearful fall.

THE STRANGER IN THE PARK.

For three weeks the Winged Man searched almost every town in England for Mary Evanson, but in vain.

Danby Druce had hidden his charge too well for even the Winged Man to track her down.

Again and again, unseen, though perhaps not entirely unsuspected, the Winged Man followed Danby Druce, hoping that the detective would lead him to the one he sought.

But, anticipating some such move upon the Winged Man's part, Danby Druce was careful not to go near the pretty little cottage in Ham, where he had left her in charge of an old servant and his wife, unless so disguised as to be sure that even the Winged Man could not follow him.

A hundred times the Winged Man had the unconscious detective at his mercy. More than once the temptation to annihilate his foe had been almost more than the Winged Man could withstand.

But the Winged Man's hatred of the great detective was now so intense, so fearful, that death alone would not satisfy him. And if he slew Danby Druce, he would probably lose for ever the clue to the whereabouts of Mary Evanson.

Brooding moodily upon what he conceived his wrongs, the Winged Man spent hours inventing tortures with which to punish Danby Druce for daring to thwart him.

To have the great detective in his power, to reduce him, by slow, cruel tortures, to a state bordering upon imbecility, would alone satisfy the Winged Man's lust for vengeance.

He panted for the hour in which he might bring Danby Druce to his knees, a piteous, hopeless supplicant for his mercy.

°**MARY EVANSON'S PRESERVER.**

Danby Druce should live, but only as a caricature of a man, without a thought of his own, without the power to do aught save at the Winged Man's bidding.

Surely no more terrible revenge than that could be desired.

Mary Evanson had soon grown very fond of the kindly-hearted couple in whose charge Danby Druce had placed her. She also looked forward with pleasure to the rare and short visits the busy detective could alone spare her, for, his mind relieved of the anxiety about the woman he loved, Danby Druce had returned to his occupation of detecting crime with renewed vigour.

As yet love for the friend who had saved her from a life of pain Yuri and want, and, more, from the clutches of the dread Winged Man, had not been awakened in Mary Evanson's heart.

She was barely eighteen, and she regarded Danby Druce, who was more than double her age, more as a father than in the light of a lover, whilst the detective, craving for love, not gratitude, refrained from pleading his cause.

Then there came a day when, walking in Richmond Park, Mary was insulted by a couple of young cyclists, one of whom, taking advantage of her defenceless condition put his arm round her waist, intending to steal a kiss. Suddenly he found himself seized by the nape of the neck and hurled into an adjacent pond.

With a cry of anger his comrade flew at the tall, clean-shaven, handsome man who had inflicted such well-deserved punishment upon his companion.

But, though the young cyclist prided himself upon his prowess with the

---

gloves, he found that he had taken on a task a little above his strength, for, whilst his blows were wasted on thin air, the tall stranger, hitting straight from the shoulder, knocked him almost silly in one round. Then, taking him up by the waist-band of his trousers, flung him to the ground, to crawl out as best he might by the side of his companion.

Mary glanced beneath her long eye-lashes at her rescuer, and thought she had never seen a more handsome man in her life.

Yet, whilst the somewhat pale, aristocratic face attracted her, Mary was at first conscious of a feeling almost amounting to repulsion, which, however, she speedily overcame.

Day after day they met, either in the park or by the side of the river, a feeling of a warmer nature springing to life in Mary Evanson's bosom, and poor Danby Druce's last chance of happiness seemed to vanish before the girl's growing preference for the stranger.

A WEIRD TRYST.

It was a hot, oppressive autumn evening as Mary Evanson, a happy smile upon her lips, a bright, joyous light dancing in her eyes, threaded her way through the bracken in Richmond Park to a large oak standing, like a monarch surrounded by its court, in a secluded part of the park.

The oak was the trysting-place where, for some time past, Mary had been accustomed to meet the tall stranger with the dark, handsome, melancholy face who had won her heart.

The oak reached, she was conscious of a slight pang of disappointment, for, usually the first to reach the trysting-place, the stranger, who, by the by, she only knew by his Christian name of Max, was not there.

The next moment she recovered her wonted spirits, as she remembered how, the last time they met, he had told her that he had a long journey to go ere she saw him again.

Yet his last words had been a promise that he would be with her at the hour named. Somehow or other, Mary's confidence in her sad-faced lover was such that it seemed impossible that he should ever be false to his word, or deceive her in any shape or form.

Besides, her watch, a magnificent, diamond-studded little gem Max had given her, showed that it yet wanted five minutes to the appointed time.

Walking slowly backwards and forwards beneath the tree, she became wrapped in happy thoughts of the future.

Max loved her, of that she was well assured. What cared she though she knew nothing whatsoever of him, and that he had begged her to keep their meetings secret—at least, for a time?

She hated the idea of even appearing to deceive the kindly old couple with whom she lived. Yet, if Max wished it, it must be right, she thought, with touching confidence in the man she loved.

Suddenly she started as a loud shout, followed by the reverberating roar of a shot-gun, fell upon her ears.

Then she glanced upwards, and her blood appeared frozen to ice within her veins, her hair appeared to stand on end, her heart almost ceased to beat.

Borne rapidly forward on his wide, outstretched, fearful pinions, his face a ghastly white mask, the features of which were indistinguishable, the Winged Man, in all his weird horribleness, swept by immediately over the girl's white, upturned face.

As he did so something warm and wet fell upon Mary's cheek.

Instinctively she brushed it off with the back of her hand, then glanced at her long, well-shape and fingers.

With a cry of terror she shrank, trembling, well nigh fainting, amongst the gnarled roots of the mighty oak, for betwixt her thumb and first finger was a dash of crimson.

"Mary, my darling, what is the matter? What has frightened you?" rang a minute later in her ear.

She felt herself raised from the ground by a strong hand.

With a glad cry Mary turned, and flung her arms round the tall stranger's neck, crying:

"Oh, Max, protect me; I have been so frightened! That awful flying demon the Winged Man!"

"Why, Mary, surely you do not believe that old wife's tale?" cried the other. "Come, dear one, look up. No harm can befall you now I am here to defend you."

"I know, Max; I feel quite safe now!" cried Mary, nestling to her lover's side.

It seemed so natural to cling to him in time of trouble and terror that Mary quite forgot that, as yet, no declaration of his love had escaped the stranger's lips.

With a happy laugh, Max bent down and kissed her fondly.

"The question I came to ask is already answered, dear one," he said, "by your actions, if not in words. Have I judged wrongly, Mary? Am I not right—you love me?"

"I think I have loved you ever since we first met, dear," murmured Mary, as her cheek lay against his; then, as she felt it was wet, touched it lightly with her finger.

As she did so a sudden thrill of horror swept through her heart. Once more her hand was stained with blood.

"What is it, dear one?" cried Max.

Then he saw the ill-omened stain, and realised what it was that had so disconcerted the girl whose love he had won.

"What a superstitious little darling it is!" he cried half banteringly, though even to Mary's love-enchanted ear his mirth seemed forced and uneasy. "I was late, and hastening through the woods a twig, springing back, caught me in the cheek," he added in explanation.

Mary glanced at her lover's face. It was perchance a trifle paler than usual, and on one cheekbone a black mark showed beneath tiny drops of red.

Ere he could speak the branches of a thicket close at hand were thrust swiftly aside, and a velvet-coated, leather-legginged keeper burst upon the scene.

His face, deathly white, he was evidently labouring under ill-suppressed excitement.

"Where is he? Have you seen him? He came this way!" gasped the keeper, as Mary cowered, like a startled fawn, to her lover's side.

"Seen who? There has been nobody pass—at least, I have not noticed anybody," answered Max calmly.

"And yet he flew over this oak, I swear," asserted the man.

"My good fellow, if you call birds 'he's,' you must expect to be misunderstood," laughed Max.

"It was not a bird; it was"—the man lowered his voice and looked with a shudder around him—"the Winged Man!"

Then he continued, speaking quickly and excitedly:

"Human, they call him; there aren't much human about him. I let him have both barrels of my breechloader full in the head, yet he flew on as though nothing had happened."

"By Jove, I begin to think there is some truth in the tales the papers have been full of lately about this flying fiend!" ejaculated Max. "If so, my friend," he added, half banteringly, half seriously, "I should advise you to make yourself scarce, and lay low for a little time. Depend upon it, sooner or later, so wondrously endowed a being will claim a full reckoning for every pellet which had struck him, and for every drop of blood he has shared."

So impressively were the last word spoken that the gamekeeper glanced apprehensively around him; then, muttering something about "seeking assistance to find the Winged Man if he was still in the park," hastened off.

LOVERS' VOWS.

As the two strolled with arm-encircled waists along a sylvan glade leading down a gentle slope into a secluded valley, Mary, fearing nothing now her lover was with her, soon became her old cheery, chatty little self.

"You are coming nearly home with me, sir, then return to Richmond by 'bus," she said, with pretty, pretended authority. "I am not going to have you cross the park alone with this fearful, flying monster about. What you said to the keeper seemed like a message of warning from the Winged Man himself."

Max came to an abrupt halt, and took her lovely, smiling little face between his hands.

"You love me, Mary?" he asked, in low, thrilling tones.

"Even at the risk of making you more conceited than you are by nature, I confess I do. I love you as I did not think it possible that I would ever love any man," was the whispered reply.

"If I told you that appearances are deceptive, and that I am a poor man, who will have to work hard to provide the bare necessities of life?"

"That accounts for less than nothing with a woman's love," returned Mary bravely.

With a happy laugh the man kissed her on the lips.

"Will nothing ever change your love, Mary?" he asked, in the tones of one confident of the reply.

"Nothing, unless I found you unworthy of my love; and that will never be," replied Mary, a world of loving trust shining from her eyes.

"Not if you discovered that I was a monster in human shape—say, for instance, the Winged Man?" persisted Max.

The trusting laugh with which Mary had greeted her lover's opening words died away.

A shadow shook her frame.

"Don't, Max!" she said, almost appealingly. "Nothing that I have ever seen, heard, or dreamt of has filled my heart with such horror, with such indescribable terror as that fearful, awful being!"

A spasm of pain shot across her lover's face. For a few minutes the two walked on in silence.

"Why, Mary," cried Max at length, "we are getting quite miserable, and that will never do upon this evening of all others. See what I have brought you! Our engagement-ring, which I wish you to wear until shortly—very, very shortly now, I hope you will wear a plain gold ring beside it."

Mary peered eagerly through the darkness at the glittering, gem-studded circle, which, despite the darkness that obtained on every side, flashed brilliantly.

"You cannot see it, dear one. Now, I must summon my magic powers to your aid," cried Max, laughing happily, as he stepped behind the girl, and, thrusting his arm over her shoulder, held the ring some eighteen inches before her face.

Then a bright light flashed from the centre of his forehead, and Mary uttered an ejaculation of delight, as its white beams were reflected from the almost priceless diamonds of which the ring was composed. Then the light vanished, and astounded, yet delighted, she turned round.

"However did you do it, Max? I begin to feel quite afraid of you. You must be a magician!" she laughed.

Max smiled.

"You are quite right, little one, I am a magician," he replied, in the same light turns. "Now, be a good girl, and don't ask questions, I will explain one day. Now, how do you like the ring?"

"It is the most beautiful ring I ever saw in my life, dear," replied Mary, thrilled with joy from head to foot, as Max slipped it on her finger. "But are you quite sure you can afford it?"

"Afford it!" laughed the other. "Now you have promised to be my wife, I will let you into a secret, Mary. I am a rich man; how rich I scarcely know myself. My wife need never leave a wish unsatisfied. Wealth, such as few women in this world can boast, will be hers. Her path will lead her amongst the highest in the land. Ay, dear one, say the word, and a mighty nation shall acknowledge you as its queen."

As he spoke Max drew himself up to his full height and gazed into his loved one's face. But Mary's cheek grew pale.

"Don't, Max, you frighten me! I am but a poor, simple-hearted girl. I do not want wealth or position, I only want to be your wife. My sole kingdom shall be your heart."

With a cry of joy Max folded her in his arms, and as they strolled, forgetful of everything but their love, and the future love would brighten, Max told her that, owing to circumstances he could not at present explain, he wished a secret, and immediate marriage, to which—though not without inward misgivings, she felt as though she was making but an unworthy return to Danby Druce, and the good old couple to whom he had entrusted her, for all their kindness—Mary consented.

DANBY DRUCE ON GUARD.

It was just as, with a last, long, lingering embrace, the lovers parted, that Danby Druce came upon the scene. Walking upon soft, springy grass, by the side of the road, his footsteps made no noise, and, wrapped in anxious thought, he might have passed the pair unnoticed, but that the inexplicable thrill, half fear, half awe, wholly ominous, which ever entered his heart in the Winged Man's presence, brought him to a halt.

"Good-night, dear one!" he heard the man whisper in low, tense tones.

"Good-night, Max! Heaven guard you, my love!" came the response, and Danby Druce felt his heart sink like lead within his bosom, as he recognised Mary Evanson's voice.

So, she had found another lover! Well, such was Fate! So long as the man proved worthy, Danby Druce's love was too great, too unselfish to grudge his successful rival his happiness.

Besides, at that moment, his whole being, his whole soul, his every sense was peering into the darkness in search of the weird horror who instinct told him was close at hand, and against whom Danby Druce had determined to protect Mary Evanson at all costs.

Therefore, instead of following his successful rival, and finding out all he could about him, as had been his first intention, Danby Druce hastened to overtake Mary, determined to remain in, or about, the house throughout the night, lest the Winged Man, having discovered her retreat, should seek to carry her off.

At the gate he overtook her, and smiled sadly as he noticed the half guilty start with which she responded to his greeting of:

"Good-evening, Mary! It is over-late for young ladies to be about alone."

"But I was not alone," retorted Mary; then, came to an abrupt halt, as she realised that she had been within an ace of betraying her secret.

"So I saw," said Danby Druce, with a forced laugh. "Am I permitted to ask who the gentleman was, and how you became acquainted with him?"

"Not yet. Please do not ask me anything yet! I will tell you all by-and-by!" promised Mary, in agitated tones, as she hurried through the old-fashioned porch into the open hall door, closely followed by Danby Druce, whose brow was furrowed with a thoughtful frown.

He did not like it at all. Mary, generally as open and frank as the day, had a secret she did not wish him to share. What did it mean? Then he remembered the silent embrace in the night, he had just witnessed, and put it down to girlish coyness in a first love affair.

Truth to tell Danby Druce had no room in his busy brain for thoughts of love, successful or the reverse. His instinctive feeling that the Winged Man was near, had rendered him thoughtful and anxious, and as he sat in the little sitting-room, listening to the praises of Mary, from her kindly hostess, a thought which had often assailed him, but which, till now, he had not allowed to remain in his heart returned with redoubled persistency.

"Yes," he thought, and heeding the good lady's voluble chattering, "it is better so. So long as the Winged Man remains at liberty my life is not worth a moment's purchase. Any day, any hour, any second, he may put his fearful threat into execution, and wipe me off the face of the earth, with as little mercy as he would crush an annoying fly. It would be a wicked sin to link my precarious life with hers, even if she would deign to look upon an old fogey like me. On the other hand, if she marries another, she would, at least, have a second pair of willing hands to protect her."

Barely had he come to this conclusion ere Mary Evanson entered the room, and, as Danby Druce rose to hand her to a seat, he marked with a joy, tempered by sadness, the bright, happy light which glistened in her eyes. Yet he could not repress a feeling of regret that it had not been his lot to call that blessed light into existence.

Realising that any confidences that Mary would make, must be voluntary, Danby Druce did not broach, even banteringly, the subject of Mary Evanson's companion in the lane. Instead, he exerted himself to please, with the result that ere long his host and hostess and the girl, who little guessed the gnawing pain of hopeless love that rent his heart, were roaring with laughter at his witty representations of some humorous scenes he had witnessed during his travels.

About ten o'clock, he rose to leave, and Mary, as was her wont, accompanied him to the garden-gate. Danby Druce, with almost fatherly gentleness, laid his hand upon the girl's shoulder.

"I do not think I would stir out after dark, Mary, if I were you," he said. "You may sleep soundly, for I will be near to guard you, but do not forget that the Winged Man has assuredly not relinquished his search for you."

Danby Druce felt the slight form tremble beneath his hand.

"I know," came in a hoarse, frightened whisper from the girl's lips. "I saw him this evening in the park."

It was Danby Druce's turn to start.

"And he saw you?" he asked anxiously.

"I think—indeed, I am sure, not!" replied the girl, trembling in every limb as she glanced apprehensively to right and left.

Then, in answer to the great detective's further questions, she related all that had occurred, omitting, however, all reference to the companion who had comforted and encouraged her.

Danby Druce heard the girl's tale out.

"Fear not, little one," he said encouragingly. "Run in, and sleep soundly. I will not go far from the cottage to-night."

"How good you are to me," murmured Mary Evanson, as, raising her graceful little head, she imprinted a sweet kiss upon the detective's cheek.

It was a kiss such as the Winged Man need not have been jealous of—a kiss that brought scant comfort to the detective's heart, for it was a kiss a daughter might have given an indulgent father.

With the stab of regret piercing his heart, the detective bade Mary a hasty "Good-night!" and walked swiftly in the direction of Ham Common.

BORNE FROM THE EARTH.

All that night Danby Druce patrolled in front of the cottage in which Mary Evanson slept; then, when dawn brought relief—for he knew that if the Winged Man had discovered where Mary Evanson had taken refuge, he would not have let that night pass without attempting to regain her—he made his way across the Common towards Ham Gate, through which he passed, intent upon searching the spot where Mary had seen the weird horror the previous evening.

As he approached the oak beneath which Mary Evanson had awaited her lover, the same strange shudder which ever heralded the Winged Man's appearance, shook his frame, and he knew that the dread aerial monster he thought was close at hand.

Diving into the bracken which lined his path, he dropped down, until the dew-laden fronds hid him from view, then he made his way slowly and cautiously towards the tree.

Presently, he sank to the ground, peering through the graceful foliage at a sight which drove the blood back into his heart with horror.

Standing close to a mighty branch, almost on the spot where Mary Evanson had crouched the previous evening, was the Winged Man, his mighty pinions hung loosely to his side, his arms were folded, a smile of evil triumphant malice lit his face as he watched the helpless struggles of the gamekeeper, whose pellets had drawn blood from his cheek the previous evening.

Surely, never had even the Red Indians of the West invented so cruel a torture as that with which the Winged Man was avenging himself upon the unfortunate wretch.

Overpowering the gamekeeper as he walked his rounds, the Winged Man had bound the unfortunate man's arms above his head, thrust a pear-shaped gag into his mouth, then, splitting open a small bough, jutting from its parent branch, had held it apart with an iron hand, while he thrust his prisoner's fingers through the opening.

Instinctively, the gamekeeper, fearing lest he should drop to earth, had clung to the jagged edge of the split branch. Then the Winged Man had withdrawn the piece of wood which held the bow apart, which, springing to, caught the man's fingers as in a trap.

Then, monster of cruelty that he was, the Winged Man left him hanging by his torn and lacerated fingers, whilst, dropping upon the ground beneath him, cried, just as Danby Druce appeared on the scene:

"It will be months, my friend, before your fingers will close round a gun-stock again. Let this be a warning never to use them against the Winged Man. He spares your life this time, but the next—"

He got no further. Even as he was speaking Danby Druce had crept, like a leopard in its native jungle, through the bracken, until within striking distance, and then had launched himself upon his foe.

Taken by surprise, the Winged Man was borne forward, but his falling body never touched the earth. His extended wings allowed him to skim over the ground, and, with Danby Druce still clinging to his throat, he rose slowly and painfully in the air.

"Fool, foredoomed wretch, let go your hold lest I fill your whole frame with pain is too great to be borne!"

"Bah, Winged Man! Save those wild threats for more credulous dupes than I. Danby Druce fears you not!" retorted the great detective.

Then he felt, with a spasm of elation, the weird horror start, as the hated name fell upon his ears.

"Aho, mine enemy! It is you!" laughed the Winged Man. "Well, you have taken me by surprise this time! What do you intend to do?"

"To cling like a leech to your throat, foul demon of the air!" retorted Danby Druce, "until I bear you weakened, and helpless, and at my mercy, to the earth!"

Loud and long laughed the Winged Man, though, truth to tell, the detective's boast was no empty one, for, whilst his wings were extended, the Winged Man could not reach him.

Again that mocking and unearthly laughter filled the air; then a ranger, crossing the park, stood spellbound, as he saw the Winged Man rising straight as a lark from its nest into the air.

Up he went, higher and higher, bearing the plucky detective further and further from the earth, until at length the two seemed but specks in the distance.

A thousand feet from the earth, the Winged Man remained poised on outstretched wings.

"Look around you, Danby Druce. See the fair landscape beneath. Turn and gaze once more at the mighty sun. It is the last sun you will ever see."

"That may be," retorted the detective, in calm, level tones. "Yet, if I fall, you shall fall with me!"

The next moment Danby Druce's hold on the Winged Man's throat tightened, as he felt the strong, muscular body beneath his knees bend inwards, saw arms and legs contracting, and the next moment a spasm of terror swept through his heart, as the Winged Man turned somersault after somersault, and fell like a falling stone earthwards.

With bulldog tenacity the detective clung to his fearful foe, whilst his legs, thrashing the air, he was swept round and round at a fearful speed.

Now uppermost, now beneath, earth, sky, heaven seemed dancing before his gaze, whilst each moment he experienced greater difficulty in breathing, and, despite all he could do, he felt his hold on the Winged Man relaxing.

So swift was their descent that in an almost incredulously short space of time they were close upon the leafy upper branches of the "Trysting Oak." Then, his back to the earth, the Winged Man shot out his broad pinions, stopping his descent with the jerk, which tore the detective's fingers from their hold, with the result that the next moment Danby Druce, a cry of despair upon his lips, was crashing through the branches.

A blow on the side from a mighty bough a violent collision with a spreading branch, and Danby Druce remembered no more.

When he came to his senses, it was to find himself laying on the greensward beneath the mighty oak. He was surrounded by a crowd of pale-faced keepers, rangers, and gardeners, who were dividing their attention between himself and the unfortunate victim of the Winged Man's cruelty.

Wonderful to relate, save for lacerations and numberless bruisers, Danby Druce was unhurt. His iron constitution and wondrous pluck prevailed over the severity of his injuries, and he was able to walk from the park by the side of the extemporised litter which bore the injured gamekeeper.

A LIFT IN THE RAIN.

Needless to say, a beautiful girl like Mary Evanson could scarcely go out without attracting a good deal of attention. Many were the admiring glances cast after her as she passed through the streets, strolled across the park, or walked along the semi-country roads around Ham.

All river resorts, especially as near London as Richmond, are haunted by a number of young fellows with more money than manners, some of whom had at times pestered Mary with their unwelcome attentions.[41]

Amongst others was a certain young millionaire, named Henry Potts, who, having inherited an enormous fortune, was seeking to dissipate it and ruin his own health as quickly as possible.

On the evening following Danby Druce's adventure with the Winged Man, Mary Evanson, who had been to visit a friend on the outskirts of Petersham, set out on a long walk from Robin Hood's Gate, through Richmond Park, to Ham Gate.

She was later, too, than she intended, because her friend's brother had promised to escort her home. But when ten o'clock struck, and her promised escort did not turn up, Mary had started boldly on her long, dreary walk.

Dreary, that is to say, to anyone but a young girl enjoying her first love-dream. Wrapped in thought of her dark, handsome lover, Mary had tripped lightly over the roadway.

So lost in thought was she that it was not until she had got a good distance into Richmond Park that she realised that dark storm clouds were gathering over the moon.

In fact, it was not until the first few heavy drops fell upon her that she knew she was in for a thorough soaking. For a moment she hesitated. To go back was as bad as pressing forward, and, drawing her cloak tighter round her shoulders, she hastened onwards.

It was about this time that Henry Potts' motor-brougham entered the park. The young millionaire was in a howling temper. He was due at a select little supper-party at the Star and Garter at ten o'clock, and now, after waiting for nearly an hour at an appointed spot on Wimbledon Common for a certain fair companion, he had driven off alone to face the laughter of his more fortunate comrades when he should arrive at the Star and Garter, the only one unaccompanied by a lady.

Cursing his ill-luck, he was laying back in one corner of the splendidly-upholstered vehicle, gazing sullenly out into the stormy night, when the brilliant glare of the car's acetylene lamps fell upon a girl's form struggling bravely against the storm.

As the car whizzed by she looked up, and Henry Potts uttered an ejaculation

---

[41] This harkens back to the original suggestions that the original appearances of Spring-Heeled Jack were attributed to a wager among individuals of "the higher ranks of life" as described in the "Resident of Peckham" letter.

of surprise and delight when he recognised the beautiful, clean-cut features of Mary Evanson.

In a moment his mouth was against the speaking-tube.

"Go back, Roberts. Offer that lady a ride. Say nothing about my being in here," he ordered.

Then he chuckled at his cleverness as the car was backed slowly down the road. A few minutes later it stopped close to Mary Evanson.

"Beg your pardon, Miss!" said the chauffeur, politely touching his cap as he spoke. "I am going to Richmond if you would like a lift."

"Oh, thank you so much!" replied Mary gratefully, as, springing from his seat, the chauffeur held open the door.

Eager to get in out of the rain, Mary jumped so quickly into the vehicle that it was not until the door had been slammed to behind her, and the chauffeur, accustomed to such adventures, had regained his seat, that she realised she was not alone.

"I am so sorry; I thought the carriage was empty!" she stammered.

"Why sorry, Miss Evanson? I am only too delighted to be able to serve you," was the unexpected reply.

An ejaculation of alarm rose to Mary's lips as she recognised the speaker's voice. Instinctively she grasped the handle of the door.

"No—no, don't do that!" objected Henry Potts. "You will be badly hurt if you get out whilst the car is moving."

As he spoke he laid a detaining hand upon her arm.

Bitterly the girl regretted her ready acceptance of the chauffeur's offer, but the distance was not far, and, with a half petulant little sigh, she screwed herself into a corner, as far from Henry Potts as she could very well get, much to that gentleman's annoyance.

Presently the car pulled up before a broad flight of steps, which Mary recognised as the entrance to a large hotel.

"Won't you alight, and have something, Miss Evanson?" asked Potts politely.

"I'd rather not, thank you!" replied Mary. "If your chauffeur will call a cab—"

"Oh no!" said Potts. "He shall drive you home. Good night! I am glad to have been able to render you a little service," he added, as, opening the door, he sprang out, and gave some orders to the driver. The next minute he was back at the door of the car.

"My idiot of a chauffeur has allowed himself to run out of petrol, but it won't take long to get a fresh supply. In the meantime, please come in, and have, at least, a cup of tea. You will catch your death of cold sitting there in your wet clothes."

The request was so politely urged that Mary felt it would be churlish to refuse. Reluctantly she gave her hand to the triumphant young man, and allowed herself to be escorted into the hotel.

A servant came forward, but with a warning frown Henry Potts waved him aside, and, with Mary's tiny hand laid gently on his arm, led the way upstairs.

By this time Mary was feeling supremely uncomfortable; her teeth chattered, and she longed for a cup of tea to put a little warmth into her chilled frame.

Presently Potts paused before a closed door, from beyond which came the silvery ripple of women's laughter, and the deep voices of men.

"We'll go in here, Miss Evanson, if you don't mind. I dare say we'll find a table unoccupied," he said, throwing open the door, and leading Mary into a brilliantly-lighted room.

The crash of a door slammed to behind her warned Mary Evanson that all was not well. Coming to an abrupt halt, she looked around her with startled eyes.

She found herself in a fair-sized room round a table set for desert, in the centre of which were seated at a number of men in evening-dress, each with a lady by his side.

A roar of welcome greeted the pale, shrinking girl, mingled with which were half jealous, wholly envious, ejaculations from the ladies, as they realised that a woman the more beautiful than either of them was in their midst.

With a white, startled face Mary Evanson looked around her.

But, with loud shouts of malicious glee the women darted forward. Two of them seized her by the arm, and one, snatching her hat, loosened her lovely, luxuriant tresses, which fell in wavy masses over her shoulders.

"Oh, don't! Please let me go! If you are women, if you have a spark of womanly feeling left in you, let me go!" pleaded Mary.

"Hold!"

Deep, clear, reverberating, the voice rang through the room.

Immediately every tongue was hushed, the laughter faded, and the colour from the men's faces.

By what means he entered the room none could tell; standing in the centre of the table, one foot crushing a fruit-laden epergne,[42] the other pressing the juice out of a dish full of peaches, his fearful wings half extended, his face partly hidden by a black mask, glowering angrily upon them, stood the Winged Man.

A shuddering moan of terror arose from the revellers' lips as they gazed, too horrified even to flee, upon the avenging form of the weird horror.

"Hold, I say! Dare move hand or foot, and shrivelled, blackened forms you will lie at my feet. I, the Winged Man, command! Let he who dare disobey!"

Save the same shuddering moan we have before mentioned, not a sound escaped the fear-paralysed lips of the well-dressed crowd.

But, with a low cry, Mary Evanson dropped unconscious to the floor.

With difficulty restraining an impulse to rush to the assistance of the girl he loved, the Winged Man looked compassionately upon her for a few seconds.

Then the fear-paralysed men and women shrank cowering back before the fearful, almost unearthly anger, which blazed from his eyes, or streaked, with

---

42 An ornamental centrepiece for a dining table.

furrowed wrinkles, his white, deathlike face.

Drawing the seven-thronged scourge from his waist, the Winged Man hovered on outstretched wings above the shrinking, frightened crowd.

"Hence, heartless, pitiless wretches! Hence, I say! Let these stripes remind you that the Winged Man lives to avenge such wrongs as hers!" he roared.

"Hence, heartless, pitiless wretches!" cried the Winged Man.

Then the terror-laden silence which obtained through the room was broken by howls and shrieks of pain from men and women, as the Winged Man, darting swiftly from point to point, brought his hissing thong down, with merciless force, upon the bare shoulders of the women, the faces and necks of the men, until he drove them in headlong flight from the room, shrieking in terror-laden accents as they ran:

"The Winged Man! The Winged Man!"

Such terror did the fearful name inspire that it was not until several minutes had elapsed that, headed by a policeman, a group of hotel servants burst into the room, to stand on the threshold gazing about them in amazement and dismay.

Of the costly glass with which the table had been crammed, not a single piece remained whole. Mirrors were splintered on the wall, pictures torn from their frames, or slashed to ribbons.

But of the Winged Man and Mary Evanson, no sign remained.

THE ELOPEMENT.

When Mary Evanson recovered consciousness she looked about her in amazement, half persuaded that the events of the previous night had been some fearful nightmare-ridden dream.

She lay in her own little room in Mrs. Dawson's lilac-coloured cottage.

She remembered everything, even to the feeling of revulsion and horror with which she had looked upon the Winged Man, though he had come to rescue her from her tormentors' hands.

Then as the weird being's fearful frame seemed to rise up before her eyes, she uttered a low cry of terror, and covered her face with her hands.

A minute later a wild, piercing shriek burst from her lips as a hand was laid upon her shoulder.

Shuddering, she opened her eyes, then flung her arms appealingly around the motherly form of Mrs. Dawson, who, hearing her charge's cry, had hastened to her side.

"Yes, dearie, don't be alarmed, it is only me!" she cried, stroking the girl's shapely head with motherly touch.

"Oh, keep the Winged Man from me! Don't let him come near me! I feel as though I cannot be in his hated presence and live!" cried Mary hysterically.

Neither heard the low, despairing wail which came from beyond the open window, as the Winged Man, clinging to the window-still, heard Mary Evanson's tear-laden appeal for protection from him.

Careless of whether he was seen or not in the early morning light, he spread his wings and flew in the direction of the river.

"The Winged Man!" repeated Mrs. Dawson, her rosy face losing its colour, as a deadly fear gripped her heart. "Was it, could it have been the Winged Man who brought you to my door last night?"

"I hope not, I trust not!" gasped Mary, in low, breathless tones. "I cannot bear to think that I have been once more in his power."

"I was sitting up for you, dear," explained Mrs. Dawson, thinking to distract the girl's thoughts from the terror-inspiring remembrance of the Winged Man, "and was getting a bit anxious because it was growing late, when I was startled by a loud, double knock at the front door.

"I rushed into the hall, turned up the gas, opened the door, and found you lying breathless in the porch.

"And now, Mary dear, try to get to sleep. You need not be afraid. I will sit with you till you drop off."

Obediently closing her eyes, Mary soon fell into a quiet, refreshing slumber, from which she awoke better in health, but still suffering from the after-effects of her night's adventure.

Great was Danby Druce's alarm when, in faltering tones Mary Evanson related all that happened.

The first thing he did was to hasten, as fast as his car could carry him, to Henry Potts' chambers, where he gave that young libertine so severe a thrashing that he wished he had never seen or heard of Mary Evanson.

This done, Danby Druce returned to Ham, and, with every sense on the alert, every nerve strung to its highest tension, mounted guard over Mary Evanson, determined to protect her, if possible, from the Winged Man.

The ordeal through which Mary Evanson had passed was not one to be recovered from in a moment, yet the thought of her approaching marriage to Max gave her renewed strength.

It had been arranged during their last interview that Mary should meet her intended husband on their wedding-morn, near the little church on Ham Common, at eleven o'clock.

At 10.45 on the fatal morning, Mary, trembling with excitement, put on her outdoor things, kissing Mrs. Dawson with even more affection than usual, for her conscience pricked her, and walked swiftly from the house, fearing each moment to be accosted by Danby Druce, whom she knew was near the cottage to protect her from the Winged Man.

But Danby Druce was nowhere to be seen.

As a matter of fact, chance had carried him to the very spot where she had agreed to meet her lover.

Seated on a tombstone, he was trying to evolve some plan by which to hide Mary Evanson more effectually from the dread being who haunted her existence. He would rather see her dead than in his power.

He had just made up his mind that he would take the girl to a little fishing village in Cornwall, when the voice of the one who occupied his thoughts fell upon his ears, and he wondered whom it was she greeted.

Striding to the wall surrounding the churchyard, he looked over it just in time to see the tall, dark stranger, whom he had before seen, bend down, and, with an air of proprietorship, imprint a kiss upon Mary's upturned lips.

A fierce spasm of jealousy pierced the great detective's heart.

The next moment he experienced the strange, weird, inexplicable shiver which ever shook his frame in the Winged Man's presence.

Instinctively he glanced up, expecting to see the weird horror swoop down, with outstretched wings, upon the girl.

Then, self-possessed calm, ever ready to face any emergency though he was, a fearful thought held him for a moment paralysed.

Once before in that man's presence he had felt the warning shoot through his frame.

As though a veil had been lifted from his eyes, he recognised the pale, handsome features of the stranger.

A gasp of horror burst from his lips, then he vaulted over the low wall, and rushed to where Max was in the act of handing Mary into a 40-h.p. motor-car.

Hearing steps behind him, Max turned round. "Mary, Mary, for the love of Heaven come back! That man is—" he got no further. Max's fist, planted full in his mouth, checked his utterance.

LOST! LOST! LOST!

St. Michael's Church, Belgravia, was filled by a well-dressed, fashionable crowd, drawn thither by curiosity. That morning all present had received, perhaps, the strangest invitation to a wedding ever issued.

It was nothing more nor less than an ordinary invitation-card, surmounted by an imperial crown, with the names of the intended bride and bridegroom left blank.

The majority, wondering at so short notice, had come to believe that the absence of the names was due to some extraordinary mistake or act of forgetfulness on the part of the sender; but, as in the crowded pews those who knew each other exchanged confidences, it leaked out that none of the cards had been filled in, and the excitement grew more intense than ever.

In vain the verger was questioned. All he could tell was that he had received notice of the marriage a week before, but that no names had been given.

The clergyman very gravely, as though the recipient of some State secret, informed those of his friends who were present in the congregation that he had simply received and noticed that a couple were to be married by special licence at his church that morning.

He did not think it necessary to add that the notice was accompanied by so handsome a present that any scruples he might have felt at uniting a couple whose names he did not know were overruled.

Punctually at twelve o'clock a motor-car stopped at the door of the church, and a tall, dignified man, who gazed around him with a certain air of patronising hauteur, and an exceedingly lovely girl, clad in a well-fitting, tailor-made travelling-costume, walked down the aisle amidst the strains of an anthem magnificently rendered by a full choir.

Eagerly all present craned their eyes to catch a glimpse of the mysterious bride and bridegroom. All felt confident that they were witnessing the romantic nuptials of some great European ruler.

Certainly the girl was English, but the man might have been of any nationality. The opening hymn concluded, the clergyman commenced the marriage service until, in impressive words, he commanded any who "know of any reason why this couple should not be joined together in holy matrimony to declare it, or else for ever hold their peace," rang out.

Barely had the last words left his lips than the vestry door was thrown open, and Danby Druce, his mouth still stained with the blood which had poured from his lips when Max struck him, his clothes dishevelled and travel-stained, rushed into the church, crying:

"I—I forbid the marriage! That being is the Winged Man!"

A deathly silence followed the announcement. Mary Evanson, her lovely eyes seeming as though they would start from her head in horror, stepped back, and gazed, terror-stricken, upon he whose wedded wife she would have been a minute later. She stretched forth her hands towards the discomfited bridegroom, crying:

"Max, tell him he lies! You—you are not—cannot be that fearful monster!"

Then, as she marked the terrible change that had come over her lover's face, converting it for the moment into that of a human fiend, she staggered back, clasping her hands to her eyes as though to shut out some fearful vision.

"I might have known that Earth held naught for me!" came in tones so despairing, so laden with grief and misery, that scarce one of the hearers but felt a momentary sorrow for the wretched being, from the Winged Man's lips.

The next moment he had drawn himself up to his full height as he cried, in tones which reverberated like thunder through the building:

"Yes, I am the Winged Man! Mary, is not your love strong enough to keep you true to your plighted word, even though I am one whom you looked upon as an inhuman monster?"

As he spoke he stepped forward as though to clasp Mary in his arms; but, with upraised book the clergyman stopped before him.

"Back, accursed being! Go! Let not your unhallowed presence longer defile this holy place!"

"Yes, go! I loathe, I hate, I abhor you!" came in gasping accents from Mary's parched lips.

A fearful shudder swept throughout the whole of that mighty congregation as, with a wail of fearful, unutterable despair, the Winged Man spread forth his mighty pinions, and, covering his face with his hands, swept over the heads of the shrinking people to a gallery at the further end of the building.

Perched on the wooden rail, he paused, and looked down, with pallid agony-torn features, upon the sea of faces beneath.

Then, despite the horror which filled every heart, a wave of pity once more swept through the hearers, as, with a long-drawn, misery-laden cry of "Lost! Lost! Lost!" he plunged through the open window, and, propelled by long, swift beats of his mighty pinions, disappeared into the cloud-laden sky.

THE TRAIL OF THE WINGED MAN.

"Lost! Lost! Lost!"

Shrill, fierce, laden with a misery too great to be borne the, the fearful cry, now heard in indistinct murmur high in the heavens, now thrilling the listeners' hearts, as the grief-tortured Winged Man sped northward close to earth.

At eve the despairing cry resounded over Hertford Castle's battlemented towers. When day dawned the early-rises of Peterborough were terror-stricken as the cry of "Lost! Lost! Lost!" fell upon their ears.

On he flew, now rising high above the clouds, now dropping like a stone earthwards, intent on avenging the grief that tore his aching heart upon the whole human race.

Like beacon lights raised to warn the countryside of an approaching foe from London northwards, the Winged Man arose, but left behind him a trail of burning ricks and cottages and mansions, set on fire through sheer hatred and lust of vengeance by the Winged Man.

A few miles outside Lincoln's ancient walls of farmer, leaning over his gate, surveyed some dozen stacks of recently garnered corn.

Times had been hard, but the golden grain would pay his rent, and leave sufficient to reward another year's toil.

Like a falling aerolite, the Winged Man alighted on the centre of a rick, and as the amazed farmer gazed in terror at his awful form the Winged Man raised his careworn visage heavenward, crying:

"Misery, destruction, ruin to the human race! Woe to mankind—woe!"

Then, to the farmer's terror-stricken gaze, he seemed to be encompassed for a moment in a ball of living fire, ere, with a laugh horrible to hear, so laden with malice was it, the weird monster opened his wings and soared heavenwards, leaving the central stack a mass of flames.

A labourer wending his way homeward, wearied with a day's hard toil, gazed along the road to the snug, thatched cottage, faced by a pretty, well-kept garden, which he called his home.

Already he enjoyed in anticipation the plain but wholesome supper his rosy-faced wife had prepared for him.

Suddenly he came to an abrupt halt in the centre of the road, his frame as motionless as though turned to stone, as he gazed upon the fearful, terror-inspiring form of the Winged Man.

For a moment that weird terror hovered over his humble home; then, thrusting his hand into his bosom, drew forth a handful of lurid flame, and thrust it deep into the tinder-dry thatch of the labourer's cottage.

Anxiety for his dear ones conquering the terror which seemed to have turned his very heart to ice, the labourer bounded forward, cursing the malice of the flying fiend who had robbed him of his humble home, his little all.

Rejoicing over the misery he was leaving ever in his wake, the Winged Man continued his fearful northward journey.

Blame him not too harshly. Sorrows greater than often fall to the lot of a living being had been the Winged Man's portion for many years past.

A chance of happiness, like a glimpse of Heaven, had visited him for a moment; then, just as a new life brightened by a woman's faithful love had seemed within his grasp, his identity had been revealed, and his last chance of peace and happiness wrenched from his grasp.

The reaction had been more than even the Winged Man's mighty brain could stand. For the time being he was mad—stark, raving mad! A madman armed with powers which rendered his temporary insanity danger such as had not threatened England since she had become a nation.

As he swept northward his bitter, despairing cry shook the air, and those who had heard that ill-omened voice before realised that a new, a more dangerous, more fearful element had entered into the Winged Man's life.

AN INTERRUPTED SUPPER.

In an old-time hostelry by the side of the old Roman road known as Ermine Street, the members of the local cricket club had assembled to celebrate the end of the season. The supper had been cleared away, and each jolly cricketer, a well-filled glass before him, had laid himself out to enjoy the evening. Louder each man raised his voice singing in the chorus of some well-known song, all ignorant of the fearful flying terror rapidly approaching.

The loud laughter which greeted a well-sung comic song caused the Winged Man to remain poised in the air over the quaint old chimneys and gabled roof of the old-time inn.

A spasm of fearful rage shook his frame.

What creeping earthworms dare to be happy whilst he was suffering the torments of the lost?

Lower and lower he dropped, until at length he was clinging to the window-sill, and peering with heat-contorted face at the revellers within.

Before Mary Evanson had been snatched from him by Danby Druce, the Winged Man would have given much to men who, as these unsuspecting cricketers were doing, were showing their appreciation of the joys of life by roars of honest, hearty laughter.

But his whole nature had altered. Remorseless where an object was to be achieved, he had never yet shown wanton cruelty. But this evening the very happiness he witnessed seemed an insult to his sorrow and when an allusion in the song to the Winged Man evoked a fresh roar of laughter, his rage broke all bounds.

A sweep of his arms, and the window, torn from its frame, crashed into the road beneath. Then, his face contorted with fury, his long arms waving frantically in the air, his headlight a brilliant red, he burst with a fearful blood-curdling yell of rage into the room.

Springing on to the table, he seized the singer by the throat, and, lifting him above his head, pressed the struggling man's body with fearful force against the ceiling.

A moment's terror-stricken silence, then, bursting the bonds of craven fear which help the motionless, the cricketers—men of the same old stock of men as that from which famed Lincoln had ever recruited—forgot their terror at the sight of their comrades' danger, and with one accord sprang forward to his rescue.

This unexpected opposition raised the Winged Man's mad rage to fever-heat. Hurling his victim to the furthermost corner, where he lay a bruised, bleeding mass of humanity, the Winged Man grappled with his nearest foe, and sent him, uttering terror-laden shrieks, on to the top of his comrades.

Undeterred by their comrades' fate, the gallant men of Lincoln sought to close with the fearful interrupter of their revelry.

As well have attacked a lion in its native lair. His weird cry ringing in their ears, those nearest the Winged Man had scarce time to strike a wildly-aimed a blow ere they were seized and held breathless to right and left.

Borne on his fearful pinions, darting like an ill-omened bird of prey, now upon one victim, now upon another, the Winged Man swept backwards and forwards across the room, until at length his last foe had been hurled, a bruised, bleeding mass of humanity, in the corner.

Then, standing with folded arms upon the table, he surveyed his fallen foes. As he did so his madness for a moment left him, and a look of intense horror crept into his face.

The next it was succeeded by an expression of even deeper resentment and anger than before.

"Listen, you who as yet live to hear the Winged Man's words. It is to Danby Druce, he who had snatched the cup of happiness from the Winged Man's lips, that you owe your present plight.

"Already he is on my track, or he is not the man I take him to be. Tell him from me that ere long a fate at which the whole world should shudder as they read shall be his. I have shed your blood. Blood for blood is my motto. With these red drops from my heart I salve your wounds."

As he spoke the Winged Man tore apart his black, tight-fitting vest, and those who retained sufficient consciousness to behold the wonder that followed saw what they took to be a huge drops of blood fall from his breast, where they lay, not forming a liquid pool, but rising a tiny heap upon the table. Then, with an indescribably pathetic gesture, the Winged Man waved his latest victims adieu, and, springing from the window-sill, continued on his voyage of devastation and revenge.

It was some minutes after the Winged Man had disappeared that, moaning with pain, the topmost cricketers rose to their feet, and helped their half-suffocated comrades below to arise.

Fearful had been the force the Winged Man had used in his conflict with the Lincoln men, yet, strange to say, save for bruises and abrasions, they had suffered but little real injury.

Presently the captain of the club—a burly young farmer, who had been the first to attack the Winged Man—glanced at the red shining heap upon the table. A shudder shook his frame as he realised whence those mysterious objects had come. Conquering the repulsion which filled his heart, he laid a finger upon what looked like a huge drop of blood. An ejaculation of astonishment burst from his lips. It was hard and slippery, like a polished stone.

Raising it from the table, he took it to the nearest lamp, and with an ejaculation of admiration, noted how it reflected the yellow beams. Like a flash the memory of the Winged Man's farewell words returned to his mind.

Excitedly he turned to his wondering comrades.

"Boys, we have heard of the Winged Man's munificence. Nobly he has atoned for the injury he has done us. This supposed blood is in reality rubies, which, if I am any judge at all, are of enormous value."

Trembling from the effects of their recent fearful experience at the hands of the Winged Man, the men clustered round the table.

It was true! What they had taken to be drops of blood were precious stones, which one of their number, a jeweller from a neighbouring town, declared to be of enormous value.

So it proved, and many a young tradesman, or farmer, in the village, lives now to bless the Winged Man, who gave him his first start in life.

DANBY DRUCE ON THE TRAIL.

It was just after the cricketers had made the standing discovery mentioned at the end of the last chapter that, with a wheezing, rushing noise, a huge motor-car dashed past the inn. Then came a jarring sound, followed by the creaking of brakes, and rushing from the house, as well as their bruised and aching limbs would allow, the cricketers found a large 40-h.p. car brought to a standstill, with both front tyres cut pieces, in consequence of having plunged into the window-frame the Winged Man had thrown into the road.

As they approached, a man who had been examining the ruined tyres on either side turned towards them.

"What place is this? How came that glass in the roadway?" he asked.

"As for the glass," continued the captain of the cricket team, when he had satisfied the motorist with the name of the village, “you must blame the Winged Man for that.”

“Has he been here?” inquired Danby Druce eagerly, for the motorist was he.

With a rueful nod the captain pointed to his bruised and discomfited comrades.

“It looks like it, doesn’t it?” he demanded, laughing. “We attacked him, but he beat us off at single-handed. But we don’t bear any ill-will for it.”

Danby Druce turned angrily towards his chauffeur:

“Make haste with those tyres, the Winged Man is on ahead!”

“All right, sir; I will be ready in a few minutes!” replied the chauffeur.

Whereupon Danby Druce accompanied the cricketers into the inn, where he listened to a narration of what had occurred, laughing scornfully as the captain of the team delivered the Winged Man’s threatening message.

Ere long the chauffeur entered to inform Danby Druce that the repairs were completed, and, accompanied by the usual rubicund, but now deathly pale, innkeeper, who had not yet recovered from the fearful events which had taken place in his house, the whole party moved from the inn.

Suddenly they were brought to an abrupt halt by an ejaculation of astonishment from the innkeeper, who was standing a few feet from the door gasping with astonishment as he pointed to a pair of upright stones beneath a spreading chestnut tree to the right of the inn door, where a few minutes before a huge horse-trough of solid stone had been standing.

“It was there a minute ago, I’ll swear it was!” declared the innkeeper vehemently.

Barely had the words left his lips ere all eyes were turned heavenwards as the Winged Man’s terrible, weird cry burst upon their ears.

It was a clear, starlight night, and, in full view of the cricketers, Danby Druce, and public and alike, the Winged Man was seen holding the enormous stone trough in his hands, as he remained poised immediately above the car.

Even as they gazed the Winged Man let go his hold of the trough, and an ejaculation of rage burst from Danby Druce’s lips as he saw the enormous mass, gathering pace as it fell, descend straight towards the car.

The next moment it had struck the vehicle full in the centre, doubling it up as though it had been made of cardboard, and reducing its delicate machinery to scrap-iron, whilst the petrol from its reservoir splashed in all directions. Uttering an ejaculation of rage, Danby Druce drew a revolver from his pocket, and, taking hasty aim, fired at the Winged Man.

A mocking laugh followed the shot, then a ball of fire let fall from the Winged Man’s hands, alighted full upon the demolished tank.

Immediately there was a loud explosion, whilst the petrol-soaked woodwork of the car burst into flame. Peal upon peal of mocking laughter bore evidence to the Winged Man’s triumph, as he flew swiftly away, leaving Danby Druce to follow as best he might, or give up the pursuit.

THE WINGED MAN’S TRIUMPH.

But Danby Druce was too accustomed to having his plans upset by the Winged

Man to allow the destruction of his motor-car to delay him. Half an hour later he and his chauffeur, mounted upon horses provided by the captain of the cricket team, were galloping towards Kirton, where the detective hoped to be able to purchase a new car.

A fresh impulse to capture the Winged Man had entered the detective's heart, and even as he rode, the memory of how, upon waking from her swoon in the church, Mary Evanson had clung to him, calling him her dearest and only friend, had brought a new happiness into his life. Yet he dare not even dream of love whilst the Winged Man remains at liberty.

First let him capture or say that dread horror, then he would ask Mary Evanson to become his wife, and, retiring from his dangerous profession, live a life of ease and happiness.

Engrossed in thoughts of the future, Danby Druce allowed his horse to drop from a canter to a trot, from a trot to walk, whilst his chauffeur, already grown stiff from the unaccustomed equestrian exercise, was too grateful for the respite from the continual jogging to awaken his master from the waking dream of a happy future into which he had fallen.

Yet, though neither of the men suspected his presence, the Winged Man was near. The destruction of the motor-car had not been an act of spiteful vengeance, but a means to an end, that end being the capture of his great foe.

As the two men rode along the starlit road the Winged Man had hovered close behind them, moving through the air in a series of gliding swoops, lest the beat of his mighty pinions should attract their attention.

Presently, as the road passed through a long stretch of low-lying, timberless country, the Winged Man soared aloft, unwinding from around his waist a long, silken lasso, such as cowboys use, as he did so. Armed with this, he descended on outstretched wings, until he hovered immediately above the unsuspecting detective, then, with a deft movement of his wrist, swung the descending loop around his head.

Chance caused the chauffeur to look up. For a moment terror left him speechless; then, with a loud shout, which was almost a shriek, he cried:

"Look out, Mr. Druce, the Winged Man is upon you!"

Too late, Danby Druce awakened from his reverie. Even as his hand sought his ready revolver, the snake-like coils of the rope settled over his shoulders, and the next moment, torn from his saddle, he was being carried swiftly through the air, whirling dizzily round at the end the lasso, whilst the Winged Man's loud triumphant laughter rang in his ears.

Glancing up, he saw the thin, silken cord stretched from the centre of his own body to a belt round the Winged Man's flying form.

"Aha, Danby Druce, I have you now!" chuckled the Winged Man. "Look well upon the earth, draw in deep breaths of the cool night air, for soon the earth will claim you as its own, the night air whistle through your whitened bones!"

Danby Druce made no reply. The weight of his body had drawn the lasso tightly round his waist, causing him intense agony, and he feared to speak lest the Winged Man should detect in his tones the pain he suffered.

As the Winged Man's fearful, blood-curdling chuckle fell upon his ears, Danby Druce watched with swimming eyes the landscape sweeping by beneath him.

On they flew, whilst the great detective's head felt as though it would indeed be burst asunder by the rush of blood through his veins. At last a merciful unconsciousness gave him relief.

The salt sea-breezes cooling his fevered brow revived his senses. He opened his eyes, to see beneath him a wide expanse of dyke-traversed marsh-land, beyond the reedy border of which could be seen the waters of a mighty estuary, and he knew that his fearful captor had borne him to the banks of the Humber.

On a point jutting into the river Danby Druce saw the broken walls and half-demolished towers of an ancient ruin. Thither the Winged Man carried his prey, and alighting on the thick wall of what had been the castle's donjon-keep, allowed the detective to rest upon the sharp, cement-embedded stones of which the ancient building was composed.

So great the relief from the ever-tightening rope round his body that Danby Druce breathed a deep sigh. Then, as his courage, which had never entirely forsaken him, reasserted itself with returning strength, he tried to struggle to his feet. But even as he did so the loose stones gave way, and he felt himself falling from the giddy height on to a rough heap of fallen masonry below.

Down, down, down he fell, until, with a fearful jerk, his descent was checked, and the terrible lasso tightened round his body once more.

"Oh ho, Danby Druce, you will have to learn to walk again, it seems!" cried the Winged Man, as, allowing his prisoner to drop gently on the ground, he alighted on a huge coping-stone by his side, and, his elbows on his knees, his pale, evil, smiling face between his hands, he surveyed the detective with eager, hate-laden eyes.

Despite the weakness consequent upon his fearful ride through the air, despite the utter hopelessness of his condition, Danby Druce met his foe's glance calmly, steadily, and unflinchingly.

IN THE WINGED MAN'S POWER.

"Well, Danby Druce, I have the inestimable privileges of your company once more!" cried the Winged Man mockingly. "It seems quite like old times, you and I being together for a friendly chat. Do you know what I am going to do with you?"

Danby Druce shrugged his shoulders.

"Kill me, I suppose," he replied calmly. "If so, the only favour I ask is that you get it over quickly."

Never had Danby Druce heard such a fearful sound as the wild, mocking laughter, full of evil triumph, with which the Winged Man responded to his appeal.

"What, and send you into the dark unknown where my vengeance can no longer reach you? Never!" cried the Winged Man, in tones so hate-laden that even the dauntless detective shuddered with horror.

"That would be mercy, indeed," continued the weird horror. "Hope for mercy from the hunger-maddened tiger of the Indian jungle, but not from he whom you have robbed of his last chance of happiness on earth. I tell you, Danby Druce," went on the Winged Man, standing over his prostrate foe with wildly-gesticulating arms, "you knew not what you did when you turned my promised bride's love to loathing and disgust by unmasking me before her. You robbed a lost soul of its only hope, and let loose upon the world a demon whose hatred will ever crave blood—blood—blood!"

Aching in every limb, his head yet swimming from its long-sustained downward position, Danby Druce, struggling painfully to his feet, supported himself against the stone the Winged Man had just vacated, as he cried:

"Though I know my fate is sealed, that I am in your power, without hope of rescue or relief, I tell you, Winged Man, that I would deem myself shamed for ever had I seen any girl lured to wed such as you and held my peace. Sooner or later she would have learned your fearful secret. Terrible indeed would be her sufferings when she found that the one she had loved was being hated and abhorred by the whole world!"

A momentary gleam of admiration flashed into the Winged Man's eyes as he gazed on the pale-faced but heroic detective.

"Fool! Honest fool, perhaps, but still a fool," he muttered, striding backwards and forwards before his prisoner. "When I entered the church with Mary Evanson"—a spasm shot across the Winged Man's white face as the name crossed his lips—"hanging upon my arm, the Winged Man was to all intents and purposes dead. Never again would the world have been thrilled by accounts of his fearful flights, his ruthless actions.

"But you—you, Danby Druce, most hated of a hated race, you have brought him to life once more! You have seen with what result. Ruin and devastation have marked my path from London, but more terrible yet shall be the Winged Man's erratic course throughout the length and breadth of Britain. Only one person in all this mighty Empire shall be safe from my vengeance—Mary Evanson.

"But enough of this. Already the morning sun tinges with red the eastern horizon, whilst the falling tide leaves bear the saltings beyond the reed-fringed marsh. There is much to be compressed into the few hours that must elapse ere that tide returns."

But Danby Druce was not the man to be led like a sheep to the slaughter. The short respite from pain had cleared his brain. As the rope tightened he uttered a rage-laden, vindictive shout, and hurled himself madly upon his foe.

Alas! the cruel strands of the rope cutting into his flesh had robbed his arms of strength, and with contemptuous ease the Winged Man repelled his wild, hopeless, but gallant attempt to break free from his all-powerful foe.

"What, still unsubdued, Danby Druce!" cried the Winged Man, his laugh tinged with venomous spite. "It is well. I would not gain too easy a victory over you. Yet the time is drawing near when, a supplicant at my feet, you will beg for mercy!"

A FEARSOME JOURNEY.

Then, without awaiting the baffled detective's reply, the Winged Man pulled him heavily to the ground with the jerk of the lasso, ere dragging the limp, almost senseless body behind him, as a child might drag an overturned toy-horse, he strode through the opening in the wall.

As he did so, worked by some concealed spring, the huge slabs of the opposite wall opened to right and left reclosing of their own accord as the Winged Man passed through.

His hands clasped over his head to protect it from contact with the rough floor over which he was being dragged, Danby Druce, too weak to struggle, felt himself being pulled along a strange, dark, awful path.

Now he was dragged down a narrow flight of stairs, the thud of his falling body being greeted by peals of almost maniacal laughter from his merciless character, now along a narrow passage, the rough sides of which tore his clothes to rags, and robbed his joints of their covering of skin.

Now in an atmosphere which made breathing difficult, he was dragged, for what seemed an unending eternity, along a passage, the floor of which was dotted with pools of foul, stagnant water.

It seemed all part of some fearful dream to the half-conscious detective, from which he dreaded to awake lest even worse should befall him.

Presently a cool, refreshing breath of fresh air told that the end of their journey was approaching. Then, more dead than alive, Danby Druce breathed a deep sigh of relief as the onward movement ceased, and, looking up, he found himself lying in the centre of the bed of rushes, with the bright, unclouded morning sun above his head. Everything around tended to soothe the horrid nightmare he had experienced.

A VAIN ATTEMPT.

For some minutes Danby Druce lay fighting against the deadly faintness that was creeping over him. Clean living and an iron constitution at length prevailed. Conquering the vertigo which caused his brain to swim, he leaned upon one elbow and gazed wonderingly around him. He was alone in a narrow circle of rank-growing reeds.

"The Winged Man thinks me unconscious and has left me unguarded; I must escape ere he returns," was the one thought ever in Danby Druce's brain.

Aching in every joint, the great detective struggled to a sitting position, then, on hands and knees, moved in the direction which he knew must lead to more open ground.

Alas! Barely had he crawled, a pain accompanying each movement, a dozen feet ere he found himself sinking into the soft, stinking mire. With difficulty extricating himself, he returned to the spot where he had first been, then, painfully, but with constantly increasing strength, sought to find some path of escape from his open, yet strongly guarded prison.

East, west, north, and south, in every point of the compass, he sought some way of escape. It was in vain. At last, a feeling of deep despair gnawing at his heart, he dropped, deathly weary, on to the trampled rushes. As he did so he was conscious of the fact that the ground upon which he lay was harder and more level than that he had previously trodden.

With frenzied haste he threw the bush rushes aside, and a flood of hope for a moment almost robbed him of the power to move as he beheld an iron trapdoor let into the carefully hidden brickwork on a level with the ground.

Here, then, was the entrance to the subterranean passage through which he had been dragged, and here lay his sole chance of escape. Attached to the trapdoor was a large iron ring. This Danby Druce grasped with his hands, tugging violently as he tried to raise the floor. It resisted his efforts, yet gave sufficiently to induce further endeavours.

Dropping for a moment on the ground, he lay to recover strength; then, with tightly empressed lips, his brave heart beating with determination to raise the trapdoor or burst a bloodvessel, he seized the ring once more.

A wild, almost hysterical shout of triumph burst from his lips when he felt the door rise slowly upwards on its hinges. It seemed strangely heavy, exactly as though it was being dragged down by some heavy weight upon the other side. Yet, realising that before him lay the only path to safety, Danby Druce put his strength into the task before him.

Wider and wider grew the opening until at length, his head bowed between his arms, Danby Druce drew the door over its centre and allowed it to fall backwards upon the reeds.

A loud, despairing cry of bitter disappointment burst from his lips. Rising slowly from the opening, a smile of fiendish malice hanging over his pale, bloodless face, the Winged Man appeared enframed in the square opening he had been at such pains to uncover.

Danby Druce, his hands clasped despairingly to his forehead, staggered back whilst the weird horror hovered above the opening, his evil face showing how keenly he enjoyed his foe's discomfiture.

"I thank you, Danby Druce," he said mockingly. "I have worked hard and quickly since we parted last. I was weary, and you saved me the trouble of opening the trapdoor."

Robbed for a moment of power to speak, to move, conscious only of a feeling of deep, unutterable despair, Danby Druce stood gazing in dismay upon the being who seemed to have the power to appear whenever his presence was least desired.

Again the Winged Man spoke.

"Listen, Danby Druce. You know that the Winged Man ever keeps his word. I have sought to break your proud spirit, to humble your pride in the dust, to avenge the wrongs you have inflicted upon me. Yet I am in a lenient mood. Kneel at my feet, swear to be my dog, my slave for life, and the tide may yet advance up the Humber, roaring in vain for the victim I have promised it."

"Never!"

The word came in clear, though low, gasping accents from the dauntless detective's lips.

"You lie, Danby Druce, you lie! Ere the tide laps the high water mark, you will, of your own accord, have agreed to my demands," cried the Winged Man, in loud, thunderous accents.

°A FIENDISH CONTRIVANCE.

A paroxysm of fury shook the Winged Man's frame. With a shriek of rage he flung himself savagely upon the detective.

Danby Druce gave himself up for lost. But instead of tearing him limb from limb, he seized him in a resistless grasp, and bore him as a hawk would a pigeon over the tops of the swaying rushes to where, in a deep channel, between huge banks of mud, the Winged Man had erected a stout post, five feet in height, with a cross-piece on the top.

At the end of one cross-piece was a brass disc, glistening in the sun. At the bottom of the post, was what looked like a black box, with two similar boxes above, each added distance of about two feet from the other. As they drew nearer, Danby Druce noticed a number of wires hanging loosely from the post.

Disdaining to engage in a useless struggle, Danby Druce and allowed the Winged Man to bind his body to the post. This done, the Winged Man remained poised a few minutes upon the muddy bottom of the tidal channel, as he gazed upon his foe, with looks rendered horrible by the cruel, malicious satisfaction which gleamed from his eyes.

"Do you realise what your fate will be, Danby Druce?" he asked at length, rubbing his thin, talon-like hands in gloating delight.

"A child could tell. You intend that I should perish a slow death by the rising tide. It is worthy of you, Winged Man, worthy of your mean, despicable, revengeful nature.

° 2 MAY 1913.

Loud laughed the Winged Man.

"Partly right, partly wrong, Danby Druce!" he replied. "Still, if your death is your portion, it will be of your own choosing. Press the brass button near your left hand, and your life will be saved, but mind, by so doing, you will acknowledge me as your lord and master."

"When I do so, Winged Man, then, and then only can you claim lordship over me," was Danby Druce's calm, dignified response.

"Look, the tide approaches! I leave you, and if the racking pain, which will soon distort your limbs, leave you power to think remember how your death will leave Mary Evanson at my mercy!"

With this last cruel stab into his prisoner's heart, the Winged Man soared over the waste of mud bank towards his rush-covered lair.

Facing the oncoming tide, Danby Druce saw the waters, heralded by tiny waves, drawing nearer and nearer. As one fascinated he marked the tide approach, and the sun beat fiercely down upon his unprotected body.

Slowly and relentlessly the tide arose, until at length he felt the waves breaking over his feet. The water covered his ankles, then an ejaculation of astonishment burst from his lips. A fierce tingling sensation thrilled his frame. Another, and another shock followed. Instinctively he looked down at the box by his side.

It was covered with water. Like a flash the truth burst upon him. Within the box was an electric battery, the chemicals in which was stirred into action by contact with the water.

As yet the shots were of a comparatively gentle nature, and invigorated his greatly-tired frame rather than inflicted pain. Higher and higher rose the tide.

With difficulty the detective repressed a cry of pain as the flooding of the second battery sent shocks flashing in quick succession through his frame.

A deadly terror gripped his soul. He understood now what the Winged Man's fiendishly ingenious torture meant. What he now endured was well-nigh unbearable. What would it be when the rising water set the third battery to work?

With every shock that shook his frame, his writhing limbs were cut by the tightly-twisted ropes which bound him to the post, and he almost longed for the time to come when the increased electric shock would render his soul from its habitation of clay in one fierce, irresistible spasm.

AT THE ELEVENTH HOUR.

As Danby Druce's wild, yearning eyes gazed around the bleak, monotonous mudbanks and the grey stretch of water took on a new beauty, for they represented to him life and all that makes life worth living.

Then, his body twitching as one suffering from St. Vitus' dance,[43] he glanced at the cruel flood mounting inch by inch up his body.

For a moment his eyes wandered to the brass switch within reach of his hand. An almost irresistible longing to buy relief from his suffering at the expense of his freedom filled Danby Druce's heart.

The next moment he banished the unworthy thoughts from his mind. Again and again his hand moved towards the switch, which seemed to have a peculiar fascination of its own, and lest his weakened frame should be tempted to buy release at so fearful a price he turned his head resolutely away.

Higher and higher mounted the insidious, death-dealing tide. Suddenly a convulsion not caused by the constantly, recurring electric shocks which were torturing his frame, agitated water round the great detective's half-covered body.

A loud, wild shriek—it could scarcely be called a shout, burst from his lips as a patrol-launch containing two men swept by the entrance to the now partly-filled channel.

With scarce beating heart Danby Druce saw the men in the launch look towards him. The next moment they disappeared, as the boat swept behind one of the miniature mountains of mud towering to right and left of him.

A cry of despair rose from the great detective. He had been seen, his situation unrecognised, and left to die.

But no! As the bitter thought swept through his throbbing brain, the launch, her gunwale almost under the water, so swiftly had she been turned, circled round, and the next moment was headed swiftly towards the imperilled man.

"Quick, quick! If the water touches the box beneath my shoulder you will come too late!" shouted Danby Druce frantically.

The launch was cutting her way through the water at a good twenty knots an hour but already the tide had more than lapped the bottom of the fatal box.

---

[43] Sydenham's chorea (chorea minor), a disorder characterised by jerking movements affecting the face, hands and feet.

Would they be in time or would he be slain as though by a lightning-flash at the very moment his rescuers stretched out their hands to save him?

A new danger presented itself in vivid colours before his eyes as he noted the high wave hurled from the swiftly-advancing stem of the launch—a wave that would sweep over the box, and sent the dread current through a frame already heavily charged with electricity.

"Slow down—for the love of heaven, slow down!" he shrieked.

But the men in the boat—the uniform proclaimed them sailors—deeming that he feared lest they should run into him, only smiled, and waved their hands encouragingly. In fact, the engines had been cut off some minutes before, and the boat was being carried on by its own momentum.

At length, the taller of the two men in the launch hastened to the bows, and dexterously thrust his boat hook into the top of the post.

Even as he did so the eddying water swirled over the detective's head, and a half-suffocated, irrepressible shriek of agony burst from Danby Druce's lips, for a more awful electric shock than any he had yet experienced swept through his frame.

The limit of human endurance had been reached, and those in the boat uttered ejaculation is of alarm as they saw the livid face of the man they strove to save hanging upon his breast.

Leaning forward, the taller of the two men, who was clad in a naval officer's undress-uniform, whilst his comrade bore upon his arm the insignia of a warrant-officer of the Navy, thrust his arm around Danby Druce's body.

He drew back with a cry of alarm, and nearly tumbled headfirst into the water as a fierce electric shock shook his frame.

Astounded though he was, the lieutenant did not pause to find out whence the mysterious shock had come, but, rushing to a locker near the launch's engine, he returned with a pair of nippers, with which, careless of the shocks which swept up his arm, he severed the wires.

It was now the work of a few minutes to release the unconscious detective, and draw him into the boat; then the launch's head was turned towards the mainstream of the Humber.

Barely had they left the fatal post hundred feet behind them ere the warrant-officer, leaning forward from the tiller, touched the lieutenant, who was trying to restore Danby Druce to consciousness, on the arm and jerked his thumb over his shoulder.

His face was deathly pale. Following the direction of his subordinate's staring eyes the lieutenant felt the blood for a moment rush from his heart as a wild, terror-inspiring, awful cry of rage burst upon his ears, and he saw rising from the reed-covered shore the fearful, ominous form of the Winged Man.

So unexpected, so fearful was the appearance of the weird horror that, stout hearted sailor though he was, the warrant-officer nearly allowed the tiller to slip from his hand.

But the next moment he had seized it in a firmer grasp, and increased the sparking of the engines to the utmost, with the result that the launch—a patrol-boat attached to a cruiser anchored in the Humber—seemed literally to glide over the water, so quickly did she fly.

Then the race began! Where would it finish? How would it end?

DESPITE SHOT AND SHELL.

Swiftly though the patrol-boat flew, the Winged Man, beating the air with his mighty pinions, soon hovered immediately above her.

"Surrender your prisoner! It is the Winged Man who commands!" thundered the dread being, as he hovered, like an eagle above its prey, over the boat.

"A British officer obeys no commands but those of his superior and his King!" replied the lieutenant dauntlessly.

With a cry of rage the Winged Man swooped down upon the man who had the temerity to defy him; but though he had left his sword on board, a more effective weapon lay ready to the young officer's hand.

Seizing a long, spiked boathook which lay over the bows, he held it pointed upwards towards the Winged Man.

A feeling of exultation swept through his heart as he saw the Winged Man descending like a falling stone upon its sharp point.

It was not until almost too late that the Winged Man saw his danger, then swerved aside just in time to avoid the officer's weapon.

With a cry of baffled rage the Winged Man darted, with lightning speed, to right, to left, in front, behind his agile foe.

In vain. From whichever point he prepared to charge, he found the long-handled iron forbidding his advance, whilst every beat of her swiftly-revolving screws was carrying the launch towards where, still but a dark speck on the broad expanse of waters of the Humber estuary, the cruiser lay at anchor.

Suddenly the Winged Man soared aloft, apparently abandoning the strife.

Pausing to draw his hand across his heated brow, the lieutenant saw him dart off at fearful speed in the direction of a large barge beating its way seaward against the wind.

The barge was about half a mile ahead of the launch, yet the loud shrieks of terror which arose from its crew, as they hurled themselves overboard at the Winged Man's approach, reached the lieutenant's ears.

Then he saw the flying monster alight upon the barge's deck, grasp something grey in both hands, and rise as easily as though he had been carrying a pebble from the shore instead of one of the heavy stones with which the barge was loaded.

A few minutes later the Winged Man hovered once more over the launch, its huge square block of stone held in his strong, iron grasp.

"For the last time! Will you surrender my victim?" he demanded.

"Never!" came in brave defiance from the young lieutenant's lips.

"Then die!" hissed the Winged Man, as he released his hold of the stone, which fell straight towards the launch.

With a dexterous twist of the tiller the steersman saved the frail craft from destruction, yet so close fill the huge stone to its stern that the boat's occupants were drenched with the spray the slab cast up as it entered the water.

He hovered over the launch grasping a huge block of stone.

Answering the sailor's triumphant cries with a mocking laugh, the Winged Man darted back to the barge, returning shortly after with a second and larger stone.

But even as he did so, a dull, sullen roar, accompanied by a burst of smoke from the cruiser's side, showed that her crew had awakened to the danger that beset their launch. A few seconds later a shell from a quick-firer hurtled, shrieking, past the Winged Man.

Again the stone fell, and again the warrant-officer skilfully avoided the falling missile.

Careless of the constant succession of shells from the cruiser's quick-firer that hurtled around him, the Winged Man, skimming over the water like a swallow, flew between the launch and the barge, dropping stone after stone, in vain endeavours to sink her.

Suddenly the vicious hiss of rifle-bullets singing in the flying terror's ears warned him of a new element of danger. Looking in the direction from whence the shots came, he saw that four launches, filled with rifle armed sailors, had left the cruiser's side, and were rushing to their comrades' assistance.

Yet it was not until a shell exploded so close against him that, but for the slab of stone he was carrying it must have blown even the Winged Man to pieces, did the weird winged monster abandon the chase, and, with fearful shrieks of rage and loud-voiced threats of vengeance, fly slowly, as though scorning the bullets and shells sent after him, in the direction of the land.

It was not until the Winged Man was a mere speck in the distance that the captain of the cruiser ordered the firing to cease.

By that time Danby Druce was safe on board the cruiser, and being slowly brought back to life by the ship's surgeon.

THE FLYING MAGNET.

Barely had the excitement consequent upon the appearance of the Winged Man settled down ere the ship's crew were once more aroused to a state of activity by a wireless telegraphic message to the effect that the Crimea was to sail northward without a moment's delay.

None but the captain knew the meaning of this sudden order, for it had been given out that the Crimea would be anchored in the Humber for several days.

The fact was that a foreign man-o'-war was cruising suspiciously near the British coast, and, though the public seldom hear of it, even a foreign boat does not appear in British waters without one of the British "bulldogs" who guard our shores being at hand, if out of sight.

Within an hour of the Admiral's order having been received on board the Crimea, she had rounded Spurn Head with Danby Druce still on board, for there was no time to send him onshore, and, as it happened, none but outward-bound vessels were in sight.

It is true Captain Dorkins offered to place his passenger on board one of these; but, on learning that the Crimea would keep near the coast, Danby Druce, who thanks to an iron constitution, was rapidly recovering from his unpleasant experience at the Winged Man's hands, decided to remain, for he made sure that the Winged Man was bound for his eyrie on the Yorkshire coast.

But it soon became evident that the Winged Man had not finished with his detective foe, for when, towards evening, still a bit shaky about the legs, but drawing in fresh strength with every breath of fresh, cool, sea air, Danby Druce came on deck he saw floating immediately above the cruiser a tiny black speck, which he immediately recognised as the Winged Man.

To one less generously endowed with courage, the fearful persistency with which the weird horror followed him would have filled his heart with terror.

Not so Danby Druce. He rejoiced that the Winged Man was near, for, thanks to his power of flight, Danby Druce knew that he could never come in touch with his terrible foe unless he put himself voluntary within his reach.

Again and again Danby Druce glanced upwards, each time to find that ominous moving speck above his head.

Fearful of betraying the fact that he was discovered to the Winged Man, Danby Druce refrained from pointing out his arch foe to the captain, who had courteously invited him on to the bridge.

Swiftly the magnificent warships sped northward, until at length the gathering shades of night enclosed her on every side.

Although he knew that nothing would be easier than for the Winged Man to swoop down upon him if he remained on deck, Danby Druce scored the thought of seeking safety below. But his fingers were ever clasped tightly round the butt-end of his revolver as he awaited the Winged Man's attack.

The moon had sunk beneath the horizon plunging the world in darkness, when the same mysterious tremors, which he had so often experienced before, warned Danby Druce that the Winged Man had approached nearer the ship. Yet nothing happened, and Danby Druce had already approached the officer in charge to bid him "Good-night!" when the lieutenant held up his hand saying:

"Hush! What is that?"

At the same time he glanced anxiously at the compass, breathing a sigh of relief when he found the ship was still keeping true to her course.

"What was it? I had nothing save the continual beat of the engines," replied Danby Druce.

"I thought I heard the sound of waves beating on the shore. Strange, I never remember to have been deceived like this before. Yet it is impossible—"

He ceased speaking as from the bows came the ominous cry:

"Breakers ahead!"

"Where?" he asked as he issued a rapid order.

"Straight over our bows, sir!" came the immediate response, the speaker's tones tinged with alarm.

"Full-speed stern!" commanded the navigating lieutenant adding, as he turned to the midshipman on duty: "Switch on the electric light, Mr. Hawtrey."

A moment later the bright beams of the cruiser's searchlight blazed forth illuminating a frowning, precipitous cliff, beneath which was a white line of surf within a cable's length of the doomed vessel.

Fearful through their peril, Danby Druce had no eyes for aught but the fearful form of the Winged Man, who, flying backwards, was holding before him a huge electric magnet, with which he held the needle of the compass in one direction, and had thus lured the cruiser to her doom.

In a stride Danby Druce was at the Marine sentry's side, in another he had snatched the man's rifle from his hands, and fired point-blank at the weird horror.

A spasmodic movement of the Winged Man's distended leg showed that the hastily-aimed bullet had touched him.

With a shriek of rage the Winged Man dropped the magnet into the sea. Immediately the compass resumed its proper direction showing that the ship, instead of preceding due north had been, owing to the Winged Man's fiendishly ingenious plot, steaming nearly west.

Then, like a stone from a catapult, the Winged Man launched himself upon

Danby Druce, who, with a brave, defiant laugh, dropped from the upper bridge to the cruiser's superstructure, just in time to avoid the Winged Man's fearful swoop.

Though in the presence of the weird horror himself, the lieutenant did not for a moment lose his self-control.

Immediately the alarm was given, the men piped to quarters, and all that human skill could do was done to avert disaster.

Enraged at the escape of he whom he had thought to have secured, the Winged Man uttered his weird, angry shriek, and started in pursuit.

It was touch and go, for, just as Danby Druce sprang at a single jump down the stairs leading into the officers' quarters, the Winged Man was close behind him.

For the time being Danby Druce was saved. A body of officers and men, rushing on deck in response to the alarm, intervened between and pursued and pursuer.

At the same moment, with a rending, sickening crash, the cruiser trembled from truck to keel as she grounded upon the rocky shore.

At first she floated off, but for the second time, with an even greater violence than the first, she struck hard and fast upon the rockbound coast.

BEYOND THE WATERTIGHT DOORS.

As the cruiser grounded, Danby Druce, having secured a revolver, returned on deck.

Perched on the warship's masthead, closing over the mischief he had wrought, the Winged Man showed black against the white face of the cliff, for the cruiser had run aground at a spot where there was deep water close to the shore.

The wild, blood-curdling yell with which the Winged Man greeted his enemy's reappearance attracted the captain's attention, who had hitherto been unconscious of the fearsome presence which, like a wrecker of old, had lured the cruiser to her doom.

A sharp, short word of command, and a body of Marines opened a brisk fire upon the Winged Man.

Whether enraged at being driven from the mast, or struck by a chance bullets, Danby Druce could not tell, but with a fierce, reverberating yell the Winged Man darted from off the masthead, and circling in the air, disappeared in the darkness above them.

His every nerve on the alert, Danby Druce watched the gallant tars darting hither and thither, yet with as perfect discipline and freedom from bustle as though the ship was still sailing on a level keel over the deep blue sea.

Suddenly Danby Druce started, and, his pale face turned heavenward, stood ready to repel his fearful foe, who, shrieking with rage and hate, was descending through the clear, starlit air straight towards where he stood, evidently with the intention of bearing him prisoner to his lair on that rockbound coast.

When his flying foe was within a hundred feet of the deck, Danby Druce opened fire; but, skilled shot though he was, he was aiming at an almost impossible mark, for even as he took aim, with an almost imperceptible movement of his wings, the Winged Man would glide to right or left, and allow the bullet to whistle past him, mockingly numbering each shot as it was fired.

"One—two—three—four—five—six!" he cried. The last word ended in a shriek of malevolent triumph as he added: "Now, Danby Druce, your weapon empty, you are at my mercy!"

But the Winged Man had reckoned without the officer in charge of the Marines.

The officer had not a moment in which to decide how to act, yet, placing himself, with uplifted sword, by Danby Druce's side, the single order, "Form rallying square!" burst from his lips.

The next moment the Marines had clustered round their officer and the detective, their glistening bayonets forming a canopy of steel through which the Winged Man could not pass.

So unexpected was the Marines' action that it was only by a hair's-breadth that the Winged Man escaped impaling himself upon the soldiers' bayonets.

But though the wind borne by the sweep of his mighty pinions swept over the faces of Danby Druce and his gallant guards, the Winged Man's wondrous presence of mind saved him, and, gliding between the davits of the starboard lifeboat, he plunged like a discharged torpedo into the sea.

Afterwards the men who had witnessed the Winged Man's plunge declared that hissing steam arose from the spot into which he had fallen.

But those on board the Crimea had no time for further thought of the weird being who had already made them pay so dearly for daring to succour the man he hated.

Calm, resolute, undaunted, though upon his shoulders lay the responsibility of seven hundred lives, Captain Dorkins gave the order: "full-speed astern!"

Immediately the mighty iron structure trembled beneath the fierce pull of her triple screws. For a moment the vessel trembled; then, as her screws gripped the water, she glided swiftly from off the rock.

For nearly five minutes a deathly silence obtained throughout the ship. Would her water-tight compartments hold, or with the sea, rushing through the jagged wound the rock had made, drag her beneath the surface?

Suddenly the question was answered by a rousing cheer as the cruiser drew, stern foremost, further and further from the shore.

At that moment a carpenter's mate hastened to where Danby Druce was standing, still surrounded by Marines.

"Beg your pardon, sir, the chief carpenter's compliments, and will you come below," said the man, saluting.

Wondering why this message had been sent to him, a civilian, Danby Druce complied.

He found the chief carpenter and two of his subordinates in a store-room beneath the men's quarters. They were leaning with their ears pressed against a watertight door, which had saved the cruiser from destruction.

Despite the fact that had the door given they would have been immediately overwhelmed by the inrushing flood, without a chance or even hope of escape, these three brave men, ready to give up their lives at the call of duty, as British sailors ever are, had stationed themselves in this lowermost cabin to watch the door upon which the lives of all depended.

Without a word, the chief carpenter signed Danby Druce to listen.

The next moment the great detective's ear was pressed against the iron door. Above the swishing whirl of the water was heard the ominous sound of a swiftly-moving brace, boring its way into the iron plates. He knew that, separated from him only by the iron door, the Winged Man was boring away the iron rivets of the protecting shield that the waters might burst through and flood the cruiser.

A LIFE WELL LOST.

"Well?" asked the chief carpenter, as Danby Druce withdrew his head from the water-tight door.

"It is he! It is the Winged Man!" declared Danby Druce, and a shudder shook for a moment even the death-defying hearts of his heroes. "No other being could live and work in the flooded ship's bottom."

"Yes, yes; I know!" gasped the carpenter, breathless with the horror of the threatened danger. "But what can we do to save the ship and our mess mates?"

"Nothing!" replied Danby Druce, in accents of despairing determination. Then he paused, adding, in a hurried whisper, lest even through the thick iron the Winged Man should hear what he said: "but we may avenge them!"

Immediately aft of the compartment in which they stood was a magazine where the loaded heads of the torpedoes were stored.

Acting under Danby Druce's orders, one of these death-dealing instruments of warfare was placed near the watertight door, in such a way that when the water burst it open it should fall upon the torpedo head, and, exploding, blow the merciless fiend at work beyond to pieces.

This accomplished, Danby Druce, ordering the carpenters to follow, hastened on deck to tell the captain what he had done.

Captain Dorkins, the aggrieved at the inevitable destruction of his ship, realised that she would not be entirely thrown away if with her perished the dread scourge who had so long terrorised all Britain.

Obedient to the captain's orders, the sailors commenced lowering the boats, securing the ship's papers, and everything else of importance that could be saved.

The minutes dragged slowly away, yet the fearful explosion did not come. Taking his life in his hands, Danby Druce hastened below to find the watertight door still standing, and that the dread sound made by the Winged Man's tool had ceased.

THE WINGED MAN'S RETURN.

Danby Druce's surmise had been correct. It was indeed the Winged Man who, entering by the huge, gaping wound torn in the cruiser's iron hull, had sought to break down the sliding iron panel that alone kept her afloat.

But endowed with almost superhuman power though he was, the Winged Man, in common with all other breathing creatures, could not remain in that water-filled compartment for an indefinite period.

Soon his swelling lungs warned him that he must return to the surface or die.

Reluctant to leave his task of vengeance unaccomplished, the Winged Man continued to press his electric drill into the ironwork until his head and breast felt as though they would burst.

With a gesture of rage he turned to leave the ship; but he had just missed the intermittent retreat of the water, and, despite his wondrous strength, was borne so heavily back against the door on which he had been working by the incoming flood that his clenched teeth were wrenched open. Immediately the air rushed out the water rushed in, and a fearful suffocating feeling told the Winged Man that he was drowning. Yet he fought with dogged, unflinching courage against the fearful fate that threatened.

Fierce indeed was the Winged Man's fight for his life. Entombed in a flooded iron prison of his own making, the fear of death gripped his heart. Still, the rare courage which had made him the terror of a mighty kingdom caused him to continue the fight until, just when he felt his senses reeling, his lungs distended almost to bursting point, his hand grasped the splintered iron edges of the hole by which he had entered.

Another five seconds and he was gasping for breath on the surface. For some minutes he lay like a log on the water, gathering renewed strength with every breath of the cool air he drew into his sorely-tried lungs.

More determined than ever that the Crimea should not escape the fate to which he had doomed her, he allowed his feet to drop beneath the surface, and, extending his huge pinions, strove to fly after the cruiser, whose rapidly disappearing lights were by this time a mere speck in the distance.

In vain. Torn during his frantic struggle to escape from the cruiser's hold, his utmost efforts only served to whirl him round and round upon the surface of the ever-moving sea.

Gnashing his teeth with rage, beating the sea with his clenched fists, as though it was some living creature whom he sought to slay, the Winged Man gave free vent to the baffled rage which filled his heart.

Soon his furious, unreasoning rage burned itself out, and he lay upon the surface of the sea as helpless as a wounded gull, waiting, with sullen impatience for the tide to carry him shorewards. He was in no danger of sinking. Making use of the many secrets his mighty brain and keen research had wrenched from Nature, he had learned to make his body as buoyant on the sea as in the air.

Just as the rising sun cast its reddened beams across the horizon, a fisherman, half dozing over the tiller as he sailed before a favouring breeze homeward with his night's catch, almost let go his hold of the tiller as his eyes fell upon a fearful, almost unearthly form seated on the summit of a large rock, jutting some fifty feet into the sea, as he watched the billows break at his feet.

It was Ghat, whom instinct had warned that the master he loved and feared was near.

Delighting in mischief, Ghat flung his long arms above his head, and laughed aloud in evil glee when he saw the terror depicted upon the fisherman's face as his boat glided past the rock. Hugging himself with delight, Ghat watched the boat until it was out of sight; then, shading his eyes with his hand, gazed apparently straight into the round, glowing orb of the rising sun.

The next moment, with a cry of joy, he rose to his feet, and, springing headlong from the rock, swam with incredible swiftness towards where the Winged Man, borne on the swift-rushing tide, was sleeping as peacefully as a child in his cot. Without arousing the sleeper, Ghat dived beneath the Winged Man, and, taking his still sleeping master on his shoulders, swam with him to where the waves rolled, foaming and roaring, into a low cave at the foot of the beetling cliff.

As Ghat gained a rocky platform within the cave the Winged Man awoke. Repaying the faithful servitor's gentle care with a blow which stretched him well-nigh senseless on the rocky floor of the cave, he rose to his feet, and strode along a torturous passage which led to his lair; whilst Ghat, picking himself up, followed his cruel taskmaster in uncomplaining silence.

A FEARFUL RESOLVE.

Within one of the many caves of which the Winged Man's Yorkshire lair consisted the weird horror slept, hanging head downwards from the dome-shaped roof. It was indeed a wondrous bed-room this cave in the heart of the Yorkshire cliff.

The rough, uneven walls remained as Nature had left them, save that every angle, every jutting crag, had been covered with a layer of sheet-gold.

Roof, floor, walls were all hidden by the same precious metal, until it seemed as though the Winged Man slept in a mine of solid gold. Though endowed with a power of going a week on end without sleep, when the Winged Man closed his eyes it was often days, perchance weeks, before he opened them again.

For three days the Winged Man slept, then awoke, refreshed in body and mind, and ready for any act of desperate evil that might suggest itself to him.

Then something happened which once more clouded his keen, active brain with the partial madness with which despair and grief had overwhelmed it on the day of his interrupted marriage.

Dropping from the pocket, in which he had carried it ever since he had met Mary Evanson, a photograph of the woman who had stirred the Winged Man's heart to love lay, face upwards, upon the floor, and was thus the first thing the Winged Man's eyes fell upon when he awoke.

Immediately the memory of all Danby Druce had robbed him of filled his heart with unbearable misery.

With a wild, piercing, bitter cry of despair, he dropped to the ground. His face, which on awakening had been calm and immovable as that of a statue, was now contorted with almost maniacal grief.

A wild, bitter cry of "Lost, lost, lost!" burst from his lips. In a single bound the Winged Man reached the curtain of cloth-of-gold which hid the entrance to his gilded cave.

Then, with wildly gesticulating arms and heartrending moans, he sped along passage after passage towards the open air. Presently Ghat, hearing his master's cries, hastened on the scene.

One glance at the Winged Man's terrible face, and, shrieking with terror, the dwarf turned and fled. But barely had he taken a dozen strides ere the Winged Man was upon him, bearing him to the floor as though he would tear him limb from limb.

A glimpse of the blue sky and restless sea through the semi-circular entrance to the cave changed the Winged Man's purpose. With a fearful, blood-curdling laugh, that chilled Ghat's blood within his veins, the Winged Man bore him, a limp, unresisting mass of deformed humanity, to the rocky ledge at the mouth of the cave.

Raising the deformed body above his head, the Winged Man hurled him into the roaring waves a hundred feet beneath. Instinct taught the dwarf to protect his head with outstretched hands. Down he plunged deeper, almost to the bottom of the sea; then, striking wildly out, rose to the surface, and, whimpering with terror, swam shorewards.

His rage increased rather than diminished by this last act of unnecessary cruelty, the Winged Man spread his black pinions, and, beating the air with swift, regular movements of his mighty wings, flew in a north-easterly direction.

A fearful resolve urged him on. Within his bosom beat a thousand wild, fierce passions. Within reach of his aerial flight was a spot, dark and forbidding, where he knew—for he had often hovered over it at certain times—Nature gave a fearful exhibition of the mighty power she wielded.

Many a time had the Winged Man contemplated the dread maelstrom, which for countless ages had been looked upon with superstitious dread by the hardy Norwegian sailors. He had longed to plunge into its depths and explore its hidden horrors, to find whither the engulfed water flowed.

His tortured spirit craved for an adventure which would bring him face to face with the death he scorned, yet had never braved.

A few hours later, smiling beneath a clear, unclouded sky, the Loffoden

Islands[44] lay before him. Slower and slower grew the beat of his mighty pinions. His goal was reached. At present the sleeping quarters looked no different to the boundless expanse of sea on either side but one. Yet he knew that a few hours would change that peaceful stream into a wild, indescribably horrible vortex of raging water.

Poised in mid-air, above the centre of the dread, though now sleeping maelstrom, the Winged Man awaited its awakening.

WITHIN THE MAELSTROM.

It was a fair scene. A stranger ignorant of its fearful character would have found it difficult to believe that he was sailing over the most dangerous and indescribably awful spot in the whole world.

Presently a dark speck was seen swimming from one of the islands which dotted the sea towards the mainland. It was a bear, and the Winged Man, from his lofty eyrie amidst the clouds, laughed aloud as he realised that ere half the poor beast's journey was performed the sleeping maelstrom would awaken, and the bear be engulfed in its raging waters.

Like a stone, the Winged Man dropped to within a hundred feet of the sea, the better to watch the coming struggle between the bear and the fearful forces of Nature.

Slowly a change came over the scene. The sleeping waves seemed to wake to life, not in a long, billowy sweep of waters, but huge masses of agitated water, tossing hither and thither.

It was as though the old Norse fable was true, and beneath those waters slept Kraken and, a huge marine monster, who created the maelstrom by turning over in his sleep, as he swallowed and ejected the sea in which he slept.

As though for the first time conscious of its approaching doom, the bear lifted its shaggy shoulders out of the water and looked around, whining with terror.

Then it commenced swimming, not in a straight line as hitherto, but taking a zig-zag course, as though striving to escape the fearful downward pull which threatened to draw it to its death beneath those seething waters.

Higher and higher rose the waves, crashing against each other with a roar as of thunder, and sending spray flying almost to where the Winged Man, hovering on outstretched wings, watched the scene with breathless interest.

At first it seemed as though a hundred tides had met, each striving to force the other back. North, south, east, west, they dashed, the majesty of the scene filling even the Winged Man's breast with awe. Gradually the confused mass of water seemed to marshal itself in broken yet decided lines, then to move round and round, like the spokes of an enormous wheel, to the centre of which the unfortunate bear was swiftly drawn, until, with a loud, fearful howl of terror, it

---

[44] Lofoten, an archipelago located towards the northernmost coast of Norway between the Norwegian Sea and the Vestfjorden. Moskstraumen is one of the strongest whirlpools in the world. It is the subject of Edgar Allan Poe's short story "A Descent into the Maelström".

was sucked into the bottomless void beneath.

Swifter and swifter moved the watery wheel, until, what we may call its rim moving swifter than its hub, the centre gradually deepened.

At first the water assumed the shape of a shallow plate, then a basin, then a cup, and finally a wide, fathomless funnel of water, whilst all around, as though lashed by a mighty wind, the sea raged and roared in fearful fury.

One glance the Winged Man cast at the sun, that he might never see again; then, intent upon exploring the fearful path to which the maelstrom led, the Winged Man took in a long, deep breath, and dived headlong into the centre of the fearful vortex.

Down and down he dropped, passing on the way the broken hulls of wrecked ships, the jagged spires of which protruded from the ever-moving wall of water, whirling round at so great a pace that had they struck him his almost superhuman career would have been entered.

Down, down, down, until the Winged Man began to think that the tradition which proclaimed the maelstrom bottomless was well founded.

Presently he reached a part of the fearful funnel where his outstretched wings brushed against the revolving stream.

Then he looked up. It was a fearful, awe-inspiring sight which met his gaze. He was at the bottom of an enormous bowl of water, the sides of which glistened like glass as it circled swiftly round and downward. Above all shone the cloud-flecked Norwegian sky.

Overawed by the magnificent spectacle, the Winged Man glanced beneath him. It was, indeed, a fearful path he had set himself to explore.

Immediately at his feet the water rushed and roared through an enormous, jagged-edged chasm, leading, apparently, into the very centre of the earth.

Even as he gazed, a sudden break in the roaring water above his head caused him to look up once more. He was just in time to see the sides of the funnel rush in upon each other, shutting out the glimpse of blue sky, as they met with a sound like that of a thousand thunders.

With an ejaculation of alarm, for well he knew that if the mass of water descended upon him it would crush him to powder, the Winged Man dived headforemost into the dark chasm at his feet.

The next moment he was conscious of a sensation as though he was being pressed forward by some giant's merciless hand, and knew that the sea, held back for a time by the whirlpool, was closing in behind him.

THE SUBTERRANEAN RIVER.

There was no retreat.

He must go on, let the consequences be what they might. But no thought of retreat entered the Winged Man's head.

He had chosen this wild, this mad, this well-nigh impossible task after many years of cool reflection, and he would not give back an inch, though death itself disputed the awful path.

The fearful weight of the waters pressing him on every side robbed the Winged Man of power to do more than allow himself to be carried forward at a fearful rate.

He tried in vain to throw the beams of his lamp ahead. The water was too thick to allow its light to penetrate beyond a few feet, but it was sufficient to show him that he was surrounded on all sides by an enormous quantity of fish, swept into the chasm by the fearful whirlpool in which he had so rashly dared to thrust himself.

Onward he was carried, until his swelling lungs proclaimed that the limit of even his wondrous insurance was near.

It was not fear, but a deathless determination to live which caused the Winged Man to exert all his mighty strength to increase the pace at which he was being carried along by a skilful spiral movement that made his body perform the functions of a ship's screw.

Suddenly, with a feeling of triumph, the Winged Man realised that the pressure around his limbs was relaxing, and he knew that he must be approaching some subterranean lake in the underground world into which the waters of the maelstrom rushed.

This idea received confirmation by the fact that each moment the strong rays of his headlight pierced further and further ahead.

Then the deadly blue of everything above his head became fringed with white spray, and he knew that by rising to the surface he would be able to take in a fresh supply of greatly-needed air.

Yet for a fraction of a second he hesitated.

What if the air above this dark, unknown seal was mixed with some deadly gas? Well, he must risk it, or perish of suffocation beneath the surface.

A moment later his head and shoulders were thrust above the wildly-rushing torrent, and he could have shouted with joy as he took in a deep breath of clear, health-giving air.

A glance overhead showed that he was being carried through some mighty, subterranean cavern.

The next moment he had dived again as the water hissed and gurgled through a rocky passage. But though he was still being carried on at a great speed, his progress was slower than before, neither was the passage so long, and when he was once more able to rise to the surface, he found that at length he was able to guide himself.

Walls of rock still hemmed him in on every side, but the roof was gradually retreating from the surface of the water, until at last even the strong rays of his headlight failed to reach the dome of earth above his head.

For half an hour the torrent bore him onward with constantly slackening speed. Around him on every side played countless shoals of fish.

Presently he noticed that the fish were trying to swim against the current, as though fleeing from some fearful danger. A regular, ever-rising, ever-falling sound fell upon his ears. It was like nothing so much as the deep breathing of some enormous animal.

Louder and louder it grew the mysterious sounds. Presently even the Winged Man's fearless heart almost ceased to beat, as the rays of his lantern fell upon one of the most fearful sights the weird horror had ever seen.

Completely filling the riverbed down which the subterranean torrent rushed was what looked like a deep, red cavern, but which, as the Winged Man drew nearer, he found was nothing more nor less than the gaping mouth of some unknown, fearful monster, into which the current was bearing countless fish.

What the strange subterranean monster was the Winged Man never knew. He had only just time to see that it was like nothing so much as a gigantic whale, when he was obliged to trust to his sodden wings to bear him over its head, or be drawn down that fearful, red, gaping throat.

Never before had the Winged Man experienced so narrow an escape from a fearful death. Had he left the water a second later he must have been hurled against the repulsive creature's upper jaw.

As it was, his soaked wings scarce sufficed to carry him over a huge, bulky, uneven body, from which emanated a fearful, almost overpowering, musty smell.

Then his tired limbs refused to bear him up longer, and he fell into the sea behind the monster. Eager to put as long a distance between himself and the fearful vision as possible, he forced his way through the water as fast as his limbs could carry him.

Once more the roof seemed to descend, until at length the Winged Man was obliged to take refuge beneath the surface.

The passage through the subterranean tunnel seemed longer this time; but at length, worn out, and well-nigh spent, the Winged Man was thrown by the eddying current on to a flat rock, to which he clung, half conscious, panting, and breathless.

A FEARFUL ENCOUNTER.

Presently the Winged Man arose and gazed wonderingly about him. Where was he? What was this strange, dark, windless land in which he found himself?

To right, to left, before, behind, as far as his headlight beams could pierce, was nothing but a black, still void.

Rising on outstretched wings, he circled upwards, doubtful whether he was miles deep in the bosom of the earth, or had returned to the upper earth again.

Soon, five hundred feet from the spot where his aerial flight commenced, his pinions brushed against a solid roof of rock.

Wonder filled the Winged Man's soul, a wonder not entirely unmixed with awe, as, inclining his body forward, he descended what, for want of a better term, we must call earthwards.

A dozen feet from earth he stopped his descent; then, standing upright in the unsubstantial air, glanced hesitatingly around.

Whither should he now wend his flight?

He had entirely lost all idea of direction, yet by a loud, clear, defiant shout, as the Winged Man flew off in the way chance directed.

Onward he flew, a deep despondency, bred by his awful surroundings, weighing heavy upon his heart. He seemed to be alone in that awful under-world. A world within a world. A world such as the most imaginative writer of fiction has never dreamt of.

An hour's steady flight and he dropped to earth, to find crumbling, scorched, and blackened rocks surrounding him on every side.

Never in all his wanderings had the Winged Man's eyes alighted upon so fearful a scene of desolation.

THE REPTILE.

With an irrepressible shutter, so weird and uncanny was the deathly silence that obtained on every hand, the Winged Man continued his flight.

Presently he started and skimmed along the ground, peering ahead, as a strange, shuffling, hissing noise fell upon his ears, and an almost unbearable fœtid odour assailed his nostrils.

Strange and mysterious though the sound was, it was evidently produced by some living creature. Eager to discover to what new danger he was flying ere he was seen himself, the Winged Man cut off the current from his headlight; then, peering eagerly forward, flew on.

As he did so, the strange sound which had so puzzled him increased in volume, until he could see sufficient of the ground over which he flew to find that its character had changed.

The scorched and blackened rock had given place to a rank kind of moss, agitated as though innumerable loathsome reptiles crept beneath it.

Presently, what looked like a bank of yellowish-grey mud loomed ahead. Wondering what this strange mound could hide, the Winged Man dropped closer to the ground.

As he did so, a long, hair-covered tentacle darted upwards, and as the Winged Man rose to elude its serpentine coils, seized him by the ankles.

In vain the Winged Man beat the air with his mighty pinions. Great though his strength, he was powerless to resist that fearful downward pull.

A cry of horror burst from his lips as a second, a third, and yet a fourth loathsome arm shot out from where he now knew must be the body of some huge, fearful, subterranean monster, and wound their sinewy lengths round arms, legs, and body.

A helpless captive, yet undaunted, even by this more than earthly horror, the Winged Man was drawn struggling to the ground, whilst the huge body rose higher and higher from the crouching position in which it awaited its prey.

The bravest man that ever walked the earth might well have shrieked aloud with terror at the fearful position in which the Winged Man now found himself.

He was in the grasp of a huge creature—animal or reptile he could not determine—such as he had never imagined possible even in his wildest dreams.

The loathsome creature's body, like nothing so much as an enormous distended bladder, was supported on four legs, larger in girth than the trunk of the biggest oak.

The monster had no neck. Its fearful mouth and horn-armed nostrils seemed to form part of its hideous body.

The Winged Man ceased to struggle. If fear for a moment gripped his heart, it vanished before the insatiable curiosity of a man of science.

He knew he was in danger of immediate death, yet his only thought, his only wish, was to discover the nature of a mysterious monster, like nothing that breathes the upper air, ere he died.

He could yet move one hand. With this he switched on his headlight, then gazed in horror and amazement straight into the gaping mouth to which the fearful tentacles were dragging him. He noted the treble row of glistening teeth; he noted the round, white balls which did duty for the monster's eyes.

The Winged Man's fearful encounter with a strange monster of the Under World.

Then, ere he could take in further details of his strange captor, he was hurled backwards, whilst the monster retreated, rending the air with a fearful bellowing. So unexpected had been the Winged Man's release that naught but his quickly outstretched wings saved him from falling heavily to the ground.

With rapidly kindling anger he prepared to avenge the rough handling he had received. But how?

There was a brace of revolvers and a keen, long-bladed hunting-knife in his belt, but what would such puny weapons avail against such a foe? Yet, even though he became imprisoned in those jointless arms again, he resolved to do battle with the fearsome creature.

Keeping just beyond reach of the countless waving tentacles that seemed to form a ring round the retreating monster's body, the Winged Man flashed his light upon it, seeking some unprotected portion of its frame upon which to descend without fear of those awful coils.

To his amazement, as the light fell upon the monster's head, a loud, deep roar of pain arose from its cavernous mouth. In a moment the Winged Man realised the reason.

Born and living in darkness, it could not bear the light. Following the clumsy brute as it hastened over the moss-covered ground, with long, ungainly strides, he focused the beams of his headlight full upon its eyes.

Looking like a gigantic bank of mud, from which sprang enormous, writhing serpents, the monster came to an abrupt halt, then its loud roars turned to a strange, increasing whine of terror, as it held its fearful tentacles intertwined before its eyes.

Gloating over his enormous foe's defeat, the Winged Man remained stationary in the air, never for a moment allowing his headlight's rays to move from one of the prostrate beast's head until, one by one, the giant tentacles dropped writhing to the earth.

Then a shudder shook the monster's frame, and it was dead, slain by the Winged Man's powerful electric rays.

A cry of triumph arose to the Winged Man's lips, checked ere it found utterance by the loud beating of a thousand wings. A number of huge bat-like creatures hurtled through the air and were soon tearing at the dead monster's flesh with long, pointed jaws, armed with spike-like teeth.

Rising high above the spot where the slain monster lay, the Winged Man watched the fearful spectacle. Now and again a sharp blow on his pinions told that he had been struck by one of the many winged monsters hastening to join in the terrible feast.

The noise of the clashing beaks and the hissing sound of swiftly-moving wings was deafening, yet the Winged Man, careless of the fact that at any moment these unknown flying creatures might tear him limb from limb, watched a scene as earthly eyes have never witnessed before.

In an incredibly short space of time the bat-like creatures completed their fearful feast, leaving nothing of the monster which had so nearly slain that the Winged Man but an enormous skeleton of white, cleanly-picked bones.

Then, as suddenly as they had come, the loathsome flock disappeared. The Winged Man heard the loud beating of their wings grow faint in the distance, ere, with a final look at the monster's skeleton, he continued on his way.

THE UNDER WORLD.

Filled with an ever-increasing wonder, the Winged Man flew on. He could scarcely realise that he was miles below the earth's surface, so boundless seemed the strange, subterranean world which he alone, of all earth-bound creatures, had been privileged to visit. The thought filled him with exultation, driving out all remembrance of the bitter disappointment in love, which had driven him to face death in the heart of the maelstrom. Even Danby Druce was forgotten by the Winged Man as he flew through that dark, wondrous world.

His path was no longer illuminated by his headlight, for he realised that its light would probably frighten away the inhabitants of this strange, unexplored subterranean world. Besides, he had already discovered that it constituted a weapon against the almost sightless beings who crawled the earth beneath him.

Hour succeeded hour ere the Winged Man became conscious of a rapidly-increasing rise in the temperature of the air through which he forced his way. It was not the invigorating, dry warmth given out by the sun, but a moist, unpleasant, clammy heat, which seemed to rob his muscles of their power.

The character of the country over which he flew had also altered. Trees, the leaves of which were a strange, greyish green, arose from the moss with which the whole subterranean earth seemed covered, through which the Winged Man caught fleeting glimpses of weird, strangely-shaped, horrible creatures, greyish yellow colour of the monster he had first encountered.

Soon he became conscious of a dull light, like the sun rising on a stormy morning, before him. Brighter and brighter grew this strange illumination, until the whole land was flooded with a bright glare as though from an enormous fire. Suddenly the Winged Man checked his onward flight, and gazed at what looked like a beehive-shaped heart immediately beneath him. Then he felt the blood course swiftly through his veins with excitement, as he realised that he was looking down upon the habitation of an unknown inhabitant of the centre of the earth.

Presently a figure emerged from an opening in the hut. Could that thing be a man? It walked on two legs, it is true, and possessed arms and a head, but the arms reached almost to the ground, and was so lean as to look like spider's legs rather than a human being's limbs. Its head was a complete oval, whilst the nose was represented by two round orifices, on either side of which, peering from two narrow slits appeared a pair of small, bead-like eyes.

The creature's head was totally destitute of hair, and its skin—for it wore no clothes so far as the Winged Man could see was a dull, livid grey.

Barely had the Winged Man taken the above in ere the man—for it evidently was some kind of human being—glanced upwards, saw the Winged Man, then, with a cry of terror, dashed into his hut; and the Winged Man, eager to explore that strange country further, continued on his way.

Brighter and brighter grew the yellow glare; and warmer and more oppressive the heavy air.

Throwing off the feeling of fatigue that was sweeping over him, the Winged Man continued his onward flight. The character of the country had again changed. The forest had given place to fields, in which a number of the strange beings like the man who had emerged from the woodland hut were engaged in agricultural occupations—ploughing with roughly-made ploughs, drawn by a small, long-snouted animals, resembling tapirs, rather than the horses or oxen of the upper world.

As the Winged Man flew onward the country became more thickly populated, and traversed by roads, along which rolled quaintly-shaped vehicles drawn by many different kinds of animals. At length his way was barred by a small range of rugged, but low, mountains pierced by numerous passes, through which a constant stream of people, in carriages and on foot, were fleeing, now and again casting frightened glances at the winged figure overhead.

BY THE RIVER OF FIRE.

Upon the highest peak of the subterranean mountains the Winged Man alighted, and gazed in wonder about the strange scene spread out before his eyes. Beneath him flowed a broad, swiftly-flowing river, a river such as human eyes had never gazed upon before. It was a river of fire, from which now and again spears of lurid flame shot through the damp, moist air.

Upon the banks of this awful subterranean stream stood a large city, its numerous buildings dyed a hundred different colours by the ever-flickering light of the rivers of fire.

For a few minutes the Winged Man hesitated; then, springing from the rocky platform upon which he stood, winged his flight towards the city. As the Winged Man approached the tall, greystone walls which encircled this wondrous under-world city, amazement that any living creature could bear the fearful heat which drew huge beads of perspiration from his opening pores as he flew, filled his heart.

He had often plunged unharmed through fire which would have shrivelled the flesh off the bones of an ordinary human being, but even he could scarce breathe in this fearful, stifling heat. Yet the sight of thousands of the strange inhabitants of this wonderful country moving without the slightest difficulty through the streets caused him to persevere in his laborious flight.

What such beings could do surely the Winged Man could accomplish! Yet, when within a hundred yards of the city wall, even the Winged Man could stand no more, and realising that at any cost his weakened frame must have rest, he glided swiftly earthwards.

Suddenly a shiver shook his frame. He felt as though he had passed from a boiling hot bath into icy cold water. A minute later he was standing on the solid ground, shivering from head to foot, and looking around him in a bewildered stare.

For some minutes he stood gasping as he gazed around, seeking to discover the meaning of this sudden change.

Then the truth was borne in upon him.

The heat from the river of fire rose to the mighty, rocky roof above his head, leaving the air nearer the ground hot, but breathable.

Barely had the Winged Man come to this conclusion ere the measured beat of running feet caused him to look up. The city gate near which he had come to earth had been thrown open, and file upon file of disciplined men, with strangely-shaped weapons in their hands were upon him.

The Winged Man's first impulse was to draw his revolver and defend himself to the end; but as his eyes took in the overwhelming numbers of his foes, he realised the hopelessness of resistance.

Drawing himself to his full height, he advanced to meet the soldiers, who, uttering cries in a tongue the Winged Man could not understand, flung themselves upon him, bore him to the earth, and bound him with a rope made of a strange, wire-like grass.

Helpless in his captors' hands, the Winged Man then was escorted into the strangest city he had ever seen. It was laid out in painfully-straight streets, rendered hideous by the fact that no opening pierced the walls of the houses, save low, narrow doors.

Throughout the whole city there was not the slightest attempt at ornamentation of any kind. The crowd who thronged the streets were clad alike in a kind of coarse, grey, closely-fitting tights.

The very soldiers wore no uniform, and the officers were only distinguished from the rank and file by superior height.

All was drab, grey, and depressing, until passing through a pair of double doors into a huge building standing in the centre of a large square, the Winged Man found himself in the presence of a strange being, who was evidently the king of this wondrous city.

Here some slight attempt decoration had been made, whilst the large, bloated figure seated upon a raised stone chair in the centre of a big pillared hall wore a plain gold circle round his head, from the centre of which blazed an enormous ruby.

On either side of the strange monarch's throne stood a number of figures clad in black tights dashed by yellow marks, evidently intended to represent flames, whom the Winged Man rightly supposed to be priests.

A fierce, angry light flashing from his bead-like eyes, the king, speaking, addressed the Winged Man in shrill, angry tones.

When the king ceased speaking, one of the priests stepped forward, and, saluting the throne with a low bow made a long, tedious speech.

The whole proceedings began to drag terribly so far as the Winged Man was concerned. Tired out with his long journey in the interior of the earth, he interrupted the priest's speech with a loud yawn.

Evidently the Winged Man had been guilty of a great breach of court etiquette, for the king rose angrily from his throne, the priest ceased speaking, and soldiers and courtiers turned with flashing eyes and half-raised weapons upon the Winged Man, who, bound though he was, gazed upon the sea of angry faces with a contemptuous smile, then opened his mouth in a second yawn.

With an angry gesture the king issued some orders to his soldiers. Immediately the Winged Man was forced on his knees, whilst one, evidently the executioner, stepped up behind the prisoner and raised a huge, knotted iron club above his head, and was about to dash out the daring yawner's brains, when a tall, gaunt priest stepped forward, and, turning to the king, said something in a tone of haughty command.

A prisoner in the Under World.

As the priest spoke the Winged Man felt the hands which held him shudder, a deadly power crept over the faces of those around him, and he fancied he detected a look of pity in their small, bead-like eyes.

A long, and at times, heated argument ensued between the tall priest and the occupant of the throne. Eventually the priest's argument prevailed, and some half-hour later the Winged Man was led from the palace towards a group of buildings at the further end of the city. Evidently this place was a temple or monastery, for, as they approached, the gates were thrown open, and a number of flame-bedecked priests issued forth, who, lining the streets, bowed low as the cavalcade passed between their ranks.

THE WINGED MAN'S REVENGE.

Presently the Winged Man found himself in a small room where a substantial meal of strangely-flavoured meat, tepid water, and a coarse kind of bread, was laid before him, to which, his hands being unbound, he did ample justice.

Seating himself on the table, for the strange people seemed ignorant of the use of chairs, he soon became lost in deep thought.

What would be his fate? Had the priests saved his life, or was he doomed to be sacrificed as an offering to some strange, unknown, subterranean god?

Whatever his fate might be, the Winged Man had no intention of submitting quietly to it.

He had already tested the ropes which held him, and knew that, at any moment he could burst free, yet was determined not to do so until he found out what his captors' intentions were.

He was not kept long in doubt. Presently his ears were tortured by the most fearful sound he had ever heard.

Immediately the priests closed around him, and he was escorted into the streets, where he found a band, consisting of a number of men blowing into weirdly-shaped instruments, awaiting him.

Heralded by this band, and guarded on either side by priests and soldiers, the Winged Man was marched along a wide, well-kept road towards a huge, flat-topped mountain a mile from the city gates.

The top of the mountain reached, the priests broke into a loud, droning chant, as they lined the banks of an enormous reservoir evidently built to supply the city with water.

His face contorted with cruel, malicious hatred, the chief priest approached the Winged Man, and, touching him on the shoulder, pointed to the calm, placid water, then made a sign to the guard, who, seizing the prisoner, raised him unresistingly above their heads, and hurled him headlong into the reservoir.

Bursting asunder the cords which bound him as he rose to the surface, the Winged Man swam calmly around the miniature lake.

The icy-cold water into which he had been plunged acted as a tonic on the Winged Man, who resolved to avenge himself upon his captors for the indignities to which they had subjected him.

Swimming to the centre of the tank he suddenly threw up his arms, uttered a loud, despairing cry, and his face contorted as though with unbearable agony, sank beneath the surface.

Ten minutes later he rose again and found, as he had anticipated, that the crowd, priests, and soldiers, were making their way back to the city.

A hard, cruel glitter in his eyes, his mouth set with a look of unfaltering determination, the Winged Man attacked the side of the reservoir nearest the city, pulling huge stone slabs from the side of the dam, and hurling them into the water.

For two hours he worked, only pausing to plunge now and again into the cold, refreshing flood, until at length the weakened embankment gave way, and, in an irresistible stream, the water rolled towards the doomed city.

Loud cries of horror and dismay startled the hot, close air as the wretched inhabitants of the city saw the ice-cold flood approaching.

Spreading his mighty pinions, the Winged Man flew to the summit of the king's palace, and struck terror into the hearts of the panic-stricken crowd with his wild, mournful cries.

Shrieks of agony arose from the thronged streets as the water flooded the whole town.

Never before had the Winged Man witnessed so fearful the scene. As though the liquid flood was molten metal, the scarce human occupants of this underground world dropped with fearful, agonised cries as it closed around them, until every street and square in that strange city was covered with a carpet of floating dead.

Presently the cries of the dying were drowned in a loud, earth-shaking explosion from the river of fire.

Turning, the Winged Man gazed in the direction from whence the fearful sound had come.

An awful sight met his eyes.

The water flowing into that fearful river was converted so rapidly into steam that the air was rent by a thousand fearful concussions. Realising that not only the people but the whole city was doomed, the Winged Man spread his wings, and flew swiftly towards the mountains.

°A WORLD IN DISSOLUTION.

As the Winged Man flew slowly over the reservoir he was surprised to find that the torrent still poured down the mountain-side as swiftly as when he had first sent it on its errand of destruction towards the city.

It was not until he stood near the yawning chasm in the masonry that the mystery was solved.

Beneath him lay a basin-like lake, from the centre of which arose a column of water which told him that the lake was fed by an inexhaustible subterranean river.

Turning, he gazed towards the doomed city once more. Even his lust of vengeance was satiated when he saw the fearful destruction that had following the flooding of that strange land.

It was an indescribably horrible scene of destruction upon which the Winged Man gazed. Half hidden by thick rolling bellows of steam, houses, temples, palaces alike rolled like ships labouring in a heavy sea, until suddenly a louder, more fearful explosion than any that had preceded it shook the earth, and the unknown city was turned to a heap of crumbling masonry before his eyes.

"Thus perish all who dare to lay hands upon the Winged Man!" cried that fearful being, as he shook his clenched fist over the steam-hidden ruins.

The next moment the mountains trembled beneath his feet ere it burst in twain, hurling a column of scalding steam into the air, then, opening into a huge, mushroom-shaped cloud, scattered a rain of boiling water far and wide.

Half suffocated, the Winged Man fled from that fearful zone of danger. As though outraged justice claimed the life of he who had doomed so many thousands of living creatures to a cruel death, the eruption followed close behind him. Even the Winged Man felt his heart sink within his bosom as his staring eyes swept over the fearful scene.

———————————————

° 10 MAY 1913.

So continuous were the explosions, but they seemed to have settled into one deafening roar. At one moment the Winged Man would be flying over a stretch of cultivated land, from which the tillers of the soil were fleeing for their lives, the next the earth would open, pouring forth heavy masses of flame-tinged smoke and steam. Water and fire had met, with the result that a fearful fight was being waged in the centre of the earth.

Presently the Winged Man reached the spot from whence, as far as the eye could reach, the earth was covered with mighty trees. A sigh of relief escaped his lips. Here surely he would find safety.

The hope was in vain. Even as the thought flitted through his brain the forest, apparently kindled in a hundred places at once, burst into flame.

To right and left the Winged Man darted in search of a haven from the dangers that beset him.

Beneath him, crashing through the undergrowth with shrill cries of terror, hundreds of strangely-shaped animals and reptiles were fleeing from the forest in a course parallel to, but several degrees to the right of, that in which the Winged Man was flying.

Realising that instinct was probably taking the animals to a place of safety, the Winged Man changed his course, and soon reached a dull, sluggish stream flowing through a bleak, marshy country.

His wild, weird cry rising shrill above the roaring flames, the Winged Man plunged headlong into the river.

A SEA OF MUD.

As the Winged Man disappeared beneath the surface of the sluggish river an ejaculation of surprise burst from his lips.

He had plunged headlong into hot, evil-smelling, sulphur-impregnated mud. Realising that beneath the surface he might hope to escape the burning air which seemed to wither everything it touched, the Winged Man dived, careless of whither the river took him so that he left the awful land of fire behind.

Presently he returned to the surface, to find the stream approaching a well of rough, grey rock. Drawing his head and shoulders out of the water, he looked around him, then gnashed his teeth in rage as he saw the fearful death-trap into which he had flown.

The river of mud passed through an opening in the rock, the roof of which seemed resting upon the thick liquid.

Yet there lay his one and only chance of escape. Soon he found himself immediately before an opening in the rock. One final glance at the fearful land through which he had just passed, and, drawing in a deep breath of the hot, cinder-laden air, the Winged Man dived beneath the surface.

Forcing his way through the thick, though swiftly-moving liquid, the Winged Man remained beneath its dark-brown surface until the need of air grew imperative, then rose to the surface once more.

A blackness deeper than any earthly night hung like a sable curtain around him. Treading water, the Winged Man blazed abroad the bright beams of his headlight. He was floating in a sea of mud. To right, to left, in front, behind, his electric light revealed nothing but an empty void of impenetrable night.

Hour succeeded hour, yet not so much as a rock protruding from that fearful sea relieved the monotony of his solitary voyage. Never before had the Winged Man realised how unspeakably awful was absolute silence. Not a single sound fell upon his strained ears. Once when he spoke his thoughts aloud, his own voice seemed so fearful that he did not care to repeat the experiment.

Now and again he would rise in the still motionless air and fly in search of some break in the fearful monotony that was quickly growing unbearable. In vain. The sea of mud seemed illimitable.

As day succeeded day, if such an expression can be used of a land in which it seemed all night, no change came to vary the fearful sameness. A black, impenetrable void obtained on every hand. Slowly yet surely numbing despair seized upon the Winged Man's heart.

Terrible thoughts flitted through his active brain. Could it be that, in punishment for the many ruthless crimes he had committed, he was doomed to wander for ever in that fearful solitude? Or had he passed unconsciously from life to death, and was wandering hopelessly through the dark realms of the after-world?

Fearful though the thought, it sapped not the more than human courage from the Winged Man's heart. This strange, weird place must have other inhabitants and he would be here, as he had ever been, king and lord of all.

At length there came a time when he had not strength even to spread his mighty pinions to the windless air, but was borne slowly, whither he knew not nor scarcely cared.

A deadly torpor crept over his heart and brain the weakness which was robbing him of power to move, or even to think. At length, for the first time in his life, the Winged Man lost consciousness.

THE RETURN TO EARTH.

With a feeling as though iron fingers were clasped about his throat, the Winged Man awoke, to find himself in the centre of the torrent of almost hot, clinging mud, some of which, penetrating his nose and mouth, had given him the sensation of suffocation which had called him back to life.

Returning consciousness brought no hope. Robbed of his enormous strength, starving, scarce able to retain his recently returned consciousness, the only part of the Winged Man's frame which still seemed able to do its duty was his ever-active brain.

How he longed to reach the upper world again, to feel the cool earth-breezes fanning his heated brow, and see once more the sun's blessed light. A great longing for life filled his soul. Would that longing ever be satisfied?

Already sparks were dancing before his eyes. Could he hold out until a relaxation of the clinging mud around him brought a moment's respite?

But even as the thought flashed through his brain, a loud, wild shout of joy burst from his lips, as a bright light flashed in his eyes.

With loud, piercing shrieks of terror ringing in his ears, the Winged Man crawled painfully up some worn stone steps to a grassy slope, over which a number of quaintly-clad figures were rushing in panic-stricken flight.

A few deep breaths of the clear, cool, strength-giving air, and the Winged Man looked back whence he had come.

It was a small pool from the muddy water, from which arose thin reefs of steam. Upon the borders of the pool were what looked like a number of enamelled baths, which the Winged Man knew were receptacles in which patients, seeking relief from rheumatic and similar ailments, sat in the mud drawn from this healing spring.

There were no patients to be seen now, however, but marks of muddy feet, and discarded garments scattered about the place, told of a hurried flight. For the first time for many weeks a smile flitted across the Winged Man's face when he recalled the extraordinary spectacle the mud-covered patients presented when he had shot unexpectedly from out the mud spring.

Rising painfully to his feet, the Winged Man stretched his aching arms. So weak had he grown during the terrible journey through the under-world, that he swayed like a drunken man as he followed, with unsteady steps, the path taken by the fugitives.

Presently he came upon a large hotel, before which a crowd of people, many of whom still wore their mud-plastered bathing-suits, were clustered, who uttered loud cries of terror as the Winged Man strode towards them.

A red-faced man, evidently the proprietor or manager of the hotel, barred the Winged Man's path. "Who are you? Where do you come from?"

With a threatening gesture the Winged Man waved him aside.

"No matter whence I came. Out of my way, or it will be the worse for you! Fool, do you not know me? I am the Winged Man!"

As the dreaded name fell upon his ears, the hotel-manager, white to the very lips, stepped back, whilst the Winged Man strode through the shrinking crowd. Fearful, indeed, he looked. So wasted his frame, so pale his face, that he seemed but a moving skeleton.

Guided by the odour of cooking meat, the Winged Man made his way into the hotel-kitchen. Cooks, scullerymaids, waiters, servants all fled at his approach.

Throwing open the oven door, the Winged Man drew forth a sirloin of beef, from which he cut huge slices, devouring the half-cooked meat as though he would never leave off eating.

At length his hunger was appeased, he strode upstairs. Crouched in the corner of the long corridor was one of the hotel menservants. Ere the terrified man could flee the Winged Man grasped him by the neck.

"Cease struggling, fool; I will not hurt you!" cried the Winged Man. "Go to the owner of this place. Tell him I have taken yonder bed-room for the night, and if any seek to enter, if a single hand is laid upon door or window, I will burn the hotel and all within it to the ground! Go; it is the Winged Man's command!"

Hurling the terrified man from him, the Winged Man entered the bed-room, closed, and locked the door, pulled down the blinds; then, springing to the ceiling, folded his wings around him, and, hanging head downwards, passed into a sound, dreamless slumber. But before he slept he laughed suddenly. Had he fallen into that state of mind during a period of unconsciousness, and had it all been a dream, his journey in the under-world, or had his soul wandered during his body's unconsciousness?

THE FLYING TERROR'S DEMAND.

It was a late sitting in the House of Commons. A newly-elected tub-thumping Member of Parliament, who had yet to learn that street-corner eloquence will not go down in the British House of Commons, was pouring out a series of commonplace sentences, which, though apparently new to the speaker, the majority of the members present had heard over and over again, until they were thoroughly sick of them.

The occupants of both the Government and Opposition benches were well-nigh bored to death; but there seemed no stopping the continuous flow of stale argument which was being dinned into their unwilling ears.

How long the House would have to put up with their colleague's so-called speech, it is difficult to say. Suddenly, even his flow of words was checked by a strange, hitherto unique interruption.

Whistling through the air, a round, globular object descended straight from the ceiling to the Speaker's table, where it lay, swaying from side to side, a thin stream of sulphurous smoke pouring from an opening in its centre.

"A bomb! A bomb!" responded in accents of terror from every side. Many of those present made a mad rush for the door, or crouched, terror-stricken, behind the benches.

But, thank Heaven, there are still men of the good, old British breed left in Parliament. These, though with pale, blanched faces, stood their ground, and calmly waited the fearful explosion which seemed imminent.

Foremost among these was the Speaker, who, rising from his chair, stood bravely facing the death he could neither avert nor escape. Five seconds of deadly suspense, then a faint, insignificant pop resounded through the spacious hall.

So slight was the explosion in comparison to the burst of the death-dealing destruction they had expected, that a loud, hoarse roar burst from some of the younger members; but a deep flush of anger burnt on the faces of those to whom the honour of the House was dear. They deemed that they had been the victims of a stupid hoax, and that the whole House of Commons had been insulted.

All eyes were turned upon the speaker.

"The honourable member for East Empstead will perhaps resume his speech," said the Speaker in calm, level tones.

There was no response. The member, who, a moment before, had been taunting his political opponents with rank cowardice, had flown at the first sign of danger.

"I rise to a point of order, Mr. Speaker," said a leading member, "and would suggest that the police be instructed to take possession of yonder rubbish, and try to bring the perpetrator of this vile outrage to justice."

As the Premier resumed his seat the member for Boulton Bay arose.

"I move, Mr. Speaker, that the papers upon the table be now read," he said, pointing to the remains of the bomb, in the centre of which was a small piece of parchment tied with red ribbon.

The Speaker hesitated. He had detected the presence of the mysterious document, but had been unwilling to call attention to it.

However, as the last speaker's proposition seemed to meet with the approval of the House, he opened the tiny roll, spread it out on the table before him, and mastered its contents.

As he did so the pallor on his face deepened, to be succeeded by a flash of anger.

"This is too much! We never to be rid of this pestilent being? Evidently, what we have taken to be a hoax, is really a serious menace to the country. Listen:

"London is held to ransom. The richest city in the world can well afford a million a year to save it from a fate at which the whole world will shudder. Two hundred and fifty thousand pounds, the first quarterly instalment of this sum, must be deposited, in notes, on the summit of the clock-tower ere sunrise. Failure to comply with my demands, or attempted treachery, will fill your crowded streets with death.

"(Signed) THE WINGED MAN."

For several minutes a deathly silence followed the reading of the strange document during which various members, who had fled at the first sign of alarm, stole shamefacedly back to their seats.

The Premier and leader of the Opposition exchanged glances. Then, stepping forward, the leader of the Opposition took the letter from the Speaker's hand, and, tearing it in half, passed the torn sheet to the Premier, who tore it into tiny strips.

The significance of this action, to which both Liberals and Conservatives had, through their leaders, pledged themselves, was not lost upon the House; and a loud, ringing, defiant cheer arose, such as the time-honoured Council Chamber of the British Empire has seldom heard before.

Again the Speaker called upon the member for East Empstead to resume his speech, but that gentleman had been far too frightened to comply, and the debate was taken by an opponent as calmly as though vague, inexplicable danger hung over the world's greatest capital.

THE TRAIL OF FIRE.

It was with a vague feeling of uneasiness that the British public, especially the inhabitants of London, read of the strange event which had occurred in the House of Commons the previous night.

There was a time when few had taken the Winged Man seriously; but now all men had learned to acknowledge and fear his wondrous powers.

In London trains bearing busy men City-wards, on the tops of trams and 'buses, in the streets, nothing was talked about but the Winged Man's fearful threat.

Many and vague were the conjectures as to the form his vengeance would take. Some suggested a simultaneous explosion of the gas-mains which undermined every street. Others spoke in loud whispers of poisoned water works, whilst many believed the Winged Man would fulfil his word by dropping bombs loaded with some fearful explosive into the crowded streets.

It was noted afterwards that there was no panic, no wild, reckless flight, save in the quarters that are inhabited by the alien scum whom England shelters.

Nor with the Government entirely idle. Barely had the sun rose ere troops began to pour into London. Infantry lined the road-ways, cavalry patrolled the streets, artillery, ready for action, were stationed in various squares.

It was as though London had been threatened by an advancing invader. Slowly the sun rose in a clear, cloudless sky. Seldom had there been such a perfect spring day. It seemed impossible any untoward event should happen on such a magnificent morning.

Slowly the hours dragged on. Save for the military in the streets, a stranger, judging from the hurrying crowd, who, engaged in business or pleasure, thronged the streets, would not have suspected that a warning, which could not be disregarded, had been given to the principal Council of the nation the previous night.

As the day advanced, and no sign of the dreaded foe appeared, a hope that it was all a great bluff, a gigantic hoax, arose in many hearts.

It was just as Big Ben boomed forth the noonday hour that a strange shudder seemed to sweep over the crowded streets. Descending in a series of circles immediately over Westminster, was a dark speck that grew bigger each moment as it dropped swiftly earthwards.

A cry of "The Winged Man! The Winged Man!" swept through the crowded streets; but it was silenced, as it became evident that the dark speck was not the flying horror, but a large airship.

A thousand feet above the earth it remained, poised in air, and the general commanding the Home District, who, with a corps of signalmen, was on the top of the Victoria Tower, saw a dark figure clad in tight-fitting, black clothes, surveying the clock-tower through a pair of binoculars.

The signaller, leaning over the tower's parapet, fluttered a signal to the troops below. Immediately a thousand rifles were levelled at the airship; but ere the impending volley could be fired, she shot out of range, where she remained stationary, as though in mockery of the feeble attempts of the soldiers to bring her down with rifle-fire.

It is true the airship was still within reach of a battery of artillery stationed in Trafalgar Square, but the general hesitated to give the orders to fire.

The segments of iron, bullets, and pieces of broken shell, falling from so great a height, could not fail to do great damage in the crowded streets. Besides, as yet their fearful foe had made no hostile sign.

Presently the anxious crowd saw what seemed like a white ball of fire spring from out the side of the airship, where it remained, sending white rays earthwards, as it moved up and down, backwards and forwards, to right and left.

What could it mean? What fearful danger did that white, glistening speck portend? was the question which tortured every awe-stricken beholder's brain.

With startling suddenness the answer came. For a moment the round, glistening object was veiled, then burst forth again, shooting a straight, white pillar of light into the open space before the Houses of Parliament.

A loud, agony-laden, piercing shriek arose from a hundred throats, as, where a wondering, excited crowd had been a moment before, lay a writhing, scorched, and burned heap.

Guided with fearful precision, the airship moved slowly through the air, the white pillar of burning light passing slowly down Whitehall, its fearful breath turning wooden pavement into a bed of fire.

It was an awful sight—a sight such as no mortal man has ever looked upon before.

At one moment the eye would take in a heavily-laden 'bus dashing towards Trafalgar Square, its panic-stricken driver lashing his horses to a mad gallop;

then that relentless pillar of light would fall upon it, and horses, driver, and passengers vanished into a blaze of fire.

Following a zigzag course, leaving a burning path six feet wide wherever it went, the awful light approached Trafalgar Square.

A dignified, grey-haired man, one of England's most notable scientists, hastened to where the officer in command of the battery stood, awaiting the order to open fire.

"Why are you stopping? Shoot! In the name of all that is pitiable, fire! Break it!" gasped the scientist.

"My orders were not to fire until I received permission from the general," was the soldier's reply.

"And you will stand idly by whilst such a fearful massacre is being perpetrated before your eyes?" ejaculated the scientist. "I tell you, man, that one single shot will suffice to smash that inhuman creature's fearful contrivance!"

"Break? Smash? What on earth are you referring to, sir?" asked the officer irritably.

"Can't you see? Are you blind? The scoundrel in yonder airship has with fiendish ingenuity rigged up an enormous burning-glass with which he is scorching the life out of a score of human beings. A splinter from a single shell would save the lives of thousands."

The officer hesitated; then glanced once more in the direction from whence the expected order must come.

The whole of the British Army did not boast a braver or more capable officer, but opening fire upon the flying terror indirect disobedience to orders might mean the entire ruin of his career.

No matter, let the consequence be what it might, he could stay inactive no longer.

Turning, he strode to where the men of his battery stood anxiously awaiting the order to open fire.

Gallantly the gunners sprang to their weapons, but ere a lever could be pulled, a screw adjusted, the airship sprang forward, its pillar of light carving a fearful death-track through the crowded square.

The next moment, in a succession of loud, a reverberating roars, the limbers of the battery, set on fire by the concentrated beams hurled earthwards from the airship's enormous burning-glass, exploded, scattering doom and destruction on every side.

THE WINGED MAN TO THE RESCUE.

That night a second communication was dropped upon the Speaker's table in the House of Commons.

This time the writer demanded an immediate payment of £500,000, swearing, unless his demands were complied with, to destroy the British Museum, Buckingham Palace, the National Gallery, and St. Paul's Cathedral.

A few members of Parliament were in favour of surrender to one they seemed powerless to resist, but to this course the frontbenchers of both the Government and the Opposition were united in favour of resistance, for capitulation would place the country at the mercy of one whom they already knew to be unscrupulous and merciless.

Punctual to the stroke of twelve the airship, which the newspapers had christened "The Flying Death," hovered once more over the Clock Tower.

Clad in the tight-fitting garments with which the Winged Man was ever associated, a man leaned over the railed-in deck beneath the airship's hull and scanned the top of the Clock Tower through a pair of powerful glasses.

"A truce to these pig-headed Englishman! Will they never surrender?" he muttered angrily. "I was wrong," he continued, speaking to himself. "Berlin or Paris would have proved an easier prey. No matter; I will read the island dogs a lesson they shall never forget. Perhaps when they see the National Gallery, with its priceless treasures of Art, burning, they may hoist the white flag of surrender."

A sharp tug at a lever, a quick whirl of the steering-wheel, and the airship flew over the blackened streets which marked her course of the previous day, until at length she hovered over the National Gallery.

Stopping his machinery, the aeronaut turned the handle of a wheel attached to an endless screw.

From a receptacle beneath the deck a huge mass of crystal, larger than the object-glass of any known telescope glided into position.

A cry of anger, rage, and despair burst from the streets below as they saw the threatened destruction of the nation's most highly-prized treasure-house.

Even the aeronaut himself hesitated, until a shell fired from a gun concealed in St. James's Park burst beneath him, but too far off to inflict injury upon either airship or glass.

Yet he dare not remain there until, by scattering the gun-squad and blowing up the limber, he had put the artillery out of action.

He turned from the burning-glass, the rays of which, as yet unfocused, fell harmlessly upon the cupola of the National Gallery, then uttered an ejaculation of rage and amazement.

Standing with one hand upon the engine's levers, the other whirring round the spokes of the steering wheel, was the Winged Man.

"So you are the impostor who has dared to masquerade as the Winged Man, and in my name have perpetrated horrors such as in my wildest moments I have never even contemplated!" cried the King of the Air, crouching over the trembling man.

Twice the aeronaut tried to speak, but his tongue seemed to cleave to the roof of his mouth with terror.

"I—I deemed you dead. I thought, as the whole world believed, you were swallowed up in the maelstrom off the coast of Norway!" came at last in gasping accents from his pallid lips.

"And dare to think that you, a mere earthworm, were able to fill my place?" demanded the Winged Man contemptuously. "Do you know what I'm going to do with you?" he added.

The trembling wretch glanced appealingly into the Winged Man's face.

As well might a drowning sailor, borne forward on the crest of a storm-tortured billow, seek the mercy from the pitiless rocks towards which he was being carried.

Stern, cold, hard, immovable were the Winged Man's fearful features.

"Cast your eyes into yonder crowded streets. Behold the men whom, from your lofty eyrie, you have terrorised, whose brothers, sons, and fathers—ay, mothers and little children—you have slain without mercy; then think what mercy you will receive at their hands when I cast you to them."

The inventor shuddered. Well he knew, if that justly-enraged crowd laid hands upon him, they would tear him from limb to limb, as hounds break up a fox.

"No, no! Anything rather than that!" sobbed the miserable man.

For a few moments the Winged Man surveyed the grovelling man without speaking.

"There is an alternative," he said.

Eagerly the wretched man glanced into his fearful judge's face.

"Yes, yes?" he asked breathlessly.

"Pshaw! Think not I offer you better terms!" cried the Winged Man.

"But you will spare my life? For the sake of all you hold dear, you—"

The Winged Man held up his hand impatiently.

"Yes; I will spare your life on condition that you surrender yourself, body and soul, to me. Be my slave—my dog—to obey my every word—to have no thought, no wish, no power of movement, save at my will."

A fearful shudder shook the inventor's frame.

Slowly he raised his eyes to the Winged Man's white, livid face.

"No! Avaunt, fiend! I will neither be your slave, nor perish at the hands of yonder mob! Death, swift and merciful, shall be my portion!" he cried. Then, ere the Winged Man could prevent him, he flung himself over the low rail which protected the airship's deck, and, with a loud, piercing shriek, plunged, whirling head over heels, earthwards.

A cry of baffled rage burst from the Winged Man's lips. The next moment, as a swimmer dives into the sea, he followed in swift pursuit of the falling man.

Like a stone fell the ill-starred inventor; like a thunderbolt from heaven the Winged Man cleaved through the air.

Halfway between airship and earth he pounced, like a hawk upon a falling bird, upon the other's body, and, seizing him by the nape of his neck, spread abroad his mighty pinions, and checked his downward flight.

Then he flew in the slanting direction towards Trafalgar Square, crowded now with a curious, terrified throng, who were examining with blanched faces the remnants of the destroyed battery which littered the torn stonework surrounding the square.

Wild, weird, fierce—yet withal wondrously mournful and despairing—the Winged Man's awful cry rang out over their startled heads.

Ten thousand white faces were turned heavenwards.

A cry of astonishment rose from ten thousand throats when they saw, not one Winged Man, but two, approaching—at least, both figures were clad in the sombre, tight-fitting garments the front pages of the illustrated papers had made familiar to the public.

But as the two drew nearer it was seen that only one was provided with wings, and he held his counterpart, a limp, trembling prisoner, in his fearful grasp.

In a deep, unbroken silence, the Winged Man alighted upon the head of one of the Landseer's mighty lions, where he took his stand, his hand raised to command attention.

He threw him into the centre of the crowd.

"Listen, men of London!" he cried in stentorian tones, which seemed to fill the whole square. "I am the Winged Man, King of the Air; he who from the realms of space visits the terror of his wrath upon the creeping sons of earth. With my own unaided arm I strike terror into the hearts of men; yet never, even in my angriest moments, have I inflicted indiscriminate slaughter upon the innocent and guilty alike. Women and helpless children had never felt the terror of my wrath.

"See this puny creature lying at my feet? Deeming the impossible had happened, and the Winged Man was dead, he sought to usurp my kingdom of the air. I he could not injure. It is you he has hurt, and to your vengeance I leave him."

Raising the shrieking man from the ground, he lifted him high above his head. Then, with a loud:

"Whoop! Tear—tear—tear! Worry—worry—worry!" he threw him, as a huntsman throws a slain fox amongst the hounds, into the centre of the crowd.

A score of arms broke the wretched man's fall, but with an indescribably terrible yell of almost maniacal horror he burst free from the men who had seized him, and, striking blindly to right and left, fled headlong in the direction of a double line of police drawn up along Northumberland Avenue.

He was mad with fear.

The cry—exultant, fierce, triumphant—which rose from the throats of the crowd as they closed round their victim, was one of the most awful sounds that had ever fallen upon human ears. Above it all arose the wretched man's appealing cry:

"Save me, Winged Man! I am yours! Do with me what you will. Save me— save me!"

In a moment the Winged Man had left the lion's head, and, forced through the air by his mighty wings, reached the struggling man's side, snatched him from the grasp of those who would have torn him limb from limb, and, with a shrill, exultant cry, bore him aloft.

Immediately the tumult ceased. Men who looked at each other with pale, blanched faces, as, a hundred feet above their heads, the Winged Man checked his flight for a moment, tossed his prisoner's limp body in the air, caught it by the heel as it fell, then, with a loud "Mine—mine—mine! Body and soul he is mine for ever!" rose swiftly in the air until he became a mere speck in the distance.

DANBY DRUCE RENEWS THE CHASE.

It was on the coast of Norway, whither he had gone to investigate the reported death of the Winged Man, that Danby Druce first heard of the airship's appearance in London.

Immediately the head of the turbine cruiser that had been put at the great detective's service by the Government was turned towards Edinburgh, and Danby Druce alighted at Euston from a special train which had brought him from the North shortly before the Winged Man's reappearance on the scene.

Springing into a motor-car which awaited him, he reached the outskirts of the mighty crowd that thronged Trafalgar Square just in time to see the Winged

Man bearing his victim aloft.

Danby Druce literally foamed with baffled rage. For some minutes he sat watching that awful flying terror disappearing in the distance, then a larger, bigger speck in the air attracted his attention.

The airship, its engine stopped, was being carried by the gentle breeze in a southerly direction.

A superintendent from Scotland Yard fought his way through the crowd to the car, in obedience to Danby Druce's beckoning finger.

A few brief questions sufficed to acquaint the great detective with all that had occurred. In a moment his mind was made up. Wheeling the car round, he started in pursuit of the airship. If he could but capture it he would be able to meet the Winged Man on something like equal terms.

Yet he was not very sanguine of success. The chances seemed a thousand to one that in its unguided descent the airship would wreck itself on the chimney-pots and roofs of outer London.

But fortune proved kind to the great detective. As gently as though steered by its master's hand, the airship, after skimming over the roof of the Royal Infirmary at Putney, and the tall trees surrounding it, came gently to earth on Wimbledon Common, just as Danby Druce dashed up the steep ascent leading to this one of London's most beautiful open spaces.

Armed only with the revolver without which he never moved abroad, he boarded the airship, and had soon mastered its ingenious but exceedingly simple engines. It was with a thrill of not altogether unpleasant excitement that Danby Druce, pulling one of three levers which stood ready to hand near the steering-wheel, felt the airship moving swiftly skywards.

A hundred feet above the earth he put his recently-acquired possession through its paces, making it rise, fall, turn to right and left, advance, retire, until, feeling confident of his capability of driving it, he set off as swiftly as the small but powerful engines could force it through the air in pursuit of the Winged Man.

Upon a rack above the levers lay a pair of powerful glasses, through which, with one hand on the steering-wheel, Danby Druce scanned the blue, cloudless expanse of heaven as the airship rushed swiftly northwards.

Presently he detected a small, black speck, which some half-hour later he recognised, with an ejaculation of delight, as the Winged Man.

Swiftly though the airship moved, they were nearly forty miles from London ere the Winged Man was overtaken.

Intent upon plans for the future, scarcely feeling the weight of his prisoner's body, whose shivering moans alone proclaimed that he yet lived, the Winged Man was unconscious of his great foe's presence, until Danby Druce's voice calling upon him to surrender fell upon his ears.

"Aho, mine enemy, you are again upon my track! It is well. Your enmity is one of the few things that makes this life worth living. It is well I had not met you ere I plunged through the gates of the maelstrom into the under-world; then my rage was such that I could have stooped to any subterfuge to get you into my power. Now, though I will slay you sooner or later, it will be as it was before you did me the last great injury, and on earth or in the air we will fight on comparatively equal terms, and let the best man win. One word ere the battle begins. The girl you robbed me of—is she well?" cried the King of the Air.

"She is well, and will soon give me the right to protect her as my wife," replied Danby Druce.

A loud, fierce shriek of rage burst from the Winged Man's lips.

"Fool! Would you dare to drive me to fury?" he cried, as releasing his hold of the unfortunate inventor, he dashed at Danby Druce.

But ere he reached the airship he remembered the man now hurtling helplessly to the earth.

"I forgot. I have need of him," he muttered. Then, with a "Remain where you are, I will return," to Danby Druce, he darted in pursuit of the inventor, overtaking him just in time to save him from being dashed to pieces on the ground.

With the unconscious man's body in his arms the Winged Man glided over the tree-tops towards where, on the summit of a small hill, stood a lonely tower, surrounded by the ruins of a strong castle.

Raising a screen of blackberry-bushes that grew at the base of the tower, the Winged Man, dragging his prisoner behind him, crept through a small, burrow-like hole in the thick wall, until the blazing beams of his searchlight illuminated a large, pillared crypt.

Passing through this crypt, the Winged Man entered a dark, noisome dungeon, scarce four feet square, in which was a rusty chain, secured to a huge iron staple, driven deeply in the wall. On the other end of the chain was an iron belt. This the Winged Man clasped round his unconscious prisoner's waist, and, as the secret spring snapped to, turned his back upon the unfortunate man, and, retracing his steps, clambered up the tower's precipitous wall.

HELPLESS IN SPACE.

A glance from the summit of the tower showed the Winged Man that Danby Druce yet awaited him. Rising in an ever-widening circle, he stood poised in air, whilst his fearful, mournful cry carried its challenge to Danby Druce's expectant ears.

Like an arrow from a bow, the airship, steered by the detective's skilful hands, plunged through space at its new owner's foe. Poised on his quivering wings, the Winged Man awaited the onslaught, a contemptuous smile parting his thin, pale lips.

It is true Danby Druce carried a revolver; that he feared to use it, lest the flame should set light to the inflammable gas which filled the body of the airship.

Yet the huge flying construction would in itself form a weapon he might be able to use with deadly effect upon his foe. The prow of the long platform that constituted the airship's deck protruded in a sharpened point a good three feet beyond the silken envelope, and it was with this Danby Druce hoped to strike his dying adversary down.

Swifter and swifter flew the airship, nearer and nearer it drew to its quarry, until, just as Danby Druce thought victory assured, with an almost imperceptible movement of his wings, the Winged Man allowed the airship to glide swiftly by.

Round swung the splendid flying-machine, darting like a swallow hither and thither, up and down, as Danby Druce sought to strike or crush his agile opponent.

It was all in vain. With a feeling of bitter disappointment Danby Druce realised that an ironclad might as well hope to ram a torpedo-boat as his flying-machine to overtake the Winged Man.

It was after one of Danby Druce's fierce, determined rushes that the Winged Man disappeared from view.

Up and down, north and south, Danby Druce scanned the clear air in search of his foe.

In vain. No sign of the weird monster could he see. There was only one place in which the Winged Man could have hid from his gaze, and that was the platform immediately beneath his feet. Besides, the clock-like instrument which recorded the elevation at which the airship flew told that they were falling rapidly, as though being dragged down by an extra weight.

Reaching forward, Danby Druce pressed the elevator-lever home to its last notch. Immediately the machine began soaring swiftly upward.

A wild, mocking laugh warned Danby Druce that in some as yet mysterious way he had fallen into a death-trap, set, with fiendish cunning, by his fearful opponent. His hand was still on the lever, and with a smart jerk he drew it back. As he did so he realised what had happened.

The Winged Man had disconnected the lever from the engine, and, do what he might, he could not stop the airship's upward flight. It is true he could stop the engines, but by doing so would doom himself to almost certain death.

A sepulchral laugh immediately behind him caused Danby Druce to turn round. Perched, like some mocking spirit of evil upon one of the quivering steel guides holding the platform to the balloon, which rendered the machine light enough to lift it, was the Winged Man.

"Aho, Danby Druce! Great shall be your rise, but great shall be your fall. I await your return to earth with impatience!" cried the Winged Man.

Ere Danby Druce could reply he flung himself backwards from the rope, and, turning over and over as he descended, dropped earthwards in a series of somersaults.

Several valuable minutes did Danby Druce waste trying to break open the hatch leading to the engine; but the Winged Man had anticipated some such attempt, and wedging in the hasp, had rendered it immovable.

The tiny apartment which did duty as an engine-room on board the airship being underneath the platform, it was impossible to reach it from the side. As he rose from his knees something cold and wet touched his cheek.

He looked up, and for a moment could scarcely believe his eyes. The balloon ropes, platform, wheels, all were encrusted with glistening particles of white frost, and a glance at the gauge told him that he was being carried upwards through the thin, rarefied air at a tremendous rate.

It was deathly cold. Bands of ice seemed to press round his throbbing temples. His fingers and toes ached as though frost-bitten, and as the full horror of his position burst upon him he stood breathing in short, quick painful gasps, as he gazed in horror around him, for well he knew now the fearful fate to which the Winged Man had condemned him. He was doomed to be carried upwards, ever upwards, until he perished miserably by cold and suffocation.

A groaning, creaking noise above his head caused him to look up. The light, leather outer skin which covered the gas-bag above his head was swelling visibly.

Now and again, with a mighty crack, a seam would give way, and a roll of gas-filled silk be thrust through the opening.

Drawing a knife from his pocket, Danby Druce took it between his aching teeth, intent on clambering to the gas-bag and cutting it open.

Too late! His numbed fingers refused to grasp the icy-cold rope, and, with a moan of despair, he sank back upon the deck. The next moment he was on his feet again.

One wild farewell glance he cast upon the fearful waste of blue that surrounded him on every side; then, drawing his revolver from his hip-pocket raised it in the air.

So intense was the cold that the first shot went wide of its mark.

Again Danby Druce cocked his weapon.

It was his last and only chance, but he would make the most of it.

SAVED BY A PARACHUTE.

Danby Druce laboured under no delusion as to what the probable outcome of his rash act would be. Better a quick death than a long, lingering existence in that icy atmosphere.

Moving immediately beneath the centre of the gas-bag, he raised his weapon above his head, and when its muzzle almost touched the leather outer cover, pulled the trigger.

The report of the pistol was drowned in a deafening roar, as the gas-bag, turning for a moment into a ball of fire, burst asunder.

Half blinded by the glare, Danby Druce was hurled on to the deck, and was only saved from being thrown into space by his body falling between the steering-wheel and the lever.

For a few seconds Danby Druce lost consciousness of what was going on around him. When he regained the entire possession of his faculties, the gasbag had disappeared, leaving a mass of torn, bent, and jagged spars above the deck of the doomed craft.

A roaring, hissing noise fell upon the great detective's ears. At first he could not make out whence it came. Then, like a flash, the truth burst upon him.

The weight of the engine and his own body had kept the flat deck on, so to speak, a level keel. They were falling through the air, but not so swiftly as would have been the case had the airship descended stern or bow foremost.

A despairing glance around showed Danby Druce a large, circular construction, rising some eight inches above the deck just aft of where he lay scarce daring to move lest he should upset the equilibrium of the vessel.

He remembered now having noticed it before, but events had followed each other so quickly since he had started upon his daring voyage that he had no time to examine it.

Cautiously he struggled to a sitting position; then, reaching out, grasped an iron ring let into the top of the circular object, and pulled it towards him.

The next moment he had flung his body in the opposite direction as he felt the deck tip dangerously forward.

Swifter and swifter dropped the deck. Already the difficulty of breathing warned Danby Druce of the approaching end. Well he knew that from the tremendous height from which he had fallen he would be dead long ere he reached the earth, unless he could find some means of checking his downward flight.

Turning slowly round he rose to his feet. Bending his body in opposition to the airship's list, he glanced down upon the folded silk lying within the cavity he had just laid bare.

There was no doubt now watch the box contained. It was a parachute to be used in case of an accident by the imperilled aeronaut to reach the earth in safety.

It was but a slender hope of escape, yet, throwing caution to the wind, Danby Druce sprang forward, and drew the silk swiftly from its resting-place.

But, alas! his indiscreet movement threw the deck of the airship off its balance, and the next moment he felt a mighty rush of air close around him as the airship's stern sank earthward.

Wildly Danby Druce threw out his clutching hand, whilst terror of what seemed a certain death drew a loud, despairing shriek from his lips.

The next moment his groping fingers closed around something. What it was he could not tell, but as a drowning man clutches at a straw so he clung to his unknown substance.

Then there came a jerk which threatened to tear his arm from its socket; but he held on like grim death, and the next moment a long-drawn sigh of intense relief burst from his lips as he saw that fortune had not entirely deserted him.

By the merest chance his fingers had closed around the iron ring, to which were fastened a number of thin but strong cords attached to the silk; whilst above his head fluttered the body of the parachute.

He was falling earthwards with fearful swiftness; but quickly though he fell a glance below showed that the wrecked airship was but a tiny speck between himself and the distant earth.

Slowly the parachute extended above his head, like some huge umbrella; then its earthward speed slackened, and he knew that once again he had escaped what had seemed certain death.

BORNE BEFORE THE BLAST.

Taking in a long, deep breath, Danby Druce, raising his body, slipped his arm to the shoulder through the ring. Confident that he could not now be shaken from his hold, he glanced earthwards, just in time to see the airship plunge into a black mass of the storm-cloud, which seemed from that enormous height to be resting on the earth itself.

Even as he watched he saw the vessel move from the straight line in which it had fallen towards the west, and realised that a sudden storm had risen in the strata of air nearest the earth.

Beneath him, in enormous billows that at one time looked like the surface of an angry sea, at others so black that it seemed as though he was dropping into the realms of endless night, dark storm-clouds rushed and tossed, and he knew that perils almost as great as those from which he had already escaped were yet to be met ere his weary body could find rest upon the solid earth.

Although the above has taken so long to describe, events followed each other with lightning rapidity. Barely had Danby Druce realised this second danger ere he had dropped into the storm area.

As the swiftly-rushing wind caught his body it bore him westward as though it would tear him from the waving parachute. The next moment it had caught the silk in its fearful grasp, and soon, like a leaf at the sport of winds, Danby Druce, dragged through the air behind the flapping parachute, found himself whirled swiftly onward in the heart of the storm.

Never will Danby Druce forget that fearful journey. Buffeted about as though by unseen hands, he was hurled hither and thither; whilst to the terror of his position was added the deafening roar of thunder and the fearful glare of lightning, which, springing from every part of the heavens at once, was lost in clouds amongst which he was being carried.

EARTH AT LAST.

Once, seized in a vortex of the storm, Danby Druce was whirled round and round until his senses reeled, and it was with difficulty he could prevent his arm from slipping from the ring.

Yet, with the dogged pluck which had carried him unscathed through so many hair-breadth escapes, the great detective held to the iron ring attached to the parachute, which alone prevented his being dashed headlong to the earth.

Once his whirling body twisted the cords which held the parachute together, so that the silk was unable to support his weight, and, with a feeling of blank despair, he felt himself falling with tremendous velocity towards the earth.

Fortunately, as Danby Druce fell, the cords unwound themselves, and a hundred feet from earth his descent was checked.

Now at length the end of his journey had surely come. A few seconds more, and the parachute would lower him gently to earth.

To be ready to let go at the moment of contact with the ground, Danby Druce withdrew his arm from the ring, to which he had clung with both hands.

But even as his feet skimmed over the bare branches of a blasted elm, a fearful gust got under the parachute, and the next moment he was being carried swiftly over the chimney-tops and roofs of some country town.

What place it was Danby Druce could not tell. So fiercely had he been buffeted by the storm, so swiftly carried onward during his fearful journey, that he had lost all sense of direction.

Borne forward on the wings of the wind, Danby Druce sought once more to regain his former position.

Alas! even his iron muscles could do no more. His failing strength would not allow him to make his position secure.

Onward he was carried; now five hundred feet above the earth, now so close to its surface that more than once he was tempted to release his hold, and risk, life, limb, and neck—anything rather than endure that fearful strain a moment longer than he could help.

But each time, ere he could put his desperate resolve into execution, he would be whirled so high above the earth as to render the expedient worse than useless.

At length, on the summit of a tall hill standing in the centre of a wide stretch of moorland, the parachute dropped to earth, and Danby Druce, releasing his hold, sank senseless to the ground at the foot of a ruined tower which crowned the crest of the hill.

When he recovered consciousness the storm had died away, and the sun was shedding its last rays upon the earth.

As Danby Druce, sore, stiff, and feeling very ill after his fearful experience, struggled painfully to his feet, he stood as one rooted to the ground, gazing straight into where the sun was setting in a red bank of clouds beyond a line of tree-capped hills, for in the exact centre of the huge red orb appeared the Winged Man.

In a moment Danby Druce had dropped to the ground.

Weary, worn, sick, he was in no condition to renew his unending fight with the Winged Man, although well he knew that if his dread enemy discovered his presence there nothing on earth could save him.

Glancing swiftly round, he saw close at hand a doorway leading into the ruined tower.

In a moment he had darted through it, and, seeing a small opening in the massive wall just inside the doorway, crouched inside it to hide until the dread horror had passed by.

HOT ON THE TRAIL.

Ten minutes went slowly by; then the same strange feeling which ever swept over Danby Druce at the Winged Man's approach, caused the great detective to appear through the semi-darkness of his cave-like retreat.

Upon the broken parapet which surrounded the old tower the Winged Man was standing, with folded arms, gazing into space.

For nearly half an hour the Winged Man stood, his tall, gaunt frame, black, dark, forbidding against the darkening sky; then, spreading his wings, he dropped to the masonry-covered floor of the roofless tower, and without troubling to look around him—for he felt confident that no human being could be near, or he would have seen him—bowed his tall form, and entered the tiny apartment, which had probably been the guard-room in the old days when the castle dominated the surrounding country.

Danby Druce gave himself up for lost.

Weary though he was, his brave spirits did not for a moment admit the possibility of a tame surrender; yet he knew the Winged Man's giant strength too well to doubt for a moment what the outcome of the struggle would be.

Realising that his only chance—if chance it could be called—would be to take the Winged Man by surprise, he was gathering his body for a spring, when he rose swiftly to his feet, rubbing his eyes as though assured that vision had paid him false.

The Winged Man had disappeared!

A moment before that weird form had stood erect before him. Now it had gone, swallowed in the darkness, or vanished into thin air.

So astonished was Danby Druce that for several minutes he remained staring incredulously at the spot where he had last seen the Winged Man, then moved cautiously forward.

As he did so the mystery was explained. In what he had taken to be solid wall was a small opening through which the Winged Man had gone.

Danby Druce's first impulse was to leave the tower and to seek safety in flight.

"No," he muttered. "I have sworn to devote my whole life to the overthrow of the Winged Man, and now that Fate has betrayed one of his hiding-places into my hands, come death, come life, I will not shrink from the task I have set myself!"

And, unarmed and weary though he was, he stole cautiously down a steep flight of moss-grown steps after the Winged Man.

Pausing at the foot of the steps, Danby Druce rapidly removed his boots, then, slinging them across his neck by their laces as he ran, hastened through the darkness, now and again bruising shoulders, head, and knees against the rough sides of the narrow passage.

Forgotten were fatigue and lassitude, for before him gleaned the rays of the

Winged Man's head-light as he strode along that strange, subterranean passage.

Now that the game was afoot, and he was hot on the scent of his quarry, the great detective felt no fear.

It was nothing to him that, should the Winged Man discover that he was being followed his life would not be worth a moment's purchase.

At any moment his life might be forfeited to his great opponent's rage. What of that? Better to die striving against his great adversary to the end than be slain by an unseen blow in the dark, as he knew might be his fate at any moment.

It was a fearful journey this dark plunge through the narrow, noisome tunnel which led with whither Danby Druce could not even guess.

Certainly it was taking him far from the ruin, as if he had been traversing a descending slope ever since the flight of steps had been left behind, he realised he must by this time be far beneath the earth's surface.

Presently a feeling of being boxed in, which had hitherto afflicted him, departed, and, stretching out both arms, he tried to reach the sides of the tunnel.

But in vain, nor, though he raised his hand above his head, could he touch the roof; yet he knew he was on the right trail, for, some twenty yards ahead, the brilliant light from the Winged Man's electric lamp led the way.

Suddenly a half-suppressed exclamation of dismay burst from Danby Druce's lips, and he plunged headlong into a pool of icy-cold water.

A few seconds' helpless foundering in the black liquid, and Danby Druce, seizing the edge of some stone coping opposite the spot where he had fallen, was about to drag himself on to dry land, when in a blinding flash the Winged Man's headlight was turned full in the direction from whence he had come.

Fortunately, the rays were directed over his head, and, loosening his hold of the stone, Danby Druce sank noiselessly back into the water.

As he did so his extended hand met no resistance, and to his joy he discovered that the action of the water had washed away the soil from beneath the stone, leaving just sufficient room for his head to rise above the surface.

Barely had he taken up his position in this chilly, uncomfortable hiding-place, when the beams of the tell-tale searchlight, after flashing backwards and forwards along the passage down which he had just come, settled upon the water.

Then he heard the Winged Man approach and come to a halt on the very stone beneath which he crouched.

"It was but a stone falling from the roof," Danby Druce heard the Winged Man mutter.

Then the light swept from off the water, and he heard his dread foe move swiftly away.

As the footsteps died away Danby Druce came from beneath the stone, and, clambering on to it, followed, dripping and chilled to the bone, though as resolute and determined as ever, after his fearful quarry.

He was just in time to see the weird horror pass through a low, arched doorway, and continue on his way along a narrow, rock-strewn passage.

THE ABANDONED COAL-MINE.

Ten minutes later Danby Druce came to an abrupt halt, as the Winged Man's head-light dropped like a falling star close to the damp, dripping roof, to disappear beneath the level of the ground.

Dropping on his hands and knees lest he should fall upon some dark, unsuspected chasm, Danby Druce advanced cautiously towards the spot where he had last seen the Winged Man.

Then the mystery of the Winged Man's disappearance was solved.

The passage ended in the shaft of a deserted mine, for, gazing upwards, he beheld as through the wrong end of a telescope a circle of the star-dotted heavens; then, looking downwards, he saw the Winged Man slowly disappearing into the depths below.

Lower and lower he fell, his descent checked by his partially outstretched wings.

For a moment Danby Druce thought that the insurmountable barrier would turn him back, but the next the blood rushed swiftly through his veins with excitement, as the beams from the Winged Man's headlight disclosed a number of beams placed at intervals of twenty feet down the shaft, each connected with the one above by long ladders, stoutly, if clumsily built, and brown with age.

Danby Druce might well have been forgiven had he elected to have given up the chase then and there, but it was not in his nature to do so whilst the slightest chance of following the Winged Man remained.

A moment's hesitation—for who could tell how long those ladders had been standing there, how rotten and unreliable they might be?—Then, undeterred by the knowledge that the chances were ten to one against the ladders bearing his weight, Danby Druce, grasping two of the rungs, swung off the solid ground, and the next moment his body was dangling over the yawning pit.

Even as he hung he knew that others besides himself had recently traversed that dangerous path.

Instead of the dust of ages upon the rungs to which he clung, his fingers closed over the pieces of grit which could only have come from the sole of a man's boot.

A couple of swings, and Danby Druce gained the uppermost side of the ladder, then he lowered himself slowly to the first beam, and, standing upon the narrow, wooden ledge, glanced to where the Winged Man's headlight was by this time but a glimmering spark in the depths below.

As Danby Druce had anticipated, the head of the next ladder was close to the first, yet he remained gazing down into the pit.

He dare not attempt the journey until the Winged Man had moved away. The slightest noise, a dislodged stone, would betray his presence, and he had not risked so much to spoil all by carelessness at the moment of success.

Presently he saw that the Winged Man's descent was stopped; then the light moved a yard or so to the right of the shaft, and disappeared.

Immediately Danby Druce was on the second ladder and clambering down it as fast as darkness and uncertainty of his terrible path would admit.

He was not entirely in darkness, but the starlit heavens only afforded sufficient light to see how difficult his self-imposed task really was.

As he stepped lower and lower he noticed that in many places the ladder had been repaired, and in others entirely new ones provided.

Brave though it was, it was with a sigh of relief that Danby Druce reached the bottom of the shaft, from whence half a dozen dark, gloomy passages converged.

But he remembered the direction in which the Winged Man had gone, and, turning to the left, had barely taken a dozen paces ere he came to an abrupt halt.

Before him stretched a large room—it could scarcely be called a cave—lighted by a brilliant white light.

Never before had Danby Druce gazed upon such an apartment. Roof, floor, walls were all a rich, deep black. Numberless pillars supported the roof, and around the wall stood statues of the same black material.

For some moments Danby Druce gazed in perplexity at the wondrous beauty of the apartment; then the truth dawned on him.

The mighty hall into which he had penetrated unbidden, the statues upon which he gazed, the elaborately carved pillars which surrounded him, were all of solid coal.

Barely had Danby Druce taken all this in then he shrank back into the tunnel, as the Winged Man appeared upon the scene, and, mounting six broad steps at the further end of the hall, the weird horror seated himself upon a magnificently-carved throne, and, leaning his elbow on his knee, placed his chin in his hand, and gazed abstractedly before him.

THE BLACK HALL OF JUSTICE.

Presently the Winged Man started as a dreamer awakened from sleep, stamped angrily on the floor, and cried:

"Bring forth the prisoner!"

As the ringing tones reverberated through that weird, black hall, heavy hands were laid upon Danby Druce's shoulder, strong fingers closed around his wrists, and the next moment he felt himself being forcibly propelled towards the black throne.

In vain he struggled. His captors had already obtained too strong a grip upon him to be lightly thrown off; besides, as his eyes encountered the hideous, distorted frame of Ghat, the Winged Man's dwarf attendant, a momentary horror seized him in its grasp.

"So Danby Druce, you thought to enter the lion's den, and escape unscathed? Ho, ho! You shall find that it is easier to force your way into the Winged Man's lair than to escape therefrom!" thundered the weird horror.

"That is as may be, Winged Man," replied Danby Druce boldly. "I am in your power; what do you intend to do with me? I know you, and fear you not, though there is no room for mercy in your black heart.

Loud laughed the Winged Man.

"Speak all ye who have felt the Winged Man's vengeance. Does he slay his enemies?"

"Would that he did! Would that he did!" came in accents laden with unspeakable despair from every part of that fearful hall at once.

Danby Druce turned in the direction from whence the nearest voice came. As he did so he beheld a small, iron grating, about a foot square, against which was pressed a white face so lined with care, so distorted with pain, that, despite himself, he shuddered.

A mocking, triumphant laugh escaped the Winged Man's lips.

"Ha, ha, Danby Druce, man of iron, though you are, the Winged Man has already made you wince!" he cried. "Listen! There was a man who sought to rob the Winged Man; sought to betray him into the hands of his foes. Dog, appear!"

In obedience to the Winged Man's command, a wild, unkempt figure, clad in filthy rags, crept across the floor to the foot of the throne. So fearfully wasted was the forlorn wretch, so matted his long, untrimmed hair, that at first glance Danby Druce scarce deemed him a human being. But when, in obedience to the Winged Man, the wretched creature looked up an ejaculation of astonishment burst from his lips, as he recognised in the wretched prisoner a man who had once been known as the smartest detective in Scotland Yard.

He remembered now how he had been detailed to run down the Winged Man, how he had gone forth one morning and never returned. All deemed him dead. Rather a thousand times would Danby Druce have seen him lying in the cold, still grave, then such a wreck of a human being as that cringing, spiritless form he saw before him.

"Whose dog are you?" asked the Winged Man, spurning the kneeling man with the toe of his pointed shoe.

"Yours, dread being—yours!" came in faltering accents from the kneeling man's lips.

"Who controls your every word, your every movement, your every thought?" said the Winged Man.

"You, Winged Man!" admitted the other.

"There is dust upon my boot; remove it!" continued the Winged Man.

Without a moment's hesitation the wretched creature bowed his head, and licked the Winged Man's high instep.

"Charles Harmand, shake off this accursed being's spell! Remember you are a man, at one time acknowledged the smartest and bravest detective in the world!" pleaded Danby Druce.

As his name fell upon his ears the wretched being started, half rose, and looked eagerly up, but at a single wave of the Winged Man's hand he crashed upon the coal steps once more.

"You see this wretched caricature of what has once been a man, Danby Druce?" demanded the Winged Man.

"I see a victim of your cruelty, unholy wretch, and be sure that every indignity you have inflicted upon him shall be repaid tenfold!" was the defiant reply.

"I hurl back your threat in your teeth!" thundered the Winged Man. "But long ere that happens you will be reduced to the same state as this man, upon whose neck I place my feet."

"Never! I know not by what fiendish tortures you have degraded an intelligent man to the level of beasts, yet there is that within my breast which tells me that in my case you can never succeed. Winged Man, I hate and defy you!" cried Danby Druce.

Moved by a sudden paroxysm of rage, he broke from his captors, and, determined to kill the Winged Man, even though he perished with him, he sprang towards the throne.

But even as his foot touched the lowest step a deep, loud, reverberating roar, as of a thousand thunders, shook the hall, and an inky darkness, deeper than that of night, swept over the scene.

Undaunted, undeterred, Danby Druce rushed up the broad steps, then hurled himself with almost maniacal fury upon the occupant of the throne.

"Now, Winged Man, the hour of your reckoning has come! Though you were fifty times the supernatural being you claim to be, you should not escape me!" cried Danby Druce, as, with frenzied strength he clasped his fingers around the other's throat, and struck his head against the back of the throne.

For a moment his victim struggled then a hollow, shuddering moan escaped his lips and Danby Druce felt the body lie limp in his hands. A wild shriek of exultation burst from the great detective's lips.

"At last, Winged Man, I have prevailed!" he cried.

"You lie!" thundered a fearful voice by his side.

The scene in the Hall of Justice.

INTO THE DEPTHS.

The next moment the Hall of Coal was bathed in light, and with a cry of baffled anger and dismay, Danby Druce removed his fingers from his victim's throat.

Pale, cold, still—could it be in death?—Charles Harmand lay, a scarce-breathing, inert mass upon the polished throne.

The Winged Man's unholy laughter ringing in his ears, Danby Druce gazed down upon the lifeless form.

It seemed incredible that in so short a time the change could have been effected. Yet, so it was. Escaping Danby Druce's avenging grasp, the Winged Man had thrust a man who had at one time been Druce's comrade into his hands.

"And did you think, Danby Druce, that your puny strength could have sufficed to knock the Winged Man senseless?" asked the weird horror, hovering between the roof and the floor as he gazed with contemptuous scorn upon his foe.

"Would that it had been you! Gladly would I have laid down my life, if by doing so I would have rid the world of you!"

"Poor fool, he must be of more earthly build who overcomes the Winged Man!" cried the weird horror; then, alighting within six feet of the detective, he stamped twice upon the floor. As he did so Danby Druce, eager to conquer one who would fain be his master ere his failing strength vanished, sprang at him once more. But even as he did so the ground opened at his feet, and he found himself falling into a black, cavernous opening of unknown depth.

Down he went, down, down, until at length his descent was stayed by plunging headlong into a pool of dark, evil-smelling water.

° 17 MAY 1913.

A TERRIBLE TRIAL.

Rising to the surface, Danby Druce struck wildly out, and soon, to his joy, his hands touched solid ground.

But even as he strove to clamber on that unknown shore, an ejaculation of horror escaped his lips, for his groping fingers had closed over a cold, slimy "something."

What it was he could not tell. Conquering his repugnance to the slimy unknown, Danby Druce renewed his attempt to escape from that black, evil-smelling liquid. The second time he was more successful. A minute later he lay panting upon a slab of rock, bruised and shaken from his fall, but otherwise unhurt.

Presently he sprang to his feet with a cry of alarm. It seemed as though deftly-cold fingers had passed over his face. Then he stepped back in horror as a moist, heavy body rolled up against his legs.

Groping, his hand touched a rough wall of rock, but even as he did so he drew it back; for his fingers had encountered something moist, clammy, and repulsive.

A momentary feeling of revulsion and terror brought a wild shriek of despair from the detective's lips, echoed by a loud peal of mocking laughter from immediately above his head.

He looked up to find the Winged Man peering at him from the edge of the hole in the floor through which he had been hurled.

"How like you your new bedfellows, Danby Druce?" cried the weird horror mockingly.

"Better they than you!" he hurled back the defiant answer.

"As the hours turn into days, the days into weeks, the weeks into months, and you find your only companions repulsive reptiles and creeping things, you will be glad, on any terms, to exchange your prison for the light of day."

"Never! My bones shall lie here and rot, mute witnesses against your inhuman cruelty, before I give in to your evil will!" cried Danby Druce defiantly.

"We shall see," returned the Winged Man confidently. "The bravest man, one of the strongest I have ever known, succumbed to a fortnight's imprisonment in yonder dark hole. Farewell, for ever, Danby Druce, the great detective, when we next meet you will be a creeping creature of my will."

As the Winged Man's awful words reverberated through that pit-like shaft, the secret trap-door rose from its place, and Danby Druce was left in darkness and alone, surrounded by a thousand unseen terrors.

Seated on a hard, bare rock, his elbows on his raised knees, his chin resting upon the palm of his right hand, Danby Druce remained for some minutes lost in deep thought, trying to retrace his late rash journey step-by-step.

But in vain. All he could be sure of was that he must be several hundred feet beneath the surface of the earth, probably hidden in the intricate maze of an abandoned coal-mine.

Not for a moment did he seek to hide from himself the fearful peril that menaced him.

IN THE WINGED MAN'S CLUTCHES.

Unarmed with not a soul on earth who knew whither he had gone, he was entombed in the bosom of the earth, at the mercy of the most fearful foeman has ever had to content against. Yet Danby Druce's courage did not fail him. He had escaped from the Winged Man's clutches before—he would do so again.

Neither disappointment, wounds, no disaster could frighten Danby Druce of the quest on which he had set his heart. Even in that black, unwholesome prison, unshared by a single ray of hope, he was as determined as ever to hunt the Winged Man to the gallows, or to perish.

Now and again Danby Druce, despite his well-tried courage, shuddered as some cold, slimy living creature sought to creep over him, or touched where, during the struggle, his clothes had been torn, laying bare his flesh.

Determined to discover the nature of his repulsive companions, Danby Druce drew a match-box from his pocket, only to find that there were but three matches in it.

For a moment he hesitated. It would be folly to throw a single chance away, and on one of those matches his life might, at some future time, depend. Yet it was above all things necessary that he should see the nature of the prison in which he was confined. Besides, he felt that if he knew by what manner of loathsome reptiles and creeping things he was surrounded, he could bear their presence better.

From his breast-pocket he drew a foolscap envelope. This he twisted into the shape of a torch, and, striking one of his precious matches, held the lighted paper aloft.

As he did so the horror of his hitherto unseen companions was replaced by disgust, for he found himself in a rough, cave-like tunnel, some twenty feet long by six broad, half of which was occupied by a dark, repulsive, slime-covered pool of water, whilst the comparatively dry ground was dotted with a number of hideous lizards, big-eyed frogs, and dark-brown, repulsive toads. The walls were covered by the largest slugs he had ever seen.

Disgusting though his companions in that fearful prison were, Danby Druce breathed a sigh of relief as he realised that he stood in no danger whatsoever from them.

Yet ere the paper burning down to his fingers forced him to let it fall to the floor, where it flared up, filling the fearful cave with light ere it died out, he saw, or fancied he saw, the surface of the slime-covered pool agitated as though some huge creature was moving uneasily in its fearful depth.

Yet he might be mistaken, for, despite his iron constitution, his fearful adventures in the more than awful place in which he found himself might already have affected his nerves.

Backing as far from the slime-covered pool as the narrow precincts of his prison would allow, Danby Druce swept a number of gigantic slugs from a huge stone that cropped up from the uneven floor, and awaited what might next betide.

AN EXPLODED TERROR.

Ten minutes passed slowly by, ten minutes of deep silence, broken only by a sepulchral croak from some disturbed frog. Gradually Danby Druce became aware of the fact that the darkness was less intense than it had been. A faint, indescribably awful light was gradually filling the whole cave.

Brighter, if such a word can be used in describing that dull, leaden glow, grew the illumination, until he could just see, through a kind of haze, the cave's huge, jagged, dripping roof, uneven walls, and the platform of rock upon which he stood, and beyond it black, forbidding in the uncertain light, the dark, fearful pool into which he had fallen.

Presently Danby Druce sprang to his feet, his every nerve quivering, his eyes filled with horror as out from the agitated waters arose the most fearful head he had ever gazed upon.

It was like nothing the pen of the writer has ever described, or the pencil of an artist delineated. Round, glistening with an unearthly phosphorescent glare, its huge blinking eyes seemed riveted upon the astounded detective, whilst its huge, gaping mouth slowly opened and shut, disclosing rows of jagged, uneven teeth.

Slowly this fresh horror drew a huge, tail-like appendage from out the water, as it was borne forward on a number of small, slowly-moving wings, similar in shape to those shown upon the fabled griffin.

Terror for a moment held Danby Druce in its icy grasp. The next he had shaken the numbing feeling from him, and was groping on the floor at his feet for some weapon with which to meet this new, this terrible assailant. His hand closed over a small flint, but as he realised the uselessness of so puny a weapon against so fearful foe, he flung it from him with a bitter, scornful laugh, and, planting his feet firmly apart, stood awaiting the weird monster's approach, armed only with Nature's weapons—his naked fists.

Swaying from side to side, now rising to the ceiling, now rebounding from the floor like an indiarubber ball, the strange apparition approached.

Breathing hard between his clenched teeth, as he resisted with all the strength of his iron will an almost irresistible desire to shrink into the furthermost corner of the strange prison, Danby Druce waited until the monster was within a few feet of where he stood, then took a step forward, and, throwing the whole weight of his body into the blow, struck the swaying "Thing" full between the eyes.

To his amazement, the cold, slimy form gave to the impact, and his fist was buried almost to the rest in the loose folds of clammy skin, then, gliding back out of his reach, the monster resumed its former shape, apparently uninjured by the fearful blow Danby Druce had delivered.

For a moment the detective stood gazing at the apparition in surprise, then a loud if somewhat quavering laugh burst from his lips.

"Pshaw, you must find some more terrible foe than this, Winged Man, if you think to subdue Danby Druce!" he muttered.

Then, as the Winged Man's strange creation bobbed and swayed between roof and ceiling, he lighted a second piece of paper, and waving it before him until it broke into a fierce flame, immediately dropped upon one the beneath the huge, distended body, and, holding the paper aloft with one hand, pressed it against the huge, ungainly form. There was a momentary fizzling as the flame touched the water, clinging to the bladder-like object, then a fearful report crashed through the narrow limits of the cave, sending the frightened frogs hurtling to the shelter of the pool—a bright, blinding flash of light dazzled Danby Druce's eyes, and the next moment the apparition disappeared from view.

Danby Druce had judged the nature of the Winged Man's attempt to frighten him right. The flying monster was nothing more nor less than an enormous gas-filled copy of a penny toy sold in the streets as "a dying pig," which with fiendish ingenuity, the Winged Man had invented to terrorise those unfortunate enough to fall into his power, that he might shatter their nerves and render them subservient to his will.

THE DETECTIVE'S RUSE.

Hours of weary waiting followed. Ever on his guard against some sudden terror, some hidden danger, Danby Druce prepared to meet his weird captor's next move. As the hours drew on the fearful silence of that awful place began to tell upon even Danby Druce's iron nerves. To add to his discomfort he gradually realised that the evil, heavy air was growing hotter and more unbearable each moment.

Seated upon a stone, Danby Druce drew his handkerchief wearily over his heated brow, then, by that faint light which still shone through the cave, he learned from whence they came. The whole surface of the pool was covered by thin, almost invisible, wreaths of steam, which, rising, soon filled the entire cave.

As the steam increased in density the water commenced to bubble, and Danby Druce, breathing the hot, scalding air with difficulty, looked in vain for some means of escape.

Thicker and thicker became the steam, hotter, and more repressive the stifling atmosphere, whilst the wondrous pool cast bubbles to the surface which bursting, added more steam to the already crowded apartment.

For nearly ten minutes Danby Druce bought the awful discomfiture of that fearful torture, then, determined to bring things to a crisis, flung his arms above his head, and, with a wild, shrill, despairing shriek, sank to the ground.

Immediately a loud, piercing whistle resounded from somewhere close at hand, then a hidden door half way up the wall near which Danby Druce lay, opened, through which the steam poured in clouds.

His eyes half closed, for his scream of agony at his fall had been but a ruse to lead his enemies to disclose themselves, he saw a dark form block up the steam-filled opening, and, with a thrill of excitement, recognised the features of the Winged Man.

A strange smile curled the fearful being's lips as he entered his wondrous torture-cave and stood looking down, with a kind of sad triumph, upon his fallen foe.

Danby Druce had closed his eyes as the Winged Man approached, lest the weird horror should see that he was shamming. Other footsteps approached.

"Again you triumph, my dear master!" said someone, in shrill, high tones, which he knew to be those of Ghat, the Winged Man's deformed slave.

"Over the body, dog, but not over the mind," replied the Winged Man discontentedly. "Others we have found whimpering on the floor. This man is overcome by heat, not by terror."

"Yet he will be, master," declared Ghat, chuckling villainously. "None can resist you are—none defy you—none!"

Still the Winged Man did not speak, but lost in thought, stood with folded arms gazing down upon the detective.

"Ho, ho, ho! I love this dainty prison of yours, master!" chuckled the misshapen dwarf. "I love to see strong men enter it, to see them come out broken in body and in spirit, slaves to do your will and mine!"

"What, dog?" roared the Winged Man, seizing Ghat in his fearful grasp. "And yours? You dare to put yourself on equality with me—to mention your evil, misshapen body in the same breath as mine? Learn that in my eyes you are but a soulless dog!"

As he spoke the Winged Man threw Ghat into the still steaming pool, as a boy hurls a dog into a pond to teach it to swim.

With a loud shriek get disappeared beneath the surface of the almost boiling water. Presently, shuddering with terror and moaning with pain, he dragged himself ashore, and crawled, sobbing pitifully, to his master's feet, where he crouched, gazing furtively into the weird horror's face, as though he were indeed the dog the Winged Man called him.

Spurning the cringing dwarf with his foot, the Winged Man ordered him to arise and follow, bringing Danby Druce with him.

As easily as though he had been but a child, the dwarf slung the detective over his shoulder.

It was anything but a comfortable position, for Danby Druce lay resting upon Ghat's misshapen shoulders, his head hanging over the dwarf's back, his legs dangling limply before him.

Still, his every nerve alert for some means of escape, Danby Druce gave no signs of life.

Presently, as he was carried through what was evidently the working of an abandoned mine, he felt his cheek rub against something hard, and cautiously groping with his fingers, they closed over the hilt of a broad-bladed knife.

This Danby Druce carefully secured, and its blade hidden up his coat-sleeve, allowed his arm to drop almost to the ground once more.

Presently the dwarf halted, and flung his burden on to a couch in a small, cell-like cave, guarded by a thick iron door.

"Lie there, Danby Druce, and recover consciousness. You may think the fact that you are not as other men for your escape from the bodily torture I usually inflict upon my foes. Yet"—the Winged Man uttered a grim, blood-curdling laugh—"you have not much to congratulate yourself about in that. I have sworn to break your stubborn spirit, to drag you down into the mire, to a deeper abasement than you have ever dream to possible. Blind, dumb, decrepit, you shall pass the remainder of your wretched life as my dog, my slave."

Then Danby Druce heard the door slam to, and he was alone once more—alone, yet with renewed hope.

He had passed through the ordeal comparatively unscathed—nay, more, had succeeded not only in duping the Winged Man but in securing a weapon with which to defend himself, if necessary.

The Spider's Web.

Leaving his prisoner, as he thought, unconscious, the Winged Man made his way through passage after passage, up countless stairs, until at length he reached a large cave opening on to a hill, its entrance shrouded by a leafy screen of tangled briars.

On one side of the entrance stood a pair of steps, upon which the Winged Man seated himself in a grotesque, crouching attitude, watching with interested eyes a huge spider spinning its web from the rocky side of the cave to the struggling branches of a small ash-plant.

For hours the Winged Man watched the little insect spinning its threads, then, rising upon extended wings, flew to a kind of shelf in the roof of the cave.

A few minutes later he reappeared, with what looked like a long box attached to his chest. From the end of this box hung a white, thin, but exceedingly strong thread of some glutinous material.

As he touched the floor of the cave the thread attached itself securely to the rough ground. Then, as the Winged Man flew to the top of the entrance, the thread spun out from the box. Backwards and forwards he flew, moving swiftly up and down, to left and right, leaving wherever he went a trail of glutinous twine, yet so thin as to be perfectly invisible half a dozen feet away.

For hours he worked, until at length, stretched across the mouth of the cave, was an imitation, exact in every particular, of the spider's web in the corner, to which he returned now and again that he might study its intricate shape.

The web completed, he built himself a tunnel-shaped home on the left-hand corner of his strange construction, and there, crouched like a spider awaiting its prey, surveyed his handiwork with every mark of satisfaction.

"Oh for a fly, a good fat fly, be it man or animal, to test the strength of my little silver web!" chuckled the Winged Man, as he peered from his cobweb-like nest.

As though in answer to his wish, a rabbit, alarmed by somebody climbing up the hillside, dashed blindly into the net.

Immediately its limbs became entangled in the merciless meshes, whilst the Winged Man, clambering from his eyrie, wound fine, weblike strands tightly round its limbs, then hurled it, bound and helpless, into the cave.

So strong with the strands of this gigantic web that, despite the rabbit's struggles, not a cord was broken; and, having assured himself that his web had borne the strain, the Winged Man crawled back to his lair, where he lay, his white, keen face peering from out his tunnel-like layer, looking like some enormous human spider.

Presently he started and looked quickly up. His quick ear had detected a movement not far away.

Clambering across his net, he leaned forward, and, putting aside the branches which overhung the top of the cave's mouth, peered through on to the outside world.

A low chuckle escaped his lips.

Hundred yards lower down the hill was a stout, cheery-faced man, clad in a rough tweed suit, his head protected by a broad-brimmed white hat, whilst his eyes were hidden behind a pair of huge blue spectacles, through which he gazed around him as though in search of something.

In his hand the stranger carried a large green net, with a handle some four feet in length; at his back swung a specimen box; by his side a bulging leather wallet.

The new-comer was Professor Omaney, a world-famed naturalist. He was searching amid the gorse and grass for butterflies, moths, or any strange insect that might stray across his path.

Pursing his lips, the Winged Man uttered an almost inaudible sound, something between a chirp and hiss. It was the cry of the grasshopper challenging a rival to fight.

The naturalist heard the sound, but, learned in natural history though he was, little guessed its meaning, or how laden with terrible possibilities for his future it was.

Again the sound rang forth. This time there was an answer to the challenge, and a magnificent green grasshopper, with black spots along the middle of its body, sprang from the grass almost under the naturalist's feet.

Despite his blue spectacles, Professor Omaney's eyes were keen enough to notice the black spots, which proclaimed the insect as being a very rare specimen; in fact, though his was probably the biggest private collection in the United Kingdom, he had not yet succeeded in capturing a great spotted grasshopper. With an ejaculation of delight he started in pursuit of the agile insect.

It is not generally known that the grasshopper is probably the most pugnacious insect in the world; in fact, the Japanese capture and train these agile little jumpers on purpose to set them against each other in specially prepared arenas.

During these grasshopper fights much money changes hands, and a well-trained fighting locust, or grasshopper, is worth its weight in gold.

Answering the challenge from the cave with a number of short, sharp, angry chirps, the grasshopper seemed absolutely unconscious of its pursuer's presence.

Again and again Professor Omaney brought his net down, as he thought, over the coveted specimen, but each time the agile little creature eluded the deadly swoop, and, clearing a good four feet at each jump, drew rapidly nearer the cave.

Mortified by repeated failure, Professor Omaney exerted every muscle to secure his prey, but, run though he might, the grasshopper still kept ahead, until at last it disappeared through the leafy screen which hid the cave's mouth.

Angry at being balked of his prey, the professor thrust his net through the leaves, hoping to frighten the insect into the open once more.

To his astonishment, he could not withdraw his net, and, thinking that it was probably caught by some thorns, he thrust his hand through the leaves.

As he did so his fingers closed over some thin, sticky substance.

In vain he tried to withdraw his hand. It was fastened tightly to one of the centre strands of the Winged Man's web.

Wondering what the strange, glue-like substance might be, and little realising the terrible danger which menaced him, the Professor moved forward to determine if possible the reason of this phenomenon.

As he did so his legs and body struck the fearsome meshes, and were immediately glued fast to the Winged Man's wondrous web.

A sudden spasm of fear chilled his heart. Raising his disengaged arm, he struck at the almost invisible bonds which bound him.

Alas! the attempt to break through only made his eventual capture more sure.

Glued tightly to the fearful web, he could only writhe frantically in a futile attempt to break free.

A slight trembling of the web caused him to look up.

He ceased to struggle. His hair seemed to stand on end, his blood to turn to ice within his veins. Coming towards him, over what he could now see was a number of tied cords stretched like a wheel from a central hub, crossed and recrossed by other cords, was a huge, black fearful monster, with a single red eye, which cast a baleful light over the imprisoned man.

Even as he gazed the eye closed, and Omaney shrieked aloud with terror, as he saw an awful white human face peering at him from the black body of what he could but believe was an enormous spider.

A foot from his miserable prisoner the Winged Man paused and surveyed his capture.

The Winged Man paused and surveyed his capture.

"Help—help! In the name of Heaven, help!" shrieked the unhappy Omaney.

But the hill was remote from the haunts of man. There was none to hear his appealing cry for help save the Winged Man, and he, gloating over his prisoner's sufferings, slowly extended one hand, and touched the fear-maddened man on the cheek.

So terrible was the Winged Man's calm deliberate movement, so icy cold the touch of the long, white hand that, in a paroxysm of terror, Professor Omaney tore his head, arms and shoulders from the restraining strands; then a loud, piercing, almost maniacal cry burst from the wretched man's lips, as, springing from the web, the Winged Man alighted upon his victim shoulders, and commenced to make sure of his victim by swathing his arms and legs in that thin, glutinous cords from the apparatus he carried fastened on to his breast, until at length, with one last despairing cry, one final frenzied attempt to break free, the Professor's tormented brain found rest in unconsciousness.

Removing his victim from the web, the Winged Man, filling the cave with peal upon peal of mocking laughter, laid him, bound and helpless, by the side of the rabbit.

"Two!" cried the Winged Man gazing down upon his captives. "Not bad for less than an hour's sport. Ho, ho! What game will blunder into my net next, I wonder? Time alone can tell." And turning on his heel, he mended the broken strands of his gigantic web, then returned once more to his fearful lair.

A MINUTE'S FREEDOM.

In the meantime, after waiting what he deemed sufficient time for his enemies to leave the vicinity of the well, Danby Druce sprang from his couch and felt with groping fingers over the rough walls of his prison.

Floor, ceiling, walls, and door he examined foot by foot, inch by inch, but without finding one weak spot, or even so much as a crevasse into which he could thrust the point of his knife.

Walls, roof, and ceiling were of solid rock, the door of heavy plates of iron, against which he would only blunt and break his weapon in vain.

Suddenly he threw himself on the couch, and, his knife up his sleeve ready for immediate action, lapsed into pretended unconsciousness, for the grating of the key in the lock warned him of a coming visitor.

A minute later Ghat entered the cell, a common white enamel jug in one hand, a loaf of coarse bread in the other.

Peering through his eyelashes, Danby Druce saw the dwarf deposit the bread and water on a tiny shelf by the side of the door, then take his stand by the bed.

As he did so Ghat's eyes fell upon a magnificent pearl and diamond pin, a present from the Emperor of Austria, which Danby Druce wore. A look of intense avarice flashed into the dwarf's eyes.

For a moment he hesitated; then, stealing softly to the door, looked cautiously up and down the passage, ere he stepped back on tip-toe to the side of the cot, and shot his thick, stubby fingers towards the pin.

The next moment and edge actuation of alarm burst from his lips, as, ere his fingers closed upon the coveted gem, his hand was seized, whilst the detective's iron fingers closed around his throat.

Staggering back, drawing Danby Druce with him, Ghat exerted his whole enormous strength to burst free.

In vain. In Danby Druce he had met his match, yet the detective soon found that he was not to have it all his own way, and for several minutes the two rolled over and over on the floor clenched in a deadly embrace.

Unfortunately for Danby Druce he had been obliged to relinquish his knife when he seized the dwarf by the throat, lest he should raise an alarm.

As they struggled, now Danby Druce, now Ghat uppermost, each was fighting for a moment's respite, that he might seize the deadly weapon and plunge it into his foeman's heart.

Once Ghat's extended fingers touched the knife's handle, but ere they could close upon it Danby Druce had jerked his arm away.

With a howl like that of a maddened wolf Ghat buried his fangs deep into the detective's arm, worrying him as a terrier worries a rat. The pain was fearful, yet Danby Druce did not utter a single cry, for, carried away by a sudden paroxysm of rage, Ghat had for the moment forgotten that, whoever was first to gain possession of the knife would prove the victor.

He was reminded of his folly by Danby Druce breaking free, snatching up the knife, and waving it above his head in triumph.

With a snarl of baffled rage and hate Ghat turned to flee. Too late! In a stride

Danby Druce placed himself between his foe and the door.

For a moment Ghat stood glaring at him as though he would fly, unarmed though he was, at his throat. Then suddenly his hands dropped to his side, and, to Danby Druce's astonishment, he sank down on the rough, comfortless bed upon which the detective had been laid, and burst into tears.

Anger faded from Danby Druce's generous heart, to be succeeded by a feeling of deep pity for the unfortunate wretch.

"Oh, the Winged Man will whip me, he will drop burning lead upon my body, he will starve me, he will rack my body with the most fearful pain!" he cried, allowing the hand with which he had covered his face to fall to his side.

"If you fear him thus, why not leave him?" demanded Danby Druce eagerly.

"Would that I could! Would that I dare!" moaned Ghat. "If I hid a thousand fathoms deep beneath the earth, if I could fly to the furthermost star which decks the heavens the Winged Man's vengeance could overtake me!"

"The why not help me to capture him? Once he is safe in prison he would be powerless to injure you?" cried Danby Druce with a wild hope that if he could once get this strange creature on his side half his task would be done, and the Winged Man would prove an easy prey.

A contemptuous laugh was Ghat's only response.

"The iron is not yet dug out of the earth which will hold the Winged Man against his will, the prison walls are not yet built which could hem him in. Think you, Danby Druce, that you would be alive at this moment had not the Winged Man doomed you to a fate worse than death. I am the Winged Man's slave, and the Winged Man has sworn that you shall be my slave."

"I pity you if that time ever comes. It strikes me the slave will soon prove master!" laughed Danby Druce scornfully.

An angry flush dyed Ghat's cheek.

"When that day comes I will bring you what you have just said back to your mind, a blow for every word!" he hissed. Then, so suddenly that Danby Druce was almost taken by surprise, he sprang, without a single preparatory movement, straight from the bed at his foe.

Swiftly Danby Druce's fist shot out, and catching the dwarf in mid-air between the eyes, clutching him back, stunned and dazed, into the centre of the cell; then, turning on his heel hastened from the cell, and, slamming the door to behind him, turned the key in the lock.

CHASED TO HIS DOOM.

"Free at last! Free! But for how long?" cried Danby Druce, as he stood for a moment in the corridor outside his cell.

Swift came the answer, but from whence Danby Druce could not surmise:

"Until you meet the Winged Man again!"

"Who speaks?" cried Danby Druce, wheeling swiftly round.

"Who speaks?" was brought to his ears from the distance.

Danby Druce breathed a sigh of relief.

"It was but an echo!" he murmured aloud.

"But an echo!" came back the answer.

A puzzled frown wrinkled the detective's brow. The second echo had been much clearer and closer than the first.

"Is it the Winged Man?" he demanded, in strong, clear tones.

"The Winged Man," repeated the echo, now apparently at the very entrance to the long rocky corridor into which the cell where Danby Druce had been confined, opened.

A wave of superstitious terror for the moment held Danby Druce dumb, but with an effort he regained his wonted courage. Placing his back to the rocky wall, he faced the direction from whence the echo had come, and, his knife advanced, cried:

"Come one, come all, seen or unseen, man or fiend, I defy you to the death!"

"To the death!"

No longer before him, but above, below, to right, to left, from the very rocks against which he lent, loud, clear, ominous the echo came:

"To the death! To the death!"

Nothing that Danby Druce had hitherto experienced was quite so awful as this echoing of his own words from a dozen different points at once.

His nerves were strung to their highest tension, his eyes glanced fearfully to right and left. Suddenly he felt icy-cold fingers were encircling his throat, and, with a gasping cry of terror, he turned, and fled, followed by peals upon peals of mocking, unearthly laughter.

Dashing blindly forward, whither he knew not, Danby Druce sped up a precipitous slope, clambering sometimes on hands and knees up broken, moss-grown stairs, until gradually his native courage drove back the panic surging within his heart, and he began to think more rationally as he ran.

"Steady, Danby Druce—steady!" he muttered reprovingly. "You have faced death in its most horrible aspects a hundred times to flee like an hysterical, terror-stricken woman, from what? Before some cunning trick of a monster, who, though his nature may seem supernatural, is yet but a being in human form."

As these words left his lips he slowed down until at length he came to a halt in a long, narrow passage cut through the living rock, down which a cool, refreshing breeze fanned his heated brow. But barely had he drawn in a second long, deep breath, ere once more the icy fingers of returning panic seemed to grip his heart.

Far away in the distance arose sounds to which Danby Druce had oft listened with joyfully beating heart on many a winter's morning, as, astride a well-bred hunter, he took hedges and ditches in masterly style when following the hounds.

But then those sounds had been ahead, now they were behind him, growing louder, fiercer, more insistent each moment.

It was the deep bay of hounds in full cry. There was no need to ask the quarry.

Well Danby Druce knew that it was he they chased.

Before him lay a bend in the long, straight passage he had just followed, beyond which appeared the light of day.

Thither he sped; then, turning, looked behind him. A fearful sight met his gaze. Their eyes gleaming green in the semi-darkness, their heads raised, showing that they were running to a breast-high scent, a pack of enormous hounds came sweeping from the darkness of the abandoned pit upon him.

In vain Danby Druce shot a swift, searching glance around in search of some ledge or jagged rock, upon which he might climb, and at least stave off the awful fate that menaced him.

But only the bare, uneven, unclimbable wall of the passage met his gaze. There was nothing for it but to trust to his feet. Turning, Danby Druce ran towards the ever-increasing light before him, expecting each moment to feel the cruel fangs of the foremost hounds fixed into his shoulder.

Yet, as minute succeeded minute, and nothing happened, he cast a frightened glance over his shoulder, to find that the awful pack were at the same distance from him as when he had first seen them.

Suddenly a wild, shrill cry of delight burst from his lips. Before him shone the bright light of day, piercing through a screen of autumn-tinted leaves.

"The outer world! Thank Heaven, the outer world!" almost shrieked the detective, as he hurled himself headlong towards the entrance of the cave. But ere the joyful words had well left his lips, he uttered an ejaculation of dismay, as he struggled fiercely to break free from the strong, sticky cords which held him prisoner.

For a moment Danby Druce struggled fiercely; then, as his eyes grew accustomed to the bright sunlight which played full into the cave, he saw to his horror, that he was enmeshed in the strands of a gigantic web.

Nor was that the worst. Barely had he made the discovery ere he saw, peering at him from round the mouth of his lair, the white, mocking face of his enemy, who, like a human spider, crept slowly, as though gloating over his captive's agony, towards him.

RECAPTURED!

In vain Danby Druce struggled to break free from the adhesive threads which seemed to wind themselves around his limbs of their own accord.

He was still armed with Ghat's knife, with which he made a gallant fight for freedom, probably for life, slashing at the threads until at length the pressure relaxed, and but a single cord held him back from freedom.

But even as he raised his knife to slash the last strand in half, something white hurled through the air, and the next moment a thread, guided with unerring skill by the Winged Man, encircled the detective's body, binding his arm helpless to his side.

Cord followed cord in quick succession, until at length, with a fearful load of despair weighing down his heart, Danby Druce realised that he was a closer prisoner than ever.

A low chuckle of intense enjoyment caused him to look up. Creeping over the strands of the web, his eyes aglow with fiendish malice, came the Winged Man.

"Aho, mine enemy! When to pass and idle hour, perhaps the chance to teach a lesson to such men as he," cried the Winged Man, pointing to where Professor Omaney lay gazing at the weird horror with starting eyeballs, "I built this web, I little dreamed that amongst the first who would blunder into it would be the great Danby Druce. I dreamed his course was run, and that he lay a closer prisoner within the bowels of the earth."

"Then you have yet to learn that even the Winged Man is not all-powerful!" cried Danby Druce defiantly. "You'd better kill me, Winged Man," he added in tones of calm contempt, "for that will be your only chance to hold me fast."

"Kill you? I would not slay you outright for all the wealth yet lying undiscovered in South Africa!" declared the Winged Man, in a sudden flash of wrath. "No, no! I have sworn to humble your proud spirit, to bring you creeping to my feet and my slightest call. When, I know not. It may be a week, a year hence; but be sure, Danby Druce, that time will come. Unwilling to lose the sport your unfaltering pursuit of myself brings, I spare your life for a time. It must be gall and wormwood[45] to your proud spirit to know that he you hate spares your life, not through pity, but in contempt. But there is a greater humiliation than any before you. The day I enter a prison door will be the most bitter in your life."

As he ceased speaking the Winged Man scrambled rapidly over the yielding web, and, seizing the helpless detective by the collar of his coat, dragged him from the web and deposited him on the floor of the cave by the side of the Professor Omaney.

All this time the hounds who had chased Danby Druce through the subterranean passage were filling the air with deep-chested bays in the furthermost extremity of the cave, their bright, angry eyes glaring like green specks from out the darkness.

---

[45] Resentment (Gall is bile and wormwood is a bitter plant).

A sharp word of command stopped their clamour, and Danby Druce heard the pattering of many feet growing fainter in the distance as the dogs returned to their kennels in obedience to their weird master's command.

Placing a golden whistle to his lips, the mouthpiece of which had been cunningly cut from out a single ruby of enormous worth, the Winged Man blew a loud, shrill blast.

There was no response, and after a minute or so of impatient delay the Winged Man whistled once more.

Struggling, despite his bonds, to a sitting position, Danby Druce gazed tauntingly into the Winged Man's face, but ere he could speak a third louder, angrier, shriller whistle echoed and re-echoed through the cave.

"Louder, Winged Man! Perhaps Ghat—for I suppose it is he you would summon—is asleep, or helping himself to your uncounted stores of pilfered gold!" cried Danby Druce mockingly.

"Silence, dog, foredoomed slave!" thundered the Winged Man. "As for he you mention, I will break every bone of his body! I will tear him to pieces with red-hot irons! I will make him curse the hour in which he was born!"

Even Danby Druce recoiled for a moment from the fierce, almost maniacal rage which blazed from the Winged Man's eyes as he uttered this fearful threat against his all too-faithful servitor; yet the detective's voice was filled with mockery as he cried:

"Perhaps it would be as well to assure yourself that Ghat can answer your summons ere wasting breath in futile threats."

"What mean you?" asked the Winged Man, frowning angrily upon his prisoner.

"I mean that unless Ghat has strength to tear down the iron-bound door of my late prison, you may whistle till you burst your throat, and he will not come!"

"Ah, that explains your presence here, mine enemy!" chuckled the Winged Man. "Yet think not that so paltry an excuse will save the dwarf from my wrath. Naught but gross carelessness could have put him in your power. Enough! Learn that the Winged Man is served by more than one slave."

Upon the same whistle he blew a number of totally distinct notes, then stood with folded arms and a mocking smile upon his lips, surveying his astounded captive.

°A Startling Discovery.

A shuffling of many feet and a number of bent, wasted, miserable-looking creatures, with gaunt, almost fleshness limbs, untrimmed, matted hair, and ever-shifting, terror-laden eyes, crept—they could scarce be said to walk—into the cave.

° 24 May 1913.

So abject was the demeanour of the new-comers that Danby Druce could scarce believe he was gazing upon human beings.

The Winged Man read his thoughts.

"Yes, Danby Druce, they are indeed of the same human race as yourself," he declared. "Once they were happy, healthy men, strong in mind and body, as you are at this moment. Even as they are shall you be when your time comes."

"Never!" retorted Danby Druce defiantly. "You make kill my body, but the soul which Heaven has implanted in my bosom shall never bow to your inhuman tortures."

"We shall see!" retorted the Winged Man confidently. Then, with a mocking bow, he continued; "But I apologise; I have not yet introduced your future comrades to you. No. 7, step to the front!" Immediately, what had at one time been a tall, well-made, middle-aged man advanced with shuffling, shrinking steps towards his fearful master. "Look up; put back the hair from your face, that Mr. Danby Druce may recognise your features," commanded the weird horror.

The man obeyed, the flush which swept across his ashen face betraying the fact that, deep within his soul, there yet lingered some sense of shame at his degraded position.

Danby Druce uttered an exclamation of astonishment.

"Lord Ferrars!" he ejaculated, as he recognised a member of the British House of Lords, who had been foremost in urging the authorities to stop at nothing to capture the Winged Man, and an account of whose mysterious disappearance had filled the papers for many days.

After listening to an all-night sitting in the House of Commons, Lord Ferrars had been seen to enter a deserted ante-room. From that moment he had disappeared from human ken, until Danby Druce recognised him as a helpless prisoner in the Winged Man's power.

"Yes, Danby Druce, it is he," admitted the Winged Man, with a ring of triumph in his voice. "Lord Ferrars, one of the most influential peers of the British Empire. Alone and unaided, I carried him from out the very seat of Government itself. Take warning by his fate. Swear to abandon all attempts to track me down, and I, on my part, will promise not to molest you."

A loud, scornful laugh, in which there was more than a ring of triumph, burst from Danby Druce's lips.

"So, Winged Man," he cried, "your words have betrayed that there is at least one man in this world you fear!"

"You lie!" thundered the Winged Man. And, snatching a jagged log of wood from the floor, he rushed to Danby Druce as though, carried away by a paroxysm of rage, he intended slaying him then and there.

Bound, and helpless to avert the threatened blow though he was, Danby Druce shrunk not nor quailed, but, fixing his eyes firmly upon his great foe, bade him strike.

A look of in voluntary admiration flashed from the Winged Man's eyes.

"I thank you for reminding me that in one angry moment I might have placed you beyond reach of my revenge for ever," he said, in tones of ominous calm.

Suddenly Lord Ferrars seemed to shake off the spell of terror the Winged Man had placed over him. Advancing towards where Danby Druce was seated, he raised his hands in appeal, crying:

"All those I loved deem me dead. Swear, Danby Druce, never to make public my humiliation. The thought of that would be a greater torture than any this cold, callous fiend has yet inflicted upon me. Pity my broken spirit, my bruised, distorted body, and keep my fearful fate from the dear ones I may never see again!"

"You may trust to my discretion, Lord Ferrars," promised the great detective. "Believe me, when I regain my liberty I will not rest until you are free."

"Lord Ferrars does not need your help, Danby Druce!" cried the Winged Man, with a scornful laugh. "See, No. 7, the way is open. Before you lies the world with all its joys, its pleasures, its ambitions, its hopes. Go, there is naught to keep you here, save your own will!"

With a cry of incredulous joy the unfortunate peer gazed for a moment almost gratefully at the Winged Man; then his bent form straightened, a look of ineffable joy lighted his face, and he sprang towards the entrance to the cave.

But even as his foot, for the first time for many weary months, pressed the soft, yielding grass, he came to an abrupt halt, a look of hopeless despair swept across his face. Striving to advance, he felt as though a thousand invisible hands were dragging him back.

"What, is your love for me so great that you hesitate to leave me?" cried the Winged Man mockingly. "Go quickly, lest I repent of my mercy, and call you back!"

"I can't! Heaven help me—I can't!" moaned the wretched man. Then, sinking to the ground, he covered his face with his hands, and burst into tears.

A HUMAN MOTH.

Fierce anger welled up in Danby Druce's heart.

"Winged Man. I would rather be yonder poor, helpless slave of your will than you, in all your pride and might!" he cried, anger and horror at the way the Winged Man had played with his prisoner's helplessness driving all fear of his own precarious position from his heart.

Deigning no answer to Danby Druce's contemptuous cry, save a shrug of the shoulders, the Winged Man called another from his band of miserable slaves.

This one Danby Druce recognised as a rich banker who had made a public offer of £10,000 to anyone who would slay the Winged Man.

A policeman who had gallantly attacked the weird horror, and had almost succeeded in disabling him, was the next. Then followed men of various classes of society, several of whom Danby Druce had known in happier days.

In obedience to a sign from their fearful taskmaster, the Winged Man's slaves raised Danby Druce and Professor Omaney from the floor, and carrying them down several flights of steps, deposited them in chairs in a large cave, fitted up as a laboratory, then leaving the two men and the weird horror alone.

Wondering what cruel fate would be his, Danby Druce watched the Winged Man as he stood for some minutes intently regarding the professor.

Presently, with a cry of well-simulated delight, he freed the professor from the glutinous threads which bound him; then, laying the terror-paralysed man upon a table, bent over him, soothing his ruffled clothes, and rearranged his tousled hair.

"A fine specimen. Not as good as I have seen, perhaps; still, a valuable addition to my collection," Danby Druce heard his fearful captor mutter.

A groan of terror burst from Professor Omaney's lips, mingled with shrieks of pain as the Winged Man twisted his limbs about as though ignorant of the anatomy of the human frame.

Danby Druce watched those strange proceedings with growing surprise.

He knew that the Winged Man seldom acted upon caprice. For all he did he had a reason, though for the life of him the detective could not understand the vague mutterings in which he seemed to be trying to classify his prisoner, as he continued stroking the professor's clothes, as a sportsman might arrange the plumage of a dead bird.

Presently Danby Druce saw the Winged Man withdraw a large slab of wood, and what looked like a huge pin, from a recess in the further end of the cave. Laying the professor face downwards upon the board, he picked up the enormous pan, and, raising it in the air, made as though he would thrust its fearful point between the prostrate man's shoulders.

The professor turned his pale, frightened face up to the Winged Man's stern, relentless visage.

"Mercy! Mercy! Do not kill me! Or, if I am doomed, let the end be swift!" came in accents of heart-breaking appeal from the pallid lips.

"Ho, ho!" roared the Winged Man. "You beg for a swift death! Professor Omaney, a few weeks back I strode through your library. There I saw a case of butterflies and rare moths, each pinned, whilst yet living, to cardboard by your hand. What was that? Have you ever given a moment's thought to the agony endured by these helpless, gaudy-coloured creatures?"

"No, no; I swear not one was living when I fastened them in the case! They had all passed through the killing bottle!" shouted Omaney eagerly.

"Say you so?" demanded the Winged Man. "Then, as you have done to other living creatures, shall be done to you. Lie there; move hand or foot, and I will pin you to the board as you have pinned many an unhappy moth. I go to prepare a killing-bottle large enough to contain you."

With these words the Winged Man dropped to the floor, and, throwing the gigantic pin from him, strode from the room.

THE FLIGHT.

Hardly had the Winged Man taken his departure ere Danby Druce leaned forward as far as his bonds would allow.

"Quick, Professor, release me! We may yet escape this cruel fiend's grasp!" he cried, in a low, hurried whisper.

"No, no; I dare not! You heard what he said. He will pin me to this board, and will leave me writhing in agony till death brings release!" moaned the professor.

"Well, it's that all the killing bottle," retorted Danby Druce. "Come, be a man! Better to die fighting than to succumb without resistance, like one of your own moths. Why, man, even a timid butterfly would fly if you left it as the Winged Man has left you!"

"Don't—don't! I cannot bear to think that probably thousands of helpless living things have suffered the same torture I have endured this last hour!" moaned Professor Omaney.

"But it is nothing to what you will endure when the Winged Man returns. Believe me, I know him well; he has never yet subjected a captive to a painless death!" insisted Danby Druce.

Acting on the principle that one nail will drive out another, he was seeking to banish the professor's fear by instilling and even greater terror of the Winged Man in his heart. "But what is the good of trying to escape from this dread horror?" objected the professor. "We will never reach the outer world again."

"We can and will, if there yet remains a single spark of manhood in your breast!" declared Danby Druce.

Emboldened by the confidence in the other's tone, Professor Omaney, glancing fearfully at the door, rose to his feet, and soon, though with trembling fingers, had set the detective free.

"That's right; the first step towards liberty has been taken!" cried Danby Druce, stretching his cramped limbs, and speaking with a greater confidence than he felt, for he could not believe that the Winged Man would have left them thus alone if there was not some fearful trap already prepared for them.

A swift glance around the cave showed Danby Druce an electric lamp standing upon a shelf.

This he gained possession of; then, looking round for a weapon, his eyes fell upon the sharpened bar the Winged Man had threatened to thrust through the professor's body.

As his fingers closed over the glistening steel, renewed courage filled his heart. At least he would not be recaptured without a struggle.

"Come, yonder door is open! Why you standing still? Come quick!" gasped the professor in terror-laden, excited accents.

Danby Druce shook his head. The very fact that the door stood wide open warned him of danger to come, yet there seemed no other means of leaving the cave; so, motioning the professor to follow, he advanced slowly along a passage cut in the living rock.

Suddenly he felt the ground tremble beneath his feet, and sprang back drawing the professor with him just in time to escape being hurled down a dark chasm which had opened suddenly at their feet.

Switching on the light of the electric lantern, Danby Druce cast its beams on to the floor of the passage.

Immediately before him was around opening, heading into what looked like the glistening sides of a glass chamber.

In a flash Danby Druce realised the trap which, with fiendish ingenuity, the Winged Man had laid for them. What was evidently a vault beneath the level of the cave had been rapidly turned into the semblance of a huge killing-bottle, such as are used by naturalists, into which the Winged Man doubtless intended the professor should fall, believing that carried away by selfish terror, he would seek to save his own life without troubling to release the detective.

Motioning Professor Omaney to remain where he was, the detective rushed back to the room they had just left, returning a minute later carrying a roll of matting from the cave's floor over his shoulder.

This, to the professor's astonishment, he dropped into the circular cavity.

Immediately the sliding door glided back into its place, and, grasping the professor by the arm, the detective led him safely over the hidden death-trap.

Extinguishing the lamp, lest its beams should lead to their detection, the two crept noiselessly through an apparently endless maze of passages.

Hour succeeded hour, and the two began to despair of ever reaching the outer world.

At length, even when Danby Druce was beginning to lose heart, a faint gleam of daylight ahead caused him to quickened his steps.

Brighter and brighter grew the light, and Danby Druce was about to congratulate himself upon having once more escaped the Winged Man's clutches, when, without a moment's warning, a loud, fierce, angry bark resounded through the passage, and the next moment a huge Russian boarhound, bearing its sharp, cruel teeth in a fearful grin, launched itself through the darkness at the detective.

Instinctively Danby Druce lowered the point of the steel rod, and the hound's growl was succeeded by a yell of pain, as the furious animal impaled itself upon the sharp steel point.

The iron had pierced his heart, and even as Danby Druce hurled the weapon which had stood him in such good stead to the ground, the boarhound died, viciously biting its hard haft to the last.

A few minutes later two pale-faced, trembling figures emerged from the cave, across the mouth of which still hung the grey threads of the Winged Man's broken web.

With subdued shouts of joy they rushed side-by-side down the hillside, until at length bursting through a hedge, they stood on a white dusty road, and peered through the branches at the awful cave they had just left, half fearing to see the awe-inspiring form of the Winged Man following on outstretched wings in swift pursuit.

But no sign of the weird horror could be seen, and, turning their faces towards where, nestled in a valley, across the roofs and chimneys of a distant town, they walked swiftly down the road.

Suddenly Danby Druce came to an abrupt halt, gazing fixedly at the bars of the gate leading into an adjacent field.

"What is it? Is the Winged Man following?" demanded Professor Omaney, seizing his companion by the arm.

"No, no! I think for the time being we have escaped that fearful creature. See, what does that remind you of?" he added, pointing to the gossamer-like threads of a spider's web between the bars of a gate from which a blue-bottle was trying ineffectually to escape.

Without a word Professor Omaney knelt down, and with tender fingers released the fly.

"I have learned my lesson," he said, as he rose to his feet. "Henceforth no helpless living creature shall suffer at my hands."

LORD FERRARS' MESSAGE.

Two days later Danby Druce emerged from a thick wood growing on the opposite side of the hill to that on which the Winged Man's cave was situated. He was clad in the velveteens and leggings of a gamekeeper, and carried a breach-loading gun over his shoulder. His eyes glittered with suppressed excitement, as well they might. Assisted by half a battalion of infantry, a squad of mounted police, and his own highly-trained staff of detectives, Danby Druce hoped this time to lay the Winged Man by the heels.

Nobly the authorities were seconding his efforts, and so well had he laid his plans that it seemed certain that the weird horror's career would at length be brought to a close.

His only fear was lest the Winged Man should leave Puck's Hill, as the acclivity was called, ere their arrangements were completed.

But evidently the Winged Man was taking one of his long periods of rest, for no sign of the dread being had been seen by Danby Druce, or by the detectives skilfully concealed around the hill.

Leaving the wood behind him, Danby Druce, taking advantage of every piece of cover, reconnoitred the ground above the cavern's mouth.

As he did so his eyes wandered eastward, and satisfy chuckle escaped his lips as he saw, close to the horizon, two round objects, like yellow soap-bubbles, which he knew were military balloons, ready to take their part in the night's work.

Suddenly the great detective crouched in the centre of a large alder-shrub immediately above the cave. His quick ear had detected a shuffling of many feet. Suddenly the sounds ceased, and a deathly silence obtained over the hillside.

Five minutes later, from the distant road, into which the detective and Professor Omaney had burst their way after their mad flight from the Winged Man's subterranean stronghold, came loud, clear, and distinct in the evening air three strident blasts on a motor-horn.

Immediately the screen of leaves which covered the mouth of the cave was thrust aside, and Danby Druce's heart for a moment stood still with anxiety, as, like some evil bird of prey leaving its eyrie, the Winged Man swept on outstretched wings from the mouth of the cave.

Were all Danby Druce's carefully-thought-out plans to be of no avail?

Time alone will tell.

Turning in a graceful circle in the air, the Winged Man remained poised before the entrance to the cave; then, drawing a short-handled, long-thronged whip from his belt, he cracked it until reports like pistol-shots echoed amongst the trees.

"Hasten, Ghat, you lazy, slovenly dog—hasten, or I'll flay you alive!" roared the Winged Man.

"I come, master; but the creeping curs move slowly. They whine that the chains gall their wrists and ankles. Ho, ho, ho!" came in tones of fiendish enjoyment from the ground beneath the crouching detective.

The next moment, chained like convicts two and two, the miserable slaves of the Winged Man's will emerged from the cave.

In the rear came Ghat, hopping with grotesquely horrible strides up and down the long line, urging on the miserable procession with blows from a whip similar to that carried by the Winged Man.

Chained like convicts, eight emaciated men emerged from the lair.

Marching to the accompaniment of clanking chains, eight dejected men commenced the descent of the steep hillside.

"On, dogs that you are—hasten!" cried the Winged Man, as, descending in a fierce, circular swoop, he passed up and down the miserable line, striking the unhappy captives with cruel, merciless force upon their heads and shoulders.

A stinging blow, which sent the cruel thong circling round his neck, and left a livid scar upon the wretched man's cheek, drew a loud shriek of pain from the foremost of the miserable gang.

With a cry of rage Ghat bounded forward, and as the Winged Man unwound his lash from his victim's throat the dwarf fell upon the culprit, tearing and scratching at him as though he would rend him limb from limb.

A movement in the rear of the procession attracted Danby Druce's attention for a moment from the cruel exhibition of fiendish hate which was taking place in the front, and he saw one of the prisoners, whom he recognised as Lord Ferrars, stumble and fall to the ground, drawing the unhappy wretch to whom he was handcuffed with him.

So natural was it that so misery-worn a wretch should stumble and fall, that Danby Druce would have thought little of it had he not seen his hand thrust swiftly beneath a tuft of the long, dry grass, and as swiftly withdrawn.

The next moment, his attentions attracted by the clanking of chains, the Winged Man, with one swift movement of his wings hovered over them, and, with cruel, skilfully-applied lashes of his scourge, soon forced them to their feet.

His blood boiling with indignation, it was with difficulty Danby Druce could restrain himself from emptying both barrels of his gun at the weird horror.

But to have done so would have been rendered useless all his elaborate precautions for the capture or destruction of the Winged Man. Well he knew that being who seemed impervious to bullets could not be injured by the small shot with which alone his gun was loaded.

"Hither, dog!" cried the Winged Man, as the mournful procession continued on its way down the hill.

Ghat hastened to his master's side.

"Guide these worms of earth to yonder van. Leave them in my various haunts. See that none escaped on the way or—well, I need not threaten; you know how I avenge failure. Go!"

Dropping upon all fours, Ghat rubbed his low forehead on the ground at the Winged Man's feet, in token of obedience; then hastened off after the departing procession, whilst the Winged Man muttering, "Now for a night's uninterrupted work in my laboratory; then to gather fresh booty once more," he, to Danby Druce's relief, re-entered the cave.

Through a pair of field-glasses Danby Druce watched the wretched procession until, reaching the road, it entered the open door of a motor-van, which bore upon its back and sides the name of a well-known firm of caterers.

Then he saw Ghat don a long motor-cap and goggles, and seat himself by the driver's side as the vehicle moved off.

Waiting until he deemed all was safe, Danby Druce crept on hands and knees from shrub to shrub, until at length he stopped close to the tuft of grass near where Lord Ferrars had fallen. Glancing apprehensively at the cave—for he was in full view of that leaf-screened entrance to the Winged Man's hidden haunt—he thrust his hand beneath the grass. His fingers closed upon a small, flat piece of wood.

Not daring to stop in so exposed to place, Danby Druce thrust it into his pocket, and, regaining the alder-shrub through which he had witnessed the departure of the Winged Man's prisoners, eagerly examined his find.

It was, as his touch had told him, a piece of wood, just large enough to be conveniently concealed in the palm of the hand. On it, in a pale, faint letters, evidently written in the wretched peer's blood, were the words:

"If D. D. would redeem his promise, he must seek me on the Falcon's Crag."

"The Falcon's Crag?" repeated Danby Druce. "The name seems familiar, yet I cannot remember where it is. No matter, I will find it out, and it shall go hard with me if the unfortunate nobleman is not restored to his weeping friends!"

Then, lest the piece of wood should fall into the hands of the Winged Man, he cut it into innumerable pieces. This done, he withdrew into the wood, and, throwing himself upon a heap of leaves beneath a spreading chestnut, he awaited, with what patience he might, the coming night.

There was nothing further to be done. Each man knew his post; and hidden away in a rutted lane, some half a mile from the mouth of the shaft leading to the Winged Man's Hall of Coal, were a number of covered carts, the contents of which were destined to play no unimportant part in the Winged Man's downfall.

THE ATTACK.

As the sun sank beneath the horizon, Danby Druce approached the outskirts of the wood. It was a beautiful autumnal evening. The sun had been shining brightly all day and, as inevitably happens at this season of the year, a thick white haze had arisen from the low-lying country around.

It was upon this fact that Danby Druce had reckoned to draw his cordon of police, troops, and detectives unseen around the Winged Man.

Save the call of a partridge in a distant field, the baying of a dog in some remote farmhouse, and the lowing of cattle in the meadows, not a sound arose to break the silence that obtained, yet well Danby Druce knew that already armed men were hastening to various points north, south, east, and west of the hill from whence they would spread out until Puck's Hill was entirely surrounded.

Nor had the great detective forgotten the Winged Man's powers of flight. Ere an hour had passed the two military balloons we have before mentioned had been drawn near by a company of Royal Engineers, until they commanded the whole summit of the hill.

In the car of each balloon was a long-barrelled pneumatic gun, capable of throwing an explosive shell a distance of a mile.

Never before had so systematic an attempt to capture or kill the Winged Man been made, and never before had Danby Druce felt so sanguine of success.

Exactly two hours after sunset a rocket, bursting in the air a mile away, showed that all was ready for the attack.

Drawing a rocket from beneath his coat, Danby Druce stuck its stick into the ground, then, applying a match, sent it soaring heavenward in reply.

Immediately a number of dark figures burst from the white mist which had by this time climbed half-way up the hill. Noiselessly but swiftly they spread a huge steel net, such as is used to protect warships against torpedoes, over the entrance of the Winged Man's cave.

A number of low, dull, thunderous roars, following in quick succession, came from the direction of the disused pit shaft, down which cart-load after cart-load of chemically-treated cotton-waste was being flung.

Hither Danby Druce directed his steps, arriving upon the scene just as the last load had been shot into the old mine's cavernous depth.

An engineer was in the act of applying a match to a bomb filled with oil as Danby Druce reached his side. Holding the bomb over the mouth of the pit, the officer let it fall.

Down it went, its flaring fuse growing fainter and fainter in the distance, until as, craning his neck over the orifice, Danby Druce followed it in its descent, he saw it strike the piled-up loads at the bottom of the shaft, then explode in a burst of flame.

Immediately the cotton-waste caught fire, and as the flames spread, they shed a lurid glow over the dark, confined space below.

Even as Danby Druce looked the Winged Man sprang upon the scene, and, trampling upon the waste, tried in vain to extinguish the flames.

Presently he looked up, and evidently recognising Danby Druce amongst half a dozen faces peering at him from above.

Leaving the fire to take care of itself, his face contorted with rage, the Winged Man shot upwards, intent upon grappling with his foe in the open.

"Quick, lads—the lid!" cried Danby Druce, springing back.

Barely was the last plate in its place air the thick iron cover shook again beneath the heavy blows showered upon it by the Winged Man.

Dropping on his knees upon the plate, Danby Druce approached a grating left for the purpose of parley.

"It is useless striving against Fate, Winged Man!" he cried, unable to repress the triumph he felt. "You are hemmed in on every side. Escape is impossible. Be wise. Surrender whilst you have yet time!"

A loud, mocking laugh was the Winged Man's fall.

"Surrender to such as you? Never!" came in tones of ringing contempt, from his lips. "Fools, you know not what you do! You have commenced that which will end in the destruction of you all. On the morrow the world shall read how the Winged Man laughs at man's puny efforts to capture him."

Then, lowering his wings, he descended, dropping like a stone down the centre of the shaft, where the chemically-prepared waste, no longer burning brightly, was a mass of red, smouldering embers, from which poured clouds of stifling smoke.

Poised in the smoke-tainted ere a few feet above the glowing mass, the Winged Man folded his arms, and gazed, half in admiration, half in contempt, upon the great detective's handiwork.

"I see your scheme, Danby Druce. Knowing that neither steel nor bullet has power to touch me, you would smoke me out like a rat in its hold," he muttered; "and," he continued, as the noxious fumes began to affect even his breathing, "to a certain point you will succeed. Then you shall learn how boundless is the Winged Man's power."

Gliding on outstretched wings from passage to passage, the Winged Man made his way to a huge cave close to that containing the boilers Danby Druce had noticed in his escape from the Winged Man's power a few days before.

It was a strange piece of mechanism upon which the Winged Man gazed. In the centre was an enormous iron cogwheel, worked by an endless screw attached to the engine. In the hub of the wheel was a hollow tube some six inches in diameter, from which a tall tongue of blue flame was mounting almost to the cave's lofty, jagged roof.

Even as the Winged Man reached the wheel, the tube disappeared beneath the surface of the iron hub. Immediately another, drawn forward by an ingenious arrangement of levers, was inserted in the almost empty hole.

Presently a mass of liquid rock shot up to the ceiling, and fell down at the

Winged Man's feet.

"Aho! My scheme works well. Another hour, and those who have dared to come in arms against the Winged Man shall rue their boldness!" he cried, in tones of fiendish exhortation.

Then, turning on his heel, he strode from the cave, leaving his machinery to do its fearful work.

Boring through the earth's crust to where the slumbering river of fire which connects Mount Etna with Vesuvius flows, the Winged Man had been at work for years sinking deep borings to tap this fearful subterranean river.

To what end? Simply to gratify his insatiable curiosity, although too well he knew that by thus tampering with the hidden secrets of Nature he ran the risk of bringing ruin upon the country-side for miles around.

THE ERUPTION.

As the smoke from the foot of the pit shaft increased in volume, faint wreaths broke through the earth in a dozen different places, thus fulfilling Danby Druce's anticipation by betraying the Winged Man's secret exits.

Keen eyes were on the alert. No sooner did a curling wreath proclaim an opening ere a stretch of torpedo netting was drawn across it.

"We have him safe this time, Mr. Druce," said Colonel Martin, the officer commanding the infantry, as his men pegged down a net over a hollow tree-stump through which the smoke had come.

"You lie!" thundered a voice close at hand. And all recoiled, save Danby Druce, as the white, fearful, rage-contorted face of the Winged Man was pressed against the stout, steel meshes of the net. "What! Think you that the Winged Man is a rabbit, that you net the place thus? Bah! I hate and defy the whole human race, asking no quarter, giving no quarter. Terrible shall be my vengeance when it falls!"

"Fire! Shoot him down!" thundered the colonel, rendered furious by the Winged Man's defiance.

A score of rifles were flung to as many shoulders, and the next moment a sharp, rattling report rang out as a score of bullets were aimed at the white, mocking face.

A loud, ringing, almost triumphant laugh followed, and as the faint smoke of the rifles cleared away they saw the Winged Man standing, untouched, behind the netting.

"Farewell, Danby Druce! We will meet again," cried the Winged Man, as, with a gesture of defiance to the astounded soldiers, he disappeared into the intricate network of the caves beneath him.

Despite his bragging words, the Winged Man was in an exceedingly dangerous position. Outlet after outlet he tried, only to find them closed with the great detective's ingenious contrivance.

Eager to leave his fearful foe no chance of escape, Danby Druce ordered every exit from the cave to be blocked up, leaving only the mouth of the cave on the hillside open, round which he gathered the greater part of his men to give the Winged Man a warm reception when he attempted to break out.

As Colonel Martin, the chief constable of the county, and one or two newspapermen, were standing some twenty yards from the mouth of the cave, watching the thick clouds of heavy, gas-laden smoke pouring through the meshes of the wire, the colonel turned to Danby Druce, saying:

"I do not think England will be troubled with the Winged Man after this. Were he twice the supernatural being he is reported to be, he could not remain much longer in that suffocating smoke. You think not?" he went on, as Danby Druce shook his head. "I'll wager the best dinner—"

He ceased speaking, leaning over, and would have fallen had he not clutched hold of Danby Druce.

"Good gracious! Am I dizzy, or did the earth indeed tremble beneath my feet?" he gasped.

Ere anyone could reply, a low, deep roll, as of distant thunder, came apparently from the centre of the hill, followed by a deafening report, as though the navies of the world had combined to fire a last, parting salute over the Winged Man.

The next moment cries of terror resounded on every side, as the whole mass of earth upon which the little party stood swayed from side to side, like a ship in a stormy sea.

Louder and louder grew the mysterious earth rumbling. At last accompanied by a deafening report, a fierce, white flame swept from the mouth of the cave, licking up the stout wire rope to which the net was made as though it had been tow, and sending soldiers, police, and detective alike reeling, scorched and burned, down the hill.

Then a strange, fearful, almost incredible thing happened. With starting eyeballs the horror-struck spectators witnessed one of the most awful sights human eyes had ever beheld.

For a moment the whole cap of the hill seemed to rise in the air; then, with a loud report, it disappeared, blown into a thousand pieces by the fearful force the Winged Man had let loose from below.

A huge, lurid pillar of flame sprang roaring and hissing, a hundred feet above where the hill-top had been a moment before, sending huge masses of burning rock and dense clouds of ash in all directions.

A report scarce louder than a pop-gun in comparison with the mighty efforts of Nature caused Danby Druce to look up. He was just in time to see one of the military balloons, its gas-bag fired by the intense heat, disappear in a ball of fire.

The next moment a shuddering cry of horror and amazement drew his attention to burning hill once more.

A feeling of awe-stricken horror swept through the great detective's frame for rising on outstretched wings, so close to the lurid pillar of flame that he seemed embedded in it, was the Winged Man.

Suddenly, what looked like a bursting star appeared in the pillar of flame a few feet from where the Winged Man flew on outstretched wings. Undeterred by the fate of his comrades in the other balloon the gallant Engineer officer had launched shell at the Winged Man.

"He is hit—he is hit!" came in accents of incredulous wonder from Danby Druce's lips.

Barely were the words uttered ere the Winged Man, who, blown on one side by the force of the explosion, had seemed about to fall into the fearful crater, recovered himself with a mighty effort, and, mounting swiftly, was lost into the black cloud, alive with tongues of red flame that hung over the crater.

Danby Druce waited to see no more, but sprang to where the Engineers were striving to hold the plunging horses attached to a waggon bearing the reel of wire which held the balloon in place. Springing into the vehicle, he commenced climbing hand over hand up the tautening wire.

When half-way up he was nearly hurled from his hold as the horses, breaking free from their driver's restraining hand, dashed forward in mad terror.

But he clung to the wire like grim death until, the off hind-wheel of the waggon striking a tree, the vehicle was overturned, and the balloon, which had been dragged almost to the earth, rose upwards, dragging the heavy windlass from its fastening as it did so.

Straining every muscle, Danby Druce climbed higher and higher, until at last he was able to catch hold of the rope hanging from the balloon. A minute later he had reached the car in safety.

A WILD VOYAGE.

As Danby Druce swung himself into the wickerwork car the Engineer lieutenant in charge of the balloon pressed the trigger of the pneumatic gun hurling a shell into the thick black cloud which was rapidly over spreading the whole land, hoping against hope that a lucky shot might reach the smoke-enshrouded Winged Man.

It was a wonderful, fearful, yet inexpressibly grand sight upon which Danby Druce looked down.

Beneath him, sending forth so fierce a heat that it seemed to parch his very bones, was a constantly-increasing mass of fire, from which large streams of lava rolled down the hillside upon the country below, setting grass and bushes on fire, and driving the force the detective had assembled to destroy the Winged Man before it in all directions.

"Cast loose the wire! We must rise above yonder cloud of smoke and ashes, or the overwhelmed!" cried Danby Druce.

The lieutenant nodded, and issued an order to the sergeant who was in the car with him.

Stooping down, the man drew out a sliding bolt, and the next moment, released from the winch's dragging weight, the balloon soared heavenwards.

It seemed as though some unseen, fearful foe was hurling red-hot stones and burning rocks at it, so terrible was the fusillade of fiery metals which assailed the round, gas-filled bag.

Fortunately, the wind had carried the balloon away from the hill, and though one or two of the fearful missiles came perilously near, they rose above the smoke-cloud unharmed.

"Look, look! Heavens above, it is no man but a fiend we have been fighting against!" gasped a sergeant, laying one hand on Danby Druce's shoulder, and pointing with the other towards where, poised upon a rolling mass of smoke, stood the Winged Man, flashes of lurid fire darting from his upraised fist.

For a few seconds Danby Druce gazed awe-stricken upon this wonder; then he turned to where the lieutenant was endeavouring to cover that awful, majestic figure with the pneumatic gun.

"Fire! One lucky shell may lay him low; and, though I fear England must pay a heavy price for the victory, it will not be dear if the Winged Man perishes!" he cried.

"I have him now!" replied the brave officer, who, though perchance his face was somewhat pale, was as steady as though watching a sham fight on the plains of Aldershot.

But ere he could pull the trigger a cry of angry disappointment burst from his lips. Seized in a vortex caused by the intense heat which obtained above the centre of the new volcano, the balloon was whirled round and round, rendering accurate shooting impossible. Round and round she spun, until first the sergeant, then the lieutenant, and finally Danby Druce sank, dazed and deathly faint, in the bottom of the car.

Danby Druce awoke with a feeling as though his body was wrapped in ice. Raising himself with difficulty upon one arm, he looked around. His companions—who were lying as though already dead on either side of him— were covered with a thin coat of frozen snow, whilst the ropes which held the car to the balloon were covered with hoarfrost.

A strange creaking sound caused him to look up. The silken cover of the balloon stood out in round bulges between the network, and he knew that it was but a question of a few minutes ere the gas, swelling in the rarefied air, would burst the outer covering and let them fall to a fearful death.

Twice Danby Druce strove to rise. His feet and hands were numbed with cold the third time he succeeded, and made a snatch at the valve-line.

Alas! his fingers refused to grasp the swaying cord, yet they were mounting each moment higher and higher. He must release the gas, or perish.

A wild look round showed that they were floating in what seemed to be endless space. In one frantic final effort he grasped the frozen cord between his teeth and jerked back his head.

The icy strands seem to burn their way into his lips, but the detective persevered, and a few seconds later had sunk to the bottom of the car, with the welcome sound of escaping gas hissing as it rushed from the valve at the top of the balloon sounding in his ears.

Lower and lower they sank, until at length returning warmth restored the lieutenant and sergeant to consciousness.

After what seemed an indeterminable time, Danby Druce, looking over the side, beheld the earth apparently springing up to meet them.

"Up lads! Out with a bag of ballast, or we shall be dashed to pieces!" he cried.

Stirred to life by his words, the Engineer raised a shingle-filled bag from the bottom of the car, and though it tested his weakened strength to the utmost, emptied it over the side. Another and another followed, until, when barely a hundred feet from the earth, the balloon's ascent was slackened, and they were saved.

Half an hour later, Frost-bitten, weak from the rapid change of attitude they had experienced, but otherwise unharmed, the three men were enabled to take a train back to the nearest station to Puck's Hill.

As Danby Druce drew near the scene of the fearful catastrophe, dark forebodings filled his heart, for the whole countryside was covered with a layer of thick ashes; and when at last a bend of the line brought them in view of Puck's Hill, a sigh of relief escaped his lips.

What might have been a national calamity had been providentially averted. Where a green-capped hill had stood arose a jagged mountain of burnt, still-smoking rock; but save a pillar of thin smoke rising lazily from its summit, and the still-seething stream of lava that had rolled over the surrounding country, no sign of activity appeared in what is now called the Winged Man's Volcano.

'TWIXT THE CUP AND THE LIP.

Of the Winged Man, Danby Druce could gather no news.

Some believed that he had perished in the catastrophe of his own raising, then shook their heads, declaring that, like typhoid and other fevers, the Winged Man was an ill the country must accept as permanent. Though, perchance, his ravages could be lessened, they could not be stopped entirely.

One man there was, a sailor, the contracted black iris of whose eyes proclaimed his long sight, who declared he had seen, from the neighbouring hills, some two miles away, a black speck fluttering like a wounded bird on to the red-hot rocks.

It was after a close cross-examination of this man that Danby Druce drove in his motor-car to the scene of the eruption.

It was night, and as the detective approached the fatal spot, the darkness was illuminated by a dull, whitish glare cast off by the cooling lava.

Presently he found the road blocked by an enormous mass of rapidly cooling liquid rock, which had flowed across the road.

Springing from the car, Danby Druce looked to his weapons, then commenced to clamber over the still smoking lava.

So hot was it that he felt the heat burning through the soles of his boots; but he persevered, and soon, the obstacle surmounted, stood ankle-deep in ashes, surveying the scene so weird and desolate that he could scarcely believe it to be the same beautiful landscape he had looked over the previous day. Hedges and fences had disappeared, giving place to a grey monotonous stretch of hill and dale, scarred by ridges of still glowing lava.

A full moon shone through a cloudless sky, its pale, silvery light giving an added horror to the fearful scene.

Slowly Danby Druce moved onward, intent on encompassing the whole of that torn and rugged mass of rock which had been Puck's Hill, hoping against hope to find some sign which would assure him that the Winged Man was no more.

His progress was slow, heavy taint of sulphur filled the air, rendering constant movement impossible, and forcing him now and again to rest upon some bare rock, or blackened stump of what had been a mighty tree.

Weary, bathed in perspiration, oppressed by the suffocating fumes of sulphur, Danby Druce persevered for two hours.

He was on the point of giving up the search until the morrow. He came to an abrupt halt, his every nerve tingling with excitement, fatigue and suffocation alike forgotten, for his eyes had fallen upon a moving object creeping over the ash-strewn ground hundred yards or so away.

The indescribable feeling which ever warned Danby Druce that the Winged Man was in the vicinity, thrilled his heart. He could scarcely believe his good fortune.

But what else could yonder slowly-moving object be? It was too large for a dog, too small for a wandering cow; beside, what would any living animal be doing in that desolate waste?

Drawing his revolver, Danby Druce started in pursuit. But barely had he taken a dozen paces ere the moving being stopped, and rose slowly and painfully to its feet.

A thrill of exhortation swept through the great detective's heart.

His instinct had not betrayed him.

Before him, covered with dust, blood flowing from a fearful gash in his forehead, his wings hanging in tatters round his body, was the Winged Man.

So dejected, ill, suffering, looked the one-time king of the air, that a momentary spasm of pity for his fallen foe shot through Danby Druce's heart.

But a single glance at the fair country-side, turned into a howling wilderness at the dread being's command, drove all softer thoughts from Danby Druce's heart, and, with weapon advanced, he strode forward, calling upon the Winged Man to surrender.

A flash of his old unconquerable spirit darted for a moment from the weird horror's eyes as Danby Druce's summons fell upon his ears. The next, with a hanging head and downcast eyes, he murmured:

"At last, oh, mine enemy, you have prevailed! Yet not you, but the forces of Nature, which, in my vanity, I thought to control, have proved my master. I own defeat, but to a power greater than either of us."

"I own, Winged Man, that fortune has befriended me, or, though I would have stuck to the task I had set myself until I died, I fear it would have been a hopeless one," admitted Danby Druce.

Ere the Winged Man could reply he was seized by a sudden faintness, and would have fallen, had not Danby Druce caught him in his arms.

"Water—for the love of Heaven, water!" came in gasping accents from the Winged Man's parched, blackened lips.

"Courage! My car awaits me upon the other side of the hill. If you are not strong enough to walk, I will carry you there, then you shall have the refreshment and medical attendance you require," promised the detective.

"And a prison!" added the Winged Man bitterly.

"Ay," admitted the great detective honestly; "I wish it could be otherwise, but your crimes are too many to hope for mercy."

"Fate is too strong!" murmured the Winged Man. "So be it. But look, there is water over yonder; carry me to it that I may drink."

Danby Druce hesitated, then gazed for a moment towards where a tiny rivulet, its course blocked up by a wall of lava, had spread over the surrounding country, forming a miniature lake.

His first impulse was to lay the Winged Man down, and, rushing to the lake, return with his hat full of the required liquid; but he dare not leave him where he was, and as the Winged Man seemed too weak to walk, he flung him over his shoulder, and struggled across the broken ground towards the pent-up stream.

As he did so a strange noise burst from the Winged Man's lips. A momentary doubt surged through the detective's heart, for the sound that reached his ears at seemed like a suppressed chuckle of malicious satisfaction.

"What! Did you speak?" he asked.

"Speak? No. I groaned. You have not yet realised, Danby Druce, that even the Winged Man feels pain," was the reply.

Somewhat ashamed of his suspicions, Danby Druce quickened his speed. Soon, the edge of the flood reached, he had seated his burden upon the ash-covered ground, and was sweeping the ashes, which covered the water, aside that he might get them clean, drinkable water, when an ejaculation of rage and amazement burst from his lips, and, feeling a heavy blow upon the head, he fell into the stream.

In a moment he struggled to his feet, just in time to see the Winged Man dived head-foremost into the deep water beyond his grasp.

Furious at the way he had been duped, Danby Druce swam towards where the Winged Man had disappeared. But, though he remained afloat until exhaustion compelled him to seek land, he failed to catch a second glimpse of his fearful foe.

Another might have deemed the Winged Man dead, drowned in the ash-covered water; but Danby Druce knew the dread being too well for that, and, his heart oppressed by a feeling of bitter disappointment, he clambered, wet and dripping, over the burned, scarred ground to where he had left his motor-car.

THE WINGED MAN'S SURRENDER.

Hitherto, Danby Druce, despite his repeated failures, had been the idol of the British public; but now a reaction had set in, and the great detective had the mortification of seeing himself held up to ridicule by the very papers that had been loudest in their praises of him.

The comic papers cartooned him; even the great dailies, forgetting his many successes, spoke slightingly of his powers.

It was the bitterest time of Danby Druce's life. He knew that he had done all that man could do; more, indeed, than the majority of men in his place would have even attempted.

It was cruelly, bitterly hard to be so treated in the moment of adversity.

Another man might have affected to have laughed at this unjust reversion of public opinion. Not so, Danby Druce.

A week after his last adventure with the Winged Man, he was seated in his room, diligently wading through the mass of correspondence with which the daily papers were filled, all without exception condemning Danby Druce, and asking if, as British detectives had proved themselves as utterly unable to deal with the fearful scourge that held Great Britain in terror, the Government would not seek help from abroad.

Danby Druce read the answer to this appeal in a late edition of the "Evening Press." which a servant brought in some half-hour later. It was but a few words—a mere "stop press" telegram—but, short though it was, the poignant words struck like a dagger to Danby Druce's heart.

"It is officially announced," ran the telegram, "that the British Government have secured the services of the great American detective, Mr. Jonas P. Falkner, to take up the chase of the Winged Man, in which Mr. Danby Druce had so signally failed."

Shamed and despairing, Danby Druce allowed the pink paper to flatter from his hand, and sat for several moments, his head buried on his breast, lost in bitter thought.

A strange chill, as though his heart had been gripped by icy fingers, caused the great detective to look up.

Grasping the arm of his chair, he rose slowly to his feet, his eyes fixed in an incredible stare towards where, in the centre of the room, a strange, enigmatical smile parting his thin, hunted lips, a look almost of compassion in his eyes, stood the Winged Man!

"You!" ejaculated the detective, with labouring breath. "You have come to exult over me in this bitter moment of defeat and degradation!"

A sudden wild anger flared up in his heart, a vague hope that already it might not be too late to redeem his name, caused Danby Druce to throw himself headlong upon his fearful foe, and, seizing him by the throat, strife to bear him to the ground.

He might as well have striven to bend a statue of stone. Firm as a rock, the Winged Man received the detective's fierce attack; then, with almost contemptuous ease freeing himself from the other's grasp, flung himself back into his chair, saying:

"Steady, man! Is this the way you receive one who comes to serve you?"

"To serve me!" gasped Danby Druce, restraining with difficulty and inclination to fly at his foe's throat once more. "You, to whom I owe this humiliation! You to capture whom I have abandoned all the world holds dear!

And this is my reward!" he added, with a fierce gesture towards the papers that were scattered about him.

"Yes," repeated the Winged Man, "this is your reward, Danby Druce—I am your prisoner!"

The great detective looked in amazement at the speaker.

"Ask me not why!" interrupted the Winged Man, as Danby Druce was about to speak. "Perchance I am unwilling that one who has made almost supernatural efforts to lay me by the heels should be robbed of the fruits of his endeavours. Perchance"—a look of unutterable misery swept across his face—"I am weary of this constant strife, this constant living at enmity with the whole world, without a creature, scarce a dog, whom I call my friend. Perchance," he continued, with a slight smile, as he pointed to the scar upon his forehead. "I feel a battered wreck, no longer equal to the strife. Be the reason what it may, I am your prisoner. Go summon a conveyance to take me to Bow Street. Be sure I will not seek to escape on the way."

It is impossible to describe the bewilderment and delight with which Danby Druce listened to the Winged Man's announcement. The darkest cloud has it silver lining. In fancy Danby Druce saw his enemies confounded, and himself hailed as the saviour of this country, when the morning papers announced that he had, with his own unaided efforts, brought the Winged Man to surrender.

"I go; but ere I leave the room, let me thank you for what you have done. Believe me, if Danby Druce's voice can yet influence men, he will do his utmost for you at your trial."

"The Winged Man needs not the advocacy of any man!" came, with a flash of his old imperious spirit, from the Winged Man, as he motioned to the man to whom he had surrendered to hasten on his errant.

Danby Druce, his brain in a whirl of excitement, emerged from the front door, he ran against a newspaper reporter, who, late though the hour, had come to interview the man whose name was on everyone's lips.

"Ah, Mr. Danby Druce, I have been sent by the 'Searchlight' to obtain your opinion on—" he began.

Danby Druce seized the young fellow by the muffler of his coat.

"The 'Searchlight' has been the only paper which has treated me with anything like justice!" he said, almost fiercely. "Therefore, I give you the opportunity of making the 'Scoop' of the year. On the morrow my foes will be dumfounded. Ten minutes ago the Winged Man surrendered in my room, and I am on my way to secure a conveyance in which to carry him to Bow Street!"

The reporter waited to hear no more. If the "Searchlight" should be the only paper to announce the Winged Man's capture, as Danby Druce had said, it would have secured, not the "scoop" of the year, but the "scoop" of the century.

In an incredibly short space of time the type was set and the announcement of the Winged Man's capture, in big, black letters, was being inserted on the front page of the great halfpenny paper.

SELF-SURRENDER!

"Good morning, Mr. Druce!" said the inspector in charge of Bow Street, as the great detective entered the charge-room. "Caught the Winged Man yet?"

A stifled laugh arose from several constables who were standing about.

Danby Druce flashed angrily, but he was in too high spirits to resent the taunt.

He had never been popular at Bow Street; in fact whilst admiring his undoubted brilliant powers as a detective, the whole police force had been a little jealous of him.

"I certainly caught a prisoner," he said good-humouredly. "By the by, unless my memory fails me, you have already had the Winged Man at Bow Street, and could not keep him."

The inspector bit his lip. The detective's reply was a home thrust.

"At any rate, we don't boast we are going to do such a lot and do nothing," retorted the inspector angrily. "Our duty is to see that our prisoners don't escape. The Winged Man is about the only one who has done so, and if we lay hands on him again you may take it from me that he won't have much of a chance."

"Then I trust you will be as good as your word," said Danby Druce, beckoning a dark figure forward, which had held back in the entrance-hall.

With long strides, the figure crossed the intervening space between the door and the inspector's desk; then, with a dramatic gesture, flung aside his cloak and cap, revealing the fearful, well-known features of the flying horror.

"Behold the Winged Man!" said Danby Druce, enjoying the confusion and dismay depicted in the inspector's face.

"The Winged Man—the Winged Man!" came in low, awe-stricken whispers from a dozen pairs of lips at once.

"Yes, the Winged Man," replied the weird horror, drawing himself up to his full height and smiling, as he noted how the stalwart policeman blanched before his gaze.

At a sign from the inspector, a constable closed and locked the door of the room.

A FRESH INSPECTOR AT BOW STREET.

For some time after Danby Druce's departure all was silent within the police-station—silence broken occasionally by a wild burst of singing from an habitual inebriate in a cell adjoining that into which the Winged Man had been thrown, and the sobbing of a young boy captured in his first theft.

At first, as the news of the Winged Man's capture was voiced abroad, the policeman on duty in Bow Street Police Station would appear through the grating at the dark, huddled heap on the floor of the cell which represented that dread terror, the Winged Man; but after a time those in reserve, who were not on duty, returned to the recreation-room to sleep or while away the hours as best they might, whilst the inspector, who was determined that the Winged Man should not escape him this time, sent his sergeant on his rounds, and remained in charge of the station himself.

An hour passed, the disjointed verses ceased from the cell of the singer, the stifled sobs of the boy grew less frequent.

Slowly the Winged Man raised his head, and listened attentively. The next moment subdued snap attracted the attention of the policeman on duty outside the cell, and he peered through the opening of the prisoner.

To all appearances the Winged Man had not moved, but was still stretched upon the floor, his white face glaring through the darkness.

The policeman, confident that his ears had not deceived him, stood lost in thought with his back to the cell.

Again the Winged Man moved, so noiselessly that not a rustle of his garments disturbed the watchful policeman. With swift deliberation he rose to his feet, leaving the handcuffs and chains which had bound him in a heap on the floor.

His limbs were at liberty, and soon he would be free—free to work his fearful will upon the earth once more.

There was something ominous in the perfect silence in which the Winged

Man worked as he pressed his white face against the bars of the grating and looked cautiously through the passage into the charge-room, where he could just see the inspector bending over his desk.

The observation-grating of the door was eight inches short by six high, and protected by for short, stout iron bars.

Gripping two of the latter in each hand, the Winged Man contracted his iron grip, and the iron bars, stout though they were, bent noiselessly inwards, allowing sufficient space for him to thrust his long, thin, strong hands through the aperture.

Some instinct of danger caused the constable to look swiftly up; but ere he could turn round the Winged Man's fearful fingers were at his throat.

In vain the policeman strove to cry for help. Taught by an unequalled knowledge of anatomy, the Winged Man pressed his fingers so tightly into the wretched man's windpipe that not so much as a gasping sob escaped his lips.

The policeman was a big man, weighing close upon fourteen stone; yet, apparently without effort, the Winged Man held him from the ground, writhing, suffocating, growing momentarily weaker, until at length his struggle ceased, and, taking advantage of any renewed outburst of singing from the inebriate's cell, the Winged Man allowed his victim to fall with a hollow thud upon the stone-flagged passage.

"Quiet that howling, Simonds!" growled the inspector, without raising his head from the book upon which he was engaged.

"Yes, sir. Be quiet, can't ye, or we'll see what the cold-water cure will do!" cried the Winged Man, imitating the unconscious policeman's voice; and the inspector, hearing his subordinate's reply, went on reading.

It was a common report, almost universally believed, that there was no lock yet invented, no bolt so strong as to keep the Winged Man in prison, and the majority of people attributed this to supernatural powers.

Could any have seen the skill and agility with which the Winged Man, armed only with small but wondrously strong tools, which he ever carried concealed about his body, unlocked the cell door and pulled back the thick iron bolts, they would have known that it was to his great mechanical skill the Winged Man owed his many escapes.

Noiselessly thrusting open the door, the Winged Man dragged his unconscious victim into the cell, then glided on outstretched wings in the direction of the charge-room.

Creeping to an eight-foot partition, with an ornamental top, which cut off the inspector's private den from the rest of the room, the Winged Man peered over.

A single noiseless beat of his wings bore the Winged Man over the wooden partition; then, like a hawk upon its prey, the Winged Man swooped down upon the inspector.

Feeling rather than seeing the fearful, black, ominous form above his head, the inspector looked up.

Terror froze the cry for help that rose in his throat ere it could pass his lips.

It was not until he felt the Winged Man's cold, icy grip upon his throat that despair lent him strength to attempt resistance.

Too late! Already the Winged Man's mighty wings were folded round his victim, blotting out all light, and plunging the panic-stricken man into utter darkness.

The inspector was no coward, or he would not have risen to his present position in the Police Force. His record told of many a fierce battle against overwhelming odds. Once, with his own unaided arm, he had captured and held till help came, two of the most dangerous burglars that infested London.

Yet so sudden and unexpected was the Winged Man's approach, so fearful his icy-cold touch, so unspeakably horrible the enfolding wings, that, brave man though he undoubtedly was, the inspector hung limp and motionless in the weird horror's arms, as incapable of crying for help or fighting for freedom as a bird fascinated by a serpent's gaze.

A noiseless yet awful chuckle escaped the Winged Man's lips. Rising to the ceiling, with the inspector in his arms, he glided over the top of the partition to the cell he had just left.

Three minutes later he reappeared, clad in the inspector's uniform and peak cap; then, a fearful smile upon his pallid face, he mounted the tall stool before the inspector's desk, and, turning over the pages of the charge-book, was soon lost in its contents.

JONAS B. FALTER.

The contents of the charge-book seemed to provide the Winged Man with a great deal of amusement, to judge by the low, amused chuckles which escaped his lips as he read.

Such documents must ever contain a record of sin, crime, folly, and weakness, and the Winged Man rubbed his long, thin hands together in intense enjoyment of the misery he could read between the lines of every page.

Presently he looked up as a voice with a decided Yankee twang, speaking to the policeman at the door of the station, fell upon his ears.

"Say, boss, is this Bow Street Police-Station?" asked the stranger, who was clad in an ill-fitting suit of rusty black, with a felt hat upon his head.

He had a long face, goatee beard, and a long cigar pointed upwards from the corner of his mouth.

"Yes, sir," replied the policeman, surveying the visitor from head to foot.

"Waal, I hear you have got the Winged Man at last. Trot the critter out, will ye?" demanded the new-comer.

The policeman smiled.

"You are an American, aren't you?" he asked, ignoring the other's request.

The man started, and looked up at the speaker in surprise.

"Waal, now, for a citizen of a worn-out effete old country like England, I call that real smart. How on earth did you know?" he demanded.

"Oh, we British police are not such fools as you Americans take us to be," explained the amused policeman.

"Oh, you're police are all right, perhaps!" admitted the Yankee. "It's your detectives that will have to come to us Americans to be taught the A B C of their business. So you have got the Winged Man—eh! It's a pity, 'cause I have come all the way from New York on purpose to lay him by the heels for you."

But the policeman was not to be drawn.

"You'll find the inspector inside, sir, though I don't expect you'll get much out of him," he replied.

"All right, boss," growled the Yankee, as, cocking the point of his cigar to a more acute angle than ever, he strode into the building.

Opening the door of the inspector's cubicle, he came to a halt before the brass-railed desk. As though absolutely unconscious of his presence, the "inspector" remained with his eyes glued upon the book in front of him.

"Say, boss, I am Jonas B. Falter," began the Yankee.

The Winged Man looked up.

Strange, unfamiliar feeling of awe, almost amounting to terror, swept through the Yankee's heart as his eyes alighted upon that deathly-white, bloodless face, from which a pair of dark eyes seemed to pierce through him as though they were fiery gimlets.

The next moment that native impudence, which Yankee school independence, asserted itself.

"Say, boss, aren't you well? You do look mighty bad, I'll allow!" gasped Jonas B. Falter.

"Never better in my life, Mr. Falter—in health or spirits," replied the Winged Man genially.

"That's good! I am Jonas B. Falter, the great American detective, of whom you have doubtless heard. Your Government has deployed me to hunt the Winged Man down, but I find luck is against me, and you have already got him."

"Yes, I am afraid you are a little behindhand this trip, Mr. Falter. However, I dare say the Government will employ you to see that he does not escape."

"Waal, as to his escape, you must be a lot of mugs if you let him go once you have laid hands upon him," opined the Yankee.

"You don't know the Winged Man, that's certain. Perhaps you would like to see him?" offered that strange being.

"That's the very identical reason I trotted along as soon as I heard he had been captured. What are those things?" he added, as his eyes fell upon a pair of handcuffs hanging on the wall.

The Winged Man explained their use.

"Waal, I had a mind they were something of that sort. No wonder you Britishers can't hold your prisoners when you use old-fashioned articles like that! Here are handcuffs that would hold anyone," said the American producing what looked like a flat bar of steel with two holes on either end, from his pockets.

The Winged Man eyed them critically.

"What do you use those things for?" he demanded.

"Hold out your hands, and I'll show you," offered the American.

Without a word the Winged Man complied, and the next moment Jonas B. Falter had slipped his wrists through the two holes of the bars of steel.

"There, if you can get them off without the key, you can lock me up with the Winged Man!" he cried triumphantly.

But even as the words left his lips the Winged Man threw his hands into the air, and the steel handcuffs were sent flying towards the ceiling.

"Bah! If you hope to hold the Winged Man with such a contrivance, allow me to inform you that you are not half as smart as we Britishers have been led to expect."

For perhaps the first time in his life J. B. Falter had not a word to say, but stood gazing at the uniformed figure in blank amazement.

"Snakes!" he gasped. "I didn't believe there was a man living who could throw off the Falter Double-Locking Make-Fast Handcuff! Say, stranger, I'd consider it a favour if you'd just tell me how you did it."

Without a word the Winged Man reached to where a police baton hung by the side of the desk.

It was a hard wood cudgel, as strong as iron, almost as heavy as lead; yet, springing from his stool, he held the baton by either end, then snapped it across his knee as easily as though it had been a pipe-stem.

"Snakes, stranger, who on earth are you—Sandow,[46] Goliath, or Samson?" gasped Falter.

For answer the Winged Man tore off his closely-fitting tunic, and, springing upon the brass rail before the desk, unfolded his wings, and glared, with a smile of malicious triumph, into the other's face.

"I am he you have come to England to seek. I am the Winged Man!" he thundered.

"The Winged Man!" repeated the Yankee, staggering back, white to the very lips, and trembling from head to foot.

"Yes, the Winged Man, he against whom you would dare to pit your puny wits! Fool, what Danby Druce has failed to do no bouncing Yankee need attempt!" cried the weird horror, towering over the Yankee as though about to crush him to the ground. "Go, leave England within twenty-four hours or you shall taste the Winged Man's vengeance!"

Shaken to his very soul though the Yankee was, he, like the majority of those who had never come in contact with the weird horror, deemed himself capable of contending with one who had so long held England in his grip.

Besides, he had published throughout the whole of America, from Canadian

---

[46] Eugene Sandow (1867–1925) Prussian bodybuilder, contemporary with this publication.

borders to Rio Grande, his intention of teaching the European police how to capture their malefactor, explaining how he would bring the Winged Man to justice within a week of his landing at Liverpool.

The thought of being held up to ridicule, as one who had been defeated and humiliated within twelve hours of his arrival in England, wounded his Yankee vanity, and gave him a courage no other consideration could have done.

Even as the Winged Man, his white face contorted with fury, pointed with outstretched hand to the door, Jonas B. Falter had made up his mind how to act.

With a swiftness borne of many a fight in a frontier saloon, he drew a revolver from his belt, and, springing forward, pressed its muzzle against the Winged Man's breast.

As he pulled the trigger, there was a loud report, and a dense black smoke filled the place. When it cleared away, Falter was alone in the charge-room, gazing with amazement at the shattered and twisted barrel of his revolver.

Of the Winged Man naught was to be seen.

As, anxious only to leave the spot where he had met with so unexpected, so astounding an adventure, Falter made for the door, he saw the policeman on duty lying stretched senseless upon the steps, his helmet battered in as though from a blow wielded with irresistible force.

°THE FIVE DETECTIVES

Jonas B. Falter's sole idea when he fled from Bow Street Police-station was to obey the Winged Man's command, and get out of England as quickly as he could.

But when he reached his hotel, and, arousing the five assistants he had brought with him to assist in the Winged Man's capture, related the events of that night, or, rather early morning, he found his companions by no means disposed to fall in with his views.

It was not only the handsome reward offered by the British Government which brought him to England, but also the reports of the enormous quantity of booty the Winged Man had acquired in his various hidden layers.

Even before leaving New York they had made up their minds to get in touch with the Winged Man, and exhort a large sum from him as ransom, or, what they would much prefer, find one of his hidden haunts, and help themselves.

Consequently, Jonas B. Falter received but little sympathy from his comrades, who told him, in as many words, that he could return to America with a fallen reputation and an open confession of failure if he liked, but as for them, they were determined not to leave as poor as they came.

"But don't I tell yer the critter aren't human! If he was, he be lying in Bow Street Station with his heart blown to smithereens at this very moment!" declared Falter, exhibiting his shattered revolver as proof of his words.

° 31 MAY 1913.

"Of course, if you go sticking the muzzle of your iron against a steel breastplate, it will bust in your hands!" cried Todd Merton, a burly Californian. "You bet if you shoved a bullet through his head you'd have had a different tale to have told us. Anyhow, you do as you like. I, for one, will remain in England."

"I am with ye, Todd!" ejaculated a tall, lean Virginian.

"Bully for ye, Merton!" added a black-browed Bowery boy, who, though enrolled as a member of the great American detective firm, was as big a scoundrel as any in New York State Penitentiaries.

The others acquiescing in Merton's determination, J. B. Falter, whose courage was returning, somewhat reluctantly agreed to remain.

"Waal, boys, I don't know as you are not right. We'll stick together. It'll have to go mighty hard with us if we don't get the better of this Spring-Heeled Jack critter," agreed Falter.

"That's all right, Jonas B.," interposed Merton, "but no more shooting on sight, if you please. The Winged Man is worth a great deal more to us alive than dead. So let's to business. The first thing we have to do is to get on the trail of this here Winged Man, which I'll allow is easier said than done. The air leaves no trail, and, for all we know, he is fifty miles away by this time."

"What of that?" growled another detective. "He must show himself some time or another, then we'll be on his track like hounds on a fox."

"Quite right, Bill," agreed Merton. "We'll lie low until we find out where the Winged Man is, then—"

"The Winged Man is here!" came in ringing tones from the furthermost corner of the room.

His nerves shattered by his late terrible experience, Jonas B. Falter uttered a yell of terror, and promptly dived beneath a large ottoman, for the consultation had taken place in a private sitting-room the Americans had hired for their stay in London.

For nearly a minute the five men who yet remained upon their feet stood gazing with bulging eyes at the weird horror.

Swiftly Merton's hands slid to his hip-pocket, but ere he could grasped the butt of his revolver the ominous cry of:

"Hands up!" burst from the Winged Man's lips.

Without a moment's hesitation the Yankees obeyed the order, for, quicker than thought, the Winged Man had drawn a large Navy revolver from his belt, which he was covering the cowed and trembling men.

"So, gentlemen, I have the pleasure of making your acquaintances a little earlier than you anticipated—eh?" cried the Winged Man, with a mocking laugh. "I understand you will not take good advice when it is given you, and intends to prolong your sojourn in England. The Winged Man never repeats an order twice. Beware, unless you have left England for ever by six o'clock this evening, you will never do so, for from that moment I forbid you to leave this country, under pain of instant death. Now turn your faces to the wall. I will excuse your backs upon this occasion. Farewell! If you obey my orders all will be well, if not, we will meet again."

Five minutes of unbroken silence followed, then very cautiously Todd Merton ventured to look round. A gasp of amazement burst from his lips. The Winged Man had disappeared!

NIGHT ON THE RIVER.

Jonas B. Falter, as he emerged from beneath the ottoman, found his comrades in the centre of the room, casting frightened glances to right and left as they spoke in low whispers.

Their encounter with the Winged Man had proved that their leader had not exaggerated his wondrous, almost supernatural powers. Yet, although half inclined to obey his command, and leave England for ever, cupidity prevailed over their fears, and when an hour or so later they sat down to breakfast, they had determined to risk all and hunt the Winged Man down.

Separating, they passed the day searching for the Winged Man in the crowded London streets.

At six o'clock they returned, dispirited, to their hotel, where Jonas B. Falter found a letter, which had been delivered by hand, awaiting him.

As he read the communication and ejaculation of triumph burst from his lips.

Thrusting the letter into his pocket, he signed to his companions to follow him.

"Boys, we are in luck; read this!" he cried, spreading out the half-sheet on the table of their sitting-room.

There was no address or signature; simply the words, in rough, ill-formed characters:

"If you would find the Winged Man, seek him amidst the shipping in the Pool at midnight."

"Perhaps it's a plant!" growled Todd Merton suspiciously.

"Anyhow, it's a clue, and will follow it for all it's worth!" declared Falter. "Come, boys, will have our hands to the plough, let there be no turning back!"

Despite their brave words and loud boasts, it was a secretly trembling and unwilling party that dropped down the river in a boat hired at the foot of Waterloo Bridge.

The six were armed, each carrying a Bowie-knife, as well as a heavy Colt revolver.

As they neared London Bridge they drew in their oars, wrapped cloth brought for the purpose around them, then, stealthily and silently, passed through the old bridge's mighty arches, and headed towards where a line of lights betokened the Tower Bridge.

It was here they first caught sight of their quarry. As though a thunderbolt had fallen from the heavens, a bright light illuminated the pinnacles and spires of the mighty fabric's towers, and, with cries of wonder and dismay on their lips, the American detectives gazed in amazement at the Winged Man.

Poised on the topmost spire he stood with outstretched wings, as though threatening them with instant annihilation.

The next moment the vision vanished, and after a moment's delay, during which their boat was rapidly carried downstream by the outgoing current, they made their way beneath the huge cantilever.

"Look, what's that?" whispered Merton, glancing fearfully over his shoulder as some dark object flapped by above their heads.

"Bah, you're as scared as a gal, Todd!" said his leader contemptuously. "It was but a gull flying seaward."

"A gull? Never—" began Todd, then added in a low, hushed whisper: "Hark, there it is again!"

The men rested upon their oars as through the darkness came the low, steady beat of huge pinions. But, strain their eyes as they might, they could see nothing but the dark, cloud-covered heavens above.

"Pull, boys! For Heaven's sake don't linger here!" cried Falter, in a hoarse, strained whisper.

Steering towards where a large steamer lay at anchor, Falter guided the boat downstream.

Five minutes past, and no sound of their dread opponent having fallen upon their ears, they began slowly to search the barges moored in big clubs on either side of the stream, or paused to cast frightened glances upon the decks of the various craft they passed.

Presently a man named Wilson, who was in the bows, uttered an exclamation of alarm.

"Steady, boys," he added, in a low whisper; "there's a dead body floating just ahead of us!"

"Let it be, Wilson," ordered Falter; "it's no business of ours! We are out after the Winged Man, not body-hunting!"

"Better haul it aboard, cap'n, and see whether it's got anything valuable about it," suggested Merton.

"All right; where is it, Wilson?" asked Falter, standing up in the stern with a filigree rope in either hand.

There was no need for the men in the bows to point out the grim object.

Floating within an oar's length of the boat was a ghastly white speck, which could only be the face of a drowned person.

Falter shuddered, but cupidity overcoming his natural horror of the dead man, he hung on to the tiller-ropes, and the boat's head swung towards the floating object.

"Catch hold of him, Todd, before we are swept by!" cried Falter, as the boat floated alongside the corpse.

Merton leaned over to obey, but ere his outstretched hand could clasp the figure he started back with a wild cry of terror—a cry echoed by all on board—for the body rose slowly from out the water, then turning its white, staring face to the six detectives, stretched forth to long, white, skeleton-like hands, as though about to seize them.

"Powers of darkness," almost shrieked Todd Merton, "it is alive! For Heaven's sake keep it off!"

"Ho, ho, ho!"

Loud, blood-curdling, came the mocking laughter from the lips of the supposed body. Then a pair of mighty wings flashed from its side, and the Winged Man—for it was he--sprang like a rocket into the inky black night above the river; whilst the detectives, taking to their oars, rode as swiftly as they could pull the boat through the water down the stream, careless of everything so that they might leave the dread horror behind them.

Suddenly they ceased to pull, as a loud voice hailed them from the darkness above their heads.

"Ho, ho! Is that you, Jonas B. Falter, the man who promised to show the London police how to capture the Winged Man? Why, you are but a cowardly woman after all! See, I await you. Capture me who can!"

Through the darkness the terrified detectives saw an ominous figure approach a number of barges moored just off the river's fairway.

With an oath Todd Merton sprang to his feet. The next moment a loud report rang over the river as he sent a bullet hurtling through the air after the Winged Man.

A cry of triumph burst from the desperate man's lips, for, with a shriek of pain the Winged Man turned a somersault in the air, then fell sprawling upon the bows of the nearest barge.

"Give way, lads, we have got him! The Winged Man is ours!" shrieked Falter, as he turned the boat's head in the direction of the barge.

BENEATH THE ICY FLOOD.

A few minutes later the Yankee detectives, tying their boat to a rusty anchor which held the barges to a buoy, swarmed onto the deck.

A cry of disappointment proclaimed that their quarry had disappeared.

"See, what is that upon the tiller of the second barge?" cried Merton, seizing Falter by the arm, and pointing to where, just distinguishable through the darkness, a black, shapeless object was climbing painfully from barge to barge.

With shouts of triumph the Yankees started in pursuit, confident that ere long the Winged Man would be at their mercy. From barge to barge they clambered, dashing wildly backwards and forwards, bewildered and dismayed, for, though the Winged Man seemed wounded nigh under death, and scarce able to drag one foot after the other, yet in some strange manner he managed to evade them.

Suddenly a wild, piercing shriek rent the air. All faces were turned in the direction from whence the sound had come.

A fearful sight met their gaze. Standing on the top of a barge's caboose, his face contorted with fiendish fury, one of their comrades held, and helpless as an infant, in his strong grasp, stood the Winged Man.

"Aho, aho!" cried the Winged Man, as he stood, a fearful black object thrown into clear relief by some mysterious light which seemed to exude from every part of his body, with the unfortunate detective held high above his head. "The hour is passed, your last chance is gone. The fate of he I hold my hands shall be that of ye all, save such as shall serve me to the death!"

With a shriek of mingled rage and triumph, he held the wretched, convulsively-writhing man into the dark, icy water roaring and hissing beneath the barges.

Todd Merton's pistol rang out for the second time that night. As before, the bullet flattened itself against the stout yet light and flexible breastplate the Winged Man wore beneath his clothes.

Placing his hand to his heart, and uttering a low, shuddering moan the Winged Man sank, apparently lifeless, across the gaily-painted top of the caboose.

With cries of triumph, the Americans, recking little of the terrible price they had already paid for victory, crowded round the prostrate Winged Man.

"Keep your pistol against his head; blow out his brains if he attempts to move!" ordered Falter, as, kneeling by the Winged Man's side, he placed a hand over his heart.

Not a flutter of his eyelids, not a beat of the heart told the American detectives that the Winged Man yet lived.

"So, King of the Air, as you call yourself, your course is run!" growled Falter adding as he rose: "now, boys, look lively, bring round the boat, and we'll carry the body home, search it for any plans that may lead us to his secret haunts, then hand it over to the police and claim the promised reward. It's been a jolly sight easier than I thought it would have been. Why, I have had more trouble running an absconding bank-clerk to earth than the Winged Man.

As Falter spoke all save himself and Ted Merton crossed to where they had left the boat. Barely had they gone air Falter, raising the Winged Man's right hand, sought to draw off a magnificent ring which sparkled on one of the fingers; whilst, eager to gain as much more than the lawful share of the booty as he could, Merton seized the other hand, his greedy eyes attracted by a single ruby of enormous value which glittered upon the Winged Man's little finger.

To their terror, the Winged Man's fingers closed upon their hands with an iron grasp. In vain the tried to break free. It was as though their aching fingers were imprisoned in the iron jaws of some deadly trap. Even as, mad with terror, they strove to rise from their knees, they found, to their horror, that the Winged Man's lifeless form was rising also. "Help, help, help! For the love of Heaven, help!" yelled the wretched men, as the body, apparently defying all known laws of gravitation, rose until level with their shoulders then moved slowly, irresistibly, towards the edge of the barge.

Both Falter and Merton were strong men; yet, though they strove their utmost, they could not break free. Drawn by those cold, clinging fingers, they were drawn nearer and nearer the swiftly-rushing water. For a minute the Winged Man hovered over the stream, then, his would-be robbers' hands still imprisoned in his own, plunged heavily into the icy-sleet-covered flood.

Immediately the detectives' cries were hushed, as, drawn beneath the surface, the water closed in upon them. Down they dropped, lower and lower, until at length their heads were plunged into the soft, yielding black mud.

Nerved by despair, terror of death driving terror of the grisly monster from their hearts, they struck blindly at the fearful weight which had dragged them down. Suddenly the Winged Man's hold relaxed, and, their heads and shoulders caked with mud, they rose, gasping for breath, to the surface, where they were speedily picked up by their comrades.

THE CROWN JEWELS.

Barely had the boat containing the American detectives pulled, with the frenzied haste of men stricken with deadly fear, up the stream, ere the Winged Man rose to the surface. Pulling himself on to the barge upon which he had feigned death, he crouched upon its blunt prow and gazed reflectively through the snow-laden air.

"Bah, the cowards are scarce worth the Winged Man's attention!" he muttered contemptuously. "Danby Druce is worth the whole six of them. He is an honourable foe—his heart beats high with true British pluck. These men's bravery is one of a kind that gold can buy. One by one they shall perish, that all the world may know how perish those who hunt the Winged Man. Now to secure a few hours' rest, then to plan some bold stroke which will strike terror and dismay into the hearts of this great people—the mighty British nation."

As he spoke he extended his broad pinions, and, soaring high above the masts of the surrounding shipping, flew westward. Presently the huge grey mass of the Tower of London attracted the Winged Man's attention.

"Why rest, when there is so much to be done?" he muttered. "Below me is a prize worthy even of the Winged Man!

"Aha!" muttered the Winged Man. And he descended upon the topmost pinnacle of the Tower Bridge and surveyed the gloomy old fortress so dear to the heart of every Englishman, the thought that has guarded London a thousand years and more.

"The Crown jewels lie there!" hissed the Winged Man—"the Crown jewels lie there!"

He rose in the air.

Descending in a series of graceful circles, he at length stood upright upon the summit of the White Tower. A few lights shed their beams over the old courtyard, here and there a sentry paste to his solitary beat; otherwise all was still as the grave; the Premier citadel of England slept secure from every foe.

For some minutes the Winged Man sat swinging to the breeze on the vane which surmounted one of the tall turrets, brooding like some black thing of evil over the sleeping tower.

To his left where the Waterloo Barracks, in which slept a battalion of his Majesty's Guards. Immediately before him, Beauchamp Tower; beneath it, the ominous black spot in the paved courtyard, where in the olden days the executioner's block stood; behind him, Broad Arrow Tower.

Whirling on the vane, he faced one and then another of the buildings above enumerators, and eventually came to rest with his eyes fixed upon the Wakefield Tower, within which reposed the Crown jewels of England.

Deep thought furrowed his brow. He was about to perpetrate an outrage which, if successful, would thrill every quarter of the English-speaking globe.

Leaving his lofty eyrie, the Winged Man dropped upon the flat top of Wakefield Tower, then clambered like some enormous spider down the perpendicular stone wall, until he came to a diamond-paned casement.

A minute's silent work, and the casement swung open to his pool. Creeping through the window, he found himself in a low, cell-like, but cosily-furnished bed-room, where slept a grey-bearded old man. On a chair by the side of the bed lay the sleeper's quaintly-shaped Beefeater's coat. The Winged Man smiled triumphantly as his eyes rested upon the recumbent figure, for he knew that instinct had guided him to the chamber of the Keeper of the Crown jewels.

With noiseless steps the Winged Man stole to the side of the bed and quickly searched the pockets of the discarded garment. A frown crossed his brow. The keys were not there. A shuddering ejaculation caused him to turn. He found the Beefeater gazing at him with distended eyeballs and ashen face.

"Who are you—what are you doing here?" gasped the old man.

The Winged Man spoke not, but raising himself to his full height, held the old man's gaze with his black, piercing eyes.

"I am the Winged Man!" he announced in low, impressive tones.

A cry of alarm rose to the old man's lips, but his tongue refused it utterance.

Yet, though in the grip of a power he could not resist—overwhelmed by a terror such as his brave old heart had never deemed it possible a man could experience and live, he thought of the Crown jewels, of which he was the custodian, and fought gallantly to throw off the paralysing horror which held him captive.

As one in the grasp of some fearful nightmare he saw the Winged Man's fearful, white face approaches own; then from the weird horror's lips came a blast of hot breath, and, clutching at his throat as though suffocating, the old man sank back unconscious upon his bed.

Regarding his latest victim with a look of satisfaction, the Winged Man thrust his hand beneath the pillow upon which lay the pale, distorted face, and drew forth, with a chuckle of delight, a bunch of quaintly-shaped keys.

Opening the bed-room door, he passed out on to a dark, and lighted passage and down a winding-stair. A moment later the glare from his head light was reflected back from the Crown jewels of England lying behind their iron cage. The regalia of the greatest Empire the world has ever seen lay at the Winged Man's mercy.

His eyes blazing with cupidity, his whole face distorted with avarice, the Winged Man grasped a stout iron bar in each hand, and, exerting to the full his wondrous strength, tore them apart. Then, smashing the glass within, he drew out King George's crown.

With a fearful laugh of inpatient delight, he placed it upon his head, and stood, with folded arms, surveying mace, orb, sceptre, and the many orders which lay ready for his grasp.

Moved by a strange impulse, he buckled on the Sword of State, then, the sceptre in one hand, the orb in the other, seated himself, as a king upon his throne, on a bench running round the room.

"Why not?" he muttered. "The King of the Air may well be king of the earth also. And what else is he who rules over the destinies of Britain but the arbiter of the whole world? Now by stealth I wear these gems, but the time shall come when I will wear them by right of conquest."

A BRAVE LASSIE.

So enrapt was the Winged Man in his ambitious thoughts that he did not see a tiny, white-robed figure gazing at him, her blue eyes distended in amazement, from the doorway through which he had entered.

It was little Maisie, the keeper of the jewels' granddaughter, who, hearing a noise in the jewel-room below, had, after trying in vain to arouse her grandfather, crept down the cold, stone stairs.

For nearly a minute she stood gazing upon the weird horror; then, her little mouth squeezed tightly with an expression of determination, she stole silently downstairs.

It was no light task to shoot back the heavy iron bolts which held the massive door in place; but, child though she was, she knew that upon her alone depended the safety of the Crown jewels, over which her grandfather had ever watched with such jealous care.

Exerting to the full her baby strength, she drew back the bolts one by one, though she had to get a chair to reach the topmost bar. But at length she succeeded, and only opening the door sufficiently to allow her small form to squeeze through, she closed it noiselessly behind her, and rushed through the snow towards the sentry on duty outside the guard-room.

The six-foot Guardsman started violently as the white-robed little figure hastened towards him. Instinctively he gave the challenge: "Who goes there?" as he brought his rifle down to the "charge."

"It's me—Maisie—Mr. Soldier!" cried the child in a low, hurried whisper. "Oh, Mr. Soldier, make haste; there's a big, ugly, black man in the jewel-room!"

The sentry allowed the but-end of his rifle to clatter to the stone in amazement.

"Oh, please be quiet, or you will not catch him!" cried the child anxiously. "Do make haste! Call the others, and come!"

"Hallo, Maisie, what's the matter? Nothing wrong with your grandfather, I hope?" asked the sergeant of the guard, coming out of the guard-room at that moment.

"Oh, no. I think—I hope not!" replied the child. "But he is so sound asleep I cannot wake him. Do come, please come, or the big black man will take the Crown jewels!"

"What black man, Maisie?" asked the sergeant incredulously. "You have been dreaming, and walking in your sleep that's what's the matter with you."

"No, no; I woke up and heard a sound as if glass was breaking, so I ran into grandad's room to tell him there was somebody in the jewel-room," explained the child. "But I saw a big black man. He had one of the crowns on his head, the ball with the dicky-bird on it in one hand, and the gold stick in the other. He was sitting on a bench, talking away to himself."

An incredulous smile hovered over the sergeant's lips; whilst the soldiers of the guard, who, attracted by the sound of voices, had come from the guard-room, laughed aloud.

"Silence!" commanded the sergeant, in a low voice; the smile fading from his lips as a sudden thought struck terror to his heart.

"You are sure there is somebody in the jewel-room, Maisie?" he demanded gravely.

"Maisie never tells wicked stories," replied the child reproachfully.

"No, no; but you may have been mistaken. Asleep and dreaming, perhaps. What kind of man was he?"

The little girl shuddered.

"An awful bogey kind of man, dressed all in black," replied Maisie, with a shudder. "There was a kind of cloak hanging over his shoulder, and his face—oh, his awful face!—It was not like a man's face, but as white as Maisie's night-gown. I could not see his eyes, but over as head shone bright, white, dazzling light."

"By heavens, it's the Winged Man!" gasped the sergeant, now as pale as the brave little girl who, forgetting her own peril, had come to warn him.

"Fall in, there! Load your magazines with ball-cartridge! Are you ready?"

A whispered murmur of assent came from the soldiers.

"Then follow me!" ordered the sergeant, leading the way towards the Wakefield Tower.

"Let Maisie come with you; she is not frightened," pleaded the child.

The sergeant shook his head.

"But grandad may wake up, and wonder what's become of me," she persisted.

The sergeant hesitated; then, realising that every moment was of consequence, raised her in his arms.

***

In the meantime, all unconscious that a child's hand was bringing peril upon him, the Winged Man, arousing himself from his reverie, had secured the valuable Crown jewels, when a sound of footsteps and heavy breathing of excited men reached his ears.

With the snarl, like that of a wolf interrupted in the act of devouring its prey, the Winged Man glanced swiftly around him. Save the door by which he had entered, there seemed no other means of exit from the room.

Yet, as the thought that he was trapped flashed through his brain, a scornful peal of laughter burst from his lips—a laugh which sent a cold thrill of terror through the veins of the approaching soldiers.

Then he commenced what, under the circumstances, would have struck an observer had there been one, as a childish proceeding. Spring around the cave, the Winged Man stepped violently upon the stern flaps with which the room was paved, as though dancing.

Suddenly he came to a halt, a look of intense satisfaction upon his face; for, not the floor, but the wall close to where he stood had rung hollow.

At that moment a loud cry of:

"Surrender in the King's name! Shoot him down if he moves a single step backwards or forwards, lads!" came from the open doorway, enframed in which was the burly figure of the sergeant; whilst behind him, the Winged Man's headlight was reflected back from a number of brown rifle-barrels.

"Who dares to call upon the Winged Man to surrender?" thundered the weird horror, his eyes flashing with suppressed rage.

"I do—sergeant of his Majesty's Guards! Move, and a score of bullets will pierce your body!" replied the sergeant, moving forward.

Defiance ever roused the worst feelings in the Winged Man's breast.

With the snarl of rage he thrust his hand into a large black wallet he carried at his belt. His fingers closed round a small glass globe, small though it was, it

505

contained sufficient explosive liquid to hurl the advancing soldiers to a swift and fearful doom.

But, even as he half drew it from its hiding-place, he saw the little child, whose golden hair fell in a rippling cascade over the brawny sergeant's red tunic.

Never yet had the Winged Man injured a child or dog. Swiftly the ball was exchanged for a small glass phial, and this, ere a shot could be fired, he hurled at the sergeant's feet.

A low, dull, muffled roar echoed through the room which was immediately filled with a cloud of dense, black, impenetrable smoke.

Coughing, half suffocated by the fearful fumes, the soldiers staggered back from the door.

The next moment the sergeant's voice rang out loud, clear, and distinct.

"Fire! Fire! Empty your magazines into the room, lads! We will have him yet!" he cried.

In one loud, resonant clap the soldiers' rifles rang out, their bullets searching every part of the room.

It seemed impossible that anything larger than a rat could have escaped that fusillade, and when, dazed and trembling, the keeper of the Crown jewels, aroused from his trance by the roar of musketry, appeared, lantern in hand, amongst the soldiers as they advanced into the room, cries of wonder and amazement burst from their lips.

The Winged Man had disappeared. The walls were pitted with bullet-marks. It seemed impossible but that one at least must have reached its mark.

A triumphant cry burst from the sergeant's lips, as he bent over a single drop of blood near where the Winged Man had been standing when the volley was fired.

At this moment the sleeping tower awoke to life. Bugles rang out, drums beat the "alert," as from the quarters of the non-commissioned officers, from the room is occupied by the Army Service Corps—in fact, from every inhabited part of the old tower, put forth a stream of excited and alarmed men, awakened by the soldiers' useless volleys.

MAISIE'S PRAYER TO SANTA CLAUS.

The sergeant and those who had seen the Winged Man decked with the crown, the collar of the Golden Fleece, and a big diamond star flashing on his breast, standing by the wall, were of the opinion that he had vanished in the smoke of his own creation.

None knew that there was a secret engine entrance in the jewel-room. Through this he had escaped just as the soldiers opened fire, but not before a bullet had struck the hand with which he was pulling to the sliding stone.

As the massive stone dropped into its place the Winged Man strode angrily down a narrow flight of steps into the thick outer wall.

In a small, cell-like compartment he halted to examine his wounded hand.

A paroxysm of rage shook his frame. His eyes flashed, his whole frame trembled, as, grinding his teeth, he struck wildly at the air, as though wreaking his vengeance upon some unseen foe.

"Death to all within this building! Death to those who dare to wound the Winged Man!" he shrieked. "With that I had power by a word to level this old pile to the dust! Power? Ay, I have the power! The world shall ring with the Winged Man's vengeance!"

Turning, he examined the walls by the glare of his headlight. His eyes fell upon a rusty nail embedded in the masonry. He pressed it inward.

As he expected, a portion of the wall slid back, revealing a flight of steps, up which he strode, until at length a secret door admitted him to the summit of the Wakefield Tower.

Turning, he gazed upon the busy scene below.

Soldiers, some bearing rifles, some lanterns, were hastening excitedly hither and thither, evidently searching for the Winged Man. Suddenly every man came to an abrupt halt as the Winged Man's mocking laughter echoed in their ears. Poised on the parapet of the tower they saw him, clad in the Royal regalia of Britain.

As a score of bullets whistled like bees about his ears, the Winged Man retraced his steps; then, after threading countless winding passages hidden in the tower's thick walls, he stood within a large, damp, low-roofed cell.

He knew that he was in one of the many lost dungeons of the Tower of London, for attached to the wall by chain and, was a faded form.

"Oho, oho!" laughed the Winged Man, in fearful mirth. "Well met Brother Doom! I Crown the King!"

As he spoke he placed the glistening diadem upon the white, grinning skull; then hung the various jewels and insignia of rank upon the dried bones, and having thrust the orb and sceptre into its fleshless hands turned to the crumbling wooden doorway by which he had entered, saying:

"These are yours, friend Doom, for the time being. Ere long I will return and claim my own."

Ten minutes later the Winged Man was flying through the large, slowly-falling flakes of snow, which were rapidly covering London as with a white mantle.

Tireless, scorning the bitter North wind, which howled and roared around him, the Winged Man flew swiftly to wear, far away in the Midlands, he had stored sufficient of a new and deadly explosive he himself had invented to level all London in the dust.

Forty-eight hours later the Winged Man returned to the world's metropolis, borne on the wings of a fierce snowstorm, which shrieked among the chimney-tops and whirled the snow from the roofs into the streets below.

The Winged Man laughed aloud with evil glee. He loved the storm; he loved the bitter cold which pinched the limbs and chilled the hearts of the race he hated. Above all, he delighted in the prospect of the evil he was about to do.

His terrible laughter struck terror into the hearts of the crowds hastening along the snow-filled streets, as he called to mind the Christmas gift he had prepared for England.

Lights shone from every window, bright fires blazed in every room of the Waterloo Barracks, as the Winged Man, alighting as before upon the Wakefield Tower, made his way, by the secret passage known only to himself, to the maze of dungeons beneath the tower's foundations.

For hours he worked, laying metal bombs here and there with such skill that each explosion would wreak terrible damage even on the solid, thousand-year-old building above his head.

On the roof of the Wakefield Tower the Winged Man deposited the detonator the explosion of which would turn the tower into a mass of ruins.

Poised upon the parapet of the tower the Winged Man drew a pistol from his belt and pointed it at the polished disc glistening amongst the snow at his feet.

Another moment and the shot which would have caused the death of thousands would have been fired; but at that moment, loud and clear through the snow-laden air, came children's voices singing a Christmas Carol.

Noiselessly the pistol dropped upon the snow-covered roof. A spasm of fearful agony contorted the Winged Man's white, deathlike face. Who could tell what memory of the past was stirring to life within the weird being's breast by those sweet, children's voices? Perchance Christmas tides long gone, almost forgotten, when he, the scourge of a mighty nation, had been a happy father, surrounded by loving, laughing, happy children, had been recalled to his mind.

"'Tis Christmas Eve, and I contemplated that!" he cried, indicating with a sweep of his hand the noble pile he had doomed to destruction.

His fearful plot forgotten, he bowed his head in his hands, and crouched upon the parapet, his shoulders shaking as though with sobs. Suddenly he assumed a listening attitude, as from somewhere immediately beneath him came a child's voice, saying:

"Santa Claus—dear Santa clause, please don't bring me any toys this Christmas! I am a miserable little girl, whose grandad is in prison; but, oh, Santa Claus, if you can, bring back the stolen Crown jewels!"

A spasm of agony as there were knife had been driven into his heart crossed the Winged Man's face. Gliding noiselessly from his lofty eyrie, he paused before the window at which little Maisie, the keeper's granddaughter, was kneeling, her white, eager face turned towards the dark void without.

The Winged Man overhears a little girl's prayer.

Without a moment's hesitation the Winged Man, descending by the path he had trodden two nights before, entered the lost dungeon where he had left the Crown jewels in the safekeeping of their grim custodian.

An hour later he stood once more in the old keeper's room.

The bed was empty. Maisie had told the truth. Her grandfather, though not in prison, was in custody on suspicion of having assisted in the theft of the Crown jewels.

Stepping noiselessly across the room, the Winged Man opened the door and peeped into the adjoining apartment. In a cot against the wall lay Maisie, her pretty little head buried in her tear-stained pillow.

Noiselessly the Winged Man deposited the Crown jewels at the foot of the cot, stole silently from the room, and, retracing his steps, turned his back upon the Tower.

CHRISTMAS EVE.

From the golden ball beneath the richly-gilt cross that adorns the top of St. Paul's the Winged Man watched the busy scene of life beneath him.

To the west blazed a long line of lights, showing the roots of crowded thoroughfares. To the east similar lights, but few in number, and divided by large black spaces, where, herded together in common mystery, the very poor eke out a precarious existence.

Releasing his hold of the gilt ball, the Winged Man allowed himself to be carried on the wings of the wind to a deserted street of Holborn. As he alighted a suppressed shriek from the doorway close at hand fell upon his ears.

A woman in clad in ragged garments was gazing in wild-eyed terror upon him. For a moment she clutched the shawl which protected the babe she held in her arms closer to her; then, with a sudden indescribable gesture of despair, rose to her feet and faced the Winged Man.

"Are you Death?" she demanded. "If so, strike!"

As she spoke she drew herself up and waited for the thrust of the keen shaft of one whom she believed to be the grim King of Terrors.

"Who craves for death on Christmas Eve?" demanded the Winged Man, in hollow tones.

"It is because it is Christmas Eve, and memory brings back the happy days gone by that I crave for the rest death alone can give," moaned the wretched outcast.

"Hold out your hand!"

Wonderingly the woman obeyed.

"I am not Death," continued the Winged Man. "I cannot give you the gift of death, but here is gold, and the life gold will give to you and your little one. Go; and remember, no matter how great your misery and suffering may be, there is one dreaded by all, loved by none, who would give all his useless wealth to change places with you."

Wonderingly, the woman clasped the purse of gold the Winged Man had dropped into her hand. In vain she tried to thank the strange donor. The spell of the Winged Man's fearful presence was upon her, and tongue-tied, she moved slowly away.

A deep sigh escaped the Winged Man's lips as his wings draped around him like a cloak, a black slouch hat hiding his deathly-white face, he mingled with the happy, jostling crowd buying presents and provisions for the morrow's festivities in Holborn.

Those who knew the Winged Man only as a devastating demon sweeping across the land, leaving murdered men and devastated households in his track, would not have believed the weird horror capable of such human feelings— such boundless sympathy with grief.

It was the children who appealed most to the Winged Man. A rare smile would cross his lips as he saw an eager-faced child, drawing father or mother after it with imperious hand, point out a brilliantly-lighted shop-window some toy he wanted to buy for brother, sister, or friend.

Again his heart would bleed—the ever-present sorrow in his eyes deepen— as he beheld ragged children devouring with their eyes the wonders stowed away in the shops, or casting envious glances at more fortunate children whose arms were laden with newly-purchased toys.

Near the plate-glass window of a large toyshop the Winged Man was standing with folded arms. It was strange how, though none knew him, none so much as suspected his presence in their midst, the hurrying pedestrians of avoided coming in contact with that all, motionless form.

The window before which he had taken his stand was a perfect fairyland of toys. Round it were gathered a number of open-eyed children from the neighbouring slums, happy if they might but see the toys they could never hope to possess.

The huge liveried doorkeeper, with a round, good-humoured face, pretended not to see the eager-faced mites who kept better-dressed children from the window.

Suddenly a frock-coated, important-looking individual strode from the shop.

"Confound you, Johnson! What you think I have stationed you here for?" he demanded of the doorkeeper. "Not to allow a lot of beggarly brats without sixpennyworth of coppers between them to block up my windows. Send them going, or, if you can't, call in the police! You understand?"

Touching his, the man moved forward to obey his employer's command.

"Stop!" thundered the Winged Man, in tones which rolled like thunder over the roar of the traffic. "I, the Winged Man, forbid!"

Unfurling his mighty pinions, he swooped down upon the white-faced, trembling shopkeeper and hurled him headforemost through the enormous plate-glass window.

"Hasten, little ones, help yourselves! It is the Winged Man's command!" he ordered.

For a moment the children hesitated; then, after casting frightened glances at the Winged Man's face, now softened by a sweet, melancholy smile, each seized the toy he most coveted, and dashed off ere the astounded spectators could interfere, even if they had felt disposed to do so.

A Spoilt Child.

It was before a toy-shop in Westbourne Grove that the Winged Man next put in an appearance. Since leaving Holborn his loud, mocking laugh had chilled the hearts of hundreds as he flew over London's main arteries. Again and again he had passed by shops, around which adults thronged, but grown-up people had little or no interest for the Winged Man. It was children he loved to watch—children's wrongs he loved to right. As he took his stand on the curb close to a well-appointed carriage-and-pair and watched the eager-faced youngsters devouring the wealth of toys beyond the plate-glass windows, his attention was attracted by a cry of pain immediately before him.

A boy of about ten, clad in warm, well-fitting clothes had just slapped the face of a ragged little mite some two years younger than himself.

"Hallo, Hallo! What's all this about?" demanded a fat, round-faced, fur-coated man, followed by a richly-dressed lady, as stout and preposterous-looking as her husband, who emerged from the shop at that moment.

"Algernon, what is the meaning of this?"

"That's a nasty street-boy asked me to show him my new horse," pouted the angry child, displaying at the same time the expensive horse on wheels his father had just given him with a lot of other toys. "How dare he speak to me? I am a gentleman, and he is only a gutter-snipe!"

"So you boxed his ears? Served him right!" chuckled the old man, as, turning to his wife, he told her what had occurred; whereupon the woman, bending down with a proud smile on her face, kissed the ill-mannered little cur.

A paroxysm of rage shook the Winged Man's frame. He was about to interfere, when a pale, thin man, his ragged frock-coat buttoned tightly to his chin, stepped eagerly forward.

"Your boy had no business to hit my child," he began.

Then a look of amazement crossed his face as his eyes fell upon the man in the fur-coat.

"Oh, sir! Oh, Mr. Scarf, I did not know it was your boy!" he added.

"Like father, like son!" growled Josiah Scarf, glowering at the man who, owing to ill-health, he had discharged from his office three months ago.

"Indeed, sir; it was only a little childish indiscretion," apologised the father. "My poor boy has no toys; he only wanted to see Master Algernon's horse."

"And got what he deserved for his cheek!" replied Scarf brutally. "Get out of the way! Can't you see I am going to my carriage?"

"Oh, sir; I am starving—my wife and children are starving! A few shillings would give us all a Christmas dinner, and we have nothing!" pleaded the man.

"Serve you right!" growled Scarf. "It is like you improvident lazy beggars to come begging of those who have earned their money by sheer hard work. Where would I have been if I had been like you?"

"Probably where I am now. There is no room in this world for honest, hard-working men!" seemed almost forced from the wretched clerk's lips as he turned away.

Josiah Scarf, his round, spotted face convulsed with rage, took a step forward, as though about to inflict summary chastisement upon the wretched man.

But probably there was something in the look Horace Widney gave him as he turned away that want the millionaire it would not be quite safe to carry vindictive spite too far, and, muttering something about:

"He hoped the beggar would die in the gutter!" he entered the carriage, and seated himself by the side of his wife; whilst his promising son thrust his head out of the window and made faces at the ragged children who had been half frightened, half interested spectators of the little scene. Still, the carriage did not move off.

"Where is Miss Amy?" growled Scarf to a footman, who still held the door open.

"Beg your pardon, sir! She is talking to the boy Master Algernon hit," replied the man.

Josiah Scarf's face grew pale with anger, for, perfectly oblivious of everyone else, a pretty, golden-haired girl of eight was bending over the still sobbing boy.

Even as Mr. Scarf's eyes fell upon his daughter she kissed the tear-stained little face. Josiah Scarf could scarce believe his eyes. His daughter, the daughter of Josiah Scarf, millionaire, was kissing a little street urchin!

With a howl of rage he sprang from the carriage, and, grasping the child by the arm, dragged her roughly into the carriage.

"Amy Scarf, I am ashamed of you!" he gasped. "Wherever you get these low, vulgar tastes from I cannot tell. You will go to bed directly we get home, and keep in bed all tomorrow."

The sobbing little girl turned an appealing glance towards her mother.

"Don't look at me, Miss!" shrilled Mrs. Scarf. "I am ashamed of you! I don't know who you take after, I am sure!" she cried, slapping her daughter's arm as the carriage rolled away to their palatial abode in West Kensington.

FROM GARRETT TO PALACE.

As the carriage moved from the curb, the Winged Man passed through the crowd with long, angry strides, as he followed Horace Widney to a grim, dirty-looking house in a very poor street off Holland Park.

Within a miserable garret at the top of the house a woman crouched over a few coals that glowed at the bottom of the miserable grate.

By her side, her little hands blue with the cold, played a little girl of eight. The mother looked up. A ray of undying love brightened her worn, wasted features, as she recognised her husband's step. A minute later Horace Widney entered the room.

"Well, dear, back again, then!" said the woman, with forced cheerfulness. "How did little Charlie like the grand toy-shops—eh?"

"Oh, mum, they were beautiful! Such good things in the food-shop windows!" cried the boy. "How is it, mother, that we have no warm clothes, no beautiful toys, not even food, when there is a lot everywhere?"

Mrs. Widney shook her head.

"Ah, dear, that's what wiser people than you or I have often asked!" she replied gravely. "It is cruel, Horace!" she continued, turning to her husband, a momentary anger flashing from her gentle eyes. "Let those who won't work starve; but it is hard, cruel hard, that you, who have never done a mortal creature an injury, who have always striven your utmost for the sake of your dear ones, should be brought to this; whilst Josiah Scarf, who, Heaven forgive me if I judge wrong, has robbed thousands, lives in luxury and wealth."

"Of course, there is no letter from him?" interposed Horace Widney.

Mrs. Widney shook her head.

"But why 'of course,' dear?" she asked. "The long years that you have been in his service should at least bring a courteous reply from one who was once as poor as ourselves."

"Ah, it is such men as he who have hearts of stone!" replied Horace Widney. "It makes me wild to hear spouters at the street corners declaiming against the callousness of the aristocracy, when it is in reality men of their own kidney, men who have risen from the ranks, who are ever the hardest, coolest, most unfeeling. Well, well! Evil thoughts of others will not help us. Come, dear, get the children to bed, and we will go for a walk. Perchance, Fortune may throw the means of getting a Christmas dinner in our way."

It seemed almost mockery to talk of putting the children to bed, when their only couch was a rough pallet stretched in the warmest corner of the almost empty room, and it was with a heart-breaking sigh she could not quite repress that Mrs. Widney obeyed; then, leaving her children sleeping peacefully in each other's arms, followed her husband down the stairs.

Barely had they gone ere the window was softly opened, and the Winged Man stepped into the room.

Tenderly as a woman he wrapped the poor little mites in the clean but ragged coverlet, and, taking them in his arms, flew quickly over the City.

It was an old-fashioned Christmas night. The storm had abated, but the snow still fell in thick, white flakes.

On the roof of Josiah Scarf's palatial residence the Winged Man alighted; then, clambering down the wall, paused before a dimly-lighted window.

This he opened without difficulty, and thus gained admittance into a magnificent room, which was full of neglected and broken, but expensive toys.

It was the day nursery in which Algernon Scarf passed many a sullen, discontented hour. The babes still sleeping peacefully against his bosom, the Winged Man passed into a cosy night nursery, where, in two white enamelled cots, covered with expensive quilts, the children of Josiah Scarf slept, recking little of the fearful being who was gazing down upon them.

Moving to the boy's bed, the Winged Man gazed at the tossing little figure. Young though he was, Algernon Scarf already felt the effects of injudicious indulgence.

Drawing a phial from the wallet at his belt, the Winged Man arrested it gently against the sleeping boy's nostrils.

Immediately the child's tossing ceased, his breathing became more regular, and he slept soundly.

Raising a little Algernon from the cot, he laid the Widneys in his place; then, as soothed by the unaccustomed warmth, their drowsy little heads dropped upon the pillows, he strode noiselessly from the nursery, along a wide passage, rich with priceless gems of art, to the room occupied by Mr. and Mrs. Scarf.

"Awake to the punishment your sins have brought upon you!" thundered the Winged Man, in deep, loud, sonorous tones.

Awakened by the summons, Mr. and Mrs. Scarf set up in bed, and gazed with white, blanched faces at the fearful apparition which stood, holding their eldest born in his arms, at the foot of their bed.

There was no smile upon the Winged Man's face now. A fearful frown contorted his features; his eyes flashed with stern anger.

In vain Josiah Scarf strove to cry for help. The words he would have uttered died away in meaningless whimpers; whilst Mrs. Scarf gazed with bulging eyes at the white-faced figure before her.

"I am the Winged Man," came in fearfully distinct tones from the weird horror's lips. "I am he whose name strikes terror to the heart of the mighty nation—he who never yet has threatened and failed to keep his word. You love your child," he added, pointing to the boy, whose head rested upon his shoulder. "If you wish to see him again, obey without hesitation, without daring to rebel, my orders."

"My boy—my boy, don't hurt my little Algernon!" came in a low, hoarse, gasping whisper from the mother's lips.

"He shall be restored to you unharmed when he has learned his lesson, and the blow he struck an innocent child avenged."

Again Josiah Scarf attempted to speak, but the Winged Man silenced him with a wave of his hand.

"Dare to attempt to summon assistance, dare to raise an alarm in any way, and never again shall your eyes fall upon your boy's face," said the Winged Man, as, confident that his command would be obeyed, he turned and left the room.

THE CHRISTMAS TREE.

Ten minutes later the Winged Man was back in the Widneys' poor garret, and laying the sleeping boy on the bare pallet, walked slowly down the stairs.

As he reached the dark, mud-stained, dirty hall, a beetle-browed, brutal-looking ruffian, whom the Winged Man recognised as one of the few human beings with whom he had had personal dealings in the past, emerged from one of the lower rooms.

A single stride sufficed to carry him to the man's side.

"A word with you, Slinky Sam!" he whispered, addressing the ruffian by the nickname by which he was known in the court.

"Well I'm blest!" was all the astounded man could say, as he allowed the Winged Man to draw him into the room he had just left.

Proceeding the conversation by drawing a handful of sovereigns from out his wallet, at the sight of which the burglar's eyes sparkled avariciously, the Winged Man entered into a low-voiced conversation—if conversation it could be called, when one commands the other lessons.

"Obey me to the letter, and these coins shall be yours," said the Winged Man, in conclusion. "Fill me, and your fate is sealed!"

Without another word the Winged Man strode into the street. For some moments after the weird horror's departure Slinky Sam stood gazing at the spot his fearful visitor had just left.

Then he hastened into Widney's garret, and, raising Master Algernon Scarf off the pallet, conveyed him to his own room.

In the meantime the Winged Man, rising to a level with the eaves of the house, flew slowly in search of Widney and his wife.

Probably there is no part of London where extreme wealth and extreme poverty can be found so close to each other as in Holland Park.

As is often the case in that district the entrance to the slums where the Widney's lived was gained through a main thoroughfare of magnificent houses.

Attracted by the light blazing from a large first-floor window, the Winged Man alighted on the balcony, and, crouched in the snow, his elbow on his knee, his chin in his hand, gazed upon a scene the like of which could have been seen in many a home of England that night.

It was a large room, evidently a drawing-room, although the greater part of the expensive furniture had been removed to make room for a huge Christmas-tree, decked with many coloured lights and laden with toys.

From a band at the further end of the room it came the merry strains of a lively measure, to which some fifty or sixty bright-faced, happy children were dancing round the Christmas-tree, their little cheeks flushed with health and happiness, their eyes shining bright with anticipation of a share in the handsome presents hanging from the tree.

As the Winged Man gazed, a look of unutterable misery swept across his face.

"Ah, for the irredeemable past—for the days when, instead of crouching here and lonely outcast, whose very name is never mentioned, save with loathing and hatred, I was a welcome guest at such bright scenes as these! Gladly would I relinquish my all-conquering power, distribute to the wind my ill-gotten wealth, if I could but feel one of those little ones clambering around my knees, to hear baby lips whisper loving words in my ear!"

Lower dropped the Winged Man's head; large tears rolled down his white, deathly cheeks. A drop that seemed to burn into the flesh like vitriol fell upon his wrist.

With an ejaculation of despair he rose to his feet, and, raising his clenched hands above his head, cried, in agony-laden accents:

"Away! The thought unmans me! Happiness, love, all human good is not for the Winged Man. They are lost for ever—lost—lost—lost!"

As the thrice-repeated words arose in a despairing shriek from his lips, the music ceased, the childish voices were hushed, and the little revellers gazed with startled eyes into each other's faces.

A man rushed to the window and looked out. There was no one there. The Winged Man had vanished.

Ten minutes later, as Horace Widney and his wife passed the house where the revels around the Christmas-tree were in full swing once more, they found themselves confronted by a tall, black-garbed figure.

"Horace Widney, follow me!"

"Why should I follow you? Wither would you lead me?" gasped the astounded man; whilst his white-faced wife clung closely to him.

"To the house wherein awaits your Christmas dinner. Ask no questions, but obey. Fear nothing. From this moment your life of toil, privation, and misery is ended. Happier days are in store. Come!"

"But the children. I cannot leave my children!" came in a low, frightened whisper from the woman's lips.

"I lead you to where your children sleep in a bed of down, covered by a silken quilt," was the Winged Man's unexpected reply.

Yet the frightened couple held back.

"Who are you? Speak, that I may know wither you would lead me!" persisted Widney.

"No matter who I am. Sufficient for you that I wish you naught but well. Follow!" was the reply.

Remonstrances rose to Horace Widney's lips; but there was that in the strange being before him which forbade their utterance, and, almost against their wills, they followed the Winged Man.

THE MILLIONAIRE'S CHRISTMAS TREAT.

Loud-voiced, silver-toned bells rang out through the clear, frosty air, awakening the inhabitants of London to Christmas morning.

Within a draughty attic at the top of Josiah Scarf's house the owner and his wife stood gazing over the snow-laden housetops, shivering with cold, white-faced, terror-stricken, anxious.

It was the Winged Man's command that they should remain there until summoned below, and lest evil should befall their petted, spoilt boy, they dare not disobey.

Presently the door opened and the Winged Man appeared before them.

"Come, breakfast awaits!" he ordered.

"But my boy—my little Algernon! Oh, dread being, surely even such as you could not have the heart to injure him?" cried Mrs. Scarf.

"Fear not. No ill shall befall him whilst you obey," promised the Winged Man. "He, like you, has a Christmas lesson he must learn. Follow, and ask no more!"

Turning upon his heel, the Winged Man led the way into a magnificent dining-room, in which blazed a roaring fire.

There a wondering butler, footman, and housemaid were setting a sumptuous breakfast upon the table.

Mrs. Scarf moved instinctively towards the fire, but the Winged Man stopped her with an imperious wave of the hand.

"Yonder are your places," he said, pointing to two common wooden chairs in one corner of the spacious apartment.

"I will not be ordered about like this in my own house!" cried Josiah Scarf, rage turning his white visage a fiery red. "Manning, Clarke," he added, addressing the men-servants, "run quick! Summon the—"

"Remember!"

Loud, clear, filled with unspoken threat rolled like thunder from the Winged Man's lips.

The warning seemed addressed not only the millionaire, but also to the servants who glanced irresolutely from their employer to the Winged Man.

"I have taken possession of this house for the next twenty-four hours, Josiah Scarf," continued the weird horror. "See," he added, pointing to the window, "upon the opposite pavement walks a policeman! Call him if you dare!"

°A TASTE OF POVERTY.

Scarf glanced anxiously at the stall what constable; then, with a moan, half of anguish, half of impotent rage, flung himself into a chair; whilst Mrs. Scarf, seating herself by his side, implored him, for the sake of her son, not to thwart the Winged Man.

The next moment the door opened, and Scarf could scarcely believe his eyes when Horace Widney and his wife, clad in warm, neat garments, and followed by the two children and little Amy, entered the room.

With a timid cry Amy Scarf moved towards her mother, but she had never been a favourite child, and, her thoughts fixed upon her missing son, Mrs. Scarf repelled her daughter with a glance.

If there was one thing Scarf loved more than money, it was the good things money could buy, and he gnashed his teeth with impotent rage as he saw his discharged clerk's family enjoying the spread he could not partake of.

Lunch was a repetition of breakfast. Ravenous with hunger, Josiah Scarf almost forgot the peril which hung over his son, in his craving for food.

Never had the little Widney's passed such a day. Bound by the threats of the Winged Man, as well as by the promise of enormous rewards, the servants did their utmost to make the little ones enjoy themselves.

Before dinner-time arrived Mrs. Scarf broke down, and, giving into the pleading of Mrs. Widney and little Amy, the Winged Man allowed her to retire to her room, where she enjoyed a simple meal of cold meat and bread, her sole Christmas fare.

Then came dinner, during which Josiah Scarf sat leaning forward in his chair, almost mad with hunger, watching, with greedy, unsatisfied eyes, the man he hated helping his wife and children to the delicacies the millionaire had provided for his own consumption.

Turkey and plum-pudding, flanked by numberless entrées, provided a feast such as the Widney's had never tasted before.

Dinner over, Scarf saw, with rising anger, yet with a strange glow in his heart he had not experienced for years, his doors thrown open, not to the children of

---

° 7 JUNE 1913.

the great and wealthy who had been invited, but to ragged, hungry children from the neighbouring slums.

THE LESSON LEARNED.

The same Christmas bells which had heralded in a day his father and mother would never forget, awoke Algy Scarf from his long, drug-imposed sleep.

"Boh, boh, boh! I am cold! Hawkins, you lazy slut,[47] you have let the fire out. I'll tell mother!" he cried, sitting up in bed rubbing the sleep from his tear-dimmed eyes.

Instead of Hawkins, Algernon's neatly-uniformed nurse, who, copying his father and mother, he tyrannised over on every possible occasion, his cries brought Slinky Sam into the room.

"Hold yer row, or it will be the worse for ye!" was that worthy's Christmas greeting.

Algy Scarf gazed at the intruder in dismay, then burst into a loud yell than before.

"Go away, you dirty, common man; I want my nurse!" he sobbed.

"You're a nice, dutiful kid, I don't think," growled Slinky Sam, "a-callin' your own father a dirty, common man."

"My father! You're not my father! My father is a gentleman! Take me out of this dirty place at once, or he will have you locked up!" shrieked Algernon.

"Shut up, you white-faced lunatic! Things have come to a pretty pass when a man is flanked by his kid. Hi, missus, here's this boy of your'n in gone dotty!" roared Slinky Sam, striding to a door which opened into the room in which the boy had found himself.

A very stout, very dirty, very untidy woman, with a big, round, pimply face, and thin, grey, tousled hair, stumbled into the room.

"Now, Billy, you young warmint, leave off blubberin', ye aggravatin' crittur!" cried Mrs. Sam, pouncing upon the astounded boy and shaking him violently.

Never having been so much as slapped in his life, Algernon Scarf flew into a violent temper, and, seizing the old woman's grey hair, tugged at it viciously.

Then followed a whipping Algernon Scarf was never likely to forget, for, loading him with abuse at every blow, Mrs. Sam slapped him vigorously, then flung him upon the palate.

"There, ye warmint, don't ye attempt any of your tricks upon your mother again, or it will be the worse for you!"

Algernon Scarf could scarce believe his ears. He looked at the beetle-browed ruffian who claimed him as his son, then at the woman who had declared she was his mother.

"You're not my mother; I'll tell pa, and you'll all be hung!" sobbed the writhing boy.

"Oh, answer your mother, aren't I?" cried the old hag, seizing him by the neck

---

47 From "Slatten", meaning a slovenly, untidy woman.

and lifting him from the pallet of straw.

"You know you are not," replied the boy sulkily.

Down came the woman's hand upon the same spot where she had already inflicted chastisement.

"Am I your mother?"

"Oh, please don't hit me!"

Another blow.

"Am I your mother?"

Another blow, then the same question repeated.

"Yes, please, ma'am," admitted the boy; and as the woman, with a triumphant leer, released him, he crouched, trembling, in the furthermost corner of the room.

But his tormentors had not done with him yet. His own warm clothes had vanished, and he found himself compelled to put on filthy rags, so full of holes that they scarcely hung together. Then, bare-footed, bare-headed, he was forced to help his supposed mother tidy up the room.

Gradually it dawned on Algernon that it was long past breakfast-time.

He could hear the church-bells ringing, and a sob rose to his lips as he remembered the cosy fire, the servants, the table laden with Christmas presents which awaited him at home.

A hint that he was hungry only brought a stale crust, flung angrily at him, which he made no attempt to pick up and eat.

Slinky Sam was evidently in luck, for at midday his wife cooked a beefsteak in a frying-pan, over the small grate.

The appetising smell increased the boy's hunger tenfold. Eagerly he watched this steak being turned out on a plate, then looked timidly at his temporary parents and edged closer to the table.

"What are you doing here?" growled Slinky Sam. "There's your breakfast. I never did see such a boy as you, allus wanting your better's food."

Algernon Scarf glanced at the hard, dry crust which had been thrown him for his breakfast, then turned sadly away, and from the corner watched husband and wife gobble up the whole of the steak.

"Here, you may lick that!" cried Slinky Sam, sliding the empty plate across the floor to the sobbing child.

And Algernon did lick it. Not only that, urged on by hunger he devoured the dry crust to the last mouthful, wondering the while how it was he had never tasted such nice bread in his life, and not realising that it was because he had never been hungry before.

Throwing himself on to the pallet, he drew some pieces of old sacking over him and sobbed himself to sleep.

He awoke with the strokes of a distant clock ringing in his ears.

It was six o'clock, the hour at which his friends had been invited to a children's party in the millionaire's house.

How he had reckoned upon it! How he had looked forward to displaying, with the vulgar ostentation he had inherited from his father, his expensive Christmas presents!

Could it be all a dream? Would he awake to find himself in his little cot at home?

Slowly he ventured to approach the windows and look out.

Immediately before him was another window, through which he saw some half-dozen children, in a bare, comfortless room, clustered round a scraggy Christmas-tree, from which hung a few spluttering candles, some coloured paper, and a few, very few, cheap, common toys.

As he looked the thought of the magnificent Christmas-tree he had seen brought into his father's house the previous day arose before his eyes.

To his astonishment, he found himself wishing that he could bring it, laden with toys, as he knew it would be, and place it in the tiny circle of white-faced, poor, but happy children he was watching so enviously.

Never had such a wish entered his heart before. The Winged Man's seed had already taken root in his little heart.

An hour later Slinky Sam through a shabby little overcoat across the boy's shoulders, and, carrying him through the streets, set him down near a doorway into which a number of eager-faced though ragged children were hastening. Then, pushing him forward, the burglar shrunk away.

Wonderingly the child allowed himself to be carried onward by the press.

Within the house he stopped to gaze around him. Then, with a glad cry, he sprang forward, as he recognised his own home.

At the entrance to the drawing-room he came to a sudden halt, and gazed about him in amazement.

There was his Christmas-tree, and there his guests, but very different guests to the well-dressed ones he had expected to find.

Ragged children, drawn from garrets and cellars, filled the room with noisy laughter. In the place of honour where he should have been was the little boy whose face he had slapped the previous evening.

By the boy's side, their faces wearing the bewildered look which had scarcely left them all day, were Mr. and Mrs. Whitney, whilst seated with buried face in one corner of the room disregarded, neglected by all, was the owner of the house, near whom stood the tall, dark form of the Winged Man.

Within Algernon Scarf's tiny bosom beat a child's loving, affectionate heart, though warped and well-nigh spoiled by never having been denied the slightest whim.

As his eyes fell upon the bowed form of his father, he forgot the glories of the Christmas-tree, and, springing forward, flung his arms round Josiah Scarf's neck.

"Dada, my own, own dada, don't cry! Your little boy has come back to you!" he cried, as he rubbed his cheek against that of his father.

With a loud cry of joy Josiah Scarf clasped his boy to his breast, then looked round for the winged Man.

But the strange being, his task done, had disappeared.

With his boy's arms clinging round his neck, Josiah Scarf strode towards where Horace Whitney and his wife had witnessed the reunion of father and son, with tears streaming down their cheeks.

"Whitney, your hand! I, who have suffered in the last twenty-four hours more than I deemed it possible any human being could do beg your pardon for the misery I have indirectly caused you." Then, reverently bowing his head, he added: "Heaven bless the Winged Man, who has taught me a lesson I shall never forget."

AN INTERRUPTED ARREST.

Whilst Josiah Scarf and his late clerk, Horace Whitney, were discussing plans for the latter's future, amidst the cheery voices of the children dancing round the Christmas-tree, a very different scene was taking place in the snow-laden street without.

As chance would have it, Jonas B. Falter, the great Yankee detective, who had been employed by the British Government to hunt the Winged Man down, and his lieutenant, Todd Merton, were walking, somewhat unsteadily, down the street in which Josiah Scarf lived.

About a dozen yards from the millionaire's house, Falter came to an abrupt halt, and, seizing his companion by the arm, pointed to where, leaning with his elbows upon a railing outside the window of the room he had just left, was the Winged Man.

"By crumbs, Todd, it's the Winged Man!" gasped Falter.

"He is a strange one, anyhow. It aren't natural for any creature with all his money to be watching other people enjoying themselves when he could have a high old time on his own," replied Todd Merton disgustedly.

"Well, well, we all have our little peculiarities, and it's for wise men to take advantage of them," said Falter. "Slip across the street and try to get on the other side of him. If we both spring at the white-faced chowl all together, we'll have him, sure," he added, in a low whisper.

Merton nodded, and, moving noiselessly through the deep snow, slunk round the Winged Man.

As silently as a pair of cheetahs stalking their prey in an Indian jungle, the two men closed in upon the Winged Man.

Nearer and nearer they came until they paused almost within touch of the weird terror. Yet, his eyes fixed upon the cheerful scene within the room, the Winged Man seemed unconscious of the danger that menaced him.

"Now!" cried Falter, springing towards the Winged Man with outstretched hands, while Todd Merton, with a loud oath, did the same.

But even as their fingers touched his outer garments, the Winged Man, who had been conscious of his foe's approach all the time, glided back, and his would-be captors tumbled into each other's arms.

Not realising what had happened in the semi-darkness, and blinded with excitement, the two men, seizing each other by the throat, struck blindly at what each thought to be the face of the Winged Man, as they rolled over and over in the snow, shouting, kicking, hitting.

"Hi, Todd, you sneaking coward, come and help me, or he will get away!" cried Falter, landing a stinging blow upon the others ears.

"Look out, boss! Don't leave it all to me!" gasped Merton, as he returned to the blow upon his opponent's nose.

A police whistle ringing shrilly near where they were fighting, fell upon their ears, and the next moment a burly constable, taking each by the collar, drew them apart.

"Now then, what are you to fellows fighting in the streets like this for?" he demanded.

The combatants did not reply, but looked at the policeman, then at each other, then round up on the deserted street with staring eyes.

"The Winged Man! Where is he? I had him a moment ago!" cried the Yankee detective excitedly.

"Here, take my advice, and go home. You have been keeping up Christmas rather too well," suggested the policeman.

"Go home yourself, you blundering fool!" growled the Yankee. "My assistant and I had got the Winged Man, when you were obliged to interfere and let him go. I had my hand on him, and had just caught him a good 'un on the ear, when you came up."

"And I had given him one on the nose!" interposed Todd Morton.

The policeman smiled incredulously.

"Oh, it's as bad as that, is it?" said Todd Merton, putting himself in an attitude of defence; but the next moment there was seized by a pair of stalwart constables, who, summoned by the comrade's whistle, had come upon the scene at that moment, and, despite their indignant protestations, were marched off to the police-station for brawling on Christmas night.

Arriving at the police-station, Falter had little difficulty in proving his identity, and they were immediately released; but the smiles of the inspector, the suppressed laughter of the policeman on duty, and the constable who had arrested them explained how he had found them fighting each other in the snow, under the impression that they were attacking the Winged Man, filled the hearts of the two men with impotent rage. They left the station vowing vengeance upon the Winged Man.

"Say, boss," said Merton, coming to a halt some two hundred yards from the police-station, "Guess this night's work has about done for us so far as the British Government is concerned. You may do what you like; I'm going after this flying horror on my own."

"I am with you, Todd," was Falter's quick reply. "I'll spend every penny I've got but what I'll be even with the slippery cuss!"

A loud peal of unearthly, mocking laughter caused them to turn swiftly round. Perched on the top of a pillared porch, the Winged Man had been an unseen listener to their conversation.

Quick as lightning the two men produced their revolvers, but ere they could pull a trigger the Winged Man had disappeared.

"LOST! LOST! LOST!

Borne aloft on his enormous pinions, the Winged Man flew slowly towards the Hotel Cecil.

The influence of Christmas was still strong upon him, changing the very expression of his face, for the usually hard, stern, cruel look had disappeared.

He longed to mix on equal terms with his kind, to throw off, for the time being, the almost supernatural attributes of the Winged Man, and become a man once more.

Again and again the thought crossed his mind. Was the power he wielded worth the sacrifice he had made to retain it?

Was not the workman, enjoying his Christmas in the bosom of his family, or the company of his mates at the workingmen's club, happier than he?

That day he had tasted the delight of making others happy, and as he flew slowly over the housetops, half-formed plans for turning his mighty power to furthering the happiness of the human race, were flitting through his brain.

"Ay, it were better so," he muttered; then, as his eyes travelled downward, he remained for a few moments motionless in the air.

Fate had directed his path to the street in which Danby Druce lived.

Yes, he would commence his new career by offering the hand of friendship to one whom, though he had hated him with a bitter, malignant hatred, he had ever admired and respected.

Eager to put his newly-formed resolution into execution, the Winged Man alighted on the parapet of Danby Druce's house, and, crawling down the wall, let himself in by one of the upper windows.

Sounds of music and laughter from the lower floor led the Winged Man to suppose that Danby Druce was entertaining friends. He passed noiselessly downstairs, until at last he stood leaning over the banisters of the first floor. Through an open door leading into the dining-room he could see some twenty couples dancing to the strains of a piano.

It needed no second glance to the Winged Man that these were not the great detective's friends, but from the conversation he overheard between two men in the hall below, he gathered that, in his absence, Danby Druce had given his servants leave to invite their friends on Christmas night.

"It is like him," muttered the Winged Man as he turned towards the door which he knew gave admittance to the great detective's den, whither he was accustomed to retire to solve the many problems that were presented to him. "Danby Druce has a heart of gold. If I find it possible to return to ordinary life as an ordinary man, I trust that Danby Druce will ever be my closest friend."

As the words passed his lips he entered the den, and, closing the door behind him, switched on the electric light.

As the bright light suffused the cosy, well-furnished apartment, the Winged Man stood as one turned to stone. The softer light faded from his eyes. The old, cruel, hard, stern expression brought back the deep, furrowed lines to his white, fearful face, his whole frame trembles, for his eyes were fixed upon a splendidly-executed portrait of Mary Evanson which hung in the place of honour over the great detective's desk.

All was changed, all kindly feelings banished at the sight of that lovely, and dearly-loved, face.

"He, the man whom I thought to take my heart, as the scoundrel who has robbed me of the only being on earth I could really love!" he muttered. "Perish all kindly thoughts! The momentary weaknesses passed, the Winged Man is himself again."

Striding towards the picture, he stood with folded arms before it, eagerly devouring every line of that lovely face, his own distorted with agony, baffled love, and undying hatred.

With a gesture of despair he turned from the picture.

As he did so a letter lying on the floor attracted his attention.

Moved by that unfailing instinct which gave the Winged Man much of his wondrous power, he picked it up. Even before he opened it he knew it was from Mary Evanson.

Yet, though the knowledge that it belonged by right to his hated rival sent the hot blood mounting to his forehead, he was not prepared for the secret its contents revealed. It was evidently in answer to one from Danby Druce asking Mary Evanson to be his wife.

As the Winged Man read the frank, honest words Mary Evanson had written, the aching misery in his heart deepened, for in the letter she owned that Danby Druce had won her heart, and had asked him to spend the Christmas and New Year with her at the house of an old uncle who lived close to Peril Castle; or, as it had been called for many centuries, Castle Perilous, in Yorkshire.

It was in the concluding paragraph the Winged Man found the poisoned dart which pierced him to the very soul.

"Even though I did not love you," wrote Mary Evanson, "gratitude to one who had saved me from being I cannot even now think of without a shudder, would—"

The Winged Man read no more.

Crushing the letter in his clenched hand, he raised his arm above his head, and a loud, misery-laden, wailing cry burst from his lips.

As that awful, indescribable, haunting cry fell upon the dancer's ears, it was as though the cry had had the fabled power of turning men to stone.

Trembling women looked into the eyes of pale-faced men.

"What is that?" demanded Danby Druce's housekeeper, in low, trembling tones.

The girl's voice seemed to break the spell of terror which had paralysed the company. The women clustered together as though for protection, the men looked inquiringly at each other.

No one answered. Then from the upper room came once more that fearful cry, fiercer, shriller, more penetrating than before, followed by a voice, laden with unutterable, unendurable misery, crying:

"Lost, lost, lost!"

Again a deathly silence fell upon the crowded room. None dare speak the fearful name which was on every lip. All knew that so fearful a cry could only have come from the Winged Man.

Ten minutes passed ere any dare attempt to leave the room, then a stalwart sergeant of the Grenadier Guards, moved towards the door.

"Hang it, I cannot stand this any longer! Winged Man, or no Winged Man, I am going to find out the meaning of those awful cries!" he cried.

"I'll come with you!" said Danby Druce's butler, bravely stepping forward.

"And I!" And I!" And I!" repeated several others.

Beckoning the volunteers to follow, the sergeant, albeit with pale face, and swiftly-beating heart, led the way towards the staircase.

The door of Danby Druce's den was open, and a bright light shining from the room told that the electric light had been turned on.

"Keep close to me, lads. If the Winged Man is within, fling yourselves upon him at once! It is our only chance!" ordered the sergeant.

Followed by his assistants, he burst into the room.

It was empty, and though his sense of duty had induced him to discover the meaning of those fearful cries, it is no reflection upon the sergeant's bravery to say that he was relieved to find that the Winged Man was not there.

"Look—look! The picture!" gasped the butler, pointing with trembling hand at Mary Evanson's portrait.

Exactly where the girl's heart would be in a living woman, protruded the hilt of an Oriental dagger, snatched, as the empty scabbard proclaimed, from a trophy of arms on the wall.

Wonderingly the sergeant and butler approached the picture.

As they did so, the former started back, clasping his hand to his forehead as he cried:

"See, it bleeds!"

It was true. As though drawn from the senseless canvas, a large patch of crimson lay immediately beneath the portrait.

None ever knew that the Winged Man, in his mad, uncontrollable rage, had plunged the dagger so fiercely into the picture that it had set his own wounded hand bleeding afresh.

THE NIGHT MAIL.

The Winged Man had entered the house softened, chastened man; he left it possessed with a great hatred of the human race, and a more fixed determination to wreak evil than ever.

His very flight as he forced his way through the air towards King's Cross told of the unquenchable fire which burned within his bosom. Now and again his fearful, melancholy wail drove all gaiety from the hearts of those who heard it.

Once he crossed a small square off Oxford Street, the singing of half a dozen merry, light-hearted lads of about seventeen or eighteen fell upon his ears.

A sudden rage burned within his heart.

What right had others to be happy whilst he was borne down by a misery almost greater than his soul could bear?

His wild, frenzied cries quieting the singing lads, he swooped like a hawk upon its prey amongst them, dashed them to right and left, kicked, cuffed, brutally ill-treated them, then, rising with a cruel, callous, mocking laugh, continued on his way.

Alighting in a distant part of the station, the Winged Man wrapped his all-enfolding cloak-like wings around him, purchased a ticket, and, entering a first-class compartment, flung himself down in one corner of the York mail.

Barely had he done so ere the door opened, and an inspector entered.

"Tickets, please, sir!" he demanded; then glanced with an irrepressible shudder at the long, talon-like hand which held the piece of pasteboard towards him.

The puzzled frown swept across his features, and he strove to scan the face of the solitary occupant of the carriage.

But in vain. The Winged Man's broad-roamed slouch-hat prevented him from seeing those fearful features. Yet he caught a glimpse of a chin of unearthly whiteness, and, almost persuaded that the unknown passenger was the Winged Man, hastened from the compartment.

Presently the door opened, and an elderly man, followed by a porter carrying a port-manteau and hat-box, entered.

At that moment the guard blew his whistle as a signal for the train to start.

The Winged Man looked up. An angry frown crossed his lips.

"Go! I would be alone!" he cried, rising to his feet, and pointing to the open door.

One glance at the white, fearful, fury-laden face, and with a cry of terror the old gentleman turned to flee, knocking over the porter and his luggage as he did so, and, after sending him hurtling on the platform, rolled on the top of him.

At the moment the train began to move out of the station, and, gathering speed with every revolution of the engine's driving-wheels, her tail lights disappeared in the distance before the old gentlemen could recover sufficiently to explain his hurried exit from the compartment.

The knowledge that the Winged Man was travelling on board the train filled the authorities with vague forebodings of evil.

It was seldom the Winged Man deigned to travel by rail in the ordinary way.

Indeed, he had seldom need to have resource to any mode of propulsion save his own strong wings.

But he was weary; more than a week had passed since he had last closed his eyes in sleep. Besides, he wanted to think out his plans for the future, for he was determined that, even though he had to slay with his own hand the woman he loved, she should never be Danby Druce's bride.

Until the train had left the houses of mighty London behind the Winged Man remained seated in the corner into which he had thrown himself; but as the open country was reached, and the train's speed increased until they were travelling at a good sixty miles an hour, he rose from the cushions, turned a half-circle in the air, then, his feet glued tightly to the roof of the carriage, hung head downwards, and, old by the swaying of the train, was soon fast asleep.

ON PETERBOROUGH PLATFORM.

The slowing-down of the train as Peterborough was reached awoke the Winged Man; yet a sneering smile curling the corners of his thin, narrow lips, he remained hanging head downwards from the roof.

As the train glided slowly into the station, the smile gave place to an angry snarl instead of the usual hurrying passengers, the platform was crowded with uniformed police-men, plain-closed constables, and detectives.

"There he is! That's him!" cried a police-sergeant, springing towards as the carriage in which the Winged Man had travelled stopped immediately opposite where he was standing.

The next moment he had flung open the carriage door and entered.

But even as he did so the weird terror swung towards him, seized him behind the arms, and, twisting as he swung back, hold the unfortunate man through the opposite window, where he fell into the midst of a number of constables who had lined the permanent way to prevent the Winged Man's escape on the off-side of the train.

Undeterred by the fate of his superior, a gallant young constable sought to enter the compartment; but by this time the Winged Man was on his feet, and met his new assailant with a blow on the chest which sent him rolling into the arms of those who followed to assist him.

Then, his fearful eerie cry, followed by a peal of mocking laughter, the Winged Man flashed out from the carriage, and, attaching himself to an iron girder, gazed with flashing eyes, his fearful headlight gleaming upon his foes.

White-faced, but determined, a superintendent of police stepped to beneath where the Winged Man hung.

"Surrender, in the King's name! The very roof of the station is guarded! You cannot escape!"

"Surrender! Fools, you know not the Winged Man!" was the contemptuous reply.

"I give you one minute to decide. All my men are armed with revolvers, and at the first movement on your part we will shoot!"

The Winged Man flashed his keen eyes over the platform. It seemed as though a crop of pistol-barrels had sprung up in obedience to the superintendent's words, for two hundred gleaming barrels were pointed at the Winged Man.

"Thirty seconds!" thundered the superintendent. "I mean what I say—unless you have surrendered within the minute, we shoot!"

"Shoot, you clustering pack of baying hounds! I defy you! Away, or I will tear you limb from limb!" shrieked the Winged Man, his voice shrill with fury.

Then, swift as a lightning flash, he descended in a sweeping flight upon his foes.

A ragged volley crashed out, then ceased, for the Winged Man, untouched by blade or bullet, was cleaving away as the plough cleaves a furrow, through the clustering police who sought to hem him in.

Fearful indeed with the blows the Winged Man struck to right and left, felling a man at every blow, now and again pausing to seize some unfortunate policeman by the throat or belt, and hurl him, a living missile, into the midst of his comrades, yet all the while skimming so close to the surface of the platform that the police dare not fire, lest they should hit one of their comrades.

A few seconds of fearful strife, and the Winged Man had reached the confines of the crowd.

Then arose an awful cry:

"The engine! Head him off! Head him off!" as the Winged Man was seen flying as swiftly as a swallow cleaves through the air, towards the enormous, many-wheeled engine attached to the mail train.

From the footplate the engine-driver and fireman saw the weird terror approaching. With a cry of alarm the latter snatched up a shovel, and, raising it above his head, aimed a fearful blow at his assailant.

But the blow was wasted on empty air, and the next moment, seized in the Winged Man's iron grasp, the gallant fireman was hurled unconscious on to the platform.

A sharp blow on the shoulder caused the Winged Man to turn round with a snarl of anger.

Armed with a heavy iron wrench, the engine-driver and flung himself upon him, but without a moment's hesitation, apparently without an effort, the Winged Man seized the gallant old man and hold him on to the permanent way.

Then with a loud, mocking cry he opened the throttle to its fullest extent, and, like a horse that feels the spur, the mighty engine bound forward, dragging the long line of carriages behind it.

Cries of terror and pain echoed through the station as many of the alarmed passengers through themselves from the moving train; but others, too terrified to move, crouched helpless in the various compartments.

A policeman held for a moment to the brass rails of the engine's, but a blow from the Winged Man's merciless fist sent him reeling beneath the wheels, and the next moment the train was dashing on with constantly increasing speed a half a mile from the station.

AN HEROIC GUARD.

Grasping the rail of the footplate, the Winged Man swung by one hand over the permanent way, his fearful, diabolical laughter rising above the roar and rattle of the rushing train as he gazed down the long line of brilliantly-lighted carriages, from almost every window of which was thrust a white, frightened face.

"We are off, ye white-faced dogs!" he shouted in stentorian tones, which fell like a knell upon the frightened passengers' ears. "Off upon as wild and mad a ride as ever yet fell to the lot of man! Pray, ye dogs—pray, as you have never prayed before, that the line may be clear, or there will be the biggest smash that ever filled a gaping world with horror!"

Then, springing back on the footplate, he flew to the furnace doors, and, seizing big lumps of coal in both hands, hold piece after piece into the blazing fire, which seemed to devour them like paper.

Swiftly, almost madly, though he worked, never once did he miss the mouth of the furnace, or throw the coal where he did not want it to go.

There was little of human knowledge the Winged Man did not know; single-handed he could have driven the enormous locomotive from John O'Groats to Land's End without a stop, safely and well.

But on the present occasion he cared nothing for safety, long for nothing but to send the engine and its load of carriages hurtling over the rails at a speed they had never before travelled.

Swifter and swifter flew the engine, the forced draught sending sparks flying like fire-works from her funnel; yet, with an eye ever on the water-gauge, the Winged Man continued to throw the coal on the furnace with skilful hands, until the sliding doors glowed beneath the intense heat which burned within.

At last, with a loud, shrill yell, fiercer and more awful to hear than the death-whoop of a Red Indian brave, the Winged Man close to the furnace doors, and, balancing himself with folded arms upon the footplate, gazed through the look-out, and evil grin of malicious enjoyment upon his lips.

"Ho, Ho, there are quaking hearts, there are trembling forms on board this train! It thrills my heart, my head worlds with mad delight to think of the well-fed, luxury-weakened men of the earth, clinging in the expectation of instant death to the soft cushions of the first-class carriages! Aho, it is a rare sport! It is fine sport!"

Instinct, or perchance his wondrous sense of hearing, warned the Winged Man of danger approaching from behind.

He turned just as the guard of the train, who, despite the fearful rate at which the train was travelling, had crept along the footboard to the engine, hurled himself upon him, crying:

"You merciless fiend, would you hurl a hundred human souls into eternity?"

"A hundred—ay, a thousand hundred!" came with a wild, blood-curdling laugh from the Winged Man's lips, as he seized his attacker in his iron grasp, and, big man though he was, held him from him as easily as though he had been but a child.

In vain the guard, careless of his own danger, thinking only of the imperilled passengers who had placed themselves in his care, struggled blindly, fiercely with the Winged Man.

But without avail. Tighter grew the weird horror's iron grip round his throat. Do what he might, the guard could not so much as bend that strong, fearful arm which held him with almost contemptuous ease.

"Speak, dog!" cried the Winged Man, shaking his prisoner. "Choose which you will—your life or those of the passengers?"

"If it must be, if nothing but blood will satisfy you, kill me and stop the train!" came without a moment's hesitation from the gallant guard's lips.

The Winged Man glanced with in admiration at the pale-faced but determined man.

"What, have you nothing to live for? What is a pack of selfish passengers to you? Have you no wife and children who will be robbed of their all by their father's death?" he asked.

A fearful change came over the guard's face.

"Pity help me, I have both!" he gasped.

"Then take your own life, and seek not to come between the Winged Man and his vengeance! Again I give you your choice—their lives or yours?"

A spasm of intense mental agony shot across the guard's face. Before his eyes arose his humble but clean and comfortable little home, the wife he loved, the children he adored.

For a moment he faltered; then, looking the Winged Man full in his eyes, he said, in low, intense, determined tones:

"I have already chosen; there are many fathers and husbands within this train. My death will plunge but one home into misery; but unless this train is stopped, scores of homes will be plunged into despair!"

A MAD RIDE.

With a cry of rage the Winged Man held the despairing man above his head, and sprang upon the engine's tender.

At that moment the train was thundering over a bridge spanning a mighty river.

"For the last time, your life or theirs," he shrieked, holding the terror-stricken, yet still determined man poised above his head.

"I will not buy my life at such a price!" declared the gallant guard; then closed his eyes that he might not see himself hurtling through space into the river a hundred feet below.

The next moment he found himself standing by the Winged Man's side on the footboard of the swaying engine.

"There are only two things the Winged Man respects—a brave man, and an honest, unselfish heart. You have both, and for your sake I will spare those who, as passengers in this train, are in your charge!"

Without giving the delighted man, who could scarce believe his ears, time to reply, he flung over his shoulder as easily as though he had been but a dummy figure, and, scrambling over the coal-filled tender dropped to the footboard of the van filled with luggage nearest the engine, then made his way to the carriage immediately behind it.

The struggle on the roof of the express.

Flinging open the door of an empty compartment, the Winged Man thrust the guard within; then, slamming to the door, crept between the carriages to the guard's van.

A minute later he had unfastened the coupling, and the creaking of brakes told that the broken air-pipe had put the automatic Westinghouse brake on.

So swiftly was the engine travelling that almost in a flash the long string of carriages had been left behind; yet the brake was on the engine as well, and her speed had grown perceptibly slower by the time the Winged Man, after a fierce struggle with the wind, regained the footplate.

The Winged Man's first care was to throw off the brake, and the engine regained its loss to speed once more.

For several minutes the Winged Man was busy piling coal upon the surface; then, with steam hissing out of the safety-valve, he climbed out of the cab, and, with a wild, fierce yell of mingled triumph and delight, seated himself astride the mighty boiler.

None but he could have borne the fierce heat that emanated from the huge, green-painted boiler, yet the Winged Man scarce felt it.

"On, on, my noble steed! Forward, my gallant iron horse!" he cried, as the engine swayed and throbbed like a thing of life.

On it dashed, bursting like a meteor through wayside stations, on the platforms of which the Winged Man saw white-faced men shrinking back in terror as they saw the grim horror astride his iron steed, and heard his fearful, blood-curdling laugh ringing in their ears as it dashed by.

"On, on! Quicker—quick!" shouted the Winged Man, throwing his arms above his head in wild gesticulations, as, like some fearful missile from the mouth of an enormous cannon, the engine dashed out of the tunnel.

Suddenly the Winged Man leaned eagerly forward.

Half a mile ahead, looking in the dim light like a huge, black serpent, a luggage-train was stretched across the line.

°THE DEATH RIDE.

The next moment the engine was upon it. There was a rending crash, a ripping, tearing, awful sound, and the mighty engine had burst through the train as easily as a bullet tears through a paper target.

Loud, blood-curdling, unspeakably horrible, arose the Winged Man's terrible laugh as the engine, steadying itself after the crash, continued upon its mad way.

On, on they dashed, now brushing aside the gates of a level crossing as though the stout, wooden framework had been a gossamer cobweb, until at last, just outside York, the engine turned into a siding, and as soon as the officials were informed of the safety of the train, plunged with terrific impact into a dead end.

The wondering spectators, railway officials, and those who had been awaiting friends at the great terminus, caught a brief glimpse of the Winged Man standing upright upon the boiler with distended wings; then came a terrific explosion, a huge cloud of steam shot heavenwards, and all was silent.

Fearful though the scene of destruction where the engine had struck the great building against which the dead end had stood, covering its mighty, still glowing

---

° 14 June 1913.

iron body with a heap of fallen masonry. A crowd of officials and spectators hastened forward, congratulating each other that at last the Winged Man's fearful career had been brought to a tragic termination.

Yet though they searched amongst the wreckage, hoping to find the weird horror's mutilated and dismembered frame, they could find nothing.

The Winged Man had again escaped unscathed!

IN THE FORBIDDEN ROOM.

Little those who hoped they had witnessed the Winged Man's end realised the fearful, almost unearthly power possessed by that strange being. Had not their attention been so riveted upon the fearful destruction wrought by the engine, they might have seen him rising at the very moment of the impact and hovering on outstretched wings above the scene of the disaster.

"The fools deem me dead," muttered the Winged Man. "Well, let them hug themselves in their folly. It is better so; it will enable me to pursue my task of vengeance upon Danby Druce undisturbed."

Then, rising slowly on outstretched wings, he flew swiftly northwards. Some forty minutes later his attention was attracted by a castellated old mansion a little to his left, every window of which was ablaze with lights.

"It is Wembly Castle," muttered the weird horror, recognising of the oldest and most celebrated mansions in Yorkshire. "His Lordship keeps Christmas in the good old style, it seems; as an uninvited guest the Winged Man shall partake of his hospitality. Besides, at such a time, and at such a place, there should be jewels worthy even of the Winged Man."

Circling in the air he alighted upon the summit of a castellated tower, then commenced to climb, clinging like a fly to the wall, down its precipitous sides.

As he did so he noticed that, although from his lofty point of advantage he had seen the old castle lit up from top to bottom, the lights seemed suddenly to have disappeared.

Not a sound, save the moaning of the dog in the adjoining stable-yard, broke the silence which hung over the castle.

"It is strange; they could not have extinguished all the lights at once, nor have gone to bed at the same time," he muttered. "There is more here than I can understand."

As he spoke he paused before a large window, and, hanging on to the sill, appeared beneath the blind, which did not come to within a few inches of the bottom.

Before him was a large, well-furnished bed-room, on a bed at one side of which was stretched a tall, aristocratic-looking old man, whom the Winged Man immediately recognised as the owner of the castle.

"Could my eyes have paid me false?" thought the Winged Man, as he moved along the wall away from the window. "It must be so; the host would not retire before all the guests had departed. However, now to investigate!"

Pausing before a second window, he soon opened it and entered, to find himself in a large, unoccupied bed-room, the hangings and paper of which were all of blue.

Yet there was something unfamiliar, unnatural about the room that the Winged Man could not quite understand, until, as the beams of the newly-risen moon filtered through the diamond-paned window, he uttered an ejaculation of amazement.

Upon the opposite side of the bed stood a huge, old-fashioned oak press, which he could see plainly, although the hangings of the bed intervened.

Wonderingly he moved towards the press. As he did so he sought to pull aside the heavy curtains from off the bed, but nothing met his outstretched hands, and his arm passed through the apparently solid bed-post.

Then he realised that he stood in an empty room surrounded by what can only be described as ghostly furniture.

At that moment the Winged Man turned towards the door, and saw the shadowy form of a lean, thin-faced man, a look of fiendish malice and cunning upon his face, entered the room and glide noiselessly to the side of the bed, which the Winged Man noticed for the first time was occupied by a young man with a handsome face, though marred, even in his sleep, by a look of hard, cruel, relentless determination, who, as the first spectre laid his hand upon his shoulder, awoke, and, springing out of bed, seized a long rapier leaning against a chair by the side of the couch.

The next moment he seemed to recognise the intruder, and an animated conversation took place although the Winged Man could not hear a word that was said.

But as the sly-faced man spoke, the awakened sleeper's eyes flashed with rising anger, until, drawing on his doublet and hose of Queen Elizabeth's time, he grasped his companion by the shoulder and advanced with long, angry strides towards the door.

Immediately the vision vanished, and the Winged Man found himself alone in the bare, unfurnished room, the walls of which were covered with faded hangings that evidently once had been blue.

Eager to follow the mystery to its conclusion, the Winged Man strode towards the door, and, flinging it open, entered a large picture-gallery, along which he strode until he was brought to a sudden halt by a loud, piercing shriek, which echoed and re-echoed through the sleeping house.

The sound came from a worm-eaten, heavily ironed open door, which appeared to swing open. A second later, and the dark man he had seen sleeping on the bed in the blue chamber, emerged, wiping the blade of his long rapier on his cloak, as he dashed with angry, horror-stricken face from the room.

The next moment the Winged Man glided swiftly behind a suit of armour, standing upon a pedestal near the open door, just as another door opened and a white-faced girl entered the landing at the moment the sword-armed spectre glided by.

The Winged Man saw the girl's eyes fixed in unspeakable horror upon the apparition, then, with a shriek of terror, she fell senseless to the floor.

In a minute the gallery was crowded with guests staying at the house, who, clad in any garment they could snatch up on the spur of the moment, hastened from their rooms to ascertain the cause of that awful cry of terror.

From his hiding-place behind the armour, the Winged Man saw a portly old dame, evidently the housekeeper, kneel by the side of the fainting girl and raise her in her arms, whilst the alarmed guests clustered about her.

"What is the matter? Who called?" et came in a loud, aristocratic voice from an open doorway on the opposite side of the gallery, and Lord Wembly, clad in dressing-gown and slippers, with a loaded revolver in his hand, joined the frightened group.

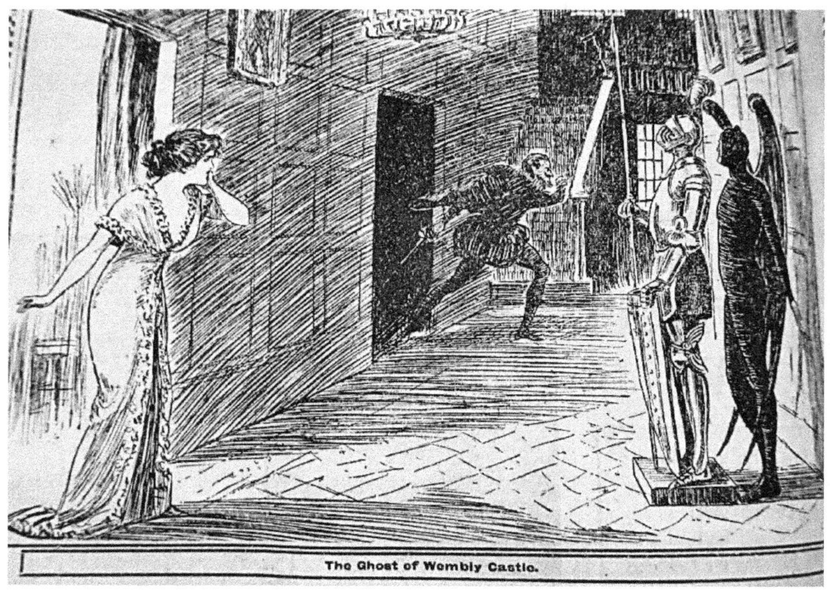

The Ghost of Wembly Castle.

"It's Miss Hemhurst, sir!" said the housekeeper, looking up. "Something has frightened her. It is Christmas night," she added, looking significantly at her master.

Lord Wembly looked very grave, but ere he could speak the girl partially recovered, and flung her arms round the old housekeeper's neck, sobbing:

"Oh, keep him away from me! Oh, it was awful! That fearful, angry face—the sword in his hand—the awful look of despair in his eyes! Oh, don't leave me!"

"Yes, yes, dearie; that's all right, nothing shall harm you now!" said the old housekeeper. "He came out of the forbidden room just as, alarmed by a shriek as if someone in deadly pain, I emerged from my room!" continued the girl, in trembling accents, adding, in low hushed tones: "And he was not alone; a tall, black, horrible, white-faced form stood near him by the door!"

Then, bursting into a peal of hysterical laughter, intermixed with sobs, the frightened lady was carried back into her bed-room.

"It was nothing, ladies and gentlemen. Miss Hemhurst had a nightmare, dream, or something of the kind," said Lord Wembly. "Kindly return to your rooms; this kind of thing upsets the servants, and fills their heads with stupid ideas!"

With a low murmur is of sympathy for the frightened girl, the guests returned to their rooms, leaving Lord Wembly standing in the gallery with a tall, handsome, well-set-up young fellow of about eighteen.

For some minutes father and son looked at each other without speaking.

"I will never spend Christmas here again, Harry," said Lord Wembly at last. "Each Christmas night it has been the same; Black Wembly's crime has been re-enacted."

"Father, I wish you could do something to lay this ghost. Tell me what is inside yonder room?" said the sun, pointing to the iron-studded door.

"You will enter at once, Harry—that will be according to the tradition of our family—on your twenty-first birthday, and it will not be opened again until your son is twenty-one. Good-night, lad; try to sleep and forget all about your unfortunate ancestor and his crime!" And the two, separating, entered a different bed-rooms.

As soon as all was quiet, save the sound of muffled sobs from the frightened girl's room, the Winged Man stepped up to the closed door, and, drawing some small steel instruments from his wallet, bent over the huge, old-time lock. Large though it was, it was simple in construction, and a few minutes later the Winged Man entered the forbidden room.

A minute later he was back in the gallery, a look of wild, wondering horror upon his face.

What he had seen there no tongue can tell, no pen can describe. It was something so indescribably horrible, so fearful, that even the Winged Man stole quietly from the old castle and flew silently and dejectedly away.

MARY'S PROMISE.

On the edge of wide expanse of rugged moorland, in the centre of Yorkshire, Peril Castle stands upon a precipitous rock, overhanging a dark, forbidding chasm, a hundred feet beneath its mighty outer walls.

In the old days Peril Castle had been the stronghold of a gang of outlaws, who, from their lofty eyrie, commanded the great north road to Scotland.

Many a tale of cruelty and lawlessness perpetrated by the robber baron and his villainous gang, was told round the firesides of the cottages clustered in the smiling valley some quarter of a mile from the gloomy edifice.

For years the robber barons held sway over the surrounding country, until one of their number had, unfortunately for himself, robbed and ill-treated a

King's messenger, on his way to the Court of Scotland.

This brought things to a head, and a large force was sent against the castle.

After a long siege, it was taken by assault, partially destroyed, and now naught remains that the West Wing and the ruined East wing, which, owing to its sinister reputation, was seldom visited by day, and never by night.

In the West Wing Lord Hawkhurst lived the life of a recluse, was hated and feared by the village that bore his name, for he was a gloomy, sour, disappointed man, who beginning life as a spendthrift, was ending it as a miser, his sole companions an old couple, as lean, dark-featured, and as unprepossessing as himself.

Within a small but cosy little house, half cottage, half villa, close to Peril Castle, Mary Evanson had found a home with an old uncle and aunt, who had retired to their native village to live on a snug little income, the result of industry and self-denial in their young days.

Here Danby Druce had found his sweetheart awaiting him the previous Christmas Eve. But the little house was locked up, and, save for a dim light burning in the hall, in darkness, the Winged Man alighted upon its red-tiled roof.

Clambering over the wisteria vines with which the walls of the little house were clad, the Winged Man peered searchingly through every window; then, confident that there was no one within, wended his flight to the topmost tower of Peril Castle.

Perched like a thing of ill-omened upon the tower's jagged summit, the Winged Man peered through the darkness, until his eyes alighted upon a farmhouse a mile beyond the village, the windows of which were ablaze with light.

Rising on outstretched wings, he flew slowly over the village.

As he did so, a farmer, bidding good-night to his friends at the door of the Red Hawk Inn, ceased speaking to gaze wonderingly into the dark, cloud-hidden heavens, as the low, hissing beat of the Winged Man's wings fell upon his ears.

A moment before a little party of some half-dozen men, who had emerged from the in to see their friend off, had been laughing and cracking jokes, but as that ominous sound fell upon their ears, they looked fearfully around.

The weird terror noted the effect his presence had caused, and a wild, melancholy, indescribable laugh echoed in deep, sonorous tones over the roofs of the houses.

"Fool that I was to contemplate, even for a moment, abandoning the power which is mine to strike terror into the hearts of men!" he muttered, rejoicing at the trail of fear he had left behind him as he beat his way through the air to the brilliantly lighted farmhouse.

Perched amidst the boughs of the mighty walnut-tree immediately in front of the farmhouse, the Winged Man gazed through an uncurtained window, upon a scene of revelry and honest, simple-hearted pleasure. Within a large, oak-beamed room some two dozen farmers, their wives, sons, and sweethearts, were dancing to the strains of the piano, all unconscious of the fearful, black, threatening form watching them with evil, hate-laden eyes, from amidst the branches of the old walnut-tree.

At first the Winged Man could not distinguish those he sought, but presently his white stern face grew dark and lowering, and he clenched his hands so tightly that his long nails penetrated his flesh, for bending over the graceful form of Mary Evanson, who was seated in a secluded corner of the room, was his hated rival, Danby Druce.

A wild, despairing cry arose to the Winged Man's lips, but, with a mighty effort, he repressed it; then, his whole frame trembling with rage, he flew away, lest he should be tempted to wreak his vengeance upon the farmhouse and all it contained.

All ignorant of the fearful peril that menaced them, Danby Druce and Mary Evanson were lost to everything save the love they read in each other's eyes. His quest of the Winged Man ended, as he thought for ever, the detective had persuaded the lovely girl to share his lot.

All too swiftly the happy evening drew to a close. Bidding their hospitable host good-bye, Mary Evanson's aunt and uncle entered a little pony trap, and were driven back to the village.

There was plenty of room in the vehicle for Mary and Danby Druce, but it was a clear, frosty night, the roads were hard and clean, so the lovers elected to walk home.

As they walked briskly down the narrow country road, Danby Druce, his arm around Mary's slender waist, proffered the request which had been upon his lips the whole evening, a request which he felt so confident would be acceded to, that ere leaving London he had secured a licence filled in with the name of Danby Druce and Mary Evanson.

As, their steps growing instinctively slower, they made their way towards a stretch of low-lying marsh-land that lay betwixt the farm and the village, Danby Druce asked Mary Evanson to marry him the following New Year's Day.

For a moment the girl hesitated, then, looking into his face with the world of trusting, devoted love in her glorious eyes, she placed her hand in his, saying:

"As you will, Danby. We have waited long, and, though the time is short, on New Year's Day I will become your wife."

With a cry of joy Danby Druce clasped his sweetheart in his arms.

"Heaven bless you, dear one; you shall never regret the confidence you have shown me," he whispered; then started back, feeling as though a cold hand had been laid upon his heart.

Was it fancy, or had a long, low moan echoed his glad cry?

Eagerly he glanced around, half expecting to see the awful form of the Winged Man hovering above him.

But he saw nothing; and, drawing Mary's arm through his, they continued on their way, talking in low-voiced whispers of the happy days before them.

THE WILL-O'-THE-WISP.

As the road penetrated deeper into the marsh, a thin, smoke-like haze overspread the scene.

Presently Mary Evanson pointed to alight some twenty yards off the road to their right.

"Whatever is that, Danby?" she asked curiously. "There isn't a single house between the farm and the village."

Danby Druce looked in the direction of his sweetheart's outstretched hand. As he did so the light began to sway from side to side, like the lights on board a storm-tossed barque.

"Perhaps it is some belated traveller lost on the marsh," suggested Danby Druce. "Hello, you there! Here's the road!" he shouted.

There was no response, but the light sprang twenty feet in the air, then, slanting earthward, commenced moving so swiftly backwards and forwards that the eye could scarcely follow its flight.

With a little cry of terror, Mary Evanson clung to her sweetheart's arm. His forehead puckered with thought, Danby Druce watched the strange light.

"Come, dear, whoever it is, let him enjoy his eccentric dance alone. It is too cold for us to act as audience here," he said at length; and they resumed their walk towards the village.

But walk swiftly or slowly, as they might, the strange light kept ever flickering close at hand—now here, now there, now high, now low abreast of them, until as they emerged from the mist it disappeared.

A low, relieved laugh escaped Danby Druce's lips.

"How stupid I was not to think of it before, Mary," he cried. "The fact of its being unable to follow us in the clear air proves the nature of the strange light. It's a will-o'-the-wisp. I have often heard of them but have never seen one before."

"I hope I may never see it again," returned Mary, with a little shudder. "It is uncanny. No wonder the superstitious peasantry regard that flickering light with terror."

"They need not," laughed Danby Druce reassuringly. "It is only a luminous gas exuded from the marsh. But now, dear, to resume our interrupted conversation. Despite my failure to run down the Winged Man"—and Mary Evanson shuddered as her lover pronounced that fearful name—"the public do not seem to have lost confidence in me, for I am very busy. A month's honeymoon in the Riviera, then I must return to work once more."

"Promise, Danby, never to do anything to bring the Winged Man's wrath upon you, dear one. I would not know a moment's peace if I thought that dread horror had again cause to hate you!" pleaded the anxious girl.

"I cannot promise that, Mary," returned Danby Druce, "for there is no telling how long the Winged Man will maintain the truce which he himself pronounced between us. Should he break it, I, in self-defence, must do my utmost to capture him."

Even as he spoke a vague uneasiness drove the happiness from Danby Druce's heart.

Would not the Winged Man's rage be intensified a thousand-fold when he discovered that Danby Druce and Mary Evanson were man and wife?

Some half-hour later Danby Druce bade Mary Evanson good-night at her uncle's gate, and, turning on his heel, he made his way towards the Red Hawk Inn, where he had engaged rooms.

But he knew he was too happy to sleep, so determined to retrace his steps, in the hope of again seeing the will-o'-the-wisp.

Like all great detectives, Danby Druce was of a scientific turn of mind, and the natural phenomenon of the will-o'-the-wisp is an unexplained mystery that has ever had a fascination for men of science.

There was another reason why the great detective sought the mist-laden marsh.

He remembered the low moan he had heard. It might have been the sighing of the breeze through the leafless trees, it is true; on the other hand, it might have emanated from his great enemy, the Winged Man, though how the Winged Man could have traced him down to that remote Yorkshire village he was at a loss to conceive.

If the weird horror was indeed in the neighbourhood, Danby Druce was anxious to have a conversation with him.

His life had now a fresh value in his eyes, and he was anxious, if possible, to come to terms with the dread being against whom he had fought so nobly and well.

THE PLOT ON THE MARSH.

As Danby Druce entered the mist enshrouded road he forgot the Winged Man, and the purpose that had brought him thither, in the thoughts of Mary Evanson.

It was walking down this lane, when the leaves were gay with the russet-gold tints of autumn, that he had first discovered Mary Evanson loved him.

Now, his long spell of waiting ended, Mary Evanson would soon be his for ever.

A flash across his path awoke him from happy dreams of the past and future. He started eagerly forward, for the elusive flame was dancing, bobbing, and twisting between the branches of the roadside hedge.

Wonderingly he gazed at the strange phenomenon; then, as, never still for a fraction of a second, it glided in an erratic course down the lane, he followed.

Presently the will-o'-the-wisp turned abruptly to the right. Eager, if possible, to thrust his hand into the flame, to decide once and for all the vexed question whether the will-o'-the-wisp gives out heat, or is merely a phosphorescent gleam, he clambered over the hedge, and the next moment was running swiftly over the rough, coarse, marsh grass.

It was a futile chase. Now and again the elusive flame would stop until he was nearly up to it, then dart away to right or left, yet ever luring the detective on with, deeper and deeper into the marshes.

The more the will-o'-the-wisp evaded him the more determined was Danby Druce to come to close quarters with it, though what he would do if he succeeded he had not the slightest idea.

On he dashed, little recking of the danger, until suddenly he felt the ground gave way beneath him, and the next moment was struggling, buried to the waist, in a quagmire.

As he strove in vain to retrace his steps, a loud, mocking laugh rang in his ears, and he beheld the Winged Man, poised in mid-air, with the false flame he had used to lure the detective to his doom burning like a tongue of living fire above his head.

"Aho, Danby Druce, we meet again! To think that you, the greatest detective of your age, the man of whom even Scotland Yard is envious, should be lured into my power by such a childish trick!" chuckled the weird horror.

Danby Druce gazed in amazement at the speaker.

"What! Is it in your power to command even this strange phenomenon of Nature?" he asked.

"It is. Behold!"

As the Winged Man spoke the flame, as though in obedience to a whispered order, floated to his outstretched hand; then, bobbing up and down like a cork in a mill-stream, disappeared in the direction of the road, in obedience to the Winged Man's cry of "Go! Lure some other fool to his doom!"

"So Danby Druce, we meet again," repeated the Winged Man, regarding his old enemy with an evil, malicious grin, which transformed his fearful face into the likeness of a snarling fiend.

"Ay, Winged Man, and glad am I that it is so!" returned Danby Druce, who by this time had recovered from the shock of finding himself in the weird terror's power. "You and I have fought a good fight. It is true the honours have been for the most part on your side, but I have done my best. Let the strife end. Let there be peace between us."

As the great detective spoke he held out his hand. The Winged Man ignored the proffered grasp.

"Twenty-four hours ago, Danby Druce, I entered your house, resolved to make amends for the past," he said, in slow measured tones. "Unwonted weakness made me ready to cry a truce with the human race. Upon your wall I saw a portrait of her you robbed me of, and a letter laying unheeded on the floor, as though a thing of little worth, I read to her promise to become your wife. In a moment my softened mood had vanished. You ask for peace. Peace let it be. The price, Mary Evanson's hand!"

"Never!" came from between Danby Druce's hard-set teeth. "Even could I give consent it would avail you little. Mary Evanson hates and loathes you!"

A fearful paroxysm of rage shook the Winged Man's frame, and for a moment Danby Druce thought the weird horror would rent him limb from limb. Confident, now that he dared not hope for peace, he snatched a revolver from his pocket and fired it point-blank into the Winged Man's white, mocking face.

A loud, nerve-racking yell of pain and rage burst from the weird horror's lips as he staggered back, and, to Danby Druce's delight, sank in a huddled heap on the soft, water-logged soil.

Rapidly re-cocking his weapon, Danby Druce remained on guard, lest it should be a trick of his wily foe to take him unprepared.

But even as he gazed the black, shapeless form sank lower and lower into the semi-submerged ground, until nothing but a white, limp, talon-like hand, thrust through the rushes, met his gaze.

A wild thrill of exultation swept through Danby Druce's heart. At last, when he least expected it, victory had smiled upon him.

Great indeed would be his triumph when the wires flashed the glad news from one end of the kingdom to the other that the Winged Man was no more.

Fortunately for Danby Druce, the quagmire into which he had been lured was not deep, and, though with difficulty, he succeeded in withdrawing his legs from its muddy grasp. Throwing down his cap to mark the spot near which the Winged Man had disappeared, he made the best of his way back to the village, freed at length from the anxiety which had ever been as a black shadow over his happiness.

Unless he could produce the weird horror's body he could not claim the enormous reward the British Government had offered for the Winged Man's destruction, so he made up his mind to keep his own counsel, until he could drain the marsh and dig out the Winged Man's remains.

Danby Druce's first care the following morning was to acquaint Mary Evanson with the Winged Man's destruction; and he noted, with a feeling of intense satisfaction, how the girl's pretty face brightened as she heard that the dread scourge had been removed from her path for ever.

This done, Danby Druce made his way to the marsh land where the tragic events narrated in the preceding chapter had taken place. It was some time before he could find his, and when he did he looked around him in amazement and ever-increasing dismay.

Close to where the cap lay was a tiny, muddy pool, scarce a dozen yards across, and all round it's not the solid, treacherous bog he had expected to find, but solid ground.

A fierce anger surged within his bosom as he realised that the Winged Man had outwitted him once more, unless, indeed, his fearful foe had sunk beneath the mud of the little pond.

Breaking a stake from out a neighbouring cattle-hedge, Danby Druce probed deep into the mud.

But in vain; and an hour later he returned dejectedly to the in, with the uneasy consciousness that the Winged Man was still at large.

Although his sojourn in the village had been so short, Danby Druce was already a prime favourite with the villagers, whilst Mary Evanson's kindly disposition, gentle manner, and lovely face had earned for her many friends.

Consequently, when, on a New Year's Day, Danby Druce drove up to the little church standing in a perfect forest of yew-trees, about a hundred yards behind the village, he found the sacred edifice packed with friends and well-wishers.

Alighting from the carriage, he walked up the trimly-kept gravel path, and, standing on the porch, was soon the centre of a laughing, good-humoured group of the principal inhabitants of the village, who were chaffing him,[48] and wishing him good luck.

Loud pealed the wedding-bells, yet, to his surprise, Danby Druce realised that he did not feel nearly so happy as he thought he would have done upon this day of days.

Striving to throw it off as he would, a dull, foreboding of evil filled his heart.

Anxiously he looked at his watch. From the church porch he could almost see the door of the house in which Mary Evanson lived. But the carriage in which his promised bride, her uncle, and her aunt should come, naught was to be seen.

Twelve, the hour at which the wedding was to have taken place, boomed forth from the clock-tower.

The white-robed clergyman stood impatiently by the chancel step, the choirboys fidgeted uneasily in their seats, whilst the organist, running his fingers idly over the keys, drew sweet, but low, wailing mournful notes, ill-attuned to a bridal ceremony, from his instrument.

Increasing anxiety weighing down his spirits, Danby Druce left his anxious friends and strode down to the old wych-gate leading into the churchyard, round which a knot of excited villagers were talking in low whispers.

"Why had she not come? What can have happened to prevent her?" he muttered.

DANBY DRUCE PUZZLED.

Danby Druce, as he glanced up the street, saw the carriage standing at the door of the distant house, and noted that the coachman's head was turned towards the house.

Even as Danby Druce gazed, the man descended from his box and walked through the tiny, well-kept garden towards the house.

For several minutes he was lost to view within the honeysuckle covered porch; then, with growing alarm, Danby Druce saw him step back from the house and gaze up at the windows.

Danby Druce could stand the suspense no longer. His soul harrowed with anxiety, and a vague fear of he knew not what, he set off at a brisk walk up the street, followed by a wondering and sympathetic glances of the crowd, who, after

---

[48] Good-humoured teasing.

a moment's hesitation, fell in behind him, joined a few minutes later by the majority of the people who would shortly before taken their places in the church.

As Danby Druce approached the house, the coachman, who had remounted his box, beckoned to him.

Immediately the detective's walk turned to run. His well-brushed silk hat fell to the ground; but, without stopping to pick it up, he pressed on until at last he stood, white-faced, panting, and breathless, by the side of the carriage.

"Where is Miss Evanson? Why has she not come? What is the matter?" asked Danby Druce breathlessly.

"Don't know, sir; can't make it out," replied the man. "Mrs. Trent came out about ten minutes ago, and said that her niece was just putting a few finishing touches to her dress. Then Mr. Trent brought me a glass of something short, to drink your health, sir, and went in, leaving the door open behind him."

"Quick, man—what else?" implored Danby Druce anxiously, for he could see from the man's manner that he was keeping something back.

"Well, there wasn't nothing else, in a manner of speaking, and yet there was. Just afore twelve o'clock struck I saw somebody, all dressed in black, across the hall. Then the door was slammed violently to, and—I can't swear to it, mind, it might have been almost anything, but I fancied I heard a woman cry out."

Danby Druce waited to hear no more; but, dashing through the garden gate, rattled the handle of the front door.

It was locked from within, and, his fears increased by the discovery, he flung himself upon the door as though it would burst open.

The stout framework resisted his every effort. Realising that he was wasting valuable time, he hastened to one of the closed windows, and, careless of the flying glass, smashed the pane with a blow of his fist.

Rapidly flinging open the sash, Danby Druce clambered into the Trent' little dining-room, in which was set out the splendid wedding breakfast.

"Mary, Mary! Where are you, dear one! Speak to me—for Heaven's sake, speak!" he cried, as he dashed into the hall.

His worst fears were concerned as he saw the Trents' little maid-of-all-work lying, gagged and bound, at the foot of the stairs.

A low moan from an adjoining room attracted Danby Druce's attention.

Throwing open the door, he entered, to find Mr. Trent stretched face upwards on the floor, and his wife seated, as though turned to stone, in the tall-backed armchair by the side of the fireplace.

She was clad in her wedding finery, which added tenfold to the fearful power of her wrinkled face, which was set and immovable as that of a marble statue, whilst from her eyes shone a look of horror such as Danby Druce had never seen upon a human face before.

Yet Danby Druce spared not a second glance for the wretched old couple. Rendered selfish by a great love he flew up the stairs two steps at a time, and, flinging open door after door, rushed from bed-room to bed-room, calling wildly upon his lost bride, until at length he reached the door which resisted his efforts to open.

Endowed by misery, with almost superhuman strength, Danby Druce drew back to the opposite side of the landing, and, rushing at the door with all his force, burst it open.

It needed no second glance to show that he was in Mary Evanson's room. The corded trunks, the little nick-nacks upon the dressing-table, and, above all, a trampled and torn leaf of orange-blossom all spoke of Mary's recent presence.

Yet whither had she gone?

Rushing towards the window, he examined the clasp, to find it closed; whilst a brief examination of the shattered door, showed that it had not only been locked, but bolted inside.

With a low moan of despair, Danby Druce flung himself into a chair, and buried his face in his hands.

A loud, mocking laugh burst upon his ears, and, looking up, he saw the Winged Man standing against the opposite wall.

Not a word escaped the weird horror's lips; but, a mocking smile of gloating hatred upon his lips, he watched greedily every spasm of pain which crossed the other's face, and Danby Druce had no need to ask whose hand had robbed him of his lost love.

A maddening paroxysm of rage driving all thoughts but those of revenge from his heart, the detective flung himself upon his exultant foe.

Even as he did so, the Winged Man glided away, allowing Danby Druce to collide so heavily against the wall that his senses reeled; a sudden pang of unbearable pain swept across his temples, and he remembered no more.

A WILD CHASE.

Not for long did unconsciousness hold Danby Druce's inactive brain. Barely a minute had elapsed ere he was up again and gazing wildly around him.

Presently his eyes became fixed upon the spot on which the Winged Man had stood.

"Even the Winged Man has not the power to render himself invisible at will. He must be concealed behind some secret panel," thought Danby Druce.

And, beside himself with grief and despair, the detective tore frantically at the paper-covered walls.

As he did so the hollow sound that answered the drumming of his fists told him his surmise was correct, and that beneath the paper were panels of wainscoting.

Wildly he looked around him for some tool to tear down the woodwork. His eyes fell upon a cast-iron bar at the foot of the bed. Seizing it with both hands, he tore at it with almost maniacal force until it broke off short in his hand; then, returning to the wall, he attacked the panels once more.

But just as the welcome sound of splintering wood reached his ears, a low, agitated moan of terror, in a score of different voices, caused him to desist.

In a couple of strides he was at the window, and looked out just in time to see the Winged Man, with Mary Evanson in his arms, a light on the roof of the garage.

It was a closed victoria,[49] but as the Winged Man alighted on it it was forced open by a fierce stamp of his powerful leg.

"Seize him! If you are men, do not let him carry off my promised wife!" almost shrieked Danby Druce, leaning from the window.

As the detective's appeal fell upon his ears, the coachman, who, paralysed with terror, had been surveying the Winged Man with staring eyes, brought the butt-end of his whip down with crushing force upon the Winged Man's shoulder, just as the weird horror arose to an upright position, after having carefully deposited Mary Evanson on the cushions.

Never will the fearful yell of pain and rage which burst from the Winged Man's lips fade from memory of those who heard it, as, seizing the brave coachman in both hands, he hurled him amongst the crowd, air, standing poised likely upon the narrow splashboard, he urged the horses on faster and faster with voice and gesture.

Shrieking with terror, the crowd opened to let him pass; but so swift was the terror-inspired gallop of the horses that ere all could get out of the way the snorting, trembling beasts were upon them, dashing men and women to right and left, leaving a trail of groaning injured behind them.

Beside himself with despair and grief, Danby Druce ran out of the house, and, though with little hope of overtaking the fugitives, rushed into the street just as a man riding on a motor-bicycle appeared upon the scene.

As the new-comer slow down, Danby Druce grasped the handle-bar of the machine with one hand, and, thrusting his arm round the astounded rider's waist, hurled him to the ground.

Springing on to the machine, he thrust forward the sparking-lever to its furthest notch and the next moment was dashing over the road in swift pursuit of the flying carriage.

A bend in the road hid the Winged Man from view; but a few minutes later, as the motor-cycle's engine got in its work, Danby Druce came in sight of the fleeing vehicle.

"Stop! Face-to-face, hand to hand, unarmed them I am, I fear you not!" shouted Danby Druce, as the swift carriage quickly overtook the galloping, swaying carriage.

A mocking laugh was the Winged Man's sole answer to Danby Druce's challenge. Then the detective saw him, bending to the right, pull on one rein with all his might.

The next moment the horses' heads had been turned down a narrow by-lane, and, though the carriage was lifted completely off its near-side wheels, it escaped disaster; whilst Danby Druce, whom the manoeuvre had taken by surprise, dashed past the turning at a good thirty miles an hour.

---

[49] A brougham carriage with a coachman's box-seat, normally open to the elements.

Careless of broken limb or neck, eager only to rescue Mary from the Winged Man's clutches, Danby Druce, setting his teeth, guided his cycle to the opposite side of the road; then, leaning on one side, steered straight for a shallow ditch and low hedge which hemmed in the road.

It was only the terrific pace at which the motor-cycle was going that carried the dauntless detective in safety over the obstruction into a field of unploughed stubble upon the other side.

Settling himself in the saddle, Danby Druce turned his machine towards where he could see the carriage dashing at right angles to the course he had taken along a narrow, little-used track across the field.

As he beheld the swaying carriage, the fearful form the Winged Man balanced upon the splashboard, and the latter-covered, terrified horses, a momentary faintness blurred his vision, a terrible, icy chill struck his heart, for he remembered now whether that lane led.

It was the old quarry, from whence the stones with which Peril Castle had been built had been taken.

Large drops of cold perspiration pouring down his face, Danby Druce did all that human ingenuity could conceive to increase the speed of his iron mount.

There was yet time to reach the unfenced track, and, hurling himself and his machine before the horses, bring them down before the quarry was reached.

But barely had he taken this brave, self-sacrificing determination ere the back wheel of his cycle, injured in its plunge across the ditch, collapsed, and he was flung heavily to the ground.

Fortunately, he felt clear of the heavy machine, and, though bruised and shaken, was able to spring to his feet and continued the hopeless pursuit on foot.

Alas! the delay was fatal. Even as he staggered blindly forward an unearthly scream of terror rose from the doomed horses. He saw them rise, as though for a jump, and the next moment of horses, the carriage, and its helpless occupant disappeared into the yawning mouth of the quarry, whilst, rendering the air with awful laughter, the Winged Man hovered on outstretched wings overhead.

Covering his face with his hands, Danby Druce stood paralysed with the greatness of the catastrophe that had ended a morning which had broken so happily for him.

MR. TRENT'S STORY.

Several minutes elapsed ere Danby Druce could steel himself to approach the quarry and looked down its steep, rugged side. Then a shudder shook his frame as he saw, fifty feet beneath him, the mangled remains of the horses lying amidst the wreckage of the carriage.

How Danby Druce clambered down the precipice he never knew. All he remembered afterwards was finding himself standing by the side of the demolished vehicle, and pulling away the wreckage with frenzied hands, fearing each moment to see the face of his stolen bride, white and lifeless, peering at him from the splintered woodwork.

Presently, with mixed feelings of relief and despair, he realised that his search was in vain. Mary Evanson was not there!

Regretting the precious minutes he had wasted in his search amongst the wreckage, Danby Druce armed himself with a spoke from the broken wheel, and, peering into a crevasse here, searching behind an enormous block of stone there, pushing apart the snow-laden leaves of a shrub which clung to the face of the quarry, or glancing about him in search of footsteps, he sought for some trace of his fearful foe.

But in vain. Save the marks his own feet had made, the drifted snow lay pure and spotless around him. Yet for an hour the detective pursued his search, until at last he was fain to own himself beaten, and slowly and sorrowfully turned his steps towards the village.

As Danby Druce passed up the village street, the sympathetic crowd, reading failure in his dejected mien, stood aside in silence to let him pass. All realised that they were witnesses of sorrow a too grateful sympathetic words to assuage.

Looking neither to right nor left, Danby Druce re-entered the little house from whence is promised bride had been torn. As he crossed the threshold a bowed, shaking form moved down the little hall to meet him. It was Mary Evanson's uncle.

Grasping the detective's outstretched hand, the old man, whose face still bore traces of an almost unbearable horror, led him into the little drawing-room, upon a table in the centre of which was set out, as though in mockery, the wedding presents.

"I need not ask. You have no news of Mary Evanson?" he said.

Danby Druce shook his head.

"Only the worst," he replied.

"She is dead?" asked the old man, tears rolling down his wrinkled cheek.

"Fear not," replied the detective, in despairing accents.

"Fear not?" repeated the old man, in surprise.

"Yes. Dearly though I love her, I would rather see her stretched in death upon yonder couch, then live to know that she is in the Winged Man's power!"

Mr. Trent shuddered.

"The Winged Man!" he repeated. "Often has poor Mary try to describe the horror of that awful being. Yet her most eloquent words failed to impress upon me the unearthly terror of his fearful face!"

As he spoke both men started as an awful, terror-laden shriek fell upon their ears. Danby Druce moved towards the door.

"It is my poor wife," explained the elder man, laying a detaining hand upon his arm.

"She was seated in yonder chair," he went on, pointing towards the armchair in which Danby Druce had seen her when he first entered the house, "happy in the happiness which she felt was assured her dear niece. I was putting the finishing touched to yonder present, when I saw her face become as one turned suddenly to stone. Heaven grant that I may never again see such a look of horror on any human being's face.

"I followed the direction of her eyes, and saw a black-garbed, awful form enframed in the doorway. Seeking to protect my wife, I advanced towards him.

"What happened next I cannot say. The weird being laid a claw-like finger upon my forehead; then, as though a fearful blow had descended upon my head, I remembered no more until I awoke to find Dr. Broome bending over me, and two kindly neighbours carrying Mrs. Trent, shrieking as you heard her just now to her room.

"Danby Druce, I pity you from the bottom of my heart, yet I would you had never crossed this threshold!"

THE MISER OF PERIL CASTLE.

Within a large, oak-panelled room, the windows of which overhung the precipice upon which Peril Castle stood, the last Lord Hawkhurst sat in solitary state.

It was a magnificent apartment, hung with priceless tapestry. Along the walls were arranged life-size figures, clad in the armour of dead-and-gone Hawkhursts, who, whatever had been their faults, and had been brave warriors, earning their living at the point of the sword, and holding what they thus obtained by the strength of their good right arms and dauntless hearts.

Different indeed was there descendent. The blood of the wild, fierce Hawkhursts flowed in the veins of a grasping old miser.

Before a table groaning beneath a heap of glittering, golden coins was the last of the bold robber race.

His lean, wasted features, his sunken eyes, glittering with an almost maniacal light, his shabby clothes, his shrunken frame, all spoke of one who had surrendered the honours and joys of life to gather together a horde of the yellow metal lying upon the table before him.

Now and again he would raise a back from an ironbound chest that stood by the side of his high-backed, richly-carved chair, and emptied it on the table, laughing with fearful glee as the golden coins rolled in a yellow stream down the side of the glistening heap.

"It is mine—all mine!" he cried, burying his arms to the elbows in the gold. "None shall take it from me; none will try, for none know that it is here. They pity me, the fools—the outside world! They speak of poor Lord Hawkhurst, debarred from every pleasure by a cankering poverty which has forced him to give up society and friends, and staff in the ruined walls of Peril Castle. Ho, ho! The fools, if they could see me now, how hundreds of fawning scoundrels would be clustering around me. But none shall have it, and when I am dead—"

He shuddered, and looked fearfully around him.

"Death! Who speaks of death?" he cried, rising, on tottering legs, looking apprehensively over his shoulder. "No, no; I am a young man still. Scarce sixty years have passed over my head. I am good for another quarter of a century spent in the company of my beloved gold!"

As he finished speaking the wretched man sank forward on the table, and, burying his face in the gold, pressed frenzied kisses upon the glittering coins.

"But what," he murmured, rising suddenly to an upright position—"what if any discover my secret? No, no; it is impossible! Judas Darbe and old Deborah are the only people who ever enter this part of the building. Yonder door is never opened, and none but myself knows the secret passage which leads from the room in which I am supposed to pass my time in scientific studies, to this banqueting-hall, in which the fools who preceded me wasted the precious gold they extorted from the surrounding country in revelry and riotous living.

"No, no. Were I in a desert island I could not be safer than I am here from curious ears and prying eyes."

Even as the words left his lips his pale face grew sallow with terror, his whole frame shook, as though stricken by a sudden ague, as he stood gazing in horror at a full-length portrait of an evil-faced, bearded man, clad in sea-faring garments, who, if report spoke truly, had led a fearful existence as a pirate on the Spanish Main.

"Those eyes—those eyes!" gasped the old miser. "I saw them move! I saw the flash with greed and avaricious desire!" he murmured, adding reassuringly the next moment: "No it was fancy; I did but dream. My eyes have been dazzled by gazing at my precious gold!"

As he spoke he raised two of the massive silver candlesticks, in which burned cheap tallow candles, for he was too mean to use wax, and with tottering steps crossed the room and held the light against the canvas.

"Ha, ha! I knew it was fancy! It must have been fancy! But, even if it was not, Red Hawkhurst could not come out of his frame and carry my gold away. Aho, aho!"

Chuckling to himself, the miser returned to the table, and, receipting himself, commenced shovelling the coins with feverish haste back into the bags.

The strange eyes he imagined he had seen peering at him from the canvas had stricken terror into his avaricious heart.

°A TREACHEROUS PAIR

Well might Lord Hawkhurst hasten to replaces gold in the strong-box from which he had taken it.

It was no fancy which had conjured up that lifelike look into Red Hawkhurst's painted eyes.

Crouched in a secret passage, near to, but entirely separate from the one by which the miser gained his secret hoard, was Judas Darbe and his wife Deborah, Lord Hawkhurst's sole companions in Peril Castle.

Like clings to like, and save for the differences in their position, and the fact that Lord Hawkhurst had gold, and his servants none, they were similar in disposition, and the grasping greed, which seems to break out like a disease in some people's souls.

Judas Darbe was a wizened, wrinkled, round-shouldered old man, whom even his wife had never known to smile, and from whose lips a kindly word had never passed.

Save for his master, to whom he seemed devoted, Judas Darbe hated the whole world. The hatred was extended even to his wife Deborah, but in this case tempered with a wholesome fear, for Mistress Deborah had a tongue that the captain of a tramp steamer might have envied.

° 21 June 1913.

She was a big, strong, masculine woman, with a harsh, coarse, evil-looking face, rendered more repulsive by the grey-streaked hair upon lip and chin.

It was her eyes Lord Hawkhurst had detected gazing at him from behind the portrait. Finding her employer's suspicion aroused, she had allowed the flap of canvas to fall back over the holes cut in the portrait's face, and grasping her husband by the collar of his frayed livery coat, she had dragged him along a narrow passage, down a steep flight of worn stone steps, into a large, many-pillared crypt which had evidently been used at one time as a chapel, for at the further end of this apartment stood an altar.

"It's a good job you have got me to take care of you, Judas Darbe," said Deborah, as she stopped for a moment's breathing space in the old chapel, on the floor of which the beams of a full moon fell through an opening in the face of the precipice from out of which the crypt had been carved.

"The gold, Deborah—the rich, yellow, shining gold! Pounds of it, hundredweights, and you and I, who have served him so faithfully for so many years, obliged to live upon odds-and ends many a beggar with scorn. Because, forsooth, he was poor—so poor that he could not afford us more.

"How does he repay our services?" hissed Deborah. "By insults, by grinding us down to the last penny. I tell you, Judas Darbe, if I was the man and you the woman, the last of the Hawkhurst would be sent to keep company with his forefathers beyond the grim gates of death."

Judas Darbe shuddered, and gazed fearfully around him.

"Hush, Deborah! You forget the secret passage the old fool thinks is known only to himself leads also to this crypt. Let us hasten, lest he should return and find us so near him!"

With a contemptuous snort, the woman strode to a massive pillar which supported the vaulted roof, and seizing a rusty iron cressit, used in the old days to support the torches which had lighted the sacred edifice, pressed it inward with all her might.

The iron sank half its length into the solid stone work, then a slight, grinding noise echoed through the crypt as half the pillar, opened like a door, revealed a flight of steps leading to the rooms above.

Five minutes later the worthy couple had regained the huge, stone-flagged kitchen, where at one time oxen and sheep had been roasted whole to supply the wants of the castle garrison.

Now a small American cooking-stove, standing in the yawning fireplace, had taken the place of the large boilers and spits, on which our forefathers cooked their simple but substantial viands.

"Judas Darbe," said the woman, as her husband seated himself on a chair and warmed his shaking hands over the open top of the cooking-stove, "what do you think of Lord Hawkhurst now?"

The man shot a swift, enquiring glance at his wife.

"If we can do so without arousing his suspicions we might get better food, higher wages, and more firing from him," muttered her husband.

"Bah, Judas Darbe? Can your thoughts rise no higher than that?" inquired Deborah contemptuously. "Listen! You heard him muttering, you know, that none besides himself and us know of his secret hoard."

"Yes, Deborah, but—" began Judas.

Then, grasping the arms of the chair, sat gazing with dawning terror in his eyes at his wife.

"I repeat that none but you and I share Lord Hawkhurst's secret with him. Should his body be found at the foot of the precipice beneath the castle wall, who has more right to his hoarded gold than we, whom he has duped to help him save it?"

"What do you mean, Deborah? Would you—" began Judas.

He paused; then seem to force the words from his parched lips.

"Would you do away with him?"

"Ay!" admitted the woman boldly. "And you must share his gold or his grave!"

With a cry of terror the old man sprang to his feet, gazing in horror at his wife, and trembling from head to foot.

"You would kill me, too—I, who have been your husband for so many years; I who have never given you a cross word, or balked you in any way."

"Because you dare not!" laughed Deborah. "Why, you miserable little shrimp, I have only put up with you so long because you dare not call your soul your own. But come, enough of this!" she added. "Which is it to be? Must I do the deed, or you? Think what the gold means to us? With it we can set up a money-lending business in London, and soon grow rich beyond the dreams of avarice!"

"We can live in a big house, and have servants at our beck and call, surround ourselves with every luxury wealth can buy!" cried Judas Darbe, his shifty eyes blazing with cupidity. "Yes, yes Deborah, I was a fool to hesitate! You and I will do the deed together. You shall hold him whilst I strike!"

"And have the deed brought home to us the next day?" sneered his wife. "No, no. Listen!" And, drawing a chair to her husband's side, the villainous couple entered into a low-voiced eager conversation, broken after a time by the ringing of a distant bell.

The conspirators glanced significantly at each other; then, as Mrs. Darbe emptied the contents of a saucepan simmering on the fire into a basin, Judas entered the coal-cellar, returning a minute later with a large, heavy hammer concealed beneath his coat.

Not a word was exchanged between the villainous couple as Mrs. Darbe, placing the basin on a cheap wooden tray, led the way from the kitchen into a barely-furnished, dirty dining-room. As she entered, Lord Hawkhurst, who was crouched over a few scarce-glowing coals, looked up.

"Your porridge, my Lord!" said the woman, without a tremor in her voice to warn the unsuspicious man of the fearful plot which had been concocted against his life.

Seating himself at the table, Lord Hawkhurst stirred the porridge with a common metal spoon.

"Good gracious, Deborah! How thick you have made this porridge! Do you want to ruin me!" he demanded angrily.

Then, hearing a slight noise behind him, turned.

Too late! With trembling hands Judas Darbe brought the heavy-headed hammer down, and, with a low, shuddering moan, Lord Hawkhurst glided from the chair on to the floor.

"Well struck, Judas! The blow has not killed him, but it will suffice. Quick, catch hold of his legs! I'll carry his head and shoulders!" cried Deborah.

Together they bore him out of the room, along a bare, unfurnished landing, to what had been the old castle courtyard.

Making their way across the yard, the guilty couple, staggering beneath their load, reached a flight of stairs, up which they dragged their senseless burden; then, laying him down on a stone platform, peered over the battlemented parapet into the darkness below.

A few minutes for rest for the woman to regain courage on the part of the man, and they carried their still breathing victim a few feet along the battlements towards a gaping chasm in the wall.

"This is the place!" chuckled Deborah. "We will tell everyone that the battlement was his favourite walk. What is more likely than that he should fall headlong through this hole in the dark? Now, then, both together! Heave-ho! Heave-ho!"

As, with brutal callousness, the woman uttered the last words, the two through the limp, helpless body into the night.

The next moment Judas Darbe had grasped his wife by the arm.

"See," he cried, "it is not falling! It hangs suspended on empty air. Merciful heavens! Look; it is coming back!" he gasped.

Then, with a shriek, he turned and fled, leaving his wife, paralysed with horror and dread, gazing at the senseless form, which, swung as though held up by invisible supports, was gradually approaching nearer the wall.

In vain Deborah Darbe tried to fly. Her limbs refused their office, and she could only stand trembling from head to foot, gazing with staring eyes at the dread phenomenon.

Nearer and nearer it came, until at last Deborah, in a wild, dread way, noticed that the darkness immediately beneath the body was of a more prominent blackness.

Scarce daring to breathe, the woman watched until her victim's still breathing body touched the wall; then a second face appeared beside the first, and, with a loud, fearful, mocking laugh, the Winged Man, Lord Hawkhurst clasped in his arms, stood beside her.

A NEW MASTER.

Gradually Deborah Darbe's stare grew less stony, she noted the mocking smile on the Winged Man's thin lips.

"If I where he whom you believe me to be what I have saved this man from death?" asked the weird horror, laying his hand upon the breast of the unconscious man.

"I have heard you take care of your own," came in hesitating accents from the woman's lips.

"Ha, ha, ha! Ho, ho, ho!" laughed the Winged Man. "Then, if he is mine, you, who would have killed him, are mine ten times over! Beware! Wander from the path I set you by so much as a hairsbreath, and you are doomed! Go! Summons that white-livered cur, your husband, Hither! Seek not to escape, for, if you disobey, the snows of the Himalayas, the fires burning beneath the centre of the earth, could not hide you from my vengeance!"

Without a word the woman hastened across the courtyard into the kitchen.

Her husband was not there. She found him trembling beneath the bed, and, drawing him forth by the heels, shook him until his teeth rattled again.

At first Judas Darbe absolutely refused to return to the battlement, but a second shaking from his better-half caused him to change his mind, and a few seconds later, her hand on his collar lest he should attempt flight, the worthy couple returned to the walls, where they found the Winged Man leaning upon the parapet, with Lord Hawkhurst's unconscious form at his feet, as, chin in hand, he gazed over the sleeping village.

As the two stood upon the stone-capped platform the Winged Man turned a bright crimson glare upon them.

A squeal of terror burst from Judas Darbe's lips. Fain would he have risked his wife's anger and fled, but he could not, terror chained him to the ground.

"Why did you attempt this crime?" asked the Winged Man, fixing the trembling couple with his awful eyes, as he pointed a long, white finger at Lord Hawkhurst.

"Please, your Majesty—" began Judas Darbe, when the Winged Man interrupted him by saying:

"Silence, worm! Let that woman, your superior in strength, your superior in brain, your superior in courage, your superior in wickedness, speak!"

THE WINGED MAN'S MISTAKE.

It was rarely the Winged Man made a mistake, but he had done so in this instance. Had he allowed Judas Darbe to continue, the man would have betrayed the secret of Lord Hawkhurst's hidden hoard.

Not so his wife. During her passage to the habitable part of the old castle and back she had made up her mind that the prize within her grasp was worthy the risk of death itself. In fact, so great a hold had the desire to obtain possession of Lord Hawkhurst's gold upon her that she did not wish to live unless she could claim it as her own.

"Speak, woman!" thundered the Winged Man, turning upon her.

"Because we were tired of the service which was repaid only by blows, curses, and insults," she explained sullenly.

"I have heard England called a free country; you could have left his service, I presume?" asked the Winged Man suspiciously.

"And have ended our days in prison."

The Winged Man nodded.

"You mean Lord Hawkhurst, realising that such as you can be ruled only by fear, held you to his service by the possession of some secret which would get you into trouble? Ha, ha, it's the way of the world! Man's chief prey is man."

The woman made a silent sign of acquiescence.

"Well, you have but exchanged a master who possesses one of your secrets for a master who possesses two. Serve me well, and perchance your service will end in a few days. Dare to rebel, and fear the Winged Man's vengeance!"

"The Winged Man!" came almost in a shriek from Judas Darbe's lips. "And I thought you were another gentlemen," he added hastily, fearing to offend the dread being glowering at him with mocking, merciless eyes.

"Ay, the Winged Man!" repeated the weird monster. "Carry Lord Hawkhurst to his room. See that he recovers health and strength, for I have need of him. If he dies, by my power, your life shall pay the forfeit! Go!"

Without a word the well-matched pair raised their intended victim from the ground, and toiled painfully back to a room adjoining the one in which they had struck him down.

Here, owing principally to Deborah's skilful care, Lord Hawkhurst slowly regained consciousness, and listened, with suspicious, shifty eyes to Judas Darbe's explanation that entering the room he had fallen, and the edge of the tray he was carrying had struck his master's head.

Lord Hawkhurst knew the man lied, but he pretended to believe him, knowing how completely he was in the power of his two servants, and, turning his face to the wall, closed his eyes.

DEBORAH'S CHARGE.

Leaving their master, as they thought, asleep, Judas Darbe and his wife retired to the bare and comfortless kitchen, where, stirring the flickering embers of the fire into ablaze, they commenced talking in low, hurried whispers.

Suddenly they were alarmed by a loud crash. Looking up, they saw that the back of the huge fireplace had parted to right and left, revealing the fearful form of the Winged Man.

"Judas Darbe, leave that chair on your peril! Deborah Darbe, follow me!" he ordered. Then, as the woman, trembling in every limb, rose to obey, the Winged Man led the way down a flight of moss-grown steps.

Sustained by the thought of the gold for which she was fighting, Mrs. Darbe followed her fearful guide, whilst opening the opening through which she had passed closed of its own accord.

As they pressed on through the darkness, their way lighted by the now white beams from the Winged Man's electric headlight, Deborah wondered at the weird horror's knowledge of the perfect maze of secret passages through which they passed—passages the very existence of which she had been ignorant until that moment.

As she walked terror greater than that of the Winged Man gripped her heart. Surely one who had such an intimate acquaintance with the castle must know of Lord Hawkhurst's secret hoard?

Doubt became certain when the Winged Man, rising through a trap door, composed of a huge flagstone, which moved aside in answer to a secret spring, stepped into the old chapel.

As she gazed around upon the familiar apartment, rendered ten times more ghostly by the livid grey beams which the Winged Man now sent from his headlight, baffled greed, rage, and despair caused a thousand varying emotions to flit across her face.

"Fear nothing. The Winged Man knows how to reward those who serve him!" cried her fearful guide.

Then, to her inexpressible relief, he led the way, not to either of the secret entrances into the treasure-chamber, but towards the tiny chancel.

Deborah Darbe did not see the Winged Man touch the wall, yet it opened, apparently of its own accord, to let him pass, and an ejaculation of amazement burst from the woman's lips as he led the way into a bare, cellar-like apartment on the floor of which lay the unconscious form of a lovely girl clad in bridal array.

"Behold your charge! Treat her, if not with kindness—full well I know that your evil heart is incapable of so human feeling—with courtesy and gentleness. A word of complaint from her lips and punishment such as in your wildest dreams you have never deemed possible of shall be yours. If she escapes, this room shall be your tomb!"

Wonderingly, the woman knelt by the unconscious girl's side, and raised her lovely head upon her arm.

"Whither shall I carry her? She cannot remain here; she will die of cold."

There was no answer, and, turning, she breathed a sigh of relief. The Winged Man had disappeared.

DANBY DRUCE ON THE TRAIL.

In the meantime, Danby Druce had not been idle. With Mr. Trent's grief-laden proof ringing in his ears, he retraced his steps to the old quarry, for it was there he had last seen Mary Evanson, and commenced a more systematic search of its jagged sides than he had yet been able to give them.

An hour dragged slowly by, and Danby Druce had almost given up all hope of success, when, lying behind a huge boulder that rested upon a ledge half-way up the quarry's rocky side, he found a single white rose.

In summer-time that delicate flower might not have been an important clue, but found amongst the winter snow, he knew it could only be one of a small bunch he had ordered from Covent Garden and sent up to Mary the previous evening.

Eagerly he searched the frozen rock, but without avail. Either the Winged Man had been concealed behind that boulder, gloating over his misery as he surveyed the wreck of the carriage, or the rose had dropped from Mary's hair as her fearful kept winged his way through the air.

Presently he ceased his search, and leant his back against the boulder as he tried to think out, calmly and collectedly, what would be the Winged Man's most probable course of action.

As he did so he noticed that the boulder moved. Trembling with excitement, he pushed it with all his might.

"Hurrah, the rock gives!" came, in an exultant shout from between his clenched lips; then, putting every ounce of strength he possessed into the task, he pressed his hardest against the rock. Slowly the huge stone rolled over, until at last it plunged with the deep, sullen roar down the side of the quarry, revealing a deep pit-like opening, beyond which all was dark.

Pausing only to satisfy himself that his revolver was loaded in every chamber, Danby Druce drew an electric torch from his pocket, and flashed its bright beams into the opening.

The next moment he plunged eagerly forward. Caught upon a projection in the rocky side of the narrow tunnel was a piece of frayed veiling.

Confident that he was on the right track, Danby Druce hastened down a sloping tunnel, until at length he found himself in a narrow, stone-flagged passage.

Wondering whither this strange clue would lead him, Danby Druce pressed on. As he forces way deeper into what seemed a never-ending subterranean passage the air grew heavy and oppressive until he felt his brain swimming, strange lights danced before his eyes, and he realised he was surrounded on all sides by poisonous gases.

Determined to leave his bones mouldering in that unknown, forgotten secret passage, rather than retreat, he staggered blindly on, and was rewarded by finding that the passage sloped slowly upwards, and that fresher, purer air was fanning his brow.

Darkness succeeded day, yet Danby Druce moved tirelessly along his strange path until presently he arrived at a spot where two ways met.

Eagerly he swept the rays of his electric torch along the flagstones which paved both passages, then moved swiftly towards where the beams of his electric torch were reflected from something bright and sparkling lying upon the tunnel floor.

Stooping, he picked it up and pressed it to his lips. It was the diamond brooch he had given Mary a few days before.

His spirits raised by his discovery, Danby Druce quickened his steps. Five minutes later allowed ejaculation of dismay burst from his lips, as the ground seemed to vanish beneath his feet, and he found himself falling through space, until his further descent was stopped by a plunge into icy cold water.

As he felt the foul, stagnant liquid closing over his head Danby Druce instinctively raised the hand in which he held his electric torch.

It was well he did so, for the water was not deep, and when at length he scrambled to his feet its rays showed him that he was in a round pit dug in the centre of the passage.

Leaning against the side of the pit was a stout post terminating in a sharp iron spike, and Danby Druce knew that he had fallen into a trap, provided by the old-time barons of Peril Castle to protect their secret tunnel.

Fortunately, the sharpened stake had been overthrown years before, or else Danby Druce would have fallen to certain death.

But now the very weapon dead-and-gone Hawkhurst had provided to ensure their foe's destruction proved Danby Druce's salvation. Climbing the thick post, he was able to scramble out of the pit on the opposite side to that from which he had fallen in.

Only pausing to draw off his coat and squeeze what water he could out of it, Danby Druce continued on his way.

But not far. Ten minutes later he found the tunnel blocked by tons of fallen earth and masonry.

A brief examination sufficed to show that there was no opening here through which even the Winged Man could creep, and a fierce flood of anger surged into the great detective's heart as he realised that the diamond brooch had been purposely thrown where he found it that he might plunge headlong into a death-trap.

Regretting the time he had lost, Danby Druce rapidly retraced his steps until he stood once more on the edge of the yawning chasm.

Anxiously he scanned its depth. There was no way round. It was too wide to jump. Without a moment's hesitation Danby Druce lowered himself once more into the pit, and though with difficulty, for the wood was waterlogged and sodden, he shifted the post from one side to the other. A minute later he had regained the brink of the pit.

But the Winged Man's cunningly contrived false trail had caused him to waste over an hour, and breaking into a run, he rapidly retraced his steps, only to realise some half-hour later that the truth of the old saying, "More haste, less speed," for he had missed the second passage, and was well on his way back to the deserted quarry.

His heart filled with bitter disappointment, Danby Druce went to the rightabout, until at last he stood at the turning of the ways once more.

On he went, plodding through the darkness with dogged determination, until at length he paused for breath by the side of a perpendicular opening, and gazed through the night upon the twinkling lights of the village below.

He knew now that, as he had before suspected would be the case, the secret passage had led him to Peril Castle.

Husbanding the rays of his electric torch, Danby Druce groped his way blindly on.

Hour after hour Danby Druce sought for an exit from the maze of passages which undermined the old castle, when finally, chilled to the bone, weary, despairing, he sank upon the topmost step of the steep flight of stairs, and, burying his face in his hands, dropped at once into the dreamless slumber of complete exhaustion.

FOUND AND LOST.

"If you are a woman, if your heart has ever been filled with love for a sister, a daughter, or a mother, have mercy, and help me to escape from this dread horror's clutches!"

Danby Druce awoke with every nerve on the alert, as the appeal, in Mary Evanson's well-remembered tones, fell upon his ears.

"It's no good, girl. I'm sorry for you, that's a fact; but if you filled this room with gold I dare not let you go," came the reply, in a harsh, grating, woman's voice.

Silently Danby Druce arose, and, not daring to use his electric torch, lest its beams should betray his presence, crept on to the landing in which the secret stairs terminated, and passed his hand cautiously over the wall.

"At least do this to me. Take a letter to Mr. Danby Druce, I have nothing but an ill-treated girl's thanks to give, but he will reward you handsomely," Danby Druce heard Mary Evanson implore.

"Would a hundred pounds be too much?" asked the other voice eagerly.

"No, I'm sure it would not. It is a large sum, but I am sure he would gladly pay it for news of his stolen bride."

There was a brief silence; then the harsh voice answered:

"I'll do it; but mind you put on the envelope 'Only to be delivered on payment of £100,' and your name."

"Yes, yes!" agreed Mary Evanson eagerly. "Quick, quick! Pen and ink—or a pencil will do! Do not delay, lest the Winged Man discovers all!"

There came a shuffling of slipshod footsteps, followed by the slamming to of a door, and a sudden click as of a bolt being shot home in a lock.

Flashing a light over the wall from beyond which the above conversation had come, Danby Druce discovered that he was standing at the back of some worm-eaten wainscoting.

Cautiously he tapped upon one of the panels.

A suppressed scream reached his ears.

"Courage, dear one; it is I, Danby Druce, come to save you!" whispered the detective. "Quick, search for a secret spring in the panelling."

"Oh, Danby, thank Heaven you have come! I knew you would not leave me in this fearful monster's power!" came back the joyful response.

"Quick, dear one, waste no time in words! Search, for the love of life and liberty, search!" implored her lover.

The subdued sob of joy which reached the ears from the other side of the panelling was the sweetest music Danby Druce had ever heard. Casting the rays of his electric torch between the joints, he searched for some opening in the panel.

It was true the woodwork was rotten, and he might have forced his way through it, but he could not have done so without noise, and silence was, above all things, necessary.

Once Danby Druce stood as still as a statue whilst he listened intently. He fancied he heard a suppressed cry, but so low that his ears might have deceived him. Not daring to speak more than he could help, lest the Winged Man should detect his presence in the castle, Danby Druce continued the search for the secret spring.

Suddenly a portion of the wall flew aside, and a bright light flooded the secret passage.

Blinded by the sudden glare, Danby Druce dashed through the opening with the name of Mary upon his lips. Even as his foot touched the bare boards of the room into which he had penetrated he came to an abrupt halt, gazing as one turned to stone, upon the Winged Man, who stood surveying him with a mocking smile of fiendish triumph.

"Mary—Miss Evanson—where is she? She was here a moment before," he gasped at last.

Loud rang the Winged Man's fearful laughter through the spacious apartment.

"Welcome, Danby Druce!" he cried, ignoring the other's frenzied inquiries. "You have come somewhat sooner than I expected yet you are welcome. Never did man greeted his dearest friend as I you, oh, mine enemy! Mary Evanson is mine! They needed but one thing to make my tribe complete, to have you in my power!"

"Your triumph is premature, hated being!" cried Danby Druce. "Either you or I shall not leave this room alive!"

Carried away by rage, despair, and misery, Danby Druce hurled himself at his fearful foe's throat. The next moment he realised the folly of his action.

It was not the first time he and the Winged Man had come to death-grips, yet each time the Winged Man had conquered him as easily as though he had been a child.

It was the same now. A few second's fierce, unavailing struggle, and Danby Druce found himself lying, handcuffed, and helpless upon the floor.

For some minutes Danby Druce writhed in despairing rage upon the floor, during which though his wrists were handcuffed behind his back he struggled to his feet. Gradually his rage evaporated before the steady emotionless, sphinx-like eyes of his fearful captor.

"Danby Druce, what would you do to save Mary Evanson?" asked the Winged Man at last.

"Do? There is nothing I would not do!" replied Danby Druce eagerly. "I would give my life, my very soul, to save her from your power! Winged Man, we have fought together, we have even met as friends. I have never known you yet to war against women."

"The Winged Man wars not against women," replied the weird horror proudly. "When a woman runs counter to his will, he sweeps her from his path. But you have not answered my question. What sacrifice will you make to save the woman you pretend to love?"

A terrible fear assailed Danby Druce lest the interpretation of the Winged Man's words which flashed through his brain should be a true one, yet, without a moment's hesitation, without a change in the tone of his low, eager voice, he replied:

"Name your conditions. I will obey them."

A look of intense triumph blazed from the Winged Man's eyes as he gazed upon his bound and helpless prisoner.

"You remember the oath I swore, that you should become my slave? I read my answer in your face. Does not that prospect chill even your courageous heart, Danby Druce?" demanded the Winged Man.

With terrible vividness, the wretched creatures Danby Druce had seen in the Winged Man's haunts, creeping, broken-spirited scarce human, creatures of their dread master's will, rose in his mind. He—he, whose intellect had enabled him to cope so long with one in doubt with almost superhuman power, was to become one such as they.

For a moment his whole being revolted against so fearful prospect; but the memory of the woman who had been so nearly his wife, forced into unholy wedlock with the dread being who held her in his power, drove all thoughts of self from the noble detective's heart.

Steadfastly he fixed his eyes upon the Winged Man's face.

"Have it as you will. Would you had demanded my life, rather than my manhood," he said.

THE OAK PRESS.

No sooner had Lord Hawkhurst found himself alone, then, dragging himself from the bed on which Judas Darbe and his wife had laid him, he stood for a moment listening intently; then, stealing to a cupboard on the wall, took from out of it a bottle of brandy, from which he took a long, deep draught. Strengthened by the stimulating liquid, he stole across the room, a cunning smile upon his lips, a look that was not good to see in his eyes.

"They would have murdered me—me, their benefactor, the man upon whose charity they have lived so long," he muttered. "But I will be even with them. One more hour spent in the company of my beloved gold, then to the village to lay information against my would-be murderers before a magistrate. Aha, Judas, in character as in name a traitor, you and your evil wife shall perish upon the gallows for your crimes!"

Cautiously opening the door which gave admittance to the room in which he usually lived, he peered in.

There was no one there, and, stealing across the floor, he turned the key in the lock of the door which communicated with the domestic officers.

Even as he did so he started, and his white, wrinkled face grew pallid with terror, for a low, indescribably horrible chuckle fell upon his ears.

Fearfully he gazed around, half expecting to see the grinning faces of the servants he had so long bullied, but whom he now feared, behind him.

There was no one else there, and muttering: "Bah! It was but fancy. I am unnerved. My gold—my precious gold—will give me strength to carry out my scheme of vengeance!" he moved to a corner of the room furthermost from the bed-room door, and, standing upright in an angle of the wall, pressed a concealed spring close to his hand.

Immediately, moving on some unseen pivot, the wall, from floor to ceiling, moved round, carrying Lord Hawkhurst with it, until he stepped from off the triangular piece of floor into a narrow, secret passage.

Immediately the double strip of wall returned to its proper position, fitting in so entirely with the rest of the room that it would have defied any eye but that of the Winged Man to have detected any difference between it and the rest of the wall.

A few minutes later Lord Hawkhurst arose, like some fearful spectre of the past, from a concealed trap door in the floor of the magnificent room that held his unsuspecting wealth.

Cautiously closing the trapdoor, he lighted the candle standing upon the table before mentioned, and breathed a sigh of relief as he gazed around him.

"I am safe here. None know of this chamber but myself," he muttered. "Ah my friends—my faithful servants—ere twelve hours have spared you will regret your attempted treachery!

"But now, my gold, let me feast my eyes upon you; let me feel you running through my fingers; Let me bury my face amidst your round, Golden discs once more; then, for a little time I must leave you!"

Crooning as though to some unseen, dearly-loved child, the old miser hobbled across the room to a large oak press, in which he kept the iron-bound chest containing his gold, and raised the lid.

A moaning shudder—it can scarcely be called a cry—of paralysing terror on his lips, his hands clasped to his brow, Lord Hawkhurst staggered back as from out the chest arose a shapeless black form.

Higher and higher mounted the apparition, its head touched the lofty ceiling, then it opened, a brilliant light flooded the room, and the Winged Man stood revealed.

LORD HAWKHURST'S PAST.

"Aho, Baron Hawkhurst, degenerate descendant of an unruly race, we meet again!" thundered the Winged Man.

"Meet again?" echoed Hawkhurst, gazing with protruding eyeballs upon the terrible apparition.

"Ay, we meet again!" repeated the Winged Man, as, dropping to the floor, he stood with folded arms surveying the terror-stricken man. "I see you have forgotten me. It is strange. Few who have once seen the Winged Man are able to banish his lineaments from their memory."

Lord Hawkhurst try to speak, but no words passed his lips. In obedience to a wave of the Winged Man's hand he sank into an old-fashioned, straight-backed armchair, where he sat, the very picture of misery and despair, his eyes following his fearful visitor's every movement, as the Winged Man seated himself on one corner of the table, his elbow on his knee and his chin in his hand, surveyed the trembling man with an expression of fearful mockery in his eyes.

"I see recollection is dawning upon you. Let me hasten your memory. Behold!" cried the Winged Man, pointing to the opposite wall.

A moan of terror burst from the unfortunate lord as he saw, or fancied he saw, the wall vanish, and in its place appear a large room containing a huge, old-fashioned four-post bed, upon which an old man lay gasping for breath.

Upon one side of the bed, looking anxiously upon the dying man's face, stood a middle-aged woman Lord Hawkhurst recognised as Deborah Darbe.

In a chair upon the opposite side of the bed sat the counterfeit presentment of himself—younger, but with his evil face already marked with dissipation and debauchery.

Unable to move his eyes from this fearful vision of the past, Lord Hawkhurst saw himself glance furtively at Deborah; then, as she turned away, he emptied the contents of a phial into a bottle of medicine standing on a table by the side of the bed.

Then, as Deborah returned to the bed once more, he rose and glided from the scene.

Presently the sick man opened his eyes, and made a motion with his hand to his mouth.

In a moment Deborah was at the bedside, and, pouring out a dose of the poisoned medicine, put it to her patient's lips, who drank it, then sank back with a relieved sigh upon the pillows.

For a moment the scene vanished. When it reappeared the patient was dead, and by the bedside stood Lord Hawkhurst, pointing to the glass, and evidently accusing the nurse of the crime he himself had committed.

The next moment the picture disappeared.

"Do you remember me now, spoilt, ungrateful son, who, when the doctor had pronounced that your father had a chance of life, robbed him of that chance that you might come into the property you coveted, whilst, lest suspicion should be aroused, you schemed to fix the guilt upon another? Do you remember how, as the frightened woman, overwhelmed by the proof you could bring against her, dropped upon her knees in the death-chamber and begged for mercy, you looked up to find the Winged Man standing by your side?"

"Mercy—mercy! I was in debt; disgrace and ruin hung over me. I had forged my father's name. Had he lived, discovery was certain," came the gasping confession from Lord Hawkhurst's lips.

"Enough of the past! Behold the present!"

In a moment another scene appeared, or, conjured up by the miser's conscience-stricken brain, seems to appear, upon the wall.

It was as though they were looking into a glass, save that the Winged Man was not represented, and the table upon which he still leaned was piled with gold which the miser was greedily devouring with eager, maniacal eyes.

Despair crept into Lord Hawkhurst's heart. His secret was a secret no longer.

"You have seen the past and present. Would you gaze into the future?" demanded the Winged Man.

"No, no; in mercy spare me!" cried the wretched man. "You know of my gold, and will take it from me. What care I what the future may have in store?"

A strange enigmatic all smile hovered for a moment over the Winged Man's lips.

"Poor worm, follow me!" he cried, leading the way towards a full-length picture which occupied the centre of one wall.

As he advanced towards the wall his foot touched a secret spring, and the canvas, opening like a door, revealed a narrow flight of steps, up which the Winged Man strode, closely followed by his trembling and confused companion.

Presently the Winged Man paused, and, slipping back a piece of wood, ordered Lord Hawkhurst to look through the opening.

Stretched upon a couch before a fire that blazed in the old-fashioned, open hearth, her luxurious tresses trailing on the ground, her lovely face pale and tier-strained, yet unconscious of the espionage to which she was subjected, was a beautiful girl.

A long-drawn, wondering sigh escaped Lord Hawkhurst's lips.

Like a flash it dawned upon him that there were other things in life with having besides gold.

"Who is she? How came she there? How beautiful she is!" he murmured.

"She's the future Lady Hawkhurst!" was the astonishing reply.

"But I am old, and she is young. Besides, a young wife like that would spend my money, and scatter it broadcast," objected the old miser.

"As well her as another. Listen, Lord Hawkhurst, unless Mary Evanson becomes your wife, your gold is lost forever!"

"No, no; it cannot be! I dare not hope—that is to say, she would never consent to be my wife."

"She will consent, for it is the Winged Man's will," was the proud response. "Yesterday morning she was to have married a man I hate. But wedding her to such a one as yourself, I doom her to a life of misery, and break my rival's heart! But why should I condescend to justify my action, suffice it that within twenty-four hours you must be a wedded man or pauper. Perchance both; but you must risk that."

Closing up the peephole, the Winged Man led the way back to the miser's room, where, with the vision of Mary Evanson's loveliness before his eyes, Lord Hawkhurst promised to obey the Winged Man.

As the words which bound him left Lord Hawkhurst's lips the Winged Man stamped on the floor, and, descending by a concealed trapdoor, disappeared from view.

A NOBLE SACRIFICE.

If the good people of Hawkhurst could have spared a thought for the gloomy ruins which towered above their village, they would have noticed that no sign of life, save the smoke rising lazily from the chimneys in the heavy air, would be seen about Peril Castle.

But all were busy discussing the strange events which had happened in the village the previous day.

Even the strange disappearance of an old hag, regarded by the superstitious villagers as a witch who had long occupied a tumble-down hovel on the marsh adjoining the village, failed to make the impression upon them it otherwise would have done.

A heavy cloud of impending disaster hung all over within the ruined castle.

Denied food and drink, unable to move hand or foot, Danby Druce, held to the stone pillar by merciless iron bands, watched the light increase and darken again, his brain clouded by a feeling of dull, hopeless despair.

In obedience to the Winged Man's orders, Deborah Darbe waited, with what gentleness her rugged nature possessed, upon the Winged Man's beautiful captive.

As for Lord Hawkhurst, implicit belief in the Winged Man's promise caused him to look forward to the time when the lovely girl he had seen sleeping upon the couch the previous night would be his wife.

But what of Mary Evanson?

Despair had laid its numbing hand upon her heart. It is true she had written to Danby Druce, and entrusted the letter to Deborah, but her hopes in that direction had been shattered by the woman's confession that the Winged Man had forbidden anybody leaving the castle.

Slowly the hours dragged on. Night fell, and Mary Evanson, having dismissed Deborah, was weeping by the fire, when a slight noise at her side caused her to look up.

In a moment she had sprung to her feet, and was gazing with terror-stricken eyes at the motionless form of the Winged Man.

The dread horror's face was set in a look of fearful determination, yet as his eyes met those of his trembling captive a tiny spark of hope sprang to life in Mary's heart, for she thought she could detect a gleam of pity in those hard, cold eyes.

Snatching at this slight hope, as a drowning man snatches at a straw, Mary Evanson dropped upon her knees, and seized the Winged Man's deathly-cold, white hand in hers.

"Why have you brought me here? Why did you come into my life to bring misery upon one who has never done you any harm?" she cried.

A mirthless laugh burst from the Winged Man.

"No harm, girl? You know not what you say! You stirred a heart to love that for years had known no emotion but hatred of its kind. You fed that love with love, then, at the bidding of another, you left me—ay, at the very altar you allowed me to be driven from you. Had your love been strong to stand firm in good report and evil, the Winged Man would by now be an almost forgotten tale, told to frighten children round a winter's fireside."

Excuses and expostulations rose to Mary Evanson's pallid lips, but the Winged Man stopped her with upraised hand.

"I know what he would say. There is not an argument in your favour I have not repeated over again and again. Through Danby Druce you left me, and I, in revenge, have snatched you from my rival's hands—ay, more! At this moment he is a chained and bound prisoner at my mercy.!"

A cry of heart-broken despair burst from Mary Evanson's lips.

"Spare him! If ever you had a spark of love for me, spare him!" she implored.

"I will spare him," replied the Winged Man, "on one condition."

"Name it. Whatever it may be, I consent. There is no sacrifice I will not make for his sake," promised the distracted girl.

"Marry me, and Danby Druce shall go free!"

Slowly Mary Evanson rose to her feet, and a look of intense mental agony swept across the Winged Man's face as he read the loathing and despair in her glance.

With folded arms, his head bowed on his breast, the Winged Man awaited the girl's reply.

Slowly, as though the words were torn one by one from her heart, Mary said:

"For Danby Druce's sake, I will be your wife!"

Solemnly the Winged Man bowed, then, without a word, strode from the room.

°**Mary's Promise.**

Cramped, chilled to the bone, a dull, leaden pain of hopeless despair gnawing at his heart, Danby Druce awaited the Winged Man's will.

Intense awareness had set it seal upon his brain, but though now and again his limbs relaxed as sleep overcame him, it was but to awaken with a moan of pain as the rough rim of the iron, which encircled his neck cut deep into the flesh.

Suddenly a loud crash reverberated from without, followed by the vivid glare of a blinding flash of lightning.

As though summoned by the roar of "heaven's artillery," Danby Druce looked up, to see the Winged Man standing before him.

"What, dejected, miserable, and the Winged Man's honoured guest!" laughed the weird horror as he leered maliciously into his conquered foe's face. "Whatever you feel, let your face show happiness in the Winged Man's good fortune."

"The Winged Man's good fortune spells evil to me and to the whole human race," retorted Danby Druce fearlessly.

"That is as may be," replied the weird horror. "Listen, even Nature itself sends music to honour the Winged Man's wedding," he added, as a loud clap of thunder than any that had yet preceded it resounded through the old castle.

Danby Druce's heart sank like lead within his bosom. These repeated references to his wedding could point but to one thing, that the Winged Man was determined to force Mary Evanson into unholy union with himself.

As though he read his prisoner's thoughts, the Winged Man beckoned

---

° 28 June 1913.

towards the shadows hiding the furthermost corner of the crypt, and a low, despairing moan escaped Danby Druce's lips as Deborah Darby and Mary Evanson walked slowly up the aisle.

"Mary Evanson," said the Winged Man, taking the girl's limp hand in his, "once more, in the presence of this man, I ask if you will become my wife?"

"No, no; for the sake of all you hold dear. Mary, do not link your life with his!" cried Danby Druce, in tones of hoarse with horror.

"It is for the sake of one I hold very dear that I consent," replied the girl, her pale face flushing as she allowed her eyes to rest for a moment upon her lover's face.

"Mary, it shall not, it cannot be!" shouted Danby Druce. "The greatest torture wreaked upon this defenceless body will be as nothing in comparison with the thought that I leave you defenceless in yonder monster's power!"

"The promises given, the compact made; you cannot draw back now," came in stern, cold tones from the weird horror's lips.

Then, at a sign from the Winged Man, Deborah laid her hand on Mary Evanson's shoulder, and let her, unresistingly, away.

"Has the iron entered your soul, Danby Druce? Does your heart swell as though it would burst with agony?" hissed the Winged Man thrusting his fearful visage close to the detective's perspiring brow.

"Fiend, monster, have you no mercy?" shrieked the tortured man.

"None!" came in deep reverberating tones from the Winged Man; whilst, as though to ratify his declaration, the stately building shook beneath a deafening crash of thunder.

Turning his back on the detective, the Winged Man stamped three times upon the stone flagged floor.

Immediately a door opened, and the stunted, misshapen form of the Winged Man's familiar appeared. Ghat's hideous face was contorted by a malicious leer as he led forward a tall, thin-faced, sallow-looking man of about fifty.

It was a registrar from a neighbouring town, whom the Winged Man had torn from his home the previous night and borne, paralysed with terror, to Peril Castle, where he had been kept a close prisoner ever since.

The registrar's eyes wandered round the crypt until at length they fixed themselves upon the Winged Man and his ironed prisoner. A loud cry of terror on his lips, he would have fled had not Ghat seized him by the wrist.

"Advance! For nothing; no harm shall be for you. You were brought here to join in wedlock to eager souls. Your fee shall be a thousand pounds," promised the Winged Man.

"And if I refuse?" demanded the registrar.

The Winged Man's whole frame seemed to swell. A look of almost unearthly rage convulsed his face, whilst, as though to add increased terror to his appearance, a flash of forked lightning swept through the window, and wound itself for a moment around his awful frame.

With a cry of terror, the registrar clasped his hands to his eyes to shut out the fearful sight, then fell upon his knees.

"Arise! You have had your answer. Fearful indeed is the fate of those who dare to disobey the Winged Man!" cried that awful being, as he resumed his former calm attitude.

Trembling in every limb, the registrar arose, and stood gazing, as though fascinated, upon the Winged Man's fearful form.

"Remain here! Move a step on peril of your life. Soon the couple whom you have to join together will come before you," ordered the Winged Man, as he strode to the apparently blank wall at the end of the crypt, which, to the registrar's horror, opened of its own accord to receive him.

THE MARRIAGE IN THE CRYPT.

It is impossible to describe Danby Druce's feelings as he awaited, helpless even to raise a finger to alter the course of events, the strange tragedy that was being enacted before his eyes.

A glance at the trembling form of the registrar warned him that an appeal to that gentleman would be worse than useless.

Besides, not for himself, but for Mary Evanson's sake, he hesitated to do aught to thwart the Winged Man, unless he could have seen a way to have done so effectually.

All seemed so blank, hopeless, and despairing, that even Danby Druce's brave spirit was subdued.

He was aroused from the bitter reverie into which he had fallen by the opening of the secret door in the end of the wall, through which the Winged Man had disappeared, and the entrance of two forms muffled from head to foot in black.

Well he knew those features were hidden by those fearful veils. The taller could be no other than the Winged Man; the other, the woman he loved so dearly.

As the strange pair walked slowly up the aisle, Danby Druce looked in wonder around. So penetrating that even the crash of the thunderstorm raging without could not drown its solemn notes, the "Wedding March" swelled from some unseen instrument through the crypt.

It was an impressive scene. The detective fastened upright to the stone pillar, the white-faced, trembling registrar standing with open book by his side; whilst, mouthing and gibbering, Ghat was crouched at his feet, his deep-set eyes flashing like sparks of light from beneath his shaggy eyebrows, and two muffled forms advancing up the aisle, followed by Judas and Deborah Darby, who were to act as witnesses.

As one in the grip of a fearful dream, the registrar went through the simple ceremony, until at length he pronounced the words which made the pair one.

At that moment an invisible hand snatched the man's black garment aside, revealing, not the stern, awful features of the Winged Man, but the trembling, half-frightened, half-excited face of Lord Hawkhurst.

"Ho, ho! He, he!" burst in a shrill laugh from Ghat's lips, as he bounded grotesquely forward, crying:

"Hearty congratulations Lord Hawkhurst! Surely the time has come when you may look upon your bride's lovely face! Unveil, sweet one!" he added, turning to the other black-robed figure. "Let your husband feast his eyes upon your loveliness."

"Yes, yes, dear; he is right. It is usual for the bridegroom to be the first to embrace the bride on these occasions."

As Lord Hawkhurst spoke he laid his head upon the clinging, black garment and moved it aside.

The next moment he staggered back with a scream of rage and disgust as the cloak fell to the ground, revealing the form of a wrinkled, grey-headed, toothless old woman.

"Duped! Fooled!" came in an angry roar from Lord Hawkhurst's lips; whilst his newly-wedded wife uttered a loud, cackling laugh which sounded almost as horrible as the peals of mocking laughter that seemed to come from every corner of the crypt at once.

"Come, deary, won't ye kiss your little wifie?" she asked, leering into her husband's face.

"Avaunt, hag! This is no marriage! It cannot be—it shall not be legal!" shrieked Lord Hawkhurst.

"I am afraid it is, my lord," interposed the registrar.

An angry retort rose to Lord Hawkhurst's lips, but ere it could find utterance the Winged Man appeared suddenly by Danby Druce's side.

"My hearty congratulations, Lord Hawkhurst," he said, with a mocking bow to the old hag who, grinning fearfully, answered his congratulations with a low curtsy.

Judas and Deborah Darby," continued the Winged Man, as he pointed to an open door, "Go! As a reward of your treachery, the contents of the iron-bound chest in the secret room are yours!"

"No, no; it is mine—the careful hoarding of years! I will not be robbed!" interposed the baron, stepping forward as though to follow his delighted servants.

The Winged Man laid two icy-cold fingers upon his chest, and the wretched man remained motionless as though rooted to the ground.

"Listen, unworthy descendant of an ancient house! The world was before you; you could have done much, you chose to do little. Lest a wife should dissipate your hoarded gains, you refused to marry until I tempted you with one of the purest, noblest women who ever walked the earth! Then, though you know that by wedding her young years to your wasted, old age you would bring misery upon her, you hesitated not a moment. See! I have given you a wife more suited to your years. One whom you once robbed of her little all, then left to live or die as best she might."

"My gold—my gold!" was all the wretched man could utter, ere, with a piercing shriek, he fell senseless to the floor.

Turning contemptuously from the unconscious lord, the Winged Man thrust a role of notes into the registrar's hands, saying:

"Go! Let this night's work be for ever a secret locked within your bosom, or it were better for you that you had never been born!"

Glad to escape with the enormous fee he had never for a moment hoped would really be his, the delighted registrar hastened from the crypt.

"Danby Druce," said the Winged Man, turning to the detective, "we will meet again!"

Stamping upon the floor, it opened, and he disappeared beneath the flag stones, whilst the thunder rolled and lurid, electric flashes lighted the crypt. Then all was dark, and a silence as of the grave obtained around.

THE ESCAPE.

Anxiously Danby Druce sought to pierce the darkness which hemmed him in on every side. What would be his fate? He knew the secret of the crypt was known only to Lord Hawkhurst and the Winged Man. Was he doomed to hang there until starvation had accomplished its fell work?

And what of Mary Evanson—the lovely, gentle Mary, in whose company he had hoped to spend so many happy years?

Despair gripped his heart. If he could but be assured that she was safe, he felt he could have met any fate with equanimity.

A deep, long-drawn moan of utter misery burst from his lips. The next moment he raised his head and listened eagerly.

"Danby—Danby! Speak to me! Where are you, dear one?"

Could he believe his ears? The voice was that of the lovely girl who had occupied his thoughts.

"Mary, can it be you?" he cried hoarsely.

The next minute a shadowy form flitted through the darkness, and a feeling of intense joy surged up in his heart, as he felt a pair of loving arms in circling his neck, and loving kissing pressed upon his lips.

"Hush! Not a word! I have escaped! We may yet escape the Winged Man's clutches!" whispered Mary.

The next moment Danby Druce felt the iron clasp which held his throat removed, and he was free.

One long, passionate embrace, and the two glided towards the door by which Mary Evanson had entered the crypt. Cautiously they threaded the tortuous passages of the old castle, until at length the courtyard was reached, and they stood hopefully before the castle gate.

It was locked, but even as they stood, undecided which way to turn, a light appeared at the further side of the courtyard. Crouched in the doorless entrance to what had been the castle's guard-room they saw Deborah and Judas Darby, carrying an ironbound chest which tested their united strength to the utmost to lift, staggering towards them.

Scarce daring to breathe, Danby Druce and Mary Evanson watched the villainous couple unlock the gate, and disappear with their prize in the darkness without. A minute later Danby Druce and his sweetheart had followed and were free.

"Quick, Danby, run; I will not feel safe until we are at my uncle's house again!" gasped Mary.

Danby Druce shook his head, but did not quicken his pace.

"You know not the Winged Man, Mary, or you would be certain that we would not have moved an inch without his leave," he replied.

"Do you think he has forgiven us, and will leave us in peace?" she asked.

"The Winged Man never forgives nor forgets!" came in deep, threatening accents from immediately above their heads.

They looked up, and there, hovering in the dark, cloud-riven sky, was the indistinct, yet fearful form of their dread enemy. The next moment he had disappeared, and the two continued upon their way; Danby Druce fearing every moment lest Mary Evanson should be torn from his grasp, for well he knew that the Winged Man took a fiendish delight in playing with the hopes and fears of those in his power as a cat plays with the mouse.

Yet nothing happened, and some half-hour later Danby Druce and Mary Evanson entered Mr. Trent's door.

Early the following day Judas Darby was arrested in York for attempting to pass false coin. Upon the police visiting the room the worthy couple had taken upon their arrival at York that morning, they found an iron-bound oak chest, filled with spurious coin.

Not daring to say whence they had obtained the chest, Judas Darby and his wife met the fate the Winged Man intended, and was sentenced to a long term of imprisonment for passing the false money which the Winged Man had substituted for Lord Hawkhurst's treasure.

A LONG FAREWELL.

A heavy, oppressive fog hung upon the river is the good ship Maori forged her way slowly down the Thames' estuary. Leaning over the rail beneath the shelter of the starboard lifeboat was Mary Evanson, beside her Danby Druce.

After a long and bitter struggle Danby Druce had steeled himself to part from the girl who, but for the Winged Man, would at that moment have been his wife. He would not allow her to link her life to his, knowing that at any moment the Winged Man might sweep him from his path and leave her a widow. She was leaving him, may be forever, on a visit to some relations who owned a sheep-farm in Australia, and Danby Druce was accompanying her as far as Dover, where he intended going ashore in the pilot-boat.

"I wish, Danby, you were going with me, or would let me stay and share your peril is with you," said Mary, looking appealingly into her lover's face.

"I can do neither, Mary; you would not wish me to turn my back on the path of duty," replied Danby Druce. "Owing to the failure of the American detectives to capture the Winged Man, the British Government have once more turned to me for assistance. Besides, dear one, even the other end of the world would not be far enough removed to secure you from the Winged Man's vengeance. Whilst you remain unmarried, I feel convinced he will not molest you, but every moment we spend together only increases your peril. Come, dear, let us forget the misery of the present moment, the unhappiness of the past, and look forward to the time when, the Winged Man is captured or destroyed, a brighter, happier time will dawn for us."

"When that time comes, Danby, you will find me ready, waiting, and true," whispered Mary.

"I know it, Mary, and the knowledge will strengthen me to do my utmost to secure this weird horror, whose very presence is a curse upon whatever land he haunts!"

The next moment Danby Druce had drawn Mary closer to him, as from close at hand came the Winged Man's fearful, maddening laugh. He looked up. Perched like a bird of ill-omen on a davit crouched the Winged Man.

"Aho, Danby Druce! Mary Evanson will be an old, old woman as she marries you, if she waits until you, a mere, paltry earth-worm, can make good your boast, and lay the Winged Man by the heels!" laughed the weird horror "it is well you leave the ship at Dover, or, by my power, I swear she should never reach her destination! Go, Mary Evanson! In your new home beneath the Southern Cross may every happiness await you; but remember that, whatever his faults, whatever crimes may be attributed to him, the Winged Man loved you as seldom has woman been loved before!"

Then, his low, wailing cry striking a deathly chill to the hearts of all who heard it, the Winged Man rose from the davit, and the next moment was lost to view in the thick fog through which the ship was slowly feeling her way to sea.

But, though unseen, the Winged Man did not leave the vicinity of the ship. Borne forward upon his broad pinions, the weird horror sword unseen above her decks, his keen eyes piercing the thick, white mist as he kept guard over the ship which contained the woman he loved.

Her syren sending its strident notes over the mist-laden river, the Maori at length reached the Nore. So slow, however, was the journey that night fell, and still the ship had scarcely rounded the South Foreland.

Fain would Mary Evanson have remained on deck, to have seen the last of her gallant lover, but it was bitterly cold, and, anxious to spare her the pang of a last farewell, Danby Druce insisted up on her retiring to her cabin shortly after dinner. Then, the captain of the steamer being an old friend, he joined him on the bridge, when, lighting a cigar, he leaned against the weather-rail and smoked in silence.

A WEIRD STEERSMAN.

During the fog is the most anxious time a ship's master can experience, and Danby Druce was too good a sailor to attempt to distract the officer's attention by idle conversation.

"Hoot! Hoot! Hoot!"

The captain of the Maori paused in his restless striding up and down the bridge, and, leaning out into the fog, tried to pierce the thick void that had the bows of the ship from view.

"Hoot! Hoot! Hoot!" replied the Maori's syren; answered a minute later by the unseen vessel which was evidently bearing rapidly down upon them.

No wonder the captain's nervous fingers closed tightly around the icy-cold iron railing which protected the bridge. Already he had signalled 'Dead slow' down to the engine-room, whilst, standing by the wheel, he tried to make his sense of hearing take the place of sight.

It was an awful moment. He had done all that human skill could contrive to avert a catastrophe, and knew that his fine vessel and the four hundred lives on board her were now at the mercy of the merest chance.

"Hoot! Hoot! Hoot!"

The sound seemed to come immediately over the port bow.

"Starboard on your life!" cried the captain, his hand on the brass handle of the telegraph.

The next moment he was held against the weather-railing, whilst the steersman, torn from his wheel, was thrown into Danby Druce's arms, who gazed in dismay as the fearful form of the Winged Man, tall, rigid, and commanding, took command of the vessel.

Twirling the wheel rapidly round until it was "Hard aport," the Winged Man reached forward, and, grasping the handle of the telegraph, pulled it with the jerk to "Full speed ahead."

Barely had the answering tinkling of the bell from the engine-room reached his ears, ere the vessel trembled beneath her mighty engines, and the next moment she began to move swiftly through the waters.

Even as she did so a cry of alarm from the bows was passed from lip to lip to the bridge. A huge, black hole had emerged from the fog, and a mighty British battleship glided past the Maori, so close that one of the torpedo-net supports swept away the stern railing.

Leaning with ashen face against the weather-rail, the captain of the Maori watched the Winged Man whirl the wheel around with practised hand, until the ship was on her proper course once more, and knew that their weird steersman had saved the ship. Had he kept upon a starboard course, deceived by the echoes which always sound in a fog, he would have plunged his ship bow foremost into the mighty mass of iron they had just seen gliding slowly past.

"Whoever you are, if you are Davy Jones himself, I owe you a debt of gratitude! But for you, the ship would be already taking her last plunge beneath the waves!" cried the captain, approaching their rescuer.

The Winged Man turned his white face upon the speaker, but not a word escaped his lips as he stood at his self-appointed post, now whirling the wheels this way, now that.

Overawed by the Winged Man's fearful appearance, the captain remained silent, until the pilot drew his attention to the fact that, though they could not see a cable's length ahead, the Maori was rushing at full speed through the fog.

He moved towards the Winged Man, but Danby Druce laid a restraining hand upon him.

"Remain still, on your life!" he cried. "The Winged Man knows what he is doing!"

And as they seemed to glide, as though by magic, from the track of all the other vessels which had filled that narrow sea, the captain held his peace.

Little the passengers, settling down for the voyage in the well-furnished saloon below, guessed whose hand was guiding them safely through the fog.

Presently the Winged Man rang the engine down to "Dead slow," then to "Stop," and, extending his right hand, uttered the single word—"Dover!"

The four men on the bridge gazed at him in amazement. Naught but fog could be seen on every side. How, then, could their weird steersman know that the town lay so close?

"Farewell, Danby Druce, or let it be au revoir, for of a certainty we will soon meet again!" pronounced the Winged Man. "Let this knowledge comfort your mind. So long as Mary Evanson and you remain apart no harm shall befall her!"

"For that I thank you! For the rest—afloat, ashore, on the earth, or in the air, I will seek you as a man seeks his deadliest foe!" replied the detective. Then, shaking hands with the captain, he descended to where a pilot-boat awaited them by the side of the vessel.

As the pilot stepped into his yawl, the sailors, who had been holding the boat off the vessel's side, looked at him in amazement.

"Hang it, Bill, it beats me how you picked us up as you did! We couldn't see a dozen yards ahead of us, yet the Maori came gliding out of the fog and stopped alongside our craft," said one. "And we here, not a hundred yards from the harbour's mouth, either! We didn't expect you down just yet."

"Only a hundred yards from the harbour?" ejaculated the pilot. "It's a mercy we didn't run into the breakwater!"

"No wonder at all," interrupted Danby Druce. "If you knew the strange being who has taken the Maori under his charge as well as I do, you would know that the thickest fog which ever hung over sea or land has no terrors for him."

"Well, I'm not saying as you are wrong," returned the pilot; "seeing the way he brought us down. Anyhow, I'm glad to be in my own boat again; yon chap is not the kind of mate I would choose for a long voyage."

In the meantime the Maori had continued on her way, dashing ahead through the fog at full speed once more. Gladly would the captain have expostulated, but he dare not utter a word. There was that in the weird being's very look which enforced silent obedience.

Hour succeeded hour, day broke, night fell; day broke, and again night spread its able mantle over the sea, yet, motionless, save when he made the spokes of the wheel revolve beneath his strong hands, the Winged Man remained at the wheel, an object of terror and wonder to passengers and sailors alike.

It was not until about eight bells on the third night, when the beams of the lighthouse on the Caskets flashed over their stern, that the Winged Man, relinquishing his hold of the wheel, rose in the air, and, uttering his loud, mournful, nerve-destroying cry, flew swiftly northwards.

BENEATH THE STREET.

Silently, cautiously, day in, day out, a dozen feet beneath the level of the busy street, the Winged Man bored with tireless energy, filling skipped after skip with earth which Ghat, breaking into dust, emptied into a sewer, that it might be carried away to the sea.

It was a strange, twisting passage the Winged Man had dug, now diving beneath a water-main, now turning to right or left to avoid some man-hole leading into a sewer, or sinking to borrow beneath the foundation of the mighty building.

A score of men could scarce have accomplished in a month what the Winged Man had done in a week, as he zigzagged his way beneath the ground towards the iron and cement bolts of the Grand National Safe Deposit Company.

A huge advertisement, placarded all over the British Isles, in which he was represented as standing, foiled and defeated, before the fire and thief-proof vaults of the Grand National Safe Deposit Co., had been accepted by the Winged Man as a challenge.

Having hired a house opposite the premises, he was burrowing his way beneath the street towards his goal, his only confidants and assistance the dwarf Ghat, and one of his spirit-broken white slaves, brought from his Yorkshire lair for the purpose, who, posing as a tobacconist, occupied the lower floor of the small shop opposite the National Safe Deposit Co.'s premises, from which the Winged Man had started his herculean task.

At the back of the shop was a bed-room where the assistant slept, and beyond that the laboratory, where the Winged Man prepared the acids and noiseless explosives he used in his excavations.

Prone on the floor at the further end of the tunnel the Winged Man lay, studying a skilfully-executed plan of the National Safe Deposit's buildings. He had already burrowed beneath the foundations of the building, as the red, tortuous line along the plans proclaimed.

Betwixt the weird horror and his booty was but a few feet of hard London clay and the iron and concrete floor of the vaults, yet the Winged Man's fingers traced a path even deeper into the heart of the building.

"It is here I must emerge," he murmured, laying the nail of his long, thin little finger upon an eight-cornered vault in the centre of the premises, "for there is stored the gold reserve of a dozen banks. Ho, ho! Bitterly shall they regret the insulting poster! Poor fools, to think that even were there treasure buried a mile deep beneath the surface of the earth it could escape the Winged Man!"

Rising, he thrust the plan into his pocket; then, armed with an instrument that looked like one of those small chemical fire-extinguishers one sees in motor-'buses, on underground railways, and many private houses, he directed the nuzzle towards the rugged end of the tunnel, and turned on a small tap.

Immediately a tiny stream of liquid spurted out. It was a recently-discovered acid possessed of the power of eating its way through stone and soil as a drill bores through rock.

It was wonderful to see the solid stone turned to liquid as this powerful acid touched it, until a hole a foot in-depth had been excavated.

Inserting a glass phial in the hole, to which was attached a slow-match, the Winged Man applied a match to the fuse and stepped back.

A noise, not louder than that made by a cork flying from a ginger-beer bottle, sounded through the tunnel, which was filled the next moment by a thin, almost invisible cloud of steam-like smoke, that made the eyes smart, and left a bitter taste upon the tongue.

Then the face of the tunnel seemed to crumble into loose soil, which the Winged Man shovelled rapidly into skips, and passed on to Ghat for removal.

A few hours later he ceased his work of excavation, and, a triumphant smile on his lips, commenced boring his way upwards.

Presently an irregular circle of smooth, grey-white cement was revealed immediately above the Winged Man's head. It was the lower floor of the Safe Deposit Co.'s premises.

Had the unseen worker been any other but the Winged Man he might well have retreated before the apparently impenetrable barrier of cement and steel above his head. But what was impossible to others was but a work of time for the Winged Man.

A shouted order to Ghat, and the misshapen little form, appeared staggering beneath the weight of a huge screwjack, which the Winged Man stood immediately beneath the centre of the cleared space; then, turning its handle, pressed its flat top against the exposed piece of flooring.

This done, he brought the acid into use once more, and, clinging to the perpendicular walls of the tunnel, as a fly clings to a window-pane, cut a circle round the cement, until at length, his work done, he lowered the powerful screw with a portion of the floor upon it. The impossible had been proved possible. A way had been cut into the most secure room in the whole building.

IN THE MIDST OF HIS TRIUMPH.

Soaring through the opening, the Winged Man gazed triumphantly around the strong-room, which was illuminated by the beams from his wondrous headlight.

To right and left arose huge iron safes, each bearing the name of some well-known bank.

Manufacturers are wont to boast that they can make safes which will defy the skill of the cleverest cracksmen, whilst, on the other hand, those who have made burglary a fine art declare that the safe has not yet been made which, given time and proper tools, they cannot open.

Truth to tell, the combined skill of the most accomplished scoundrels in Europe would have been taxed to the utmost to have opened even the simplest of safes upon which the Winged Man gazed, yet within twenty minutes the dread being had the first safe open, and its golden contents at its mercy.

The Winged Man chuckled softly as, unfastening one of the bags of specie, he plunged his hand to the wrist amidst its golden contents. Then he stabbed twice upon the floor, and Ghat appeared, bearing on either hand a pail, one of which was empty, the other filled with round pieces of metal about the size of a sovereign.

Emptying bag after bag into one pail, the Winged Man refilled them from the other. By the time this was done Ghat had returned with two similar receptacles, then hastened off, bearing the filled pails with him. For hours the work proceeded, until two of the saves had been emptied, and though Winged Man was richer by over half a million sterling.

There was little chance of interruption. Save at stated periods, when representatives from the banks examined their saves to assure themselves that they had not been tampered with, and on the rare occasions when the reserve gold was needed, nobody entered the room, whilst the very thickness of the walls and doors made it impossible for sound or light to penetrate from the interior.

Presently there came a pause in the work of robbery. Ghat was longer than usual on his errand of emptying a pail into rough packing-cases in the laboratory at the back of the tobacconist's shop.

"The dog grows lazy!" muttered the Winged Man. "No matter, I can utilise the time by opening the other safes."

The third and fourth safe opened, the Winged Man desisted from his labours for a moment, then strode angrily towards the hole in the floor.

"Ghat, you dog, stir your clumsy limbs, or it will be the worse for you!" he cried, in a low, hoarse, angry whisper, confident that the tunnel, acting as a speaking-tube, would carry his voice right across the street to his other entrance.

There was no reply. Muttering angrily, the Winged Man snatched up the filled pail, and, descending into the tunnel, made his way, with fierce, angry strides, down, muttering threats of vengeance against his lazy servant as he did so.

Half-way betwixt the Grand National Safe Deposit Co's buildings and the shop, he stopped, puzzled, before what looked like a slender rope drawn across his path.

With an ejaculation of annoyance he seized it to throw it from him. The next moment he felt as though a thousand exultant demons were pulling at his very nerve, twisting his every muscle, whilst shock after shock swept through his contorted frame.

A wild, fierce, angry yell burst from the Winged Man's lips when he realised that what he had taken to be rope was an unprotected cable bearing the current for the electric tramways which thundered overhead.

The fearful shocks which rent his frame would have slain any except one so wondrously endowed as the Winged Man; but he, bringing his wondrous knowledge of electricity to bear, rapidly disengaged himself from the deadly grasp of the highly-charged cable; then, diving beneath it, continued on his way.

Presently he came to an abrupt halt, and looked searchingly around. He was in a narrow chamber immediately beneath the shop. Instinct warned him of danger, and the presence of foes.

A triumphant smile upon his lips, he moved cautiously forward. Barely had he taken a couple of steps air a noose fell over his shoulders, he was tripped up from behind, and the next moment four pairs strong hands were thrown around him.

In vain the Winged Man struggled. Ten minutes before he could easily have thrown off his would-be captors, but now, his muscles still quivering from the fearful force of the electricity which had passed through them, he could offer little resistance, and a few minutes later he found himself lying, bound and helpless, on the floor of the tunnel, with Josiah B. Falter, Todd Merton, and two other American detectives bending triumphantly over him.

THE PRISONER.

"Wall, I guess you're fairly copped this time, Winged Man!" said Falter exultantly, kicking his prisoner in the ribs.

The weird horror deigned no reply, but the look he cast upon the speaker caused the triumphant smile to fade from Falter's lips, and he moved instinctively back from the presence of his bound captive.

"Come, boys," he continued, rapidly recovering himself, "Haul the flying cuss along; he shall lie on his gold until we have made up our minds what to do with him!"

Beckoning Todd Merton to follow, he clambered up the rough wooden steps that gave admittance through a trapdoor into the apartment at the back of the shop, where they paused, and, bending down, assisted the other two men to raise the Winged Man's bound form through the opening.

As the Winged Man gazed round upon a number of packing-cases, many of which were filled almost to the top with sovereigns, he discovered the cause of Ghat's mysterious delay stretched upon the floor, a nasty bruise in the centre of his forehead, was the Winged Man's faithful but hideous friend.

As he looked round, the door was softly opened, and the man he had put in charge of the shop stole silently and, casting fearful glances at the Winged Man as he did so.

The weird horror transfixed the man who had proved a traitor with his fearful gaze.

In vain the wretch, his nerves already shaken by the fearful treatment he had experienced at the Winged Man's hands, tried to withdraw.

The Winged Man's gaze held him fast. A low, shuddering moan burst from his lips. Suddenly his knees gave way. He fell upon the floor, and raised his outstretched hands appealingly towards his dread master, who, although bound, and helpless, and a prisoner had exercised such fearful influence over him.

"Mercy! Forgive! Anything but that! Kill me! Tear me limb from limb, but not that—not that!"

"Why, you coward, what's up with you? The Winged Man can't hurt you!"

"He can; he will! I am lost! Why didi you ever tempt me with hopes of freedom from his power? I am doomed—doomed to the fearful torments of the ice-hole!"

"Pshaw! The man is mad! Pay no attention to him!" growled Todd Merton contemptuously.

"Mad? Would that I were! The Winged Man never allowed his victims the luxury of forgetfulness!" shrieked the man. "Be warned, release him, and on your knees beg his forgiveness, or dread his anger!"

Loud, contemptuous laughter burst from the four men.

"Not much, sonny! I guess I am top-dog this time!" laughed Falter. "Here, stop! Where are you going?"

The man who had moved towards the door turned a pair of lustreless, despairing eyes on the speaker.

"Back from whence I came—back to the fate which is ever that of a traitor to the Winged Man!"

"Seize him, Jake! Don't let him go! He'll give the whole show away!" cried Falter, in alarm.

One of the Americans seized the man by the arm, but he flung him off with a strength which sent him rolling heavily against the wall, then glided into the street.

"Quick, Merton, after him! If he blabs we are done!"

Then for the first time, the Winged Man spoke.

"Stop!" he ordered, in the tones of stern command. "Fear not; he will turn neither to the right nor left, nor speak a word until tortures such as you cannot dream rack his frame in the ice-hole!"

Falter gazed in a species of terrified surprise at the Winged Man.

There was an air of confidence in every word he uttered, which told the Americans that he spoke the truth.

"Kind of mesmerism, I suppose," he surmised. "No matter if it is, the poor beggar will be set free before he reaches Yorkshire—that is, if your power ceases with your life.”

A low, chuckling laugh was the Winged Man’s sole reply to this ominous speech.

“You may laugh, my flying friend, but we have had too much trouble to catch you to risk letting you go!” continued Falter, shiveringly, he scarce knew why.

“Aren’t you going to hand him over to the British Government and get the reward, Jos?” asked one of his companions.

“What, and give up our share of the boodle?” laughed Falter. “Not much! We’ll just make sure Spring-heeled Jack here can’t return to interfere with us; then we’ll scoop in the rest of the gold and clear off rich men for life!”

A fearful spasm of rage convulsed the Winged Man’s frame, and the cords which bound him creaked until his captors feared he would break them asunder.

It was not that he feared their threats; it was the insulting name—Spring-heeled Jack—which, though he knew it not, had doomed Josiah B. Falter to the worst the Winged Man could inflict upon him.

As suddenly as they had risen all signs of rage departed from the Winged Man’s face, and he lay perfectly motionless, whilst his four captors consulted in low, excited whispers.

°THE CREMATORIUM.

Shortly afterwards one of Falter’s subordinates left the shop, and disappeared amidst the crowd of clerks, assistants, and others hastening homewards after their daily toil.

About nine o’clock a motor-lorry, driven by Falter’s messenger, drew up at the door of the shop, and a long packing-case, in which the Winged Man had been roughly thrust, was placed in it.

Then Falter looked up the shop, and slipping the key into his pocket, joined the other three men in the lorry.

An hour later Falter and his companions stood before a large, dome-shaped building, from which radiated a soft, subdued light, showing the intense heat which raged within.

It was a crematorium, recently erected on the outskirts of London, around which were bare, deserted fields, already marked out in streets and roads, showing that the jerry-builder[50] had already fixed his evil grasp upon what was yet smiling country.

“Waal, Falter, you take the cake!” growled Merton. “Why you have gone to the expense of coming here and bribed the man in charge of this shanty to try and experiment, as you call it, to get rid of the Winged Man, when we could have knocked him on the head, and chucked him in the river without half the trouble, is more than I can say.”

° 5 JULY 1913.
[50] Slapdash construction, built with poor quality materials.

"And perhaps have him swim ashore, and work havoc on us all!" replied Falter. "No, no, Todd Merton! I have had enough of the Winged Man to last me a dozen lifetimes. Now I have got him I mean to make an end of him. Winged Man, or no Winged Man, there won't be much of him left after he has been in that raging furnace a few seconds!"

"Waal, perhaps you are right, Falter! Phew! It wouldn't be healthy for us about here if he escaped!"

"Nor, though you searched the world through, will you find a spot to hide you from my vengeance!" came in loud, deep, threatening accents from the Winged Man's lips.

All started, so still and quiet and he lain that they had deemed him unconscious.

"I'll take my chance of that, my friend!" laughed Falter triumphantly.

Todd Merton bent forward, and whispered something in the other's ear.

Falter's eyes flashed avariciously.

"Look here, Winged Man, I am not a cruel man by disposition. Live and let live is my motto! You swear to add a hundred thousand pounds to the little haul we have secured already from the Grand National, and perhaps we will content ourselves with keeping you a prisoner," he suggested.

Loud laughed the Winged Man.

"Why should I buy that which I possess already, and which you have not to sell?" he demanded. "Fool, do you think that even yonder furnace can rob the Winged Man of life?"

"Wall, I guess it'll go a good way towards it, anyhow!" laughed Todd Merton. "So you refuse?"

The Winged Man deigned no reply, and, after waiting a few minutes for an answer, Falter turned to his companions, crying:

"Perhaps it is better as it is. We'd never be certain of the fellow, no matter how we bound him down. Bring forward the trolly, Joe," he added, addressing the youngest of the four men, who moved to a small house, from which ran a pair of stout iron rails some ten feet from the ground.

Along these rails Joe drew a stout wire platform, and, depositing the Winged Man's unresisting form upon the rails, they bound him hand and foot to the platform; then Falter and Merton flung open a pair of heavy iron doors.

As they did so they started back, blinded by the fierce white glare revealed beyond the doors.

"Let him go!" ordered Falter.

As the clutch which held the suspended trolly motionless was removed the Winged Man shot forward into the white, glowing furnace.

A moment's silence followed.

J. B. Falter was the first to speak.

"Good-bye, Winged Man!" he cried mockingly. "We'll never meet again!"

His words were drowned in a loud explosion. Staggering back, the four men saw, to their horror, the dome of the crematorium burst into about a hundred pieces. A white pillar of intense heat flashed into the sky.

"What was that?" demanded Falter, clutching Todd Merton's arm.

"Something gone wrong with the works! The whole concern has bust up. But look, what is that? It is the Winged Man!" he added, pointing with a trembling hand to where, poised on outstretched wings, the weird horror hovered above the destroyed building.

THEIR DOOM PRONOUNCED.

In vain the American detectives drew their revolvers. The weapons fell from their nerveless grasp, as, uttering his wild, weird cry, the Winged Man swooped down from the dispersing cloud as though intent upon tearing his would-be murderers limb from limb.

Gladly would they have given all the gold in the Grand National Deposit's safes for power to have fled. Fear held them spellbound.

A shuddering cry passed from lip to lip, as, poised on widely outstretched wings, some twenty feet above their heads, the Winged Man surveyed his victims. Folding his mighty pinions, he dropped to a huge mass of masonry, torn by the fearful force of the explosion from the elaborate the decorated front of the crematorium, then, elbow on knee, chin in hand, gazed contemptuously upon the four men.

"On your knees, Yankee dogs!" he thundered.

And, eager only to avert the anger of the fearful being whose destruction they had sought to encompass, the four men cast themselves on the ground before the Winged Man.

"Listen to your doom, you cringing curs!" thundered the Winged Man, rising, extending his hand threateningly over them. "Listen, were the representatives of a braggard nation, you who have dared to lay your hands upon the Winged Man; you who, in your folly, and pride, thought to slay him and seize his treasure! What, did you think the task which proved too great for the greatest detective of his age, Danby Druce, could be accomplished by such as you? Hear, doomed wretches, the Winged Man's sentence: Joseph Dent, stand up!"

Trembling in every limb the youngest of the party obeyed.

"Doomed wretch, trembling at the bar of the Winged Man's justice, go! Upon the twenty-first of March next, you shall pay the penalty of your presumption."

Casting a terror-stricken glance at the Winged Man, Dent walked swiftly away until the outer gate of the crematorium reached, he took to his heels, and ran as though pursued by a thousand imps.

"Zachariah Dyson," continued the Winged Man, turning to the next man, "make what use you can of the next two months, upon the twenty-first of April my vengeance will crush you to powder go!"

Dyson needed no second order, but, fearful lest the Winged Man should change his mind and strike him down then and there, fled at the top of his speed in an opposite direction to that taken by his companion.

"Todd Merton, go!" hissed the Winged Man between his clenched teeth. "Hide where you may, bury yourself in the thickest forest of the South American Continent, or in the boundless steppes of Northern China, the sun which rises upon the twenty-first of May will be the last you will ever see!"

Dismissing the panic-stricken and trembling man with a wave of his hand, the Winged Man descended from the heap of masonry which had formed his throne of justice, and, striding to where Falter knelt, white to the very lips and trembling in every limb, stood gazing at him as though he would read the very secrets of his soul.

"Ho, ho Josiah B. Falter, you who sought to teach the British detective a lesson, are about to learn one which, if you lived a thousand years, you would never forget! Mark well the twenty-first of June. On that date, like a thunderbolt from the lurid storm-cloud, my vengeance shall overtake you."

Then answering the unspoken question in the wretched man's eyes, he continued:

"You deem yourself favoured that you have been allowed four months in which to hide yourself. Fool, he who has but a month is happier than you. His anxiety and anguish will soon be over, yours will linger over you, robbing you of sleep, and rendering your very food hateful to your lips. Farewell— remember the twenty-first of June!"

Opening his wings, the Winged Man rose from the ground and soared through the darkening twilight towards the city.

Left to himself, Josiah B. Falter followed the Winged Man's departing form until he disappeared in the mist-laden sky.

A deep sigh of relief burst from his lips, followed by a shudder which shook his frame from head to foot.

"The twenty-first of June," he muttered; "only four months! Surely within the wide bounds of earth and ocean there is some spot where even the Winged Man cannot find me!"

Ere accompanying the Winged Man on his return journey to the shop whence the subterranean excavations, bored under the National Safe Deposit's building started, we will follow, in their flight, the four men whose doom he had pronounced.

Each had taken a different way.

Careless of all else, save to leave England and the Winged Man behind them as soon as possible, wealth untold could not have induced them to return to the secret tunnel, for they felt convinced that thither the Winged Man would proceed them.

Twenty-four hours later the four men were making their way to different parts of the compass.

Joseph Dent was on board a liner bound for New Orleans, Zechariah Dyson had already shipped as an able-bodied seaman on board an Australian sailing-vessel lying in the London Docks. Todd Merton was in Paris on his way to Algiers, whilst Josiah B. Falter was being borne, as swiftly as an express engine could carry him, towards St Petersburg. Siberia, the land of immeasurable distance, was the place he had hit upon as a refuge, until the date named by the Winged Man had passed.

Yet, widely separated though they were, the first intimation they received that their flight was in vain came to each man at the same time.

Falter, sleeping in one corner of a first-class compartment, awoke with a start.

An unseen hand touched his shoulder.

"Remember the twenty-first of June!"

Seated in a third-rate café, in a small, unfrequented street of Paris, Todd Merton was trying to drown his terror with strong drink, when the same voice, and the same fearful warning, caused him to spring from his seat and dash madly into the street.

In a cabin of a liner, and in the fo'c's'le of a sailing-ship, Dent and Dyson each received a similar warning. Nor was that the worst. At regular intervals undeniable proof that in some wondrous way the Winged Man was keeping in touch with their most secret movements, drove the four unhappy wretches almost mad with despair.

GHAT'S ARREST.

To return to the Winged Man.

Night had fallen, and as the Winged Man remained poised unseen over the street in which the tobacconist's shop was situated, a spasm of fury shook his frame.

A large crowd had gathered round the building, kept back by a cord and of police, whilst men, whom the Winged Man recognised as Scotland Yard detectives, passed swiftly in and out of the little shop.

Alighting on the roof of the house, the Winged Man, clinging like a fly to the wall, crawled down it, until he reached the window that gave light to the little back room. As he pressed his face against the pains, he ground his teeth in fury.

The room was filled with police, between two of whom was the handcuffed form of his assistant.

The Winged Man's first impulse was to dash through the window, seize Ghat in his iron grip, and carry him off.

But the thought that Ghat had allowed himself to be caught, trapped, and filled by the American detectives, caused him to hold his hand.

As he gazed through the window his eyes passed lightly over the chests of gold.

They had a twofold interest for him now. enormous though the sum which had been at his mercy, it was not for gold, of which he possessed such enormous stores, that the Winged Man had undertaken single-handed a task which would have taken a small army of workmen to have accomplished in the time.

The poster we have before referred to had been proved a pictured lie, and his end was achieved.

Suddenly he started. The keen expression found on a fencer's face when he finds himself confronted by a foeman worthy of his steel flashed from the Winged Man's eyes as he saw Danby Druce, accompanied by a Commissioner of the City Police, enter the room, and he knew that he owed Ghat's arrest to the great detective.

Turning swiftly from the window, the Winged Man disappeared into the night.

When morning broke a cry of wonder flow from one end of London to the other. Working with the skilled touch of a true artist, the Winged Man had so changed the obnoxious posters that, instead of the Winged Man being depicted standing, baffled, before the safes in the strong room, he stood before an open safe, grinning with triumphant scorn upon the wealth at his mercy.

Then, for the first time, the directors of the Grand National Safe Deposit Company realised that it had not been their gold the Winged Man sought, so much as to prove his power and wondrous skill.

Alighting in a side street, the Winged Man mingled with the crowd, smiling sarcastically to himself as he listened to the exaggerated rumours that passed from mouth to mouth. Rumours of a whole army of winged men who had been engaged in digging the tunnel which the police had discovered, etc.

In the evening paper the Winged Man read that Ghat, who was known to be an accomplice of the flying terror, would be brought before the magistrates the following day, and undoubtedly committed for trial.

At the bottom of one column was a brief account of the explosion at the crematorium, which, however, none seemed to attribute to the Winged Man's agency.

Amongst the crowd that poured into the police-court the next morning to feast their eyes upon the one who was so nearly attached to the Winged Man as his faithful servant Ghat was the weird being himself.

None recognised in that quiet, retiring figure the man whose name was on every lip, none save Ghat, and he cast one swift, appealing a glance at the Winged Man, then kept his eyes sullenly cast down on the floor, whilst the Public Prosecutor went over the charge the police had brought against him.

Ghat had been taken red-handed; consequently, after a comparatively short sitting the magistrate committed him for trial at the criminal courts; and the Winged Man, passing out with the crowd, wandered thoughtfully about the streets.

THE TRIAL.
The court was crowded on the day when Ghat was brought before a judge and

jury on a charge of having, together with a certain notorious character, known as the Winged Man, made a burglarious entrance to the premises of the Grand National Safe Deposit Company.

A strange silence pervaded the court, outside which was paraded a battalion of guards, whilst the corridors and ante-rooms were patrolled by a strong force of police.

An air of expectancy, half of fear, hung over the building, for all realised the wondrous powers wielded by the weird being whose creature they were about to try.

The very ushers issued their orders in hushed, awed tones. Counsel and lawyers alike shared the feeling of uneasiness which hung like a black cloud over officials and public alike.

The only one who seemed wholly unmoved was Ghat, and he, from his place in the dock, scaled from beneath his bushy eyebrows upon the expectant crowd, as though, if he had the power, he would have slain them with a glance.

There was no defence, forget had angrily refused the services of an aspiring young barrister who had offered to defend him. Indeed, when the judge asked the usual question: "Who appears for the prisoner?" Ghat had thrilled the court by seizing the front of the dock in a paroxysm of rage, shaking it as though he would tear the stout wood to pieces, as he cried:

"He who served the Winged Man scorns to be defended by a worse robber than himself. Poor fools!" he added, glancing contemptuously round the court. "Think you that your soldiers or your police can injure the Winged Man's favourite slave! From the judge on his bench to the lowest menial in court, I scorn and defy you!"

Then he sank into sullen silence, and seemed scarce conscious of the fact that the trial affected him in any way.

To the disappointment of the public, there was little or no excitement throughout the whole proceedings.

The police had the case cut and dried, and the majority of those present was somewhat surprised, when the jury retired to consider their decision, that they had not given a verdict of "Guilty" without leaving the box.

As the jury filed out of the court the judge retired to his private room, and there, dismissing his attendants, spread out some papers upon a table, and was soon immersed in their contents.

A quarter of an hour later an usher informed the judge that the jury had returned.

It was remembered afterwards that the judge returned to his seat, his head bowed as though lost in thought, his face partially hidden by his wig.

"Gentlemen of the jury, have you arrived at your verdict?" he demanded.

"We have, my lord," replied the foreman.

"Guilty, or not guilty?" asked the judge, dipping his pen in the ink stand before him.

"Guilty, my Lord! The jury desire to add a rider 'that they trust ample provision will be made that one so closely connected with the hideous, black-hearted monster, the Winged Man, should not escape. And we further wish to express our gratitude to Mr. Danby Druce for—'"

"A doctor—quick! His lordship has fainted!"

The interruption came from the doorway of the judge's room, on the threshold of which stood a white-faced usher.

A momentary silence, broken by expressions of astonishment, and, here and there, titters of suppressed laughter followed.

"What do you mean, Mr. Nesbitt, by this disturbance?" inquired one of the officials, looking anxiously at the usher.

"What does it mean? I cannot understand it!" stammered the usher. "A minute ago, on entering the judge's room, I found his lordship stretched on the floor, unconscious, and breathing heavily. See?" he added, as he pulled the man towards him, and pointed with trembling hand into the room. "There he lies still upon the couch as I left him!"

Even at that distance there was no mistaking the judge's clear-cut features.

Both men hastened towards where an inspector of police was standing, surprised, and somewhat scandalised, by this unseemly interruption of the course of justice.

The counsel for the prosecution joined them.

"Who with yonder man?" he demanded, pointing to the judge upon the bench.

As the inquiry reached his ears, the judge rose from his seat, flung aside his wig and ermine robes, and the Winged Man stood revealed.

"I am the Winged Man!" he thundered.

Poised on outstretched wings beneath the embroidered canopy over the judge's seat, the Winged Man presented a fearful sight to the astonished spectators.

From each extended finger burned a steady flame, so bright, so intense, that it robbed daylight itself of half its power, whilst the bright glare from his fearful headlight now flooded the court with ruby red, now turned the pale faces of the alarmed spectators an ashen grey beneath its green beams.

It seemed as though the whole mighty concourse gazed upon the fable Gorgon's head, which was said to have the power of turning men into stone, for all gazed, paralysed with terror, at the weird horror.

For nearly a minute the Winged Man remained motionless; then, in response to an appeal from an inspector, a dozen policemen and twice as many civilians, rushed from the benches to seize the fearful apparition.

Motionless as a rock, the Winged Man awaited the attack. But just as a dozen hands were stretched forth to seize him, he raised his hands above his head as though in malediction, uttering his piercing, blood-curdling cry, and the next moment his attackers recoiled, thrilled in every vein by the fierce electric shocks which flashed from out the Winged Man's frame.

A loud, shuddering cry of terror burst from the spectators; then, seized in the maddening grip of unreasoning terror, they fled, shrieking and howling, fighting desperately towards the doors, which were soon to become blocked with a mass of struggling humanity.

Throughout the turmoil the inspector kept his head.

"Remove the prisoner!" he ordered. And the warders, whose attention had been concentrated upon the strange events taking place so close to them, turned to obey the order.

But Ghat had vanished.

Unnoticed in the excitement, he had slipped out of the back of the dock, and was already lost amongst the panic-stricken fugitives.

"Come on, inspector! Are you not going to arrest me? Or are you overawed by the majesty of this most puissant judge?" cried the Winged Man mockingly.

"If you were fifty times the supernatural being you are, you shall not escape this time!" cried Danby Druce, taking up the challenge. "Surrender! See, you have put yourself into a trap, from which there is no escape!"

As he spoke he indicated, with a sweep of his hand, an officer and a file of Grenadier Guards, who had gained admittance by way of the witnesses' door.

At the same moment a loud, sullen, angry roar burst from without for word had reached the gathering crowd in the street that the Winged Man was about to rescue the prisoner.

"Ho, ho!" laughed the Winged Man. "Fire, gentlemen of the King's Guards! A thousand pounds to the man who can shed so much as a single drop of my blood!"

A ragged volley rang out, followed by the patter of bullets upon the walls, the fall of plaster, the rending of wood, and the splintering of glass.

Yet, though it seemed impossible that any living creature could withstand so fearful a volley, at so short a range, a mocking peal of laughter showed that the Winged Man remained unharmed.

"Try again, gentlemen of the King's Guard!" he cried mockingly. "But, stay! Perhaps you are too good sportsman to aim at a stationary mark; see what you can do with flying game!" And, rising from the bench, he soared almost to the top of the lofty building, into the ceiling of which the bullets from the soldiers' rifles pattered like hail.

For a moment he clung to the ceiling, from whence he grinned deadly defiance at his foes, then a cry:

"He is hit—he is hit!" arose from the excited spectators as his feet released their hold of the ceiling, his body hung limp by the arms for a moment; then he dropped like a stone headforemost to the ground.

But even as his body touched the echoing boards, a deep, sullen roar filled the building, a brilliant ball of fire shone with dazzling brilliancy from the place where the Winged Man had alighted, to change the next moment to a thick, black column of smoke.

Half expecting to feel the building falling about their ears, police, soldiers, and officials, and the few spectators who had stood their ground, gaped in wonder and horror upon the black, impenetrable cloud.

Slowly the smoke dispersed; then cries of wonder and baffled rage echoed on all sides.

The Winged Man had disappeared!

GHAT'S ESCAPE.

In the meantime, using his long, misshapen arms, endowed with fearful strength, upon those pressing around him, Ghat had fought his way through the crowd into the Strand.

The exploding rifles within the building told that the Winged Man had not yet made good his escape, and, eager to make his way, unseen, to a place of safety, the dwarf was slinking through the crowd which blocked the whole of the open space near the church, when a man seized him by arm, crying:

"Look out, mates, this is Ghat, the Winged Man's accomplice."

With the snarl like that of an outraged beast, get turned upon his would-be captor, and, seizing him in his own grasp, hurled him, bruised and senseless, to the ground.

Then arose the angry roar which had reached the Winged Man's ears, as, with a loud shout of "Kill him! Out him! Tear the little wretch to pieces!" the mob flung themselves upon him.

The very fury of Ghat's assailants saved him. So eager were the crowd to strike one whom, as an associate of the Winged Man, they hated, with fist or stick, that as many blows were expended upon themselves as upon the snarling, foaming, animal-like form of the Winged Man's slave. His broad shoulders rising and falling, his bosom heaving with rage, his hideous head rolling from side to side, his face red eyes glaring savagely upon his foes, his huge, fang-armed mouth opening to hurl insults at his attackers, or closing to grind his misshapen teeth in fury, Ghat faced his foes like some fierce animal at bay.

Anger banished all thoughts of danger from his heart, and he fought with a fierce intensity which, for a moment, drove his assailants back.

Realising how great the odds were against him, Ghat sprang with the agility of the monkey he so much resembled, to the foot of the fire-escape which is always standing near the church, and a minute later was perched upon its swaying summit.

With yells of derisive laughter, the mob seized the handle of the escape, and began to lower the clinging Ghat into the outstretched arms of their companions, when a cry so wild, so fierce, so threatening, that it struck terror to all who heard it, from the summit of the Law Courts, caused them to release their hold.

"The Winged Man—the Winged Man!" came in a shuddering a moan from every lip, as the weird horror himself, diving from the top-most parapet of the magnificent pile of buildings which ornament the Strand, sped swiftly through the air, seized Ghat in his strong arms, and, ere the mob could recover from the consternation into which his sudden appearance had thrown them, had disappeared in the direction of the Thames.

Rending the air with loud, angry cries, the mob started in pursuit; but, though sweeping aside all opposition, they invaded the quiet precincts of the Temple, searched every house from cellar to garret, while the outskirts, overflowing to the Embankment, kept watch and ward over the Thames no sign of their dread foe and the one he had snatched from the hands of justice, could be seen.

That evening many who had witnessed the Winged Man's flight from the Law Courts were drawn to the Eldorado Theatre by the announcement that cinematograph pictures of the stirring events which had taken place in the heart of London that day would be exhibited.

They were, perhaps the most successful pictures the Eldorado management had ever produced. Spellbound, the audience saw the entrance of the Winged Man, disguised as one of his Majesty's judges, saw the dramatic interruption, which terminated in the Winged Man's disappearance in the pillar of smoke.

Then pictures from outside the Law Courts were shown.

There was the old church, the sea of faces filling the open space at its base, the sudden tumult that followed Ghat's discovery, the fight with the crowd, the swift rush up the fire-escape, the lightning-like sweep of the Winged Man, and the audience cheered to the echo as, with Ghat in his arms, the Winged Man flew from off the scene.

The picture vanished, leaving naught but a white, shimmering screen.

There was a slight commotion on the staging from whence the cinematograph was worked, but the audience paid little attention to it, all eyes were fixed expectantly upon the screen.

A strange thrill of excitement swept over the audience, as a tiny black speck, growing momentarily larger and larger appeared in the centre of the screen. Presently wings flashed from either side of the black speck, and with breathless excitement, the audience realised that it was a picture of the Winged Man himself coming towards them.

Nearer and nearer it grew. A shudder shook the audience from stalls to gallery, as, with every line of his clean-cut features, every fold of his wings, every line of his body, thrown out in clear relief, the Winged Man filled the centre of the screen as he gazed with a mocking smile on his lips, upon the breathless, astounded crowd.

The figure ceased to move; then gradually a cold chill of apprehension settled upon each heart, when all in that closely-packed audience realised that it was no living picture upon which they gazed, but upon the Winged Man himself.

Held mute by the wondrous power of those baleful eyes, the whole audience awaited, breathless and trembling, what new evil the Winged Man's unexpected presence might portend.

The silence was broken by a loud shriek of hysterical laughter, as a woman in the auditorium, unable to bear the fearful suspense, sunk into a chair, overcome with sudden hysteria.

As though the laugh had broken the fearful spell the Winged Man had placed upon them, the audience rose to their feet. But only to recoil as the Winged Man stepped to the footlights, ere, uttering his mournful, thrilling, nerve-racking cry, he rose slowly in the air, and with steady beats of his mighty pinions glided upwards to the moving roof, which opened to let him pass, and disappeared in the blackness of the night beyond.

The Winged Man suddenly appears in a cinematograph theatre.

THE TWENTY-FIRST OF MARCH.

On the north of the Panhandle district, in Texas, a mob of between four and five thousand steers were about to commence their long journey across the Indian Territory to Kansas City.

It was one of those fearfully hot, oppressive evenings, which, in the great American Continent, are always the precursors of a fierce electric storm.

The cattle felt the disturbing element in Nature as much as their human drivers, for they were restless, and the "boss" looked anxiously at the lowering skies.

Experience had taught him to dread these stormy evenings, when the slightest unusual sound would send the cattle under his charge rushing across the prairie in mad, headlong flight—a flight which no human being could control, for once cattle break they never stop till too exhausted to go another step.

Woe, then, to the luckless horse or man borne to the ground before their fearful charge. Sudden and hopeless as their fate. They are literally torn to pieces beneath the hooves of the galloping steers.

Consequently, when the day shift came off duty he ordered them to feed and water their horses, and return to assist the night-shift in keeping the herd from breaking.

Needless to say, having already been twelve hours in the saddle, the cowboys grumbled at this further extension of duty, although, as they knew how imperatively necessary the order was, they addressed their complaints to the weather instead of to the "boss."

There was one cowboy, however, who said nothing; and, having watered and fed his horse, he took his place in the long line of cowboys who were constantly riding round and round the outskirts of the herd.

Although he had only joined the party at the outset of the "trail," he had already earned for himself the nickname of "Sullen Joe," for he never spoke, save when addressed, and then only in monosyllables.

Though he had given his name as Joe Tenby, the reader last saw him slinking away from the crematorium on the outskirts of London, the doom pronounced by the Winged Man ringing in his ears.

Yes; it was Joe Dent, and the following day would be the one on which, unless he had successfully hidden his track, the Winged Man's vengeance would overtake him.

Needless to say, Dent felt little inclined to sleep, and, as night advanced, and the muttering of the rising storm grew nearer, he almost hoped that the cattle would break, and give him something to occupy his thoughts in place of the constant terror gnawing at his heart.

He had his wish. About midnight the storm broke in all its fury. Scarcely had the first clap of thunder died away ere it was echoed by a deep, and, in the cowboy's ears, more ominous roar, as, seized with mad terror, the cattle broke towards the south.

Joe Dent had craved excitement; he speedily realised that he was in for more than sufficient excitement for he was on the side on which the cattle broke, half-way between the horns of the herd.

Wheeling his horse round, he settled himself in the saddle to ride for life, casting now and again frightened glances over his shoulder at the countless fierce, shining eyes, wide, terrible horns, and red, open mouth of the steers, the whole frightful sight borrowing additional terror from the almost continual flashes of lightning which rent the darkening sky.

On he dashed, on and on, that mad charge of swiftly-beating hooves ever thundering in his ears, ever drawing closer and closer to him.

But though terror brought streams of cold perspiration running down his pallid cheeks, the thought that his death beneath the bullocks' hooves would balk the Winged Man of his vengeance, brought a strange kind of comfort to his heart.

Suddenly a wild cry of terror burst from his lips. His horse had thrust his hoof into a prairie-dog's hole, and had fallen heavily to the earth.

Scrambling to his feet, Dent ran hopelessly on. The thundering of the steers' hooves grew louder and louder each moment.

He threw a terrified glance over his shoulder. The long, black, threatening line was almost upon him.

Panting, he ran, until at length, with a cry of despair, he flung himself headlong upon the grass and awaited the end. Even as he did so, he felt himself seized in an iron grip and borne aloft!

Wonderingly, he saw the ever-moving bodies of the cattle pass beneath him; then he gazed upward, and, with a piercing cry of despair, strove to burst from the iron grasp which held him, for he had looked straight into the deftly-white face of the Winged Man.

A flood of hope filled his heart. The Winged Man read his victim's thoughts in his kindling eyes.

"You—you have saved my life!" muttered Dent incredulously.

"Because your time has not yet come. Tomorrow is March the twenty-first," replied the Winged Man.

Then, as the last of the cattle passed beneath them, he deposited the trembling man upon the ground and disappeared in the darkness.

For a few minutes Dent watched the disappearing herd of cattle, followed by swiftly galloping cowboys; then, clasping his hands despairingly to his brow, he strode off, caring not whither, so long as his trembling legs bore him far from the spot where he had last seen the Winged Man.

On and on, with stumbling steps and fear-laden eyes, he pressed. On throughout the night. On even when the sun rose and beat with pitiless fury upon his head.

Suddenly he came to an abrupt halt, and looked around with terror-laden eyes. His wandering steps had carried him far into the great alkali desert of North-Western Texas.

He turned to retrace his steps. As he did so his attention was attracted by what he at first took to be a vulture. A second glance sent the blood rushing swiftly backwards to his heart, and, with a low moan of terror, he plunged deeper into the desert, for well he knew that what he had taken to be a vulture was his inveterate foe, the Winged Man.

Terror-stricken, mad with fear, the wretched man stumbled on. Now trying to turn to the right, now to the left, but each time driven back by the fearful apparition, which was driving him deeper and deeper into the desert, as a sheepdog herds a wandering sheep.

At length, worn out, parched with thirst, baked with the heat which seemed to arise with redoubled strength from the ground, Joe Dent flung himself on the white, parched ground in the centre of a clump of cacti, or prickly pear-trees.

Even as he did so there was an ominous rattle, and a huge, diamond-eyed rattlesnake launched its fearful, fang-armed head at him.

But ere the reptile could plunge its fangs into his body a white hand clasped it round the neck and hurled it aside.

For the second time the Winged Man had saved his victim's life.

Despair gave Joe Dent courage. Staggering to his feet, he faced his fearful foe.

"To what awful fate am I doomed, that even death is forbidden me?" he demanded.

The Winged Man answered not a word. Drawing a long-bladed knife, such as is used for cutting sugar-cane, from the folds of his wings, he hovered over the thick stem of an enormous prickly pear, and commenced hacking away at it until he had scooped out the middle. This done, he lifted the unresisting man from the ground and dropped him into the hollow trunk.

"You fiend, you mean to leave me to perish miserably in this fearful prison?" gasped Dent.

"Do not be impatient to anticipate your fate," sneered the Winged Man. "Live and learn. Had you been wise you would rather have thought to thwart the tiger in its native jungle than the Winged Man," replied the weird horror, as he thrust his prisoner so far into the trunk of the tree that only his head showed between its quaint, thorn-surrounded branches.

With mocking words of farewell he rose in the air, and flew away, muttering as he did so:

"Farewell, Joseph Dent! You will never cross the Winged Man's path again!"

Finding himself alone, Dent strove to clamber from his prison. His heart almost ceased to beat as he realised that, though he had entered so easily, the top of the tree had already shrunk, so that he could not get his shoulders out.

In vain he sent piteous cries for help ringing over the desert. At first he deemed that he had been left there to perish miserably of thirst, but he very soon found that the Winged Man had been more merciful.

The sun's rays acting upon the sap left in the trunk of the prickly pear caused it to contract with irresistible force. Within an hour of the Winged Man's flight the first of his four foes had paid the penalty of his crimes.

°THE WINGED MAN'S VENGEANCE.

The Pacific Ocean was as smooth as a sheet of glass. Not even a catspaw ruffled the surface of the sleeping water, or played with the limp sails of the good ship Yukon, outward bound from San Francisco to Melbourne.

A huge ball of fire, the sun shone with fearful force from a cloudless heaven, scorching the deck until the tar bubbled from between the planks.

Seated in the shadow of the starboard lifeboat was Zachariah Dyson. Anxious only to escape from the Winged Man, he had fled half-way round the world, cleverly hiding his track as he went, until in San Francisco he had shipped as a deck-hand on board the Yukon.

Surely the forecastle of a sailing-ship in mid-Pacific would be a safe hiding-place from his fearful foe?

Yet so great was his terror of the Winged Man that it was not until they had passed the Golden Gate and had left the Californian coast well over their stern that Dyson began to breathe freely.

The morning of the Day of Doom had dawned. The fatal April 21st, upon which the Winged Man had sworn he should die, was upon him, and as, rising from the deck, he gazed around upon the boundless expanse of ocean, a feeling of elation filled his heart.

Not a living thing was in sight. It seemed as though the ship floated in an unknown, untraversed, uninhabited sea.

"Wall, I calculate the Winged Man is pretty considerably out of it this time," muttered Zachariah Dyson.

Even as the words escaped his lips a cry of horror sent cold chills chasing each other up and down his spine.

He looked in the direction from whence the cry had come, to see the second mate grasping the shroud of the mizzenmast with one hand, whilst with the other he pointed over the sleeping sea.

Despair eating at his heart, Zachariah Dyson followed the direction of his mate's extended hand, expecting to see the fearful form of his remorseless enemy swooping upon him from the cloudless heavens.

Instead, he saw a sight scarce less to be dreaded than the Winged Man.

Their spreading tops reaching almost to the sky, their huge, round stems, like elephants' trunks, swaying to and fro, their tapering ends gliding over the surface of the waves, three enormous waterspouts were approaching the doomed ship at express speed.

The mate's cry of horror had brought the crew, who, gasping for breath, had been stretched on the scorching planks on deck, or in the stifling cabins below.

All gazed in horror at the awful peril which had sprung upon them, as it were, out of nothing in the twinkling of an eye.

° 12 JULY 1913.

Rising, descending, contracting, expanding, moving now this way, now that, as though engaged in some fearful, weird dance, the waterspouts approached the Yukon.

Nearer and nearer they came. Helpless to raise a finger in their own defence, the crew awaited the end with blanched, terror-stricken faces.

A sigh of relief rose in one huge, gasping sob from the lips of the terror-stricken spectators, for when it seemed as though naught could save the vessel, the waterspouts had swept by with a roar as of a thousand thunders.

The next moment terror, wonder, and superstitious awe drowned their rising hopes, for, as though at the word of command, the mighty masses of whirling water had swept round, and were dancing towards the ship again.

A shriek, terror-laden, despairing, hopeless, rang out over the ship. The startled mariners turned to gaze with wondering, panic-stricken eyesas Zachariah Dyson, who, his mouth agape, eyes bulging as though they would start from his head, his hair on end, his face ashen-grey, was pointing with a hand that shook like an aspen-branch at the centre waterspout.

Curiosity conquering dread, the sailors followed with their eyes the direction of his outstretched hand; then, accustomed to the terrors of the deep though they were, each felt his heart sink like lead within his bosom, for, towering aloft upon the outer edge of the waterspout's extended summit, arose a tall, black, dark-clad, white-faced, majestic being, with pinions spread, his white, skeleton-like hands stretched towards the ship, as though he would draw her to her doom in the whirling waters.

Slowly the Winged Man—for the weird apparition was the flying horror—fixed his flashing eyes upon Zachariah Dyson; then, allowing one hand to drop by his side, beckoned the wretched man with the other.

A second fearful scream burst from the doomed man's lips.

"No, no! Mates, help! Hold me back! Don't let me go!" he cried, in tones of such a hopeless despair that the sailors shuddered as they listened.

The captain and two sailors would fain have gone to the wretched man's assistance, but horror held them as though turned to stone.

"Come Zachariah Dyson, for it is the twenty-first of April, and the Winged Man claims his prey!" came in thunderous accents from the weird horror.

Clambering on to the bulwark, Dyson paused to cast one last, appealing glance towards his mates.

"Come!" came in loud, reverberating accents of thunder from the Winged Man's lips.

None who heard the fearful cry with which Zachariah Dyson plunged into the sea will ever forget it. Rising to the surface, he was drawn as a magnet draws steel to the waterspout upon which the Winged Man stood enthroned.

A cry of horror burst from every lips as they saw the waterspout hover over where the wretched victim half swam, half floated on the agitated surface; then the huge, trunk-like cone descended, and sucked him up to its revolving interior.

The next moment the horrified witnesses of this fearful scene saw the struggling man appear on the outside of the huge column of water, then he was whirled swiftly upwards, ever upwards, until at last, with a cry of fiendish triumph, the Winged Man seized him by the arms and held his limp, panting, yet living form to his fearful side.

For nearly a minute he stood thus, whilst the fearful column of water roared and rolled around him. Rising on outstretched pinions, he soared a hundred feet in the air; then, his loud, mocking laughter sending spasms of icy terror through the spectators' veins, he dropped the writhing, struggling man into the centre of the waterspout.

As Dyson struck the massive column of water, it burst with a roar as of a thousand thunders ere it fell, a fearful mass, into the sea.

The next moment the sailors on board the Yukon were clinging to shrouds, belaying-pins, and masts for their very lives, for the vessel was lifted on the summit of a mighty wave, and then sank deep into the trough of the tempestuous sea, until her frightened crew thought she would never rise again.

But though tossed hither and thither like a cork on a mill-stream, she kept a level keel, and outrode peril.

Presently the water settled down, and many an anxious eye was cast over the troubled sea; but Zachariah Dyson had disappeared. The Winged Man's vengeance was complete.

THE TWENTY-FIRST OF MAY.

It was night on the boundless Sahara. As far as the eye could reach the pale beams of the African moon shone brightly over a level expanse of silver sand, broken here and there by tiny hillocks, where the wind had gathered the tiny grains together.

A mysterious, low, musical note, caused by innumerable particles of sand rubbing against each other, was the only sound which broke the deathly silence.

All else was still, save where a continuous fountain of sand rose in the air to leeward of one of the small hills we have before mentioned.

It was the Winged Man digging, digging, digging, as though engaged in the, even to him, impossible task of clearing the sand-submerged soil of the desert.

Hour after hour he laboured, ceaselessly, tirelessly, until at length he stood in the centre of the pit a good twenty feet in depth, its sides composed of shimmering sand.

Away to the north, hidden by a dip in the apparently level ground, a small oasis of palms grew round a tiny well, which bubbled like liquid silver beneath the rays of the steadily-shining moon.

In this oasis a man was encamped, his horse sleeping by his side.

The man was clad in the flowing burnous of an Arab chief; yet, as he tossed in sleep, the hood fell back from his head, revealing the crime-marked face of Todd Merton.

Once before he had visited the boundless desert of the Sahara, and, deeming it the safest hiding-place the world can produce, had fled to escape the Winged Man's vengeance to an oasis known only to the Arab chief who had directed him in his path across the desert. He was sleeping peacefully, as he thought, safe beyond the reach of the Winged Man's deadly grip.

Morning dawned, the fatal morning of the twenty-first of May. With a start he awoke, to find the sun lying, a red ball, in the Eastern horizon.

Suddenly he started. Shading his eyes with his hand, he gazed, trembling in every limb, straight into the fearful splendour of the glowing orb of day.

Had fancy painted it? Was it a vulture, or, indeed, the Winged Man that he had seen portrayed for a moment against the centre of the sun?

He rubbed his eyes, and looked again.

The form—it had seemed nothing more than a tiny speck—had vanished.

"Pshaw! The Winged Man has got on my nerves! I reckon even he will not seek me in this waste of baking sun," he muttered.

As he spoke, he drew a handful of dates from his saddle-bags, and commenced eating, grumbling at having to content himself with such scanty fare, but drawing comfort from the reflection that, after that night, he could wend his way back to civilisation, confident that the Winged Man's curse had failed.

His dates finished, he dropped on his hands and knees by the fountain to drink of the clear, sparkling water.

As he did so, his muscles grew rigid, his whole frame seemed turned to stone. Peering at him from the liquid stream, was the deathly-white face of the being from whom he had fled so far to escape.

A cry of terror burst from his lips. He sprang to his feet, for the surface of the fountain had burst like a shattered crystal, and the Winged Man poised upon the surface of the agitated water, stood, with folded arms, calmly surveying his victim.

"Oho, Todd Merton, had you forgotten May twenty-first? Did you think that even the desert of the Sahara could hide you from my vengeance? Fool, Earth itself is not large enough to hold one whose destruction the Winged Man has sworn."

Throwing off with a mighty effort the terror which held him speechless, Todd Merton, covering his face with his hands, turned to where his horse had been contentedly nibbling the grass beneath the trunks of the palms shortly before.

It was gone. Terrified by the Winged Man's fearful presence, it was already speeding as fast as fear could force it over the ground, across the desert.

Maddened with terror, Todd Merton sought to draw the revolver which hung in its holster at its side.

It was gone, and, gazing frantically around him, saw it lying on the spot from which he had recently arisen.

AT THE MERCY OF THE SAND.

The Winged Man smiled mockingly, as, striding towards where the weapon lay, he ground its deep into the sand with his heel; then, pointing towards the spot where he had laboured so strenuously throughout the night, he cried:

"Go, dog! Crawl to the grave the Winged Man has provided for you!"

In vain Todd Merton strove to resist.

He would have given even life itself for power to strike but one blow in self-defence. But in vain.

Strengthless as a child, he turned, obedient to the Winged Man's order, and staggered rather than walked over the yielding sand.

Presently the Winged Man ordered him to halt.

"Had you been at the beginning of life instead of at its close, I might, perhaps, have advised you to spend your spare time in natural history. You would find it both instructive and useful," he declared.

Todd Merton looked in wonder at the speaker.

"Ants are the most intelligent of insects," he went on, as though chatting with an interested friend. "See, at your feet, is the pit of an ant lion, and, approaching its brink, an unsuspecting beetle. Watch it! Ah, see, it has fallen into the trap the clever insect has constructed. Yet the ant lion does not move. Well he knows that the beetle cannot climb up those banks of sand, and when it is too exhausted to fight for its life, he will throw itself upon it and obtain an easy victim."

"Why do you tell me this? What awful meaning underlies your words?" asked Todd Merton, gazing fearfully at the Winged Man.

An unfathomable smile hovered for a moment over the Winged Man's thin, cruel lips.

He made no reply, but stood watching the struggles of the beetle to escape from the pit so intently that Todd Merton was emboldened to steal off. Slowly at first, then, as the distance between himself and his fearful captor increased, quicker and quicker.

The next moment he was flying swiftly over the sand.

A wild, angry cry caused him to cast a frightened glance over his shoulder. The Winged Man, poised in mid-ere, was flying swiftly after him.

Well he knew the struggle was hopeless, yet it was better than awaiting death without an attempt to escape.

On he dashed, in blind, mad, unreasoning terror, until presently he came to an abrupt halt on the verge of an enormous pit.

In a moment he understood why the Winged Man had drawn his attention to the ant lion's pit.

He tried to stop himself. In vain! Already the yielding sand was giving way beneath his feet, and the next moment, with a cry of despair, he rolled head over heels down the sloping bank.

Mad with terror, he strove to regain the surface of the desert. For every upward step he took, he fell back two.

At length, worn out, half-suffocated with a blinding sand which rose in clouds around him, he flung himself down at the bottom of the pit, and gave way to the utter despair which filled his heart.

Higher and higher rose the sun, until at last it shone with scorching beams full upon the wretched man.

"Ha, ha, Todd Merton, it is hot within there, eh?" came in mocking tones from his self-appointed executioner's lips.

"If you have a spark of human pity, kill me!" moaned the wretched man.

"Pity! Who speaks of pity to the Winged Man? Surely not he who doomed him to a fearful death. Ha, ha, Todd Merton, the heat in the crematorium was hotter than that which oppresses you, but it was more merciful, for, could you have slay me, my end would have been quicker!"

"Mercy! Mercy!" came in gasping, broken accents from the wretched man's lips.

But the Winged Man's sole reply was a contemptuous laugh, as, seated upon the edge of the pit, he watched his victim's frantic struggles to escape, until at length, overwhelmed by sand, choked, suffocated, his wretched victim's movements ceased.

THE ANARCHISTS' DOOM.

Glancing furtively to right and left, a man knocked on the door of a moderately well-to-do house in a side street of St Petersburg.

It was Jonas B. Falter, who, seeking an asylum from the Winged Man, had thrown in his lot with Russian Anarchists, deeming it impossible that his great foe would seek him in the ranks of those desperate fanatics who would overthrow the tyranny of the Tsar to provide for the suffering Russian people and even greater tyranny.

He had already found out that he had but jumped from the frying pan into the fire for the band he had joined consisted of the most reckless and daring Anarchists in Russia. They had spies everywhere, and now, when one of the greatest outrages they had ever conceived was on the point of being enacted, he found himself unable to withdraw.

The outlook was not a pleasant one. If the outrage succeeded there was a great probability of the "Band of Twelve," as they called themselves, being blown up themselves.

If it failed, immediate execution or Siberia would be the certain price.

On the other hand, he knew that if he turned from the house whilst there was yet time, watchful eyes, backed by ready hands, were upon him, and he would not leave the street alive.

A few seconds and the choice was no longer his, for the door opened and he found himself confronted by the burly custodian of the gate.

"To-day a traitor lives!" cried the man, as he opened the door.

"To-morrow a traitor dies!" replied Falter mechanically; and the watchword having been given, he passed down a well-furnished hall, and, descending a flight of stairs leading into a basement, entered a small room, where he donned a shapeless cloak, over the centre of which had been sewn a hood.

Arranging the hood so that he could see through to slits cut for the eyes, he entered a large cellar containing a table round which was seated ten hooded men, whilst an eleventh occupied a chair at its head.

"You're late, brother," said the last named, as Falter entered.

"I was detained, most worshipful president," replied Falter.

The president bowed, and signed to a vacant chair, into which Falter dropped.

For some minutes not a figure stirred, not a word was spoken. Presently the president raised his hand.

Immediately every cowled figure sprang to its feet, produced a revolver, raised it above its head, then laid it on the table before him.

Again the president raised his hand, again the hands of the conspirators fumbled beneath their cloaks, and, reappearing, each grasped a long-bladed knife by the hilt.

This, with a flourish, they left quivering in the uncovered boards.

"The revolver and knife are but weapons of self-defence. Bring forward the dread missile with which, ere another day has passed, we will strike terror into the hearts of our foes!" thundered the president.

Without a word two men disappeared through a distant door, reappearing a few minutes later bearing a wooden tray, on which were piled twelve glass globes filled with a dark-coloured liquid, which Falter recognised with a shudder as the most deadly explosive known to science.

The bombs, for such they were, were arranged in a pyramid, surmounting a white, grinning skull.

Carefully placing the tray with its fearful burden upon the centre of the table, its bearers resumed their seats. At that moment the man next to him laid a long, white, talon-like hand upon Falter's shoulder, whispering:

"Remember the twenty-first of May!"

A shriek of bewildered terror burst from the Yankee's lips as he realised that his neighbour was none other than the weird being from whom he had sought to hide himself in vain.

Despair lent him courage. Turning, he met the stern, inquiring face of the president.

"There is a traitor in our midst—we are betrayed," he cried.

"A traitor? Impossible! Yet if it be so, it is your duty to name him, and ours to see that he does not leave this cellar alive," thundered the president. Their eyes flashing fiercely through the slits in their black hoods, the conspirators grasped their weapons.

The next moment, hardened villains though they were, their blood ran cold as a wild, mirthless, fearful laugh echoed through the cellar. The next moment, his cloak thrown aside, the Winged Man stood revealed.

The Russians had scarcely heard of the weird horror, yet, as their eyes fell on that white, glowering, expressionless face, their hearts sank like lead within their bosoms.

"Who are you?" demanded the president, after a few minutes silence.

"I am the Winged Man come to claim my own!"

"No, no; he lies. I am not pledged to him in any way!" shrieked Falter, scarce knowing in his terror what he said.

"But I am pledged to you!" said the Winged Man, with a grim smile. "Upon the twenty-first of May, not a day before, nor a day after, I have sworn that you shall die!"

"Comrades, help! Let me not be drawn from your midst by this fearful being!" pleaded Falter.

"Nor shall you," returned the president. "Fear nothing, if you be a true man. This Winged Man, as he calls himself, has come as a spy upon us, and the penalty of his crime is death. You laugh," he added, as the Winged Man's weird laugh drove the colour from the listeners' cheeks once more. "Know then, that we are sworn brethren, bound by the most fearful oaths to stand by each other."

"I would not separate so worthy a company for the world!" cried the Winged Man mockingly. "Therefore, gentlemen, adieu!"

"Guard the door—seize him!" commanded the president, as the Winged Man, his hand upon Falter's shoulder, moved by the table.

As the president's words fell upon his ears, the Winged Man turned with the snarl of an enraged tiger upon the men advancing to seize him.

He raised a chair from the floor, as though in self-defence, but instead of striking his adversaries down, threw it with crushing force at the pyramid of bombs.

There was a loud explosion, a fearful burst of flame, and men for a mile around stood paralysed with horror, as they saw a pillar of lurid flame shooting heavenwards from the midst of the city.

There were those who afterwards declared that ere the light faded from view they had seen a fearful, weird, winged figure borne upwards on the summit of the flash.

°A JONAH ON BOARD.

A few hours later Josiah B. Falter found himself in a dark, evil-smelling, ever-moving prison. It was some time before he realised where he was. Gradually it dawned upon him that he was in the hold of a ship at sea.

Wondering how he had escaped from being blown to pieces, in an explosion which must have carried destruction far and wide, he lay still for several minutes, not daring to open his eyes lest he should see the fearful form of the Winged Man glowering at him. At length hunger, and a desire to find out where he was, induced him scramble over the cargo-filled hold, until he came to a bulkhead, against which he hammered with all his might.

It was some time ere the unhappy man's signals were answered, but at length a flood of light flooded the hold as the hatchway was removed, and Falter, dazed, bruised, parched with thirst, faint with hunger, was hauled on deck.

In vain Falter tried to explain how he came on board the break on which he found himself. His explanations were received as clumsy lies. The name of the Winged Man was greeted with roars of incredulous laughter by his auditors.

"No, no, my lad!" declared the captain, when Falter had ceased speaking. "Such a tale as that won't go down with me. I dare say you have been mixed up with Anarchists, or some other disreputable people; I have nothing to do with that. All I know is that you were found stowed away on board my ship, and as I happened to be a man short, you must work your way to Hull."

To this Falter readily agreed, rejoicing at having got so easily out of the trouble he had seen looming ahead.

Josiah B. Falter was not destined to have a very happy time on board the Highland Lass. His discovery in the hold, the strange tale he told, his white, blanched face, the way he started when addressed, the wild, fear-laden glances he cast around, got upon the nerves of the superstitious sailors. They made no secret in their belief that Falter was a stowaway who would bring them bad luck, and the result that, bullied by the officers, avoided and driven from the sailors'

------

company by blows and curses, the next few days were probably the most miserable of Josiah B. Falter's life.

Then came a time when the superstitious fears of the sailors seemed well-founded, for, the North Sea reached, the Highland Lass encountered the full force of a south-eastern gale, before which she was obliged to run with bared poles in a northerly direction.

Day after day the storm continued, during which Josiah B. Falter dare scarce close his eyes, lest the sailors, believing him because of their misfortune, should throw him overboard.

His appearance grew more morose than ever as he clung to a frozen shroud, or sheltered, trembling, to leeward of the little cuddy, for he preferred the open deck to being shut up in the small fo'c's'le with men who hated whilst they feared him.

For three days and nights the storm raged furiously.

About two o'clock in the morning of the fourth day, Falter, who, worn out with several sleepless nights, was sleeping like a log in his bunk, was awakened by a sharp blow in the ribs.

"Turn out, you Jonah!" cried the bo'sun, who was leaning over him. "Serve you right if we left you to go down with the Highland Lass!"

"What's happened?" growled Falter.

"What else could happen, with such as you on board to bring bad luck to honest sailor men? We have sprung a leak, and the water is coming in like a torrent!" replied the man, hastening on deck, without Falter followed, to find the crew hard at work at the pumps; but the labouring of the ship told even a landsman like Falter that the end was near. Barely had he taken his place at the pump ere the skipper decided to abandon his craft. Soon the pumps were deserted for the boats, of which there were but two—a long-boat on blocks between the brig's two masts, and a dory swinging from davits at her stern.

But this caused little uneasiness, as the long-boat was big enough to hold the crew.

"Now, lads, in with you! What are you stopping for?" demanded the captain.

"Beg pardon, sir, the men say they would rather remain aboard then go in a boat with that chap!" explained the bo'sun, pointing to Falter.

"Nonsense, man! We can't leave him behind!" remonstrated the captain.

"He has sunk the Highland Lass, and he'll sink the long-boat!" declared one of the sailors, with an angry glance at the trembling stowaway.

"There's the dory, let him go in that," growled another.

Falter glanced from the tiny boat swinging from its davits, to the lowering faces of the sailors, and feeling he would be safer alone, offered to take his chance in the dory if they would lower it.

Willingly the sailors sprang to the davits, and Falter was lowered into the troubled waters; then the blocks were cast loose, and he pulled away from the doomed vessel.

ALONE WITH THE DEAD.

Even as he did so, a wild, despairing cry broke from the sailors. Without a moment's warning the Highland Lass had plunged, bow foremost, beneath the waves, drawing the brig and her whole crew into the hungry depths.

Overwhelmed by this fearful catastrophe, from which he had so narrowly escaped, Falter, keeping the head of the boat to the waves, gazed through the darkness towards where, a few minutes before, the Island Lass had floated.

A wild cry for help rang in his ears, and he saw a sailor battling with the waves.

His first impulse was to turn a deaf ear to the cry for help.

The men had ill-treated him, and had sent him adrift in the boat alone. Why should he raise a finger to save one of them from death? was his first thought. His second, how much easier to could manage the boat than one; and not through humanity, but for his own sake, he guided the boat to meet the struggling sailor.

He reached his side just as the man raised his hands above his head, and would have sunk beneath the waves had not Falter caught him by the wrist, and, after a severe struggle, drawn him into the boat, where he lay motionless, as though already dead, in the bottom.

A wave beating over the boat warned Falter that he must keep the boat's head to the waves, or be swamped.

As day dawned the wind dropped, and the sea going down, and allowed him to turn his attention to the rescued man, but only to find that the poor fellow was already dead.

AN EXCHANGE.

For some minutes Falter gazed at the dead body. Gradually something approaching a smile crossed his haggard face.

"By Jove, I see daylight!" he muttered. "Anyhow, the body had better be removed. But the clothes and papers may be useful. Ha, ha. The Winged Man, I see a chance of escape after all!"

With trembling hands Falter drew off the rough pea-jacket, jersey, and trousers. These he donned, a triumphant chuckle bursting from his lips as he felt the papers in an inner pocket.

"So, I am Charles Able, of Bristol, am I?" he muttered. "Good! The body had better go overboard."

Taking the body in his arms Falter consigned it to the deep.

Falter's position was still a precarious one. Save that he was in the North Sea, he had no idea where he was.

As the day advanced he crouched for shelter from the piercing wind in the bottom of the little dory.

He could not, he felt sure, survive the rigours of another night, and, rising, he gazed wildly around him.

A wild, almost hysterical shriek burst from his lips. Coming swiftly towards him, under full sail, was a fishing smack.

Ten minutes later Falter found himself on her deck, surrounded by a group of sympathetic, kind-hearted, Scotch fishermen.

ON BOARD THE WHALER.

When, a week after the events described in the previous chapter, the whaler Arctic Queen steamed from Dundee, Josiah Falter, alias Charles Able, was in her forecastle.

The smack which had rescued him had taken him to Dundee, where, hearing that the Arctic Queen was bound for a whaling voyage, he had shipped on board her, thus helping to throw the Winged Man off the scent. Robbed of the constant horror of his foe's presence, which had hung like a fearful nightmare over him so long, he looked forward almost with pleasure to the voyage.

His satisfaction was short lived. They passed the Faroe Islands just as the sun sank in a red bed of clouds behind the rugged peaks. A pipe between his lips, Falter was drinking in the beauty of the scene, when he started, and, shading his eyes with his hand, gazed full into the glare of the setting sun.

Contentment fled from his heart for ever, peace would never more rest upon his soul.

On the jagged peaks sat the Winged Man, his elbow on his knee, his chin in his hand, calmly surveying the whaler as she passed on her northward journey.

Chance might have led him there, yet Falter new, in his inmost soul, that the Winged Man had never lost sight of him, and was now silently tracking him to the end.

Three weeks later the Arctic Queen was steaming slowly through an iceberg-dotted sea.

So far the voyage had been a prosperous one. Early though the season, they had already secured several casks of oil, and all hearts beat high with the hope of an early return from their perilous voyage.

Suddenly the look-out in the crows-nest uttered a warning cry. Immediately the men, who had been lolling about the decks, sprang eagerly to their feet, swept the ice-dotted sea, or shot enquiring glances up at the man in the cask at the masthead.

A moment's excited pause, then, loud and clear from the look-out, came the welcome words:

"There she blows!"

Following the direction of the look-out's out-stretched hand, the sailors caught a glimpse of what looked like steam shooting up from a black mass a mile or so away.

Soon the boats were launched, and Falter took his post in the bows of the port whale-boat, alongside the harpoon.

Swiftly the long, double-stemmed boats glided over the waves, each crew eager to be the first to reach the wail.

It was a close race, but the boat which carried the American ex-detective won, and soon a loud, strident:

"Back, boys—back for your lives!" told the crew that the harpooner had plunged his weapon deeply into the enormous mass of flesh and fat before them.

The next moment the whale dived, and the rope ran out with lightning speed, whilst Falter, kneeling in the bows, axe in hand, fixed his eyes upon the harpooner, ready to sever the cord at the first sign of danger.

Presently the tension on the rope grew less, and as the harpoon and his assistant pulled in the slack their victim rose to the surface.

For a few minutes the huge beast lay motionless on the top of the water, until the boat stole close up to its huge side, and the harpooner punched a spear into it.

A fountain of blood and water pouring from its air-holes the whale dived a short distance below the surface, then spread northward.

On, on its bed, straight towards where a magnificent iceberg, with towers and spires, like some enormous floating cathedral was stretched, an island of ice, across their path.

The harpooner's face grew very grave. He had sailed those seas for many years, hundreds of whales had fallen victims to his unerring harpoon, many a mile had he been dragged in the exciting whirl of the monster's death-struggle over the Arctic seas, and only twice had he known a whale escaped by diving under ice, especially such an enormous berg is that before them.

Its topmost peak rose two hundred feet above the surface of the waves, and its base must have been several times its height beneath the surface.

By every artifice known to his craft, the harpooner strove to divert the whale's course. As though intent upon the death of its foes, the whale headed a straight course for the berg.

Nearer and nearer to the mighty mass of ice the chagrined whalers were dragged until, a cable's length from the berg, the harpooner turned to Falter, crying:

"Cut the rope, man—quick, on your life! She is about to dive!"

There was no response. His companion was gazing with fixed, horror-stricken eyes up at the topmost peak of the iceberg.

Swift as lightning the wondering man's eyes followed Falter's frozen gaze.

A cry of amazement burst from his lips. Perched with extended wings upon the summit of the crag was the awe-inspiring form of the Winged Man.

But even in that fearful presence the harpooner did not lose his presence of mind. Bending, he snatched the axe from Falter's helpless hands; then with one sure, strong blow severed the rope just as the flukes of the dying whale's tail shopped upwards in the air.

Too late, unchecked by the bending oars, the boat sped onward with fearful force, and the next moment came in contact with the hard, frozen mass with a force which splintered the stout craft to matchwood.

A wild, despairing cry burst from the sailors; but louder, wilder, more awful than all, arose Falter's death-shriek, as, raising his hands above his head, he deliberately sought to sink beneath the foam-capped waves dashing around the base of the enormous berg.

In vain Falter sought refuge in death. His wild, weird laughter striking terror into the sailor's hearts as they struggled in the icy waves, the Winged Man dropped like a stone from his elevated perch, and plunging into the sea, arose a minute later bearing the limp, motionless, terror-paralysed form of his foe in his fearful grasp.

So awful was the Winged Man's appearance that the sailors, clinging to oars and wreckage of their boat, gazed upon him paralysed with terror.

"To the iceberg, men!" thundered the fearful apparition. "I war not with you. It is this doomed wretch upon whom alone the Winged Man would wreak his vengeance."

Relieved of a greater terror than even that of a seaman's death beneath the waves, the sailors watched the terrible apparition disappear on the floating mountain of ice.

One by one the shivering sailors reached a flat shelf at the base of the berg, where, glancing apprehensively up at the towering peaks above them, they awaited rescue by the second boat.

The whale, unable in its weakened state to dive beneath the iceberg had run with headlong fury against its submerge base, and, stunned and dying, was floating on the surface; but the sailors did not stop to secure their prey.

Rowing as they had never rowed before, they regained the shelter of the ship.

As they did so a fog hid the berg from view.

Her steam syren sounding, the Arctic Queen moved slowly towards the east, for in that direction alone had appeared the chance of escape.

Night fell, day dawned. As the sun rose, the fog was dispelled. A cry of amazement from a sailor brought the captain to the side of the bridge.

He could scarcely believe his eyes. Moored to the vessel's side was the dead whale, the harpoon still protruding from its enormous back.

How it got there none could tell until the harpoon, dropping upon the whale's broad back, saw burnt deep, as though with a red-hot iron, into the haft of the weapon, the words:

"The Winged Man wars not with honest sailor-men."

The same sun which disclosed the Winged Man's gift to the wondering eyes of the Arctic Queen's captain shone upon a strange, fearful seen some twenty miles below the western horizon.

Embedded deep in the ice face of the enormous berg, a look of unutterable horror on his face, lay—or, rather, stood, for it was in an upright position—the body of Josiah B. Falter.

Above him, gazing with folded arms upon the last of his American foes, was the Winged Man.

For nearly an hour the weird horror remained motionless as though he had become part of the mighty berg; then, sweeping like an eagle from its eyrie, he rose until he became but a tiny speck in the clear, cloudless air, and flew southward with lightning speed.

A Flight Across the World.

With slow steps the Winged Man paced a room in his magnificently furnished retreat amidst the caves on the Yorkshire coast.

"It is done! My work here is finished. I return whence I came. Yet ere I go those who, willingly or unwillingly, have served me must be rewarded," he muttered.

He struck a deep-voiced gong as he spoke. A door opened. Ghat entered.

"Whose dog are you?" demanded the Winged Man, in the well-known formula in which he often addressed his slaves.

"Yours, master—in life and death, yours!" returned Ghat submissively.

"Ay, a faithful dog, and shall receive the reward you deserve!" said the Winged Man.

Ghat looked wonderingly at the Winged Man. He had spoken in gentler tones than he had ever heard him use before.

"Faithfully and well you have served me for many years, Ghat. What reward do you ask for your services?"

"Only that I may be ever near you, my master," replied the other.

"That is impossible. Listen, my one and only friend! I go, whither you need not ask. Where I go none may follow. See"—he handed him a bunch of keys— "these keys command the whole of my wealth. Save that it is my will that you distribute a portion amongst the many slaves imprisoned in my various strongholds, it is yours to do with as you will."

"I want it not, if its possession robs me of the only friend I have in the world!" sobbed the dwarf.

"With it or without, Ghat, we separate here and now."

"But will you not return? Well I never look upon your face again?" demanded Ghat, his face humanised by a look of dog-like love, as tears chased each other down his wrinkled cheeks.

"That I cannot say. Fate is stronger than the Winged Man. It may be I will return; but if you knew all, loving me as you do, you would not wish me back. Go," he added; "I have fasted over-long. Bring food and wine!"

Ghat, with a lingering glance at his master, obeyed, and when he returned the Winged Man had vanished.

In vain he searched the countless maze of his master's splendid subterranean palace. He was gone, and in his heart Ghat knew it was for ever.

A desire to look once more upon mighty London induced the Winged Man to travel from his Yorkshire cave to our great metropolis.

Seated in one corner of a fashionable restaurant just off Piccadilly, he ate alone, and in silence, watching through half-closed eyelids the gay throng at the tables around him.

His dinner finished, he called for coffee and liqueurs. Lighting a cigarette he open opened an evening paper, and skimmed lightly over its contents.

He smiled as he read an alarmist report that the Winged Man had been seen hovering over St. Paul's. Then his eyes fell upon a tiny paragraph in one corner of the paper.

He started. His face, in which a deep-seated melancholy had driven out all other expression, became convulsed with rage as he read aloud, though in so low tones that none near heard him:

"Mr. Danby Druce, whose plucky attempts to capture the flying fiend known as the Winged Man have earned him the respect and admiration of all the world, was this morning married at the cathedral in Melbourne to Miss Mary Evanson. We understand that Mr. Druce has decided to rest upon his laurels, and has bought a charming estate at the base of the extinct volcano Tarakmido."

Suddenly the diners were terrified by a long-drawn, piercing wail of agony, anguish, and rage.

All eyes had turned in the direction from whence the cry had come.

A low, shuddering moan swept from one end of the long room to the other, as, his face convulsed with fury, his fearful pinions outstretched, mad rage flashing from his eyes, the Winged Man flew like a baleful meteor over their heads.

Crash!

Flying with blind fury, he had come in contact with an enormous chandelier. Snapping the stout stem which held it in two he dashed it to the floor. Resuming his mad flight, he thrust aside, as easily as though they had been but children, the stalwart doorkeeper is who would have seized him, and dashed into the street.

Horses reared, men shouted, women screamed, yet, heeding not the outcry on either side and below him, the Winged Man disappeared in the darkness.

"A thousand curses alight on Danby Druce's head! The compact ran: 'Whilst he kept from her, I should leave Mary Evanson in peace.' It is he who has broken his word. Upon his head be the consequences! Twelve hours, and Britain would have been free from my presence for ever. It is he, and he alone, whose hand has unloosed the terror of my hate upon a devoted people once more!" muttered the Winged Man, as he flew swiftly southward.

Since his return from the Arctic regions the melancholy on his face had perhaps increased, but there had been a look of peace, as of one resigned to his fate. Now, his face was convulsed with rage, his eyes flashed with mad hate, his thin lips were pressed tightly together with cruel determination.

Southward he flew—southward, ever southward—until, on the outskirts of Paris, weariness compelled him to seek the earth.

A rattle of wheels, a roar of steam, and the Lyons express thundered towards him. Rising, he soared over the line, then dropping like a stone from out the darkness of night, alighted upon the footplate of the engine.

His laugh, more reckless, more awful, more maniacal than ever, rose above the rattle of the wheels, and the deep third of the swiftly-working piston.

Recklessly, the Winged Man forced the train through the night at ever-increasing speed. Tearing through stations, rushing by level-crossings, thundering over bridges, dashing madly through towns and crowded junctions; whilst the officials, unable to account for the mad rush of the express, telegraphed frantic orders to stop it up and down the line.

Suddenly lights appeared ahead. Lyons was reached.

Almost as soon as the town appeared in sight the express plunged into the station.

The driver of a crowded local train made frantic efforts to draw his charge from the onrushing express's path.

In vain. With a rush and a roar, the express was upon it, and the next moment the engine, hurling carriages to right and left, reared like a maddened charger, then rolled over on its side.

His mocking laughter rising above the din of the escaping steam, the Winged Man rose on outstretched wings, and, leaving the scene behind, flew, refreshed by his long rest, southward.

A warship ploughing the waters of the Mediterranean reported that the Winged Man had been seen to leave her fighting-top with the first rays of dawn.

From islands in the Indian Sea came strange reports of the Winged Man's progress, whilst several ships' captains noted in their logs the appearance of the flying horror, soaring with tireless wings over the Pacific.

THE WINGED MAN'S FAREWELL.

Hand-in-hand Danby Druce and his wife wandered along the shores of a sleeping sea.

Above their heads cowered the cone of Tarakmido, upon the shores of which stood the commodious but a homely mansion in which the great detective hoped to pass the remainder of his life, far removed from the stirring scenes which had made his name a household word throughout the world.

To right and left stretched inexhaustible pastures filled with lowing herds and flocks of sheep, interspersed with a well-cultivated plantations.

It would be difficult to have found a more peaceful spot than this in the whole, beautiful world, yet, as Mary, her head resting confidently on her husband's shoulder, strolled by his side, a cloud hung upon her brow.

"What is it, dear one? You are thoughtful?" asked Danby Druce, stooping to imprint a kiss upon her white forehead.

Mary laughed.

"Perhaps I am. I cannot banish from my mind thoughts of the Winged Man," she replied.

Danby Druce started.

He had carefully kept the fact from his wife, that once or twice during the past week he had felt the inward shudder which had ever warned him of his dread foe's approach.

"You are nervous, Mary, and out of sorts," he replied. "Report has it that he is dead. Even if he were living I do not think we have cause to fear him now."

Mary was silent for a few moments.

"I do not think it is exactly fear, Danby," she said after a time. "It is not that. I saw him in, perhaps, a different light to what you did, in those days when he—you must not be jealous, Danby, for you have known it all along—when he won my regard, if not my love. What know we of his past? What know we of the wrongs which may have made him what he is? I feared him when I knew his true nature, I trembled at his approach, yet, strange though it may seem, there is only one thing wanted to complete my happiness, and that is, to meet the Winged Man once more, and to hear the admission from his own lips, that we are friends."

"Your wish is granted."

With a startled cry Mary clung to her husband, whilst Danby Druce, throwing his arm around her waist, instinctively thrust his hand into his hip-pocket, where until the last few happy weeks his faithful revolver ever rested; for, barring their path, a strange, unfathomable smile upon his lips, stood the Winged Man.

Mary was the first to break the silence with which the three, whose adventures we have followed so long, regarded each other.

Gently disengaging herself from her husband's protecting grasp, she advanced towards the Winged Man with outstretched hands.

A spasm of pain flitted for a moment across the Winged Man's pale, strongly-marked features, then, taking the proffered hand, he dropped upon one knee and pressed it to his lips.

Rising, he held out his hand to Danby Druce.

"Long have we fought, bitter has been the struggle, but you have won, and the Winged Man grudge is not your victory. I came, maddened with rage, to slay. To-morrow night, fire from yonder volcano would have overwhelmed you and yours. Unseen, I hovered above you in your walk this evening. Where I thought myself an object of hatred and scorn, I found kindly feeling, forgiveness.

"Danby Druce, worthy rival of one whose part you can never know, whose nature you may never fathom, farewell! And you, gentlest, sweetest, loveliest of mortal women, adieu! I go! I thought that none would ever mark my departure, for all the teeming millions in this wide world, I deemed the Winged Man friendless and alone. Come!"

Turning, he led the way along a winding path to a tiny land-locked bay, the entrance to which was guarded by sloping tree-covered promontories.

"Farewell! Wealth, happiness, love is yours! Weep not, Mary!" continued the Winged Man, for tears were falling fast down the tender-hearted girl's cheeks. "You have gained your kingdom. I go to mine."

At that moment the moon, rising slowly from the unbroken horizon of the distant ocean shed a silvery path of light through the entrance into the bay.

Waving his hand in farewell, the Winged Man glided along this silvery path, until the entrance to the bay was reached, when, pausing, he held his hands above his head with a gesture of farewell then sank beneath the waves.

Was it fancy, or was it but the sighing of the sea breeze through the trees, but it seemed to the watching couple as though a burst of distant triumphant music had fallen upon their ears.

Then, as a rising cloud enveloped the low moon, they left the bay and walked home in silence.

The End.